I0772363

A SANCTUARY FROM SHADOW

The Larkspur Curse Series Book 1

Laura Irwin

CONTENT WARNING

This is a dark romantic fantasy. Some may find its contents disturbing, as they include: profanities, violence, sex, attempted rape, blood, death, murder, animal death, fire, PTSD, sexism, slavery references, and brief references to human trafficking. There are also references to recent politics, and a retelling of a Bible story. This book is not meant for anyone under the age of 18.

For Mom and Daddy
There are no words. Only memories.
And love that will never be matched.

MAG MELL
Fionnara
(Winter Court)
The Peaks
Angel Oak Portal
The King's Road
Tamsyn's House
Avenshire
Thorny Rose Tavern
Spring Palace
Fomorian Isles
The Nixie's Cave
Evereostre
(Spring Court)
island
(Autumn Court)
Blackvale Portal
Morrigan's March
Humwater Dell
Harbinger Camp
Glynlea
Goblin Market
Dagda's Passage
Dragoner Kill
Shanerie
Crowcairn Bridge
Kirk of Cara
The Owenfen
Kaidoscope Post
Summer Palace
Keitha Ronan
Shadow Palace
Lithalaly
(Summer Court)
Brigid's Trail
Woebegone wood
Covenlen
(Shadow Court)

Pronunciation Guide

Names

*Aengus: Ain-gus
*Amaranthine: Am-uh-ran-thin
*Arbutus Colwort: Ar-byoo-tus Cul-wert
*Balor: Bay-lor
*Boderg: Bod-eerg
*Buxus: Bucks-uss
*Cermait: Ker-mit
*Cernunnos: Ker-noo-noss
*Cissus: Sih-suss
*Cornelian: Cor-nee-lee-en
*Domhnall: Dough-null
*Dando: Dan-doh
*Erybos Gentian: Air-uh-bus Jen-shin
*Eulalia: Yuh-lay-lee-uh (Aylie: Ay-lee)
*Fianna: Fee-ah-nuh
*Freesia: Free-shuh
*Glashtyn: Glash-tin
*Ilex Howlite: Eye-lex How-lyte
*Imogen: Im-oh-jun
*Laurustinus: Law-rus-tin-us
*Liatris: Ly-at-ris (Lia: Lya)
*Loosestrife: Loos-stryf
*Lugh: Loo
*Luxovious: Lux-oh-vee-us
*Morus: Mor-uss
*Myrrdin: Mur-din
*Nimue: Neem-weh
*Novus: Noh-vus
*Olea: Oh-lee-uh
*Oxalis: Ox-uh-liss
*Pavonia: Pav-oh-nee-uh
*Polkweed: Poke-weed
*Riordan: Reer-din
*Rhamnus: Ram-nuss
*Rhoswen: Hroz-wen
*Sionna: Show-nuh
*Sedge: Sej
*Tansy: Tan-zee
*Viola: Vy-oh-luh
*Zahra: Zah-ruh

Places

*Aisland: Ash-land
*Avenshire: Ay-ven-shur
*Evereostre: Ev-er-oh-stra
*Fionnara: Fin-nah-ruh
*Galena's Farm: Guh-lee-nuh's Farm
*Glynlea: Glin-lee
*Lithalaly: Lith-uh-lah-lee
*Kirk of Cara: Kirk of Kar-ruh
*Timbermoor: Tim-ber-mor
*Tír na nÓg: Teer-nah-nog
*Shanerie: Shay-nair-ee

Creatures

*Bogeybats: Boh-ghee-bats
*Cantir: Can-teer
*Dealan-dhè: Dee-lan-duh
*Fleecer: Flee-ser
*Púca: Poo-ka

Other

*Anam cara: Ah-nem Kar-ruh
*Beyn: Bayn
*Ceyla: Kay-lah
*Chronopath: kron-noh-path
*Drey: Dray
*Feyr: Fair
*Fomorian: Foe-mor-ee-an
*Milesian: Mil-ee-shun
*Nemedian: Nem-ee-dee-en
*Ryan: Ree-an
*Ryn: Rin
*Scian: Shkee-un
*Sylph: Silf (Sylphen: Silf-en)
*Tuatha Dè Danann: Tu-ah-ha Day
  Dah-nun
*Zephyrist: Zef-er-ist

PROLOGUE

May, 2018 M.M., Evereostre

He awoke in a cloud of mist beside the Thorny Rose Tavern, sprawled shirtless in a flower bed. Cotton filmed his tongue, his head as heavy as the hogshead of honey mead he'd polished off in last night's carousing. His morning glory throbbed in his leather trousers, straining to one-up the tulips surrounding him.

Clearly, he hadn't gotten that ride with sweet-lipped Freesia. He briefly wondered why before loosing a monstrous groan and rolling onto hands and knees, hocking phlegm into the soil. More on instinct than on sight, he reached aside to graze a horn tankard and smirked through his hangover.

Auld Jade—always looking out for him.

After draining Jade's disgusting dandelion tonic, he belched, expelling his toxins in a pungent mustard haze, which floated off to rankle some unlucky shrub elf.

The rising sun and the spring mizzle battled for supremacy as he rose, trudging toward the fluttering woods to wrangle his pisser and relieve himself. He was reveling in the sweet release of a full bladder when the shutters of the nearest tavern window banged open. "Watch you don't wee on my crocuses, Pete," a voice rasped the mild breeze. "You kill them, and I'll make you pay your tab for once."

His head already clearing after the tonic, Pete chuckled. "Such a pleasure to hear your silky tones first thing upon waking, my lovely Jade."

Jade giggled like a schoolgirl who'd been smoking cigars for 20 years. In her case, it was more like 500. "Lay off the sweet talk, you scoundrel. Business arrived for you not an hour ago."

Yawning, he waved. "I'll be in shortly." First, his tadger needed tending. "In the meantime, care to whip me up some of your delectable oat cakes?"

"Bah! You'll get the porridge already cooking and like it." He heard her hobble from the window and smiled.

Oat cakes and elderdeer sausage links awaited him as he lumbered into the tavern. Its hearth, a hollowed tree lined with bricks, crackled with fire. Inside sat a hefty cauldron simmering that porridge Jade had threatened him with. Mossy wisteria hung from the ceiling beams, lending the smoke a musky sweetness. Scratching his bristled chin, Pete wended through the tree trunks supporting the second story of the large public house—the only one at the juncture of the King's Road and the Dagda's passage.

Other patrons had long since retired to their rented rooms. The poorest travelers snored upon bedrolls within the common room. His own sat in a corner by the side staircase, untouched.

Little wonder Freesia had spurned his advances if he'd lacked the wherewithal to prepare a suitable bed for her. Rather high-minded for a tavern wench, she was. He'd have enjoyed a drunken roll in the tulips, but she treated her cunny like a damn gold box. He wondered whose bed she'd graced with her soft tits and lavender tongue the night before. Sedge's, he guessed. The lucky sod.

Pete winked at the hefty Middling peering at him over a row of sudsy horn tankards. The piercings along her arched ear glinted in the light breaking through the open window.

"I knew you had a soft spot for me, Jade." He padded to his breakfast. "Can't deny it now."

Before Pete sat to eat, the meaty hand of a Troll fae with a domed, blond head and mocking blue eyes snatched the trencher away. "I'd say her soft spot is more for your mongrel, human." The Troll set the trencher on the floor beside his enormous sandaled feet and whistled. A nimble mutt of black and tan origin trotted over in response, feathery tail a-wagging.

Sionna devoured the entire meal in three chomps, then licked the trencher so clean it sparkled. Pete only stared at the empty plate, disappointed at the least.

Jade smiled, teal cheeks dimpling. "Sit yourself down, Pete. Reed, take a break from your washing and find something to fill his sour belly." Smirking, the Troll dropped his rag into a sudsy bucket and wiped his hands on his stained apron. He swaggered toward the kitchen, ducking under the lintel. "And fetch the parcel what was delivered for him!" Jade shouted into the passthrough. "That ghoul nearly spooked the living shite out of me, bringing it here. Must be fair important."

Exhaling, Pete rested on the bench where he'd meant to eat. It creaked in protest, bowing under his weight—not made for someone of his stature. Most fae weren't distantly descended from Vikings. Though they wished.

"Did you drink the whole of my tonic?" Jade asked. "You're still green around the gills."

Pete swiped a hand through his mussed brown hair. It badly needed shorn. The longer it grew, the fluffier it got. "Yes, mam. Every drop."

She grunted and set a dried pitcher upon one of the shelves behind her, where she kept the coveted imported spirits—from other courts and Earth. After Pete's more profitable bounties, he'd treat himself with jiggers of his favorite Irish whiskey. This could cost him; Jade made him pay for the good stuff up front.

Imports from Earth were rare since the moronic king had closed the portals to traders. Still, some of the best human wares strayed into the fae realm through the black-market—and the black-market portals. He'd yet to find one of these outlawed portals himself, though he'd never stopped looking.

"I'd best fix you another draught." Jade set her towel on the bar. "Reed won't take kindly to replacing the moss so early in the day should you retch." She waddled off to join Reed in the kitchen. Sionna, always a welcome guest, was permitted to follow.

Pete swiveled to hunch over the table. He was rubbing a dull throb from his temples when Reed returned, brandishing a plate piled with hash and a tankard of Jade's tonic. Under his arm glared a bright purple scroll sealed with the Shadow Court insignia. "Bloody Christ," Pete growled as Reed set down his burdens.

"What?" Reed griped, dropping the scroll on the table beside the plate. "You don't want hash, and you don't want porridge. Where is it you think you're eating, your majesty? The Spring Palace?"

Pete laughed despite his clenching wame. "I've no complaint with your fare, fella. My qualm is with the message."

Reed eyed the parcel. "Doesn't look too wicked."

Sighing, Pete grabbed it. "Regardless, it is." He whistled, long and high, and Sionna skittered from the kitchen on cue, scampered straight to him as trained. He stroked her dutiful head, her chocolate eyes blinking up in anticipation, her tan brows wriggling to and fro.

Reed stepped back, gasping. "Is that one of your assassination ordinations?"

"No, those are color-coded black. These are far worse."

Reed scoffed. "What's worse than death?"

Pete broke the scroll's seal, the delicate fragrance of morning dew and pears wafting up his nose. *Bollocks,* he thought. *A female mark this time, and Seelie to boot.*

Pete watched Sionna's nostrils flare at the distinct scent, her keen mind committing it to memory. "Violet missives mean I must deliver my mark to the Shadow Prince." Pete couldn't quite keep the blackness from his voice, remembering his own imprisonment in the Shadow Prince's clutches. "It's worse than death, I assure you."

The Troll frowned. "That sounds terrible, Pete. For your mark—and your soul. I don't envy your lot—or the punishment for failure."

Pete tossed the scroll aside, shutting an iron door on the do-gooder within. He could damn him eternally this time. There was too much at stake—his hard-earned freedom aside—to show mercy to one Seelie snob. If she were anything akin to the others he'd encountered at the Shadow Palace, then he could see her pealing with laughter and feasting while bleeding men stood in cages around her, starving to death.

Fuck them, Pete thought, squaring his shoulders. *Fuck them all.*

He grabbed his spoon and dug into his breakfast. "Such is the nature of life as a harbinger," he answered Reed, mouth full of hash. "Better them than me."

PART ONE

"Doubt truth to be a liar."
—Hamlet
William Shakespeare

ONE

They called the tree Angel Oak, and *damn*, was it enormous. On a small island just off the coast of Charleston, South Carolina, its limbs sprawled across the ground, curling in spirals. Ivy festooned its branches, which splayed open, welcoming as an old friend's arms. I stood upon red clay on the edge of its park with my two college buds, breathless.

"This is the coolest thing we've seen all week," I said.

Grace scoffed, honey-dew eyes glinting. "We toured the Biltmore two days ago, and this *tree* is the coolest thing you've seen on our trip?"

"Yes." I lifted my digital camera, snapping a picture. "By far."

Olivia laughed. Her highlighted curls ruffled around her shoulders as she remarked to Grace, "Why have we been spending money on admission fees for Amy? We could've left her with some shrubs—done the historical stuff without her."

I rolled my eyes. "Did you read the board at the gate? This tree is the oldest thing we'll see on our entire road trip. It's thought to be 500 years old. I'd say that makes it an artifact. And by the way, this artifact isn't behind a velvet rope or under glass. We can touch it."

Grace's laughter bubbled, oak leaves casting lacy shadows on her cherubic face. She gestured at the various signs hammered between roots. "There are literally 20 plaques saying, 'Don't touch the tree.'"

Olivia zipped her fuchsia fleece. An academic whose weedy body had little to no fat, she found the 67-degree weather too brisk. Whenever she complained, I reminded her it was snowing back on campus in Johnstown, Pennsylvania.

"Signs didn't stop us at Fort Sumter," Olivia said.

"Yeah, and we almost got kicked out," Grace reminded us.

I recalled the livid, red-faced ranger who'd sputtered at Olivia and me to, "Get your asses off the cannon!" Our fellow History Club members would appreciate that anecdote at our next meeting.

"There aren't any rangers around to yell at us." I scanned the other marveling tourists traipsing between roots—not a brown shirt in sight. "Here." I handed Grace my camera. "I'll do it myself. If I get kicked out, pretend you don't know me."

Olivia chuckled.

Accepting my camera, Grace sighed. "All right."

I strode into the open, my glaring deformities a magnet for other tourists' eyes. Their gawking wouldn't harsh my mellow, though. Not during spring break. Though I was an inch shy of six feet with blindingly pale skin, long bright-red hair, and pointy ears that stuck out from my head, I wasn't a bigger anomaly of nature than Angel Oak.

Touching any tree was like grazing the veil of history. If the sun kept shining and the water kept flowing, trees could flourish for millennia, remaining steadfast and solid as the world changed around them. But Angel Oak—she was something extra.

My fingers tingled to connect with her, the way they had when I was a child, pretending I could commune with plants. Like it was my superpower. And Danu, my religion's deity, had always welcomed me into her network of greenery.

Wind gusting me toward the nearest branch, I faced my friends. Grace held my camera to her eye; Olivia checked for rangers. I tugged down the hem of my Pitt tee, just a smidge short for me, and grinned. Placing my hand on the branch.

In my past communing with nature, Danu had always extended herself in friendly greeting. Gently, placidly. Afterward, she'd recede back to her proper realm, expecting nothing in return. This time, however, as I imagined sinking into Angel Oak's capillaries, into its rushing, branching lifeforce, the tree also sank into mine. Weighing me down, gripping me in place as a gaze, invisible and eternal, peered through me like glass. *Ah, it's you*, its essence seemed to say before energy, kinetic and sizzling, jolted through my fingertips, zinging along my arm, into my heart. Igniting something both wild and dangerous.

Abruptly, the grip freed me. I hopped like I'd been goosed and whirled to gape at the towering tree, its leaves now flittering like jazz-hands.

My superpower was only childish fantasy, but I hadn't imagined that shock. Danu had just revealed herself to me in a very real way, stealing something intrinsic from me in the process. And I already knew—she'd never give it back.

I struggled to focus for the rest of that day. My friends couldn't hold a proper conversation with me at lunch, none of the other historic sites we visited held my interest, and I'd gotten no enjoyment out of our ghost tour through Charleston. Because I just couldn't stop thinking about what happened at Angel Oak, that shockwave still echoing.

That night, I couldn't sleep. Not just because I'd crammed myself into a full-size hotel bed with Olivia, but because I couldn't quiet my mind, things I always kept anchored from my thoughts bobbing to the surface.

I dozed off sometime after 3 AM, but still, I didn't rest.

Something happened in my sleep. Something that had happened many times before, though not since I was in pigtails and Polly Flinders dresses.

I'd forgotten my night terrors, as I'd forgotten many things from early childhood—memory of my first years, an intricate conflation of both reality and fantasy, mashed together by an overactive imagination hell bent on coping with tragedy.

Tragedy the night terror always poached.

As the dream begins, I'm tiny, no older than four, and the scent of honeysuckle clings to my every breath. I sit upon satin cushions in a gilded carriage bedecked by carven runes. I graze tiny fingers over the one by my head, somehow gleaning its meaning—Larkspur—my family name.

The head of my family stands outside the carriage in finery not of modern design. A smile lights my father's long, oval face, the floral breeze ruffling the ebony curls beneath his crown of golden twigs. A motley assortment of men in shiny, engraved armor and horned helmets chortle with Daddy before his midnight gaze catches mine. His grin spreads, his eyes crinkling as he points into the mountainous distance at a black, foreboding crag. I just *know* he intends to climb to its desolate peak. And I just *know* if he goes up there, the world will end.

I'm too little to warn him, any of them, and frustrated, I cry.

My tears usher me into another setting. When my vision clears, I'm with my mother. At least, that's who I sense she is; she died when I was four.

On a feathered carpet, she kneels over me, her copper hair cascading in silken sheets. She has a lovely heart-shaped face with a broad, round nose and a voluptuous mouth, but she isn't smiling. Her expression is strained, her orange-green eyes intense and hypnotic as she chants something beyond my understanding. I'm shaking, near to wetting myself, but can't look away.

Static electricity crackles in the air, and my mother becomes a supernova of blinding amber light.

When my vision returns, I'm on the cold floor of a glass corridor, my knees tucked to my chest. Moonlight streams down on me from an unknown spring as I rise to my bare feet. My father's crown sits atop my head. It doesn't quite fit.

I call for my parents, my voice tinkling down the hall with no response. Because they're both gone. I'm alone. Orphaned.

A burning frenzy builds in my chest, and I wail to the fates who've forsaken me until the most beautiful voice I've ever heard responds. Singing, an invisible woman chucks my chin high, guiding me forward. *Follow the trail of my song*, she croons. *You'll find home in the end.*

Weeping, I scamper after the music. The closer I get, the sweeter and louder it grows until it's a swelling symphony accompanied by ghostly panpipes and fiddles, and there's only one place left to go.

I reach for a glowing door at the end of the hallway, but it opens before I make contact.

The music quiets to a poignant hush as I step into a grand bedroom brimming with toys, books, and frilly pillows. Flowers garland the vaulted ceiling. The subtle fragrance of Sweet William tickles my nose.

I know this place. It's my room. Moonlight pools in from the tall arched windows behind my scrolling bed, where my baby sister and brother sit, entwined and weeping for all we had lost.

I rush to them. One step, a child, the next, an adult. I sweep them both into my arms, promising to take care of them, that we'll take care of each other.

Their small fingers grip me when a shrouded figure appears in the doorway.

The looming specter embodies shadow—siphons the remaining light from the room. My hairs prickle as onyx streams of oblivion reach to engulf me. I've always been afraid of the dark.

Despite an overwhelming compulsion to run for my life, I rise to shield my siblings. I'm the only thing standing between them and certain doom. And I don't know if I'm enough.

TWO

April, 2008, Johnstown, Pennsylvania, USA

The cafeteria was a buffet with a two-story, vaulted ceiling from which flags of various nations hung. Its back wall featured staggered windowpanes and flaunted the beauty of the forest without. Nestled in the Appalachians among lush forests and sprawling farmlands, my college closely resembled a ski-lodge. Winters were horrendous, but I loved every minute I spent there. Usually, anyway.

Sitting slumped at my lunch table, squeezing an abominable amount of ketchup on my steak fries, I watched the sun outside shine upon barren trees. Ice from the last storm clung to budding leaves despite the oncoming warmth's best efforts. Thankfully, the cold couldn't hold on forever. Fighting a yawn, I watched a robin hop through the sparkling puddles upon the walking paths, the bleakness of winter already yielding to the aurora of spring.

"Another bad dream last night, Amy?" Zahra, my roommate, took a seat beside me at our table, her lunch tray toting leafy greens and lean lunchmeats. Healthy food—something I rarely partook in, despite what my lanky frame suggested.

"You could say that." My eyelids drooped, though it was 11:30 AM, and I'd already made it through one class.

Zahra slung her messenger bag aback her chair, rolling up her cardigan sleeves. She repositioned the polka dot headband reining back the raven halo of ringlets fanning her face. "What does that make now? The third nightmare this week?" She grimaced, forking a carrot. "Something traumatic happen on your trip down south?"

I glanced toward the entrée bar, where our other two lunch buddies ladled food onto plates. "*Please.* I went with Olivia and Grace. The only drama we encountered was a rude waitress at a diner in West Virginia."

"Then what's causing the tossing and turning at night? And the noises?"

"Oh, damn." I massaged my forehead, cringing. "Was I screaming, too?"

Zahra's lips hitched in her creamy sepia-toned face, her button nose bunching. "Only sometimes. It didn't keep me up—for very long, anyway."

"I'm so sorry. I hoped I was keeping quiet this time."

"This time? Have you had nightmares like this in the past?"

"Yes."

Her russet eyes brightened; her mouth opened around a question.

"And no, I don't want you to analyze them, Dr. Zahra," I beat her to the punch, smirking. "Thanks for the offer, though."

She crunched into her carrot. "If you change your mind, you know where to find me."

"Change your mind about what?" Olivia sauntered to a chair at our table. Casual in a gray hoodie, her curls pulled back in a tight pony, she set her tray on the table and slid into her seat, pushing her glasses up the bridge of her straight nose.

"She had a nightmare," Zahra answered before I could stop her. "And she doesn't want to talk about it."

I shot her a look asking, *Then why did you bring it up?*

"Another one?" Grace remarked as she plopped into the seat on my other side, her cheeks wind burnt. "What's that make now? The fifth one since we left Charleston?"

"Just about," I replied.

"What's causing them?" Olivia asked.

"Nothing much," I said. "Just stressed out, I guess."

"Mm," Grace hummed, sipping pop through a straw. "Stressing about your Women in Lit paper?"

We had the same class at separate times, for which a ten-page term paper was due during finals. A five-minute presentation based on our chosen thesis would follow. The task in its entirety sounded arduous, but I wasn't feeling the heat because my thesis impassioned me, and I knew just how to frame my supporting arguments.

Olivia chuckled around a bite of fried fish. "Have you decided on a new thesis yet?"

"Nope. Sticking with the one I had, regardless of your opinion."

Grace faced me. "What's your thesis, Amy?"

"I'm actually writing about romance novels—about how they empower women."

Her dark brows rose into her hairline. "That sounds—good."

Zahra's eyes twinkled with dubious humor.

Olivia gestured toward them. "See. You don't want your feminist professor to have the same reaction."

Olivia and I were both literature majors, but she preferred chaste Regency novels by authors like Jane Austen, where the subject of sex was all but glossed over. I, on the other hand, wanted to know what Mr. Darcy was packing in his trousers. My literary entertainment required spice. My real life sadly lacked it.

I laughed. "Look, I've read hundreds of romance novels." I had the proof stacked on my dorm dresser. "And I have yet to encounter a heroine I wouldn't like if I met her in real life. They've all been strong women, struggling for independence in a male-dominated world. They've all been kindhearted and intelligent. They've all had principles and ambitions and wit—"

"Yeah," Olivia agreed. "They have no physical or personality flaws. Like real women do. What message does that send? That you must be perfect to be worthy of love and romance?"

"No!" I gasped. "They're flawed."

Olivia scoffed.

"Maybe not physically flawed," I admitted. "But definitely flawed in character. In the last book I read, the heroine was unbelievably selfish before she fell in love with an indentured servant."

Grace giggled. "Let me guess—the man turned out to be secretly wealthy, and everyone realized how worthy he was of her in the end."

I pursed my lips. "Well—"

"The men are always stinking rich," Grace added.

"And they're always tall, handsome, and jacked as hell," Zahra remarked.

"If you were a heroine in a novel, would you be attracted to an uggo with warts?" I asked her. "Keep in mind, I've never seen you bring anything but studs back to our room."

Zahra considered the prospect. "He'd have to have a killer personality."

I grinned. "Uh-huh."

"He doesn't have to have warts." Olivia's blue eyes rolled. "But he doesn't have to be a prime male specimen either. With a prime male—*you know.*"

We all laughed.

"Whatever." I lifted a stubborn chin. "I stand by my thesis. Romance novels empower women to be who they are, to go out and forge their own fates. They celebrate female sexuality, instead of insisting we repress our carnal natures. Tell me, what's not feminist about that?"

Grace nearly choked on a piece of fish.

Zahra snickered into her tea.

Olivia's thick chestnut brow arched. "I'm sure your professor will explain it to you."

I waved her off. "*Anyway*—" I grabbed a steak fry, slathered it in ketchup, and took a honking bite. "Who wants to go shopping tomorrow?"

"Why?" Zahra winked. "Looking for ways to express your carnal nature?"

"Maybe."

"Well, I can't," Grace replied. "I'm only halfway through *my* paper."

I didn't confess I hadn't even started mine.

"I'm out, too," Zahra said. "My bank account's running low after my car payment, and my dad's refusing to give me a cash infusion until next week."

I turned to Olivia. "And you? What's your excuse?"

She shrugged. "Yeah, I'll go. I need some new shorts."

"Great." I smiled. "And I promise to limit talk of paperbacks and their dripping honeypots while we're out—unless you make fun of my thesis again."

I expected laughter in response. What I got, instead, were three pairs of dancing owl eyes.

"Hey, ladies," a male voice jarred me to my core—a crisp, friendly voice I placed immediately. Briar Hawthorne, my longtime family acquaintance—the epitome of those handsome romance heroes Zahra had just described—stood behind me. I strangled my fork. "How's it going?" Briar asked.

Mortified that he might've heard me say *dripping honeypots*, I cursed my big mouth. And my apathy at not putting on makeup that morning. At least I'd pinned my bangs back and changed out of my nightclothes. My snow boots scraped the salty gray carpet as I faced Briar.

He stood before us in a black button-down shirt over a heathered gray tee. A pair of gray suede sneakers peeked out from under his fitted dark-washed jeans. The guy knew how to dress, but I liked him in much less. In high school, he was on the swim team. He'd worn nothing but a Speedo at meets. Which I'd gone to religiously, just to watch him—this dreamboat of a boy I could never have.

Today, his short auburn hair was gelled, his chiseled face clean shaven. His lime-green eyes creased at the corners as he smiled at me under a dignified Greek nose.

We shared many traits—arched ears, sharp cheekbones, and slightly slanted eyes—because we were Danann, a surviving tribe of the ancient Celts. Briar's Danann features lent him an air of exoticism. Not so with mine.

"Sorry to interrupt, Amy." His smile crooked, I decided he hadn't missed my untimely promise to Olivia.

Damnit.

"That's fine," I almost squeaked. "Did you need something?"

"Not really. Was just hoping we could talk."

"Oh—uh—sure." I nodded him on. "What's up?"

Briar glanced over my head.

"Oh." I remembered my friends, who weren't even trying to hide their interest in this exchange. "You mean talk privately."

"If that's okay."

I just blinked at him.

Briar waited several awkward beats before saying, "So—?"

Zahra elbowed me. "Go on, girl," she whispered in my ear. "*What* are you waiting for? Go talk to the pretty man."

Gulping, I rose from my chair.

Briar led me to a secluded section of the cafeteria—an additional seating room yet to be used that day. The solitude unnerved me as much as the full weight of his gaze. I turtled my hands into my sleeves, knowing I'd fidget.

"So, when's your last class today, so we can get on the road?" Briar asked.

I blinked, wondering if this was code for something. "Huh?"

"When will you be ready to leave today?" He blinked back when I didn't speak. "So I can drive you home?"

I wracked my brain for an answer, only coming up with, "I never asked you to drive me home."

"Your uncle did. He called and asked if I'd bring you home for the weekend—said you wanted to see your dad, since you were away all spring break and haven't been home for three weeks."

I bristled, my neck burning. "Sorry, Briar," I sniped as politely as my tightening mouth allowed. "I wasn't planning on going home until after finals. I'd love to see my dad, but I need time to study." *And to exist outside my family*, I thought, having told Uncle Neel this the last time he'd called to hound me. "Please tell my uncle to do his guilt-tripping on his own." I spun on my heels and started back to my friends.

A strong hand grabbed my arm. "Amy, wait."

I stopped, jarred. Briar Hawthorne had just touched me!

"I'm sorry." Briar patted his heart. "I didn't know. I assumed you *wanted* to go home when your uncle called and asked me to drive you. I didn't think he was manipulating you. I wouldn't have been cool with that."

I frowned, having been manipulated similarly too many times before to trust him. "Didn't you wonder why I didn't ask you, myself?"

Briar bit his lip, contemplating me.

"What?" I tried not to snap.

"I just thought—you know how shy you can be."

"You thought I was too shy to ask you for a ride home?" I asked, even as my mind rejoindered: *Probably would've been.* "That I needed my uncle to do it for me?" *Never would've stooped so low.* I would've taken the train before I did that. And I hated taking the train.

"Well, yeah. You've always been so timid." He shrugged, fittingly sheepish. "I always thought it was sort of cute."

Were my ears broken? I usually had impeccable hearing.

"Please don't take offense. I was obviously wrong."

I digested his apology, relaxing. "Not completely," I admitted. "I know I'm not the most outgoing person you'll ever meet."

Briar's smile softened his chiseled face.

"Sorry my uncle roped you into his scheme."

"It's a shame his scheme failed, though. I was looking forward to a two-hour car ride with you."

"Why?"

Briar laughed at the question. "You're fun to talk to, Amy. I mean, whenever you feel comfortable enough to speak."

Right then wasn't one of those times.

"Hey, so if you don't need a ride, then I don't have a reason to go home either. I know you want to study tomorrow—but are you free on Sunday?"

I stared at him like he was a spider monkey emerging from a vending machine. "I am, but the chapel still doesn't have a Danann service, Briar."

Sure, he'd attended circle week after week with his parents when we were children, but he'd never seemed the devout type. That he might've sought out another parish for weekends he remained on campus bemused me. "Did you find one in the area? I didn't think there—"

"No, Amy." Briar chuckled. "This isn't about circle. I'm trying to ask you out."

"*What*? Are you joking?"

His brow furrowed. "Why would I joke about that?"

"But—what about Laurel?"

Laurel Woodrush was another Danann we'd grown up with. One of the lucky few whose Danann features were blunted to the point of normalcy. She had thick, wheaten hair with a voluptuous figure. And she'd always made damn sure I remembered my flaws, nicknaming me Sasquatch as a child.

"Laurel and I have been broken up for months now," Briar answered. "We tried long distance. It didn't work."

"I'm sorry to hear that." I wasn't but thought I should say something.

"The stars just didn't align for us."

Dananns, as a people, were big believers in fate, while I thought my future a sum of my choices—like the romance heroines I'd glorified to my friends. I so wanted to emulate those fearless fictional women, but I couldn't quite muster the courage to transform my desires into reality.

Lucky for me, I didn't need to.

Briar's grin returned. "So—about that date—?"

Minutes later, I returned to my lunch table, triumphant.

My friends' eyes all shone, mirthful and curious. "What did the walking Harlequin cliché want to talk about?" Olivia asked.

"Not much." Smug as hell, I smashed a fry into my ketchup. "But I'm glad we're going shopping tomorrow. I need to find something to wear on a date."

THREE

"Don't get me wrong, I'm hardly a recluse," I said the next afternoon as Olivia and I perused the racks in Peregrine Patriot. "I've been on my fair share of dates."

The mall store was popping, but most congregated around the summer collections. We bargain shoppers had beelined straight to the clearance racks for last year's leftovers.

"Just not ones I *wanted* to go on."

Olivia scrutinized a maroon tee-shirt. "What does that mean?"

"It means they were all blind dates set up by my aunt—with guys only there to get in good with my uncle." That truth still tasted bitter. "They weren't really interested in me. Mostly, dates were a series of awkward encounters I couldn't wait to end, so I could go home and read."

She emitted a dry chuckle. "I'm guessing your aunt didn't consider your personal tastes in boys before she set you up."

"*Please.* The only thing she considered was their Danann heritage."

"You weren't into any of her prospects?"

"Meh." I made a face. "The only Danann boy I've ever had a thing for was Briar. So, not really."

"As much as you and Zahra talk about guys, it's hard to believe you limited yourself to just one of them."

"I didn't. The others were all Christians from school, though. Or members of the Bayview Boys."

Olivia snorted.

"Unsuitable for me."

"You never went after the ones *you* found suitable?"

I shrugged. "Wouldn't have mattered who *I* liked. Nobody wanted to date Sasquatch."

Olivia clicked her tongue. "Amy, you look nothing like Sasquatch."

As my friend, she was obliged to pretend I looked normal.

"Regardless, any guys I approached wouldn't have seen past my giantism."

Usually, Olivia sympathized with this plight. We often joked that we'd never find a husband who wouldn't feel inadequate whenever we crouched to kiss him. Yet right then she appeared doubtful.

"You've never actually asked anyone out?" she asked.

"Have you met me? I'm not the type to subject myself to the pain of guaranteed rejection."

"But you never gave anyone the chance to prove you wrong. How do you know you'd have been rejected? You never did the field research."

"Trust me." I recalled high school in a series of scornful looks, laughter behind my back, and chucked parking lot pebbles. "I knew."

"Well, Briar obviously likes what he sees."

I grimaced, wondering if the dude needed glasses.

"Ready to try on?" Olivia segued, disregarding a rack of jeans after surveying their prices.

"Ready."

Minutes later, Olivia asked, "What about this?" Her slatted dressing room door juddered open.

I threw on a linen shirt, then emerged from my own fitting room to opine on her khaki shorts, the third pair I'd judged since we'd started the fashion show. "I like them on you. Are they comfortable?"

A whimsical ringtone interrupted Olivia's answer. I turned toward my dressing room, where my MulBerry's screen radiated in my canvas purse.

"Go answer it." She waved me on. "I'll try on the other three pairs, then you can help me decide."

So, I scurried into my dressing room, grabbing my phone and accepting the call.

"Hey," I greeted my sister. "What's up, Vi?"

"Nothing, really," her bright voice answered, the faint thrum of pop music in the background. "What are you doing today?"

I smirked at myself in my changing room mirror, enjoying the way the linen shirt fluttered about my hips. "I'm studying—like I told Uncle Neel."

"Yeah? What's the subject? Dresses? Shoes, maybe?"

"I don't know what you're talking about."

"You know, Uncle Neel checks your bank statement to see what you spend your money on. And when."

"Then it's a good thing there's an ATM in the student union, isn't it?"

"Sneaky, Amy."

"This ain't my first rodeo."

"When are you coming home again, though?"

"After finals."

Viola was probably sick of being the only niece around for Aunt Aylie to harangue about—everything. Or everything she deemed unladylike behavior.

I took a seat beside my purse on the dressing room bench. "How's Dad doing?" I asked, my throat tightening.

"Not great. He's been almost too tired to get out of bed this week."

So, Daddy had lied when I'd called home the night before. He'd said he was doing great, that I needn't worry about him.

"He's still acting like he's feeling fine, but he barely ate last night, and he keeps losing his breath when he walks."

"Maybe I'll come home next weekend," I thought aloud, though that was the true time for hardcore studying. Finals were just around the bend, regardless of this weekend's slacking.

"Coming home early won't improve his condition, Amy. You might as well stay there until after finals like you planned. By then Aunt Aylie and Uncle Neel will be too busy prepping for Beltane to chew you out for being gone so long, anyway."

"Hopefully. You know how good Aunt Aylie is at multitasking."

Vi giggled. "Hey, do you want to talk to Dad? He's just watching the news."

"Sure, put him on."

It took Vi a minute to bound down our creaky staircase and reach the family room, where my father always lounged in his Lazy Boy, sipping coffee despite his doctor's orders that he drink water.

"Hi there, Amy," Daddy's friendly tenor greeted me after Vi gave him her phone. His voice was always higher pitched than one would assume by looking at him. Today, his consonants lolled. "How goes the studying?"

I grimaced, guilt gnawing at me. "It's going. How's the news?"

"Dismal as always." Daddy laughed like a chugging car. "The presidential race is heating up. Any thoughts on what you'd like to happen?"

Daddy often talked politics with me. We leaned the same way on many issues—generally opposing Uncle Neel.

Growing up, Daddy had played a game with me, charging me with solving real world political problems. At first, I'd think up the most ridiculous answer possible, just for fun. As I aged, though, I got so good at posing legitimate arguments that I almost joined the debate team in junior year. Aunt Aylie had put the kibosh on that, saying women in politics were no better than meddlesome bitches. Regardless, if I hadn't loved books so much, I might've majored in political science.

"I like Obama," I answered. "He's got a good head on his shoulders and a big heart. I think he wants to serve the public. I don't think he's just power hungry."

"Some say his big heart might spell disaster for the economy."

"Could it be any worse than it already is?"

"Yes, Amy, things could always get worse."

"If it comes down to saving money or helping sick people get the care they need, I'll choose the man with the big heart. Every time, Daddy."

"It's not always so cut and dry. You need a balance."

"But balance can be—insufficient. You try to make everyone happy but end up pleasing no one, doing no good. Sometimes to be effective, you should just pick the best side, knowing you'll anger people on the other."

I pictured Daddy grinning. "Well, my dear, if you're ever confronted with a policy decision that puts your head and your heart at odds, I hope you still find action so easy."

"Wouldn't be hard. In this fantasy where I'm leading the free world, I'll just make Jamie the Cricket an advisor." Nowadays, I saved the ridiculous answers for the end. "Carrie Bobbin can be VP."

"That would make—"

My phone fuzzed with digital snow, and the fitting rooms went black. The punch of teen rock from the store's speakers stopped. The attendants' chatter ceased. Even the caress of air against my skin stilled to inertia.

Intangible murk boxed in my limbs, jolting my pulse into a gallop. I inhaled a sharp, calming breath, reminding myself, *Darkness can't hurt you.* I clutched my phone, the void devouring its glow. The MulBerry illuminated nothing past its screen, which inconveniently read, *No Service.*

"Olivia!" Arms outstretched, I rose from the bench, bungling into walls and hanging clothing. "I can't find my doorknob!"

She didn't reply, but my dressing room door rattled.

I followed the noise until I touched a smooth metal knob. I turned it and opened the door. "Does your phone have a spotlight? My screen's pathetic." I reached for Olivia but grazed only inky oblivion. "Where'd you go?" I reached again, my hand meeting nothing. "Are you dodging me? Why are you being so quiet?"

My phone flew from my fingers, sailing along an obscure gully until it fell into a hand. I started, the glow sketching the face of a boy—or a raisin left out to bake in the sun too long. His blue-lit skin crimped around a leer, his eyes more like chasms. A snaggletooth protruded from his mouth as he snickered, impish as the small child he was.

Was he some sort of cosplaying pickpocket? Impressive, if he was. Nothing about him looked human.

"What the hell, dude?" I grabbed him, started at his unnatural boniness, then stumbled over my own snow boots when the kid wrenched back. I wound up flattening him to the floor, where we scrabbled for my phone.

"Knock it off," I growled. "This prank wasn't even funny when it started!" I gripped the boy harder than I meant to, fisting his rough shirt.

The thief reeled back, snarling, before something hard and edged stamped me like a bead of hot wax. My breast instantly throbbed, a bruise upwelling.

"Learn to fight harder, Amaranthine," the child rasped. "For all our sakes."

He knows my name?

"And warn the king—the portal's open—before something wicked steals through."

WTF has this kid been smoking?

Whatever it was, he and the light of my phone vanished, darkness swallowing me like a crumb. My throat constricted, my eyes seeking focus. All my joints locked for an eruption of something horrendous.

The track lights above flared, brilliant as stars. Life resumed, angsty music riffing away, inane chatter continuing. The scent of cotton meandered onward in a particulate ocean. The thief—and my MulBerry—were gone.

"Fuck!" I pounded the floor. Uncle Neel would kill me for losing my phone, even to a thief. MulBerrys were hella expensive.

"These look a bit snug," Olivia surprised me, "but they have a good stretch." My friend stepped from her dressing room in a new pair of khaki shorts. Unworried and unruffled, she arched a brow at me. "Why are you on the floor?"

I tossed up a hand. "Didn't you hear me being mugged?"

Her eyes rounded. "What?"

I pushed to my feet, scrubbing my wound. "When the power blinked! Some little shit in a monkey mask stole my phone! He kicked me like a freaking goat when I tried to get it back." I tugged down the collar of the linen shirt and grimaced at a cloven blemish on my pale skin.

"What am I supposed to be looking at?" Olivia asked, deadpan.

I blinked at her.

"There's nothing there, Amy. You're the only freckle-less ginger I've ever met."

I scurried into my dressing room, my reflection freezing me. My "bruise" shone like flawless alabaster, the purpling welt I'd spied just seconds before a phantom in the mirror, though quite visible when I peered down at myself again. My pain was sure as hell real too.

"And the power never went out." Olivia leaned in my fitting room doorway as I gawked. "Is your blood sugar low? We should stop at the food court next."

I shook my head. *General Tso's won't fix this.*

A whimsical trill chilled my soul. Slowly, I turned toward the bench where my purse sat. A glowing MulBerry sat in its front zipper pocket, mocking me.

FOUR

For a week in seventh grade, Briar Hawthorne, my burgeoning schoolgirl crush, had seemed to return interest in me. Inexplicably, the Crombee Bros. poster boy began meeting me in the hallway after Social Studies, where he'd take my armload of books, though he had his own, and walk me the whole way to the cafeteria on the other end of our large school. We'd always separated there, went off to eat with our respective peer groups—him the popular crowd, me the outcasts. But no matter their length, our friendly, leisurely strolls set my sappy heart aflutter.

I'd still been shy, fearful of saying something uncool and repelling him. But by the end of that week, his casual charm had relaxed me into feeling like we'd always been closer than sporadic family acquaintances. And I wondered if his eagerness to take those walks with me meant he craved even more than friendship, despite my homeliness.

That hope became heartbreak the following Monday. Excited to meet Briar again after my next class, I'd sauntered to my locker to change up my books and grab my lunch money. I'd just reached my destination when a gigantic body slammed me face first into it, so hard its grated vent sliced my cheek.

"Stay away from Briar, you worthless skank," said Todd Degarmo, the biggest, meanest boy in our grade. He'd often bullied my group of friends, but he'd never gotten physical with us before. To say I was startled by his sudden violence was an understatement. "He'll never like you, squatchy, so stop kidding yourself and leave him the hell alone."

Shoving off me, he'd swaggered away, snickering with his buddies.

Trembling in both terror and embarrassment, I'd opened my locker and hid behind the door, trying without success to stem my pouring tears. When I'd finally mustered the courage to grab my stuff and turn around, blood seeping down my stinging cheek, I found Laurel Woodrush and her three closest minions smirking at me. Laurel with sordid delight in her blue eyes.

Her perfect face had twisted as our gazes met. "Ew," she snarked to her friends. "It's even uglier when it cries."

Laughter heckled my retreat to the restroom, where I'd collapsed in a stall and broke down sobbing, shards of my heart in my tears. Why had I ever thought I could be something special to Briar Hawthorne? Or anyone of his caliber? Me, the redheaded freak of Colter K-8. I'd probably read too much into Briar's kindness, anyway. How stupid of me?

I'd *never* be that stupid again.

Humiliated as I was, I decided against telling anyone what had happened. Not my teachers, not my friends, not my family. Especially not Briar. I simply pulled myself back together and arrived late to Social Studies. I stayed after to apologize to my teacher—"missing" my meeting with Briar. I'd straight up evaded him the next day. And the day after that, he didn't wait. In fact, he never waited for me again.

He'd started dating Laurel in eighth grade, and though the flame I held for him had continued burning, I'd never again imagined we'd be anything other than distant acquaintances.

Yet now, there I was—preparing to go on a date with him, staring into my dorm room mirror at a pair of wide, up-slanted eyes embellished with mascara.

Depending on my mood, they could be any color of the rainbow—one of my lesser oddities—but gold always ringed my pupils. That late Sunday morning, my eyes were hazel flecked with amber, the color of a sunrise meeting Ireland's bluffs—how Daddy sometimes described them.

I added a second coat of balm to my lips, frowning at how my canines gleamed like fangs amongst my other teeth.

"Quit your fussing," Zahra chided from the archway of our vanity alcove. She sported her Sunday best—a pair of yoga pants and a punk band tee-shirt. "You look amazing. Lover boy's tongue will mop the floor when he sees you."

I grunted, examining my every facet in our mirror. Since I'd made up my face to the extreme, my outfit was casual—a lavender tank under a plain white cardigan with blue jeans. My copper hair hung loose to my waist, my bangs framing my forehead.

I looked okay. But what if Briar saw things differently? What if he thought I was trying too hard? Or not trying hard enough?

I'd never measure up to Laurel Woodrush.

"Are you sure I don't need more mascara?" I rubbed my chest. The bruise there was still purple—at least to my eyes—but my pain had faded.

"For heaven's sake," Zahra grumbled, yanking me from the sink. "Chill."

A knock shook our door; I jumped out of my skin.

Laughing, Zahra squeezed my forearm. "That's not chilling."

"No crap!"

She flitted me toward our main living area. "Put on your boots. I'll greet your gentleman caller."

Since our debate two days before, we'd been talking like historical romance characters. It wasn't getting old either.

I zoomed through our privacy curtain of nylon string to my wooden desk chair. My phony Buggs boots stood beside it.

The door opened. Zahra said something welcoming, to which a crisp male voice replied something equally schmoozy. And unintelligible. My heart pounded too hard to hear above it.

Get your shit together, Amy, I scolded myself, then sucked in a deep breath and shoved one foot in a boot.

As Zahra and my date small-talked, my eyes roamed our room. Zahra's side was minimalistic and mature—orderly and logical. She'd even made her bed, her monochromatic sheets and comforter tucked neatly around her mattress. Her only hint at abandon was in her series of colorful Rorschach Test posters. In contrast, I'd cluttered my side of the room in splashes of paperbacks, snow globes, Hinerz memorabilia, high fantasy artwork, and posters of the Bayview Boys.

It looked like a preteen lived there.

Cursing, I rammed on my second boot, then scurried to tidy my rumpled bed, where so many throw pillows amassed there was hardly room for me. I only had moments to toss my ruffled comforter over them, hoping Briar wouldn't notice the lumps.

"Here she is." Zahra led Briar through our curtain of strings. She beamed, swept her arm toward me. "All dolled up and ready to go."

I clenched my teeth in embarrassment, wanting to pinch her.

Briar's striking good looks were so out of place in my dorky, hodgepodge world. In a long-sleeved graphic tee and a pair of fitted jeans, he paused to take me in. I couldn't gauge his appraisal of me, but whatever it was, he smiled. So, I relaxed—a little—when he held out his hand. "Come on, Larkspur. Let's get some grub. I'm starving."

After lunch at Chili's, Briar took me bowling. Many scents hung in the air of Richland Lanes. Admiring the typical hokey décor, I took a deep whiff, my keen olfactory sense identifying what it could. The pungency of oil. The astringency of shoe disinfectant. The sweet tang of the pizza being eaten by the squealing troupe of children at a birthday party.

"Those kids are monopolizing most of the balls." Briar chuckled as he returned to our lane, opposite the party. "But I think I found two that'll work for us."

Tying my clown shoes, I watched as he set his findings on our rack. One ball was a swirly green and weighed 13 pounds. The other, a 7 pounder, was neon pink. I rose from my seat at the control panel, nearly sneering at the girly ball.

"I think your fingers will fit." Briar sat to remove his suede sneakers. "The holes aren't too small."

At least he got that right, I mused as I assessed my hold. My long fingers fit without sticking, but I doubted I'd get many strikes off a ball filled with cotton.

"Do you bowl much, Briar?" I examined his heavier ball. Were its holes too large for me?

He shrugged, tying his rental shoes. "Every once in a while. You?"

I bit back a smirk. "Same."

"I didn't know what you'd want to do today," he confessed, finished with his shoes. "There aren't any good movies out this week, and I didn't think you'd be psyched for a hockey game."

I wouldn't have minded hockey but shrugged.

"Mini-golf or bowling seemed like our best options, given the limitations."

I clicked my tongue, knowing he didn't mean the weather. "And those games are kinder to the chronically uncoordinated."

Briar grinned. "Just looking out for you, Larkspur. I remember how skittish you were in gym."

I *had* been skittish in gym class and had never joined a single sports team in high school. Because I'd known my potential teammates wouldn't welcome me—a beanstalk with the temperament of a mouse. Outside of school, however, I was an athlete. First in gymnastics, then in volleyball, but I was best at bowling.

I considered finding myself another ball but didn't want Briar thinking me ungrateful for his help. He was only trying to be sweet, after all. So, I'd just use Briar's ball on my second turns. At least I'd get spares if I couldn't get strikes.

"Holy shit," Briar said after my third spare in a row. His gaze narrowed as I glided back to my seat. "You only bowl every now and again, huh?"

I chuckled. "It's true."

Since the start of college, anyway.

"Am I being hustled?"

"By *me*? I'm too skittish and inept to hustle you."

His eyes flashed, his tongue rolling inside his mouth—an adorable tic of his. I'd always *loved* the way his jaw worked when he did it. Made me wonder how he kissed.

"I guess I misjudged you yet again." I held my breath when his hand touched mine. "You're not the clumsy girl I thought you were. You're actually very graceful. And pretty damn cute."

A heat wave surged through my face. "I think you're the only one to ever call me cute."

"Well, you are." Briar squeezed my knee. I fought the urge to squeal when his free arm snaked my shoulders, pressing me close. "More than that. Don't you look at yourself in the mirror every morning?"

"Nah, I keep that sucker covered up. It's not good to be startled first thing in the morning."

Briar licked his lips, smooth as hell. "I think I'd like to see you first thing in the morning."

I practically squawked, making Briar flinch, though he laughed. Upon calming, we just smiled at each other.

I fisted my hands in my lap, my heart thundering. *Kiss me*, I wanted to say. *Rock my fucking world!*

Mournfully unable to read my mind, Briar watched me like an abstract painting he could contemplate for hours. I craved action, however, wanting to grab his arched ears and smash my mouth into his. I couldn't, though. I just couldn't.

Right as Briar's eyelids lowered, and I thought he was about to make his move—

"What are you doing here, Hawthorne?" a jocular voice whooped.

Damnit!

Briar and I broke apart.

Three lanes to our right, four guys were prepping for a game. I recognized two from UPJ, though I didn't know their names. They were all well-toned, probably jocks like Briar, and wore similar outfits—jeans and graphic tee shirts.

"Hey, Carson," Briar greeted the one who strode toward us, his hand outstretched. Briar caught it in a clasping dap. "How's it going?"

"Good," Carson answered. "Not much going on today. Thought we'd knock some shit around."

"Same." Briar's hand regained my knee.

Carson's gaze passed over me. Judging me.

"This is my date, Amy," Briar introduced me. "Amy, this is my frat brother, Carson."

Carson extended his hand. "Nice to meet you."

I grimaced politely, shook his hand. "You too."

Carson kept our handshake going for much longer than necessary, his amiable smile hardly masking his scrutiny. I withdrew, trying not to care what he thought of me.

Seeming to come back to himself, Carson expelled a breath. "Enjoy your date. I can't promise we won't heckle you, though." He gestured toward our scoreboard. "Looks like you're coming from behind, dude."

Briar chuckled. "That's how I like it."

Carson having returned to his lane, I faced Briar. "I didn't know you were in a fraternity."

"I pledged last spring. I don't live in the house, but I go to the parties."

"Are you one of those rowdy drunks I pass when I'm walking home from the library on Saturday night?" I was semi-teasing. Truthfully, wading through drunkards at the party zone harrowed me. At least sober people attempted to mask their morbid fascination at my strangeness. Drunks lacked the same manners.

Briar's brows met. "What the hell are you doing at the library on Saturday nights?"

I shrugged. "Reading."

"Can't you do that in your dorm?"

"Yeah, but I like the peace and quiet, and I love the smell of books." I didn't mention that I had my own reading nook reserved in the library. The head librarian knew me by name and let me keep pens and notebooks there.

"I like reading too. But not on Saturday nights. Saturdays are for debauchery and indulgence, Amy."

Clearly, we had different literary tastes if he wasn't finding those things in his books.

"You know, this year we're both old enough to attend the Beltane festival," Briar reminded me. "I'm looking forward to seeing you drunk and uninhibited."

I wrung my hands. "I'm not getting drunk."

"Oh, yes you are. It's part of the rite of passage. All youngbloods must drink from the Beltane cauldron, and whatever's in that thing gets you smashed in a heartbeat. Everyone else drinks from it, but not nearly as much as us. My cousin broke the rules and told me a bit about last year's festival. He said shit got wild."

I cringed, remembering Uncle Neel's green face when he and Aunt Aylie had returned home the afternoon after last year's Beltane celebration. Because of my father's deteriorating condition, they wouldn't spend more than one night away for the festival. Disheveled and dirt-smudged, grass in their hair, they'd trudged into the house and right up to bed without speaking to any of us. Concerned, we'd questioned my father about it. He'd told us to keep quiet the rest of the day. If the Beltane brew was potent enough to bring the devil out of my conservative relatives, I feared what it would do to me. And I knew Uncle Neel would drag me to the festival by my hair if I refused to go.

Maybe sensing my anxiety, Briar squeezed my knee again. "I'll take a wild stab in the dark, Larkspur—you've never gotten drunk before."

I scoffed. "Nope." But I'd never really wanted to.

"Don't worry." Briar rose with a wink to resume our game. "I'll be there to guide you through it."

Funnily enough, that wasn't soothing.

"Thank you for the date, Briar. I had fun." We stood together by my desk, the sun setting beyond my double windows. Zahra had gone to dinner, and I wished she'd waited for me.

Briar glanced away from my laptop's screen saver—a slideshow of pictures I'd taken on spring break. "I had fun too. We should do it again. Soon."

My heart soared. "Yeah, I'd like that."

"After finals, of course."

"Of course." Demanding to see him tomorrow would come off clingy.

"Guess I should leave you to study."

My breath shook as he stepped toward me. "Homework is—" I gulped. "Waiting."

Briar smiled at my nonsense, then cupped the back of my head, leaned in, and kissed me. Soft and gentle, his lips caressed mine. There was no tongue. No heat or passion. Just sweetness. And shortness. I knew I looked downright dazzled when he pulled back. A grin spread across his face.

"I'll give you a call." His thumb stroked my cheek. "I think I have your number."

I giggled. Before we'd left the bowling alley, Briar had insisted I save my cell number in his contacts.

"I better get yours too," I said, remembering my glitchy phone. "Something weird happened to my MulBerry, and now all my contacts are misidentified. Last night, I tried calling home and wound up calling my bank."

"That's weird."

"It was." I grabbed a notepad and pen off my desk and handed it to him. "We were at the mall yesterday—"

Briar paused, smirking over the notepad. "I thought you were studying yesterday."

"Er—well, we needed a break."

"A *mall* break?"

I shrugged.

He chuckled, jotting.

"My friend and I were in the dressing room when the power went out. Some weird little ten-year-old took advantage, came out of nowhere, and tried to steal my MulBerry."

Briar arched a disbelieving brow.

"He did, though, and I wrestled him for it."

"In the dark?"

"The brat kicked me like a donkey, said some weird-ass shit, and ran away." I rubbed the fading wound on my chest. "At least, I thought he did. When the lights came back on, the phone was in my purse. Guess he thought better of stealing it."

"And now your contacts are scrambled," Briar said, more commenting than questioning. "What did this kid look like?"

"Freaky. I think he was wearing a Halloween costume—a monkey mask with a fur suit under his clothes."

"In April?"

"I'm sure he had his reasons."

"Hmph." Briar's tongue rolled inside his mouth.

"It was just a stupid practical joke."

Briar grimaced. "I'm sure that's exactly what it was."

He handed me back my pen and notepad, his phone number inscribing its top page. "Well, I'll call—" His farewell died on his lips, his eyes fixed on something behind me.

I glanced back at my screen saver slideshow, now the photo Grace had snapped of me at Angel Oak. Lovely, but with one glaring flaw—a rainbow of light leaks loomed around my smiling face, making it look like the trunk's largest hollow had cracked open, sunlight slivering through from its other side.

"Where was that taken?" Briar demanded.

"At a park in South Carolina." Why had his whole body stiffened? "I traveled south over spring break for History Club. That tree is rumored to be 500 years old."

"It's much older than that, Amy," he returned, harkening Aunt Aylie during a lecture. "How did you miss all the signs warning you not to touch the tree?"

He was chastening me? For such a benign transgression? Fraternity hazing usually consisted of much harsher mischief. "I barely put any weight on the branch. I just wanted to touch something that old."

Briar groaned, massaging his forehead.

Why the hell was he so stressed? "You've been there before?"

"Has any other bizarre phenomena happened since then?"

"No, just the phone thief."

His gaze hardened. "Are you sure?"

"Yes." I withdrew. "What's the big freaking deal?"

"Don't you pay attention to any of your uncle's sermons, Amy?"

I scoffed. "Spare me the righteous indignation, Briar. I've watched you sleep through plenty—"

"I'm not judging your piety. There are just things we need to remember about trees that old. They're energy hubs. Getting too close to one is like inviting trouble into your life. Bad luck."

Why was he ruining such a perfect date with bullshit Danann superstition? I'd thought that, like me, the frat-brother party boy saw our Pagan religion as more a mythology—as moral allegories not for literal interpretation. Sure, he believed in Danu, the power of communing, and maintained a healthy interest in our religion. But did he believe all our tenets and customs must be followed to the letter? Wouldn't have thought so.

"Nothing abnormal happened while we were there," I snapped. "Just some static electricity. So, what do you want from me? I'm sorry I touched the damn tree."

Briar exhaled, tempering to my mood. "I only want you to be careful." He rubbed the tension from my arm, his touch apology enough. "I know it's mostly irrational, but I was raised to fear places like that. I panicked. Forgive me for worrying about you."

"That's—I mean—you were worried about me?"

"I've always liked you, Amy. I've always tried to look out for you."

When?

Briar squeezed my arm again. "Just watch your back for me. Okay?"

I should've asked what I'd be watching for but simply promised him I would.

FIVE

"Look who it is, Neel! The prodigal niece has returned!"

I tried not to sneer at Aunt Aylie, bungling into the foyer of my family brownstone, maneuvering two suitcases past the mahogany, glass-inlaid door. A duffel bag hung from my neck, the bulkiest necklace ever devised.

Aunt Aylie stood on our creaky staircase, one hand on the banister, the other holding a basket of laundry against her wide hip. Her stern, angular face stared down at me, her toffee hair cascading over her seersucker button up.

Uncle Neel emerged from an archway on my right, a glass of iced tea in hand. He wore a plain gray polo on his barrel-chested frame, pleated slacks hugging his lean legs. His short brown hair parted to the right, he leveled me with a displeasured scowl.

I towered over both my aunt and uncle, yet they still managed to make me feel small.

"Hello, Amy." Uncle Neel clinked his spoon against his glass. "I see you remembered the way home."

It took effort not to roll my eyes. "Thank Briar for that," I said just as my road trip partner pushed into the house with two banker's boxes leaden with books. "He drove me." In fact, Briar had rented a small trailer, so we could cart our lives home after finals.

Briar dropped the boxes on the hardwood floor with a thump. The heat outside had flushed his neck, spring having finally prevailed. I was also spritzing in my new denim capris and Old Navy boatneck.

Shoving the sleeves of his black tee up his forearms, Briar teased, "Who knew books could make you work up such a sweat?"

I laughed, freeing myself of the duffel bag.

Uncle Neel cleared his throat. "Thanks for driving Amy home, Briar."

"Weeks later than requested," Aunt Aylie reminded us, her mouth shoelace thin as she clomped down the stairs in her Crocs. She must've been working in the garden earlier; dirt smudged the apple of her slanted cheek. I hoped she hadn't pruned the roses already—my favorite spring garden chore to tackle.

Appropriately wretched, Briar bowed to her. "I'm sorry for that, *beyn an ciorcal*. Fate worked against us."

Aunt Aylie's blue gaze narrowed at me. "I suspect it had less to do with fate and more with someone's disordered priorities."

I gritted my teeth on a scream. I expected her criticism—but not in front of Briar.

A warm hand brushed my back, dispelling my umbrage.

When I didn't spew an impertinent diatribe as she'd expected, Aunt Aylie flipped her hair over her shoulder. "Well, go see your father. He's in the garden." She swept past my uncle, her voice carrying as she ordered, "Neel, put down the tea and help Briar bring in the rest of Amy's things. I'm sure his parents are eager to see him too."

Muttering under his breath, Uncle Neel returned to the dining room to set down his drink.

"Thanks for the ride," I whispered to Briar. "Sorry about them."

"It's fine. Believe me, I know what they're like."

I smiled at him—my confidant. For once, a boy wasn't there just to impress Uncle Neel. Briar was there for *me*.

"All right." Uncle Neel stormed back into the foyer. "Let's take care of this quickly. I've a sermon to finish."

After Uncle Neel stomped out the front door, Briar hooked my waist and kissed me, soft and brief. I goggled when he withdrew. "See you tomorrow?" he breathed beside my ear.

A chill skied down the slope of my neck.

Winking, Briar followed in my uncle's footsteps.

Happy to leave my belongings where they were after loading them in Briar's trailer that morning, I forged into the pastel florals, mauve voile, and impressionistic paintings decorating our family room. Mismatching woven rugs covered the hardwood floor of the cluttered, cozy room.

Our two cats—Fianna, an orange tabby, and Kell, an enormous Maine coon—were both sprawled on the rug closest to the double French garden doors, completely indifferent to my arrival. I greeted them by scratching their chins, then stepped over their fuzzy bodies.

A tall wooden fence enclosed our garden, where every square inch of ground served a specific purpose. We'd devoted most of the yard to raised herb and vegetable beds, but there were also fruit trees, berry bushes, creeping vines, my rose bushes, and two flowering dogwoods. In the right-hand corner sat a large, sided doghouse where our giant blonde mutt, Novus, napped in a bed of buttercups.

He'd been around since we'd moved to Pittsburgh when I was little, but his curly coat hadn't whitened with age. Novus was my favorite pet, although his heart and soul clearly belonged to my dad.

Draped in a plaid blanket, Daddy lounged in a distressed Adirondack chair by our fire ring, his dark-circled eyes closed upon a sunbeam. His skin, once as creamy as milk, now hung loose from his crescent moon profile, gray and jowly. Even the arches of his Danann ears lacked the mettle to stand.

I froze at the sight of him. Had it only been a little over a month since I'd last seen him? How could he have become so weakened and enervated?

I had trouble remembering when my father was the stalwart athlete Uncle Neel told stories about. Whatever illness he'd contracted when I was a preschooler had been slowly eating at his strength for years, but his vibrant spirit had always transcended his frailty. Now, however, he reminded me of a guttering flame.

Daddy's brittle voice squeezed through cracked lips. "Don't just stand there." His nostrils flared, taking in my scent, his sense of smell acute, though his body was failing him. "Come and sit with me, Amy. I've been waiting to see you."

Battening down fears that could rock my soul, I sauntered to the chair beside his. *He'll rebound*, I soothed myself. *Uncle Neel's specialist will find a new treatment. It'll work.*

Daddy's gaze glimmered at me like moonlit oceans. "Ah, I've missed that face—and those lovely eyes—amber today, like your mother's."

I clasped his skeletal hand where it rested on the arm of his chair. Silver hairs dusted his knuckles. "What are you reading?" I gestured toward the open book sitting in his lap. A pile of other cloth-bound books sat on the ground beside him.

Daddy dog-eared his page, showed me the cover. "The Social Contract—Jean-Jacques Rousseau."

Admiring the cover's gilded font, I took the book from him. "What's it about?"

"Oh, Rousseau had this idyllic notion that no monarch is divinely entitled to create and enforce laws on his—or her—people. That only the people themselves can do that."

I chuckled. "What a novel idea."

Daddy grinned as I thumbed through the pages. "It's a fantastic idea. Especially in this—country. Of course, it's not a universal fit."

"Where wouldn't it fit?" Nowhere would've been my answer.

Daddy shrugged. "Anywhere that the public has been deceived, or immorality has too much influence. When those immoral few start using the masses as a tool for their own selfish gains, fearmongering them into believing what's best for them is bad for them—and vice versa. When the tide of public opinion becomes detrimental to the common good, that's when a strong, well-meaning sovereign is necessary. Corruption can poison even the strongest government, Amy. We should never forget that."

"I thought democracy was meant to weed out corruption."

"It's meant to." Daddy grimaced. "That doesn't mean it always will."

"*That's* depressing." I closed the book, blowing bangs from my eyes.

His chuckle sounded too dry, too harsh. "It's logical."

Preferring my idealism to logic, I handed him back his book.

Daddy shook his head, tousling his silver hair, once as black as a raven's wing, against his seat back. "Keep it. I want you to read it." He motioned to the pile on the ground. "I want you to read all of these, actually."

"*All* of them?"

"Yes."

Shaking my head, I hefted several of the tomes onto my lap, reading off their illustrious authors, "John Locke. Machiavelli. Karl Marx? Voltaire. *Plato*?" I gaped at him. "I thought I was done with school this year."

He waved dismissively. "Some light summer reading."

"There are 20 books here!"

Daddy's expression slanted, accentuating his gaunt cheeks. "You'd have no trouble reading twenty of your beloved romances."

I soured. "It's easier to comprehend a simple love story than complicated political philosophy."

"Don't you disparage my daughter's intelligence. She's capable of comprehending anything—if she wants to."

"But I don't want to. You want me to."

"I promise it won't occupy too much of your time with Briar."

I stilled, no doubt blushing. "How do you know about Briar?"

"Your sister isn't exactly Fort Knox when it comes to gossip, Amy."

I bit back a curse.

"I think the whole neighborhood knows about you and Briar."

That meant Laurel Woodrush knew about me and Briar. I gulped, figuring spirit circle would be tense on Sunday. Perhaps Laurel's semester hadn't ended yet.

"Do you like him?"

I bit my lip. "He's—nice."

Daddy's brows, bushy as our hydrangeas, rose in amusement. "Just nice?"

"Yes." I rolled my eyes. "Just nice."

He studied me, making me squirm. "He's not the one."

I gasped. "What makes you say that?"

"Because he's not." Daddy shrugged. "I can tell these things."

"From looking at me? Daddy, that's crazy."

"It's not. You're my daughter. I know you. And I know love. There's a certain spark missing from your eyes. Briar Hawthorne's not your match."

"But why not? He's kind, smart, and very likable. He's studying to become an engineer, so he's bound to be successful. And he's Danann! I thought you'd be over the moon that I'm even interested in him. I know Aunt Aylie and Uncle Neel are."

"But you don't love him."

"Of course not! We've only been on two dates. One of which took place in a car on the way here."

"You've known him since you were four. I'd think love would've set in by now."

"We've been acquainted since I was four. That doesn't mean we know each other as people. We're just starting on that." I eyed him. "Is *this* you being an overprotective father? You decide to start being critical of my dates when I finally find one I'm attracted to?"

"Ah, attraction!" Daddy wiggled. "The heart of the matter."

I hid my face.

"Attraction is important, daughter, but there must be something more." He nudged my hand from my face. I met his dry gaze with one of my own. "Of course, there's no harm in testing the waters. If you have a taste for him, then—"

"Oh, please stop right there!" I exclaimed, making him laugh so hard he coughed.

"I like Briar, Daddy," I stated after he'd stopped hacking, mirthful tears in the corners of his eyes. "And that's where we'll leave this conversation."

"Fine, fine. But allow me to say one last thing."

I exhaled. "Yes?"

Daddy's bony fingers grasped my hand. "I want you to end up with someone *you* love. Not someone you think your aunt and uncle will love. Not someone you think I'll love. He—or she—"

I snorted.

"You never know."

"*Daddy*—"

"He should be someone you can't live without. Someone you'd trust with your soul. Be he Danann or not."

"Yes, yes, yes." I waved a hand.

He'd told me all this *many* times before. Usually right after one of Aunt Aylie's rants about the importance of maintaining a pure Danann bloodline. Once, after she'd grounded me for suggesting this encouraged inbreeding, Daddy had added that my future husband should love me so much that he was willing to put up with all the shit Aunt Aylie and Uncle Neel would give him.

"I just want you to be with someone who makes *you* happy, Amy."

I squeezed his fingers. "Don't worry, Daddy. Remember, I always think with my heart."

"**Y**ou brought that rodent?" I whispered to my sister as we knelt in the grass on Avalon Green, a private park amid the mountains outside Pittsburgh—our local place of worship. The grass was cool and damp against my bare knees, the sun warming my head. Clean, brisk morning dew perfumed the air I breathed. Uncle Neel's voice droned from the center of the large ring of solemn Dananns, Aunt Aylie drumming rhythmically beside him.

Viola petted the twitching head of her new guinea pig, Sugar. "Dad thinks she might be pregnant, so she needs exalted."

Uncle Neel always set aside time in his service to bless expectant mothers, allowing the All Mother to bestow gifts on the unborn—a sweet idea but merely ceremonial, in my opinion. I'd met many "gifted" people whose mothers weren't exalted.

Sometimes we included animals in this ritual—horses, cows, sheep, goats, dogs, and even cats. But never a guinea pig—a cuter, noisier rat.

Vi cooed at her shivering pet, her straight light-brown hair fluttering in the breeze. Her slanted gray eyes twinkled. Vi was much shorter than me with a more delicate frame, adorned that morning in a blue cotton dress and a knitted cardigan. A diamond sparkled in the crease of her broad, round nose. When she'd gotten the piercing, Aunt Aylie had had a conniption.

She might've ripped the stud right out of Vi's face had Daddy not proclaimed she could keep it.

"You're ridiculous," I muttered to Vi, who smooched Sugar like a baby.

She shrugged. "You're just jealous because you don't have something so sweet to cuddle."

Briar sprung to mind.

He knelt across the circle with his parents in a blue oxford shirt and a pair of khaki shorts. His glowing eyes lifted to meet mine, his lips curling upward.

My stomach fluttered. What would he do when we reached the communal prayer, a custom of meditative bonding? Who one chose to commune with was significant. It meant a special relationship had formed—or was being formed.

But I shouldn't get my hopes up. Briar and I weren't committed, not even close, and suggesting we commune together might weird him out. Besides, the beseeching glances Laurel Woodrush kept shooting Briar from further down his quarter of the circle suggested he already had a bond to meditate over.

Beside me, my brother, Ace, gripped his stomach. At sixteen, he was just an inch shorter than me with thick reddish-brown hair and matching stubble. He had my dad's crescent moon profile but with my pointed nose. Vi joked that the girls at school ogled him like the movie star, John West. Watching him suffer through his decision to binge on Taco King the night before, I questioned his appeal.

"Will you make it through the service?" I whispered to him.

Ace muffled another belch, clenching fists. "I think so." His mouth hitched at one corner. "Although, when we get home, I'm for sure heading straight to the bathroom to fornicate."

I blinked at him. "Please don't."

Daddy hacked with laughter on Ace's other side, rattling his lawn chair. Clearing his throat, he flexed his fingers upon the hook of his varnished cane. "I think you mean defecate, Ace."

"Yes," I agreed. "That sounds more appropriate."

Ace shrugged. "Uncle Neel said I should work on my vocabulary."

Daddy rapped him on the back. "Valiant effort, my boy."

"You might want to brush up on your definitions, though," I suggested. "Just saying."

Ace chuckled, drawing a censorious glower from Uncle Neel, who continued his slow, measured chant to the cadence of Aunt Aylie's drumming. My brother sobered, clutching his gut again.

Minutes later, Uncle Neel moved onto the exaltation. There were two expectant mothers at circle that day. Poppy Polkweed was 25 and had married her high school sweetheart two years ago. She beamed with joy as Uncle Neel drew the symbol of the goddess—a triskelion—on her bulging belly. Myrtle Speedwell, on the flip side, was merely 15 and happily oblivious as to who the father of her baby was. It could've been any one of the four studs there to celebrate her that morning. Haughty as Uncle Neel blessed her, she cast smug gazes on the many other girls with woefully empty wombs.

I snorted when her conceit found me. Good for her if she was ready to be a mother at 15, but my only goal right then was to find a summer job, so I could buy a car with my own money. Motherhood wasn't even on my radar.

Once Uncle Neel had finished exalting all the pregnant bellies—including Sugar's (which he did with a grumble amid laughter)—he raised his arms, robed in rough-spun hemp, and addressed us worshippers. "As our sacred ceremony comes to a close on this holy spring day, let us join with those dearest to us in a communal prayer." Uncle Neel knelt before his round stone altar and took Aunt Aylie's hands. Their foreheads touched.

Friendly murmurs sounded throughout the circle as people joined with those they cherished. I switched off who I communed with every time I attended circle. Last time, I'd communed with my father. This time, my sister automatically crawled toward me, setting Sugar beside her in the grass, where the guinea pig devoured a blade of fescue. Maybe she *was* pregnant, as Daddy suspected.

A shadow darkened the earth around me. My sister and I gaped up at a breathtaking boy with gelled auburn hair and a kind smile.

"May I?" Briar asked my sister, gesturing to me.

Vi's brows rose, her lips spreading. She scooped up Sugar and scuttled to my father and brother.

I stared like an idiot when Briar knelt before me on his grass-stained knees, offering his hands. "Amy?" he asked, his hopes laid bare.

Shaking myself, I entwined our fingers. My heart stuttered, and my breath shook as our foreheads met over our hands. I closed my eyes tight to focus on him.

Communing with someone new was like trying to find a radio station. You needed to twist the knob several times before finding the one you desired. But once you found that station, things came through crystal clear.

When Briar found my frequency, I sensed his satisfaction.

The first sensation he sent along was gentle, welcoming, and warm. Friendship. Which put me at ease, made me forget the surreality of our pairing. And once that happened, I sank into his wavelength—so kind, bright, and masculine—without a hitch.

And, man oh man, communing with Briar Hawthorne was nothing like communing with family, no matter their moods. Because before that prayer was over, he had me blushing like a fresh picked rose in full bloom.

My eyes darted from one word to the next. My heart pounded. My breathing accelerated. I reclined in my bed, reading a love scene in the latest novel I'd bought, *Sea Temptress*. As the temptress had her way with her pirate captor, my fingers alleviated what Briar had stirred up in me while communing.

"Did you see Laurel Woodrush glaring at you after circle?" Vi barged into my room without knocking, banging my bedroom door into my scarf strung mirror.

I screamed and yanked my peach sundress back down my thighs, scrambling to sit up.

"What are you *doing*?" Vi squealed, shielding her eyes.

I threw my book at her. "Never mind what I'm doing! Why didn't you knock?"

"I never knock!" She cackled, skirting my book, then a volley of throw pillows. Having spent many of her childhood nights sleeping in my bed with me, too scared to sleep on her own (she was prone to random seizures until age nine), Vi now denied me all privacy. "Next time, lock your door!"

"What's going on?" My brother peeked his head around my doorframe.

I eyed Viola. "Nothing."

She tossed a pillow back at me, keeping quiet.

"Ooo-kay." Indifferent to the ruckus he'd interrupted, Ace swaggered into the room and over to the canvas armchair beside my bookshelf, now bursting with the books I'd collected over the school year. "What's the deal with Briar?" He fell into the chair, hiking one of his long legs over a padded armrest. He had yet to wash the grass stains from circle off his knees, but he seemed in no hurry as he grabbed another of my books off the end table beside him. "You two took everyone by surprise."

Took myself by surprise, too, I thought, squeezing my legs together.

"Everyone was talking about it after circle," Vi informed me, toying with the floral curtains ornamenting my tufted window seat, where I'd set the small library my father insisted I read. "And Laurel looked like she wanted you dead."

Having caught a glimpse of Laurel's sapphire rage before I'd helped Daddy to our car, I gulped.

"Aunt Aylie's on cloud nine," Ace said. "I think she's already booked Uncle Neel for a fall wedding."

"*Please*," I said. "Briar and I have been on two dates and communed together once. We're not even officially together."

Ace sneered at the lovers on the book cover he held. "Looked pretty official to me."

"Well, I'm only 20 and in college. A wedding's not happening."

"You might want to tell Briar." Vi grabbed a purse off a hook on my dark plum wall. She draped it over her shoulder, then sauntered back across my striped woven rug to slam my door and admire her appearance in my standing mirror. "He and Uncle Neel were talking after circle. I couldn't hear what they said, but I saw Uncle Neel hand something to Briar. It was in a tiny box, whatever it was."

"Briar does *not* want to marry me." I had better chances of winning a Grammy. "He's a frat boy who's having far too much fun being young and irresponsible to settle down."

"Then what did Uncle Neel give him?" Vi challenged.

"How should I know? It could've been anything. Why would you assume it was a ring?"

"Looked like a ring." She shrugged, admiring her image.

My blood still singing the song of seduction, I glanced down at the paperback by her feet. *What's happening with the pirate captor's throbbing member?* I wondered. "Don't you guys have homework to do?"

Vi's eyes glittered. "Mine's all done."

I cursed her, then turned to Ace, who now played with the red yarn hair on the head of my favorite childhood belonging—my Raggedy Andy, my favorite character from my favorite movie.

Ace's mouth twisted. "Come on," he grumbled like I'd badgered him for hours. "I'll get it done. Doesn't have to be now."

Vi hummed, twirling over to rehang my purse. "He has a big physics test tomorrow."

Ace tossed up a hand, glaring at her.

I eyed him. "What's your current physics grade?"

He harrumphed, "D."

"What?" I pointed at the door. "Acer Larkspur, get your ass to studying!"

Ace glowered. "Relax, *Mom*. I'll pass."

His remark didn't cut the way he'd intended. We all knew I was more of a mother to my siblings than Aunt Aylie was. She lacked the nurturing gene.

I chucked another pillow. "You'll pass because you're going to study."

"Later." He caught the pillow, wedging it between his elbow and the chair. "First, tell me what's going on."

"What do you mean?"

"That answers that." Vi cast our brother an I-told-you-so glance.

"You haven't heard anything about the meetings?" Ace continued. "I thought Dad might've filled you in. He always tells you more than us."

I shook my head. "What meetings?"

"A group of five men has been coming to the house after midnight for the past few weeks," Ace said. "Dad and Uncle Neel lock themselves in the dining room with them for hours."

No wonder Daddy looked so haggard. "What men?"

"Two elders." Vi sat down at the foot of my bed, hugging my chenille bunny. "Clem Polkweed, Poppy's grandfather, and Arbutus Colwort."

"The rest are younger," Ace added. "Ash Loosestrife, Sy Rockrose, and Cole Hawthorne."

I jolted. "Briar's father?"

Ace nodded, picking at a maple syrup stain from breakfast on his polo. "I've tried eavesdropping," he confessed, knowing we'd never tell on him. "I can hear them—sometimes they're shouting—but I never understand what they're saying—like the words are jumbled."

"Or you just have terrible hearing," Vi teased. Ace had fine hearing, but he also had the smallest ears of us Larkspurs.

Ace sniffed, grinning. "Whatever."

"Why the hell would they gather here in the middle of the night to argue?" I asked. "Daddy doesn't even like Arbutus Colwort. He called him a crotchety nitpicker after the Yule feast."

"I asked Aunt Aylie if she knew what was happening." Vi's face puckered. "She said, 'Don't stick your nose in men's business, Nebby Nancy.'"

I snorted, her impression dead-on.

"Well, I'm a man," Ace griped. "But you don't see them inviting me into their meetings."

Vi and I shared a smirk but refrained from mentioning that the *man* before us still couldn't wash his own laundry.

"Is that why you want to know what they're discussing?" Vi guessed. "You feel left out of the boy's club?"

"Partly." His amber eyes clouded. "But I'm more concerned that they're talking about Dad."

My heart lurched. "Why would they be discussing him?"

Such gloom had no place in my little brother's mind. Yet, there it was, evoking flashes of a sad dream in mine. "You see how he is, Amy. He keeps getting worse. What if they're in there deciding what's going to happen after he—"

"*No*," I cut him off, gritting my teeth. "That isn't going to happen, Ace. Not for a long time. So, don't you speak those words and tempt fate."

"But what if they're making decisions about us? Without consulting us?"

My anger roiled at just the thought. "They wouldn't do that," I bit out.

They better not.

"Dad's in there with them every night," Vi reminded Ace. "He wouldn't *let* them do that."

Ace chewed his lip, wanting to believe her but doubting that he could. "I don't know. Just—something doesn't feel right."

My intuition agreed, but I put on a brave face. "I'm sure it's nothing major. They're probably just meeting about Beltane. Maybe their caterer fell through, and they're struggling to find a new one on short notice."

"That would explain the shouting," Vi said. "Can't put 70 drunk Dananns in a field with nothing to feed them. They might relapse to the old ways—human sacrifice."

We all laughed, our tension lifting.

That night, after my brother and sister had gone to sleep—in their own beds—I meandered around my room, housing my dorm belongings.

Fianna slinked along my surfaces as I reorganized, marking my new collectibles as her own. After she knocked over a set of standing picture frames, I lifted her Creamsicle body off my bookshelf. "Go find one of your hidey holes," I tutted, setting her in the hallway with a scratch behind her ear.

She'd made personal retreats out of numerous nooks and crannies throughout our old house. We didn't know what she used them for, but sometimes she was willfully lost for days.

Meowing, Fianna strutted off.

Frilly lamps lit my room as I padded across my rug. I wore a pair of Soffe shorts and a V-neck tee, quieting my mind with Rusher and other R&B artists. Humming, I clipped my iBloom Shimmy to my shirt and grabbed one of the posters out of the bin I'd used to transport my wall art home. Careful that the sticky tack on its back didn't deface the glossy image on the front, I unrolled it and pressed it to the wall beside my window seat. My vision blurred upon the Bayview Boys' smiling faces as I tugged them flat. Just as I affixed their bottom edge to the wall, something beyond my latticed window caught my eye.

Sucking in a breath, I peered around my jacquard curtain panel to find Danann men emerging from a group of cars parked along the curb of our Squirrel Hill street. I recognized Sy Rockrose and his long silver hair. Head bowed, he chatted with Ash Loosestrife, a stocky man who'd worked with my father at the bank before Daddy retired. They opened the iron gate barring them from our front yard.

Behind them walked the other gatherers on my siblings' list. Arbutus Colwort wore an aged bowler hat and a tweed coat, scowling in the fog. Clem Polkweed trudged across the lamplit pavers leading to our house, almost dozing as he went. He seemed the type to don his nightcap at sundown, so I figured he rarely saw midnight. After Clem came Cole Hawthorne, a handsome man with graying brown hair, the source of his son's appealing form and lime-green eyes.

Seeing Cole's progeny taking up the rear, I could've cartwheeled. Something in me tightened—something I hadn't quelled earlier. He looked *yummy*, dressed in a zip-up sweater and fitted jeans. Was he there to see me? Maybe he'd sneak away from the others, find me in my room, and—

I shivered at the detailed scenario playing out in my head.

Yet, Briar didn't glance toward my window, didn't sense my gaze upon him. Creases bracketed his mouth, his shoulders carrying some invisible weight as he walked into my house. He didn't come to find me. When he called the next day to ask for another date, he never mentioned being there the night before. He didn't say why he'd come.

SIX

Briar grinned above his ooey gooey sundae, the setting sun highlighting his hair scarlet. We sat hip-to-hip on a knotty log outside the local ice cream shop. "How's your gelato?"

"Good," I answered, downing another lemon lavender spoonful.

"I'm surprised you're not tired of lavender already," he remarked. "With how much you've planted these past mornings."

I shrugged. "Well, that's why I planted so much—because I like it."

Winking, Briar ate another fudgy spoonful.

We'd spent almost every waking moment together for the past week. Some nights, our dates went so late that I barely had time to catch up on *The Workplace* and grab a snack before Aunt Aylie banished me to my bedroom, another midnight meeting commencing.

Like Ace, being out of the loop drove me nuts. What were the men saying? Why did they quarrel? I wanted to ask Daddy, but I knew he would've already told me if he wanted me to know. I'd get more answers from a brick wall than I would Uncle Neel, so my only probable source of information was Briar.

He hadn't admitted anything about the meetings, even to suggest they existed. Yet, he was there every midnight without fail. Even when I didn't see him walking in with the other men, I'd spy his silver Ford Fusion parked outside my house. I wanted to demand he tell me everything but hadn't found the guts.

After Briar finished his ice cream, he set his Styrofoam bowl down on the macadam by his feet and leaned in close, wrapping an arm around me. His embrace was a brazier in the cooling breeze, though I couldn't relax.

Watching me eat, Briar asked, "What are you thinking?"

I cleared my throat, considering him. "About the last book I read," I lied.

"What about it?"

Licking my spoon, I digested a devious thought and acted on it before I second-guessed myself. "For most of the book, the heroine and her lover are fighting because she finds out he's keeping secrets from her. To protect her, he thinks. But her ignorance only endangers her, risks her life."

When I stopped babbling, Briar was chewing on his lip, his gaze razor-sharp.

I worried he thought I was passively rebuking him. Although, I totally was.

"My friend says he's not to blame since he's only trying to protect her, but I say that's no excuse. His heroine is a big girl. She can handle the truth, even if it's not something she wants to hear."

I watched his gears shift from wariness to charm. "Maybe the truth was just being held for safekeeping—to be revealed at the proper time."

Well played, I thought, picturing us on a relationship chess board.

"Did she forgive him?"

Wow, I'd already lost the upper hand.

"The heroine," Briar clarified. "Did she forgive her lover?"

Oh, you're good. "Wouldn't be a very worthwhile romance if she didn't."

His grin broadened, his eyes singing, *checkmate*.

"**Y**ou feel untouched?" Zahra giggled the next morning during our phone call.

I'd been trying to call Briar to firm up that afternoon's plans, but my glitchy cell had called Zahra instead. So, we chatted while I laid half-dressed in bed, petting Kell, who stretched, purring, beside me.

"How do you make out with someone and still feel untouched?" she asked.

"I don't know, but that's how I feel."

Briar hadn't admitted anything about the meetings, but when he'd brought me home after ice cream the night before, he hadn't gone home. He'd come up to my bedroom with me to hang out. For five minutes. Then we'd curled up on my bed and started kissing. Just before midnight, he'd pulled away, said he had to go. Two hours after he'd left, though, his car still sat outside my house.

"Has he at least slipped you the tongue?" Zahra asked.

"For the first time last night, but only a few flicks."

"Did you slip him yours back?"

"Uh-huh, but only in response."

Zahra clicked her tongue. "Next time, you do it first. See how he reacts."

"Okay," I said but knew I wouldn't be brave enough.

"Did he start rounding the bases?"

"His hands never strayed from my back or my face, but he was so sweet and gentle." I released a soft breath. "He treats me like fine china."

"And you're wondering why you feel untouched?"

I smirked. "Good point."

"Listen, if you want him to be more comfortable touching you, then you need to take the lead, Amy. Show him you're not a porcelain doll. You're not fragile, honey bunny."

My phone beeped in my ear. I glanced down at my screen to see I was receiving another phone call. From Briar.

My stomach aflutter, I held the phone to my ear. "Hey, Zahra, I'm getting a call from him now."

"Oh! Well, I'll talk to you later!"

I pushed the call accept button and Zahra dropped away. "Hey, there," I cooed into my phone, giving flirtation a try—we'd made out the night before, after all. "Care for another trip up to my room? You can dust my teacups."

"*What*? What does that mean?"

Gasping, I shot up to a sitting position. Kell meowed, irritated that I'd stopped petting. "Aunt Aylie! I thought someone else was calling—one of my friends."

"I know who you thought I was, Amy."

I cringed into my fist.

"Never mind that. Are you dressed?"

"Almost."

"Finish up. Your sister and I are heading back from the grocery store. Once we put the food away, we're going to your fitting."

"My—huh?"

"The fitting I've been talking about since you finally deigned to return home from school. For Beltane. You need a dress to wear to the festival."

I stared at my overstuffed closet. "Can't I just wear one I already have?"

"*No*! This will be your first Beltane. It's your coming of age, Amy. You'll need a special dress."

I exhaled. "But Briar—"

"He can make a trip up to your room some other time. We'll be home in fifteen minutes. Be ready to leave." Then she hung up.

An hour later, I stood on a pedestal in a downtown Pittsburgh shop called Pavonia's, pink and bashful beneath a swath of baby-blue silk.

"Whoa," Vi gasped when I'd emerged from the fitting room—against my better judgment. Lemur-faced, she'd shot up from her seat on a tufted chaise lounge.

Yep, it's as bad as I thought.

Now, Aunt Aylie and the store owner, Pavonia, beamed while I silently blasphemed at my reflection.

The "dress" was a negligee with a sweep train, hanging loose about my body, barely covering my breasts. Pearls were all that kept it from falling off my shoulders, their crisscrossing strings forming sleeves and embellishing my back in a scanty net. Its open back came to a deep V, the point of which met my tailbone and the dimples flanking my spine. I wished I could hug my arms around my back.

"You were right, Eulalia," Pavonia praised my aunt, squeezing her wrist. She was a lean, elegant Danann with delicate features and long black hair fashioned into a rigid chignon.

Her tight sheath dress revealed much less of her body than mine did. "This was the perfect shape for her."

"It's breathtaking," Aunt Aylie said, a satisfied customer.

I gaped at her. "You can't be serious. I can't walk out of the house in this!"

"You'll put it on when we get to the festival." Aunt Aylie tapped her glossy mouth, then remarked to Pavonia, "I think it'll need hemmed."

Nodding, Pavonia knelt to examine said hem.

"And what kind of underwear am I supposed to wear beneath this? You can see everything!" The bands of both my bra and panties were glaringly on display.

"Don't be silly." Pavonia folded the dress at my toes. "Darling, you don't wear anything beneath this dress."

"I'm supposed to be *naked*?"

Aunt Aylie exhaled, swatting a tuft of my copper hair off my shoulder. "If you're wearing a dress, you won't be naked."

"But—"

She quelled me with a look. "This is not up for discussion, Amaranthine. This is your Beltane dress. It's a far more modest dress than any other youngblood will wear."

Then I didn't want to see the other girls' dresses.

She set a hand on her wide-set hip. "You're twenty years old now, niece—high time you relinquished these childish insecurities. Embrace your body as it is."

This was an order, not an encouragement.

"You do look nice, Amy." Vi bit her thumbnail, looking me up and down. "Even though—"

"Even though everyone will be able to see *my ass*?"

Aunt Aylie smacked me, right on the ass of note.

"Hold still, please," Pavonia requested when I jumped.

"Ladies do not say *ass*," Aunt Aylie hissed, baring sharp teeth.

Fuming, I rubbed the welt on my posterior.

My aunt's snub nose twitched; she wagged her finger at me. "You'll wear this dress. You'll stop worrying about what everyone thinks of you. You'll eat, drink, and be merry like a proper Danann youngblood on Beltane. Is that clear?"

"Yes," I bit out, hands fisting.

Silent and glowering as my fitting progressed without my input, I saw my eyes in the mirror—blazing infernos.

"**W**hat's wrong, Amy?" Daddy asked, bundled beneath down-filled brocade and heavy knit wool, the slightest chill clinching his waning flesh. He contemplated me through dark hollows.

I sat in the padded rocking chair beside his bed, washed in dim lamplight. Novus snoozed soundly upon my feet, and *To Kill a Mockingbird* was cracked open on my lap. Daddy thought reading aloud a lost art and often solicited my mellow tones for bedtime stories. That night, however, my voice barbed Harper Lee's iconic words. Internalizing my dress fitting disaster had failed.

Exhaling, I glanced at my father. "Daddy, you should see the dress Aunt Aylie expects me to wear on Beltane."

"It's just a dress." His words scratched like rough wool through chapped lips.

"It's not really about the dress—if you can even call it that. It's about me not being allowed to pick it, about not being able to choose *anything* for myself."

Understanding though he looked, Daddy shook his head. "You've not lost all your battles, Amy. You won the most important one."

I gasped, about to argue.

"Are you not currently a student at the college of your choice?"

"Well—yes."

"Well—" He tossed up a hand.

"But you just said the key word, Daddy—battle. That's all I seem to do with Aunt Aylie and Uncle Neel. They've made my whole life a series of battles."

And I only win them when you step in.

I swallowed hard, willing myself to take in the rawness, the reality, of his pitiful state. Even with the window cracked and a fragrant candle burning on the dresser, the odor of sweet, putrid sickness wafted through his room. What would happen with my battles when my father's illness finally got the best of him? My protector and champion, the one person who, without doubt, loved me unconditionally.

I immediately routed the thought.

"Why can't they just accept that I can make my own decisions? That I don't want to live by their design." I slouched. "Why do they have to make everything so damn *hard*?"

"Who told you life was meant to be easy?" Daddy frowned. "There are millions the world over with lives much harder than yours. Be grateful for all you have."

"I am, Daddy." I pouted. More at myself than his scolding. Wardrobe debates were trivial compared to poverty, famine, and war. Shameful, that even in my enlightened, bleeding-heart liberalism, those concepts were still abstract in my middle class shelter.

"Okay, maybe I'm being ignorant, but my personal freedom is always under fire. I have no control over my own life!"

"Yes, you do. You just have to fight harder than most to maintain it."

This remark recalled the dressing room thief from weeks ago. *Learn to fight harder, Amaranthine*, he'd advised. *For all our sakes.*

Daddy's mouth tightened, his gaze growing pointed. "You're not a passive person, Amy. Don't act like one."

I finished another chapter before Daddy was halfway asleep. After making sure he was warm enough, I blew out his candle, switched off his bedside lamp, and padded out into the upstairs hallway, his condition foremost in my thoughts.

I pondered several family portraits decking the papered walls, my favorite always the one of Daddy and me swinging at a park when I was five. He'd already sickened by then; I could tell from his cane. Yet, he still looked virile, his shoulders broad, his hair dark and wavy. I cheesed hard at the camera, my copper hair a ridiculous mess about my dirty face. Daddy smiled down at me with such pride, such devotion—

Tears welled in my eyes. Who would look at me that way when he was gone?

Wiping my cheeks, I moved onto other photos. There were none of my mother. We'd never had any of her.

I'd just opened my bedroom door when an embittered rumpus broke me from my melancholy. I spun toward the shadowy staircase.

As Daddy was too weak that night to stay up past ten, I'd assumed that night's secret meeting canceled. But no! Uncle Neel and the others had locked themselves in the dining room, discussing important matters—whatever they were—without him!

Maybe Ace was wrong, and they weren't hashing out what would happen after Daddy's—I couldn't even think it. But if they were, then we Larkspur children would damn well have a say!

Gritting my teeth, I stomped down the stairs, too incensed for stealth. Not like the men could hear me, anyway, as obnoxious as they were being.

Ace was right about one thing. Though I had no problem hearing them, my ears better than most Dananns', actual words were indecipherable—a spoken cryptogram. Puzzling, I strode through the dark foyer to the dining room. I pressed my ear to its beveled door. Even that close, the gist of their argument eluded me. I clenched my eyes shut to concentrate, touching the panel.

A shattering tumbler heralded the pocket door banging open.

All the men, including Briar, jumped in their seats around the table, flummoxed by my intrusion. I gulped as all eyes darted to me.

His pajamas rumpled, his face lined and weary, Uncle Neel shot up from his dining chair and barreled toward me. "Amy, you should be in bed."

When he grabbed my elbow, I wrenched free, squared my jaw.

You're not a passive person, Amy. Don't act like one.

"I'm not going anywhere until someone tells me what's going on in here." I sounded as commanding as I could with my voice trembling and glared down at Uncle Neel.

My uncle's brown eyes flared at my insolence. His lips curled back on the promise of a tirade. I almost flinched in anticipation.

"How did she get in here?" Arbutus Colwort rumbled beneath his bowler hat, scowling across the table at Ash Loosestrife, who scrutinized me, interested. His curly black hair glinted blue beneath the chandelier light.

"Look," I choked out, my heart pounding. "Yinz have been meeting here at my house for weeks—"

"It's your father's house," Uncle Neel coldly reminded me.

My gaze narrowed. "Yes, and he's not here right now, is he?"

"I'm here for him," Uncle Neel answered, both his voice and his demeanor yielding.

"You don't need to know what we're discussing, child," Sy Rockrose dismissed me, almost sympathetic as he brushed his shiny, silver hair off his shoulder. "Go on, now."

Fury burned in my chest. "*I'm* a child?" I pointed at Briar, sitting before Aunt Aylie's massive oak hutch, where he met my gaze, pleading. "He's my age, and he's here!"

Briar opened his mouth to speak, but his father cut him to the chase.

"He's here because I made him come." Cole Hawthorne frowned. "That's all."

Briar's tongue rolled inside his mouth.

"Are you in here talking about my father?" I asked, my voice too thin. "Because if you are, then I deserve—"

"You don't make demands of us, girl!" Clem Polkweed blustered, his jowly face reddening.

Arbutus sputtered his agreement. "Cornelian, this is just what I've been arguing! Laurustinus has been too lenient with her! She's too unruly to—"

"You've been talking about *me*?" I reeled, nothing making sense.

Uncle Neel's hand clamped my arm. "Amy, go to your room. Now."

I held my ground when he tried to push me out. "Why are you talking about me?"

"See? This whole notion is preposterous!" Arbutus exclaimed.

"Shut up, all of you!" Briar roared, rising from his seat. The men fell silent as he pushed past his father, who'd risen to stop him. His eyes green steel, Briar grabbed me from Uncle Neel.

Huh? I thought. Because Uncle Neel backed off.

Briar glared at the others, warning, "Remember who you're talking to."

The others subsided, several resenting Briar's reminder.

Sorting through all the questions I needed to ask, I let Briar whisk me from the dining room.

"She shouldn't have been able to barge in like that," Arbutus grumbled under his breath. "Unless she has the—"

The pocket door shut behind us, its lock jamming into place.

Briar tugged me toward the stairs, but I dug my heels into Aunt Aylie's prized Persian rug. "Please just tell me why they were talking about me." I hated to beg, but I *had* to know. "Please."

Briar massaged his scrunching forehead.

"It's about my father, isn't it? They all think he's dying, don't they?" My soul shrunk in just saying the words. "They don't want me to know?"

My eyes teared, and Briar cursed. He took me by my arms, gentle as ever, and whispered, "The Danann elders have convened to discuss matters pertaining to your father. My father has been dragging me along, sworn me to secrecy. I wish I could say more, Amy, but I can't."

Not comforting, dude!

I choked back a sob. "So, they *do* think—?"

"It doesn't matter what anyone in there thinks. None of them went to medical school. From what I know, none of your father's actual doctors have told him to get his affairs in order."

That's more like it.

Breathing again, I collapsed into his body, needing solace.

He hugged me, rubbing my back in circles. "Sorry that I can't say more. I promise if any decisions like that need making, we'll consult you first." His lips skimmed my cheek. "I'll make sure."

Praising Danu for him, for how he had my back, I wiped my tears and squeezed him—a bit tighter than he was squeezing me. "Thank you."

It never occurred to me that Briar might be lying.

SEVEN

Dusk descending, I emerged from my Beltane festival tent. Roasting meat and lighter fluid perfumed the breeze, pigs rotated on spits, and pyres flamed in a wide circle on Avalon Green. The maypole stood at its center, wreathed in ivy glory, lustrous ribbons floating from its finial. Traditional Celtic music played, the beat of the bodhran pumping in my blood. Mantled in flora, a band performed on a festooned stage near where the gigantic Beltane cauldron hung, fire lapping at its cast iron belly. Inside, a cider potent enough to souse an army brewed.

Alcohol hadn't yet dulled people's awareness when I stepped into the fading sun. No matter what they were doing, or to whom they were speaking, every reveler paused to scrutinize me. As far as I saw, however, I should've faded into the background.

The other women wore dresses much scantier than mine, several half naked, their breasts almost completely exposed. Such immodesty made me downright conspicuous. My dress was the only one whose hem met the ground, the only one not transparent in firelight. I wrung my hands, my crown of pearls and tulips itching.

"Look at you." Briar grinned beneath a birch tree, eyes gleaming. Leafy shadows dappled his toned, naked torso, his bottom half clothed in a pair of black silk shorts. He wore what every other man at the festival wore, but Briar looked damn extraordinary.

Which made me want to slither under a rock like a snail.

I hunched, realizing he'd already seen my open back, and tucked a tress defying my Heidi braid behind my ear. My bare toes gripped the turf.

Briar approached, stroking my cheek like an eggshell. He winked at me. "Ready to party tonight, Larkspur?"

I'm readier to swan dive onto one of the pyres.

I managed half a smile. "Not really."

Briar grasped my hand, surveying the green. "If I'm being honest, I'm a little nervous about tonight too. None of us youngbloods knows what to expect. Will you stick by me? Keep me company? Keep me calm?"

I doubted he thought himself the one in need of comfort. "Of course," I agreed anyway.

"Thank you." He lifted my hand to his lips and kissed my knuckles. "There's no one else I'd rather spend my first Beltane with."

Breathless, I whispered, "Me either," meaning it.

Briar led me around the green, the twilight overhead becoming stelliferous and sparkling. We chatted with many boisterous Dananns. Some we'd known for ages. Others were visiting from sister circles, there for networking and merriment. Though they gawked at first, the newcomers delighted at meeting me. Some seemed weirdly honored. When a tubby stranger introduced himself as Bay Veratrum, Herald of the Marsh, and bowed to me like a serf before his betters, Briar cleared his throat and steered me clear of the throng.

"What the hell was that?" I gasped as we walked hand in hand toward the buffet, where hungry guests heaped plates with traditional Danann food, flavored like nothing else.

"No idea." Briar clicked his tongue. "I think Mr. Veratrum pregamed before he got here." I giggled.

Briar and I ate together at a picnic table, gluttonous as pigs. Somewhere amid scarfing, Briar turned to me, eyes like sugar glaze, and asked, "Ever have one of these?" He held up a deep-purple berry.

Licking sauce-stained lips, I reached for it, *needing* to taste it.

"Uh, uh," Briar teased, drawing back, firelight a corona around him. "Answer the question first."

I smiled, not at him but the berry. "No, I haven't. What is it?"

"It's called a moonberry—sweeter than honey. They make the Beltane cider out of them."

I glanced toward the cauldron, where Aunt Aylie stirred said cider—dressed in something I'd never wanted to see my aunt in. My eyes were burning when Briar's breath misted my cheek. I turned, facing him nose to nose.

"They're tiny but potent," he murmured. "One berry's like drinking a bottle of wine by yourself."

"Really?" I eyed the berry again. Intoxicant or not, it looked scrumptious.

He grinned. "Want to share it with me?"

The hairs at my nape prickled. "Y-yes," I stuttered, my pulse surging.

Briar pressed the berry between my lips, and my heart took wing as he leaned in and kissed me, delicate as someone handling vintage lace. We tasted the berry, the most ambrosial morsel I'd ever eaten, on each other's tongues.

Giddy after our kiss, I didn't expect the pit that formed in my stomach when I locked eyes with someone across the green. Laurel Woodrush stood alone amongst other youngbloods, half-clothed and painted with runes, tears forging mascara rivulets down her globed cheeks. No, I didn't like Laurel; she'd tormented me. Yet, I'd never wanted to torment her back. So, I'd refrain from kissing Briar for the rest of the night. At least when I knew Laurel could see.

Then the moonberry kicked in, and the deep need to feel Briar against me eclipsed all discretion.

When the Beltane ritual commenced, I knelt by the maypole, Uncle Neel funneling an entire jug of moonberry cider down my throat. Briar remained my tether to reality as the night exploded around me in a hazy, scary mess of color, laughter, and fire. Compelled by invisible forces, I danced in tangling ribbons, sung songs I'd never heard, and watched people

I'd known my whole life debauch themselves upon the altar of Cernunnos—the horned god of wild things.

By midnight, the bacchanalia raged in flashes of starlight and jewel tones, and I was on hands and knees, gripping the sod to regain control. I tried escaping the gyrating, the cackling, but closing my eyes only awakened nightmares.

Now, I faced a towering phantom. Folds of darkness cloaked his face, though his gaze burned through the purest parts of my soul. *He's coming for you, Amaranthine,* a woman's voice echoed just before the man's shadows slithered out to consume me.

I shrieked when arms swept me off the ground.

"You're okay," Briar slurred after I opened my eyes upon his lazy smile. "I've got you, Amy."

Moonberry essence still pumping through me, I clutched him—his firm, sweaty skin. "Where are we going?" The forest bordering the green seemed to march toward us.

"Somewhere more peaceful." His chuckle soothed me, and I melted into him.

Our fellow Dananns' ebullience had faded into the forest's woodnotes by the time I saw where Briar was taking me.

A ramshackle cabin stood between two rowan trees in the woods. As moss blanketed its roof, and ivy strangled its walls, I thought the place abandoned to nature, who seemed content to claim it as her own. Then I saw its chimney smoking and noted its windowpanes, orange and aglow.

"Why are we here?" I asked.

"I could tell you were done with the party, but I figured you'd struggle to sleep with the racket outside your tent."

Uh—yeah.

"So, I rented this place for you." Briar climbed the rickety stairs to the cabin door and kneed it open.

Inside was cozier than the outside made it seem. Fire crackled in the wood burner, and a fruit basket sat on a café table, as did a full Brita pitcher and two glasses. To my right, a door led to a bathroom with a shower, fluffy towels hanging on the wall above the toilet. And right before us—a full-size bed clad in fresh white cotton. Candles flared on its flanking nightstands.

My toes touched the floor, my breath shallowing. Briar's fingers stroked my nude back as I met his gaze. "You rented this just for me to sleep in?"

"If that's what you want." He caressed the nape of my neck. "Then yes."

My body tautened, liquified, my breath shaking as I asked, "What do *you* want?"

His fingers tugged at my flimsy pearled sleeves. "You."

Soon after, my Beltane dress was a puddle of silk on the floor, and I was being carried to the bed.

"The second time will be better," Briar murmured against my collarbone, reminding me of the 10-year-old who'd donkey kicked me. I lay quiet in the spoon of his warm body, still rattled by what had happened.

I just had sex. With Briar Hawthorne.

Briar's mouth tantalized me as it brushed along my neck. "How do you feel now?"

My cheeks flamed, and I giggled into my hand. "I'm good." Although I was a bit achy, my body craving a release it hadn't found. I thought about asking Briar to finish what he'd started, but I couldn't form the words. "How about you?"

Chuckling, Briar tightened his hold on me. "Incredible."

"Are you still drunk?"

"Yeah." He laughed. "You?"

"Not as much now." Penetration had sobered me up.

He kissed the place where my ear met my jaw, waking frissons throughout my body. I gripped the mattress to steady myself, rocking in a storm of unexplored pleasure.

Having no idea what he'd just done to me, Briar yawned. "I'm also bone tired." He groaned, resting his head on the pillow behind mine. "Are you ready for sleep?"

"Um—yeah." My body rioted at my betrayal. "I guess."

He squeezed me close. "Good night, Amy."

I wriggled back against his body, content to snuggle with him for the rest of the night. Intimacy would mask any physical dissatisfaction. "Good night, Briar."

During sleep, Briar withdrew from me, yanking the comforter partially off me. Cold danced down my spine without his heat, and I dreamt of a bed full of throw pillows.

My second time *was* better than my first. I adjusted to Briar faster, and I did enjoy myself.

Sort of.

Beyond the awkwardness of getting to know each other's bodies, we also lacked the one integral thing prevalent between all new lovers in my favorite romances. Passion. But we could still develop some.

I refused to believe its existence was a myth.

Morning birds twittered outside as I lay against Briar's body, my head on his hairless chest, a warm slickness between my thighs.

"Do you think anyone will notice we're gone?" I feared my aunt or uncle would come looking for me and find me like this—ruffled, naked, and in bed with Briar.

"Maybe, but I doubt they'll worry about us." He played with a tuft from my bedraggled braid. "They know we'll turn up when we're ready."

I blinked at him. "You don't think—" I felt myself blush. "They wouldn't guess—"

"They might." He grazed my cheek. "Would it be so bad if they knew?"

"I just don't want them getting all excited for a grand-niece or nephew." I bit my lip, knowing they'd heap blessings upon me—then demand I drop out of college.

"Why not?" Briar smiled. "It's a possibility."

I just stared at him, his leisurely acceptance of said possibility quite unexpected.

The night before, my inebriation and rising hormones had exiled contraceptives to an afterthought. That morning, things had happened while I was drowsy, hardly sentient. Yes, Dananns were all about the blessings of fertility, but in my mind, we'd been unforgivably irresponsible. Twice. So, I knew what I was doing that day. As soon as I could, I'd hitch a ride to the nearest pharmacy and buy myself some emergency contraception.

On Monday, I'd make an appointment with a gynecologist. Before Briar and I did any more canoodling, we needed a birth control plan.

Maybe Briar wasn't as casual in his Danann beliefs as I was—since he held stock in superstitions like bad luck trees—but I'd still assumed his views about children were as contemporary as mine. Kids would be great—when we were older. Of course, upon seeing the inexplicable hope in the frat boy's eyes, I knew it would be a touchy subject.

Which I settled on broaching *after* I'd procured and taken the morning-after pill. Because I was *not* getting pregnant at 20, no matter his views on the matter.

That my actions would get me shunned by the whole Danann community if anyone found out barely crossed my mind.

Perhaps sensing my aversion to premature parenthood, Briar stiffened against me.

Ugh, I thought. *Just rip off the Band-Aid, Amy.* "Briar, I'm sorry if I don't seem—"

"No, no." He relaxed again, though the glint in his eyes had dimmed. "It's not you, Amy. There's something I have to do." Without elaboration, he kissed me—another artform of tenderness—and stroked my hip. "Why don't you freshen up? When you're ready, we'll get breakfast."

A shower sounded amazing right then, so I slipped from bed. The floorboards were cold as I plodded to the bathroom, but the shower was piping hot. Its steam thawed my skin as I plucked bobby pins from my updo.

Somehow during the festival, Briar had procured my tee-shirt, jeans, and undergarments from my tent. He'd folded them neatly and set them on the vanity counter along with my hairbrush, toothbrush, and toothpaste.

How sweet is he?

I barely cared that his toiletries were scented—lemon lavender body wash and coconut shampoo and conditioner. I didn't know why I assumed he'd realize that I never used scented products on my sensitive skin. No perfume. No fragrant moisturizers. Not even scented laundry detergent. I guessed even Danann boys with heightened senses could be clueless about such things.

When I wafted back out of the bathroom in a vaporous cloud, dressed in clean clothes, my skin scrubbed raw beneath them, and my hair wet, Briar wasn't there. He'd probably gone for more firewood, so I sat at the café table to brush my hair. I hummed a new ballad by Delaney that I'd recently downloaded, relaxing as trees budded, wildlife chirped, and leaves rustled in the breeze beyond my window. And in this tranquility, a pair of voices rose. Briar's. And Laurel Woodrush's.

I shot to my feet, clattered to the second window, and gripped its cobwebbed sill.

I found the pair fighting in a distant copse of pines, barely obscured. Laurel wept, her cheeks blotchy, as Briar frowned, aging himself. Tying his shorts' drawstring, he glanced over his shoulder at the cabin, reassuring himself that they weren't being watched.

By me, I presumed.

Guess he didn't know how far I could hear.

"You must stop doing this to yourself," Briar said to Laurel. "Sweetheart—"

All my breath escaped in a rush. *Sweetheart?*

"I can't take this, Briar." Laurel clutched her riotous hair. Leaves stuck out of it. Had she slept on the ground? "Please, come back to me. This doesn't feel right. Nothing's been right."

For a moment, Briar looked as heartbroken as she did. "We both knew this was coming, Laurel. We both knew it must end."

"I never actually thought you'd go through with it!" Laurel wailed. "I always thought you'd decide against the whole thing in the end. Because you loved me. Because you wanted to be with *me*!"

Briar's jaw worked, ineffable emotions warring for control of his face—emotions I never saw when he looked at me. "I can't withdraw from the pact, Laurel. That would be—"

"Damn you! I don't care about that! All I care about is us!"

His Adam's apple bobbed. "There's no more *us*, Laurel."

She sobbed at those words, clutching her heart—a heart I *felt* shattering. "That's it? All these years together, and now I must watch you parade around with Sasquatch like some adoring clod? And I'm just supposed to pretend it doesn't *kill* me?"

"*Stop* calling her by that rotten name. Jealousy doesn't become you, Laurel."

Shaken, Laurel choked on a fresh batch of tears. "How did you think I'd feel? Just because she's a Larkspur, she's set to get everything I've always wanted. And in all my ages, Briar, all I've ever wanted was *you*."

He turned from her, anguish etching his features, the set of his shoulders. "It's too late, anyway, Laurel." He gulped deep in his throat. "Last night—she was ready, and I slept with her. We might conceive a child."

Fury flashed in Laurel's bloodshot eyes. She bared her teeth in a snarl. "Congratulations, Briar. I'm sure Cornelian will be pleased to hear you've finally come through on your end."

Her words a gut punch, I staggered into the table and toppled over my chair, taking it with me to the floor. Numb, I sat there with one leg sprawled over the seat, staring at nothing.

You should've known, I thought, infuriated with myself. *How could you let yourself fall for it?*

When would Briar have had time to set up the cabin? To go into my tent, retrieve my clothes, and bring them to the cabin? He'd been with me for damn near the entire festival. The cozy fire, the neatly made bed, the basket of fruit, the pitcher of water—

Besides the toiletries, the whole fucking cabin had Aunt Aylie stamped all over it.

I didn't realize Briar had returned until he touched my arm. "What happened?" He knelt to my aid. "Are you all right?"

Through my daze, I met Briar's solicitous expression and saw Uncle Neel's shade over his bare shoulder. I wrenched away from him and rose to stand, my heart splintering.

"Was any of it real?" I snarled.

Briar goggled, rising as well.

"You and me. It was all just a fucking farce, wasn't it?"

Gasping, Briar reached for me. "Amy, I promise what you saw outside with Laurel—it wasn't what it looked like."

I shirked his hand before he touched me again. "I'm angrier about how it sounded."

Realization setting in, he scraped his face. "You *heard*?"

"As much as I needed to."

"Fuuuuck," he growled. "You must have exceptional hearing, even for a Danann."

"Sorry I didn't warn you it would be harder to enact my uncle's schemes with me around."

"There's no scheme."

"So, you didn't ask me out that first time because my uncle told you to?"

He flinched.

"*Answer me!*"

"You don't understand! Yes, I asked you out at your uncle's suggestion, but he barely has anything to do with it. I *wanted* to go out with you!"

I scoffed. Why the fuck would I believe him now?

"Listen to me!" Briar pled. "I've loved being with you these past weeks. Every moment. *Especially* last night."

I cringed at what I'd done with him last night. "You're so full of shit!"

"No, I'm not." He clasped his hands, begging. "There's just so much you don't know, that I've been wanting to tell you for years but haven't been allowed to!"

I started toward the door. Briar caught me, and this time his gentle touch made my skin crawl.

"Please hear me out."

"Let me go!" I had to get out of there. If tears were brewing, they were falling. And I'd be damned if they'd do it in his presence.

"Not until you hear everything." He palmed the back of my wet head. "I'm not your enemy. Neither is your uncle. We care about you—*I* care about you more than you realize. I've been waiting—for forever, it seems—for you to be ready to be with me."

He made me sound like a muffin that was too slow to bake.

"Laurel was just a diversion, one that went on far too long. She and I were never going to amount to anything because I knew I was meant to be with you."

Mist blurred my eyes, and I tried pulling away, but he wouldn't let me go.

"If you only knew how special you are—" he breathed. "How sweet and kind and funny. If you only realized how everyone else sees you—"

"As Sasquatch." A tear slipped past my eyelid. "Your nasty girlfriend made that abundantly clear just now."

"She's not my girlfriend. I told you—"

"Right," I snapped. "She was a diversion."

"Yes!"

"Did you love that diversion?"

Briar stared at me, his mouth opening around nothing.

When I pulled back this time, he didn't stop me.

"What I felt for Laurel was—a mistake."

I bit down on my trembling lip, trying to stem the rest of my tears. "Do you still love her?"

Stricken, Briar looked away. "Amy—"

Goddess help me, I didn't want to ask my next question, but I needed the answer. "Do you love *me*?"

His eyelids lowered. "I'm trying."

Nope, that's not what you want to hear.

Stunning, the sting of those two words. I wasn't in love with Briar either. Yet, I'd thought we'd been building a bridge to that end. I hadn't been forcing it. Evidently, he had.

I couldn't be with someone who had to *try*.

Briar gasped as my tears sprung free. He reached for me again. "Amy, I'm sorry. That wasn't—"

He shut up when I raised my hand. To slap him, to *hurt* him. But I completely lacked the nerve. Instead, I curled my fingers in so hard I gouged my palms.

"Stay away from me," I hissed, then barreled out the door.

EIGHT

After storming to my tent on Avalon Green, ignoring the speculating glances from those awakening in the sunshine, I brushed my hair in a fury, cursing my relatives and their supposed pact the entire time. What had they promised Briar in exchange for seducing me? Was this how they'd rein in my ambitions? Get me knocked up and married?

Screw that!

I rifled through my belongings until I found my purse, wiped my tears, and shot from my tent to beg a ride to the nearest pharmacy from a group of youngbloods on their way to brunch.

The disheveled girls blinked at one another but quickly assented to drive me. Minutes later, we stopped at my requested destination. I thanked them for the ride and said they could head on without me.

Zinnia Ninebark watched me through the driver's side window of her orange mustang, her chestnut hair curling around her angular face. "Sure you don't want us to stay until you're done? We could drive you back."

"No, but thank you," I replied, rocky-voiced, eyes still swimming. "It's not that far. I'll just walk back."

Besides, I didn't want them knowing what I was doing. They'd definitely frown on me for it.

Uncertain though she seemed, Zinnia sighed. "As you wish."

The bushy-browed pharmacist was more than discreet when I whispered that I needed emergency contraception. He bagged my pills and instructed me on how to take them. I paid him forty bucks with my bank card, then bought a bottle of water at the front counter. After that, I trudged back out into the rejuvenating breeze and plopped down on the sidewalk alongside the building.

Weeping, I dangled my purchase between my legs, then retrieved my MulBerry from my purse and called the first person I thought of. My phone dialed the right number for once, and Daddy picked up.

"Hello, daughter," he greeted me in a knowing voice. "I'm surprised to hear from you so early after your first Beltane. Thought you'd be down for the count."

I smiled through my tears. "Naw, I'm doing all right. I can handle my moonberry cider better than Aunt Aylie and Uncle Neel."

"I'd say you're right. They returned home half an hour ago, and I've seen corpses who look livelier."

So, my aunt and uncle had left me at the green, expecting Briar to drive me home now that we'd become intimate. Something they wouldn't know if they hadn't been all up in my business.

Daddy must've heard my breath shudder. "Something wrong, Amy?"

Clearing my throat, I glanced down at the bag between my knees. "Daddy, if I did something awful, something that would break the Danann sacrament, would you still love me?"

He clicked his tongue. "What kind of a question is that?"

I gnawed the inside of my cheek. "An important one. To me."

"Why do I get the feeling this isn't a hypothetical?"

I sniffled, wiping my nose. "I just really need to hear your answer right now."

My father exhaled. "Amaranthine Ginger Larkspur, I would love you even if you massacred a village. Even if you ate babies for breakfast and puppies for dessert."

I laughed, my heart lightening.

"I would love you if you brought about the apocalypse and ended the universe as we know it."

My tears blinded me.

"I love you because you're a part of me—a part of your mother—and that will never change, even if you do."

Wishing I was home, so I could hug him, I took a calming breath. "Thank you, Daddy. I love you too."

"Now, are you going to tell me what you're up to, so I can talk you out of it?"

I sputtered another laugh. "Goodbye, Daddy. I'll see you at home later."

"Amy, please be care—"

I ended the call and dropped my phone in my purse. Steeling myself against the paralyzing fear of my kinsmen's castigation—and reminding myself of the trap Briar and my uncle had laid for me—I opened the box securing my right to my own body and popped out the first of two pills. I downed it with a gush of mineral water before I second-guessed myself.

The forbidden action done and over with, I relaxed back against the cool brick wall. I watched a set of sparrows fight over a cracker left on the blacktop by the garbage can. They twittered and flapped, their pudgy bodies hopping.

Then they started spinning.

Stabbing chest pain followed, and I struggled to breathe, my tongue suddenly too big for my mouth. I tried to get up, alleviate things somehow, but my legs wouldn't work. And I crumpled to my hands and knees.

Something was wrong. Terribly wrong!

I'd heard of women having adverse reactions to the birth control pill—which was all the morning-after pill was—but nothing like this. This was more like anaphylaxis.

Freaking out could only worsen matters, but my heart was thundering by the time things got blurry. I rooted in my purse for my phone in vain. Spots blotched my vision, and I couldn't see my keypad, let alone dial 911.

He's coming for you, the woman's voice from my drunken Beltane hallucination sung in my head.

Before the darkness I so feared overtook me, I swore I heard Briar cursing in my ear.

When the light returned, I wished I were still in darkness. I was too hot, too cold, too sick to be alive.

A ceramic mug pressed against my lips. Again. I used all my strength to fight it.

"You have to drink this." Someone squeezed my cheeks until my mouth popped open, then a bitter, searing liquid seeped past my bloated tissues. I coughed and sputtered, my guts following suit.

Eventually, my stomach muscles ached from hurling. That's when torrents of water splashed over my parched tongue, now shrunk back to normal. After the noxious drink, the water felt like medicine.

My maladies thus eased, gentle arms lifted me, laid me on a bed beside a crackling wood burner. "You'll be okay now." Fingers stroked my hair. "Rest."

When I awoke, night had fallen, and I was back in the cabin, the stench of vomit, herbs, and woodsmoke thickening the air.

Briar hunched at the café table. His auburn hair shot out in all directions, his face waxen. He'd changed into jeans and an army-green tee-shirt. Telling wet spots mottled his top, like he'd scrubbed himself clean many times.

"Oh, Goddess," I moaned, covering my eyes. "I threw up on you!"

When I finally dared to make eye contact, Briar looked ready to wring my neck. "I found you near death in the parking lot of a drugstore, and *that's* your first thought after waking?"

I frowned, ashamed of nothing.

Briar stomped over, grabbed my face in his hands. "For the love of all that's sacred! Do you really hate the idea of having my baby that much that you'd rather end your life?"

I pushed his hands away. "I wasn't trying to kill myself! I didn't know I was allergic to the pill. I'd never taken one before."

Briar rubbed his temples like he might have a stroke. "You think you're *allergic* to it?"

I blinked. "Yeah."

Swearing, he sat at my hip and squeezed one of my hands. I lacked the energy to disengage. "Amy, you're not allergic to the pill. It's toxic to Dananns."

"What? It's just hormones."

"Right, but hormones your body can't process. No Danann female can. It's like poison to you."

"And I'm only hearing about this now?"

"You've been warned not to take the pill or any other hormonal contraceptives hundreds of times!" Frustration flushed his face. "Starting from when we were 12! Remember? Your uncle had midwives take over Sunday circle lessons for two weeks to warn you and the other girls of its dangers!"

"But they said *nothing* about Dananns being any different from other women! And you know they sounded like all those religious zealots who think it's a crime against nature to prevent pregnancy! The ones who claim the pill will cause birth defects or infertility! Well, guess what, Briar—I looked up their weak-ass claims on the internet. Even at 12, I knew how to fact check."

He swore into his palms.

"The science wasn't in their favor! So, if they wanted to protect me, then why didn't someone give me specifics?"

He stiffened. "I guess nobody expected you to go out and revenge abort our baby!"

I shoved myself up to sit against the paneled headboard. "Two things!" I blustered. "First, the morning-after pill doesn't abort *anything*. It's just a heavy dose of the birth control pill. If a baby had already been in the works, it wouldn't have harmed it."

"Again—Dananns are different, Amy."

"Second, I didn't take it out of revenge, Briar. I decided to do it before I even knew you were faking our whole relationship."

He shook his hands at me. "*Why*?"

"Because I obviously don't want to get pregnant! Duh!"

Jerking away from me, Briar dropped his head into his hands, stewing.

I might've stewed along with him—I had more right to do so, after all. But he'd just saved my life. Perhaps I shouldn't be so hard on him.

"How'd you find me?" I muttered.

"Zinnia—she circled back to tell me where you were."

I should've been grateful to her, but I felt betrayed. "What was that stuff you made me drink? It tasted awful."

"An herbal antidote made of mugwort, wild garlic, and a few other things." He swiped a hand through his hair, demonstrating why it was so mussed. "It's used to purge the stomach and counteract the effects of poison." His gaze dropped to my stomach. "At least some of the effects."

I scowled. "*Anyway*—thank you for helping me. I know you think I was reckless and stupid, but—" *My body, my choice, butthead.*

"I don't think you're stupid. You're just ignorant, and that's not your fault."

Funny he should think me so unenlightened. Aunt Aylie and Uncle Neel complained I was over-educated.

"I wasn't faking anything," Briar said after another weighty silence.

I wished for spontaneous deafness, twinges rippling through my heart.

"The start of our relationship was rigged, I'll admit that. But the rest—everything between us—that was real. My feelings for you are genuine, Amy."

I *so* wanted to believe him. But I didn't.

"You expect me to buy that you weren't using me to please my uncle? That you don't care what he thinks of you?"

"Of course, I care what he thinks of me. And your father."

My gut spasmed. *Daddy played no part in this sordid mess!*

"But I'd never use you, Amy. I care more about what *you* think of me." He stroked my arm, giving me chills despite everything. "You, who's so funny, witty, and beautiful—"

"Quit it with the compliments on my beauty. That's how I know you're full of shit. Nobody looks at me and thinks beautiful."

Briar's brows leapt. "*Come* on, Amy."

The bitterness of his herbal remedy suddenly refilled my mouth.

"This is why I waited so long to approach you romantically."

"And how long has this oh-so-romantic pact been a thing? How long have you been waiting around for me?"

Briar frowned at my derision. "Years. I waited years because you just weren't ready to be loved."

Of all the ludicrous things said about me, this was number one! I'd been ready for love my whole life, reading fairy tales, then love stories like a junkie!

He doesn't know me at all!

"You *weren't*," Briar insisted. "Listen, whenever I tried getting close to you, you'd slip away from me. You were so convinced that no one could want you, that no one could be even remotely interested in you, that you shut down every advance before it could happen. After a while, I stopped trying altogether because I feared I'd scare you off forever. That's why your aunt started setting you up on all those dates."

My whole teenage love life was a ploy?

"She was gauging your receptivity to men—to see when you'd be open to my affections. We didn't realize it until you left for college—that her efforts might've done more harm than good. Without our interference, you came right out of your shell."

"No shit it harmed me! How would you feel, knowing every date you ever had was more into your uncle than you? Those boys might as well have gotten paid for taking me out!" Some of them certainly were. No normal teenage boy should have enough money to take his date to the Melting Pot. "At the end of those dates, I'd get a pathetic peck on the lips. No one ever tried to touch me, or hold me, or—"

"Because they knew I'd kick their asses."

He's got to be shitting me.

"So, what did you do?" I fumed. "Follow me around on all my dates? Hide in the background, so you could keep an eye on me?"

He didn't even blink. "Yes."

Lava churned in my belly.

"It was my duty. Still is."

I wanted to smash his handsome face into the wall. Instead, I smacked my own face into a pillow and screamed until my voice ran ragged. When my lungs had emptied, I dropped the pillow to find Briar watching, waiting for my conniption to run its course.

"Don't look at me like that," I snapped.

"I can't help feeling bad that you're upset."

"You're the reason I'm upset!"

"No, Amy, I'm not."

"Then who's responsible for this shit show?" I'd place my bets on Uncle Neel. "And why does us getting together matter so goddamn much?"

So much that Briar had abandoned his first love.

His silence was answer enough.

"You're not telling me something."

Briar slumped, then exhaled. "I'm not the one who should do this, but I have no choice." He sandwiched my hands between his. "Amy, we Dananns—we're different—as I think you've always known."

I sulked, regretting that my insecurities glared as brightly as my flaws.

"And there's a major reason for that. We're not from this place." He paused, debating his words. "Some might say we're from an entirely different world."

A whimsical ringtone pealed above the pop of a log in the wood burner. I was willing to ignore it, needing further clarification on Briar's outlandish metaphor, but he wasn't.

"You should get that." He gestured at my MulBerry on the nightstand. "I promised your uncle I'd have you home by dinner. It's past nine now; he's probably worried something's wrong."

The ID display on my phone read Olivia, but I figured someone else was calling.

"Amy!" Ace exclaimed when I answered. "Where the hell have you been? I've been calling you all day. Every time—right to voicemail."

"I—uh—I'm still at Avalon Green, cleaning up. My phone's glitching, remember? I never heard it ring."

Briar shook his head. It really hadn't rung.

"Get it fixed already!" Ace ordered. "How else can we reach you when things happen?"

I stiffened. "What's going on? Is Dad all right?"

"Dad's fine. It's *Vi*. She spaced out this morning, and her eyes glazed over. She was unresponsive for two minutes!"

Memories of Vi as a child resurfaced. Her laughing. Her in mid-jabber. And then suddenly blank-eyed, vacant, lost to me. Over and over, this had happened. It couldn't be happening again!

"But she hasn't had a seizure since she was nine," I said, more to myself than Ace.

"Well, she did today, and Uncle Neel won't let us take her to the doctor. Aunt Aylie rushed us out of the house, and now we're locked in Ash Loosestrife's basement."

"*What?*" I gasped. "Is Vi all right?"

"She seems fine now, but she's got to see a doctor. Right? I'm not overreacting!"

"Take her to the ER! Where's Aunt Aylie? Put her on the phone."

On Ace's end, a brief, muffled argument ensued. Jumbling followed. "I'm okay, Amy," Vi assured me. She'd stolen Ace's phone; he now griped in the background. "Honestly."

She sounded fine, thank Danu. "Are you sure?"

"Yes." She exhaled. "Listen, this will sound nuts, but I had—I had a vision."

"Huh?"

"Like a premonition. An omen."

My willies swiftly rebounded. "Yes, I know what you mean, Vi."

"I think something bad is going to happen. Soon."

"Stop it, Vi," I snapped, my pulse accelerating. "I'm not in the mood—"

"No, listen, Amy! You were in it! With fire and—screaming—and our home was *trashed*. I don't know what any of it means, but it felt—scary."

So, she wasn't doing as well as she sounded. "Vi, did you tell anyone else about this?" Why hadn't they rushed her to the hospital, as altered as she was?

"Yeah! And right after Uncle Neel heard what I'd seen, he sent us all packing. Except for Dad. He's still home."

Briar's face hardened, his Danann ears honing-in on my private phone conversation. I hit my speakerphone button, saving him the strain of eavesdropping.

He arched a brow at me, silently remarking, *Hypocritical much?*

Okay—he had a silent point.

"Uncle Neel didn't say why your—vision—freaked him out?"

"No, he just told Aunt Aylie to take us somewhere safe—said he'd call Briar and tell him to bring you here."

Cursing, Briar rushed to the café table. He snagged his phone off its surface and speed dialed his voicemail. My cell wasn't the only one malfunctioning, adequate reception rare in the woods.

"Maybe you should just stay where you are," Vi advised. "I mean, you were in my vision. If you stay away, maybe the scariness won't happen. We're fine here. We—"

Her voice faded to snow. Another call popped up on my screen, and my heart frosted.

Seeing the blood drain from my face, Briar silenced Uncle Neel's voicemail directives. "What is it, Amy?"

"It's me," I whispered, staring at my own name on my screen. "I'm calling my own phone."

Briar strode over. "You said your phone was stolen, right?"

"I thought so, but then the lights came back on, and it was back in my purse."

He took my phone from my slackened hand. "No, it wasn't." He answered the call, setting my MulBerry to speakerphone.

"Hello," Briar spat, almost disgusted.

"Amaranthine."

I shivered at the child thief's grizzly voice.

"She can hear you." Briar raised a hand to calm me—and silence me. "Say what you must, Kobold."

Did he know the fricking phone thief?

"I've a warning for you, Amaranthine." The thief's line crackled. "They've found him."

Him who?

"He's beyond saving now, but you can still safeguard his totem. It's what the Shadow Prince covets most."

My dream phantom billowed to the forefront of my mind, paralyzing me. Briar, however, scrambled into action, dropping my phone to gather our belongings.

"The Shadow Prince?" I repeated the surreal title. Was I being punked?

"Make haste. Before it's too late."

The line went dead.

"Wait, no!" Crawling to the phone, I redialed without success. "He didn't say who's in trouble!"

Briar swooped down and clutched my shoulders, jolting me. "Your father, Amy. We thought we'd thrown the beasts off his scent, that he was safe, but we must've failed. If they've found Laurustinus, then—"

Why was everyone talking like Tolkien characters? "Then, *what*? What the hell are you saying?"

"I'm saying I'm sorry, Amy," Briar replied. "Your father—he's not going to make it."

NINE

"**A**re you *crazy*?" Briar shouted from the front bumper of his Ford Fusion.

Ten seconds after he'd promised to take me some place safe, where the enigmatic "beasts" hunting my father wouldn't find me, I'd stolen his car keys and hightailed it through the woods back to Avalon Green—and his parked car.

"You don't understand what you're doing!" he exclaimed.

"My father's in danger!" I jammed his key into the ignition. "I'm not hiding! I've got to save him!"

"*You* won't be able to save anyone! The guards your uncle has surrounding your house may have a shot, but not you!"

What guards? I wanted to snark. *Clem Polkweed and Arbutus Colwort? Those old farts couldn't guard a cup of coffee without falling asleep!*

"You said my father wouldn't make it! You implied he was going to *die*!"

"I'm not clairvoyant. I made a snap assumption. I could be very wrong. The guards might keep your father safe. I pray that they can!"

"Stop back-peddling, Briar!" I turned the key in the ignition. The Fusion thrummed to life.

"Damnit, Amy!" He slammed his fist down on the car hood, making a sizeable dent. "It's not worth risking your life!"

"The hell it isn't! He's my *father*!"

He was worth the risk of everything.

"Amy, *please*! This is like strolling into the shootout at the O.K. Corral, and you don't have a fucking gun!"

Gritting my teeth, I set my hand on his leather gear shift. Determined. "You can either get in and come with me, or I can leave you here. Either way, Briar, I'm going home."

Cruising the car-lined streets of Squirrel Hill, I slowed Briar's Fusion, my earlier moxie to rush into danger giving way to queasiness. The closer we came to my house, the more substantial the prospect of certain doom became.

Seeing me wavering, Briar released the oh-shit bar and turned to me. "Amy, you don't have to do this. You can turn around and go somewhere safe."

Hands sweating, I strangled the steering wheel. "I won't just leave him there to die. I'm his daughter."

"Which is why we should turn around. If he knew I was letting you get this close to danger, he'd have my head."

I shook off his hyperbole—so oddly earnest. "You're not letting me do anything. I stole your keys."

His mouth twitched into a momentary smirk. "Yeah, you did, and it's my own damn fault for leaving them out on the table. That won't win me any points with him. I'll probably get dressed down for this."

"What? Like you would in the army?"

"Exactly. Only Dananns call it the Old Order, and punishments for misconduct are much more severe."

I so wasn't in the mood for make-believe right then. "You sound like a nutjob, Briar! Quit trying to guilt me into turning around. You think I care if you get in trouble?"

Briar's expression turned boyish. "Do you?"

A little, I thought and groaned. "Just tell me what to expect of the bad guys when we get there."

Briar massaged the furrows off his forehead. After the past day with me, he was going to need anxiolytics. "They're not guys, Amy. They're flying monsters who are really, *really* hard to kill."

I almost ran into a parked car, distracted as I was by his nonsense. Briar cursed, flattening against his seat just before I swerved to miss it.

"Are you mentally ill?" I asked, concerned for his wellbeing. "We don't live in Oz, Briar—flying monkeys don't exist."

"They do, actually, but these are more like bats."

"Shut up and be serious! This isn't funny!"

"I'm not joking! You wanted the truth—this is it. We're not from this world, and neither are these assholes you want to fight. They're fast and lethal, and if they catch you, they'll *kill* you."

My guts clenched, but I wheeled onto my lamplit street, rejecting his portents of doom.

"How gullible do I look?" I snarled, hysteria mounting. "You can't scare me away from helping my father with a child's campfire story—"

An object hurtled down on Briar's car, the Fusion's roof crunching upon impact.

I stomped the brake pedal, yelping, and we screeched to a halt two houses away from mine. Propelled forward, Briar gripped the dashboard.

The debris rolled off the roof and banged down on the hood. Dead weight.

I screamed reflexively. Every atom in my body poised to flee, registering that the mangled bulk before me had once been a Danann man—Sy Rockrose, his remnants dressed in black.

Sy's throat flapped open, his bloodless silver head hanging by a stringy tendon. His severed bottom half, gnawed on like gristle, slammed down onto his torso. Rocking our world. Popping the Fusion's front tire and robbing us of escape too.

"Shh," Briar hissed, muffling my scream. His breath misted my face as a series of strident squawks pierced the quiet. Something whooshed overhead as we trembled in our piss-poor shelter. "They have impeccable hearing. They hunt by scent, though. We're lucky we smell so bad, or we'd be under attack right now."

I clawed his arms, damn near hyperventilating. "We need to get to my house!"

"No, *we* don't." His breath sawed. "You're going to stay right here and keep silent."

When I made to protest, he re-clamped my mouth. "Yes, you damn well will. I'm going to sneak over to your uncle's car. If he followed protocol, the keys should already be in it. I'll back up, so the passenger's side lines up to your door, and you'll jump in. Then, I'll drive us the fuck out of here and hope the bogeybats don't follow us."

Bogeybats? Could he have picked a more menacing term?

"But what about my dad?" What happened to Sy couldn't happen to Daddy. Someone needed to reach him. Now!

Briar looked ready to shake me. "Amy, these creatures came here for one purpose—to kill your father."

Fuck if I'll let them!

"They won't stop until they've done what their master sent them to do. If they're here, we're too late." His eyes pled for reason, but I had none.

"*No!*" I yanked away from him. "He's still alive, Briar. I can *feel* it. You've got to get him out of there!"

"No, Amy, I don't!" Briar wrangled my flailing arms. "Your father made it abundantly clear that my only duty is to keep *you* safe, and I'm not compromising that for anything!"

"I don't fucking care about your supposed duties!" *Goddamn*, we were wasting valuable time! "I won't fucking abandon—"

We heard the squawk before *it* happened, the sound penetrating my skull. Then razor-sharp talons punched through the Fusion's ceiling. And wrenched us off the ground.

Briar didn't even try to contain my shriek. In fact, he joined in with me as we rose above the houses with the flap of what must've been effing ginormous wings. Our screams only ceased after the bogeybat tossed our car like a steel shot, and we crashed into the ground with the force of a 70-mile-per-hour headlong collision.

When I came to, I lay sprawled on the blacktop road outside my front gate, glass in my hair, my joints scraped raw, and Sy Rockrose's mutilated torso draped over me. Blood dripped in my eye. Mine or Sy's, I couldn't tell, but it stunk like rust.

Briar's Fusion was a hunk of gnarled steel, the trunk now in the front seats. Its airbags had deployed and burst open, its horn stuck on a steady blare.

I should be dead. An impact like that should've killed me.

But I was alive, shaken more than injured. And Briar—he was more than alive and scuffling with a nightmare—a flying hobgoblin with pallid, membranous wings. Jabbing a freaking *sword* at it like a video game paladin.

"Protect the princess!" Briar roared above the din.

What princess? I thought, wondering when reality was sucked into the chasm of delusion. I glanced about to find this princess but saw no one until a group of other Danann men in black emerged from the shadows.

Clicking like the spokes on *Wheel of Fortune*, the mammoth creature Briar battled leapt in my direction—to my gut-clenching fright. The group of Dananns swarmed it. They somehow hedged it back, the ground vibrating as it stomped.

Blood sprayed like rain on the road. Another Danann, Mica Polkweed, went down, gullet skewered by a talon.

Recoiling from the sight—from the bedlam happening around me—I clamped my ears and curled into a ball, wishing myself away, anywhere but there. Then I heard it—a ragged outcry from the upstairs of my house. It jarred time back into movement.

Daddy!

I crawled out from under Sy's corpse and snatched the short sword from Mica's limp hand. "Sorry," I croaked, hoping he'd hear me in heaven. Somehow, I'd repay his sacrifice to Poppy and her unborn child.

Tears pooling in my eyes, I scrambled past the wrought iron gating my house and up the front stoop.

"Amy, stop!" Briar bellowed, but I didn't look back as I barreled into my house.

My shoes crunched on glass in the foyer. I stopped, holding my breath.

The family room was ransacked. A massive hole now stood in place of the double French doors—where the bats had busted in, I guessed. And the dining room door hung off its track, parts of it splintered into toothpicks. Aunt Aylie's priceless hot chocolate set lay scattered in pieces in her battered hutch.

Gouges in the staircase led my eyes to the second floor. Talon marks. They'd gone right through the plaster into the studs.

Upstairs, something clattered. Something clicked. And my instincts told me to hide from the beasts making those noises. But Daddy was up there, alone with them. And *nothing*, not even winged creatures from hell, would keep me from reaching him.

Shaky yet determined, I took the first step toward the stairs. And my sword lit like a freaking lightsaber.

I blinked at it, its glow as warm as sunlight, then tiptoed on.

Our electricity flickered to pitch blackness halfway through my journey upstairs. I stopped, gripped the banister. *Of course!* I bit back a rumble. *Why wouldn't the power go out right now?*

My lightsaber illuminated the rest of my path up, thankfully.

On the landing, I stumbled over something small, fleshy, and fluffy. And I knew before I saw him—Kell lay in a pulpy heap at my feet. The bats had eviscerated him, bit his great swishy tail clean off. I clamped my mouth on a howl, bursting with tears.

They'd killed him. A harmless housecat, who'd posed no threat whatsoever to their gruesome quest.

Click, click, click. Click, click.

The noises echoed from the hallway murk—Ace's room, maybe. It was too dark to tell. But I held my breath, heart hammering, and slinked to Daddy's bedroom.

His door lay on the floor, ripped off its hinges. I stared at it, afraid of what I'd find beyond.

Please let Daddy be okay! Please*!*

The ruin I found when I stepped through the doorway frightened me. Jagged scratches grooved the wall where Daddy's dresser stood. It had taken a hit and was now bowtie shaped. Some of its drawers hung open, clothes littering the floor. Daddy's rocker lay scattered like mulch, and his bed rested, overturned, on its side. Daddy himself was nowhere in sight.

Damnit! Where is *he?*

I hoped he wasn't already swimming in some bogeybat's digestive fluids.

My ears perked at a wet, thin wisp of breath from the other side of the bed.

Daddy was still alive!

I rushed over to make sure I was right. I was—but barely.

Daddy lay sprawled ignobly on the floor, blood saturating the sheets wrapping his midsection. Gray ringed his clenched eyes, his mouth bunched and quivering.

I'd never seen a person I loved in such a grievous condition. Someone who was mine.

This just couldn't be happening. My people died of old age, sleeping in their beds after meeting *all* their grandchildren. Not of violence. Not so suddenly.

And Daddy wasn't going out like that, either.

Shaken, I fell to my knees beside him, touching his frail shoulder. His eyes flared open, and he looked more horrified by the sight of me than he did at the blood oozing out of him.

"Daddy." I tugged his sodden sweatshirt sleeve. "We've got to get out of here."

He clasped my wrist, his fingers cold, trembling. "You shouldn't be here," he rasped, his face drawn in the moonlight filtering in through his window.

"Well, I am. So, let's go."

"Amy, no." He flopped back down when I tried to heft him up. His hand twitched over his wound, his face contorting. "I can't move. You're wasting time."

"*No!*" I ignored the pool stretching on the floor between us. "You're coming with me, or I'm not leaving! Do you hear me?"

"*Scraaaaaaa!*"

I could've pissed myself when I peered around the mattress to see a living gargoyle lumber into Daddy's room. I froze, scared to stone.

Holy mother of shit*!*

Its details hit me at once. The leathery skin like ancient bones; the heaving ribs; the sinew, veins, and ears lancing from its fleecy head. The bat's spine was curved and knobby, its wings folded, bony. Eyes like blood and fangs the length of railroad spikes protruded from its gothic muzzle. Talons splayed out from its four enormous paws, its limbs—disjointed and unnatural, almost arthritic—tensed to spring. Its breath polluted mine, notes of festering sewer and gingivitis coating my tongue.

Daddy caught the back of my shirt, tried to yank me down beside him. To shield me. But his negligible strength was no match for my obstinacy.

The bogeybat had come to finish him off. No way in hell was I letting that happen without a fight.

Against Daddy's pleas that I hide, I strangled my sword hilt and rose. Then, I screamed bloody murder and flattened to the floor, the beast vaulting itself at my head, fangs glistening.

My assailant crashed through Daddy's window and into the night. Glass shattered around me, something long and wooden smacking to the floor by my head.

Daddy's walking stick. Why had he hidden it in the curtain panel—the one I'd tangled myself in?

Daddy spasmed around his wound. "Amy, take my staff and get out of here."

"I'm not leaving you!"

His fingers marked my arm, blood seeping from his mouth.

He'll be okay, I denied what my eyes saw. *He'll need immediate medical attention, but he'll survive this.*

"Take the staff to safety," Daddy rattled, his eyelids drooping. "Please, Amy. They mustn't find it. It's—" He broke off, hacking. "It's important."

I shook my head. "It's just a freaking cane!"

"No, it's not. It's ma—"

Click, click, click. The bat was coming back.

Daddy pushed me toward his cane. "Take it and go!"

I grabbed the cane and scurried toward the door, intending to lead the bat away from Daddy. It landed in a distorted hunch on the shard-dusted windowsill, glaring. Clearly, it resented my trickery.

"That's what you get for killing my cat!" I dashed to the door.

I didn't make it. Instead, I bungled back as three more bogeybats squeezed into the room on bowed legs. I kept them at bay with my weapon, panting as I searched for a second escape route. I didn't find it before the first bat flapped onto the floor with a tremor, and I shifted, not knowing where to point my blade. All four beasts closed in on me.

"Stay back!" I snarled with jittery bravado. Did they even understand English?

"Amy—" Daddy choked.

Shivering, I thrust my lustrous blade at the first bat—keeping its attention off my father. "I'm not afraid to use this, you flying wart!"

It sprang toward me. So they *did* understand English.

I screamed, hacking at it with the sword. Somehow, I made contact and opened a gash in its flank—a gash that oozed blood like crude oil. Railing, my attacker spun and walloped me with a skeletal wing.

I soared into my father's closet door, my cheek cracking against its frame, then splatted onto the hardwoods, my sword skidding out of reach. But I landed on the cane and clung to it.

My head spun, so I was only partly aware of the bat screeching, its spittle misting my cheeks. But I latched onto the flail of its uvula, its teeth gleaming in a play for my throat.

One moment, I was awaiting decapitation. The next, I was gaping up at Briar, black gore smattering his olive shirt. He'd leapt out of nowhere and onto the bat like it was a horse, and he, its trick rider. The bat roared as Briar stabbed it with a blade double his size, compelling it into the wall, plaster cracking in a web.

A feral growl followed. From my father's most loyal family member.

I questioned my own eyes when Novus, his tawny hair standing along his rigid back, bounded into the room through a wild stramash in the hallway. He gnashed at the bats by the door, several Dananns wielding sabers against them.

Briar whirled to help them. His serrated sword cast a blue glow over the ferocious brawl, one the bogeybat Briar stabbed didn't engage in. Not because it was dead—although Briar probably thought it nearly finished—but because it hadn't forgotten me.

I whimpered, squirming, when its soulless red gaze darted my way.

Briar whooped. Dodged more teeth. Kicked me my weapon.

I snatched the sword just in time to sever a slashing paw. I sobbed at what I'd done as the bogeybat deafened me. My bangs fluttered above my forehead, saliva smelling of offal beading my skin.

That's when the real fight began.

I screamed the whole time, parrying for my life, and got distracted. I didn't notice another bat hulking toward me—until its fangs fastened around my father's cane to wrench it out from under me.

"*Fuck!* No!" I dropped my sword and gripped the cane's hook with both hands, digging my nails into its varnish. I wailed for strength as the bat yanked, dragging me.

I didn't know why these flying shysters wanted Daddy's cane, or why he needed me to keep it from them, but the phone thief had mentioned protecting a totem. As badly as the bats wanted it, I'd have bet my flat ass the cane was it.

I wrenched the cane, also pulling the bat to my surprise. Little good that did me, though. Irritated eyes still bored through me, promising pain.

My jeans were poor protection against the first bat's fangs. They clinched my leg like a bear trap.

I'd never made the sounds I made then. Tears burst from my eyes, my nails gouging deeper into the cane. Somehow, I held fast as the bogeybats took turns thrashing me.

Novus pounced on the one gnawing me raw, knocking it off me. My blood dripped from its mouth.

"Hold on, Amy!" Briar sabered his foes as mine whipped me in an arc across the hardwoods, slamming me against the closet frame again.

White-hot flames flared in my tailbone. But I was more stubborn than my pain. I would *not* relinquish that damn stick if Daddy needed me to keep it.

My blood painted the floor, frenzying Briar. He no longer fought to kill but to reach me in the fray. "I *will* get you out of here, Amy!"

That was the last thing he said before he tripped over Daddy's motionless ankle and stumbled backward out the shattered window.

"Briar!" My cry rang to the stars as he plummeted, probably to his death. But I couldn't spare another thought for that trauma. Not as a jarring whack preceded Novus's plaintive yelp.

I shuddered to find a bogeybat impaling my beloved dog on his side, its hideous muzzle grinning, drooling. Novus skirmished for survival, his caramel eyes rounding.

I looked to the hallway for help, but the other Dananns had disappeared, their shouts of combat now distant. There would be no swooping savior. I was all Novus had.

I strained for my sword. Nabbed it. "Get off my dog!" I cried, then pitched the glowing blade like a javelin. Embedding it between a set of crimson eyes.

The bat slammed down in its death, burying Novus, still writhing, under its girth.

My triumph was short-lived. In winning one battle, I'd lost the other. My one-handed hold on the cane didn't cut it. The bat trying to steal it tossed me off like a ragdoll. With a screech that split my brain, it flapped into flight with the stick—now anointed in my blood.

"Goddamnit!" I whined, then forced my body up off the floor. I jerked my sword out of the thing I'd killed, baffled at the thought, and hobbled after the bat with the cane.

The torn flesh of my leg bawled in torment. As did I when I sprang, snagging the crook with one hand. I whacked my blade into the shaft with the other.

Before the bat pulled me through the window, I anchored my feet on both sides of its frame. My searing calf and my battered ass bleated, but I clutched that damn stick, gritted my teeth, and leaned back with all my weight.

The bat railed at my interference, its wings flapping double-time, gaining force.

The walls fissured around my sneakers as I beat, and sliced, and sawed. Each swing sapped my adrenaline but conceding defeat *wasn't* happening until—

The shaft broke apart!

The bat catapulted into the night, and I somersaulted back to the wall across from my father. My cane fragment, bloodied and jagged, fell beside me.

My sword clanged feet away. Just as the last two bats lurched back into the room.

Cornered, exhausted, and wounded with no weapon and no strength, I had no chance of survival. The bogeybats doubtless said as much in their bestial chatter.

Now facing my imminent death, my temperature rose like the burning sun in Phoenix. Sweat pooled on my skin as I snarled, "Just get it over with! Kill me already, so I can get away from your stank!"

Taking my advice, they dove for me together.

I cringed away, hands raising to deflect, and some hidden current within me blasted from my finger bones. Like dynamite dwelt in their tips.

The ghastly howls that followed would haunt my dreams for the rest of my life, and I wept into my forearms until I noticed just that—I was still alive.

I peeked, then gaped at a raging inferno engulfing the bats. They staggered, burning effigies, until they were nothing but charred hunks of meat on my father's bedroom rug.

Hyperventilating their ash, I bleared around for the source of the fire.

What the fuck *just happened?*

My heart thundered in my ears when something thumped to the floor. Briar stood by the window, winded but unharmed. I stared at him through the rising flames, wondering how he'd survived his fall.

Briar met my eyes, his own as wide as the bats were dead.

"I-I d-don't know what happened." I bungled an attempt to stand, my hand meeting the splintered cane at my side.

Trembling, I lifted the hunk of burnished cherry, now bleached like driftwood. With all I'd seen that night, believing the walking stick could start a fire wasn't too huge a leap.

"I think it was the cane," I croaked.

Briar's expression softened; his shoulders relaxed. He raised one hand and waved in a fluid swipe. Mist issued from his palm, dousing all the flames faster than an extinguisher.

I could've vomited amid the steam and smoke.

"It wasn't the staff, Amy." Briar strode toward me through the brume, kneeling to inspect my punctured leg. "I've seen what that thing can do." He took my hand, running his thumb along my palm. "It does a lot, but it doesn't make fire. *That* was all you."

"**D**addy, wake up!" I bent over his inert form in the smog, shaking him. My own wounds had faded to insignificance, his life my only concern. "Please wake up!"

Briar knelt beside me, one hand on my back. I didn't dare look at him because I knew what his face would say.

My sore fingers gripped Daddy's sweatshirt, willing him back to consciousness. He was still breathing, albeit faintly and rarely. If we could get him to the hospital, they could fix him. They could save his life! "I need a phone! We need to call 911."

Briar gulped deeply. "A healer is already on her way, but I think it's too late."

"I don't care what you think!" I shoved his hand off me. "You don't know anything!"

"Amy—"

The sound was as brittle as chicken bones, but I heard it and wept in relief.

"Daddy!" I flattened beside him so he could see my face.

The moonlight washed his features of all color. His wrinkled eyelids lifted partially, the midnight pools beneath gazing upon me.

"Someone's coming to help you," I quavered, squeezing his fragile arm, bolstering him with a smile. "Just stay with me for a little while. Everything's going to be all right."

More blood trickled between his colorless lips. His hand, cold as winter's grip, twitched as he pressed it to my sweaty cheek. "*Amy—*" he breathed—then didn't.

The world stopped spinning and time stood still.

"Daddy? No! No, no, *no!*"

Lightheaded, I rose on my knees and began hapless chest compressions, trying to remember *any* of my health teacher's instructions for how to perform CPR. But I couldn't think straight. Not when the one person who'd always love me, even if I ate babies for breakfast and puppies for dessert, was leaving my life before his time.

The tapestry of fate unraveled around me. This wasn't fucking supposed to happen! Daddy wasn't supposed to die! Not then. Not like that.

"Give him back!" I shrieked at the All Mother. *"Danu, give him* back!*"*

But my prayers went unanswered, and I lost so much more than my father in that wretched moment when Briar pried me off Daddy and tried to hug me.

I broke into wracking sobs and fell out of Briar's arms to the floor. I squeezed Daddy until his body lost its warmth.

Briar remained, rubbing my back. I wished he'd leave me alone, but I lacked the fortitude to ask him to go. My heart had just been gutted, its contents spilling across the floor.

"You'll be okay," Briar promised.

But I knew. As deeply as I knew my own heart, I knew nothing would ever be okay again.

Not an hour later, Novus died from his injuries, and I didn't even struggle as the darkness I'd always feared consumed me in a pitiless abyss.

TEN

Daddy's dead; Novus is dead; Kell is dead; Fianna is missing; my home is destroyed.

These were the thoughts I awoke to on a bed in an unfamiliar place—a small, cluttered room doubling as a storage closet. A ceiling fan spun above me, cooling me. The scent of eucalyptus soothed my raw throat. But for my underwear, I was naked beneath a sheet, my wounds trussed up like Christmas presents. The pain associated with those wounds had mostly faded. Either that, or I was too numb to feel it.

Beyond the door, Uncle Neel and Briar waged a war of words. After what I'd endured, I didn't care why they argued. I just wanted them to shut up. They didn't, of course.

"Why in the Isle of Apples would you bring her home?" Uncle Neel scolded. "Didn't you get my voicemails? I told you to take her to Loosestrife's as soon as possible!"

"*She* wanted to come, Cornelian."

"You shouldn't have told her!"

"I had no choice, Neel. She got a ghost call from that Kobold, warning her of the bogeybats' attack. I did what I could to protect her, but I can only do so much when she refuses to take orders."

My indifference burnt up in a quick flash. *Who did he think he was that I'd take his orders?*

"She won't refuse once I'm done with her," Uncle Neel growled.

"Not unless you tell her the truth! She thinks she's an everyday woman, entitled to make her own choices. She isn't aware how dangerous that is for her."

"Rus raised her that way." Uncle Neel's voice cracked saying Daddy's nickname. "I always warned him it was a bad idea."

"This must end. The ruse isn't protecting them anymore. We must tell them everything. We must take them back."

Back where?

I heard a deep, mournful exhalation. "I promised Rus I'd let Amy finish college before we—"

"Are you mad? After tonight, we can't keep her here. The bats have her blood, Neel. They'll come back for her—they'll find a way now that they know *where*. Either them or something worse."

Chills crept along my naked skin. *What in hell could be worse?*

"I thought you'd killed all the bats."

"One got away. With the staff."

"*What*?"

"Relax. It only flew off with part of it. Amy somehow managed to hack it in half." There was definite pride in his voice. "They can't use it while it's broken."

"Neither can we," Uncle Neel grumbled.

"We have part of it. That should serve until we retrieve the other half."

Uncle Neel harrumphed. "Colwort will surely take issue."

"If he does, he can take it up with me. I'd be happy to shove his head up his ass."

I would've laughed, but grief dulled any amusement.

"There's another reason we must tell Amy the truth," Briar continued, softer, so nobody overheard his next point. Either he'd forgotten my eavesdropping prowess, or he thought I was still asleep. "I didn't kill all the bogeybats in Laurustinus's room. Amy did."

I pictured Uncle Neel staggering. "*How?*"

"Fire, Cornelian. She's a fire sylph."

A fire what?

"That's impossible," Uncle Neel sputtered. "No fire sylphen have been born in millennia."

"Except Amy. Didn't the prophecy say the Aurora would possess rare, powerful gifts?"

"Enough with that, Briar. We don't know Amy's the Aurora!"

"But Ginny—"

"Ginny only predicted Amy would be special. She never went into specifics."

I sat up at mention of my mother's name, so rarely spoken. Why had Briar done the mentioning? By her nickname? Yes, he and Uncle Neel spoke as if Briar were ancient, but he was only 20 years old, a little boy when my mother died.

"Maybe because she didn't want anyone knowing how powerful her daughter would be. With great power comes great reverence—but also great fear. And you know the Shadow Prince would move mountains to eradicate that threat. Or worse—to abduct her for his own use."

Uncle Neel swore.

"Whether we like it or not, her gifts are awakening—on their own—without a summoning ceremony. I can already smell them in her blood. We need to get her back to Evereostre and find her a muse before she melts down like a nuclear reactor."

Bewildered, I glanced down at my hands—slender and ordinary. The most disturbing thing about them was the blood outlining my broken nails, but the fire that consumed the bogeybats had come from somewhere.

Briar seemed convinced that it came from me, and if the human vaporizer thought so, who was I to argue?

"How will we keep them safe in Evereostre?" Uncle Neel challenged.

I'd never heard of Evereostre, but I would've bet money it wasn't in North America, let alone within commuting distance to UPJ.

"Gentian breached our defenses once before," Uncle Neel said. "What's to stop him from doing so again?"

"We weren't expecting an attack the first time. Now, our forces are always prepared—trained for such things. Amy will be much safer there than she will be here, where we simply don't have the resources to guard her. Besides, she can receive a much more extensive education in Evereostre, and she'll—"

Seeing red, I grabbed a magazine off the nightstand by the bed and threw it at my door. My education was my decision, nobody else's. So was where I lived.

The men hushed at the fluttery thump, and I inwardly yelped as footsteps approached, having only meant to shut them up. As frayed as my nerves were right then, a confrontation could utterly unravel me.

I shut my eyes and burrowed back under my covers. My breaths evened just before the door creaked open, casting light across my eyelids.

"Amy?" whispered Briar.

When I didn't answer, he moved closer, caressing my cheek. I fought the urge to jerk away. After a moment, his shadow shifted. Something rustled, then merciful solitude embraced me again.

Opening my eyes, I found the mag I'd tossed at the door sitting on the lid of a Tupperware crate.

I was sure discussions on my future continued. Just beyond my earshot.

I slept for mere minutes and awoke to Aunt Aylie sitting over me, teeth clenched. Her hair was a frizzy nest, her fuzzy bathrobe gaping as she restrained my flailing limbs.

Adrenaline twitched through my muscles as I bleared up at her, dawn breaking through the window blinds.

She brushed back my sweaty bangs. "It was only a dream."

No, it definitely wasn't, I thought. Because I'd been fighting for my life when she broke me from the terror—from the shadows strangling me—and it was just as painful as any other licking I'd ever taken.

"Is she all right?" Ash Loosestrife stood in the doorway, his curly black hair disarrayed. Eyes sunken in the thin light, he wore a pair of creased dockers and a zip-up sweater. His stubby hand flexed around a saber hilt.

"She'll be fine." Aunt Aylie flitted him away as I gripped my sheet. "Leave us."

He grunted, rubbing his forehead with the heel of his hand. "Cornelian says this door should never go unguarded."

Huffing, Aunt Aylie barreled toward the door. "Then stand outside." She slammed the portal in his face, then tromped back to me, arms folded.

"Have you calmed down?" she asked with much less tenderness. I'd known the compassion couldn't last.

I nodded, still shivering.

"Good. Now that you've woken the whole house, I suppose it's time to rise. When I leave, I'll send the healer in to check your bandages, then I want you to clean up and get dressed—there's a bathroom two doors down. Once you're presentable, meet me in the living room. There's much to discuss."

The promised healer, Shasta Milfoil, a pudgy Danann elder in black calico, examined my injuries with quiet efficiency. At first, she only spoke to tell me to turn, and that I smelled hypoglycemic. After rubbing something camphoric into my battered tailbone, which felt remarkably better, she left to return with a plate of cookies and a glass of milk.

I'd have bet money she was the world's best grandmother to somebody.

While I devoured my breakfast in unrepentant piggishness, she removed the green, gooey bandage from my calf. A cookie between my lips, I contemplated my affliction. All the puncture wounds from the bat's bite had healed. Shiny pink polka dots replaced them. Shasta pressed upon one of the dots—no pain.

She smiled at my widening eyes, her pride more than called for. "How did you do that?" I mumbled around my cookie.

"We hedge healers put a little something—extra—in our poultices, darling, to speed healing. They don't normally work this quickly, mind you. Unless—" She trailed off, considering me.

"Unless what?"

"Unless a patient has what we call the warrior's skin. Beyond accelerated healing, it also makes a body harder to injure—harder to kill."

I swallowed, chocolate chips scraping my throat. "You think I have it?"

"I'd say so. It's not an uncommon gift among Dananns, although most will be mystified to hear you possess it." She paused a beat before answering the question in my eyes. "Because it's not something typically found in females."

Rare and powerful gifts. That's what Briar had said I might have (if I were the nebulous Aurora). Was the warrior's skin one of them?

I bit my lip, thinking, *What the hell am I?*

Before Shasta left me, I snatched her hand. "Please don't tell anyone."

While at first bemused, she eventually set a cool hand over mine. "Wouldn't dream of it."

Minutes later, I wore a peach sweater and a pair of heathered sweatpants, my freshly washed hair piled atop my head in a damp, haphazard bun. Ash Loosestrife led me into his uber-masculine living room. Vestiges of cigar smoke clung to his paneled walls.

Vi and Ace awaited me on a scuffed leather couch in the center of the room, both in their night clothes. Vi sat curled into the arm rest, her eyes red-rimmed, haunted. Tears streamed down her cheeks as she gnawed her thumb raw. Ace sat hunched, elbows on his knees, tapping one heel in a frantic beat. His eyes were bloodshot, his hair standing on end. The moment they saw me, they wilted in relief.

Ace surged up when I rushed them. "Thank Danu you're all right," he said as I strangled him in a hug, needing to hear the heartbeat of someone I loved.

Vi mewled like a baby when she joined the embrace, her mussed hair soft against my cheek. "We should've made him come with us." She hiccupped against my shoulder. "We shouldn't have listened when he said he'd be all right."

I wished I could tell her it wasn't that simple. Briar had warned me those assassin bats hunted by scent. They'd have followed Daddy's scent to any hidden refuge. In joining everyone at Ash Loosestrife's house, he would've led the bogeybats right to Vi and Ace.

"What happened last night?" Ace asked, hours of being left in the dark stressing him. "All Aunt Aylie told us was that Dad passed on, and that you were hurt."

I stared for a moment, the horrors I'd witnessed indescribable. Knowing wouldn't ease his mind and telling would obliterate me. I'd been trying so hard not to think about what I'd seen, though unwanted images kept flooding me. An especially graphic one of Daddy, cold and gray, had caused me a mental collapse during my shower. I'd balled up beneath the spray and sobbed into my knees.

Part of me needed to tell someone what I'd been through—needed to call my friends and unleash every sordid detail upon them. Like the telling would purge the memories. The rest of me, though—it refused to speak a single word about it. It didn't want their pity or their Hallmark condolences in the mail. Because admitting last night had happened made everything real.

I didn't want it to be real.

Aunt Aylie, Uncle Neel, and Briar's arrival saved me from having to sicken and dismay my younger siblings. Perhaps one day I'd confess what happened the night our father died, but that day was far in the future.

"I'm fine," I assured Ace before he turned to our uncle.

Lines cut across his 16-year-old brow. "Will someone finally tell us what's been going on? We deserve to know."

Uncle Neel inhaled like he was preparing to drop a meteorite on us. "Sit down, all of you." He massaged his temples. Little sleep and dismal circumstances ringed his eyes.

In the same weary state, Briar fell onto a dining chair before me, his seat no doubt placed there in preparation for this talk. He'd changed his clothes, ridding himself of oily bat blood, but ash still speckled his neck. His sweat caught me as I sat on the couch between my siblings, squeezing their hands in my lap.

Aunt Aylie reposed on the armrest of the couch, petting Vi's unkempt hair. I wondered what she'd eaten for breakfast, as motherly as she was being.

Uncle Neel plopped into a leather recliner beside Briar, facing us Larkspur kids. "I'll just start from the beginning. You three—you're not what you think you are. You weren't born where your father said you were."

Ace chewed his bottom lip. "You mean Philadelphia?"

Sniffling into a tissue Aunt Aylie had pulled from her cleavage, Vi shook her head at Uncle Neel. "Then where were we born?"

"You're all from a place called Evereostre," Uncle Neel stated. He templed his hands over his stomach. "As was your father, your mother, me, your aunt, Briar—and most of the other Dananns you've ever met."

The three of us blinked at him—absorbing.

Finally, I asked, "Why would he lie about something like that? So, we aren't originally from Philly? Who cares?"

"Philadelphia was just the cover story your father chose. He had a fondness for the place." Uncle Neel shook his head, rolled his eyes. "Something I'll never understand. In truth, he could've chosen any city and named it as your origins. You children were too young to doubt him."

Of course, we wouldn't doubt him. We were kids. How foolish of us to trust that our father wouldn't deceive us.

"He did it for your protection," Briar answered the burgeoning fury on my face. "He didn't want to lie to you, but he needed you to believe you were from this place, so you'd all act like normal American children—so you wouldn't draw unwanted attention."

Why the hell was he talking as if he'd been a wise old adult when my father had made his bullshit decision? We were born in the same fucking year!

"But *aren't* we normal American children?" Ace asked.

"No, Acer, you're not," Uncle Neel declared. "You're all part of an ancient mystical race known in our world as the Tuatha Dé Danann."

My siblings mentally stumbled over the phrase *our world*. I could sympathize, thinking Uncle Neel should've started by explaining other life-sustaining worlds existed in the universe.

Ignoring our stupefaction, Uncle Neel continued, "Translated, it means the Children of the Goddess, Danu. Now, there are many subsets of our species, but our Danann race is the most complex. We're known here on Earth by many names—*The Good Folk, The Fair Folk, The Golden Ones,* and *The Auld Ones*—but in our world, we simply call our expansive species fae."

We froze because—what the hell had he been smoking?

Ace turned to me, sneering. "Is he saying we're *fairies*?"

Vi's streaky face scrunched. "Like Tinkerbell?"

"Humans' notions of us fae have drastically changed throughout time," Uncle Neel answered. "But obviously we're not thimble-sized—at least not Dananns—and we don't fly around sprinkling dust on people. Although, some *can* fly."

"Your knowledge on Dananns is patchy," Aunt Aylie assumed the tale. "We altered your lessons to conform to human cynicism. Excepting children, they rarely believe in magic now. Which, as you might imagine, makes living here challenging—more dangerous—for us. So, before us, fae hadn't resided on Earth for centuries. We had extenuating circumstances, however."

"Fairies used to live here before?" I asked, not ready to use the word *we* yet.

"Long ago," she answered. "We existed long before the Goddess Mother created this world. She tasked us with looking after the humans, with keeping order among them. We exerted Her powers, bestowed rewards and punishments as needed. We awed humankind with our magic, and many ancient civilizations worshipped us as deities. The Greeks, Romans, Norse, Celts, Egyptians, Native Americans—they all offered us adulation and love. I don't think we have time to delve into the dynamics—" She glanced at Uncle Neel, whose mouth turned down in agreement. "But you should know that there's an important link between mankind's adulation and the strength of our powers."

Vi shifted to gape up at our aunt. "Do *I* have powers?"

"Most fae do," was her cryptic response.

Briar's eyes flicked to me. "Some more than others."

My grip tightened on my siblings' hands.

Aunt Aylie sighed. "Anyway, in the biblical era, some humans started calling us angels, depicting us as virtuous, saintly creatures—which we aren't. We're not infallible. Certainly not sinless. We're more like the vengeful, self-interested gods and goddesses they once believed in. So, when we failed to live up to their ideals, they began associating our magic, prurience, and penchant for mischief with evil.

"But we're no different than humans. Some of us are good, others bad. Although, some of us struggle with gluttony of the polar magics—opposing ends of the prismatum."

We blinked, not comprehending.

"You'll learn all about it some other time," she said. "For now, just think of it as a magical spectrum—like a rainbow, but the colors change vertically, not horizontally, from lighter to darker. And spending too much time indulging in either of the poles is just like becoming hooked on drugs."

Said so nonchalantly, my mind almost skipped over the easy danger she'd described. Almost.

"Anyhow," she continued, ignoring my consternation. "The majority of us knows it's best to follow Danu's tenets for a fruitful life. Hers and her son's."

Uncle Neel had preached about Danu and her son many times at spirit circle. Finding out their religious parables were historical recountings was like discovering Paul Bunyan and his ox had truly created the Grand Canyon.

"You should remember her son from circle lessons," Aunt Aylie remarked in the manner of a schoolmarm. "The Dagda—the All Father—the first Danann king. His descendants are still in power today."

Good for them, but I wasn't in the mood for a history lecture right then.

So, I almost groaned when Aunt Aylie cleared her throat and chronicled, "The Dagda had many children, including five sons: Aengus, Nuadu, Ogma, Cermait Honey-Mouth, and Boderg the Red—all of whom he loved just as any father loves his sons—even while knowing one of them differed greatly from his others.

"Cermait was a charming, handsome fae prince with a proclivity for greed, gluttony, and void magic—an addictive, corrupting polar magic—like a drug. Though the Dagda warned him against all these vices, Cermait couldn't stop himself.

"When the Dagda grew weary of his time as ruler, he decided to split our realm between his sons, who'd govern the world and its people together. Aengus was granted reeveship of all the lands to the north—"

"Yes, yes," I grumbled. "Where there was perpetual winter, and everything was covered in snow and ice. Can we get to the part of the story we don't already know?"

Aunt Aylie glowered at my interruption.

"Amy, you need to hear this," Uncle Neel chastened.

Heat flared into the arches of my ears. "Then maybe we should've been told years ago!"

"Well, you weren't," he retorted. "It was your father's right to decide when you learned the truth. It wasn't our place to question him. Now, listen to your aunt."

I slammed back into the couch.

Aunt Aylie lifted her chin and skipped ahead. "As the Dagda's favorite son, Boderg the Red received the throne and the fertile eastern lands, where it was always spring. He named this place Evereostre."

The mention of that place subdued me, even if Uncle Neel couldn't.

"But for Cermait, the Dagda granted nothing," Aunt Aylie stated. "He recognized what Cermait had become—an entitled, selfish tyrant, far too prone to wickedness to serve nature or our people. The fact that he'd gambled away all the magical guilds' sacred jinxes—think of them as enchanted pets—was proof enough for him.

"Cermait was granted a lower title—a place in Boderg's court—but his jealous nature spurred him to scorn his father's offer—and Boderg for being given the power he craved.

"So, Cermait withdrew from his family and set off on his own. He settled in a wasteland beyond the mountains bordering Evereostre and the Summer Court, Lithalaly. He named his barren climes Covenlen, but we've always called them the Shadow Court."

The hairs prickled along my nape. Both the phone thief and Briar had mentioned something about a Shadow Prince the night before.

"Some followed Cermait to that forsaken land, as hooked on the void as he was," Aunt Aylie said. "His court refused to pay Boderg or his descendants homage. Boderg didn't care; he looked at Cermait as little more than a fly on his neck. However, Cermait Honey-Mouth was cleverer than his brother knew.

"He began subtly disrupting order, spreading fear and doubt over Boderg's right to rule. He sowed propaganda, inciting dissent—most of which the crown always managed—and clung to his self-appointed reeveship well after his brothers moved onto the next life, passing their titles and the throne to their sons. He even changed his name, so younger generations wouldn't associate him with Cermait Honey-Mouth's misdeeds."

"What did he change it to?" Ace asked.

"Gentian. Erybos Gentian."

I frowned, having also heard the name Gentian while eavesdropping last night.

"He still lives, running—"

"Wait." Vi gasped. "How can this man still be alive? Wasn't his father the first Danann king? Back before we—I mean, mankind—even existed?"

"Yes," Uncle Neel answered. "But in our world, time and aging don't work the way they do here. In our world, time pockets are everywhere—some move faster, others slower. In some instances, time doesn't move at all."

"Then how old are you?" Ace grunted.

Aunt Aylie's sharp glance was as good as a swat aback the head. "That question is just as rude in our society as it is here, Acer."

Ace scowled.

Uncle Neel eyed him but continued without scolding. "And some lucky fae are gifted with the ability to revert to an age they've previously lived, so they can renew their life over and over again."

"Are we immortal?" I asked.

Briar leaned forward in his seat, resting elbows on knees. "No, we can still die of old age—if we allow it to happen. Of course, with the many ways to slow age progression, we can live a very long time. Most of us eventually *choose* to move onto the next life."

I met his solemn gaze, supposing he wasn't as young as he looked. The liar.

Uncle Neel cleared his throat, moving along. "Gentian is by far the oldest fae in our realm. He now runs several businesses throughout the kingdom, amassing great wealth and political power. He claims he doesn't covet the throne, but sources say he secretly works against the ruling family, hoping to foment rebellion. He wants the people to revolt and install him as king. His efforts, unfortunately, are quite effective, and he causes great unrest in the lower classes. He's convinced the people he cares for them, but he cares for absolutely nothing but himself and his revenge. If king, he'd eat the people of our world for breakfast to sate his greed."

"He wants revenge?" Vi asked. "On who? His father?"

Uncle Neel nodded. "Yes—and on Boderg."

"But aren't they both dead?" she reasoned. "I mean—they moved onto the next life."

"Millennia ago," Aunt Aylie confirmed.

Talk about holding a grudge.

"I don't know what Gentian's ultimate plan for revenge is," Uncle Neel confessed. "But I know it involves the royal family—Boderg's descendants."

"What's he trying to do to them?" Ace asked.

Uncle Neel's Adam's apple bobbed. "Kill them off."

"Why don't they just kill Gentian?" Ace suggested. "If they know what he's doing?"

"They've tried numerous times," Uncle Neel groused. "But the weasel's grown too powerful—politically and magically. His fortress is impenetrable, and his guards are ruthless, some demonic. Gentian has defiled his soul with the void, but he's also manifested strong, dangerous abilities, including the ability to craft blood curses."

Well, that couldn't sound more ominous.

"A blood curse is like an incurable, communicative disease. It starts by destroying a patriarch, then progresses down the line until all that share that patriarch's blood are dead. It only stops when the line is eradicated from existence. Several years ago, Gentian cast this curse on the royal family, starting with the reigning king."

"How the hell was that allowed?" Ace demanded of our uncle. "Wasn't the king being guarded? Or is this the kind of thing someone can do from miles away? Psh! If it is, then I'm glad we aren't there anymore."

Uncle Neel swiped his hand down his face. "I'm not fluent in curse lore, but I believe it can be done from anywhere. The curse seed will find its host—wherever they are. However, Gentian still invaded the Spring Palace to cast his curse on the king."

Uncle Neel took a breath, shook his head. "Let me back up. Before he broke into the palace, Gentian first invited the king to his court. He sent him a message stating that he wished to mend fences, that he was willing to swear fealty to his brother's line, to his rightful king. So, the king—a trusting man—took Gentian's word for it and journeyed to Gentian's Shadow Court to forge a peace treaty."

I pictured the desolate crag from my nightmare.

"During the king's visit, something happened to dash the prospect of familial bonding to hell. Something was said or done by either Gentian or the king, and the king left without a peace treaty. When the king returned home, Gentian waited until well past nightfall, when the king would be least prepared for an attack. Then he conjured an interstice, a wrinkle in space, and stepped through it into the Spring Palace. Think of it like teleportation."

"Like on *Star Voyager*," Ace clarified for himself.

Uncle Neel laughed. "Anyway, in doing this, Gentian managed to skirt all palace security details. He and his henchmen then cast the blood curse—when the king was too weak to fight the seed."

"Like an actual seed?" Ace repeated, doubtless wondering the same thing I was—how something so innocuous could annihilate an entire bloodline. "Like the seeds we plant and eat?"

Uncle Neel cleared his throat. "In our world, seeds can be catalysts for great magic. See, some magic is inherent, developed at birth. Some is so simple that you can learn it. Other magic, however, is germinated—like a plant. Magic seeds are what our civilization revolves around—the impetus of fertility and life. Ingesting one is to absorb a new ability—like the power to make rain or create light. It's usually temporary and usually contains a spark of the harmless gray magics. Regardless, all seeds draw our kind—as you three probably already know because we've never had to badger any of you into gardening. Probably the *only* chore we've never had to badger you into."

Aunt Aylie clucked in accord.

"But I'm digressing." Uncle Neel shook his head. "The point is, we fae thrive on fostering seeds, on using their extraordinary abilities to either sprout new life or influence the world around us. We're drawn to them because—well, they really are astounding in all they can do—seeds."

I was starting to think Uncle Neel had an addiction too.

"Now, *curse* seeds have the strongest draw because they've been voided, then manipulated. And the king couldn't fight his compulsion to grab Gentian's seed. Curse seeds instill a physical *need* to touch them. I've heard they cause an internal sensation—something like chicken pox in your blood."

I'd never had chicken pox, but plenty of my friends in grade school had, and they'd been miserable.

"So, the king touched the seed, and it planted itself in his body—where it would grow like a cancer. It also summoned a harbinger to kill the king."

"I thought harbingers were just signals of something to come," I remarked. "Like robins—they signal spring."

"On Earth, that's how they're known," Uncle Neel agreed. "In our world, they mean something more sinister."

I gulped. "So Gentian's harbinger came to—*assassinate*—the king?"

My uncle's frown deepened. "Yes. But unluckily for Gentian, the queen was there at the time."

Vi blotted her runny nose. "There's a queen?"

Aunt Aylie's sky-blue eyes clouded. "There was."

"There's a second reason Gentian sought revenge on the king," Uncle Neel added. "Something that made things more—personal. Gentian felt the king had stolen his intended bride—the young daughter of one of Gentian's closest allies. She had a rare gift that he yearned to control. Soon after she was born, she was affianced to Gentian. The king was promised to someone else too.

"I should explain that true Danann marriage ceremonies are much, *much* different from the ones you've witnessed. The bride and groom are both blindfolded. The intended bride is placed in a line of other females, and the groom must find her using only his secondary senses. Sometimes, mistakes happen, and the groom winds up marrying the incorrect woman."

Who the hell had thought that *a good idea?*

Uncle Neel shrugged. "We fae enjoy mischief and trickery. It certainly makes a wedding more exciting. Sometimes scandalous."

"I'm guessing the king's wedding was one of the scandalous ones," I said.

Uncle Neel snorted. "The most. Gentian's intended was there just for fun, but the king accidentally chose her instead of his actual bride. Once a choice is made, no one prevents it. Even if it's wrong. We prefer to think of fate as a better matchmaker."

"Gentian didn't see it that way, of course. He was livid, claiming the king had chosen wrong on purpose. The king denied this, but when he and his new queen happened to fall madly in love, Gentian thought his suspicions confirmed. It only fueled the bad blood.

"Anyway, the queen was there the night Gentian cast the curse. She stayed the assassin and saved her husband's life, though she couldn't lift the curse."

"Good for her," I said.

The corner of Aunt Aylie's mouth trembled as she faced me. "She used her entire store of power in saving her husband. There was no time for it to regenerate before Gentian killed her for thwarting him."

I stiffened, recalling a vision of a tall, slender woman with copper hair disintegrating around me in blinding stardust.

"Ow!" Ace yanked his hand from mine, shaking it. "Jeez, Amy. It's a hand, not a stress ball."

I patted his shoulder. "Sorry. I—I'm just—"

"What's wrong, Amy?" Briar asked.

"Nothing." Sleep deprivation had me drawing insane conclusions. "It's just—well, what happened to the king?"

"He fled the realm," Uncle Neel said. "Went somewhere he and his family would be lost in a crowd. They went somewhere they could hide from Gentian and his harbingers. They came here."

We froze again, doubting our ears.

"You mean, they came here—like to the human world," Vi rationalized.

"I mean they came *here*." Uncle Neel grimaced, watching his meteor land. "To Pittsburgh. The king—and his three children."

ELEVEN

"You can't be serious!" Vi screeched. "We're *royalty*? I'm a fairy princess, and you won't even let me have my own car?"

"This is fucking bullshit!" Ace erupted, his ears pinkening.

"Acer Larkspur!" Aunt Aylie glared. "Watch your language!"

Ace's amber eyes nearly popped from his head. "My language is called for! You made us go to school, knowing most of the stuff we learned here won't mean shit where we're from!"

While my brother and sister argued in tandem, reality stampeded me. My night terrors weren't just intricate phantasms. They weren't fantasies a child therapist could reason out of me. Because they weren't just dreams. They were memories.

"I was there," I uttered more to myself than anyone else. "I saw it happen."

"Enough, children!" Aunt Aylie hushed my siblings. "What was that, Amy?"

I blinked at her, everyone staring at me. "I was there in the room—when the queen saved the king." The full weight of what I was saying clobbered me. My hands shook as I wailed into my palms. "Ohmigoddess! I was there! She was my *mother*! I watched her die!"

"That's impossible," Uncle Neel said. "If you were there at the time, Gentian never would've left you alive—the heir to the throne."

I sat bolt upright again.

Ace collapsed in relief, looked ceilingward in silent thanks to Danu.

"I thought you said the throne was passed down to the son," I argued, gouging my own thighs. "That's Ace!"

Twitching, Ace gaped at my betrayal.

"Relax, Ace," Uncle Neel said. "The heir to the throne has always been a son because that's just how it always worked out. Technically, all the royal charter states about succession is the heir must be the ruler's firstborn."

Vi's features screwed. "No other king has had a female firstborn?"

Uncle Neel shrugged. "The Goddess never made it so, but we've had some mighty powerful queens in our history. The Dagda chose the most powerful, who we call the Morrigan, as one of his last wives. She led a war for him against the Fomorians—a race of fae Dananns don't get along with." His mouth twisted. "You should remember them from Sunday circle lessons."

Indeed, I did. Who could forget such awful stories of carnage? That I'd thought were mere allegories.

"Anyway, we won because of the Morrigan," Uncle Neel extolled.

Had she had the warrior's skin as well? I really didn't want to be the only woman in history to have it.

"What made her so powerful?" Vi questioned.

"She was what we call a triple goddess," Uncle Neel answered. "A term we use for females blessed with multiple principal powers. Most fae only manifest one, two if they're lucky. The Morrigan was the most multi-faceted triple goddess our people have ever seen. There were two others before her—Danu Herself, and Brigid, the Dagda's daughter. Every time one is born, she's more powerful than the last."

Aunt Aylie waved in dismissal. "You'll all receive a thorough history lesson in the near future."

"Sounds like we could've done without those *human* world history classes," Ace snarked under his breath.

Aunt Aylie's gaze narrowed at him. "Right now, the present is more important. Amy, your father, the king, took his final breath last night, so that makes you the queen."

All eyes locked on me. My mouth dried out. A pit formed in my stomach. "I can't be a queen!" I squeaked. "I don't know how!"

"You'll learn," Aunt Aylie retorted. "And you'll have a more than knowledgeable king to guide you."

Mouths opened on both sides of me.

Surely, I'd heard wrong. "Huh?"

Uncle Neel and Briar shared a pointed look as Aunt Aylie rose from her place on the couch armrest and clicked her tongue. "Viola, Acer—go fetch yourselves breakfast while we talk to Amy." She then ushered my shell-shocked siblings from the room.

"Why can't they stay?" I wanted them nearby. They were like lamp posts, and I was lost in a fog.

No response came, and when I turned back around, Briar sat beside me. He took my hand, his fingers warm and dexterous as they entwined with mine. His gaze brimmed with both compassion and duty. Suddenly, I realized who my king was.

"Oh, my Goddess," I muttered into a hand. Briar murmured something soft, rubbing my back.

"I don't know what you're upset about," Aunt Aylie chafed, rounding back toward me. "There are plenty of fae ladies who'd be thanking Danu on their hands and knees for a betrothal with Briar Hawthorne." Her pinch stung my shoulder. "Now, sit up and face your future husband."

"Ow!" I whined, jerking up.

Briar only adjusted his hold on me.

Rubbing my shoulder, I stared down my relatives. "So, *that's* why you've put so much effort into getting Briar and I together. To satisfy some agreement you made."

Neither expressed guilt at being caught in their manipulations. Which dissatisfied me to the point of outrage.

"We didn't make the agreement," Uncle Neel replied. "That was your parents' doing. Before you were born, they promised you to Briar. Your mother knew you'd be a girl."

"*Why* would they do that?" I whined. Wasn't it Daddy who'd taken one look at me and declared Briar wasn't the one? Why would he say that if he knew he'd already offered my hand in marriage to the man?

Damn, I wish he were here, so I could ask him.

The thought triggered instant sorrow. My eyes misted.

"Because they trusted me," Briar answered my spoken question for Uncle Neel, who'd had a heated rejoinder on the tip of his tongue. "I was your mother's closest friend. When she married your father, I joined her at Evereostre, became a member of the Old Order and a royal guard. They knew I'd protect and honor you."

My stomach knotted. "How old are you?" I cringed in anticipation of Briar's answer. We both ignored Aunt Aylie's austere hiss.

"I'm 366 Danann years old," Briar confessed. "I'm one of the fae who can revert to any previous age I've lived. When we rushed you here to safety, I reverted to your age, so you'd grow up with me."

And so I wouldn't be creeped out when you tried macking on me.

"What about the other Danann kids? Were they all old farts too?"

My word choice rankled Aunt Aylie, but Briar just chuckled. "A few were, yes, but most of them were actual Danann children, brought here with their families to create a true Danann community—so you'd feel like you belonged somewhere."

Mission failed!

"What about Laurel?" I contemplated our joined hands, picturing hers wedged between them. "What was she?"

"She—uh—she's a reverter too. But she isn't that much older than you. She was about twenty when we crossed the portal."

Was he already in love with her then?

Aunt Aylie harrumphed. "For heaven's sake, Amy. Why do you look like you swallowed a lemon? I thought you liked Briar."

Yes, I liked Briar. I always had. Was I attracted to him—*hell* yes. Did I enjoy talking to him, spending time with him? Very much. He was sweet and patient and cared about me. Just not exactly in the way I wished he did. Could that change?

Maybe. If he *tried* hard enough.

My aunt gusted with frustration. "Didn't you sleep with him?"

Holy mother of mortification!

"Aunt Aylie!" I flapped, my face burning.

"Oh, knock that off," she sniped. "I'd swear you were a Puritan. Honestly, I'd be alarmed if you'd fought off the urge to mate on Beltane. Sex is part of life, not something to be embarrassed about. You need to embrace your sensual self."

I chewed my lip, wanting to emulate all my favorite romance heroines' freedom of sexual spirit. But did I really have to do it in front of my family?

"You should better acquaint yourself with it, Amy," Aunt Aylie harangued. "One, because sex and the having of it are openly discussed topics at court, and you wouldn't want to come off prudish to your subjects. And two, because you'll need heirs—as many as those narrow hips can hold."

Words failed me. All of them.

"Goddess willing, there's already one sprouting in there." Uncle Neel nodded at my middle.

I hiccupped on my appall.

Clearing his throat, Briar squeezed my hand. "Actually, there won't be a faelet just yet."

Oh, shit, I thought, *Please, please*, please, *Briar, don't tell them about the morning-after pill*. The last thing I needed right then was their castigation for breaking the sacrament. And for poisoning myself.

Though Briar's mouth slanted at me, he turned to my relatives and admitted, "I wore a condom both times we had sex." He bowed his head, the epitome of contrition. "I broke the sacrament, and I beg the Mother's forgiveness."

I started in surprise. He was shouldering the blame for me?

Uncle Neel's mouth wriggled, an angry worm.

Aunt Aylie balled her hands, stomped her foot. "*Briar*! Why in hell would you do that?"

"We all agreed impregnating her as soon as possible was best!" Uncle Neel blustered.

Who the fuck was we?

"Yes, I remember, Cornelian. But Laurustinus raised her to think like an independent American woman." He glanced at me, exasperated. "She wanted to practice safe sex, and I figured it was better for me to further our relationship than to argue and get nowhere."

Aunt Aylie and Uncle Neel stewed.

Trying to wrap my brain around all I'd learned in the past fifteen minutes, I scratched my dampened head. "I'm sorry. I really don't see why it's so damn important that I get pregnant right now."

"Ladies don't say damn," my aunt snapped at me.

I bit back a scream.

Briar exhaled. "There's tension at court about being ruled by a female—as it hasn't happened before. We thought we'd alleviate the peoples' concerns if you were pregnant—or if you had embraced motherhood already."

I stared at him, still lost.

"Because that would assure them you intend to be a traditional queen."

"What's a traditional queen?"

"A traditional queen is her king's companion and lover." His voice was smooth, gentle. "She supports him, raises his children, oversees the running of the palace, and acts as a diplomat in many ways at court. She's a beacon of decorum, charm, and beauty for the people."

Has anyone here actually met me? I'm a beacon of none of those things.

"But she doesn't actually rule?" I clarified, getting to the heart of the matter. "That would be the king? That would be you?"

Briar shifted, clearing his throat. "Well, yes, Amy. That's what that means."

Super sensitive to even kindly judgment, I withdrew from him. "Do yinz think I'd make a bad ruler or something?"

My aunt and uncle stammered in response.

"Of course not, Amy." Briar regained my hand. "That's not what we think. It's just—well, you said it yourself—you don't know how to be a queen."

That was very true.

"We knew the transition would be difficult for you, but your father insisted you inherit the throne. So, we thought my being the sovereign would be a satisfactory solution for all. I've been groomed for this, you see. First with my father, who's the reeve of Lithalaly, the Summer Court, and then with your father, after our betrothal. I've no great desire for power, of course, and if you feel prepared to rule—"

Was this all for real? How could I answer that question? I hadn't even had time to weigh my options.

"You'd be taking on the troubles of an entire world, niece," Uncle Neel warned me. "And the various courts—they're more like this realm's continents, not its countries."

I gulped at the thought of such oppressive responsibility.

"And I hate to say it, but your burden as a sovereign would be much heavier than the one your father carried. Because you're a female. Just like this world, ours is male dominated. You'd be ridiculed as weak, ineffectual, hysterical, dimwitted—" Uncle Neel trailed off. "Need I go on?"

Aunt Aylie softened toward me, knowing I feared public scorn. "As I've always said, Amy—females and politics shouldn't mix."

That unsettled me more than anything. Aunt Aylie had to be wrong. Just so I could sleep at night.

Daddy clearly hadn't agreed with her, otherwise he wouldn't have handed me his crown. However, to imagine ruling an entire world of people whose interests and issues I had no notion of—I couldn't even grasp the onus of that.

Plus, there was the whole matter of the life I'd always wanted—to be a career girl at a major publishing house. My education, my friends, and my career—I was pretty sure all that was over with if I took up ruling a fairy realm.

Would I stand a chance of staying my course if Briar took the throne for me? As a secondary figure at the Spring Court, there'd be no good reason I couldn't remain in the only world I knew to achieve my ultimate dreams. Even if Briar and I did get married—as everyone assumed we would—things could still work in my favor. We'd just see each other on weekends or something, and I could live my normal human life.

Except, you were meant for much greater things than that, Daddy's voice chimed in my mind.

"Oh, I can't." Indecisiveness wasn't in my nature, but this pickle had thrown me for a loop. My heart didn't know what it wanted to do. "Yesterday, I was just a college student who needed a summer job. Now—this choice—I *can't*."

Briar set a hand on my shoulder. "Hey, that's okay, Amy. It's settled then."

"What—but I—you don't—that's not—" I couldn't form the proper words to explain the misunderstanding. I hadn't abdicated. I just hadn't made up my mind.

"It's fine, Amy, really. I'll do the ruling, and your only concern will be courtly life."

Uncle Neel scoffed. "And staying alive."

I turned to Uncle Neel. "What?"

One of his bushy brows arched at me. "The blood curse, Amy."

I shook my head, dense with all my thoughts on Briar's error.

A great furrow split Uncle Neel's forehead. He leaned toward me. "I thought you understood, Amy. The curse sent those beasts last night. It killed your father." His voice roughened on his last point. "Now, you're its next victim."

All my aspirations for a normal human life flitted right out the damn door.

A tear dripped down my cheek as I stood in my ravaged bedroom. My belongings lay scattered everywhere, some of them broken or shattered beyond recognition. Posters hung in tatters, the plaster beneath shredded. The bats had disemboweled my hordes of throw pillows; stuffing now coated my bedding. Somehow my headboard remained upright despite the giant crack splitting it in two. The curtains framing my window seat dangled off the wall on one side, its rod reposed in an awkward diagonal, shrouding the neat pile of complicated political philosophy books I'd set on the window seat only a week ago.

Tramping down debris, I ran to the books and scooped them all into my arms. Heavy, they may have been, but I didn't care. They were the last gifts Daddy would ever give me. Now that I knew why he'd tasked me with reading them, I'd start as soon as I was able. Maybe they'd even help me make the hardest decision of my life.

The fate of my father's crown was *not* settled. Regardless of what some assumed.

When I heard footsteps, I wiped my tears.

"I know this is hard," Briar murmured. I faced him, still embracing the books, as he stepped into the room. "But we don't have time for sentiment. We must gather your essentials and move out. The first squadron has already crossed the portal with your father's body and staff. We need to hurry after them before something unsavory finds you."

I sighed, resigned to my exodus. Knowing my life was at stake had made me quite amenable to relinquishing my dreams. What good would they do me if the curse found me? I couldn't publish novels from the grave.

"These books." I coughed, grief thickening my throat. "They've got to come with me."

"They'll be too heavy, Amy." Briar failed to hold back a harrumph. "And you don't need them. I'll make sure they're gathered up and taken by royal caravan to the Spring Palace, though. I promise your books will find you there."

He padded toward me, glass and plastic crunching beneath his sneakers. He'd dressed in all black, a thick hoodie beneath his lined leather vest. To most, he'd resemble a heavy metal enthusiast, but I knew the truth. He'd dressed for battle like all the other Danann warriors awaiting me outside my childhood home.

Their goal—to whisk me back to Evereostre before Gentian acquired the bogeybat's staff fragment. That would be evidence enough of Daddy's demise, giving Gentian the go-ahead to sic his harbingers on me. Before they reached me, my protectors wanted me ensconced in a guarded palace, so they'd have a shot at keeping me alive.

Shaking off my dread, I set down the pile of books and took the large black backpack Briar handed me. "Thanks."

He surveyed my room. "It's best if you pack lightweight items—underwear, a sweater, gloves, warm socks—"

"I thought we were going to the Spring Court." I went to my top dresser drawer, which lay overturned on my armchair beside my toppling bookshelf. "Won't it be warm?"

Briar knelt to sift through the damaged trinkets littering my floor. "The days are warm, but the nights can be nippy."

Supposing that made sense in spring, I began a hunt for the items he'd listed.

"What's the deal with the cane?"

"It's a staff," Briar corrected, rummaging beneath my bed. He found my off-brand Buggs and considered them. "Are these comfortable to walk long distances in?"

I nodded before he tossed them to me, advised me to put them on. As I was now wearing a pair of jean shorts and my favorite UPJ tee, I was glad certain celebrities had made it fashionable to wear snow boots with anything.

"Okay, what's the deal with the *staff*? Why did the bats want it so badly?" I assumed that's why the ugly bastards had plundered the house instead of just killing Daddy and moving on.

"Because it's got powerful magic." Briar nabbed my hairbrush from behind my headboard, raised it in triumph like a hard-won trophy. "It was originally the Dagda's staff."

Of course, it was.

"It's been passed down to all the Dagda's successors. Now, it's yours. Although, since you hacked it in half, its magic is sort of—broken."

I cringed. "Leave it to me to destroy something eons older than the goddamn earth."

"It's all right." Briar laughed. "Trust me, it's good that you broke it. I don't even want to know what Gentian would do with the staff at its max. It wields crystal magic—the polar opposite of void—and it's a fearsome weapon."

"What could the staff do? You know, before I broke it."

"Many things—some I don't even know of—but its principal power is the power of change. And, yes, that's a very vague concept. Change can mean many things, and it doesn't always work out exactly as the staff holder wishes it, so requests must be worded carefully."

He shrugged. "Some fae find joy in trickery, especially against their enemies. The staff was probably *made* complicated—in case it fell into the wrong hands."

"The phone thief called it a totem." I stashed a handful of panties in the book bag. "What did that mean?"

"A totem is a personal object that embodies a fae. Everyone has one. Not all of them are magical, but all of them are significant. Harbingers take them to indicate a cursed host's death. It satisfies some payment to the void used to conjure the curse."

"If it's so important to the curse, then why the hell didn't Daddy hide it somewhere more secure than the dang curtain panel?" Would things have gone differently last night if the staff were stashed somewhere safer? "Was he planning to use it as a weapon against the bogeybats?"

By the Goddess, then why didn't *he?*

"I'm sure he tried to use it before they attacked. He'd been trying to use it since we learned the bats were here on Earth. But as weak as he's been lately—" Regretful, Briar clicked his tongue. "You need a certain level of stamina to wield a weapon like that, and your father just didn't have it in him anymore."

"Then why have it there at all?" As tired and emotional as I was, my frustration was on a hair-trigger. My hands shook as I demanded, "*Why* didn't someone take it somewhere else, so the bats couldn't fucking find it?"

"Not that simple, Amy. Totems like that—heirlooms—they smell like their owner. And there were so many damn bogeybats. At least one of them would've followed the scent of the staff—would've killed the person who had it and taken it—whole and functional. And that would've been much worse than what ended up happening. Trust me."

Says the man who's been lying to me my whole life.

"Anyway, the curtain panel should've kept it safe. We'd had it specifically enchanted years ago to keep the staff secured—like a lockbox. Plus, we thought it would confuse any searching harbingers—having it disguised so close to him, where his scent was so concentrated."

Guilt pierced me straight through the heart. If I hadn't been there—like Daddy had wanted—then the staff might've stayed hidden. And maybe someone else could've used it to heal Daddy's wounds.

"The curtain didn't do its job very well." I flinched at the memory of the bloodthirsty bat vaulting itself at my head, at the sound of the staff slamming to the floor. "It fell right out of the panel when the bogeybat crashed through the window."

"Then something wasn't fastened right. Maybe Rus didn't say the incantation properly. Or maybe we should've checked the panel to ensure the spell had held all these years." Exhaling, he shook his head, found my gaze again. "Either way, Amy—I know what you're thinking—and it wouldn't have prevented your dad's death."

I swallowed a fresh onslaught of tears.

"What happens if a harbinger doesn't find someone's totem?" I asked after I'd recomposed myself.

"The search continues until it's found. Otherwise, the darkness will reclaim some of the caster's powers as compensation. Sometimes, it'll actually claim a harbinger."

"And I'm guessing you don't want to lose them."

Briar shook his head. "Wouldn't think so. Imagine the harbingers as military drones. They make it possible to do your dirty work while you're far, far away, safe from immediate retaliation. Plus, it probably takes some effort to find good ones."

"Oh, so the curse doesn't provide harbingers."

"No, a caster's got to find them himself. Fae like Gentian, who cast curses like it's their fucking job, collect them. Or, I should say they indenture them."

Indenture? I didn't like that antiquated word. "From where?"

Briar shrugged. "From the dregs of fae society. Don't shed any tears for them, Amy. No caster wants a harbinger with a heart."

I exhaled, forcing myself to continue packing.

Boots padded in the hallway. I turned to find a stout, pot-bellied Danann with a large, buzzed head bowed in my doorway. "Paragon Hawthorne—may we speak?"

I arched a brow at the strange address as Briar rose. "I'll be right back," he promised, then went with the living tank. To a distance out of my auditory range, I guessed.

I continued gathering essentials, pausing over my more sentimental belongings—photos of my friends, my Hinerz ketchup bank, the framed stubs from the last Bayview Boys concert Vi and I attended. I even paused over one of my old high school notebooks, which, ironically enough, contained the proper CPR procedures I'd failed to perform the night before.

Frowning, I committed my scribbles to memory—30 chest compressions, 2 breaths; 30 chest compressions, 2 breaths. That mantra now graven in my mind, I moved on from most of my life's debris. But there were two things I *couldn't* leave behind.

The first was my iBloom Shimmy. I questioned the practicality of bringing it. Did the fae world even have electricity? If not, I'd at least get a few hours out of the tiny device before its battery died, perhaps a small modicum of comfort in my darker moments.

The second item was Raggedy Andy. He lay on the floor beneath my shredded armchair, smooshed under a pile of hardbound books. I plucked rubble from his red yarn hair, then hugged his cotton body to my heart. His little blue sailor hat still smelled like my childhood—crayons, bubblegum, and jelly sandals—instantly reminding me of the day I got him.

At five, I'd gone through a difficult phase. With nightmares plaguing me, the prospect of sleep terrified me, which meant I was always tired, unreasonable, and churlish. And whenever one of the adults in the house tried forcing me to go to bed, I'd throw such wild tantrums that I'd injure myself. And them.

After a particularly harrowing night wherein I'd kicked Aunt Aylie in the eye, Daddy had taken me for a car ride. The warmth from the heater and the steady hum of the engine had successfully lulled me to sleep. Daddy had driven me around for four hours before finally stopping. When I'd awoken, Raggedy Andy sat beside me in my booster seat.

Not only was I enamored with Andy as my favorite character in my favorite movie, but Daddy had given me a second reason to love my new doll. He'd said that Andy wasn't just a toy, that he was also a sleep charm—that he'd protect me from all the ugly, mean monsters in my bad dreams. While he couldn't prevent my nightmares from happening, so long as I held him tight while I slept, Andy would never let the bad guys in them hurt me.

Being me, I was more than happy to believe in a magic dream guardian. Every night after that, Andy joined me in the Land of Nod, and bedtime became a much easier affair. For everyone.

As I aged, I realized that Andy wasn't magic, that Daddy had concocted the story of him being a sleep charm, so I'd feel secure enough to get my rest. Partly because I was disrupting the entire household, but mostly because he loved me and wanted me to feel someone had my back—even in my grimmest dreams.

Now as an adult, I knew that that someone had always been him.

I choked on tears I hadn't realized were falling and stuffed Andy into my backpack.

The upstairs bathroom was just as trashed as the rest of the house was. The medicine cabinet mirror lay in sparkling shards in the marble sink. Cautious, I collected various soaps from amid its remnants. I was just depositing a travel size bottle of conditioner in my backpack when I heard a rustling behind me.

I whirled around, heart racing, with a huge blade of glass in my hand. There was nothing there to fight, but the susurrus continued. The linen closet door shook, and something inside toppled over. I held my breath, waiting for an attack. Until a plaintive meow rang out.

Gasping, I dropped the glass and my bag and scrambled to the closet. My hope swelled as I wrenched open the rickety door and found a slender orange tabby cat crouched on the middle shelf of the closet surrounded by Vi's nail polish collection and a bucket of men's shaving supplies, alive and frantic for freedom.

Fianna's celadon eyes rounded as I screamed for joy and scooped her fuzzy body into my arms.

"You clever girl," I mewled, Fianna purring like a lion. She was the smallest beacon in the doldrums, but she'd do. "Thank heaven for your hidey holes!"

"**F**ianna will be fine," Briar assured me again as we bumped along in the back of a rented SUV. Ours was the center of a caravan of other tank-like vehicles stuffed with Danann bodyguards, heading to the portal to the fae realm.

I'd been staring out my window for the past fifteen minutes, watching the sun set above the white oaks bordering the road we traveled. Whatever good feelings I'd felt at finding Fianna had flown the coop the minute our plane touched down in Charleston—a place I'd so recently visited. This second trip couldn't be coincidental.

"She was placed in your sister's arms ten minutes after we left." Briar set a hand on my knee, his touch dampish. May was raging hard in the south, dewing my skin even in my tee-shirt and shorts. "You'll see your cat and your family again once they reach the palace. They won't be too far behind us, but we'll move faster without them."

Finally, I peered over at him. His eyes glowed like orbs within his black hood. "Why are we here?"

Briar deliberated, his tongue rolling inside his mouth. Finally, he expelled a heavy breath. "Because this is where the closest portal is, Amy. It's Angel Oak."

I gaped, unable to breathe.

"We never thought you'd find it on your own. Without guidance. Without prompting. We moved your family hundreds of miles away from it to be safe, never once thinking one day you'd go on a spring break adventure with your friends and accidentally stumble upon the damn thing." He shook his head, looking skyward. "Maybe it was fate."

My skin prickled as it had when I'd touched Angel Oak. So, that jolt hadn't been just my imagination.

My tongue grew sandpapery. "Did I do something to the portal when I was there?"

I'd never seen someone so somber. "You opened it, Amy, when you touched it."

The meager fast-food dinner I'd eaten started coming back up. I swallowed it down, but stomach acid stung my throat.

"Only two people can open a portal like that." Briar spoke with deference to my apparent distress. "The ruler of the realm, or his heir. If they step through, the portal automatically locks again."

"Then how will my family and the rest of the caravan get through the portal? If I go through, there's no one left to open it for them."

Was he fooling me into leaving my family behind? Briar and his men were desperate to safeguard me as the heir to the fae kingdom. I could totally see them lying about my family's ability to make it to Evereostre, aware I wouldn't abandon them if I knew they couldn't follow. Briar had admitted to deceiving me my whole life, so trusting him right then seemed risky.

"They can unlock it without you—with a sanctioned key." He unzipped his backpack, retrieving a little black box typically used to house rings.

I nearly recoiled. *Please don't propose to me in a speeding car on our escape from certain doom.*

My heart rate slowed when Briar pried the box open to reveal a tiny skeleton key, a combo of iron and brass. A smooth round ruby gusseted its blade.

I could only guess at the frivolity of my court if it wasted time and money on bedazzling mundane things like keys.

Briar plucked the key out of the box, held it up to a ray of fading light. The ruby looked more fuchsia in the sunset. "The gem is filled with your father's blood, allowing others to open and close the portal without either of you. Your dad gave me one after we first crossed—just in case I ever needed it. But I never had a reason to use it until I saw you'd touched Angel Oak. You opened the portal but didn't step through, which meant the door to our realm had been standing ajar for more than a week. Gentian's lackeys would notice it was open. They're stationed everywhere, watching for things like that."

I squeezed my knees, an inch from teetering over the edge of an unmitigated freak out.

"I left school the night I saw that picture on your laptop and hopped on a plane to Charleston with the key, so I could lock things back up, but I couldn't reach it." Regret shone in his lime eyes. "The bogeybats had already come through."

My fingernails gouged my kneecaps. "So, I let those *things* into this world? I let them in to kill my father?"

Briar's hand took mine. I didn't want to be touched but didn't withdraw. "Yes, you let them in."

So, now when I need comfort, you choose brutal honesty?

"But what happened to your father wasn't your fault. It was ours."

Huh?

"Before I reached the portal, a group of bogeybats attacked. They were perched in the woods around the park, like they'd set up camp. They weren't on the move. They were waiting."

"For what?"

"For someone stupid enough to lead them to your father."

My breath caught. "Do you think those demons stalked me and my friends?"

Briar shook his head. "No. I think they came through the portal days later. And just to clarify, bogeybats aren't exactly demons. They're mean, nasty, dark sons-of-bitches, but they're not demonic. Demonic beings have black eyes to match their empty souls. Unfortunately, a lot of black eyes are showing up in our world."

If the bogeybats weren't demonic, I never wanted to encounter something that was.

"Anyway, I managed to escape—drove for miles in all directions to confuse the beasts when they followed me. I lost them somewhere in the Smoky Mountains and called your uncle to let him know. That's when the meetings began—strategy councils to hash out a plan to deal with the bogeybats."

I chewed my lip, knowing bogeybat extermination wasn't all they'd been hashing out. Daddy's declining health, the status of my uterus, and whether Briar should take the throne from me when my father passed were probably every night topics.

"We worried the bats might split up and spread themselves out over the country. The chances that they might find your father were too great. Bogeybats have astounding noses. Plus, if a human were to spot one—"

"How could they not?" Those bats were so huge and hideous, they'd stick out like sore thumbs no matter where they tried camouflaging themselves.

"That's complicated to explain, but most modern humans can't see bogeybats. Not unless they believe in mystical things like magic, the fae, and Danu. Of course, some, like children, still believe and would be vulnerable to attack."

I paused to ponder that. "Is that why none of the neighbors called the cops last night? Why none of them came to see what had happened to our house today?"

He nodded. "They couldn't see or hear any of the commotion last night, and your house looks the same as ever to them."

"Then how can they see *us*? We're mystical, aren't we?"

"They can see us because the Mother made humans similar to us, so the human gaze looks at us and sees something familiar, which makes us real to them. Otherwise, their cynicism would veil us—and our magic."

"Then why couldn't they see us Dananns last night? We were part of that commotion."

"I suppose they could see and hear you and me. We would've looked like crazy people, though."

What would nebby Mrs. Crankle across the street have seen if she'd stuck her schnoz through her lacy curtains? A pair of college kids acting like children, fighting a make-believe battle against imaginary foes in the middle of the street at night? It was a wonder she hadn't called the police just for that.

"They wouldn't have seen the damage done to my car because a bogeybat did the damaging, and the guards wore clothes like this." Briar extended his arms, modeling his black garments. "Our fighting gear is enchanted, so humans can't see us when we don't want them to." He tapped a spot on his vest by his collarbone. "If I press here, I'm invisible to the human eye."

I eyed his vest. "When do I get an invisibility suit?"

Briar smiled. "We can have one made for you at the palace, but it won't do you much good in our world. Invisibility against other fae is a fleeting tactic, since there are so many spells and potions to counteract it."

Of course, there are.

"Anyway, your father decided we'd send a squadron of warriors down to Angel Oak to terminate the bogeybats. They departed right after your uncle gave me another key." Briar set his key back in its tiny box and clicked shut its lid. "They were to either kill the bats or force them back through the portal, which they'd then lock."

"I'm guessing it didn't work."

Briar exhaled. "During the first battle, more bats crawled out of the portal, so the key-holder ran to the door and tried to lock it. One of the bats bit off his hand, and the key with it."

I winced, remembering the feel of those fangs in my leg. Had the warrior's skin saved me from a similar amputation?

"He'll be okay," Briar assured me. "Once we get him back to the Spring Palace. Missing limbs can be easily restored with a skilled healer's help."

"So, they couldn't lock the portal?"

Briar shook his head. "Not then, anyway. They killed all the bats they could find, dug through their innards, but found no key. So, we sent another squadron down with another key, and they finally managed to lock shit up. Our men remained at Angel Oak for three more days to be sure no other bats were lurking. Then they called to ask for further orders, and the council decided it was safe to bring them home. They were back by the Beltane festival."

"Then why are you rushing me out of here? If the portal's locked, then the bat with Daddy's totem can't give it to Gentian. The curse can't progress."

"Amy, that staff was coated in your blood. That's all the bat needs to reopen the portal—and to know what scent the harbingers should track next. And they will come back for you."

Damnit! I scraped my face. *Will I ever feel safe again?*

Briar unbuckled his seatbelt and scooted over until he was flush against me. He wrapped an arm, light as a feather boa, around my shoulders. This time, I wanted the contact. I just wished he wouldn't be so goddamn gentle about it.

"I'm sorry we failed you, Amy," Briar murmured.

I wondered what more the Danann warriors could've done to fix my mistakes. "You didn't."

"Yes, we did." He swallowed, looking sick. "The men we sent down assumed they'd terminated all the bats, but there must've been a bunch of them hiding—waiting. When the squadrons started home, the bats followed. That's how they caught your father's scent." His Adam's apple bobbed. "We led them right to him."

I didn't know what to say. My grief hung too heavily to assuage anyone else's pain. At that point, assigning blame was beyond my capacity, for everyone and everything seemed at fault. Even Daddy.

Angel Oak Park was closed when we arrived, steel gating the passage in. I watched, stupefied, as a hand emerged from the lead SUV's window and snapped. A tremor rippled through me like an aftershock, the gate opening of its own accord.

"Well, that's cool," I remarked to myself as we accelerated.

"You'll learn how to do stuff like that. You'll have a muse—a teacher—at the palace."

I sighed. "At least that's something to look forward to."

Briar didn't reply to that thoughtless remark, but his tight expression confessed that I'd wounded him.

"I'm sorry. I didn't mean to imply that I wasn't looking forward to—to marriage and all." Honestly, I hadn't made up my mind on that front, but I didn't need to hurt his feelings while I decided. "It's just—"

There weren't words to express my conflicting emotions.

Briar patted my hand. "I understand all this has probably placed a pall over what should be a happy time in our lives. I'm not offended that you're not stoked for our engagement. We'll give it some time. Maybe in a few months."

Or decades.

When we parked, I said a silent farewell to my old life. To the home I'd grown up in. To the city I'd lived in. To the dreams I'd leave unfulfilled. To all my friends, who I regretted losing almost as much as my father.

I'd individually texted each of them before we hopped on the plane in Pittsburgh, saying my heartfelt goodbyes. I couldn't say where I was going—they wouldn't have believed me anyway—but I wanted them to know I'd be okay. Even if it wasn't true. I wished them all long, happy lives and told them I'd never forget them.

Two seconds after I'd sent the last text, my phone had blown up with responses. Briar had taken my MulBerry and dumped it in the nearest trash can.

Once the park's perimeter was scouted, a guard with a cleft chin approached Briar. After a brief discussion, Briar placed his key box in the guard's hand, then grabbed his backpack. "Ready?" he asked me, shrugging on the pack.

Not at all. "Yep."

Minutes later, my feet stepped once more upon red clay, Angel Oak rising before me in the periwinkle dusk. Briar guided me toward the tree.

"Don't be scared." He clasped my arm as we stopped by the branch nearest the largest hollow. "It's just like walking through a door."

I frowned at the door in question.

"It's a small climb. You walk along this branch until you reach it." He touched said branch, shook it. "It's pretty solid."

"Am I even going to fit?" The hollow was an oblong hole in the tree, half my size. How had those monstrous bogeybats slipped through it?

"It's a magic portal. It'll expand for you. Don't worry."

Yeah, okay. I wanted to roll my eyes.

"What do I do? Just touch the tree and head for the door?"

"Since the portal closes when you go through, the guards will pass first. But they'll move quick—"

At first, I thought I imagined the distant clicking. Then I heard it again, closer, and the shouting started.

"*Go, go, go, go, go!*" one of the guards bellowed, drawing his sword from his hip.

Briar grabbed my hand and pressed it to the branch. I spasmed as Angel Oak's life force surged through me—an electric shock to my core—then gasped when Briar vaulted himself onto the branch and yanked me up with him by my backpack straps. "Come on, Amy! Stay on your feet."

My heart pounded as Briar dragged me along the ivied branch. My snow boots skidded along, slowing our progress as the clicking soared closer.

"Faster, Amy!" Briar yelled, shoving me in front of him.

Somehow, I came face to face with the hollow, nearly stumbling back as the large oak's bark warped, becoming Amy-sized instantly. I didn't even have time to marvel at it. A body shoved me through it, and I sucked in a long breath like I was swimming headlong into a tsunami.

PART TWO

TWELVE

S unlight cracked through dewy tree limbs when I awoke with a shake early the next morning, a damp hand clamping my screaming mouth. Panting with the adrenaline of a nightmare, I bleared up at Briar, who gritted his teeth. The forest of blooming dogwoods and mammoth oaks, which had serenaded us with phosphorescent nightingales and the pleasance of peepers over the night, was dead silent.

Seeing I'd awakened, Briar swore and rolled onto a cushion of spring-green moss, ruffling his hair. "Mother save us," he muttered as I sat up, still trembling. "We've got to find a way to stop these nocturnal premonitions, or we'll wind up dead."

I stared at his profile, blinking. "Nocturnal premonitions? My night terrors, you mean?"

"They're premonitions. Night terrors was the best medical explanation your father could find to mask the truth. He didn't want you believing in magical powers. You'd have been tempted to use your gifts."

If my night terrors are a gift, then I want to return them. "But—the therapists—"

"He thought they'd still be able to help you cope with your ability." He shrugged. "Must've worked."

Clutching Andy's cloth body to my heart, I frowned. I *really* didn't want to think of the dark-cloaked figure from my dream as some inevitability in my future. "But—"

"They're premonitions, Amy," Briar cut me off, cranky from too little sleep. He'd stayed up all night, keeping watch for danger—and for any squadron survivors who might use his blood key to cross through Angel Oak. "Your mother had them. Her screams would wake me when we were faelets."

I chewed on this remark, curious about how long he'd known my mother. And in what capacity. He'd said he was her closest friend, but—

After a silent stretch, Briar met my gaze. "What?"

I bit down on my question but couldn't keep it in. "Did you ever have a—thing—for my mom?" Briar's eyes rounded, his shock unchecked. "Did she look a lot like me? If we were too similar, wouldn't it be kind of like—?"

"Amy, I was never infatuated with your mother. She was more like my sister. And before you ask, no, that doesn't mean I've had sex with someone I should consider my niece. I've never seen you as anything other than my future wife. Sure, you resemble your mother in many ways. In others, you don't."

"How—how am I different from her?"

Briar's irritation softened at my curiosity. He scratched the back of his auburn head. "Appearance-wise? I suppose you're a tad taller than she was. Slenderer too. She had a few more, uh, endowments than you." I could've cringed, hearing this as a judgment of my B-cups and barely-there booty. "But you're both suited to what Danu gave you. Although, Ginny would've killed for your nose."

I touched its sharp tip. "Really?"

"Mm-hm. She thought her nose was too wide, too undefined. I always thought it was cute, like Vi's, but Ginny wanted her mother's. She was ecstatic when you inherited it."

Somehow, knowing my mother had insecurities made me feel better about myself. "Did her eyes ever change color?"

Briar's brows touched. "Change color?"

"Yeah, like mine do."

"You mean they aren't always hazel?"

I stared at him, unable to breathe. Had I given my virginity to someone who didn't know the true nature of my eyes? I bet he'd notice Laurel's eyes changing colors.

"Huh," Briar grunted, scrutinizing me. "I wonder what that means."

I shifted, uncomfortable beneath my damp, woven blanket, and huddled into my knees. The dawn was crisp, mist chilling me in my lightweight clothes.

Groaning, Briar pushed to his feet. "Looks like we're traveling alone." He sounded more casual than I presumed he felt, his squadron still AWOL—probably dead. "We'd better get moving soon. I'll forage for breakfast." He grabbed a brown paper bag out of his backpack. "You stay here—rekindle the fire."

As Briar plodded into lush flora, I stared at our ashen rock circle, wondering why he assumed I knew how to rekindle a fire. I knew nothing about fire—except that I could spray it from my fingers like a blowtorch. Maybe I'd try that.

When Briar returned, I knelt over the fire ring, trying to ignite kindling with my mind, swearing up a storm. He laughed, took a knee beside me. "So, not only do you look like your mother, but you curse like her too."

I met his dancing eyes, smiling despite my failure.

After Briar restarted the fire and cooked us a berry energy drink using camping supplies from his pack and fresh water from thin air, we readied for our journey. After tackling the basics (thank Danu, Briar had packed toilet paper), we discussed our problematic wardrobes.

Briar pondered my modern Americanness. "The problem we'll face now, Amy, is blending in."

I peered down at my grass-stained shorts and damp tee. I'd never blended into the human world. Was he now saying I'd stick out even in fairy land? "You didn't seem to care about blending in while we were packing."

"We had no shot at blending in with a full cavalcade under a royal banner. It didn't matter, though. You'd have been protected."

Mentioning that the cavalcade had probably been wiped out in one fell swoop seemed tactless. Regardless, one attack in the fae realm, and we'd be in similar straits.

"If we journey on dressed like this, Gentian's spies will easily detect us. Guaranteed, no other fae we encounter will be wearing shorts and UPJ tee shirts."

Do they even have colleges here? "What do you propose we do?" I asked. "Buy new wardrobes at the local mall?"

Briar chuckled. "Not exactly, but I know someone who lives nearby. She can help us." He sliced his hand through the air above the fire, dousing it with a bucketful of water. I marveled as steam hissed from the coals.

Briar grabbed his pack, shrugged it onto squared shoulders. "Let's get moving, Larkspur. Time to meet your first Witch."

"**H**oly shit," I gasped, tripping over my own feet when we broke through the forest line. I forgot to be winded. Forgot that my feet hurt. That my legs were tired from hiking along uncut paths through dense woods. That I was frightened of every strange new creature I encountered. I lost control of my jaw as a storybook world of verdant fields, vibrant wildflowers, blooming trees, and sparkling streams sprawled before me. The sun—or suns, as I was flabbergasted to see (one brighter and closer than the other)—rose above distant lavender mountains in starbursts of magenta and gold, outlining cotton candy clouds. I stood on the edge of Avalon; its magnificence thieved my breath.

Briar nudged me. "Welcome to Evereostre, Amy." His pride gleamed against a backdrop of emerald and blush. "Or should I say welcome home?"

Home, I thought, gazing upon a wonderland words failed to describe. Recalling brownstones, coffee shops, and shelves of romance novels, a pit formed in my stomach. I forced a smile for Briar. *This isn't my home.*

"Come on." He forged into the springy sweet pasture, looking not the least bit weary, though he hadn't slept. That energy drink he'd made must've worked wonders for him. For me, the effects wore off midway through our trek. "Tamsyn's house isn't far from here."

Sneering, I jabbed the ground with the walking stick he'd fashioned for me. "You said that an hour ago," I uttered more to myself, then forced my aching legs onward. Thank Danu I had the warrior's skin. I'd never have kept Briar's breakneck pace with a leg injury.

Hedged by bald cypresses, the Witch's shack sat in a reedy swamp abuzz with insects of impossible colors and melodious spring peepers, who backstroked through the mud amid our squelching. Constructed of loose stones and thatched with bark shavings, smoke trailing from a hollowed toadstool in its roof, I wondered what rodent had built it.

A short, lissome woman with a young, round face and reddish-tan skin met us at the sturdy front door. She'd barely covered herself in patches of moss with twine. Her long hair, the shade of black coffee, lay over her shoulder in a matted braid, her arched ears peeking out through flyaways. Pitch-black shadowed her dark eyes, her eyeliner crossing over the bump in her nose bridge. "You," she grunted, sultry as summer, upon seeing Briar. She set a red-stained hand on her hip.

He smirked. "Me."

Lips twisting, she scrutinized us—me, especially. Finally, she pushed off her doorjamb and stepped aside. "In you come." She spoke in a peculiar accent somewhere between Spanish and French, and I doubted I'd ever heard her native tongue before. "Afore someone see you."

I wondered who'd see us in this remote countryside, hers the only home I'd seen on our trek.

Briar guided me into the shack. Sunlight broke through gaps in the thatching, illuminating the clutter of dried herbs, hanging cookware, and cobwebbed shelves littered with containers of unidentifiable substances. I coughed upon smoke and the metallic reek of blood, cringing as the central butcher-block island came into view. A sheep-like creature with peach wool and a horned snout lay half butchered upon it.

"Would my home offend you, princess?" The Witch sashayed past me to the carcass and snatched the cleaver stuck in the block. "I'd have done to clean up the gruesome had I known to be receiving royalty."

I flushed at my rudeness. "I'm—it's not—I'm fine." I choked down a deep breath, calming myself, and whacked my bangs from my eyes. "How did you know I was royalty?"

One of the Witch's thick brows arched, her lips uplifting, but she didn't reply. Was the answer just that obvious?

Instead, she embedded her cleaver in the animal's flank. "I figure you portal through any day now when bogeybats swarming my flock." She hacked again, and I jumped. "Devoured half my fleecers these past days."

Before my eyes, Briar transformed into Prince Charming—head bowed and all. He was too damn good at that. "I apologize for your damages, Tamsyn. We'll, of course, ensure you're repaid."

"Ha!" She whacked the carcass so hard the island tremored. "I see the day the royal coffers do charity to the likes of Witch."

Despite her acrimony, Briar smiled. "If you do us a favor, Tamsyn, I give you my solemn vow you'll be handsomely compensated for your lost livestock."

Tamsyn dropped the cleaver, wiped her bloody hand on a rough-hewn rag tucked into her twine belt. "Favor you how?"

After Briar explained our anonymity plight, Tamsyn's penetrating eyes bored through me. "Clothes be only half the worry with this one. She have too much the look of Ginny."

I perked up. Had the Witch known my mother?

"Folk about still remember her."

Briar chewed his lip. "Can that be resolved?"

Tamsyn continued her scrutiny. Her unblinking eyes burned through my skull, making me flinch.

"Tamsyn," Briar warned. "I'll thank you not to violate the princess's mind, or you'll force me to do something quite *uncharitable*. Her memories are her own."

Huffing, the Witch broke our eye contact.

I stepped closer to Briar, heart now galloping. Why would she want my memories?

"Will you help us?" Briar asked, steepling his hands. "Please?"

Tamsyn considered us, lips pursed. Finally, something in her demeanor mellowed. "I give help." Shadows flickered through her eyes. "For Ginny."

Yeah, she totally knew my mother.

Briar exhaled. "Thank you."

I watched, fascinated, as Tamsyn flitted about her shack, gathering items. Her shortness didn't hinder her. Though her shelves were out of even my reach, she had but to look at a canister, and it flew into her hands. She was scooping a handful of bright blue seeds from one of her hollowed gourds when she noticed my gawking. Stern-mouthed, she pointed to her stove across the space—a giant boulder filled with fire. "You be useful—do boil."

Ugh, Amy, where are your manners? I shrugged out of my backpack, handing it to Briar.

"You overstep your bounds again, Tamsyn," Briar snapped. "She's the Larkspur crown princess. She doesn't take orders from Unseelie—"

"It's fine!" I eyed Briar, already scurrying to grab a large kettle. "She's doing something nice for us. I should help."

Briar frowned, but Tamsyn smiled. Had I impressed her? "Clean water well behind home. You top kettle."

I headed back into the swamp. When I returned, Briar and Tamsyn were in mid-discussion.

"I seen no other harbingers near." She ground fragrant herbs and seeds with a mortar and pestle upon a large stone table disarrayed with various utensils. "Just bogeybats. I hear no other words on it. Quiet out here."

Mud caked up to my shins, I skirted Briar and the mutilated animal, squishing over to the stove. I set the kettle on its surface; it immediately simmered.

"How you route?" Tamsyn opened a drawer in her worktable and produced a small muslin bag. She dumped the crushed contents of her mortar into it. "You take King's Road, be better. Back roads take thieves and bandits these years. Few protection."

"Then the King's Road would be best." Briar bowed his head. "Thanks for the guidance."

Tamsyn stepped toward a giant spider web in the corner of one shelf. Standing on tiptoes, she plucked the neon orange spider from its silken canvas and popped it in her mouth like a mint.

I cringed. Less so from the way she gnashed the arachnid, more so because she did it with spotted teeth. *Guess good dental care is hard to come by here.*

Tamsyn grabbed the web and rolled it between her hands, chanting something low and foreign. She stuffed it in the little bag with her other ingredients, tying it shut before shaking it. Less intense now, Tamsyn faced me. "You bring the boil."

I chose the cleanest rag I could find by the stove, so I wouldn't scald my hand, then grasped the steaming, sweating kettle and toted it to Tamsyn's workspace.

She reached out her hand, and a tall wooden cup leapt off its shelf and into her soiled fingers. Taking the kettle from me, she poured the bubbling water into the mug and dropped in her personalized tea bag.

We stood in silent observation as her blend steeped, slowly turning blue. After a bit, the quiet stretching between us forced my tongue. "How did you know my mother?"

Tamsyn hummed a meandering tune, studying me.

I shifted, wondering how that answered anything.

Finally, Tamsyn chuckled. "I muse for her—one of them. Learned her to wield her voice."

"Wield it? Like a weapon?"

"Unlearned of your mother's power?"

I sneaked a glance toward Briar, who'd dozed off on a stool, his head bobbing. Clearly, I'd overestimated the pep in his step. "No, I haven't been told much about anything. I—" I turned back to Tamsyn, shrugging off a flare of something hot, something choleric. "I only learned the truth about *myself* yesterday."

"Hm." She tilted her head. "I think further truth will uncover."

I wished I could say I looked forward to that.

Still watching me, Tamsyn lowered smoky eyelids. "I take that father king gone to blood curse?"

Words impossible, I bit my lip.

Her shoulders slumped. "Well, we safe you, and when you take queen, you integrate my folk. Restore to haven in Timbermoor. See rights where rights due."

Having no clue if I could do any of what she wished, I only nodded like a simpleton.

Moments later, Briar shook the rafters with a snore, waking himself and drawing our amusement. He straightened upon his stool, blinking the sleep from his eyes. "How much longer will this take, Tamsyn? We've got a lot of ground to cover today."

Her mouth slanted. "Suppose potion will be right ready. We bandy the garb for now."

Fingers poised for conducting, Tamsyn then chanted something ancient sounding and conjured a barrage of figment hands—hands made of mammatus clouds with intermittent lightning. They enveloped me, dour as a seamstress in their prodding, cinching, and measuring, until they'd contoured my body.

After minutes, Tamsyn reeled back her storm, leaving me horripilated and encumbered by a rough-spun getup fit for the PA Renaissance Faire. Her creation consisted of layered beige linen. Its loose sleeves cuffed my arms just beyond my elbows, its long, pleated skirt swishing like a bell above the toes of my muddy snow boots. Overlaying the bodice was a form-fitting vest of scuffed black leather. Twine laced it closed in an outline of my bust. Topping off the whole ensemble was a heavy gray cloak, fastened by a single wooden toggle.

I'll pass as a milkmaid, if nothing else.

"Hope you like earth tones," Briar remarked before Tamsyn sent another hand storm his way.

When she'd finished with him, he sported a hooded sack, a thick leather belt shaping it around his narrow hips. A cape like mine mantled his shoulders. His pants fit the same but were now of umber leather instead of black denim. Antiqued, knee-high leather boots replaced his suede sneakers. I assumed most common fae lacked regular access to department shoe stores.

"Armor still be protection beneath," Tamsyn assured Briar, who analyzed his new duds. "I know important." Then she offered me the potion. "Ready for drinking."

Reluctant though I was to ingest a mysterious blue tea made from a spider's web by a Witch with blood under her fingernails, I took it from her and drank. Sweet and delicate, the potion tasted downright delicious. I drank the whole thing in two gulps as Tamsyn instructed, then burped so loud Aunt Aylie would've pinched me.

"That'll be." Tamsyn snatched the cup from me, set to cleaning it.

Feeling no different, I chewed my lip. "How long does it take to work?"

She tittered in response.

Briar rose from his seat and strode toward me, assessing. "That should do it."

I goggled. "Something already happened?"

Chuckling, he grabbed a tarnished plate off Tamsyn's table and blew off its dust. "*Scáil*," he uttered, waving his hand over the dish, which transformed into a mirror of ice. He held it up for my inspection.

I grabbed a lock of my hair. It was brown! Brown as mud. As were my eyebrows. How funny that I'd always wanted to dye my hair brown—such a common color. Aunt Aylie had forbidden such defacement of nature, of course. Finally seeing myself as a brunette, though, I was underwhelmed. The change had dulled the features I'd always thought too exotic to be pretty. I didn't just look normal now. I looked—plain.

Satisfied, Briar set down the plate and handed me my bag. "Let's get on the road, Larkspur. Daylight's waning."

Before we departed, I thanked Tamsyn for her help. She didn't look at me as she puttered, her smirk a nebulous taunt. She just hummed the same trailing tune she'd hummed at mention of my mother. The haunting refrain followed me back into the swamp and wove itself through my head like a weft to its warp.

Not until that night, after collapsing into a meadow of buttercups, did I realize the Witch's tune was the same one in my night terrors.

THIRTEEN

Birds twittered overhead as I trudged along the endless dirt road behind Briar, my walking stick holding me up. The suns soared high in the cerulean sky, the noon heat melting me like a candle in my layers. I'd long since removed my cloak and stuffed it in my backpack, but sweat pooled between my breasts, making me wistful for the stinky, damp swamp.

"Aunt Aylie's title—*beyn an ciorcal*—does that actually mean lady of the circle?" For the past two days, I'd been playing a game of 200 questions with Briar, distracting myself from my extreme exhaustion and discomfort—and familiarizing myself with my new kingdom. I figured the more I learned, the closer I'd come to deciding if I could rule. "I heard you call the farmer's wife beyn yesterday when we stopped to buy those weird potatoes."

Briar stabbed his walking stick into the dirt again, forging our way. "We made up that title when we settled in Pittsburgh. Here, Aylie has another title. But beyn is still an important word to remember. It doesn't mean lady, though. It means fae female. As woman means human female."

I stared at him, my stomach lurching. "I—I'm not a woman?"

"Nope." He didn't catch my unrest at the notion—at my identity's capsizing. "And I'm not a man. I'm a feyr. Young males are ryns, young females ryans. Fae children are still called children, although faelets is a more apt term. Teenagers are called striplings, and 20-somethings are youngbloods—but you knew that last one."

I blew out a breath, knowing my brain would stagger at addressing people properly. "Are pronouns different too?"

"No. He, she, they—all good. Oh, and—I almost forgot—there are many genderfluid fae. They can be either female or male—or both at once. We call them dreys, unless they have another preference."

"Anything else?"

"Let's see—" He clicked his tongue. "Spouses call each other ceyla, regardless of gender. There are no husbands and wives."

I massaged my sweaty forehead. "Ugh, I'm so going to bungle every social interaction because of this shit."

He chuckled. "You'll get the hang of it. Your mind will adapt."

I certainly hoped so.

"Okay—well, now I'm almost afraid to ask but—what does Unseelie mean? You called Tamsyn Unseelie."

"It's a kind of class division. Basically, Dananns, Nemedians, and Milesians compose the Seelie class. Fomorians were once Seelie, but since the war they've been downgraded.

"The Unseelie—they're known for being less in control of their powers—less in control of their animal urges."

Like savages? I wanted to snark, knowing that was the term often imposed upon those the aristocracy—in any time in history—sought to subdue and oppress for their own benefit.

"Which is why your Seelie subjects are leery of allowing them into the higher ranks at Court," Briar continued. "Your father thought he could change that by bringing Unseelie fae into his inner circle, giving them public service positions, but his efforts were wasted. Mostly thanks to Gentian."

Teeth in my leg—membranous wings—bloody last breaths—

I shook myself from spiraling into another depressive funk, wishing Briar would just stop using *that name.*

"What are Dananns then? The upper class? The Brahmins of the fairy caste system?"

"That's a great comparison." Briar peered over his shoulder. "That might change one day, but for now—I'm afraid there's a major culture shock coming your way."

He seemed content to accept the order of things, but I'd already be making plans to dismantle such an unfair system. Wasn't that the one virtue of an absolute monarchy? No red tape to prevent immediate change. A decree from me—or Briar—would become instant law.

Surely, Briar wouldn't allow discrimination like that to stand unchecked if he were king.

Briar paused as we rounded a curve, wiping a trickle of sweat off his cheek. Peering around him, I spied distant vines of smoke. Smoke meant chimneys, which meant houses, which meant a town. And food.

"It's up to you," Briar said, spitting. "We could soldier on, eat off the land later. Or we could take a small break in that borough, buy something warm to eat, and rest our feet."

"Is that really a question?" I hadn't had a semi-decent meal in days. Survival in the fae realm still wasn't as easy as conjuring a turkey dinner with a snap of the fingers. Magic had limits, which ended just before conjuring biological or agricultural substance. Briar said those gifts were Danu's alone, sustenance only attainable through traditional means.

Dust outlined the slant of Briar's grin. "I'm asking because it's risky. There's a chance the villagers might notice we're different, that we'll stick in their memory."

I frowned down at my dirty dress. If it wasn't enough to fool the masses, then why couldn't I just wear my shorts and tee-shirt? They'd be much less cumbersome.

"It's your accent." Briar rested his filthy hands atop his walking stick. "America was still in its heyday when the portals closed, so your dialect hasn't taken root in this realm yet."

"Hate to break it to you, bud, but you sound exactly like me."

He scratched the space above his lip—whiskerless, despite him not shaving. "I had to learn that way of speaking, lass." I reeled at his perfect Scottish burr. Briar shrugged. "Bet you wouldn't have guessed that most Germanic and Celtic languages originated from auld fae dialects."

I guessed that made sense if I believed my insufficient history lesson three days before. "Well, I need a rest, so we'll have to chance it." I lifted my chin. "Besides, I can mimic you well enough."

"Okay. Let's hear it."

My lips slanted down. "You just did. That was it."

His eyes widening, he swung his walking stick forward again. "Okay, then—let's pretend you're mute."

Avenshire—what Briar named the borough—was a veritable half-mile long metropolis straight from a *Berenstain Bears* book. I'd never seen a place so picturesque.

Thick trunked trees as tall as redwoods served as buildings, rope-strung bridges connecting the upper stories. All were trimmed with windows, doors, and identifying signage. Most looked residential, like apartments. Businesses occupied the rest—quaint but thriving if their foot traffic were any indication.

An assortment of fae flitted around us as we hobbled the main promenade. All shapes, all sizes, all ages, all colors. I marveled at their differences—some subtle, some glaring.

Many had arched ears like me, some more elongated than others. Several had animalistic ears reminiscent of foxes, hounds, or fauns. Some ears were notched, others pierced, and more than a few were humanesque.

Ears weren't the only attention-snagging features to blink at. Uncle Neel hadn't lied about the flying. The number of ethereal beings shouldering wings amazed me. Some wings were robust and substantial, others diminutive, adorable. Yet, big, small, leathery, moth-like, feathered, or shimmering, holographic extremities grown through magic, they all served the same function—lifting one skyward.

I envied the multiple fae fluttering past us. According to Briar, our journey to the palace would take three weeks at our sluggish pace, and I could've killed for a set of wings to spare myself the radiating pain in my heels. Plus, having wings looked hella cool.

When I nearly stumbled into a female cyclops with plaited green hair, too busy ogling someone's iridescent butterfly wings, Briar whisked me out of harm's way. "Blending in means not looking like you just stepped off the goddamn boat."

"I don't." *I look like I just walked through a goddamn tree!*

"Just stop gawking."

I glowered, figuring I had a right to give as good as I was getting. Regardless of how my new brown hair dulled my features, I'd become the butt of many a rude and curious stare. Especially from faelets.

Discovering I belonged to another world, another species, had given me hope that I'd finally belong somewhere, fit into my new surroundings. That hope was now circling the drain.

"What's wrong?" Briar whispered once we'd taken seats in the smoky, crowded tree tavern called the Beaky Ladle. Concern furrowed his brow. "You seem upset."

I sat on a stiff bench under a striped boar head, brooding because I was a foot taller than most of the fae surrounding me. "I'm all right."

A serving wench with bug eyes and antennae—the breed of fae Briar called Middling—grand-jetéd to a table, a tray of tankards balanced on her shoulder. Her barely covered breasts bobbled with her graceful landing. She was the only other female in the place, but that was our only similarity.

Show off.

"Are you jealous?" Briar whispered, leaning across the table to take my hand. "I only peeked for a second, I swear."

Leave it to a guy to dig his own grave. Would he be this forthright with me when we next saw Laurel Woodrush?

"No," I answered, letting him pet my hand. "I'm just *so* damn tired."

He relaxed back in his wobbly seat and propped his foot upon the bench beside me. "Me too." He groaned, stretching. "It's nice to rest."

"Speaking of rest, why don't we do something to make traveling easier? I think it's safe to say there are no Enterprise Rent-A-Cars nearby, but I saw a stable down the way. Couldn't we buy ourselves some horses to ride?"

Briar folded his hands behind his head. "And when did you learn to ride a horse?"

"You could teach me."

He grunted. "We can't spend our meager cache of seeds on something unnecessary. We might need them for more important things." He gestured indistinctly. "Like food. Like shelter when it storms."

Why did he have to be so damn sensible?

"Anyway, common Dananns usually can't afford beasts like horses. Mules, donkeys—maybe. Not horses."

"I could ride a mule," I said, hopes soaring. "People do it at the Grand Canyon."

"All right. After lunch, we'll ask the stablemaster if he has any mules. *If* they're a reasonable price, I'll *consider* buying you one. Okay?"

Now beaming, I clapped.

He laughed, pleased that he'd pleased me.

Moments later, the dancing wench pirouetted over to take our order in a childish squeak that would've cracked me up had Briar not nudged his boot into my hip. In a charming Scottish burr, he requested the cook's heartiest stew for us both.

After that, I sank down into my seat and continued interrogating him. "Tell me, Briar—if the fae have been in existence so much longer than humans, why is Earth so much more advanced?" I scanned the tavern's quaint townspeople, the olden décor, the rustic furniture. "Where's the technology, the electricity, the science?"

Scraping dirt from beneath his fingernails with the pocketknife he hid in his boot, Briar grunted. "You should be asking: where's the pollution, the smog, the global warming?" His eyes sharpened. "Where are the oil spills? The companies raping the ground of natural resources? The orange streams? The endangered wildlife? The plagues of plastic bottles?"

My cheeks burned. Rightfully too.

"Humans aren't more advanced than us, Amy. We just know where to draw the line. Nothing is more important to us than the sanctity of nature."

Impressive, I thought.

"I can't believe nobody has ever tried to industrialize. I mean, the temptation—" I shook my head.

"I didn't say that. There's a faction who'd love nothing more than to destroy our pristine ecosystem for profit, but we have strict laws preventing them."

His eyes roamed the tavern, his voice lowering. "Gentian has tried numerous times to repeal the environmental laws—mainly for propaganda. If we had electricity, television, and an internet, he could badmouth your good family name on a much broader scale."

My heart seized. "How can he repeal anything? Isn't this a monarchy?"

"Yes, but the monarch isn't absolute. There's a set of high clerics that we call the Divine Cadre. Subjects can appeal to them if they feel the monarch is violating the Goddess's doctrines. Gentian claims the environmental laws are violating his potential profitability—and subsequent happiness—something Danu would invariably wish for all her children. So far, his arguments haven't swayed the Cadre, but he'll keep trying."

I ground my teeth, simmering with the need for retribution. *Whether I take the throne or not, if the Cadre ever bends to any of that murdering asshole's demands, this semi-absolute monarchy will become full-on absolute real damn quick!*

Jostling the table, Briar dropped his knife and hopped up from his seat to grab my wrists. Smoke wafted from my fingers.

I gaped down at them, shaking. Out of control.

"Shh," Briar soothed, his touch misty. "Just take a deep breath."

Sparks began snapping even as I inhaled.

On my right, I felt the wary gazes of nearby diners, wondering what mischief I was making.

Looking as if he were counting the steps to the exit, Briar lowered his hands to mine and levied pools of chilled water. Dousing my flames before they flared.

Something dampened in my chest.

Briar dropped back into his chair, wiped his brow.

I stared at my hands. They looked so normal. But they *so* weren't.

Briar grimaced. "I'm sorry, Amy. Mentioning Gentian was thoughtless. Just—for a moment, you seemed like your upbeat self again, and I—I forgot. Though, I'm surprised I didn't have warning your powers were breaking through. I didn't smell it."

"I don't even know what happened."

"When the dam on a fae's powers begins breaking, strong emotions can set them off. I'd hoped we'd get you to a muse before that started."

"I think it's safe to say we're too late," I croaked, scared of myself. "There's at least one crack."

"We need to quicken our pace." He exhaled. "Looks like you'll be getting that mule after all."

The stablemaster was a slender male with intricate, coiling cornrows, creamy brown skin, and a set of housefly wings. Our cheap duds notwithstanding, he sensed Briar possessed more seeds than he let on and refused to sell us the one mule he had. Instead, he steered Briar toward his horses, which looked like they hailed from Emerald City—every color in a crayon box.

Keeping his cool, Briar dickered with the gruff voiced fae, and I wandered from the stable to catch a fresh breath. Excrement smelled the same in the fae realm as it did on Earth.

I was resting back against a fence rung outside the stables, watching a pair of pastel pigeons bicker over a worm in the ground, when a commotion drew my attention. A churlish woman, the color of salmon with a ring through her septum, beat a threesome of wraithlike, gray-skinned faelets from her shop with a broom.

They were dressed in rags, their ebony hair hanging in greasy tangles around their gaunt faces. The littlest of them stumbled to the dirt in tears. The older two bent to soothe him.

"No beggars allowed!" the shopkeeper screeched. She shook her broom at the faelets before stomping back into her tree shop.

Acting on instinct, I rushed to help the kids. The oldest was the height of a ten-year-old. Her clear blue eyes hardened at my approach. She quickly stood, her skeletal limbs stiffening for a fight, protecting what I assumed were her two little brothers.

Hit with an image from a dream where an older sister braced to battle a shadow man for her little siblings' lives, I slowed my pace, raised my hands. "I won't hurt you."

When the faelets' mouths dropped at the sound of my voice, I remembered my accent. Clearing my throat, I strode forward and spoke my next words in the best imitation of Emmeline Wilton I could muster. "I just want to make sure you three are all right."

The smaller faelets rose to their feet behind their sister. She regarded me like a bee who might sting her. "Since when do Dananns care a wit for us Middlings?" She fisted her hands to hide their trembling.

I stopped before her. "Since now."

The oldest blinked, rubbing the shoulder of her weeping brother. Dirt smudged his cherubic gray cheek after his fall.

I knelt to his eye level. "Are you hurt?" He didn't seem injured. Had he just gotten scared?

His lower lip protruded as he wept, "Mm fine, Lady."

"Where are your parents?"

The eldest's face twisted. "Why should you care?"

Ignoring her hostility, I scanned the vicinity. No other gray Middlings in sight. "Why did that woman chase you from her store?"

She blinked at me. "*Woman*?"

I shook myself. "I mean beyn."

I needed to get my couch potato mind in gear and start talking *and* thinking like I belonged in my kingdom. Maybe then I'd start feeling like I fit in.

"She says we were begging," the middle faelet peeped, peering at me through a greasy fringe of black bangs. "We weren't. We just came to see if she'd give us credit for the debt she owes Mama. But she says she doesn't owe Mama anything, that Mama's a lying lush."

The oldest socked him. "Shut your trap!"

He bristled, rubbing his arm. "It's what she said, Gail!"

I chewed my lip again, assessing the situation. If their mother was, indeed, a drunk, it was safe to assume they were in town by themselves. Probably neglected. Maybe abused. Definitely hungry.

"You three, stay here." I made my way into the grocery shop.

I yearned to ream out the nasty shopkeeper who'd batted needy faelets from her store like mice in her cupboards, but I held my tongue as I paid for a bundle of sweet rolls and something resembling jerky with a couple good quality pumpkin seeds Briar had given me. He'd said one of those was the equivalent of a five in the USA. Easy to come by and proliferous.

The shopkeeper barely managed a grimace for me before I departed, carrying my new linen-wrapped food out to the faelets.

"Here you go." I set the parcels in Gail's frail arms. "If you ration that wisely, you'll have food for a week. And I left a few pumpkin seeds in there for you. Plant them, don't spend them."

The faelets continued goggling.

"We plant seeds all the time, lady." Gail looked both frustrated and sad. "Nothing grows. Mama's soil has gone to pot since the river was diverted to Covenlen."

The Shadow Court?

Wasn't the Shadow Court a wasteland? Who'd allowed a whole river's diversion? Obviously, it held importance as a water source if families like Gail's depended on it.

"Gads!" the middle child exclaimed, lemur like. "Your eyes, lady! Colors ripple through them as they did in the sky last night."

"The sky changed color last night?" Briar and I had camped in a bower again, which had obscured the sky from sight.

"It's changed colors for the past few nights," Gail corroborated her brother's tale. "Mama says it's the calling of the Aurora."

My throat constricted. That name again?

I considered asking the faelets to explain what the Aurora was but figured I'd better pretend I already knew, so I wouldn't blow my cover. Any more than I already had. By the way Gail spoke, I sensed the Aurora was a story *every* fae had heard, just like *every* human had heard of Cinderella.

So, I just smiled. "Maybe she's right."

A return smile flitted across Gail's hollows.

"You there!" a voice bellowed. "What do you think you're doing?"

I spun about to see a smocked fae man—or feyr—with arms as thick as ham hocks standing outside the grocery shop. The shopkeeper who'd taken my money stood beside him, lips pinched.

"Thank you, lady!" Gail and her brothers took off running with the food. "We'll pray to Danu for you tonight!" They scurried under the fence by the stables.

I waved goodbye as a vice of fingers seized me, wrenching me about. The smocked feyr was irate, his pointy yellow ears flushing orange as he rattled me. "What are you about, lady? Aiding beggars with food from my shop?"

I pushed him, which did nothing. I might've been several inches taller, but he clearly had me on muscles. "Get the hell off me!" I shouted, my phony accent slipping. "What's your problem?"

"My problem?" the feyr snarled, his sharp canines gleaming in the sun. "It'll be your problem when we fetch the magistrate."

"For what? Giving food to hungry faelets?"

He huffled. "Aye!"

I staggered. "*What*?"

A second later, the grocer staggered too. The shouting had drawn bystanders, Briar included. "Unhand her at once!" He whisked me into his arms. "By what right do you accost this beyn?"

Sputtering, the grocer gestured toward the stable fence the faelets had escaped through. "My ceyla alerted me that this meddler was feeding the beggars what bother my shop! Blatantly disrespecting the law!"

"The *law*?" I exclaimed.

Briar's jaw tightened. "Aye, well—please forgive her crime, good fellow. She's simple, you see—doesn't know any better."

I glared at Briar, wanting to kick him.

The female grocer strutted over, arms folded. "Hmph. Didn't seem simple to me. Seemed to know right what she was about."

I sucked in a breath to tell her exactly what I knew, but Briar smacked a hand over my mouth.

"I assure you, she's quite addled." He adopted that infernal charmer act again. "She has the mind of a child. It's my fault, really. It's my task to watch her, but I wasn't paying the proper attention, and she wandered off."

Am I a wayward puppy? I flailed out of his hold.

The male grocer loosed a breath, considering Briar's tale.

Cold to her core, the beyn sniffed. "Simple or no, the magistrate should be informed of her doings."

"Surely you have more mercy in your hearts for a harmless fool and her caretaker," Briar said. "What can I do to make things right?"

Flexing his paws in and out of fists, the grocer wavered. "Return us the food she wrongly gave, and we'll forget we ever saw her."

I paid for that food, you greedy assholes! I can give it to whoever I damn well please!

"Consider it done," Briar agreed to my devastation.

Mere minutes later, he returned to us in a streak of leather and homespun with the bundles of food I'd given those poor faelets. Stony-eyed, he placed them in the beyn's hands. "It's all there," he said, then spirited me away before we drew further unwanted attention.

Our journey continued. Without a mule and less a handful of seeds.

My anger was a living thing, threatening to engulf anything I touched. So, Briar waited hours before he dared to speak to me. Even then it was too soon.

"Amy, listen." He snatched my wrist, stopping me in my dirty tracks. Pity for my ignorance brimmed in his gaze. "It all goes back to the laws protecting nature. It's a natural selection, survival of the fittest thing—Darwinism."

My mind spun at such bullshit. "You took food from little kids, Briar! Food I'd given them!"

"Yes." His tone bore no apology, only resignation. "If I hadn't, those grocers would've summoned the magistrate, who'd have thrown you in a jail cell. Feeding beggars is outlawed here. It's our ideal that all who thrive here do so on their own merit, without depending on their communities."

"But they were *kids!* Kids are always dependent!"

"On their parents. Faelets are solely their parents' responsibility. There are no welfare checks. No food stamps. Parents are expected to keep their faelets fed and clothed through their own means, no one else's."

My head hurt. "But isn't birth control *also* outlawed? We force people into having babies, but then we won't aid them in raising them? That's asinine!"

He sighed. "You know rejecting the blessing of a child from Danu is sacrilegious."

"And if the parents fail at raising these faelets?"

Briar's mouth turned down.

"If the parents *die*? Are the kids just expected to pull themselves up by their bootstraps? Begin running the household?"

"Of course not. If they had no other family to take them in, they'd become wards of the kingdom—they'd be adopted into servitude."

I reeled back, the truth worse than I'd guessed.

Briar reached for me again. "I know it sounds harsh—"

I shirked him. "It's not harsh, Briar. It's *cruel*."

"Amy, those children will be fine. I guarantee you, if their parents don't get their act together, the magistrate will step in and remove them from their situation. Now, I'm not saying it'll be an easy life for them. They'll grow up in servitude, yes, but they'll also receive food and clothes and a warm place to lay at night. They'll grow into productive members of society, and they hopefully won't repeat their parents' mistakes."

Close to tears, I sneered. "Yes, productive members of society—who grew up without a *mother*. Because we just couldn't find it in our hearts to give them a little bread."

Briar stilled, maybe realizing the horror he so easily accepted. The shame on his face might've been genuine this time. "Amy, I—"

"What if it were me?" I'd seen myself glaring out of Gail's eyes, after all. "And Vi and Ace? And that curse had killed both our parents? And there was no Uncle Neel or Aunt Aylie. Would you have pressed us into servitude?"

He gasped. "Of course not."

"Because we're royals, right? Or because we're Danann?"

His lips parted, but no sound slipped through them.

"We're no better than those Middling children, Briar." My fingertips almost ignited again. "If I deserved love, comfort, and mercy at a rocky time in my childhood, then so do they."

"I'm not a snob, Amy." Briar's cheeks had flashed red at my scolding. "I'm a devoted champion of the people. I'd do anything to save *anyone* from harm—regardless of their race—within the bounds of our laws."

"Then where do we draw the line?" I wiped away a tear. "You can save a family from a burning building, right? But not from starvation? Don't both catastrophes qualify as natural selection? If the family isn't strong enough to escape the fire—"

"Amy, we could spend years debating the ethics of our ways."

You bet your ass we will, buddy!

"But it's just—life."

I could've kicked him in the balls. *What a defeatist copout!*

He scuffed a boot in the dirt. "If it makes you feel better, I told those kids you were mad I was taking the food back."

I scoffed, nauseated. "You want to know the worst part? They weren't even begging. I *decided* to buy them that food. They didn't ask me for a thing."

His eyes fell shut on a curse.

"And their mother can't provide for them because their soil's dried up." My lip curled. "Someone diverted the river to the Shadow Court."

Briar's eyes bulged, his shock a small relief.

After a charged silence, I gathered my skirts in a petulant bundle and stabbed my walking stick into the dirt. Dirt notably drier than what I'd seen thus far in our journey. "Let's keep moving. Without talking."

Taking me literally, Briar didn't respond as we trod along in doleful discord.

Later that night, after I'd bathed the grime from my skin with a pitcher of Briar's magic, and we'd made camp under a bower of violet pear trees, my caustic mood finally broke. Crippling grief replaced it.

Nestled between a pair of roots under a blanket, I wept upon Raggedy Andy's permanent smile. Gail and her siblings had invoked thoughts of my own brother and sister. Where were they? Were they safe? Would I see them again before the harbinger found me? No number of tears could answer my questions, but they gushed on regardless.

Briar stirred from across the crackling fire. His shadow moved toward me, and I held my breath—desperate for a simple hug.

I wiped my clammy cheeks as Briar set a gentle hand on my arm. His gaze caressed my face. For one second, I thought he might climb under my covers with me, snuggle me against his chest. Yet, he simply tucked my covers tighter around me and padded back to his spot by the fire.

I fell asleep still weeping, wishing for that hug.

Though the suns continued shining the next day, I dwelt in a rain cloud. My feet hurt, my back ached, and dust filmed my lips. I missed everyone and everything I loved with a debilitating intensity.

Just before noon, Briar led us off the road. "You look like you could use a break."

To this, I only shrugged.

His skin glistened with sweat at he searched my face. "Well, it's close enough to lunch. Why don't you head down that hill and take a load off? Maybe gather some kindling. I'll scare up something to eat." He squeezed my arm. "You okay?"

"I'm fine," I lied, then trudged down the hill as suggested.

At the bottom was an idyllic glen, where I sat in swaying grass and wildflowers and removed my boots and socks to let my throbbing feet breathe. I'd gather twigs when I was good and ready.

Reclining in the grass, I unzipped my backpack and rummaged until I found my iBloom Shimmy. Its pink metal was smooth and cool against my fingertips, so sleek and otherworldly now. Since crossing the portal, I hadn't removed it from my bag, hoping to conserve its battery. I'd determined to use it only for a pick me up, and right then, I really, truly needed a little *"I Like it Our Way"* in my life.

When the notes written across my heart skipped sweetly in my ears, I choked back tears and closed my eyes to escape my abysmal life. Finally finding peace in my new daily recitation—30 compressions, 2 breaths—I refused to look whenever something tickled my arm. Smacking it did nothing, as it returned moments later. With a posse.

Finally, I looked, expecting ants, or something similar. Instead, I found winged people the size of locusts crawling up my body. Caterpillar green, they had slits for eyes and manic, blood-chilling smiles. They were also buck naked. *Everything* hanging out.

I popped up to sit, yanking out my earbuds. The creatures flapped into the air, displaced—swarms more than what had landed on me. I switched off my iBloom. "Hello," I croaked at their unblinking scrutiny. "Can I help you?"

The closest beyn flew into my face, leering for an uncomfortable length. My being a million times her size did little to intimidate her.

I inched back, quashing a squeal as several of her brethren crawled through my hair. "Has anybody told you it's rude to stare?"

The tiny beyn's lips took an evil slant. Snickering like a stuttering wasp, she pointed a willowy finger at me.

I didn't even have time to scream before the bombardment. I screamed during, though—until my throat was raw.

Thrashing at the tornado of pulling, prodding, and scratching fae, I blindly scrambled back up the hill, wailing for Briar's help.

"Amy!" I heard a crack, the rustling of leaves, and then the infestation thinned as Briar switched the miscreants off me.

When I was all but free, Briar clung to me, his face stark white. "Run," he rasped, then yanked me down the hill, my sore feet bungling over hidden bramble.

The swarms regrouped, bulleting after us.

"What the *hell* are those things?"

"Sluaghs!" Briar shouted. "Wicked little shits who get their rocks off by pranking travelers!" His distress hinted their pranks weren't always harmless.

"How do we lose them?" I asked, then tripped over a stump hidden by wildflowers, straining my ankle. I hissed, rippling in pain.

Briar whirled back to help me.

He should've kept running.

The swarm pounced on him before he reached me, latching onto his trappings like clothes pins. I gawked as an army of beating wings hefted his writhing body into the air, tearing his switch from his hands.

Briar roared, thrashing as they winged him away.

"Briar, *no!*" I lumbered after him. "Please, you can't leave me!"

Growling, he stretched to reach me. I leapt to wrestle him from the sky, but the sluaghs played keep-away, lifting him just out of my grasp.

"Fuck!" I shrieked, pulse pounding.

"It's okay, Amy!" Briar's voice trembled through a forcible calm. "They can't carry me far. I'm too heavy!"

"No, damnit!" My strained ankle hobbled me, though I tried to keep pace. "Put him down! Or take me with you!"

My desperation only made them snicker again.

"Amy, you must keep moving!" Briar called through the rising swarm. "Stay on the King's Road! You'll reach a tavern—the Thorny Rose! Stop there tonight, and I *will* find you!"

"*Briar!*"

"Don't be afraid, Amy!" He'd drifted much too high, his voice an echo on the wind. "You'll be fine!"

After he and the sluaghs disappeared beyond the timberline, I collapsed to my knees in the wildflowers, cooing birds and peeping frogs accompanying my sniveling.

A frightening new page had just turned in my story. For the first time ever, I was on my own.

FOURTEEN

Rain pelting my hood, I slogged along the muddy King's Road. A spring tempest had broken out an hour before sunsdown. At the first clap of thunder, I'd scowled up at the billowy sky. "*Really?*"

Now, I was close to a second nervous breakdown.

As soon as my ankle pain receded, and I'd gotten my shit back together—after my first nervous breakdown—I'd dashed down the King's Road. I *would* reach the Thorny Rose Tavern that night. At all costs. I prayed to Danu that Briar was already there awaiting me. I didn't know if I'd survive another day on my own.

Besides my general lack of food and water (Briar usually provided both), I just *knew* harbingers were hounding me. I saw evil in every shadow, heard the ominous clicking of bogeybats in every woodnote. I'd passed one other traveler on the road, and mother save me, he must've thought me insane.

He was probably a simple farmer, but at the time I was certain he'd been sent to kill me. When he got within speaking distance, I scrabbled up a flowering magnolia like a squirrel, weirding him out if his expression were any indication.

Now, I rounded another sodden bend in the road, my dress having absorbed every puddle I'd crossed. Being so drenched, the symphony of fiddles, drums, and raucous laughter cutting through the rain was Goddess sent.

"It's here, it's here, it's here!" I stumbled past a copse of overgrown boxwoods into a clearing, where an ivied tavern of rustic stone construction stood before me—a beacon of salvation. The wooden sign above the arched door clattered in the wind. A sign marked by a red rose with one thorn. I squelched toward the tavern, its windows aglow.

When my feet shuffled over the threshold, the merriment I'd heard from outside dulled to an awkward hush. Eyes turned on me in a mix of reactions: shock, distress, awe, and scorn. None of them belonged to Briar. A once-over informed me he wasn't there.

Relax, I commanded my hammering heart. *Just because he's not here now, doesn't mean he won't show up. Just be thankful for the shelter.*

The party crasher that I was, I burrowed into my dripping cloak, lending timorous greetings to those I passed on my way through the smoky-sweet tavern.

Suspended orbs of light (magic, I guessed) glinted amongst cascades of wisteria hung from the rafters, illuminating passage to the bar. Muddy moss mottled the floor planks, my soppy boots only worsening the mess. The troubadours fiddling by the blazing fireplace muffled my squishing. Their song—about someone named Bluebell Shanty and something called bane bonnets—was like coffee after a mid-terms all-nighter.

By the time I reached the bar, most of the tavern patrons had forgotten my presence and returned to their earlier revelry. The few who continued watching me did so with unrepentant distrust.

Trying my best to ignore them, I peeled off my hood and wedged myself between a pair of husky, bearded feyrs. If not for their average heights, I'd have assumed them two of the seven Dwarves. Both muttered and inched away from me, hugging their tankards like I might snatch them. But I wouldn't let that offend me.

"Excuse me," I peeped to the wench behind the bar. Her skin was a gorgeous shade of teal with eyes to match. She'd pulled her pitch-black tresses into a bun, which was stuck through with a spray of wheat. In a dress like mine, an apron clinging for dear life to her bulging waist, she turned toward me, rusty springs in her throat as she laughed at some ribald feyr's naughty joke. Her bulging cleavage jiggled as her mirth subsided. By the time she addressed me, her mouth had flattened into a tight line—all humor gone from her dimpled face.

She bowed her head. "How can I serve you, lady?"

Why does everyone call me lady when I'm dressed like a pleb?

I leaned on the bar, exhaustion striking me like a mallet. Somehow, I retained the where-withal to change my accent. I went British again, confident I wouldn't screw it up. "Have you seen a feyr with short auburn hair and bright green eyes? Tall. Handsome. Pale like me. Danann like me."

One of her thick brows arched as she swabbed her knotty bar top. "Not that I recall, lady. But I ken why you'd be looking for a fella what looked like that."

I managed a smile in return.

"What I can't ken is how you let him slip through your fingers in the first place."

I would've laughed if I'd had the energy. Instead, I exhaled and leaned harder onto the bar, making the Dwarf to my right stomp away with his drink.

"Never mind Bogpie," the wench tutted, swatting my hand with her damp rag. "A right auld curmudgeon, he is. Tell me more about how you lost this pleasant fella."

"He's my travel companion. When we stopped on the King's Road today, we were attacked by sluaghs."

She sucked in a harsh breath. "*No.* Sluaghs, you say? In these parts?"

"Yeah. They swarmed him and carried him off. He called out that I should find this place, that he'd meet me here tonight."

"I suppose that promise depends on how far the sluaghs carried him, lady."

I swallowed hard, wanting to guzzle a river. "How—how far could they have taken him?"

"I can't say for sure, o' course, but I've heard they've flown folk to whole other courts."

Goddess, no!

"But I'm certain that had to have been a plague of sluaghs what did that. Your fella must be on his way to you. Only—he may not make it tonight."

What the hell was I going to do if Briar didn't reach me that night? Sleep in the rain?

The wench side-eyed me, wringing her rag. "Will you be needing a room tonight?"

Impressive, how she'd finagled that question into our conversation—casual, like a hairdresser pushing designer product.

I chewed my lip, picking at a hangnail I'd developed climbing that damn magnolia tree. Thanks to my bungled attempt at charity, I had one measly pumpkin seed to my name. I doubted that would cover a room rental. I couldn't very well beg for a free bed, either. Doing that was outlawed. My pride forbade it anyway.

"Um, well, I think I should stay down here. In the open. In case he does show up."

So much for sleep tonight.

"Then can I fetch you something to eat? Something hot and savory on this blustery night?"

My mouth salivated at mention of food. Despite my reluctance to look the pauper, I dug into my pocket and set my paltry pumpkin seed on the counter. "What can this buy me?"

I guessed not much as she stared at the seed, speechless.

The susurrus of a dog shaking rain off its fur saved me further embarrassment. Distracted, the wench beamed at what she saw behind me.

I glanced back to find a slender black and tan beauty traipsing toward me through the crowd, nose to the moss. She was taller than a beagle but had that adorable hound face with floppy ears and big brown eyes. Scampering straight over, she sat, regal as a queen, and offered me her paw like she knew I needed a friend. Her feathery tail swished in the moss, her tan eyebrows aloft. Her muzzle opened in a smile to reveal a black spot on her pink tongue.

I sank to pet her damp, sable fur. "Aren't you pretty?"

She nuzzled my hand, and memories of Novus geysered. Oh, how I missed him. When she licked my chin as he always had, I ruffled her ears and giggled. Giggled like the old me—the girl I'd been, a hologram now darkened.

I rose, and my breath caught upon a mixture of mist, musk, and citrus. Just three paces behind the dog I'd been loving on stood the biggest male I'd ever seen in person.

This is new, I thought as I gazed up at him. *Up.* Not down or straight ahead. *Up.*

He was damn near over a half foot taller than me with limbs solid enough to support such long bones. His hands were like bear paws, his shoulders linebacker broad. He wore all black, a dripping, fur-trimmed cloak tied at his sun-kissed neck. A short beard of brown whiskers covered his jaw and surrounded a wide mouth—soft, full, and upturned at the corners. The dark hair on his head, more fluffy than curly, was unintentionally mussed, making him unintentionally sexy. His heavy eyebrows angled toward the long bridge of his sloping, round nose. His narrow-set eyes reminded me of warm molasses cookies. Those eyes now gazed at me in quizzical consideration as he closed the space between us and bent to pat the dog's head.

"Good girl, Sionna," he praised her in a deep Irish brogue. His mouth quirked up on one side. "Very good girl."

Sionna wagged double time.

If I had a tail, I'd be wagging it too.

Realizing I'd been staring for far too long, I spun back to face the bar wench. She smirked at my dazzlement, scrubbing her counter.

"Hello there, Pete," she said to the stranger, who sidled to my right, untying his cloak. Her gruffness didn't fool me. I could tell by the warmth in *her* eyes that she was quite fond of Pete. "Finally come to pay your tab, have you?"

"All in due time, Jade." He chuckled and draped his cloak over the barstool beside him, revealing a studded jerkin and a close-fitting pair of leather trousers. He'd sheathed a dagger on his left hip. A scabbard hung on his right. He looked dangerous, but I didn't feel in danger.

Jade sighed as though she'd heard his excuse a million times. "What'll you have then?"

"How's the mead tonight?"

"Absolute shite."

"Hm." He stroked the hair at his chin. "That won't do." I could've jumped out of my skin when he nudged me—a bit rougher than he'd meant to, I guessed. "What are you having, darlin'?"

Blushing for sure, I set my hand over my pitiful pumpkin seed. "I—I'm not—"

"She's having an ale and a trencher of Reed's fleecer stew," Jade interrupted, smiling at Pete. "Sound appetizing?"

Pete took a seat. "Sounds perfect, Jade." He settled a benign look on me. "Add the lady's meal to my tab, would you?"

Jade grinned as I goggled. "As you say." She winked at me before waddling away.

Humbled, I stuffed my pumpkin seed back in my pocket. "You didn't have to do that but thank you."

I couldn't bring myself to meet the gaze surveying me. I sensed interest, but surely not the kind I wanted. I just looked like a street urchin, and he felt sorry for me.

"Think nothing of it." He paused, his gaze grazing my mouth. "Looks as if you've had a rotten day."

I scratched my unkempt head. "You don't know the half of it, bud."

"No, not bud. Pete." He extended his massive hand. "Happy to meet you."

Finally, I faced him, smiling. "Me too." I shook his warm, rough hand, transfixed by how his healthy tan made my skin gleam like pearl.

He waited. Expecting something from me?

I snapped my fingers, remembering myself. And to know to lie. "I'm Rose."

Pete seemed nice, but anonymity was imperative—as I was alone, unprotected. I needed to be cautious and wily.

"Rose, huh?" He withdrew his hand, smirking. "Sounds like an alias to me."

So much for being wily.

Pete rested an elbow on the bar. "I'd think you'd grace a man who's buying you supper with the blessing of your true name, *Rose*."

Though he was calling me out, his kind eyes disarmed me, and my thoughts tumbled from my mouth without permission. "Maybe. But I'd think a man who's simply adding my supper to his ever-expounding debt would settle for whatever name I choose to give him."

Pete's thick brows jumped up.

Whoa, there, sassy pants. Where the hell did that come from?

"That was a joke." I knew I'd sounded like an ass. "I wasn't really being ungrateful."

A full grin lit his whole rugged face. "Well, your joke just earned you a second ale."

I bit down on a grin of my own. "Sure you're not breaking some ridiculous law against buying beyns drinks in taverns?"

He leaned in and whispered, "Even if it is, I won't tell if you won't, darlin'."

His charm was effortless, spellbinding, and I nearly missed something he'd said. Had he called himself a *man*? Not a feyr? My eyes darted to his ears—as round as his cheekbones.

"Holy crap! You're human!" My voice carried above the troubadours' drumbeat, drawing criticism.

Grumbling, the Dwarf to my left hopped off his stool and tottered away with his tankard. I was too excited to care. At last, I'd found something familiar in this foreign world. I wanted to hug it.

I didn't, of course.

"Aye. What of it?" Pete asked, eyeing me.

"Nothing." I cleared my throat, regaining my Britishness. "I—I just had a lot of human friends once." *Last week, actually.* "And I just miss them, I guess. Sorry."

Something flickered through Pete's gaze, but it happened so fast I couldn't pinpoint it. Regardless, he eased back into congeniality and leaned down again. His nostrils flared. "What's that alluring scent you're wearing?"

I snorted. "I call it eau de mud and sweat."

"That's not it." He breathed me in. My heart played hopscotch until he straightened, serene as anyone who'd just inhaled ambrosia. "You smell of pears. And morning dew."

"Wrong on both counts. I never wear perfume."

"Hm. Then I must detect your natural scent."

Flustered by his intensity, I stumbled back into the Dwarf's abandoned stool. Pete grabbed it before it slammed to the floor, nudged it under my bottom. I yipped and grabbed the bar when he dragged me toward him, the stool scraping the floor. We wound up bumping knees, his hand finding my thigh. The touch burned straight through the layers of my dress.

I should've smacked him. Gregarious though he was, he was still a stranger and shouldn't feel free to fondle me.

Right?

And then there was Briar to consider. *Where the hell is he?*

Sionna saved me from having to oust Pete from my bubble, rearing up to rest her paws on his leg. Not one to be forgotten, I mused. Shifting back, Pete scratched her floppy ears. To her great enjoyment. She basked in his attention, her tongue lolling.

My insides went gooey as Pete murmured endearments. Daddy always said you could judge the heart of a man by how much he loved his animals. "You have a beautiful dog, Pete."

He chuckled down at Sionna. "Aye, and she knows it."

Moments later, a brawny fellow with a blonde-dusted, domed head dropped two wooden trenchers of stew and bread hunks before us. He barely glanced at me before rumbling to Pete, "I'm surprised you've darkened our doorstep before concluding your business."

Pete shrugged. "Business brought me here, Reed. Hunters must follow their game."

Reed searched for meaning in Pete's comment until understanding dawned—an understanding well beyond me. His blue eyes swiveled my way for a heartbeat, then back to Pete. "Mother save us," the sturdy feyr uttered before stalking away.

Brushing Sionna off him, Pete rose. "Don't forget our ales!"

Waving in allayment, Reed disappeared into an archway. Sionna scampered after the sullen fellow.

"What's his deal?" I asked, bemused.

Pete settled back onto his stool. "He's a mite touchy about my profession. He'll be fine in a lick."

He grabbed his spoon and dug into his steaming stew, meat hunks and strange fae vegetables swimming in a bath of shimmery gravy. I almost drooled at its aroma—Thanksgiving in a bowl. Without taste-testing, I started scarfing, not caring at all if Pete thought me unladylike.

"Mm!" I grunted around a mouthful seasoned with something like thyme, wiping my overflowing lips on my cloak. "So good!"

Pete raised his spoon in salute. "Wise choice then, darlin'."

Laughter was tough after I'd gobbled another spoonful, but I managed. "What do you hunt?"

Pete dunked his bread. "Animals, mostly."

I rolled my eyes. "Duh."

His brows drew together. "Sounds like you've familiarized yourself with black-market vernacular right well. Expecting the powers that be to open the portals, are you? I'd wager you'll be holding your breath for a while." He took a mammoth chomp out of his bread. Goddess, his mouth was huge. "They spare no thoughts for the common folk."

I stilled for a second. Wasn't I the powers that be? Or would be if I chose that path.

Emerging from momentary mystification, I found Pete's gaze on me again. "Enlighten me, *Rose*—" He truly wouldn't believe that was my name. "What's a beyn like you doing out on a bleak night like this? By your lonesome, it seems."

"What do you mean—beyn like me?"

"I mean that you're Danann. Have you not noticed you're the only one of your kind here?"

I scanned the tavern, and, damn, he was right.

"Dananns don't usually mix with us Unseelie lowlings." His voice carried humor, but his message was heavy. "Not by choice, anyhow."

Now I understood the frosty glances I'd received upon entering the tavern. Everyone assumed I was a racist snob, though I looked like one of the masses. Did even poor Dananns act like their shit didn't stink?

Taking another bite of his bread, Pete talked while he chewed. "Most Dananns who stumble upon this place would sooner dine alone in their quarters upstairs than mingle with a Troll fae like Reed or a human like me."

I raised my chin. "Well, I'm not like that."

"You are a bit different, aren't you?"

Funny, but that didn't seem a negative comment coming from him.

"Now, what nasty trick of fate brought you to this place?"

I exhaled a breath and regaled him with that day's ordeal—excluding my tree hugging stint. That was irrelevant.

When I finished, Pete clicked his tongue. "Sounds like you had a dose of a day."

If that meant bad, I agreed. "Now I'm just waiting around to see if my companion will show up. Did you happen to pass another Danann on your travels today?"

"Can't say as I did."

"Yeah, that would've been too easy."

"Where were you headed? Just the two of you?"

I shrugged. "Home, I'm told."

He arched a brow at my abstruse answer, but I knew better than to elaborate.

"Two ales for you." Jade placed two horn tankards between our trenchers. She pursed rosebud lips at Pete, ignoring me. "Just had a word with Reed. You'll pay your tab tonight, hear?"

Inclining his head, Pete sobered. "Yes, mam."

Sniffing, Jade waddled off to tend other customers.

"Did you do something I don't know about?" I wondered at his friends' mood swings.

"Not as of yet." He swigged his ale, winking. "But they ken me well enough to figure I will."

That night, Pete bought me more than a few ales, and by the time midnight cuckooed, my skin fit much better than it usually did.

Briar still hadn't arrived, but I'd forgotten about him midway through my second round. That's when Pete had led me to an empty dining table, where we chitchatted while playing cards.

"You're not the only one fond of the black-market, darlin'," Pete lilted, dealing me two cards from his prized Bicycle deck. He must've noticed me eyeing it. "I picked up this fine manmade treasure at the Goblin Market last year. I always find the best baubles there. Bartering's a sticky venture, of course. Goblins can be right underhanded, and you must mind your phrasing, else you'll get naught but ash."

"Ash, huh?" I chuckled, swigging my ale. It went down sinfully smooth. "Sounds like false advertising to me. Call the Better Business Bureau."

"The what now?"

I snorted down at my tankard, so tickled by my own joke, I didn't give a shit that he didn't get it. Pete laughed anyway, doubtless at my peculiarity.

My mirth ebbing, I considered my cards. He'd been teaching me bachram—a popular fae card game comparable to Texas Holdem poker. The only major difference between the two games was that bachram employed the jokers. They were higher than aces and could ruin a good hand in a blink. If a joker was dealt, that hand's big blind would pick it up, then discard one of their original cards. A new card then would be dealt in the joker's place. Barring that, the rules were simple. I still sucked at it, though—beaming whenever gold appeared to me.

"Are you thick, darlin'?" Pete teased, his judgments hurtless. They were more like badges I'd pin to my breast. "Christ, if we were playing a true game right now, you'd have cost yourself a hefty pot. Aye, I'm holding a queen and a ten, but that smirk on your face just warned me to fold."

Humming, I shielded my lips with my cards. "How about now?"

"With you batting your lashes at me?" Exasperation heightened his pitch. "Now I don't just suspect you of pocket aces but think you might've also robbed me."

Days of pent-up misery erupted from me in laughter, a necessary release that disrupted the peace descending on the tavern.

Other patrons had either retired to their rented chambers or taken up bedrolls by the banked fireplace. Sionna scavenged leftovers amid the dirty plates while the troubadours collected their tips. Jade, Reed, and several others ambled about, closing up shop. One wench—a petite Middling with pouty lavender lips, a lovely set of feathered wings, and a bird tattoo on her left cheek—glared at me. I'd distracted her from gathering tankards.

Also noticing her, Pete clicked his tongue and took my cards from me. "Ignore Freesia. She's the type who wants the things she can't have. Until she can, of course. Then she can't be bothered with them."

Emboldened with ale, I stared back at the scathing Middling. Her pout only deepened. "Are you the thing she can't have?"

"For tonight, it seems."

"Well, you know—" I bit my lip. "You don't have to stay here and keep me company. It's been fun hanging out with you, but if you'd rather—"

His smile crooked, he leaned in. "I'd rather be right where I am, making you laugh 'til your cheeks fair burst."

Those bursting cheeks flushed.

"Besides, you deserved a drink and a good time tonight." He raised his tankard to me, the brightness of his eyes dimming. "As Jade's already put the former to bed, I hope you get your fill of the latter."

I clinked my tankard with his, watched as he drank. "Thank you. I—I really needed someone to be nice to me tonight."

His Adam's apple bobbed like something was stuck in his throat.

Not long after that, my head grew too heavy to lift. My surroundings were fading in and out when Pete rose from his seat, the card deck fanned out beside my backpack, which I'd shrugged off my shoulders when we'd begun playing. Next thing I knew, I was floating toward a cozy spot beneath the tavern stairs, cradled in capable arms.

The crack of a knee brought me back to awareness. I gasped through my haze as Pete laid me on a leather bedroll. "I don't do one-night stands," I mumbled, curling into the musty pillow waiting there.

"Do I look the sort who beds dozing beyns?"

"Just thought I'd make that clear." Then I lost myself to slumber's pleasant grip.

PETE

At least now that his damned Danann mark had succumbed to his sleeping potion, Pete could drop the caring stranger act. Lying always weighed on him, despite its necessity.

Exhaling the night's tension, Pete strolled to where Jade and Reed stacked trenchers behind the bar, pretending they weren't watching him. He cleared his throat, laid a handful of orange seeds on the counter—they'd cover his tab.

"Thank you for not blowing my cover," he murmured.

Reed frowned once more at the sleeping Danann.

Jade braced her ponderous body on the counter. "It's no issue, Pete. We all do things we'd rather not from time to time." She pinched Reed. "Aye?"

Reed grumbled, "Aye."

"Did you find out who she was?" Jade asked.

Pete shook his head. "She told me her name was Rose, but I kent she was lying."

"Aw." Jade grimaced. "What could the Shadow Prince want with a sweetie like her?"

Pete toughened his heart, softness something he could ill afford. "She can't be that sweet, Jade. She's Danann, ken. Even being as cordial to her as I was, just before she fell asleep, she warned me against ravishing her. The Unseelie scum that I am, she assumes me prone to rape."

Jade clicked her tongue bitterly.

"Has Gentian ever cast curses on his own kind before?" Reed's brow furrowed in morbid interest. "That seems unnatural."

"It's rare." Pete shivered in remembrance of another Danann cursed by Gentian. He blocked the images. No good ever came of rehashing the darkest moments of his life. "But aye, it happens."

"But why *her*?" Jade prodded.

Pete shrugged. "Damned if I know. I didn't scent power in her, and even though she gave me a false name, I find it hard to believe she's important. What titled Danann beyn travels with just one companion and no mount?"

"Speaking of her companion," Jade said. "You'd best be gone with her by the time he shows. There will be no bloodshed in my tavern, you hear?"

"Yes, mam." Pete bowed his head.

Pete hadn't survived years as a cage fighter and become Gentian's most successful harbinger for nothing. Fighting was always secondary to using his wits. Starting out before his mark's companion arrived was step two in his plans.

Step one was sleep.

Unfortunately, now that the Danann was snoozing on his bedroll, he had nowhere to lay his head for the few hours left in the night.

As if telepathic, which she wasn't, Freesia stomped to his right and plopped her tray of tankards on the counter. She pouted, her tiny nostrils flaring. The wings of the bird birthmark on her cheek fluttered the way they did when she wasn't the center of everyone's attention.

Angling her way, Pete lazed against the bar. "Care to share your nook for the night, darlin'?"

Her luscious pout transformed into something seductive. She'd gotten what she wanted and bested another beyn—albeit a sleeping one. Her ego thus boosted, Freesia's gaze promised naughty bed-play.

Pete hated to tell her he had about five minutes in him before he dozed off atop her. He doubted that would satisfy her, but he'd worked miracles before.

She grabbed his collar in her spindly hand, tugging him toward her.

"I'll wake you at dawn," Jade rasped as Pete shuffled off with Freesia. "And you'd best pray trouble doesn't come knocking at my door before then."

FIFTEEN

Amy

Shadows billow around the hooded figure in my nightmare, his purposeful footsteps echoing. I fall back to shield my little sister and brother. I might be able to save them. I know I can't save myself.

The shadows shackle me, haul me toward the harbinger. His breath hisses against my cheek. Darkness, pervasive as a black hole, swallows me until, for the first time, the hood masking his face falls away.

"He's found you, Amaranthine," the eternal voice of my dream sings as I stumble in my shadow cage. A cage that feels much like the arms that laid me down that night.

Darkness flickers in a pair of narrowed molasses eyes. A wide, upturned mouth curls in a sneer.

It's Pete! I realize to my horror. *It's Pete! It's Pete. It's* Pete!

My own voice screams a warning to me from the shattering windows of my bedroom. "Run!" it shrieks. "Just *run!*"

Morning had barely breached the night when I awoke, adrenaline poising me to fight. I was no longer in the cozy nook behind the stairs at the tavern. Instead, I lay sprawled in a rickety, rattling wagon. Spoked tires splashed through puddles from last night's storm, each pothole jarring my bones. I blinked in the pre-dawn mist at the ambling hindquarters of a dappled ass led by a massive man in a hooded leather jerkin. Not Briar. A nimble black figure tramped beside him, panting.

Waking this way, I had no reason to doubt my dream's warnings. Confused though I was. Why was I still alive if Pete was a harbinger sent to kill me? Why had he stolen me like a thief in the night instead of slitting my throat while I slept? Whatever the reason, it couldn't be good.

Because I could only distinguish shapes in the transitory haze, I lay still and quiet, scared to make any noise until the suns shed light on my backpack. A hasty escape plan was already forming, but I couldn't abscond into an unknown wilderness without my stuff. What little I had in my bag could mean the difference between death or survival.

By the time the sky ignited in orange, my panic had risen to manic levels. At last, I scanned the wagon and found my book bag slumped in the back-left corner, zippers jangling.

Praying for stealth, I wriggled my way to the back of the wagon, gritting my teeth the whole way. I crawled past a leather quiver of feathered arrows and an etched longbow fit for Robin Hood.

Why had Pete left the weapons in the wagon with me? I could potentially turn them against him. Which I, of course, considered. Although, I decided against it real quick.

Not only was the terrain too rough beneath the juddering wagon for me to aim true, but the bow was secured to an iron bolt in the wagon's lip by an intricate knot beyond my patience. Untangling it would take time I couldn't waste.

I caught my book bag, slipped its straps over my shoulders. Thank Danu, Pete hadn't heard me yet.

Before I second-guessed myself, I rose on my feet, lost my balance when we hit a divot in the road, and flopped over the side of the wagon into the mud with a heavy splat. Somehow, I landed on my hands and knees, unscathed.

The warrior's skin? I wondered.

I wasted no time debating my constitution. A muttered oath heralded the wagon's rolling stop.

I sprang to my feet and sprinted to my left. The woods were dense enough that Pete might lose me in a chase. And as big as he was, I assumed myself faster. Even in a heavy dress, cloak, and Bugg boots. Sure, he'd sic Sionna after me, but I couldn't picture her hurting a fly. I thought my odds of escape were pretty dang good.

That's why I squawked when, upon gaining the tree line, something wrenched me backward like a yoyo on a string, bruising my shoulder blade. I lay sprawled in a damp patch of grass when a pair of sturdy, leather-clad legs stopped before me.

Pete squatted, his bearded face wry. "Run if you like."

He reached down between us and grabbed something invisible off the ground. With one tug, a smoky rope materialized around my ankle. A rope connecting me to Pete's bear paw.

His lips slanted when I gawped in horror. "You won't make it fifteen feet before you come bouncing back to me, darlin'. My shadow tether will see to that."

Squealing, I ripped off my boot, thinking the tether might slip off my bare foot. Of course, that would've been too damn simple. Instead of slipping off, the loop shrunk like wool in a dryer. Evidence of its existence disintegrated like dust, but I still felt it around my ankle—a velvety shackle.

I smacked my boot against the ground. "Oh, you fucking *son of a bitch!*" My voice echoed, making birds squawk and flap from their nests—freaking Sionna the hell out. She skittered beneath the wagon, taking cover. Not exactly the behavior I expected of a harbinger's dog.

Pete's brow arched. "I'll have you know my mother was a fine woman."

Fuming, I gritted, "Couldn't have been too fine if her son ended up a harbinger."

"Ah, so you *do* realize there's a curse on your head. I wasn't sure you were aware at first, what with the way you were flirting with me—a stranger in an unfamiliar place. I'd understand such a thing if you didn't reckon yourself hunted. Now, I just think you're foolish."

"Wha—" I choked on my voice, aghast as I was. "*Flirting?*"

He smirked. "Aye."

"I don't even know how to flirt, you dumbass!" Was Danu out to get me? "I'm a quiet bookworm who—"

"Oh, save me the humble innocent shite," he snapped. "I won't buy it now any more than I did last night. I don't give a wit how you're dressed, or that you couldn't buy yourself supper. That proves nothing. Your companion the sluaghs carried off was probably hauling your purse for you—because it was just too bloody heavy for your dainty highborn shoulders to heft." At my shock, he spat into the dirt. "You're a Danann. You surely grew up on a massive estate, surrounded by gold ingots and seeds from the Hanging Gardens. Your da probably owns land in all four courts." He sniffed, lip curling. "Look at me and tell me I'm wrong."

I looked at him but couldn't form words. Did being king of everything mean Daddy had owned *all* the land?

"Thought so."

"You don't know anything about me!"

"Oh, no? Tell me what house you hale from, and I'll ken all I need."

Like fucking hell will I fall for that! "I'm not telling you a damn thing. My name doesn't dictate my innocence. I don't need to prove myself to you. I *know* I'm a good person. Unlike you."

"Hm, yes. Good enough to call your slaves friends."

I joggled. "*Slaves?*"

"Of course. How else would you have come by 'a lot' of humans, as you said? Purchased them at auction, you did. Or did your da purchase your *friends* for you?"

Had I hit my head or something? Was this shit for real?

"It was also sweet of you to repay my kindness for feeding and entertaining you last night by assuming I'd rape you while you snored."

"What are you talking about?"

"Just as I was tucking you into my bedroll, like a gentleman—"

The memory of that brief exchange slammed into me, shattering my remaining reserve against confrontation. And I lost my shit.

"Are you fucking *kidding* me?" I exclaimed, jerking to my feet, boot still in hand.

He rose as well, towering over me. "Christ, the mouth on you—"

"You're standing there all self-righteous, accusing me of being a racist snob because I warned you I wasn't a slut?" I hopped like a flea. "That I didn't want to sleep with you?" I threw my boot at him. It hit him square in the chest and dropped.

He rolled his eyes.

"You were laying me down in your fucking bed, dude! Where I come from, girls have to question any guy who gets too close too quick, regardless of his social standing. They hand out rape whistles in health class, damnit!"

"And where is it that you come from? Sodom and Gomorrah?"

"Nope. Just America."

The set of his shoulders stiffened. "That's a crock of shite if I've ever heard it."

"No, it's not. I grew up in the good ole US of A. Pittsburgh, Pennsylvania. In a middle class neighborhood with lots of true, *free* human friends. Friends I loved with all my heart and am downright lost without."

His throat constricted, his Adam's apple bobbing. "That's not possible. They closed the portals so long ago, and you can't be more than—"

"*Twenty.* I'm twenty years old. My father found a way through a portal when I was four. Probably to escape the curse of *you*."

He sneered.

"I've lived as a human for the past 16 years, thank you very much. Honestly, I only learned I was fae a week ago. Didn't know anything about the curse until then either."

He narrowed brown eyes at me. "If you speak true, then why in hell would you have returned? You were safer *there*."

I flinched, the carnage of my father's death flashing back to me. "Isn't it obvious? Other harbingers found us. They got through the portal. And—" I choked back tears.

You won't *cry right now! Not in front of the harbinger!*

I shook myself, cleared my throat. "Anyway, once they'd found us, no place was safe. Daddy thought I'd be better off surrounded by my own kind. Before he—" I couldn't say it. "He told me to find our old home."

From my captor's softening expression, I realized I was much better at altering the truth than I was at outright fibbing.

"And the fella you were traveling with?"

I huffed a deep breath. "I guess I'm supposed to marry him." I paused, still ambivalent about that. "He was guiding me home—since I know nothing about this place."

Pete exhaled, crooking his thumb in his belt beside his dagger. "For now, we'll say I believe you, although it's not on account of your woeful tale." His gaze sharpened. "It's because you're so peculiar, and because your accent last night was so wonky. You sound more natural this morning."

"Whatever," I grumbled. "Just stop thinking of me as some heartless racist."

He tilted his head, considering me. "Baffling, that you should care what I think of you—the man charged with delivering you to the Shadow Prince's doorstep."

I stared at him, relief washing over me. Intense trepidation followed. "Wait. I thought you were supposed to kill me. Isn't that the point of a blood curse?"

"Oh, eventually the blood curse will take your life." His matter-of-factness clenched my guts. "But that's not what my orders are. I'm to capture and deliver a Danann beyn with a particular scent to Gentian—the scent of morning dew and pears."

"I don't smell like that." Wouldn't my own superior nose have seized on those notes long ago if I did?

"Aye, you do." His nostrils flared. "I have uncommonly keen smell. The fragrance is in your blood, darlin'."

"Don't call me that."

"Even had my power failed to convince me—which it didn't—my snuff hound confirmed last night that you're my mark. Aye, right now she's fair aquiver behind a wagon wheel, I know." Sionna peered through the spokes in said wheel, her ears back, her head down. "She scares easy, but her nose is never wrong. So, rest assured, you're the lucky one Gentian's after."

"Why? Does he want to kill me himself?" Did the jackal want the thrill of offing the heir to the throne he coveted?

Pete shrugged. "Potentially. Or maybe he wants a rare power you're harboring."

I gulped, the phrases *fire sylph* and *the warrior's skin* coming to mind.

"Not that I can sniff out any great magic in you." Pete studied me. "Makes no matter to me. My only task is to deliver you. You and your totem."

I swatted my rustling bangs from my eyes. "I don't have a totem."

"Everyone has a totem."

"Hmph. If I do, I bet you anything it's still in Pittsburgh where I left it." I grinned as his gaze froze on my face. "With the rest of my earthly belongings."

After a moment, Pete relaxed, his hair ruffling in the sweetest of winds. His handsome features were more distinct now that the sky had brightened. "You mustn't ken what a totem is to say such a thing. It's an extension of the heart. A person would carry it with them no matter the journey."

The asshole looked too damn certain. "Again, I had to travel light. Must've left my heart at home."

Expelling a long-suffering sigh, Pete reached into his pocket and produced a pink iBloom Shimmy, dangling it by the earbuds like a pendulum.

"You invasive prick!" I snarled. "Give that back!"

"Why?" His gaze mocked me. "Is it important to you?"

I glowered, folding my arms. I wasn't playing this game. "You know what—keep it. Once its battery dies, it's worthless anyway."

"This is a finite comfort, is it? And you've resigned yourself to its loss?"

I shrugged, still glaring.

"Then here." He tossed the iBloom back to me. "It can't be your totem."

Praising fate for the return of my prized possession, I stuffed it deep in my pocket. When I glanced back up, Pete was combing Raggedy Andy's red yarn hair.

Rage, pure and unadulterated, seized me.

He gleamed at me over my ratty doll. "How about this little poppet, though, darlin'? Would you care if I ripped off his head right now?"

My lip curled. "Don't you fucking dare." Half booted, I advanced like a misaligned bull. Horns out.

Andy his red cape, Pete backpedaled. "Oh, this is it, isn't it?"

I leapt at him. He darted away.

"I'm not joking with you," I rasped, something ferocious pulsing through me. My hair stood at my nape. "Give me back my doll!"

"Your doll?" He clicked his tongue. "That doesn't sound right. He should have a proper name, shouldn't he?"

"His name's Andy, asshole! Give him back!"

"Andy." Pete ignored my fury. "Nice to meet you, chap."

Baring my teeth, I advanced on Pete. "You *will* give him back to me. Right now."

He brushed me off, then turned and stuffed Andy into the scuffed leather satchel strapped diagonally across his broad back. "Don't rightly think so." He craned his neck to buckle his sack shut, readjusting it to his comfort. "The only person I'll be giving this bit of fluff to is Gentian himself. Sorry, darlin', Andy's—"

He barked, flying backward on a gust of wind so powerful it bowed the younger trees growing across the rocky dirt road—a gust that had whooshed out of me in my surging wrath.

My only thoughts for reacquisition and revenge, I descended on Pete with all my weight, snatched the dagger from his waist, and pressed its razor edge to his bobbing throat. Hard.

The blade glinted against his gullet, reflecting the golden morning suns. Pete's eyes blazed in amazement. And fury. Squirming down into the dirt to put space between his carotids and the knife, he raised his hands.

I heaved, desperate to maintain control of the situation. "Now, you jerkwad, I'm going to say this one more time." Sweat slicked over the engraved dagger's handle. "Give. Andy. Back. Or I'll slice your throat like a hunk of cheese."

I tightened my slipping grip on the dagger hilt. Pete hissed as the blade nicked his skin, and the sight of his welling blood shamed me. "If you want him back, you must let me up." The cords of his throat pulsed. "I can't very well reach my bag with your knee in my chest, now, can I?"

I gritted my teeth. *What the hell should I do?*

Pete was right. In our current position, I could only retrieve Andy by letting him go, his satchel smushed beneath him, tightened to his massive body. But if I eased up even a fraction, he'd dance away from the blade. I'd no longer be a threat.

Chaotic emotions triggered my powers, so I couldn't hope for another gale-force wind to knock him on his ass.

You could just slit his throat, reasoned a stone-cold part of me. *Once he's dead, recover Andy and run to safety. Problems solved.*

Trusting that Pete wouldn't kill me was idiocy, no matter what he said. He was a *harbinger!* Even if he kept his word, let me live, he'd still hand me off to the evil fuck who wanted my entire family exterminated. Death would be a mercy then.

And what about the shadow tether problem? What if killing Pete didn't nullify the power of that damn leash? If I killed him, would I be forever bound to a rotting corpse? His replacement would surely catch me if I had to drag his dead ass around.

Stop wasting time with what-ifs! You know what you need to do!

My heart hurt just imagining it.

Pete seized on my doubt, heaving up with a roar. I cried out as he clamped my wrist, twisting my arm behind me at such an unnatural angle I had to drop the dagger. The blade sliced into the grass as Pete's gruff hands bit into my flesh, slammed me facedown into a mud puddle. I sputtered, squawked, and flailed in an all-out wrestling match with him and a threesome of snaking shadows.

Suffice it to say, I lost.

I wound up hog-tied and gagged, tossed in the wagon like a bale of hay. Standing over me, Pete shook mud from his arms as I cursed him through my invisible gag. Gibberish was all I managed, but he got the gist.

I wrenched back into the boards when Pete sank to a crouch before me and dabbed his neck. Blood coated his dirty fingertips; he grinned at the sight. "Should've killed me when you had the chance, darlin'." Then he smacked my ass.

I screeched as he burst into laughter and bounded away from my writhing filth.

T wo hours after waking, I was parched, hungry, aching, and in grave danger of peeing my pants. At first, I would've rather soiled myself than acknowledge Pete's presence. Of course, as my pangs intensified, I realized my pride would recover from deigning to speak to the man who'd tied me up like a farm animal. It wouldn't if I pissed myself before him.

After minutes of squealing for Pete's attention, the wagon finally slowed on the rocky, narrow passage through a fertile, towering woodland. We might as well have been in Germany's Black Forest, a setting featured in many of my favorite romances. Right then, of course, it was anything but romantic.

Pete folded his arms upon the wagon ledge. "Need something?"

I fought the gag to speak.

He arched a brow. "Enunciate, would you? I can't understand you."

I willed fire to spray from my eyes. Nothing so violent happened.

"*That's* a nifty little talent there—the way you make your eyes change color. I thought it was a trick of the fae asters last night, but here we are in broad daylight, and they just shifted from hazel to amber—almost red."

My eyes would only get redder.

"A word of advice—don't let Gentian see that happen if you can control it. If he doesn't ken what it means about you, he'll do whatever he must to figure it out."

My guts quavered, my bladder following suit. Moaning, I kicked, seconds away from wetting myself.

Pete chuckled and opened his fist. A set of shadow tethers materialized, extending from his fingers. He grabbed one with his other hand and yanked. The binding between my teeth slackened, then slithered back into his hand.

Blood rushed back to my lips.

"So, what is it you want?" he asked, almost bored.

I lifted my nose. "I need to go to the bathroom."

"Are there privies in the woods where *you* come from?"

"You know very well it's just a turn of phrase." I wriggled in my bindings. "I have to pee. Like, right now."

His mouth quirked. "I suppose you want me to untie you."

I glowered. "Unless you know of some other way I can do it."

A witty retort twinkled in his eyes, though he refrained from voicing it. "Fine, but if you even so much as look like you're plotting another foolhardy attack, I'll tie you up again, and you can stew in your own waste until we reach the Shadow Palace. Is that clear?"

I bared my teeth. "Yes."

Prick!

He grunted and opened his hand again. Moments later, all tethers had recoiled from me—save the one around my ankle. Pete snorted at my aggrieved look. "Oh, that one's staying. If wind tarries in your blood, you may be able to fly."

I nearly laughed. *If only—*

"Don't mistake my kindness for stupidity."

"*Kindness*?"

His lip curled. "Perhaps I should give you a taste of how other harbingers would treat you after that stunt with my *scian*." He clasped his dagger hilt. "Maybe that'll teach you some gratitude."

Gulping, I stuck my bare foot back in my boot and scurried from the wagon.

"That's what I thought," he said as I dashed into the ferns.

I went as far into the brush as I could before that damn leash grew taut. Which wasn't far at all. I could still hear Pete shuffling on the road, talking to the donkey and Sionna, who'd begun snuffling the ground like a possessed hog when we'd stopped. The trees made a pathetic barrier between me and Pete's searing gaze.

"You better not look!" I warned, pressing my legs together in a desperate search for privacy.

"Or *what*?"

"Just—*argh*!"

"Go already!" he groused, doing something that rattled the wagon. "I've no interest in watching you piss!"

Flushed, though the forest canopy did wonders against the spring heat, I hiked up my skirts, yanked down my panties, and hunkered down by a mossy tree stump to release a small, glorious flood upon the crunchy leaves at my feet.

"Have you finished yet?" Pete shouted from the road after five solid minutes. "You can't have a drop of moisture left in you!"

"I'm almost done!" I'd finished a minute after I'd started, but without toilet paper—and damned if I'd ask if he had any—evaporation was my only means of cleanliness. Scrounging for hygienic leaves was the second item on my to-do list. The first was escape.

I'd just recomposed my clothing when the berry bushes to my left shook, and a creature I'd never seen before stuck its head out of the branches to blink at me. With the slanted blue eyes of a cat, the jowls of a dog, and the fluffy brown mane of a lion, it was a hybrid the likes of which only a child could imagine. And the coolest one I'd ever seen. I giggled when it chirruped like a robin.

"Oh, *look* at you," I cooed. "Don't be scared. I swear I'm nice."

The creature loped out from the bush on four fluffy paws, its small, brown, bearlike body as plush as a stuffed animal. My initial instincts were to squeeze the stuffing out of it. Instead, I patted my knees to entice it nearer.

"Can I pet you?" I asked, already reaching out.

Examining me with wide, guileless eyes, the beast neared in stunted zigzags. Feeling me out.

"I won't hurt you."

Lifting its shiny black snout, the hybrid whiffed me. Then sneezed, fur ruffling.

I laughed. "I don't smell very good, do I?" I was caked in dried mud and stunk like it. It didn't help matters that I hadn't had a proper washing in almost a week.

Morning dew and pears my ass.

"I had a rough morning." Arm still outstretched, I tramped nearer. The hybrid crept to meet me until my hand hovered just above its forehead.

Holding my breath, I caressed a patch—glossier than chenille—between the animal's feline eyes. It purred as loudly as Kell ever had, nuzzling into my palm. "Do you like having your ears scratched? My cats always—"

I didn't even hear the arrow until it ripped through the creature's neck. Its tip protruded just spaces from my chin. Blood splattered my face.

Shrieking, I floundered away from the gurgling animal, choking on my heart. The animal's eyes blazed, the look in them burning into my brain. They shone with great surprise. And betrayal.

Longbow in hand, Pete emerged from the shadows, grinning. He might as well have strangled a bunny before me!

Sionna sat at his heels, smiling skyward for approval. Pete clucked and bent to pet her head, merciless with cheer. "Good work." He dropped his bow and unsheathed the sword at his right hip. "You snared us a delicious supper."

"What are you doing?" I shrieked, flapping like a bird when Pete brought down his sword, decapitating the twitching creature. Carnage stained the leaves.

I trembled as Pete knelt before me, inserting his blade under the creature's furry jowl, revealing a set of long, needlelike fangs—sharp, transparent, and glistening like a rattlesnake's.

I sucked in a harsh breath, wrenching back.

"You see those teeth?" Pete no longer smiled. The heartless hunter had vanished. "Do you reckon any animal with teeth like that won't use them?"

Shuddering, I shook my head.

"This beast is known as a cantir—one of the most charming, most deadly predators in all the fae realm. Its venom is potent enough to paralyze a beyn of your stature in several heartbeats. They usually don't wait that long before they start devouring their prey, of course."

Why are we traveling through places with predators like that *around?*

"You were about to become its breakfast." Pete shifted to wipe his blade on a stained wool cloth tucked into his belt. "You're damn lucky Sionna scented the thing, that I found you in time. Be more mindful of your surroundings, would you? And don't make to befriend wildlife until you ken their nature. It'd be a crying shame if you were to die before I collected my bounty."

Glaring, I wiped my cheeks and stomped away. Back to the wagon. What was the use in trying to go anywhere else?

Darkness having fallen, I sat across from Pete in a cherry-tree copse off the path, hating life as the cantir roasted in chunks on a spit over a roaring fire. The animal's blood coated my captor's giant hands. The *scian* he'd used to butcher it sat on a stone to his right.

Sionna lay to his left, crunching on a leg bone while the donkey, whose name I'd learned was Bob, grazed on buttercups and grass, intermittently swishing his tail and braying like—well, like an ass.

"What's your real name?" Pete broke the silence that had stretched after he'd murdered the cantir. He waited for my answer, turning the spit. Grease dripped off the meat, sizzling on coals.

A chill breeze mussed the hair at my back, and I yanked my hood over my head. "I told you last night—it's Rose."

"We've already established I don't believe that, so why don't you try a different lie?"

I huddled into my cloak, denying him reply.

"Have it your way. Since a long journey together is in our future, I'd prefer to call you something other than, *You there*." He raked my length, and I flashed back to middle school, where even my minor flaws were fodder for crows. "So, how about—Shorty?"

I had a visceral reaction to that nickname. Which he'd intended, his smirk a stick and my scowl the circus sideshow.

I fixed my gaze on the fire, refusing to play his game. "Whatever."

Pete chuckled deep in his throat, stirring the glow within his fire ring. Another silence spread before he pulled a crispy morsel of meat off the spit. "Here." He held it out to me. "Have the first bite."

My stomach turned, and I shook my head.

He withdrew. "Where is it that your meat on earth came from? Thin air, was it?"

"Hardy har har. It came from dead animals, just like it does here. I've just never been present when one was killed."

Never wanted to be either.

"Did your da do all the hunting in your family?" He took a mammoth bite of the hunk he'd offered me. "Or your fella traveling with you?"

"Neither." I scratched my cheek. I'd washed my face hours ago when we'd happened upon a stream, but I couldn't shake the feeling of blood on my skin. "Hunting's more a sport than a necessity where I grew up. I knew some boys in college who hunted, but in my family, we'd just go to Wegmart and buy whatever meat we needed."

Deadpan, he said, "What's Wegmart?"

"A popular superstore chain." What person from Earth had never heard of Wegmart? "Did you grow up here?"

His mouth tautened. "No." He didn't elaborate, but I needed more.

"Are you from Ireland?"

Gnawing his meat, he cut me a sharp look. "I was born there, aye—in Ulster. I spent much of my childhood in a town outside Philadelphia, however. My family emigrated when I was five or six."

I stared at him, stupefied. "You're from Pennsylvania too?"

"Aye."

I sat straighter in my patch of grass, thinking, *Small worlds.* "And you don't know what a Wegmart is?"

"Don't believe they existed when I lived there."

"Huh? Of course, they did."

"I assure you, they didn't. We didn't have chains of anything in 1778."

My mouth opened, but no words came out.

"That's the year I wound up here. If you were going to ask."

"But—but shouldn't you be dead?" I goggled at him, doing mental math. "Or really, really, *really* old?"

Pete examined his food, debating what to tell me. "I spent most of my days here in time pockets. I was nearly 25 when I was—when I came here. Now, I think I've aged to about

28." He shrugged and took another bite. "Hard to say. Do you truly ken nothing of this place?"

I sidestepped the subject. "You're Irish, but you keep using the word *ken*. I thought that was a Scottish thing."

His mouth took a terse cant. "The Scots dialect was quite prevalent in Ulster when I was a lad. Ulster Scots, they're called. What's more, I've spent a goodly portion of my time here in a place where Scots is the vernacular. The word slipped into my vocabulary. You're the only one who's ever cared enough to comment on it. Evading my question?"

I sniffed, admitting, "I don't know much about this world, no. I was told about the time pockets. Guess I just assumed they wouldn't work the same for humans."

Pete fed his last bite to Sionna. She wolfed it down, then sniffed his empty hand for more. "They work for anyone with magic."

"And you were given magic," I stated for myself. *By Gentian*, was what I couldn't say.

"I was given some extra gifts when I became a harbinger, aye." Pete soured at my assumption. "But I've *always* had magic."

When this bombshell sank, I nearly went with it. "*Humans* can develop magic?"

Laughter rarely sounded so barbed. "Christ, you Dananns—doesn't matter where you were reared, hauteur must taint your blood." He ripped another morsel off the spit. "Might you consider that Danu loved us pathetic humans as much as she loved you? She was our creator, just as she was yours. She bestowed her gifts on some of us, just as she did you."

Sparks from the fire spiraled skyward—along with my hackles. I snapped my cloak tighter about me. "That's not what I was implying by my question."

"Oh, no, of course not. And you can't be held accountable for unintended prejudices, can you?"

That's it! I thought, baring my teeth. Danann canines and all. "You can stop that at any time," I snapped, blood roiling. "I know exactly what you're trying to do."

"You do, do you?"

"Yeah, I do." I stared him down, refusing to blink. "You're painting me in your mind as some heartless Danann snob to justify this awful thing you're doing to me."

His cruel amusement withered before my eyes.

"Well, guess what, honey—that holy man whose name you keep taking in vain—he ain't going to forgive you for this any more than your own conscience will. Because I'm not the bitch you want me to be. I'm a good person whose only real hatred in life is sad endings in books. I love and respect *everyone* until they give me cause not to. Because that's how I was raised—by a wonderful, loving, open minded Danann feyr, who your evil boss had *killed*!"

Pete gulped as my eyes welled, my rage and sorrow brimming over, unconstrained.

Let him see. He deserves these tears.

"And for *what*? For some petty grudge?" I ratcheted to my feet and kicked dirt into the flames, sending embers his way.

Pete flinched back. Sionna skittered aside, wide-eyed and blinking.

"How dare you judge *me*!" I fisted my hands. "You—*harbinger*!" I then stalked from the fire—as far as my damn tether allowed.

That night, I wept for hours into my book bag—the only thing I had to use for a pillow, as Briar had shouldered all our bedding supplies. I didn't even have a blanket.

My stomach burned in hunger, and my bones shuddered with cold inside my cloak as I whispered my sorrows to the brilliant stars above, hoping they'd tell Daddy how much I missed him. I imagined his protective arms hugging me in my pain, comforting me in my desolation. Then a chill would creep up my spine, and I'd know I was alone. So alone. My tears gushed anew each time.

Then, amid my misery, came a rustling in the grass.

"Sionna." Pete turned in his bedroll by the banked fire. "Lie down."

Her claws scraped over tree roots, crackled through leaves.

"*Sionna,*" Pete hissed. "Come back here."

She ignored him, and he kept hissing. I wondered where she was going until I felt the pressure of her nose on my boots.

I gasped, peering from my cloak to find reflective eyes watching me.

Sionna sniffed me from my feet to my face, then lapped my pouring tears, her tongue warm and wet.

More tears squeezed past my eyelids as I giggled, grasping her furry face. "You're just the sweetest," I sniffled. "Did you come to check on me?"

She responded with another lick, settling in the grass beside me.

"Turncoat." Pete harrumphed, snapping his cloak back over his shoulder.

We both ignored him.

"You know, I'm a good snuggler." I opened my cloak to her. "At least that's what my dog, Novus, used to say." Another tear trailed down my cheek—for him. "You want to see why?"

The tip of her tail fluttering, Sionna army-crawled into my bubble and relaxed.

I finally fell asleep that night, my eyes swollen, my face chapped, but I was toasty and warm in my heart—where the snuff hound's head nestled.

SIXTEEN

hen I awoke the next morning to the resolve on Pete's face, I knew my guilt trip the night before had failed. He was taking me to Gentian, no matter his shame. Which was totally gnawing at his peace-of-mind; he wouldn't meet my eyes.

So, I resolved myself to something too—a tactic this self-conscious, socially anxious beyn would never consider unless driven to it. Simply put, I was going to irritate the *fuck* out of Pete until he couldn't stand being near me. Because the more time I spent away from him, the more time I'd have to plot an escape.

So, after relieving myself that morning, I plopped down by the fire he'd rekindled and whined in my most maudlin voice, "I'm *huuungry.*" The complaining progressed from there. About everything. For days.

The suns were too hot, the nights too damp. He never fed me enough. I was habitually thirsty. My back ached from riding in the wagon but walking only gave me blisters. Talking to him exasperated me, yet I hated the incessant quiet. At meals, I whined incessantly about the woeful blandness of his food. When once he finally barked that I should quit bellyaching and eat, I'd retorted, "I'll quit when you find me some ketchup, you scrub!" Because of the cantir incident, I made him run a perimeter check every *single* time I peed—which happened as much as I could physically manage given that he was such "a Scrooge McGoose with the water canteen."

The colonial remnant that he was, Pete had no clue what that meant, but by the way he slapped his water skin into my chest, I could tell the reference annoyed him to no end. He probably guessed it a cultural epithet against the Irish. Guzzling the entirety of his water as I skipped along beside him, I snickered to myself.

If he only knew—

By the fifth day, at least one of my complaints was genuine. We hadn't encountered a real stream or river since the first day of my captivity, and I—someone accustomed to daily showers—abhorred the grime coating my skin. Dirt had embedded itself under my nails, my clothing was dusty and grass-stained, and my scalp was so itchy I feared I might've contracted lice—or the fae equivalent. My long hair had also knotted into what Aunt Aylie had termed rats' nests—great matted tufts that she'd attack with a wide tooth comb when I was little. Under her tender ministrations, I'd learned quickly to keep tangle-free. But doing that required adequate conditioning, which required water.

I spent most of that fifth day bemoaning my unbearable shape from the back of the wagon. Pete spent it stalking alongside Bob over the uneven forest path, his shoulders hunching with my every grating note.

"Oh, Sionna." I smoothed her fur over her head as we sat in the wagon. We'd become besties in the past few days. To Pete's growing vexation. "How can you even stand to be near me? I smell so bad, I'm surprised you haven't already keeled over and died. I'm surprised *I* haven't keeled over and died.

"Of course, all your insensitive master would need to do is detour toward the closest water source, so I can wash the dirt away. But will he? No, because it's out of his way, and there's no time to spare. He wants his bounty, and he wants it *now*. What does he care what state I'm in when he hands me off to that jackwagon who killed my father? What does he care how many germs are crawling on my skin?

"You know, poor hygiene leads to infection. And disease. But Pete doesn't get that. In his time, popular medical science stated you got sick because God hated you, and the go-to cure-alls were leeches and bloodletting." I scratched Sionna's chin. "Spoiler alert—neither actually helped. No, they didn't. Not one bit."

"Oh, would you just *shut your bleeding trap*?" Pete's roar assaulted tranquility itself. Birds flapped from their perches as we clattered to a stop, Bob blaring his displeasure.

I popped up to my feet to give Pete attitude. Hand on hip and everything. "Excuse me?"

Pete's brown eyes widened, noticeably blackened. He snarled at the goading in my voice, and I was glad Bob and the wagon were between us. "*Excuse* you? I will *not*." Days of repressed aggression rasped out of him. "You're nothing but a writhing pain in my arse! You ceaselessly harass me from every dawn until every midnight, and I cannot, for my health, endure it a moment longer!"

Mission accomplished, I thought. "It's not my fault I'm uncomfortable. How would you feel—?"

"Bollocks! I've weathered the same conditions as you, and I'm not suffering half as badly as you claim you are."

I found my reserve toward avoiding conflict lessened the stronger my B.O. got, and I bent to seethe in Pete's face. "Might that be because you've prepared for this trip, and I didn't? Because you'll gain from it, when I'll lose *everything*?"

Pete's eyes burned like the darkest of coals. "You'll lose your fecking tongue if you don't quit your griping."

"I'll do as much griping as I want," I hissed. "And you can just fucking deal with it."

Pete took one menacing step toward me, hand on the hilt of his *scian*.

Sionna pounced on the wagon bed ledge beside me, hackles raised in a vicious snarl. At him.

I shuffled aside in deference to her disposition, her sweet face downright feral.

Pete faltered, gaping at her. She'd probably never growled at him before.

I folded my arms. "See, even your own dog thinks you're being a prick to me."

Pete's tan face flashed red before he rumbled and stormed back to his place beside Bob. Grabbing Bob's bridle in one meaty fist, he wrenched the donkey and the wagon over a muddy ditch at an abruptness neither I nor Sionna expected. We both lost balance and plummeted to the rigid wagon boards. My funny bone cushioned my fall.

I thrashed, my arm splintering. "*Ow*, you dickhead!"

"You keep whining, then rest assured, I'll give you just cause!"

Empty promises didn't seem Pete's thing, but if I was angering him enough to elicit threats, then I'd keep it up. Threats meant my plan was working. Even if he gagged me again, I could still make noises with my nose that would drive him up a tree. For the sake of his own sanity, he'd eventually seek refuge from me. Then, I'd have time to act.

My plan was simple. Just because my tether was invisible—and magic—didn't mean I couldn't sever it. I didn't figure I'd ever get my hands on one of Pete's blades again, so I'd fashion my own. I'd already collected two flat stones on one of my many potty breaks—one to use as a knife, the other to sharpen it. Now I just needed a bit of time and water to hone something with a shot at sawing through my tether. If that didn't work, then I'd have to test the tether's vulnerabilities. The damn thing couldn't be indestructible.

If it was, I was screwed.

Ignoring every instinct warning me against prodding the bear further, I continued lamenting my discomfort to a comical degree. For two more days. On the eighth day, Pete snapped.

It was almost noon. Sionna and I had dozed off in the wagon bed, cushioned by the makeshift mattress I'd crafted from grass and fern fronds to avoid future injury whenever Pete's temper spurred him to quicken Bob's pace over ruts and rocks. I didn't even notice we'd stopped until my eyes fluttered open to blear at a dusty, black leather jerkin. I was dangling like a deer carcass over the harbinger's shoulder.

"What the hell are you doing?" I squawked, pummeling Pete's back. "Get your grubby hands off me!"

Pete leapt to the ground with a grunt, squeezing me as my face rammed his spine. Seeing stars, I fought to regain my bearings—and my freedom. Pete's scowling that morning said enough; he had rotten things in store for me.

"Hold still or these grubby hands will drop you," Pete gritted out on his hike through the woods, Sionna prancing at his feet. She must've thought we were playing a game. "This is like trying to carry a swarming hive of bees."

"Why would anyone *do* that?" I joggled into his back again—a wall of solid muscle. The spicy musk of man sweat and citrus overwhelmed me. "Just put me down, and I'll walk to wherever you want."

The hell I will.

"Oh, no, no. I'd feel a right lout leaving such a pampered priss to navigate this treacherous footpath on her own, what with your brittle ankles and weak fettle. I'd surely never hear the end of it if something infelicitous befell you."

I writhed anew. "Let me go or something infelicitous will befall *you*!"

A tic crawled through his shoulders. "Funny you should say so. These past days have me wondering who Gentian cursed—you or me."

I screeched, feral as a stray cat.

Moments later, Pete finally stopped, and I held my breath for whatever came next, picturing heinous things.

Thank the Goddess I held my breath.

Pete dropped me headfirst into a pool of crisp, opaque water. Chills zinged through my bones, radiated through my lungs. I sputtered to the surface, anchoring myself in a sandbar. I glared through my dripping bangs to find Pete standing on the beach of a lake, euphoric as a clown.

"You son of a *bitch*." I struck the water rippling against my breasts.

Vendettas danced in his eyes. Their color, damn near black over the past days, had lightened back to warm molasses. Was I imagining it or was his eye color as changeable as mine?

"Come now," Pete chided, leaning against the trunk of an enormous elm like he'd nothing else to do with his day. Sionna sniffed along the shoreline, completely unconcerned for me. "You've already used that one. Where's the ingenuity, Shorty?"

I gritted my teeth on another screech at *that* nickname. Admitting it bothered me would only ensure it stuck.

"Why the insults at any rate?" A smirk twitched on and off his lips, his face ill-suited to innocence. "I thought you'd be pleased. Here, you've been wailing for a bath for more days than I can count, and now I've found you one. How about some appreciation?"

I trudged through the fathomless lake back to shore, water tumbling off me. "I'm sorry, do you usually bathe with your clothes on?" I wrung out my sopping hair. "Or—do you bathe at all?"

Pete examined the dirt caked beneath his blunt, uneven nails. "Once in a blue moon."

I rolled my eyes, the scent of his sweat lingering in my nose. "What color's the moon tonight?"

He chuckled. "Bathing's a pointless venture with so many miles still ahead of us. You'll be filthy again come sunsdown. If you had any sense, you'd wait until the end of our journey."

"Then I guess I don't have any sense." I was already unlacing my vest.

"I assumed not." He tossed me my book bag, which I hadn't realized he'd brought. "I also assume that holds all your necessary sundries."

Kneeling in the sand, I unzipped and dug through sweaters and socks for my assortment of scentless Dove products. The sight lifted my heart, if only a little.

"Get to it." Pete pushed off the tree. "We don't have all day." I watched him turn and head back the way we'd come.

I froze. He was leaving me alone! But for how long? *What should I do?*

I felt my skirt pocket—both stones were still there. I could use this alone time to hone my blade—the sensible choice. Of course, if Pete were only leaving me for moments, wouldn't my time be better spent washing? Progress on my knife would be insignificant. And I really did want a good bath.

Fuck it. Hygiene won out. I gathered my toiletries, then stripped off my clothes and laid them out on various sunny rocks. Maybe they'd dry before I reclothed.

Crunch!

I looked over my shoulder to find Pete lounging between two fallen trees, not three yards from me, chomping away at one of the yellow apple-like fruits I'd foraged the day before.

He waved his snack at me. "Carry on!"

Now in only my sweat-stained tee-shirt bra and hipster panties, I snatched up my water-logged dress to shield myself. A breeze tried whipping it from my hands.

"Shouldn't you be tending to Bob?" I snapped, wanting to throat chop him.

"Bob's an enchanted beast. He tends to himself." He took another honking bite.

"Then go find something else to do for a while."

"I'm quite content where I am, thank you."

"I don't care. Go away."

He smirked, admiring his fruit. Maybe he'd choke on it. "I'd much prefer to stay put and assure myself that you wash every insidious—germ, was it?—right off your mollycoddled skin. I fear the rant you'd subject me to, should you take ill."

"Whatever. Then cover your eyes until I'm in the water."

Chewing, he scratched his whiskered jaw. "No, I'd rather not."

I burned, stomping. "You can't really want to see me naked!"

Malice tainted the grin slanting across his face. "Oh, aye, I do, Shorty. If my watching rankles you half as much as you've been rankling me, then I want to see every bare speck of you."

"Oh, come on!" I hopped. "You're being unreasonable!"

"And you're wasting my time." He gestured at the lake. "Best set to bathing before I change my mind about stopping."

So, I could either wash with him watching or not at all.

Mother effing pervert!

"*Fine,*" I growled and chucked my dress behind me. Pete had another thing coming if he thought he could use my modesty to cow me out of my bath. "You want a show?" I taunted, unhooking my bra. "Then I'll damn well give you one."

My undergarments divested, I suppressed the urge to dive into a bush as I stood brazen before Pete. In my birthday suit. Not even my hair shielded me from his gaze, a warm zephyr blasting it off my breasts.

Pete's last bite lulled in his cheek. The tan of his face heightened, his darkening eyes roaming my form. His Adam's apple bobbed.

Afraid to breathe, I stared him down, daring him to look away.

When he finally did, something tight loosened within me. Something in Pete's eyes—the way they'd scorched—had liquefied me. My heart thumped as he rose to his feet and tossed his core over his shoulder.

Eyes averted, Pete cleared his throat. "On second thought, I've a few personal matters to attend to. It'll be heaven to enjoy a nice long shite without your voice harping at me in the background."

Blushing, I watched him pelt through the sand toward the tree line. *There you go, Amy. All this time, all you had to do to drive him off was get naked.*

Clearly, I'd misjudged that look he'd given me.

Pete emitted a sharp whistle, and Sionna sprinted back down the shoreline to him. Waiting for her, he met my gaze once more. "I'll give you some slack on your tether. But don't forget who's in charge, aye." He grabbed the invisible link between us and snapped it like a whip—wrenching my ankle, nearly unbalancing me.

Sure, I'd beaten Pete at a staring contest, but I'd never truly gain the upper hand. Not as he marched me to my doom like a filly on a lead.

Pete swaggered away with Sionna, snickering, and my slighted pride sparked with the promise of fiery retribution.

Luckily, so did my fingers.

I didn't notice I was flickering like a misfiring lighter until I smelled smoke. When I glanced down, spots of brilliant orange already burrowed into my tether, eating it for lunch.

"Ohmigoddess, yes!" I knelt over the embers and strangled the tether, keeping the damn thing visible. I cupped my hand around the glowing flecks and blew and blew and blew.

Nothing wondrous happened. If anything, I barely prevented the sparks from dying. To have any shot of severing the tether right then, I needed more fire.

"Come on, Amy. You can do this." I shook out my arms and closed my eyes to concentrate. On everything that could rile my most powerful negative emotions.

I thought of Pete baiting me into stripping, about him dropping me into the lake. I recalled how he'd fooled me that first night, playing the good Samaritan before he'd kidnapped me like a jackwagon—knowing someone who cared was coming for me.

I thought of Briar, and his panic upon arriving at the Thorny Rose Tavern to find I wasn't there. Would Jade and Reed have lied for Pete, told Briar they'd never seen me? Their terse interactions with the harbinger that night hinted that they'd known I was his target. The notion had displeased them, yet neither had warned me. So, I doubted they'd betray their friend and tell Briar I'd been abducted when he showed up to claim me like his lost puppy.

Of course, Briar would've known a harbinger had found me when I wasn't where he'd told me to be. He'd probably assumed the worst—that I was already dead. I prayed he'd search for my body before abandoning hope, but my gut said he wouldn't look *too* hard.

He's probably counting his blessings that you might be dead, my dark side suggested. *Counting as he skips right off to Laurel Woodrush's bed.*

And to the throne he was so quick to assume you'd handed him.

Stop that, I berated myself. Regardless of his feelings for Laurel—or his buried aspirations to be king—Briar wouldn't forsake me so quickly. He'd loved my mother like a sister, after all. Even if he didn't love me.

I'm trying, Briar's voice tolled.

I flinched, then embraced my disquiet as sparks flew again, smoke flavoring the breeze.

"Keep it up," I breathed, desperate to harness my escape.

Until my memories rioted, wanting out of the box I'd stuffed them in.

No, I thought at the odor of charred flesh. *Stop,* I demanded as jagged teeth gnashed my leg. *Please, no more!* I begged Sy Rockrose's pieces and Mica Polkweed's dead eyes. I winced as I flew into my father's closet, then hurtled from the sky to blacktop.

Daddy's face, pasty and gaunt, whispered my name. For the last time.

Fire exploded from my hands, its force propelling me back on my ass. The world ignited around me.

"Shit!"

Flames rained onto nearby shrubs, consuming mushrooms, ivy, and saplings alike. Smoke billowing toward the sky, I scurried around like a sand-fried chicken, trying to douse various brushfires with handfuls of water before they converged into one gigantic blaze.

Thank heaven the lake's plant life was moist and healthy. Several fires began dying without my trivial aid.

Heaving in relief, I looked down and saw my new anklet—a scintillating crust of ash. My shadow tether was burning!

Now attached to a flaming rope, I yelped in surprise rather than pain and dove into the lake, headfirst. Soon after, I knelt, dripping, on soppy sand, examining my ankle.

The fuming tether clung looser to my blackened flesh. Its mist appeared sparser, featherier. Fully expecting to cause myself torment, I gritted my teeth and prodded the anklet.

If anything, I experienced sweet alleviation as the tether withered to nothing but a circle of soot in the sand. Fresh air caressed the scab I'd given myself.

My lungs filled with a smoky breath of triumph. Freedom!

My heart pounding, I scrambled to dress. Bathing would take a backseat to simply getting the fuck away. Although, I hated leaving both my totem and my new bestie behind.

"Goodbye, Sionna." I blew her a distant kiss, squishing along the shoreline in my soppy boots and saturated clothes, following the horizon toward sanctuary. She was a sweet dog, despite her owner, and I'd miss her with my whole heart. I would've taken her with me if I could. Alas, she was a harbinger's snuff hound, and if I never saw her again, I'd consider myself fortunate.

"**D**amn you, Aunt Aylie!" I chucked a stone in my tantrum. It sprung off a wall of damp rock, plunking to the ground. "I told you I should've joined Girl Scouts!"

When pure concentration and painful memories had failed at sparking another fire, I'd tried using the two flat stones in my skirt pocket instead. They'd failed me, too.

My frustration bounded into the darkness beyond the five-foot swath of fading light filtering in through the mouth of the cave I'd chosen as my camp. The suns would soon abandon me, leaving me to my fears.

The cave had seemed a haven when I'd discovered it, obscured by creeping ivy in a mossy fairy hill. But what lurked in its abyssal caverns? Did Evereostre have bears? Or predators resembling bears? I guessed yes but prayed they dwelt outside caves in the land of perpetual spring.

Resigning myself to a night of paranoia and teeth-chattering sleep, I layered myself in my cardigan, cloak, and woolen socks. Without a fire, the dank cave would chill me to the bone. The walls around me beaded with cold sweat, which I'd already licked multiple times to combat my cottonmouth.

At least there's probably water nearby, I gave optimism a shot. My throat could scrape wood after my non-stop sprint through thickets and alder. I hadn't paused for any bodily pangs since that tether had disintegrated. Until I found the cave. I knew Pete would chase me and couldn't risk slowing. Now, of course, my thirst bordered on unbearable.

What good will a water source do without light, idiot? You can't wander blindly through a dark cave. If you wanted to kill yourself, you could've let Pete hand you off to Gentian.

Briefly, I wondered if I was better off as Pete's prisoner. He certainly didn't want to kill me—or at least he hadn't before I'd begun irritating him. Either way, his job prevented him from doing so. Maybe that meant Gentian wouldn't take my life upon delivery.

But what the hell else could he want from you? the dark side of me countered. *You probably don't want to know.*

Disgusted by my fatalistic attitude lately, I grabbed my other stone to beat the horde of rosenuts I'd gathered. They didn't grow on earth, but I knew they were edible. Pete kept a stash of them in his satchel as well as in a small, locked chest in the wagon. He'd begrudgingly give me a few each time I bitched that I was starving, so I knew what they looked like—oval with a rich burgundy shell. They weren't the most appetizing, but they'd tide me over until morning.

"You won't die tonight," I comforted myself, splintering shells left and right. "You'll be cold, miserable, and scared, but you won't die. In the morning, you'll try another fire. If it works, you'll search for that water."

I grabbed one of the shelled rosenuts and popped it in my mouth. It tasted the same as it always did—like a buttered lemon. I closed my eyes and imagined biting into hot steak fries doused in ketchup, followed by chocolate cake topped with ice cream. I almost fooled my taste buds. Almost.

My nutty supper concluded, I curled up on the driest bit of cave I could find, using my backpack as a pillow, and watched the last traces of light fade.

Giving myself license to listen to two full songs on my iBloom, I popped in my earbuds and closed my eyes, hoping Tanya Quick would croon away my fear of the dark, so I could find some much-needed rest. I couldn't very well outrun a harbinger on zero energy.

After I'd shut off my iBloom, I opened my eyes again, expecting the night to swallow all sight. Instead, an emerald luminescence brightened my surroundings. Some type of lichen thinly coated the walls in spatters, like lightning bugs dwelt within. How had I missed it earlier?

Breathless, I pushed myself to sit, my gaze following the path of an electric-green galaxy leading into distant caverns.

My sandpaper throat constricting, I staggered to my tired feet. *Time for a little bravery, Amy.* Fisting my hands, I removed my cloak, squared my shoulders, and went to irrigate my internal desert.

I moved slowly, my boots scraping the stony ground as I plodded between neon stalagmites, ducking their counterparts from above. I went carefully, lest I fall into a hole or trip and impale myself. It was just like navigating an after-dark mini-golf course with all its obstacles and divots. Or that's what I told myself.

I didn't encounter any vicious, carnivorous beasts. Just a few beetles and melodious katydids—all of which flared with vibrant phosphorescence.

"You know," I conversed with one flashing red beetle, ducking into another tunnel. "If all bugs glowed in the dark like you, I might've been friendlier to them."

Flashing, the beetle flitted down the narrowing passage. I instinctively followed him, the dead ringer for the Google Maps pin that he was. He led me straight to the loveliest sound in the world—the distinct trickle of water. I hiked my skirts and hustled onward.

Finally, I collapsed on my knees at the cusp of a rippling grotto, the large basin of which glowed as green as a shamrock. The cupola above me glittered, constellations embedded in its stone.

I didn't think twice before guzzling, slurping from filthy hands. Luckily, the water was as fresh as a spring day, though a bit like bathwater. The expansive chamber housing the grotto maintained a balmy warmth, mellowing my aches and strains.

At a chirp, I glanced left. The beetle who'd led me there played in a tiny puddle of my making.

"I should just spend the night down here with you." I offered him a finger. He stared for a moment before hopping aboard, his threadlike legs tickling me. I lifted him to eye level, watching his antennae twitch, his ruby belly flash. His green eyes met mine, more sentient than a bug's should be. "Would you mind that?"

The beetle chirped again, which I assumed meant, *Be my guest.*

Yawning, I struggled back to my feet. "Let's get my stuff. Then we'll come back here for a good night's sleep." I scratched an incessant itch on my scalp. "Maybe a long bath in the morning."

My tromp back was relaxed, the beetle directing me with bright flashes whenever I made a correct turn. "Glad you're here, or I'd already be lost."

Being lost would've been better.

Wracking my brain for ways to fashion a canteen, so I could journey on without the looming threat of dehydration until I found another water source, my guard slipped. The overpowering, out of place scent of sea salt should've alerted me that something was wrong. So should've the way my new beetle friend suddenly took wing and hid in a rock crevice.

By the time I heard the voices, my fate was sealed.

I sucked in a breath, preparing to run, just before a massive hand snatched me by my matted hair and yanked me toward my original camp, a yoyo on a string.

"Lookie what I caught, Tacker," said a voice like grinding metal. "Told you I scented someone."

My horror rippled along my skin as the hand shoved me into the glow of the first cavern to face a threesome of giants in briny leather britches and nothing else. Their long, lean muscles flexed beneath varying shades of gray skin as they surrounded me, armed on their hips with knives and spiked clubs.

They appeared mostly fae—pointy ears, exaggerated angles, and teeth as sharp as razors. From their brows to their napes, however, they were sleek as stingrays, domed and speckled.

The shortest stood a foot taller than me. The tallest hunched beneath the luminous ceiling, his long-lashed eyes gleaming at me as I backed into a cold wall.

"Well done, Scully." The tallest—I assumed him Tacker—crooned to the handsy feyr who'd caught me, whose left eye was bisected by a striated scar. Tacker grinned, dropping my backpack. His huge bare feet crunched upon the scraps of my dinner. "A Danann youngblood. Balor will be ecstatic."

The shortest chortled. "Oh, aye. He'll be more than that, I'd wager." The odor of fish tinged his breath as he leaned toward me, fungi-light enhancing the striking planes of his face. "She's got such pure, smooth skin—and see her eyes?" He held up a tremulous hand, tracing my features in the air. "Behold how they transform." His childlike delight shone like mania as he glanced at Tacker. "May I keep them, cousin? As a trophy? After?"

After what?

I wished for the wings Pete had feared I might sprout.

Tacker exhaled heavily. "We'll talk about it, Fletch. You're trying to prove your self-restraint, remember. Balor should get the first pick of spoils."

My stomach clenched. "Or *I* could just keep them." I inched along the wall toward the deeper caverns. If I could just get past Scully—

God, what I wouldn't give for pitch blackness right now.

"You know, since they're already mine and all." I gulped so hard it hurt.

Fletch's wild eyes widened further, his jaw dropping. "Oh, she speaks queerly too! Might I also have her tongue?"

I smacked his hand when his frigid, dry fingers touched my mouth.

He jumped back, rubbed his smarting hand, and eyed me like a pet who'd bitten him.

"High-handed Danann bitch!" Scully backhanded me. "You've just struck the crown lord of the Fomorians!"

Lightning splintered along my jaw as I floundered to the unforgiving stone at Tacker's massive feet. He knelt, smirking, as I struggled to my hands and knees. Iron welled in my mouth, as I'd bitten the tongue Fletch wanted to poach from me.

"I'm sorry." I wasn't, and I glared. "I didn't know who he was. Regardless, I have a right to my personal space."

"Do you now?" Tacker asked. "Who gave you such a right? Your pathetic king?"

I spat, blood and saliva pooling by my dirty fingertips. If I'd had the strength, I would've ripped out his fangs for calling Daddy pathetic. "Danu—she gives all her children the right to themselves." I rose on my knees to eye him. "Even you."

"I'd say Scully hit you harder than it looked if you think we're Danu's progeny," Tacker said. "We Fomorians are her sister, Domnu's, children. A much fiercer goddess, who endowed us with the right to take what we want—if we're mighty enough to subdue it."

I knew he meant me and shivered.

"You said you were Fomorians?" I recalled Uncle Neel's teachings on their civilization. Though I'd originally thought them religious parables, I guessed the stories I'd heard of their cruelty and warmongering were based in fae fact. "I've heard about you."

Tacker tilted his head, scrutinizing me like produce at Giant Eagle. "I presume that means you're frightened?"

You think? Tacker's weapons were way too close to me, Scully had just cracked me across the face, and Fletch—their future leader—was completely off his rocker. I had no reason not to be frightened.

Still, I kept my shit together. Panic would do me no favors. "Should I be?"

Tacker's lips hitched. "I'd think any lone, defenseless Danann beyn who finds herself trapped in a cave with three strange feyrs of any race should feel frightened. But with Fomorians—"

Keep calm. Keep calm.

I wobbled back to my feet. Tacker rose too, towering over me.

"Look, I know all those awful stories I was told about your people can't be true." I rubbed my throbbing jaw—damn sure to bruise. "I'm certain not every Fomorian in that war was to blame for the thousands of rumored hate crimes." *Against beyns—and faelets,* I reminded myself. "Which must be an exaggeration. I've never thought it okay to judge a whole race of people by the actions of a few. So why should I assume right off the bat that you three gentlefeyrs would hurt me?"

Besides the fact that the crazy one wants to put your eyes in a mason jar on his bedroom bookshelf?

Surprisingly, it was the crazy one who expressed shame at my artifice. The other two—they remained stone.

"Have you not considered the general hatred we Fomorians must feel for your kind?" Tacker replied. "Your war bitch, Morrigan, swindled us out of our homeland, forced us onto an island."

My fingers fisted at the insult against that famous goddess. Her parables had always been my favorite. "Sorry, I was told your leader retreated there—to escape capture and execution. Maybe I heard wrong. Even so, that doesn't mean you should have a beef with me."

Tacker's brow arched at my word choice.

"I mean, I wasn't even born yet. You can't blame me for the faults of my ancestors."

"Why not?" His slender nose flared. Sniffing me. "Their blood runs through your veins."

I took a step toward the mouth of the cave. Tacker parried to block me.

"Blood doesn't determine the kind of person you are," I said. "It's all about the choices you make."

Fletch's bright eyes dimmed. He pouted. "Maybe we should let her go."

My heart soared.

Irritation rippled through the squared line of Tacker's jaw. "Fletch—"

"I think I'd feel bad." Fletch regarded me like a lamb. "She seems friendly. Eating her would feel wrong."

My heart plummeted to my bowels.

A memory from Sunday Circle years ago flitted back to me. Uncle Neel's lecture on the Fomorians had somehow succeeded in engrossing Ace, a kid who often fell asleep during religious lessons. In between bites of an ice cream sandwich, he'd raised his sticky hand to ask Uncle Neel for the gory details on what the Fomorians had done to their victims.

Stern, Uncle Neel had answered, "They ate them."

Ace and our other classmates had rumbled, amazed. I'd nearly snorted at the time, assuming Uncle Neel had named a tamer crime than rape, mutilation, and torture, one the young'uns at circle could understand. But now—cannibalization seemed an imminent and terrible fate.

When I heard the scrape of metal against a scabbard, my hackles raised to emit a shriek. Tacker bent over me, his sharp teeth flashing as he fisted his long, hooked blade—the kind used to gut fish.

"Don't fret, Fletch. She's no friendlier than a sea-dragon." He grabbed my bicep when I tried to run, wrenching me into him. "She's just a clever talker."

"No, I'm not!" I appealed to Fletch, struggling. "I honestly believe there's good in you!"

Scully scoffed, but Fletch's brow remained bunched in doubt.

"That's enough, Fletch." Tacker shook me. "If you want your father to see your worth as a leader, you can't fall for every sweet lie you hear from the likes of her. She can't possibly see good in us, and she shouldn't."

Tacker's low laughter was a death knell, tolling through the cavern. "We Fomorians earned our reputation, little Danann. We feel no guilt in it. Do we, Fletch? Unless you've a quarrel with your father's ways."

That rattled the morality right out of Fletch, and the hope right out of me. "Of course not, cousin."

"Good." Tacker offered his knife to Fletch. "Then you'll be the one who takes her heart."

Undiluted joy glowing once more in his eyes, Fletch took the proffered knife, and I screamed for mercy, prey in a snare.

SEVENTEEN

Pete

Pete had laughed when he'd returned to the lake to find smoke, ash, and his prisoner gone. While Shorty had been resourceful enough to make fire (how she'd known she needed fire to break her tether, he couldn't say), she'd neglected to cover her tracks. Through the sand. Her footsteps led his eyes down the shoreline, the direction from which her now familiar scent beckoned. Like a fecking curling finger.

He'd glanced down at Sionna beside him, her floppy ears perked. "Shall we go fetch Shorty before she kills herself?"

The spoilt babe he'd come to know wouldn't make it far in the deep forest without help. He'd wagered she'd go but a mile before she opted to rest her legs, assuming a good hiding spot would thwart him.

He'd been bemused—and impressed—to find he was wrong. Shorty hadn't stopped to rest. She hadn't stopped for *anything*. The pace she'd kept was breakneck, to the point where Pete and Sionna became winded.

"Christ," he'd muttered to Sionna, whose tongue wagged as they climbed another mossy hill. "She keeps this up, she'll break her bloody ankles."

That he hadn't already stumbled upon her mewling over some minor injury amazed him. The beyn he'd been carting around in his wagon couldn't walk a snail's pace for a quarter of an hour before begging a reprieve.

By the time Pete had finally caught sight of Shorty, he was damn sure he'd been duped. She'd covered fifteen miles before she'd chosen to hide for the night—in a cave concealed by ivy.

Not exactly the feat of a coddled fussbudget, is it? he'd judged from where he and Sionna hid amid surrounding brush, watching Shorty skitter around the forest floor, foraging nuts like a paranoid squirrel. *But why act the princess? How would that benefit her?*

She goaded you into leaving her unattended, now didn't she?

His gaze narrowed upon Shorty as she glanced once more over her shoulder, her matted brown hair catching on a sapling. "Clever minx." His predatory magic writhed in anticipation of a challenge. "Not clever enough."

At nightfall, Pete loped to the cave and peered through the vines to find Shorty huddled beneath her filthy cape, curled into a shivering ball on the cave floor. Eyes clenched, she fisted her favorite tiny pink device. Two white laces carried the faint drum of music to her arched ears.

Why hadn't she made a fire for warmth and light when she'd done so earlier to burn her tether? Perhaps she realized the glow might draw him. Perhaps she knew most caves in Evereostre produced Luna moss. Regardless, the damned beyn could withstand discomfort in stoic grace for the sake of survival, after all. Her constant bellyaching was a damned ruse.

Pete, you daft clod. He grinned at the trembling waif in the cave. *Can't even tell the difference between a sniveling mouse and a wily vixen, can you? Jaysus, Sedge'll fair bust his gut if you're ever scuttered enough to unspool this yarn.*

Pete hunkered down in the grassy shadows, petting Sionna's sleek back as they waited for Shorty to sleep. Though he'd relish another hands-on scuffle with her, especially after she'd shredded his nerves to hash, taking her unconscious was wiser. Which is why he'd twitched in annoyance when she silenced her music box and opened her eyes, shocked and awed at the patina walls sheltering her.

So, she hadn't known about the Luna moss. That made sense if he believed her origins.

Instead of sleeping, though she resembled a wilting flower, Shorty rose and forged further into the cave like Jeanne Baret herself.

She'll return, he knew. *She left all her belongings.* He wriggled into the moss, prepared to wait.

Pete had nearly dozed off after hours of non-stop pursuit when Sionna whimpered, prancing at his side.

He knew his hound well. Beneath her black and tan fur was a yellow belly, and a swift breeze often sent her into hiding. Yet, when he whiffed the dissonant brine of sea salt, he agreed with Sionna. Trouble was afoot.

Fomorians, he realized, enveloping Sionna and himself in his shadow cloak. Just as predatory as himself, the Fomorians would easily sniff them out. If they blended into the dark, however, the monsters might abandon their search. They lacked Pete's patience, though they were the most vicious fae he'd encountered in this world.

Gentian had forced him into the ring with one of the wankers once. Despite being half-starved, Pete had been the prince's only fighter who'd even come close to matching the Fomorian's size. Pete had won the brawl but nearly lost his life to the poison of his opponent's razor-sharp bite. The fiend had tried to gnaw off Pete's leg. So, he'd panicked and crushed the Fomorian's great domed head with his own battle club.

Pete killing Gentian's prized Fomorian acquisition had enraged the ancient Danann. He'd let Pete suffer with fever for days before one of the gaolers, who often bet on Pete in the ring, had sneaked a stem healer—and fellow Forgotten—into his cage to save his life.

At the time, Pete had begged Olea to leave him to the almighty. He'd endured enough of the endless captivity, violence, and starvation in Gentian's court. But her glowing hands had spread over his rotting leg anyway. "You're a fighter, Pete," she'd said. "You're going to fight your way out of here one day."

And he had. In a manner of speaking. Yet, when he spied three enormous Fomorians climbing the hill, noses high, he knew his prowess meant nothing. One Fomorian was risky enough to fight. Three—that was suicide.

So, he stayed put, clutching Sionna's panting body, and prayed to Danu for their deliverance. Not until he heard the rustling within the cave did he spare a thought for Shorty. Then his innards tightened.

While the cunning beyn had deceived and bedeviled him, he knew she'd only done so for freedom. Relatable motives. She had some lofty opinions, aye, but she seemed good at heart, and he couldn't simply sit on his laurels and listen whilst those brutes raped or devoured her like mutton. If he did that, she'd be right. He'd never again be worthy of the lord's love.

And there was the ordination to consider.

His blood pulsing, Pete dug his fingers into the ground. He heard the scratchy voice of one in the threesome declare, "There's prey to be had here."

Faith and begorrah, darlin'! Please stay hidden!

He bit back a furious oath at Shorty's chattering in the distance. Who in bleeding hell was she jabbering to, anyway? Did the eejit have no intuition for looming danger? How in Christ had she made it to a score in age?

Then they caught her, and Pete scraped his face. Praying for divine intervention.

When Shorty seemed to sway the young crown lord to her plight, Pete thought that Danu had heard his prayer. Of course, then talk of taking her heart disillusioned him.

At her ghastly screams for help, Pete vented a frustrated rumble, whipped off his shadow cloak (it only served him in darkness, anyhow), and leapt to his feet.

He found Shorty flattened to the ground, a Fomorian's hand around her throat. She writhed, frantic for breath, as the mental goliath above her knifed her bodice laces. The older Fomorians stood in the background, assessing his work.

Pete surged through the ivy and rammed the kneeling Fomorian in the gut with his shoulder, tackling him to the glowing stone floor. The Fomorian's domed head cracked against a stalagmite, and he slackened beneath Pete, unconscious. The knife clanged into another cavern.

Hacking for breath, Shorty bleared at Pete, her milky skin flushed red, her large eyes as pale as custard. The hue of her fear, he assumed. But at least she was still breathing.

Pete righted himself, drew his sword, and stepped over Shorty as her shield. He flexed his fingers around his sword pommel as the remaining Fomorians turned on him, seething. Because he'd dared attack their crown lord. The crown lord who'd meant to skewer an innocent youngblood's heart.

Pete squared his jaw, cracked his neck, his prowess fiending for a fight. "There now," he growled at his remaining opponents. "Fancy a tangle with someone your own size?"

The Fomorians drew spiked war clubs heavy enough to smash bone.

That wouldn't do.

Pete's tethers horsewhipped the air, lassoing the clubs. He yanked them from the surprised Fomorians' grips, then sent the weapons that might've dented his skull soaring into the night.

He considered binding his foes in shadow, a spider with flies. But they were strong enough to use his tethers against him—to start a tug of war. So, he'd wield his shadows like striking serpents instead, never allowing the fiends a firm grip on them.

"A harbinger," the shorter one rasped, eyes narrowed to slits. "Sold his soul to the void, he did, Tacker!"

Pete's mouth twisted. "On the contrary, it was stolen from me. But fret not, I got it back."

Tacker's gargantuan fists were nearly as intimidating as clubs. "Allow Scully and I to rid you of it once more. You'll be supper." He pointed at Shorty, who struggled upright. "She'll be dessert."

The attack was vicious and sudden, and Pete couldn't escape. Fancy footwork wasn't his forte. Like the Fomorians, he was partial to brute force.

Pete's sword was little consequence to Tacker, who drove him back with a resounding battle cry. Shorty mewled, barely evading the charge. The Fomorian Pete had subdued couldn't evade anything, however, and Pete lost his footing when he and Tacker barreled over him. A blessing, it turned out, for then Tacker also tripped, giving Pete the chance to use his weapon.

He aimed for the stomach. Tacker shifted. Pete's blade glanced off a rib.

Bollocks!

Pete's staggering strength customarily rendered ribs immaterial. But as he'd well learned, Fomorians' ribs were iron. Which was why they were so *fecking* hard to kill!

Pete pummeled Tacker to free his sword, now jammed between their bodies. The enormous Fomorian barely noticed—too busy giving as good as he got.

Tacker landed an oblique punch, and Pete snarled like the beast he could be. He forgot the pain, however, when he spied Scully unsheathing another hooked dagger from his hip. He went straight for Shorty, who'd only just regained her footing. She wailed something unladylike when the dastard snared her straggled hair.

Spurred by her pain, Pete barreled into his power reserves and wrangled the strength to kick Tacker off him. A kick that sent the Fomorian sprawling across the cave. Into the wall. Cracking it. Stunning him.

Pete sprang to his feet, his primal magic coursing.

Scully, damn near astonished by Pete's might, fixed to cleave open Shorty's slender throat. She wailed as Pete speared the air with a shadow and seized the knife from Scully's meaty grip. Pete retracted his tether until he fisted the hooked knife. Then he rushed Scully, blades hot. Shorty yelped and balled up to avoid a trampling.

This time, Pete's aim was true. Forcing Scully to the wall, Pete bared his teeth and drove his sword through Scully's stomach. He never hesitated when he had the upper hand.

Scully roared, sinking to the ground. The feathery lines of his scar writhed around a vengeful eye as he grabbed Pete's blade and refused its withdrawal.

Pete was about to open Scully's throat with his own knife when—

"Watch out!" Shorty shrieked.

Pete narrowly sidestepped having his kidney punctured. Tacker, the rotter, had snatched Pete's own *scian* off his hip. Pete appreciated Shorty's warning. Although, he hated that he'd relinquished his sword.

Nostrils flaring at the fishy stink of Scully's blood, Pete flung out a tether for retrieval, but Tacker was quicker. The behemoth deflected the tether with a swipe of the *scian*. Pain like a bee sting juddered down the shadow and into Pete's hand, numbing his fingers.

Bloody fecking hell!

Tacker wrenched Pete's sword from Scully's gored belly. Scully groaned, frothing at the mouth, his entrails tumbling into his lap.

Oh, Pete had dealt him a fatal blow, all right.

Despite his impact with the cave wall, Tacker's grin promised bloodshed. Savage bloodshed.

Shorty whimpered at that grin, her eyes darting for an escape she was too shrewd to attempt right then.

Scully muttered through a rattling breath, raising a shaking hand. A gesture Pete would've heeded had he not made an imprudent mistake. Prudence helped nothing without his bloody sword, after all.

The moment feeling returned to Pete's fingers, he dispatched his every shadow straight for Tacker's throat, wrists, ankles, knees, elbows—toward any place he might cripple the monster.

Danu didn't reward his risk. And Pete wanted to throttle himself when the cosmos rippled around him, a binding spell knotting his tethers.

A *Fomorian warrior* had learned the restrictive arts? Their race wasn't known for spellcraft!

"Ready to die, Harbinger?" Scully frothed, leering. "Now that you must fight like a feyr?"

Well, then, Pete mused, squirming against the constraints of sorcery. *Now you're fucked, boyo.*

"You'll have to tell me how it feels to be flayed alive by your own blades," Tacker said, assessing how best to attack—a cat toying with its supper.

Pete clenched Scully's hooked knife, his pulse thrumming.

Survival's unlikely, chap. Might as well make it count.

Shorty quivered in a wretched pool of skirts, her torn bodice exposing the gentle swell of her breast. She wrung her hands, terrified. With good reason. If he fell, there was nothing stopping Tacker from butchering her like a sow.

Pete nodded her toward escape, his voice harsh with sacrifice. "When you reach the road, call for Bob. He'll see you and Sionna to safety."

She gaped as if she'd heard him wrong, then sprang up. She scrambled past Tacker, then evaded Scully with a screech when he made to trip her. Pete watched her flee into the night with a bittersweet pang. At least *she'd* live to see another day.

Tacker snickered, raising Pete's sword against him. "I hope she's worth your life, harbinger."

You and me both, Pete thought, then charged, a berserker with nothing to lose.

AMY

Sionna and I ran until Pete's roar overwhelmed the wood notes. I skidded to a halt by a flowering rowan tree, and Sionna turned back to pant at me, her eyebrows drawn together as if questioning my sanity in stopping.

I clutched a handful of my wild hair. The chill night caressed the tender space between my boobs, the jagged edges of my shredded bodice gaping open. My heart thundered, thankfully still inside me.

How long would Pete's stay inside him, though?

"Damnit!" I stomped at the now familiar irritant of indecision.

Pete was a harbinger. A harbinger who wanted to sell me to a jackal for a fistful of seeds. If I kept running and allowed the Fomorians to kill him, I might just succeed in getting my ass to the safety of the Spring Palace before Gentian tasked another harbinger with finding me. Especially with a wagon, a bow, a slew of arrows, a snuff hound, and an enchanted donkey at my disposal.

On the other hand, Pete had just saved my life.

Granted, he'd done so only to secure his paycheck. There must've been some good in his bad, though, as he'd pretty much traded his life for mine in the end. Harbinger or not, I couldn't just leave Pete to die. If I did, I might as well have gifted my heart as a meal to the Fomorians. Because it would ache from what I hadn't done for the rest of my life.

"Ohmigoddess, Sionna." I hopped at another howl on the wind. "We *have* to help him."

Untucking her jowls from her mouth with her spotted tongue, she gulped like she tasted something sour.

"No, I don't know how," I went on like she'd asked.

Not true, Amy.

"Or I do." I frowned. "But I'm afraid it won't work."

Yes, my powers were erratic, but they existed all the same. And barring a round-trip sprint to fetch Pete's bow at the wagon—and who knew how far the road was—my powers were the only weapons at my disposal. Plus, before Pete had burst into the cave and tackled Fletch like a football player, I'd felt something hot and dangerous already roiling beneath my skin. Fearing for my life obviously kicked up my flames. If I focused hard enough, I could still feel the fire burning.

Sionna whimpered at my side. She probably heard Pete's softer exclamations. I assumed he was struggling.

I smacked an already smoking fist into my other hand. "Come on, Sionna. We're going in."

Her ears dropped back, but she followed me as I raced to the cave.

When I shot through the ivy vines, I found Pete trapped to the floor, snarling up at Tacker, who had Pete's *scian* poised to pierce his throat. Where the other blades had gone, I didn't know.

Blood trickled from Pete's round nose, and a great gash in the arm of his shirt sleeve seeped like the walls of the cave. Had Tacker *bitten* him? Pete's muscles quivered in his effort to survive, though I doubted they'd hold out much longer.

Scully still clung to life. *Damnit.* The only reason he didn't see me when I burst back onto the scene was because he was leaving a trail of ichor along the cave floor, crawling to where Fletch lay. Doubtless to jar him back to consciousness, so he'd help Tacker end Pete's life.

That'd suck, I thought as Sionna skittered away.

She'd been brave enough to stick her nervous snout through the ivy, but that was as far as she'd venture. Which was best. She couldn't handle the can of whoop-ass I was going to open.

"Hey!" My voice bounded like a jackrabbit through the caverns. Both Scully and Tacker started, goggling my way.

Pete looked downright exasperated by my reappearance, huffing from the exertion at staying that dagger.

"Stay low," I advised him, then threw out my hands with a spectacular flourish.

Nothing happened.

Everyone blinked.

Biting my lip, I tried again. Still nothing.

Pete rolled his eyes as Tacker redoubled his efforts to stab him.

Scully guffawed what would assuredly be his last laugh, blood bubbling from his lips as he reached Fletch's foot. "Halfwit bitch."

That was the exact wrong thing to say to me.

Anger jetted to my fingertips, sweat beading my skin like a boiling tea kettle. "Nah uh," I gritted out. From the flash in Pete's eyes, I bet my own were spitting sparks. "I think you mean halfwit *fire sylph*."

The blast blew me back into the wall, but I managed to stay on my feet, though my hands shook with such ferocious power I feared losing control of it. Fire of every color sprayed from me in untamed bursts. Flames engulfed everything in view, scorching even the walls of the cave and its glowing lichen. An animal yowl flew from one of the Fomorians, and I bit down on my lip, perspiring oceans.

That'll teach you to call me a bitch.

I should've been prepared for retaliation, but I wasn't.

A bellow cut through my churning blazes before a monster vaulted himself at me, crushing me to my book bag and cloak.

My fire sputtered as Tacker pinned me. Flames danced along his back, his contorted face something straight from a horror movie. I flailed beneath him, knowing he'd eviscerate me if I didn't escape.

"Fire *whore!*" Not even billows of smoke masked the hatred born in his gaze. Nor did they stay the grip claiming me like an item at auction. An item he was free to scrap if he felt the whim, which is exactly what he did to my vest and bodice as we fought. "You'll die like the cunt you are!"

I cried when his bruising grip found my throat. Then again when his other found the split in my bodice. Yanked it wide. Clamped my boob until it hurt.

"*No!*" I shrieked. Bucked. Grappled. Scratched. All to no avail. Tacker only further swamped me, assaulting my welting cheek with his fishy breath.

"We'll crush your every brittle bone like a boiled bunkle-crab before we eat your beating heart," he promised, licking my quivering lips—making my skin crawl. "And once you're dead, we'll take turns fucking your broken corpse until you're too stiff to spread your legs. Then we'll leave your remains for the night wolves—"

The force of a boot cut off the rest of Tacker's revolting threat. Right before he sailed into the brume like a tossed sandbag.

I was still sobbing when gruff, callused hands swept me back to my feet. Through the smoke, I found a pair of wide molasses eyes.

Pete coughed. "Let's go, Shorty!"

He'd just grabbed my wrist when he was shoved back into the corner. I stumbled as he pulled me against his musky warmth, shielding me.

Before us stood Tacker, fangs out as he clutched his sore ribs, his back still smoldering. I cringed as his flesh crackled like Rice Krispies in milk, then gulped down my own tongue as Fletch staggered beside him, wiping soot from his baffled face.

"What happened?" Fletch gasped.

Tacker spat a wad of ashen phlegm at my feet. "They killed Scully."

I trembled against Pete, Fletch's madness possessing him—turning him into a devil that would no doubt haunt my dreams. If I lived to go to sleep, that was.

"You know how your father wishes us to deal with those who kill our own," Tacker rumbled.

Fletch's fangs gleamed in the green haze. "We'll piss on their decaying bones."

They both moved toward us.

Pete shoved me behind him, prepared to fight for my life again.

Not that it was necessary.

Luminescent stone exploded everywhere as an arm—a *feminine* arm—from another cavern punched through the wall beside us. Screaming, I covered my eyes, shielded my jugular from ricocheting shrapnel. Pete forced me to the ground, his body my fortress. I felt the soft scruff of his beard on my forehead as I peered around his shoulder at the naked beyn slinking through the hole in the wall.

She was tall and buxom with flowing black hair and a gorgeous, round-featured face. Water cascaded off the curves of luscious breasts and an ass superstar, Jessica Hernandez, would envy. Had she just come from a swim?

"*Christ!*" Pete urged me flatter to the ground. "Cover your ears, Shorty."

I clapped hands to ears without question.

"Fear not, noble harbinger," a voice chimed through my fingers. I stared in awe as the dripping enchantress turned a set of earthy-green eyes on me. She smiled, and I instantly loved her. Every inch of her.

Pete and the Fomorians gawped as she sashayed between them.

"I only enthrall sinners. In saving each other, you've proven yourselves worthy of not just freedom, but also my help."

Facing the thunderstruck Fomorians, she sang a trilling note until ensorcellment glazed their gazes, then took one docile hand from each. "You feyrs, however—you'll serve me all the days of your lives." She traced a finger across Tacker's collarbone. "Won't you?"

As if struck by Cupid's arrow, he murmured, "Yes, my nymph."

"Yes," Fletch echoed, blinking like a robot with damaged system files.

The beyn led the fearsome Fomorians toward the deeper caverns, leashed like puppies. Never to feel the spray of the sea again.

Before she steered them out of sight, the ethereal beauty turned back to flash me one last smile. "If all the other fae I'd met in my life were anything like you, I'd have been friendlier to them, too."

All my breath rushed out of me, chills crawling up my spine. "*You're* the water beetle?"

"I'm a Nixie. I live in the grotto." She winked at me, all sauce and spice. "But sometimes a change of skin is nice."

Being able to morph into a bug would certainly solve a lot of my problems.

The Nixie sighed. "Pity you're so pure-hearted, sweet Danann. I'd quite enjoy your company in my lair. Our conversation would never run dry."

I supposed good girl talk was hard to come by within the confines of a cave. "Thanks?"

"Word of advice." Her glittering eyes grazed Pete, whose cheeks had flushed. From the heat of the scuffle or at just the sight of the naked Nixie, I couldn't say. "Stay with this one. There's something unique in his sacrifice for you."

Huh?

With a flourish of her hand, the Nixie revealed the foggy knot of Pete's tethers. She unbound them with a song of farewell, strutting away with her new chattels.

Pete's hard breaths of relief pressed into my back as a shell of freed shadow tethers undulated about me.

Why the hell was I comforted by that?

EIGHTEEN

Pete and I didn't speak as we trudged the forest floor together, Sionna at our heels. Maybe neither of us felt the need to say I was coming with him, my independent survival in that brutal world a big question mark, or maybe we were shell-shocked.

When we finally reached the road, Pete barked for Bob, then plopped to the ground. He waited there, silent, for nearly twenty minutes before a braying donkey leading a wagon clopped into view.

"I know," Pete muttered to Bob, pushing to his feet. He dabbed his nose on his linen shirt cuff, blood leaking from his nostrils like a dripping faucet. "Took longer than I'd anticipated."

When Bob came to a cantankerous halt before us, Pete heaved himself into the wagon. Sionna leapt in after him.

Moving like I wore a 50-pound dress underwater, I struggled to join them. When brusque hands wrenched me into the bed by the back of my ripped dress, I was more thankful than peeved for the help, however rudely given.

Bob trucked ahead as I wrapped myself in my smoke-suffused cloak. I conked out sitting up in one of the back corners of the wagon.

When I awoke, I lay on Pete's bedroll by a crackling fire in a thatch of moss, Sionna curled up and dreaming beside me.

I turned over to find Pete sitting shirtless on a large rock by a babbling brook. Midnight sketched his profile as he tested the area around the black gashes in his muscled forearm—a ring of fang marks. He hissed at the whisper of a touch.

Not good.

I rose from my nest in the chill to rummage in my backpack for the insurance policies I'd stashed. Twisting my bruised neck back and forth, I slipped my chosen items into my skirt pocket, then slogged from the wagon over to Pete.

My breath caught when I drew near enough to gander the details of Pete's smooth, broad back. Healed scars of all shapes and sizes etched his skin, silver filigree under moonlight. They were beautiful on him now, though they must've been ghastly when first dealt. Much like the one currently crusting his arm.

"Go back to sleep." A cobra had less venom than his voice did. Then he exhaled, his eyes falling shut. "Please."

I closed the distance between us. "If we don't do something quick, those germs you mocked me about earlier are going to set up shop in your arm."

He massaged his forehead, doubtless throbbing from having his nose crunched in. It didn't look broken, though, and the bleeding had slowed. "I'm certain I have some variety of fortifying potion that could see me to a bonafide healer." His lips canted aside as I blinked toward the wagon. There weren't any potions in there that I'd seen. Did he keep them in his satchel? "Someone who might truly aid me."

"A *fortifying* potion? Is that like drinking cough syrup when you have pneumonia?" I made a face back at him. "Look, if you want to wait that long to get actual help, then be my guest. But I think that's a stupid move on your part."

"And just how do you propose we oust them?" he grumbled. "The germs?"

I produced a bottle of rubbing alcohol, a sterile gauze pad, and a pill bottle of old Penicillin that Ace had gotten when he'd faked Strep to get out of school for a week. He'd never taken a single dose.

"Black-market products." I rattled the pill bottle. "Otherwise known as medicine."

"Medicine," Pete grunted, probably wondering if I was trying to poison him.

"Mm-hm." I ignored his suspicious glower and set my items down on the rock beside him. I tore open the packet of sterile gauze. "So you don't get infected."

"You think these things will prevent that?"

I popped the lid on the alcohol. "Nothing's guaranteed, but it's worth a shot." I glanced at his wound, the skin surrounding it already angry. "Can't make it any worse."

Pete stilled as I saturated the gauze with the alcohol. He breathed in the astringent aroma, stiffened as I moved closer.

I lifted the pad for his inspection. "This is to clean the wound." My eyes dipped to the bite, the alcohol doing little to mask the tang of breeding bacteria from my Danann nose. "I'd bet those Fomorians have never even heard of a toothbrush. Goddess only knows what diseases were incubating in Tacker's mouth."

Though Pete's brow arched in question at my word choice, the corner of his lips quirked up. He'd taken my meaning all right. "Likely right about that. If they wanted to eat the filthy likes of me—" He opened his hands, letting my mind finish the joke for him.

Laughing felt good after the night I'd had. "See, I told you to take a bath."

His mouth twitched, reminding me of the handsome stranger I'd met on that blustery night at the Thorny Rose Tavern. The man who'd warmed my cold belly with playful banter. The man whose warm eyes had turned me to goo. The man who'd made me forget, if for only a while, that my life was in shambles.

The harbinger, *you mean*? I shook myself, backpedaling down the path I'd unwisely taken.

"All right," I coughed, concentrating on the task ahead. Not the washboard stomach and soft curls mottling manly pectorals. The term *Burly Man* came to mind. I met Pete's dark eyes with all seriousness. "This will sting."

He grimaced and proffered his injured arm.

I had to give him props. His wound was deep, probably blistering, but he sat still and let me clean every fang mark as thoroughly as I could, only hissing once or twice.

"What's a Nixie?" I asked to take his mind off his pain. I wet my bloody gauze pad again, trying to hide my disgust.

Pete glanced up like he'd forgotten my existence.

"You seemed to know about her." I blotted a glob of sticky, dried blood. The stench of Tacker's fishy mouth clung to it. "When she appeared, I mean."

"Nixies are a breed of siren. A dangerous breed."

"So, that's why you told me to cover my ears. Her voice—"

He nodded. "A siren's song is a *deadly* weapon. With but one note, she could have you merrily slitting your own throat."

I blinked at the thought, reminded of Tamsyn's hints about my mother's magic. Could she have been—?

"Mind you, not all sirens use their songs for ill," Pete gritted out, breathless after I'd finally pried that saliva coated scab from his flesh. "I've met only one other siren. They're quite rare, like." He held his breath while I dabbed the next fang puncture. This one downright gross. "She—uh—she helped me. I was in a terrible state—thought myself lost for good. But she—she managed to shake me from it. I'll be forever grateful—"

I stumbled to my knees and vomited the few rosenuts I'd eaten for supper into a thatch of reeds. When I finished, I sat back on my heels and wiped tears from my eyes, my face tingling, my muscles quaking.

"You'd make one hell of a field nurse."

My hand trembled as I wiped my nose. "Shut up," I snapped, then crawled to the brook to rinse my mouth. For long minutes, I sat hunched by the water, its flow hypnotizing.

Exhaling, Pete rose and grabbed me. "Get up." He lifted me by my armpits.

I yelped and jumped back.

He'd brushed past my cloak to help me, and his knuckles had grazed the side of my breast where my bodice flapped open. The feel of his hot, rough skin upon such tender flesh sizzled to my core.

Pete's eyes twinkled in the moonlight as I glared. "Settle down. That was but an accident." Holding hands skyward, he reseated himself. "Now, please sit before you swoon into the stream."

Yanking my cloak closed, I wobbled over to drop onto the rock.

I felt Pete's gaze on me as I slouched beside him, trying to rub sensation back into my face. "You need rest, Shorty. You should go back to sleep."

"I'll go to sleep when I'm finished with you." I shook myself. "Man! I don't know why I'm so woozy."

I'd endured worse sights and smells in my life. I'd survived the bogeybats' breath. Of course, I *had* passed out that night—after I'd lost Daddy.

Pete's brow furrowed when I turned his way. "You're—woozy, as you say—because you used too much power in too short a time tonight. Doing that weakens you, ken."

"No, I didn't *ken*."

His mouth bunched in judgment. "You must learn to better control the flow of your magic, or it'll erupt in immense torrents like that, leaving you weary, powerless. Someone *really* should've taught you that. Control takes practice—"

"Dude, what do you even care?" I bristled. Yeah, he was right. I should've been taught how to control my powers long before that night, but someone like him had no right to criticize my father's parenting choices. "Aren't you still the guy who wants to sell me off to Gentian like I'm—"

"I don't *want* to do anything of the sort."

Had I heard right? Was he letting me go?

"I'm not taking you to Gentian because I *want* to."

My hopes plunged.

"Shorty, I'd love nothing more than to set you free and never hear your nagging voice again."

"Then *why* don't you? Do you need the money that badly?"

His lips pressed together. "I've seeds aplenty, thank you."

"Then I don't get it."

"I've no choice." His gaze hardened. "I deliver you, or my freedom is forfeit."

I waited for more. If he wanted me to understand, he'd need to elaborate on his past this time. I wasn't a mind reader.

"I'm a slave, Shorty," he finally confessed. "I didn't come to this God-forsaken realm willingly. I was taken, plucked from a battlefield during the revolution by two of Gentian's Milesian slavers. They said they scented my power from ten miles away."

I figured his shadows were the extra gift he'd claimed Gentian bestowed on him when he became a harbinger, but I hadn't seen him using any other powers during our journey. Or I wasn't aware he'd been using them. "What are your powers?"

Pete gnawed his lip, the strain of voicing this tale apparent. "At birth, I was blessed with what they call predatory prowess here.

"Long ago, I thought I was just a damn fine hunter—damn fine fighter too—but now I see the differences between me and the other men I knew. I'd always been able to smell things others couldn't, hear things miles down the road, and I could track anyone, no matter their stealth. And my strength—" He shook his head. "Always knew there was something more than human about it. My vision was so sharp, I never missed when shooting. I became an acclaimed marksman in General Washington's army. Though I spent the bulk of my time fighting under the Marquis de Lafayette. He was actually quite fond of me."

I stared. "You knew *Lafayette*?"

"Aye, I did. Good-humored chap, he was, with a brilliant mind for strategy and a gallant heart. I hear he became something of a legend after he helped defeat the redcoats."

"You could say that."

His memories of a better life faded to bleakness. "Rightly so."

I watched him for a loaded beat before I pried, "So, you were on the battlefield when they found you?"

"The battle of Monmouth Courthouse, New Jersey. An erratic, poorly organized battle—so hot I was sweating my bollocks off. Didn't know what the feck was happening half the time. I was stationed with Major General Greene on a hill where I could snipe at the redcoats. Things went mad. I was dodging musket balls when I was lassoed and hoisted into the air by what I first saw as a seraph. I thought maybe I'd taken a bullet and was being winged to Jesus's arms. Might've been better off if I had."

"Didn't anyone try to help you?"

"In the heat of battle, nobody noticed me being carried off. Not that they could've saved me anyhow.

"I wasn't the only human they took that day, but I was by far the largest. One or two tethers easily controlled the others. Me—they bound me in chains of morgana silver to drain my power and forced paralytic potions down my throat. I lay trapped and powerless for weeks before we reached the Shadow Palace.

"Gentian paid handsomely to add me to his stock of cage fighters—fodder for his blood sport, treated worse than livestock. His gaolers threw me in a cage I barely fit in with no blanket to keep me warm or pillow to rest my head upon. Not even a chamber pot to piss in."

I winced.

"When the paralytics wore off, and I'd eaten what they thought passed as a meal for a man my size, they prodded me into the ring to fight like a cock—the very thing they did to me every week for the next 224 years."

WTF! Pete had suffered for a horrendous amount of time in a place that sounded like one of Dante's nine circles of hell.

"How many other cage fighters were there?"

Pete shook his head, peering off into space. "Hard to say. There were new ones every week to replace the losers."

I stilled. "When you say losers—?"

Pete met my gaze dead on, hating the truth while refusing apology. "Draws happen, but rarely. Cage matches generally don't end until all but one fighter are dead."

My throat tightened to a painful degree. "How—how many men did you kill, Pete?"

He shook his head. "Not only men, Shorty. There were women. There were feyrs of all races, beyns of all races." His voice roughened. "In the ring, I took nearly 20,000 lives—so I could live to see another day."

I stifled my shock. He'd killed off the population of Johnstown! My heart ached for all who'd met their end at his obviously lethal hands.

It also ached for him.

"When a fighter achieves 15,000 kills, Gentian *honors* him with a position as a harbinger." He sneered. "When he first honored me, I turned him down—kept doing so for years.

"At least fighting in the ring, I knew my opponents were bought for some strength, agility, or aggression. They were already inclined to combat in some way. But to think about turning my prowess on the innocent world, about becoming Gentian's pawn?" He shook his head. "I preferred bondage to that."

Was it weird that I wanted to hug him? "What changed?"

Something awful eclipsed what small light remained in his eyes. "Gentian hated that I'd refused him. He deplored me as it was—mouthy as I am. He'd bet against me in every match, hoping I'd lose. Well, my rejection of his offer made him downright barbarous toward me. He changed my fighting schedule to multiple matches a week, randomly, too, so I'd have no chance to prepare myself—to know when to rally my power. And he decreased my rations by half—making me eat the meat of the fighters I killed."

Goddess, I was going to puke again.

"He moved me to a cage in the middle of his throne room, so his wealthy guests could heckle or tease me during gatherings—so I could watch them commit gluttony at every meal—while I starved."

My soul twisted inside me.

"But I held out hope that one day things would change." Pete cleared his throat and went on. "I prayed that someone, somewhere would learn how Gentian abused his slaves and stop him, if they didn't abolish slavery outright."

His face screwed in a way that made me shiver. "And then one day, our wondrous King Laurustinus strolled into Gentian's Shadow Palace in all his finery and regalia."

I gulped down an onslaught of tears. *Daddy, no*, I pleaded with his ghost.

"And I thought—here he is, at last! My savior! My angel from heaven, sent to end my eternity of enslavement—to break me from my living hell!"

I couldn't bear to hear the rest.

"But the angel took one pained look at me, starving and dirty in my cage, and moved along to the feast."

No!

"He didn't so much as glance my way, didn't speak of the atrocities before him, though Gentian made certain to rectify any ignorance. He boasted of all the horrid things he did to his Forgottens—that's what he called us—and implored our good king to watch a match.

"To his credit, the king declined, but he lifted not a single finger to help us Forgottens. He issued no royal decrees. He walked away from the Shadow Court, away from us, as if we didn't matter. Didn't exist at all. And I knew then that I *was* forgotten. That I'd die a slave in a cage or a mutilated hulk in Gentian's fighting ring. And no moral I'd ever had seemed to hold its weight anymore.

"The next time Gentian offered to break me from my cage and make me a harbinger, I agreed."

I swiped a river off my cheek, hoping he hadn't seen.

"Then—"

How is this horror story not over yet?

"Gentian required something more of me—if I wanted the freedom of a harbinger. Since I'd resisted his will for so long, he didn't trust my loyalty. So, he made me drink a tonic he claimed would ensure my good behavior. I was in such a despairing state, I didn't give a bloody shite." His mouth quivered. "I did care moments after I drank the thing—when I felt my soul drowning. He'd not given me a simple tonic to keep me in line. He'd drugged me with death poppy. The oil from that plant is rife with void magic, and it unbalanced my internal system of power—sucked the light straight out of me and turned me demonic within two heartbeats."

I hopped up from Pete's side like a scorpion had stung me.

Pete rolled his eyes. "Fret not, Shorty, I'm not demonic now."

I studied his face like I might find Satan there. "How? Is there a cure for demonic possession? You got exorcists here?"

"In a manner of speaking. That good siren I spoke of—"

"Yeah?"

"Her song shook me out of the death poppy's grip. Saving my soul. Saving me."

"How would a song do that?" If my mother had been a siren, wasn't it possible I'd inherited her gift? I'd gotten her nocturnal premonitions, after all. *Thanks, Mom.* Did a magic voice lay dormant in my throat? *Maybe it can carry a tune better too.* "I know you said a siren's voice is a weapon but—"

"At least *that* siren's song was like a healthy dose of burning hot crystal magic. Anyhow, hers was strong enough to upset that void within me—so heavy it was crushing my spirit."

"If she cured you, why do your eyes turn black sometimes?"

"Ah, so you've noticed that minor detail, have you?" He shrugged. "I suppose it's a bit like the alcoholism I've heard tell is a common malady in the human world these days. Of course, in my time there, an abundant fondness for the drink just meant you were a jolly craic."

I assumed *craic* meant a fun time.

"Anyhow, I've subdued the poison, aye, but it still skulks about within me. Ready to take the reins. So, I must maintain a careful balance, lest I feed the void too much."

"How do you watch your balance?"

"By making good choices that create light magic as well as my usual dark."

"You can create magic?"

"Certainly." His mouth bunched again at my lacking education. "Everything you do in this place creates some type of energy—some of which can be internalized if you ken how to siphon it."

"And making good choices helps you stay balanced?"

"Aye."

"To overcome your evil darkness?"

Pete shifted on the rock. "You'll want to be careful with your distinctions, Shorty. Death poppy is unequivocally evil—its void magic can poison a person's soul. Plain auld dark magic on the other hand—well, there's nothing innately wrong with it. It's just a color of the rainbow. It's only when you let it consume you or use it with ill intent that it can unbalance your internal magics. Using crystal magic wrongly is just as bad."

"Hm. So, doing things that create light magic keeps your darkness in check. Like a yin-yang."

"Well, bugger me! I've actually heard of that one, and aye, that's precisely what it's like."

Relaxing, I reclaimed my seat beside him. "How does Gentian feel about your regained balance?"

Pete clicked his tongue. "That's the rub, Shorty. He doesn't know about it."

Oh.

"I wasn't merely speaking of bondage when I said I'd forfeit my freedom, though that threat always looms. I'm more in fear for the freedom of my soul. You see, failure to follow a direct shadow ordination would get me called before Gentian for a reprimand—which isn't a wholly terrible thing. Samhain's Passion—what us harbingers call the source of Gentian's powers—it requires harbingers, so we're too valuable to dispense of lightly. Most who displease Gentian get fifty lashes and a night outside naked in the cold."

I cringed. *How is that not terrible?*

"But with me—" He shook his head. "I fear facing an inquest means he'll realize I've undone his void."

"He hasn't seen you since he made you a harbinger?"

"He has, but I try not to linger when he's near—usually just for the space of time it takes to collect my bounty once I've met his ordination."

"But your eyes—"

"I've learned to unbalance my magic just enough, so that the poison takes a small foothold. My eyes turn to pits, but the void can't swallow me."

"That sounds dangerous, Pete."

"Aye, but no more than defying Gentian, Shorty. If I fail to deliver you, the bastard will interrogate me. If he so much as *suspects* I've loosened his hold on me, he'll make me drink from the Well of Sincerity and uncover every act I've done in disobedience against him—including helping you get away."

He'd done things in disobedience? He wasn't always Gentian's compliant goon?

"Why are you so sure he'd suspect you'd defied him? Why wouldn't he believe you'd just screwed the pooch?"

Pete laughed, rubbing his face. "I'm his best harbinger. I've never failed an ordination before. Apart from one, that is, but that was on account of his poor planning. Anyhow, if I fail again after so long, he'll suspect me of defiance straight away."

His gaze gentled as I frowned, unsettled by our shared predicament.

"Please understand—Gentian knows I hate him, that I have no allegiance to him other than the blasted tether that binds me, and that I'm not a cold-hearted killer. If I'm not in demonic thrall, then I'm just a liability."

Briar's words flitted through my mind: *No caster wants a harbinger with a heart.*

"He'll force more death poppy down my gullet, and I'll be lost to that demonic void forever."

I swallowed hard, tasting the poison.

"You can't ask me to endure the horror of losing my soul again, Shorty."

I choked back my sorrow for him as I folded suddenly shivering arms over my chest. "That's not fair, Pete. You know that's not what I—"

"But that *is* what you're asking of me, whether you wish to see it that way or not."

"But *you're* asking the same of me! You're asking me to take your place. To sleep in a cage, to fight like a dog. To be subservient to the man who *murdered* my father. You're dragging me to a place that sounds worse than hell. And I do *not* deserve it."

Pete met my eyes in the night, his ringed with silver. Sad. But not sorry. "I know."

NINETEEN

A new tether tugged on my ankle when I awoke the next morning to the smell of fired meat and a pot of rosenut coffee. Ten times the thickness of my last, it fettered me to the shirtless man by the fire.

Glowering, I sat up. "*Really*?"

Pete's mouth wriggled into a smile. He stoked the campfire's coals with a stick, his hair mussed from sleep. "Really."

I folded my arms over my chest. "*Someone's* sore that I escaped him yesterday."

"I'm not sore about that, truthfully." He took a seat in the moss and turned the spit over the fire, where two freshly skinned squirrels roasted in the morning mist. The wound I'd bandaged with clean leaves and a freshly scrubbed shred of my underskirt seemed less bothersome than it was last night. "Can't fault you for doing something I'd have done myself. And while it was sporting good fun dogging your trail through the woods—you should really learn to cover your tracks, Shorty—I think I'll do without a chase today." He sighed, resting his elbows on his knees. "I'm a mite sluggish after getting my arse battered last night."

I ignored my guilt. "I'll just burn it off, you know."

"Thought you might." His eyes twinkling, he jostled the tether connecting us. Fuming tendrils of vibrant green shot through its shadowy fibers. "That's why I've reinforced this one with ossified emerald—which won't take a flame if you were curious. I rooted the strands up just for you, Shorty."

I knew I was giving him the sour puss face Aunt Aylie had tried swatting out of me and didn't give a crap.

My churlishness only delighted him further. He seemed to pride himself in outsmarting me, like I was a video game boss he'd been trying to beat for ages.

"Gentian provides us harbingers flame nullifiers for fae such as yourself. Although, I've never had to use one before. Fire sylphen were to have gone extinct centuries ago." He arched a brow. "You're an anomaly, Shorty."

Dude, what else is new?

"At least now we ken what the Shadow Prince wants with you."

"How could he know I'm a fire sylph? I didn't even know until just before I went through the portal."

Pete shrugged, turning the spit again, patting Sionna's head when she tramped over to him—something furry, fuchsia, and squirming in her jowly mouth. "Perhaps the harbinger who found your father told him."

I winced in remembrance of the hideous night my father died. "The one that must've done that—it didn't see my magic."

Pete stilled, his gaze narrowing. "The *one*? How many harbingers were sent after your father?"

"Not sure. At least five that I know of. There were definitely more."

His gaze rounded like an owl's.

"Bogeybats," I explained.

"*Christ*. What the hell did your father do to Gentian?"

I scowled at the flames. "He existed."

And married my mother.

His bafflement slow to fade, Pete shook his head and took the critter Sionna had hunted. With a brittle crack, he broke its tiny neck and unsheathed his *scian* to gut its flopping corpse for her. She laid down beside him, watching him work.

I watched too, cringing. Yes, we all needed to eat, but I was still too bougie to accept how the sausage was made.

"Your fire didn't erupt for you that night?"

"It did." I plucked a blade of tall grass, peeled off one of its leaves. "At the end, when they were going to kill me."

"Yet you assume none of the bats brought news of your powers back to their master?"

"Well, they couldn't. I killed them all."

His eyes lifted to meet mine—froze. "You killed bogeybats?"

"Three of them." I tore off another leaf with a satisfying slice. "Didn't mean to. The fire just came out of me."

Pete's brow knit as he tossed Sionna's breakfast's innards onto the coals. They sizzled and popped—as the bats' charred bodies had done on that terrible night. I recoiled from the memory. From what I'd had to do last night.

"Shorty, you were defending yourself." Pete's voice mellowed. "You shouldn't feel badly about that."

I gulped a mouthful of emotions and asked, "Is that what you used to tell yourself?"

A small smile lifted his mouth. "Aye."

"Did it work?"

He loosed a breath. "No. Never."

His words hung heavy between us, but I appreciated his bluntness after a lifetime of lies.

"Thank you," he murmured. When I blinked back at him, his molasses cookie eyes were warm, friendly—the eyes of the man in the tavern. "For coming back for me even when you had every reason to let me die. Still, you did, and I'm breathing today because of you and your fire."

I flushed, his gratitude unexpected. "Well, you risked your life to save me first—after I aggravated you every minute of every day." I giggled at his beleaguered look. "Figured I owed you one."

Blading Sionna's meat off her catch's bones, he asked, "Does that mean you'll quit harrowing me?"

"Of course not. If you're still carting me to the Shadow Palace, then I'll whine the whole damn way. I won't make this easy on you, bud."

He gusted with laughter—and exasperation.

"I don't think you want me to, anyway." I smirked sideways at him around my twirling blade of grass.

Pete's grin spread like honey butter on warm buns. So delicious. So decadent. "Thought you said you didn't know how to flirt, Shorty."

My face flashed hot. *I'm not flirting.*

Am I?

Pete snickered, handing Sionna her breakfast. She chomped it down in two bites.

"Why don't you go cool those blushing cheeks in the stream?" He pointed his knife toward my backpack. "Wash all that grime off while I finish cooking breakfast."

Desperation for a bath banished any embarrassment, and I leapt for my backpack—then stopped just short.

Pete raised a hand to heaven. "I promise I'll keep my back to you."

After several more beats of narrowed staring, I snatched my bag and scurried toward the brook. It babbled over smooth rocks under a breathy cloud of mist. Glorious and refreshing.

"But I can't promise I won't peek."

Stumbling, I glanced back to find Pete grinning over his brawny shoulder.

I smothered my self-consciousness and kept on. Though I couldn't help pouting at his soft, galling laugh.

Two days later, I got my period. At first, I was ecstatic. I'd almost killed myself in preventing pregnancy, but it had done the trick. No baby for me! Yes, yes, *yes!* Then I realized I'd have to suffer my period without the aid of motrin or tampons—because I'd been too scatterbrained when I was packing for my new life to think of anything but death. I tried padding my underwear with leaves, but they absorbed little, leaving me damp and belligerent. I spent the next two days moaning in the back of the wagon, my insides a mass of tangled snakes. The mere sound of Pete's voice made me want to strangle him, and even sweet Sionna was like a fly buzzing around my head.

On the third day, my condition had rubbed me ragged, and I got in a fight with a tree.

In my defense, the tree started it. I'd merely been gathering more leaves for another makeshift maxi-pad when the great elm branch I'd been plucking sprung back and whacked me in the mouth. My lip smarting and blood welling, I'd screeched like a crazy woman and throttled the assailing limb.

Little did I know, but on the other side of that tree was a fairy ring of overgrown toadstools—where a troupe of mini-fae dwelt. I didn't spy their blanching faces until Pete bounded over at my outburst and wrangled me.

"Sorry to have bothered you fine folks," he apologized to the trembling teacup fae. To them, I must've appeared a roaring giant there to rampage their peaceful village.

Pete shoved me toward the road. "She was stung by a cankerwasp, ken."

"Ohhh," the gnomes chimed together in comically nasal tones, nodding heads topped by leafy hats.

"We'll be shoving off." Pete bowed his head. "Have a fruitful day."

I stomped back to the wagon and whirled on him when he met me there. "I don't need you to make excuses for me, thank you very much."

Bob brayed at my tone as Pete glowered. "I didn't hear *you* voicing your reasons for acting absurd."

I shoved my bangs from my eyes, wanting to rail at the wind, and stomped away to crawl back into a ball of misery in the wagon bed.

"Won't you at least tell *me* what's chafing your arse?" he growled, following me. "Aye, you've sworn to vex me until we reach Gentian's throne room, but you're taking your threat to unholy lengths."

Biting my tongue on a hateful rejoinder about which of us was more unholy, I grabbed the ledge of the wagon bed and yanked myself up. "What's *chafing my arse* is none of your business," I mimicked him, popping up to stand in the bed. "So, just head back to your place beside Bob, and let's get moving."

Pete arched a brow, staying put.

Sionna blinked up at me from our nest in the wagon bed as I clumped over her. I stopped at the front of the wagon and clapped my hands at our driver. "Go on, Bob! Move out!"

Bob didn't listen. Instead, he peered back with soulful black eyes and bared a set of long, yellowed teeth. He blared something along the lines of, *you ain't my boss.*

"Bob won't be budging an inch until I give my say so," Pete said. "So, unless you'd like to make camp in the village of Fern Gnomes you've scared the piss out of, you'd best explain your ill humor, Shorty."

"Don't call me that!" I snarled, then clapped again, stomping. "Come on, Bob! Gentian's awaiting! We don't want to be late!"

Rolling his eyes, Pete exhaled and set a bear paw on the wagon ledge.

"*Goddamnit!*" I barreled back over to him, but he remained unmoved by my temper.

Sionna, however, cowered into our grassy mattress.

"Would you stop being a jerkwad and tell Bob to move?"

"When you stop being a raving b—"

I swooped down and clutched him by his jerkin collar, heat flaring up the length of my neck. Surprise glinted in Pete's widening eyes, his lips curling at the corners.

"*What* were you about to say?" I hissed into his handsome, bearded face.

"I was about to use an apt term for someone behaving as you are," he replied, seemingly fascinated by the sparks doubtless flying in my eyes. "If you don't like to hear it, then comport yourself better."

Who made him the manners police? He sounded like Aunt Aylie.

"Fuck you."

His smirk broadened into something rakish and alive. "Thanks for the offer, darlin'. Can I get a rain check on that?"

His response was better than a pinch. I jerked away from him.

"Maybe when you're calmer. Right now, your cunny's in danger of starting a wildfire."

"Knock it off!" My cunny was off limits to his commentary. "You know that's not—I wasn't—I'd never—"

Pete chuckled, enjoying my perturbation. Clearly, he'd only said what he had to ruffle my feathers. He didn't really want to sleep with me.

How could he?

Well, he wasn't disgruntling me without getting thoroughly disgruntled back.

Jamming hands onto hips, I wagged my head at Pete. "You really want to know what's bothering me?"

"Oh, I'm just *dying* to know, Shorty."

"I'm bleeding."

Pete snorted, his eyes falling to the new scab on my bottom lip—where the damn tree had whacked me. "That's barely a scratch. Nothing to cry over, and it only just happened to you. You've been a wretch for—"

"I'm bleeding from my vagina, you idiot!"

Pete faltered back a step, his cheeks flushing.

"And I'm cramping, my back is hurting, I'm dead tired, and I don't have *anything* from home to make it better! Not even chocolate!" Suddenly close to tears, I gripped my hair. "So, *there*—that's why I've been so miserable. I don't know how beyns manage these things in this awful place, and unless you've got some way to help me, which I sincerely doubt, you'd better keep your head down, your mouth shut, and let me be how I'm going to be. Got it?"

His startlement passing, Pete firmed his lips, then strode to Bob's side. "Giddap," he clicked.

Drained, I sank into my herbal bed, the wagon rolling on.

Not long after that, Pete turned us down a side road that led us out of the forest and onto meandering grasslands, and I counted all the ways my current life sucked, the distance between me and the Shadow Court closing.

Brooding beneath my cloak in the wagon bed, I felt the wagon clatter to a stop and blinked back to awareness. Amiable voices conversed with Pete as dogs barked, Sionna leaping from our nest to join them. Who Pete spoke with and why we'd stopped before sunsdown, I had no clue. Didn't give a shit either.

I feigned sleep to avoid socialization. Until snapping fingers made that impossible.

Expecting to find Pete smirking, I opened one eye and glared.

Two Middling beyns stared back at me.

"Oh, aye," the taller, sultrier of the two cooed, her lined eyes sizing me up. Her skin was pearlescent, her hair hanging in ebony waves down a broad, curvaceous back. "She's Danann all right, Olea. See those knives in her look?"

Olea shushed the first beyn, a closed lip smile spreading across her round face—the color of terracotta, a few shades lighter than Zahra's. "Hello. Welcome to our camp."

Rubbing my eyes, I sat up to scan my surroundings. Olea had welcomed me to a caravan of four vardo wagons of eclectic design and vibrant color. A fire pit smoked in the camp's epicenter, brewing something in a hefty cauldron hanging above it. Two rough-looking feyrs worked beside it, chopping wood. Pete stood with them in jovial discussion. So, we hadn't stopped there by happenstance. My captor knew these people.

Did they also know he was a harbinger? How did he explain my miserable, filthy presence?

"Pete said you could use our help," the first beyn said, blinking at me when I didn't respond.

"Why don't you come with us?" Olea rapped the wagon, more direct. "I'd wager you'd enjoy a hot bath."

That perked me up better than a shot of espresso. "That sounds wonderful. Thanks."

They shared a glance at my accent, but neither of them commented as I made my way to the back of the wagon.

The bowed-top vardo they led me to was tiny but functional, full of character and color. The exterior was a deep viridian and decorated by flowering herbs, warbling wind chimes, and a clothesline replete with fluttering clothes, both a male's and a female's.

Inside was rife with the aroma of lavender. A sizeable bed, neatly made with bright, quilted bedding, spanned the entire width of the back wall. Above it, mounted shelves hugged the wall, housing books, trinkets, tins, and decorative plates. Several steps down was a minuscule kitchen with a woodburning stove, a quaint dining area before the only window, and—well, that was it. I toured the place with one glance and wondered where I'd be getting that bath Olea mentioned.

"This is cute. Small, but cute."

"Thank you," Olea said as she passed me on her way to the kitchen. She was small and stout but walked with a purpose. With a flick of her wrist, her long brown hair twisted itself into a bun atop her head. I was still admiring her convenient magic when she turned back to her friend.

"All right, Tansy." She rubbed her little hands together before grabbing an apron off the wall hook between the stairs and the kitchen. She quickly tied it around her waist to protect her clothes—well-fitting pants and a jerkin shaped for her round figure. More the gear of a blacksmith than a country peasant.

Tansy wore a similar getup, although hers was much tighter and left no curve to the imagination. Her breasts threatened to burst from her top as she, too, tossed up her hair with a magical twitch.

"I'll prepare the tincture; you draw the bath," Olea charged Tansy, already pulling things from cupboards.

"Straight away," Tansy agreed, snapping fingers.

I jumped back as the floorboards by my feet slid into nothingness, revealing a wine tub full of water beneath the wagon. Her eyes falling shut, Tansy uttered the word *teas,* and the tub's still water bubbled and steamed.

Tansy glided around the tub to one of Olea's cupboards. "What oils do you prefer?"

"Oils?" I squeaked, still amazed by the tub. What heated it? I didn't smell a fire.

"Scents," Tansy clarified, peering at me over her shoulder.

I shook my head. "Thanks, but I don't use scents when I bathe. They make me itch."

Olea shook a jar of desiccated herbs onto her wooden counter. "Use essence of chamomile on her. Add a shell of ground oats as well. Both soothe delicate skin."

Tansy added these ingredients to the ever-bubbling bath, creating a scintillating hiss.

"No cars or computers in the fairy world," I remarked. "But at least there are Jacuzzis."

Neither beyn asked what I meant, though they looked confused.

"Anyway, what would you like me to do?"

"Just have a seat." Olea gestured toward the dining table. "We'll have this sorted in a lick."

So, I eased my aching bones on a stool at said table, admiring the basket of mauve eggs placed atop it until Tansy glided my way. To unknot my cloak.

"Something wrong?" Tansy asked as I stiffened in the realization that she meant to undress me. Was privacy when bathing rare in this world?

Flames lapped my cheeks. "Well—I—where I—you know—"

"Are you embarrassed of your courses?" Sympathy undercut Tansy's dispassion. "Don't fret. Pete told us all about your troubles."

Of course, he did! The fricking big mouth!

"We're happy to help. It's nothing what we haven't seen before. All beyns are blessed with the same monthly scourge."

I managed a grimace of appreciation, then stood so she could remove my cloak. As she did, my hands rose to close my torn bodice before both beyns got a gander at my left boob.

Olea's grave eye assessed my garb as Tansy pared the layers off me. When I stood completely bare before them, shivering from awkwardness more than cold, Olea sniffed and returned to her tincture. "Might as well throw those rags into the stove," she told Tansy. "They're worthless in that state."

I squelched a complaint when Tansy swept my soiled garments off the floor.

"We'll see you attired again," Olea chuckled at my bereft expression when Tansy lit a giant match on the wall and tossed it into the stove with my dress. The fabrics caught immediately, the heat from the blaze flaring through the wagon.

I observed my hostesses. One petite, the other voluptuous. I doubted either of them owned a single article of clothing that would fit my string-bean figure.

"Now, please do settle in," Olea requested, grinding her herbs. "Try to relax."

I was stepping into the tub when Tansy giggled. "My word, where's the rest of your arse?"

I would've scowled had the milky water not already loosened my weary legs, effervescing like Alka-Seltzer. Instead, I feigned dismay and twisted to look at my non-existent booty. "Well, damnit, it must've fallen off again."

Both Olea and Tansy laughed, and I plunked myself chin deep into the glorious water.

My ailments mellowed within seconds, the water soothing me better than a deep tissue massage and a mood music CD. I might've dozed off after weeks of arduous travel had Tansy not grabbed a scrubber brush and knelt to scour me like a greasy pan.

"You guys give new meaning to the word hospitality." I curled into my knees. "Where I come from, bathing's usually a solitary experience."

"How boring," Tansy said. "And what a waste of time for one blessed with the dimples of Venus."

I assumed she meant the indents flanking my lower spine. "Guess baths aren't supposed to be fun."

"Pete did tell us the human world was a mite priggish."

My gaze froze on the bubbles around my knees. "He told you I was from the human world?"

"Aye." Tansy scrubbed my shoulder. "He told us everything. Apart from your name. That, he said, was Shorty, but I think we all ken that doesn't suit you."

I sniffed. "No, really?"

She and Olea chuckled.

"Pete doesn't know my name." I exhaled, the brush bristles on my neck like rebirth. "I refused to give it to him."

"You refused him your name?" Olea set a hand on her wide hip, turning to me. "And he didn't force you to reveal it?"

I blinked at her. "He—he can do that?"

"Aye," she said. "All harbingers carry a vial of water from the Well of Sincerity."

That answers that. "So, you do know he's a harbinger."

She and Tansy shared another conspiratorial look.

"And you don't have a problem with it?" I tried not to sound as judgy as I felt. "I mean, it's all right that he brought his prisoner here?"

"We'd hardly grouse about it," Olea said. "It'd be mighty hypocritical of us."

"You—you're harbingers too?"

"Everyone who lives here is," Tansy said. "This is a harbinger camp."

Lost for words, I stared at them.

"Is it the fact that we're beyns what surprises you?" Olea asked. "Or just learning that harbingers aren't all solitary creatures?"

"No, uh—" I cleared my throat. "I just feel bad because I know if you're harbingers, you were once cage fighters."

Tansy stopped scrubbing. Olea's smile dropped from her face.

Their reactions told me I really shouldn't know that. Maybe they liked to keep *some* things private.

"Pete ex-explained—" I stammered. "He told me what it was like."

"Did he?" Olea glared toward the drapery entrance, then turned a rigid back to me. She picked up her pestle and continued grinding. "He must've taken a liking to you to be divulging buried histories."

I chewed my lip. "Trust me, he doesn't like me. I've done nothing but sass him since he straight-up kidnapped me. He probably thinks I'm the most annoying person he's ever met."

The tension subsided when Tansy sighed. Her brush began moving in firm circles again. "I daresay Pete enjoys a bit of sass."

I grimaced, still afraid I'd just committed some egregious faux pas. "I'm sorry I reminded you of—"

"It's not likely something we'll ever forget," Olea cut me off, bracing her hands on her counter. The stiffness in her shoulders eased with one great breath. "Never you mind, anyway." She angled to look at me, not smiling, not frowning. "We all survived the Shadow Palace, and we do what we do now to protect ourselves from that goddessless place. Though, if it's any consolation to you, we don't like it."

I grimaced. "Wouldn't imagine you would."

"To be sure, most harbingers feel pride in being what they are," Tansy said. "They revel in lording their power over the weak. Some are just as callous as Gentian himself. If they weren't cruel to begin with, Gentian broke them—made them that way."

Like he'd tried to do with Pete.

"That's why we've created our own camp," Tansy said. "Away from the others."

"And that's allowed?"

"Where we live is of no concern to Gentian, so long as we obey our ordinations. Besides, if he wants to know where we are, he has but to follow our tethers." Tansy expelled a weighty breath. "Our freedom is an illusion. We'll never be completely unbound."

Thinking, I tucked my face into my knees as Tansy exfoliated me raw.

That Briar—he just can't tell the truth to save his goddamn life.

Gentian didn't cull his harbingers from the dregs of society—as Briar had claimed—if kind people like Olea and Tansy wound up in his cages. On the contrary, all of them were victims of a society that allowed slavery. How many harbingers were truly innocents—there was no way of knowing.

But I did know something drastic needed done about Gentian. And I worried that Briar, as king, wouldn't do it.

TWENTY

We emerged from Olea's wagon, heralded by a catcall.

Olea smirked at the burly Middling swaggering toward us. He had a scruffy beige beard and wore a dirty homespun shirt. His scuffed black leather trousers were in much the same state. He gestured at me with his left hand, where two fingers were shorn in half.

"She shines up like a new pair of boots," he remarked, giving me a once over.

Clean, I now sported a set of my own leather togs (what Olea and Tansy had termed my new outfit). The set had been Tansy's, but after several snippy disagreements between my hostesses, and more than a few magical alterations, Tansy's hand-me-downs now fit. The vest formed to my torso, snugging a soft linen shirt with a ruffled neckline into my refreshed skin, and the pants were comfortable while hugging my legs in all the right places. Their tan leather was breathable, elastic—perfect for travel. Plus, my new gear made me look kind of badass. Or the closest I could come to it.

I cracked a smile, flattered by the feyr's compliment.

Olea nudged him toward her vardo. "Why don't you do your own shining? Hurry, though. Supper's near to ready."

A pair of brown eyes dancing in his green-tinted face, the feyr bent and smacked a kiss upon her lips. "Won't be but a minute, lovey." He pinched her hip and duly received a good swat. Whooping, he swaggered up the wagon steps and disappeared behind the curtain.

Olea's eyes glimmered. "Seeing as he's forgotten his manners today, I'll just tell you—that was Ox." The way she said his name belied her ribbing.

"Is he your husband? Er, your ceyla?"

"My mister. We harbingers aren't permitted to wed."

"Gentian fears marriage would soften us." Tansy uncoiled her waves from atop her head. "Like most powerful fools, he sees love as a weakness."

Olea's button nose twitched. "And commitment to anyone other than himself as an insult."

I scoffed. *What* is *this guy? The anti-Amy?*

"That's enough talk of Gentian." Olea jutted her chin toward the fire. "Let's see how far along supper is, shall we?"

Strategically placed logs wide enough to fit a substantial bottom surrounded the fire ring. Two were already occupied. One, by a sinister looking fae with close-cropped black hair, bloodless skin, and a strong jaw. The other, by Pete.

Water clung to Pete's tousled hair and freshly trimmed beard, sparkling beneath the setting suns. His skin looked reinvigorated, the filth of who knew how long bathed away. He'd also changed his clothes and now sat in amused discourse with the other dark fae, who chortled despite his appearance of—well, a harbinger of doom. Instead of his dusty black togs, Pete now sported a loose, untucked linen shirt and a fresh pair of black trousers. His shirt collar was untied, exposing the dark curls furring his expansive chest. I found myself transfixed by the hollow between his clavicles.

How would it feel to rest my head there?

Startled at myself, I sidestepped that path toward disaster.

Of course, I circled back moments later when Pete sensed our approach. He glanced up and our eyes met. His gaze was as wicked as a smack on the bottom. He mentioned something to his friend, who laughed so hard his broad shoulders bounced.

"What's so funny?" Tansy whined, reposing on a log.

"I was just regaling Sedge with the tale of how Shorty here gave me the slip," Pete replied. "When I went to recover her, she got my arse walloped by a band of Fomorians."

Tansy and Olea gasped.

"*Fomorians?*" Olea set hands on hips. "Didn't you learn your lesson the first time? How in the Isle of Apples aren't you dead?"

I stiffened where I stood. Sure, Olea and Tansy seemed nice, but I'd only known them for two hours. And torture could loosen the lips of even good people. The fewer people who dealt with Gentian that knew of my powers the better.

"We had a stroke of luck." Pete shot me an expressive glance—*I'm not telling*. "A Nixie intervened on our behalf."

"A *Nixie?*" Tansy asked.

"Aye," Pete said. "I killed one of the fiends. The two others, the Nixie took to her lair."

Olea bustled over to Pete. "Right—then what parts need healing?" She clapped a hand to his forehead. "At least fever hasn't gripped you this time."

Pete batted away her examining hands, which now glowed with a shimmering white light. Even the healer, Shasta's, hands hadn't done that. "I'm fine, Olea, truly."

Olea's hand auras dimmed, though her eyes probed him.

"After the scuffle, Shorty doctored the one bite I suffered."

Olea faced me. "You have healing? Hedge or stem?"

"Well, I—I—" I cleared my throat. "I don't know to be honest." I paused, curious. "Mind if I ask what the difference is?"

Olea shrugged. "Hedge healers imbue magic into herbs and medicinals. They're experts at potioning too. Stem healers, like me, can heal with touch." She raised her hands, and they glowed again for several beats. "Our magic is swifter, though it doesn't reach as deeply unless we use great stores of power. We're good in a pinch to stave off death, but hedge healers' magic works to the marrow—only slower." She studied me. "If you do have healing, I'd be glad to give you some pointers."

I pondered how to respond. Did I want instruction on a power I didn't even know I had?

Tansy's delicate nostrils flared. "I don't smell any power in her, Olea."

I bit my lip. *Thank Danu for that.*

"You can't smell the stem healing in me, can you?" Olea said, still scrutinizing me.

"Because you masked it," Tansy returned. "Shorty seemed astounded by the *teas* tub. I doubt she kens how to mask a power like healing."

"I smell something in her," Sedge noted. His brown eyes bored into me, his bulbous nose sniffing. "Though I can't distinguish it."

"Have you all foresworn common courtesy?" Pete harrumphed at his friends, snapping them out of it. "Stop sniffing her."

I almost laughed at the absurd order.

"Christ, you're as bad as the hounds."

The hounds of note—two mammoth yellow labs, two freckled beagles, and Sionna—scampered about the camp, barking, baying, and chasing another fuchsia rodent. I hoped this one would get away, but I was realistic.

Sedge chuckled. He was a stocky, average sized feyr, but the strength radiating from him screamed lethal. I wondered what breed of fae he was. Not a Middling, I guessed.

"If you don't have healing, then how did you doctor Pete's wound?" Olea questioned me, assessing whether her friend needed further medical attention.

"I cleaned it with rubbing alcohol."

"Which bloody fecking hurt," Pete grumbled.

"And I gave him Penicillin," I said. "Antibiotics."

"Aye. She makes me choke down a chalk tablet twice a day."

I soured. "Would you rather die of infection?"

He and Sedge grinned together, probably unaccustomed to being backtalked by their captives. But this captive was becoming comfortable with speaking her mind, less concerned that people wouldn't like her for what she had to say.

"Penicillin," Olea repeated. "That pathetic human medicinal?"

The discovery of Penicillin was seen as one of man's greatest accomplishments on Earth. Yet fae healers deemed it pathetic?

"Might I remind you *again*, Olea, that I'm human," Pete said. "If Shorty's chalk was made to heal a human body, then it'll work just fine on mine."

Olea grunted, then sauntered to a seat by Tansy, leaving me standing before them all like a keynote speaker.

I considered the log beside Olea, then felt a tug on my ankle tether. My neck flared with the heat of outrage. Until I saw the appeal in my abductor's eyes. The tug wasn't an order, but an invitation.

Did I want to sit beside him?

No, you definitely don't, reason insisted.

But—I've got to sit somewhere. Might as well be beside him.

Olea clicked her tongue at Pete as I ambled to the log beside his, keeping my gaze averted. "Pete, I'll examine your wound later. If it's all the same to you, Shorty."

"Be my guest," I said. "I'm no doctor."

A trivial conversation about Tansy's latest excursion to a place called Glynlea began, and I fell into a daze. My mind and body now at ease, I was ready for a yummy meal and a good sleep. I suspected both were available to me that night and couldn't wait.

"Glad to see you're in brighter spirits," Pete's deep voice pervaded the chatter.

"I am," I admitted. "Thank you." Not only had the hot bath eased my cramps and silkened my hair, but Olea had given me three large vials of her tincture, assuring me a drop a day would stave off my period for a year—if I wished. Which I did, considering my tumultuous situation.

Noting Pete's cleaner complexion, I arched a brow. "Is there a blue moon tonight?"

"Just thought I'd save myself the pain of listening to you further carp upon my odor." He leaned closer, his expression wolfish. "Am I more to your liking now?"

Uh, yeah.

Sexy in a haphazard way, he smelled more of oranges and oak moss than sweat. Even as I scooted aside—distancing myself—my core fluttered. "I don't know if you're more to my liking, but at least I can breathe around you now."

Pete's laugh dissolved any tension I might've felt. By the time Ox joined us, and Olea began doling out stew, I was so at ease I could've been dining with my friends in the student union.

"*Mm.*" I devoured another sip from my soup bowl, my hosts having deemed utensils unnecessary. "This is so good."

Olea smiled, sitting with her own steaming bowl. "Thank you."

"What's in it?" I slurped down another mouthful, giddy. This was the only satisfying meal I'd had since the stew at the Thorny Rose Tavern. Savoring the richness of the vitamins and minerals lacking in my diet, I swished the soup between my cheeks before swallowing. "Chicken?"

"Riggit," Olea answered.

I hoped they wouldn't judge me for not knowing what riggit was.

"It's similar to a hare," Pete told me—my living survival guide. "Riggits are much bigger, of course."

"Don't tell me they're also carnivorous." Remembering the huggable cantir, I glanced aside at Pete. My supper nearly slopped to the ground when I caught him slicing open his own wrist with his *scian*.

What the hell are you doing? I damn near asked, but then Pete squeezed a trail of blood into Sedge's stew.

Pete didn't notice my horror. Sedge did, though, and fixed me with a chilling grin. In the rising moonlight, his canines glinted, much longer, much sharper than I'd seen on any other fae. "I take it you've never supped with a Vampire before."

"No," I croaked, wanting to run for the hills. "I thought they were fictional." I swallowed hard at the preternatural gleam in his eyes. "Should've known, though. If there are Nixies and Witches in this world, why not Vampires too? Why not Werewolves or Franken-monsters? Is Santa Claus real too?"

Still focused on his dribbling wound, Pete smirked at my babbling, truly enjoying my flusterment.

As did his friends. Ox chortled into his dinner, Tansy tittered like a tickled mouse, and Olea looked at me like I was a kitten batting butterflies.

"Calm your heartbeat, lady," Sedge said. "Before it bursts."

I blinked. "You can hear it?"

He nodded.

Ox snorted. "Golly, Vampires have such keen senses, Sedge can hear me mustering up a fart before I let it fly. No question he can hear your heart racing."

Sedge's chuckle somehow enhanced his dangerous mien. "You've no need to feel ill at ease with me. I've never had a taste for Danann blood—smacks too much of sour wine."

Is it weird to hope I don't taste like that?

Tsking, Olea rose from her seat, set her bowl on her log. "That's enough, Peter." She marched over to him.

"I can spare a bit more," he argued.

"He has enough stored away." She clamped her suddenly glowy hand around Pete's wrist, jerking it away from Sedge's stew. Pete frowned as her light intensified, concentrating itself around his self-infliction. "We lucked into an icebox of human blood at the market last we went. He has all he needs for now."

When Olea released Pete, his wound now a thin pink scar, he tersely thanked her. They both returned to their suppers.

I watched Sedge dip a stout finger, stirring the garnish of Pete's blood into his soup. "So, Vampires do eat regular food? As well as blood?"

Sedge nodded, sipping his supper. His cheek wriggled as if the taste wasn't quite to his liking. Were the bacteria of Tacker's bite still present in Pete's bloodstream? Or did Sedge taste the Penicillin? Either way, he didn't complain.

"Do you only drink human blood?" I inquired, both curious and disgusted.

"We can subsist on other bloods," he said. "In fact, Elf blood was our staple before humans existed—and before we signed an alchemical treaty with the Elves, banning us from feeding on them. Human blood is by far the most nutritious, howbeit—keeps me the strongest."

I glanced down at my stew, praying for my appetite's return. "How—how do you get it? I mean, is it always available in the market? Or do you solely rely on your friends to—donate?"

"Is that your diplomatic way of asking if I hunt it?"

I swallowed hard. "Yes."

Sedge eyed me above his bowl. "Hunting's been tough since the portals closed. Where once we were free to slip into the human world and freely slake our thirsts, now most of us turn to less-fortifying blood—weakening us—the strongest of Danu's races."

Vampires running amuck on earth, killing with the same resignation Pete displayed when hunting us dinner? The portal closures were a blessing in that respect.

"We Vamps are mostly sensible, lady," Sedge continued as if he'd read my mind. "We take what we must from our prey, but we oughtn't kill them. That's wasteful. When humans can regenerate their blood supply, it benefits us to let them live. In fact, back when keeping humans as pets was legal, one adult could feed a family for many years."

Pets?

"The practice was outlawed, of course, though the slave trade expanded. Then the portals closed. Now we rely on secondary methods of feeding or hope we stumble across free humans—a rarity these days. Slaves are hoarded under lock and key by their masters, who sell their blood to my kind at extortionate rates only the wealthiest of us can pay."

"Aye," Ox concurred. "And since Galena's farm shut down, Gentian and his allies have all but taken over the blood market."

Galena's probably hadn't been a typical farm.

Sedge's mouth twisted. "They starve my kind into a mad state, drive them to desperate acts of survival, and then make the rest of the realm afraid of us with their ballyhoo."

Conversation lulled, the topic at hand clearly an onion of political turmoil in my kingdom. I yearned to peel away its layers, yet I held my tongue. So far, I hadn't offended Sedge by prying, but I didn't want to press my luck.

Finally, Sedge gestured at me, seeming also to unbind himself from some invisible weight. "As to your earlier questions, lady—yes. Werewolves exist, though if you ever cross one's path, be assured you're in mortal danger. Run."

"I'll remember that," I said. "Thanks."

"There are monsters akin to Frankenstein's, though they aren't as gruesome as the book describes. Wonderful read, by the by."

"A bit macabre for my tastes."

Sedge and Pete perked, shared a glance. Impressed that I'd read the book, maybe?

"And Santa Claus," Pete said. "Unfortunately, Shorty, good ole Saint Nick passed well before even my time. You won't find him climbing down your chimney in this world. Although, I'm certain he's a right craic to be around at Yuletide in the Isle of Apples."

"What's the Isle of Apples?" I asked, bringing things once again to a hush. "Olea mentioned it earlier. I just thought it was a turn of phrase."

"My Goddess," Tansy breathed. "You really know *nothing* of faekind."

I huffed. "Well, I—"

"It's not her fault," Pete, the same person always bitching about my ignorance, defended me. "She was raised to think she was human."

"Even so," Olea said, "she should've been taught the true religion."

"I was." At least, I thought so. "But I've never heard of that place."

"Of course, you have, Shorty." Pete angled toward me, his eyes warming. "It's heaven."

"Oh, I didn't know it had a different name here."

Ox clicked his tongue. "It's not precisely heaven," he corrected his friend, louder than necessary. "Heaven's for humans. The Isle of Apples—called Tír na nÓg in auld Faence—is where the deities reside. It's where the fae who Danu deems worthy live in eternal harmony—a much finer place than heaven."

Pete's dark brows drew together. "You ken well humans have passed into the Isle, Oxalis."

"So few it hardly bears mentioning."

Pete rolled his eyes.

"Ox and Pete like to argue over which is the superior species," Olea informed me between sips of stew. "Mostly for fun." She shrugged. "Sometimes they quarrel."

"More than a few humans have passed to the Isle," Sedge confirmed Pete's assertion.

Pete turned a smug look on Ox, who waved him off.

"But they must've led impossibly heroic or extraordinary lives," Sedge added.

"Or be soulmates," Tansy said.

My hopeless romantic heart did a cartwheel. "Soulmates exist?"

Pete shrugged. "Aye." He wiped his mouth on his sleeve. No wonder his clothes got so dirty. "Though they're rare nowadays."

"*Why?*"

He glanced over at the urgency in my voice, interested. "Several reasons. First, only crystal magic fae can mate souls, and they're not being born as frequently as they once were. Second, with the portals closed, it's difficult for those fae to find humans with the proper bond for mating—and only humans can be mated. And third—" He sighed. "As with anything in this place, politics muddles the proper way of things. Thanks to complaints from many void fae, any crystal fae wishing to mate a pair of humans must petition the Divine Cadre first, to ensure a proper mating and a proper balance of power. In the past twenty years, those stuffy old Cadre members—all affluent Danann males, mind you—have approved precisely zero petitions."

How dare they!

"I don't get it," I said. "Why would people complain about soulmates? Too much love in the air or something?"

Pete smiled. "Truly, yes."

There could be no such thing as far as I was concerned.

"You ken what I told you of power? That everything you do creates some form of it—on the prismatum? It's the same for Earth. Actions there generate residual magic that we in the fae world use to enhance our powers. Many fae rely solely on those residuals to work magic, their only gifts the capacity to reap what's given to them. And soulmates—they generate the purest form of crystal magic ever reaped."

I almost clutched my heart like a doof reading a sappy scene in a romance novel.

"Love itself is a potent magic." Olea reached over and took Ox's disfigured hand. "A soulmate's love—that's the elixir of life."

"And that love—it spreads like wildfire," Sedge said. "I've only ever encountered one mated pair in my life—the original pair—Adam and Eve."

My jaw dropped to my bowl.

"Before they found the Isle, I happened upon them on the road. Their love was a thriving thing. Their passion as well." He made these points like a mathematics professor, lacking any wistfulness. "Both were unparalleled in intensity. Within moments of being in their presence, they unbalanced me—disarmed my dark magic for days."

I shrugged. "Couldn't you just use the crystal magic instead?"

Sedge shook his head. "You can't wield crystal magic that potent, lady—renders you little more than a besotted oaf, your mind adrift in the joy of it. Which is why crystal fae must stay balanced. One can lose themselves to crystal just as easily as the void."

Pete grunted at that. "Point is, a mated pair's love affects those around them, as well as the cluster of reapable magic. And when Danu first sent the crystal fae to mate the humans, they mated them in droves. Any spiritually bonded couple became eternally bonded."

I didn't break into song at those beautiful words, but I wanted to.

"But besides their bond," Pete continued, "soulmates are also gifted magic—evidence of Danu's greatness and love, which should amass hordes of worshippers. The humans' faith in Danu is what tips the scales toward crystal magic."

"Their children do much the same." Tansy smirked at Pete. "Or they once did, before humans vilified magic."

I glanced at Pete, questioning, "Is her look suggesting you're a child of soulmates?"

"Aye, I believe it is, but I tell you again, Tansy, my parents were no such thing. Their love wasn't a divine thing."

Tansy's dark eyes twinkled. "Then you must've had a pair of mated ancestors."

"Perhaps," he admitted, turning to me. "Many believe magical humans, such as myself, unless touched by a crystal fae, could've only gained their magic through the bloodline of soulmates."

"It's not as simple as just being born of the line," Olea interjected. "A descendant of soulmates must then be presented to Danu for the bearing of gifts—a baptism."

Pete took another sip of his stew, ruminating. "I know my granny still believed in *The Auld Ones*." He shrugged. "Perhaps she performed Danu's baptism on me when I was a babe in Ulster."

"But isn't your principal power dark?" I remarked. "I thought soulmates only had light magic."

Pete shook his head. "No, soulmates *produce* crystal magic. The powers Danu allots them—they could be any color she deems fit for them."

I exhaled. "Wow. This is—complicated."

"Aye," Pete agreed. "Magic's a science, ken? And what science isn't complicated?"

That reminded me of the C- I'd gotten in Chemistry last year. How I hadn't gotten lower still boggled me.

"Anyhow, the crucial bit is: all that crystal magic produced by Danu's worshippers threw off the balance of power, strengthening lighter magics, and the dark and void fae felt slighted, being ill-equipped to use it."

"They said it was unfair," Tansy said. "That the collective magic from earth should be doled out evenly and balanced accordingly."

Magical communism, huh?

Pete licked stew from the corner of his mouth. "So, the reigning king created the Divine Cadre to appease the dark fae leaders. Matings became rare, worshippers on earth dwindled, crystal magic decreased, and now less crystal magic fae are being born."

"But void magic is certainly surging," Ox said. "You don't hear them complaining of that."

"Certainly not," Sedge said. "Not with Gentian being the most powerful void fae of them all."

I glowered. Fucking Gentian—he seemed dead set on ruining everything I held dear.

Maybe it was the homemade wine Ox broke out, or all the talk of soulmates, but something had put my hosts in an amorous mood. Tansy started the raunchy anecdotes, and everyone else followed suit, trading accounts of their best boudoir exploits. Detailed accounts. Things not even my closest BFFs and I had ever discussed.

I listened as I finished supper, trying not to blush.

Oh, knock that off, Aunt Aylie's voice harangued me. *I'd swear you were a Puritan.*

So, I listened—without choking on supper—as Tansy discussed her favorite experience with anal. I giggled in all the proper places as Olea and Ox narrated the tale of their first hook-up—somehow, they'd managed through the bars of a cage. And I didn't make a peep as Sedge described screwing a tavern wench on the back of a galloping horse. However, when Pete regaled us with the tale of how Gentian whored him out to two of his friends' ceylas, I couldn't withhold my appall.

"He *what*?" I spat, clenching my bowl.

Pete waved Ox's wine bottle in disregard. "Fear not, virtuous youngblood, it did me no harm. I got to sleep in a bed, for once, aye. And the company, though not the sweetest, suited me fine."

Ox snickered. "Those overweening beyns certainly were fond of you."

Pete opened his hands. "What can I say? I deliver."

His friends groaned at his boasting.

"Of course, they might've liked me for the simple fact that I'm human." He glanced over at me. "Fae and humans can't conceive, ken? So, they could enjoy a nice romp on me without the concern of offspring."

"You mean—you weren't—didn't you feel—used?"

Everyone laughed at the notion.

Pete's expression slanted. "I suppose I did, but I was quite happy in the using. Besides, I used them right back, didn't I?"

My face burned. "How should I know?"

He chuckled, eyes dancing. "I suppose you wouldn't, virgin that you are."

I gaped at him.

"Oh, that's not nice, Peter," Tansy chastised, flashing me a sweet, mildly condescending smile. "She's old enough to have fed the kitty."

I fought the urge to ball up like a hedgehog.

"Aye, she is," Pete agreed, ignoring my disconcertion. Maybe relishing it. "But she hasn't. Have you, Shorty? Otherwise, this conversation wouldn't put you in such a dither."

Oh, how I resented his certainty.

"Stop it, Pete," Olea said. "You're making her uncomfortable."

"Precisely my point," he returned.

Such arrogance! I couldn't let it go unanswered. "For your information, you asshole, I'm not a virgin. I was just confounded by your cavalier attitude toward being raped."

Pete's brows rose. "*Raped*?"

"Yeah!" I goggled at him. "You were raped, you dumbass."

He scoffed, sitting straighter. "That's ridiculous. I—"

"Did you have a choice in the matter?" I flung the question at him. "Did you even like the beyns Gentian lent you to—like you were some goddamn lawn tool?"

He blinked at me, sobering.

"If you'd said no, struggled, what would've happened to you?"

His hardening eyes were all the response I needed.

"That's what I thought. You were a slave, Pete, which meant your will to make your own choices had been taken from you. Which meant any sexual attention Gentian sent your way was foisted. It was imposed. You were forced."

I watched Pete's eyes darken like oil for a moment, but then he rebounded, brushed off his disquiet with a gruff, "My, my, my." He handed Sedge the community wine bottle. "Views on that account have certainly changed in America since I was last there."

I sniffed. "Most views have changed since then, you old geezer."

The insult lightened the pall I'd dropped upon the group. Everyone chuckled.

"Well, tell us about it, Shorty," Tansy took me off guard once their amusement faded.

"Tell you about what?"

"The sex." Her supper finished, she set her bowl at her feet. One of the beagles panted over to lick it clean. "What was your best time like?"

I pursed my lips, astounded again.

"Go on, Shorty." Pete swatted my arm. "Tell us all about it—if you've had it."

Be a romance heroine, I ordered myself. *Don't be ashamed of your sexuality.*

"Fine." I turned from Pete. "I don't have much to tell you, though. I've only had sex twice."

"See, I told you," Pete said.

Olea pointed a finger at him. "Pipe down, you."

"Anyway," I continued. "I—uh—well—his name was Briar. He was very attractive—cute face, muscles, height—the whole package. We did it the night of Beltane."

"Beltane of this year?" Tansy asked. "That was only weeks ago."

"Yeah. We'd been dating—er, courting—for a short while, and he and I spent the entire Beltane festival together."

"I didn't think Beltane was still celebrated in America," Pete puzzled.

I gritted my teeth, knowing to divulge too much of my actual life might blow the cover off my identity. "The festival was really just a barbeque between our two families. Not a very big event at all."

Liar, liar, pants on fire.

"Anyway, we were having fun, drinking, eating moonberries—"

"*Moonberries?*"

That exclamation had issued from everyone.

"Yeah." I peered around, put off by their amazement. "So?"

Pete snickered into a hand, shaking his head before meeting my clueless gaze. "Shorty, moonberries are a potent aphrodisiac."

I gulped. "Huh?"

"They make the animal urge to copulate almost uncontrollable. Jaysus, and you think *I* was raped. He drugged you."

I shook my head, unsettled once more. "No. No, he didn't."

"Sounds like he did," Sedge noted, passing the bottle to Ox.

"Then he drugged himself too," I said. "Because he was eating them."

And drinking them by the gallon.

When Tansy cringed, I realized I'd made it seem like Briar needed the moonberries to get in the mood to screw me.

"It's just a custom. Okay?"

"Dananns," Ox muttered. "Can't even let Beltane happen naturally."

Right then, I shared his contempt.

I set my supper bowl beside my seat, Sionna already there to gobble my leftovers. "Anyway, toward the end of the night, Briar led me from the party, took me to a pretty little cabin he'd rented."

Aunt Aylie rented, you mean.

I forced a dreamy smile. "He'd lit candles, brought us a fruit basket, some wine. And—uh—that's where it happened."

"Who initiated it?" Tansy probed. "And how?"

"He did." I swallowed again. "He told me he wanted me, then he—uh—stripped off my clothes." If I continued much longer, I was going to spontaneously combust.

Tansy wasn't afraid of fire, however. She grinned, settling into the story. "Smashing. Then what happened?"

"Then—he kissed me, lifted me up, and laid me on the bed. He undressed himself and then—" My hand shook as I smoothed an eyebrow. "Then he laid down on me and, uh, just—" I made a flustered hand gesture, clicked my tongue. "Into me."

The silence that followed was worse than the personal inquiries.

"He didn't spend any time petting you?" Olea finally spoke, balancing the wine bottle on her knee. "Touching you? Readying you for such a pivotal moment?"

How could I say that I'd had sex but had never even felt my lover's lips on my breasts? "Well—"

"Did he even check to make sure you were ready?" Tansy clutched her bulging cleavage, bereft for me.

"I—I don't remember."

Another lie. He totally hadn't.

"My goddess," Tansy breathed. "I imagine it must've hurt then."

I coughed. "Yeah, it did." Didn't a deflowering always hurt? "But it didn't last that long, so it wasn't that bad."

Their horror only compounded.

Olea looked sad. "You didn't get the chance to learn the full joys of your body?"

I laughed at the verbose euphemism. "Not with Briar, but I'd already learned the full joys on my own. Trust me."

That last spoken thought immediately embarrassed me. Nobody else minded, of course.

"Ah," Sedge remarked. "Then you knew what you were missing. More's the pity."

I exhaled, seeing no point in disagreement. "Yeah."

"Would this Briar be the bloke you were traveling with?" Pete's voice sounded deeper, rougher.

I couldn't bring myself to look at him as I nodded.

"The one you're meant to marry?"

I nodded again.

"That explains it," Ox said. "This wanker obviously doesn't feel the need to woo you, as you're promised to him already. There's no risk of losing you."

"Or, he doesn't truly want the betrothal," Sedge supplied. "From the look on your face, lady, I reckon you don't want it either."

I tossed up a hand. "Yeah, well, does it even matter now? Can't hardly get married as a prisoner in the Shadow Palace!"

At that, I hopped up from my seat and snatched the wine bottle from Olea. The tangy sweetness of blueberries poured down my throat as I clomped back to my seat. I coughed at the spicy aftertaste and plopped down. Everyone watched me for an uneasy space while I hunched there, brooding.

I assumed I'd destroyed the good vibes from dinner until a bear paw swiped the wine from me. "You call that a bad sex story?" Pete downed a hearty swig. "Why, that's hardly the worst in this bunch. I know Ox here has accidentally fucked a Greenie. More than once. And appearance-wise, they're truly just one step above toads."

Everyone burst out laughing.

Ox's green face flashed orange. "You ken their kind shape shift! The conniving goon started out a nymph! Bobbling tits and all! Next thing I know, it had bulging eyes and webbed feet! And I was scuttered off my arse both times!"

Sedge chortled. "Off the Greenie's arse too, it seems."

I just about fell off my log, my pathetic deflowering all but forgotten.

The friendly gathering was still thriving when the exhaustion of weeks caught up to me. Concentrating on not falling asleep, I felt a warm hand on my shoulder and heard a deep voice murmur, "Olea, will you please show her to bed?"

I rose when prodded and followed Olea to another of the wagons, this one less decorated but still homey. While Olea unlocked the rear entrance of the wagon, the only one whose doors weren't already spread wide in welcome, I leaned back against its deep purple body and gazed up at the sky.

My eyes rounded to saucers as I caught rainbows rippling in the stars. "Oh, wow!" I stepped further into the night. I'd seen pictures of the northern lights on the internet, but none of those images did the actual show justice. "That's gorgeous!"

Olea joined me a moment later, smiling up at the spectacle as if it were a distant dream of hers. "More than gorgeous, I'd say. The aurora majesta is a portent of hope for those like us."

I glanced down at her, curious.

"There's a prophecy, aye? About the birth of a new triple goddess. The Aurora is what the prophet named her. She's meant to be a savior, to break the shackles of those enslaved, to ease the toiling of those living in squalor and poverty, and to bring justice to those suffering oppression."

My throat dried out. "She's supposed to do all that, huh?"

"And more."

If I was truly the Aurora, as Briar had suspected, then I'd be a mighty big disappointment to those who expected miracles.

"Are the lights supposed to signal that this goddess has been born?"

"Possibly." Olea shrugged. "Or maybe it signals that she's come of age, that she's started down fate's path."

I grimaced, my path leading me straight to doom.

Olea took my hand. "Come. Let's settle you for the night. If I don't return soon, I won't get any more wine. Pete and Ox will surely drink the rest."

I followed her to a night of restful sleep among the faint scents of orange blossoms and oak moss.

TWENTY-ONE

T he dream changes again. This time, I instantly recognize the ominous shadow man as Pete. A strange but welcome tension accompanies his presence. My heart races as he and his shadows plume toward me, but not with my usual terror. Instead, I'm excited. I'm relieved. I'm—safe?

I don't even struggle against capture, though I demand my immediate release. Of course, Pete ignores me, cloaking me in ebony velvet. His gruff hands take me, draw me close.

There's no need to fear his dark.

The mocking eyes from my last dream soften, warm like fresh ginger snaps. His rough fingers graze my neck, shivers erupting on my skin.

I meet his gaze, breathless for a long, tender moment.

"Run!" my own voice shrieks in the background. "Just *run!*"

I ignore the warning as Pete's smiling mouth descends on mine.

I awoke just before the kiss and popped up in bed, clapping a hand over my thundering heart. "What the hell was that?"

I stared at the tattered yellow flag nailed to the wall ahead of me. I'd noticed it last night, but in the dark, I hadn't made out its coiled, hissing rattlesnake. Now, bright sunlight broke through the hemp curtains beside me, highlighting the reptile, the warning beneath: *Don't tread on me.* The rebel motto during the American Revolution.

My mouth fell, my eyes darting about the wagon. A framed copy of The Declaration of Independence hung above the woodstove. Another tattered flag that read "join or die" was stuck with knives into the wall behind me, proudly sporting musket ball holes and gunpowder stains. A wooden rosary hung from the haft of one of those knives. Clothes of a large male lay piled by the dining table, more stuffed into a nicked armoire beside the bed. Dusty boots and rumpled trousers cluttered the floor in various places. A high ledge trimmed the entire wagon's perimeter, housing history books, classic novels, and references on every subject, including weaponry and wildlife of all worlds.

Breathing in the aroma of oranges and oak moss, I swore into my hands. Pete hadn't just crashed his friends' camp the night before. He lived in this wagon. I'd spent the night in his bed.

Loud banging signaled an intrusion. I shielded the thinness of my shift with a musty quilt as Pete bounced into view, back in his black togs, though they'd been scoured clean over the night. Rakish charm oozed from his scruffy face.

Stop it, I scolded my heart, which had accelerated at his morning dishevelment. My eyes fell right to his lips. So soft, so damn generous. They curled at the corners.

"Glad you're awake." His voice was still groggy from sleep.

Oh, Goddess, how sexy.

Knock it off!

Pete tossed me some type of biscuit. It bounced off my forehead and landed in my lap. "Get dressed," he ordered, taking a bite of his own. "The road awaits."

I sneered as he swaggered away.

An hour later, I wore my new travel gear and trusty off-brand Buggs. Pete and I hiked on either side of Bob in the sunshine across sprawling sweet pea fields.

Sionna scampered ahead of us. Having spent the night with her canine clique, she was clearly in better spirits. A good rest and friendly interaction had done likewise for Pete and me.

For the brief time we'd been back on the road, neither of us had spoken. Pete was focused on the horizon, and thoughts of home engrossed me, arousing memories of a simple ballad.

"What's that?"

I glanced over Bob's back at Pete. "What?"

"That melody you're humming."

I hadn't realized I'd been humming.

"It's bonny."

His approval weirdly flattered me. "It's just a new version of a song—'Know My Love.' I downloaded it just before I had to leave."

"Sounds incredibly sugary."

"It is. But that word describes most of the songs I love. I'm kind of a sap."

Pete grunted, his high spirits faltering. "He's all right, ken."

My brows drew together. *Who?*

"Your fella." I'd exasperated him again, it seemed. I was getting good at that. "Briar."

I stared. How would he know of Briar's welfare?

"Sedge encountered him at the Thorny Rose Tavern the morning after we met." Pete cleared his throat. "Said he was raising Cain over your whereabouts, threatening to flood Jade's larder with tainted water if she didn't tell him precisely where you were and what had become of you."

Briar can do that? "Did she tell him?"

"Not in so many words. Sedge said Jade played the fool—told Briar you were there, asking after him. She claimed she was keeping an eye out for your feyr until she saw you getting friendly with one of her patrons. She assumed him to be the chap you were waiting on and didn't think twice when you and the unnamed patron were gone before she woke."

"Great! So, not only does Briar probably think I'm dead, but now he also thinks I might've been macking on some other dude."

You kind of were, my inner voice scolded me.

Pete's pointed expression mimicked my thoughts.

"Oh, shut up."

He laughed.

Despite myself, I grinned.

"Be at ease, Shorty. He may have thought you fickle, but he didn't seem to think you dead. After Jade's account, he stormed from the tavern, declaring his intent to track your trail."

I sucked in a sharp breath, my hopes soaring.

Pete's amusement softened. "Sorry, darlin'. Neither I nor Sionna has picked up on another's scent. Your betrothed may be a right powerful bugger, but he's no tracker."

"You don't know that. Maybe he's just keeping far enough behind us, so you can't smell him. So he can rush in and rescue me when you drop your guard."

"Playing the long game, is he?"

I scowled, eliciting more laughter.

"Besides, if he were any good at tracking, he'd have scented me long before I sent those sluaghs after him."

I stopped dead.

Pete and Bob moseyed on, the former shamelessly smirking over his shoulder.

My leather pants squeaked as I scurried to jump in Bob's path. The donkey tramped to a stop, braying at me. I ignored him, my glare solely for Pete.

"You *what*?"

Pete faced me, hands open. "I needed him out of my way, and the sluaghs were the easiest solution. Would you rather I had killed him?"

My whole body went rigid, my hands fisting. "How long were you stalking us?"

Pete ran a hand down Bob's neck when he railed again. "Sionna and I caught your scent just after you passed through Avenshire. Did you realize your scent grows stronger when you're angry?" He sniffed the air. "Aye, you're as ripe as a pear tree at dawn now. Just as you were then."

Heat crept up my neck. I was beginning to smolder.

"I did wonder why you were so irate." Pete raised a hand, and Sionna stopped dead like a statue of a pointing hound. "I had to keep fairly far behind you to remain undetected, so I couldn't hear why you were arguing."

"Good! It was none of your business!"

"My marks' lives are never my business. Still, I listen, and I did catch something important on the wind—*Amy*."

I gaped, more than startled. *What the hell else had he heard?*

"If you knew my real name this whole time, why the hell didn't you just tell me that? Why go around calling me Shorty all the damn time?"

He snickered, leaning to get in my face. "Because I could tell it nettled your knickers."

Pete ducked just in time to escape the fireball that exploded out of me. It flew over him, bursting like a firecracker when it hit the knoll we traversed.

Rattled to my core, I trembled when Pete surged back up, clasping my wrists. "That was good, Shorty," he praised, all provocation gone. "You managed to stay on your feet that time, and you didn't blaze until you guttered out. Your aim is fair too."

"You—you did that on purpose?" His touch was as rough and warm as it had been in my dream. "You just said all that stuff to rile my fire?"

"Aye—although, I spoke true."

I ripped my wrists from his hands, stepped back.

Pete stroked his beard, studying me. "For now, it appears your fire is triggered by anger, which isn't the best news. Anger's too volatile an emotion. Too hard to control. Too unreliable when you need it."

"Well, that's the only thing that brings it on. That, and when I'm facing death."

He clicked his tongue. "A last defense is handy, indeed. But it's insufficient when we need your power for offensive measures."

I folded my arms across my chest, considering him as closely as he was considering me. "What's this *we* stuff? And why are *we* needing offensive measures?"

He exhaled. "I've been thinking, Shorty."

Why the hell are you still calling me Shorty when you know my real name?

"You're right."

I eyed him. Was he being sarcastic?

His gaze was open, genuine. "You don't deserve the fate I'm lugging you to, and I want to help you out of it."

I reeled back another step. "Are you—are you serious? You've changed your mind about delivering me to Gentian?"

"No, I'll still deliver you."

I was going to punch him in his nuts.

"So you can help me kill him."

Say what?

He paced, a wily gleam in his eyes. "See, if you're right, and Gentian doesn't ken you're a fire sylph, then he won't be prepared to contain you. So, if you gain control of your power, when we get that first audience with him, you can—you can just annihilate him and his cadre. They'll *never* see it coming."

Has he lost his mind?

"Doesn't Gentian equip his harbingers with fire retardant tethers? Why wouldn't he have a contingency in place for someone like me at his palace?"

Pete chewed his lip. "He might."

Again, his blunt honesty was refreshing. Startling, but refreshing.

"But even if he does, I'd wager the weapons to stop you won't be readily at hand. Gentian's too confident in his informants—he assumes they know all and tell all. If they don't have the knowledge of you to warn him, he won't prepare his men for such an onslaught.

"Besides, ossified emerald is damn expensive." Pete gestured at my invisible shackle. "He may supply his harbingers with several strands of it, just in case, but there's no way he wasted seeds on emerald armor. Not when he believes fire sylphen are extinct. Gentian's hardly a miser where defense is concerned, but he *is* a pragmatist."

I massaged my forehead, trying to wrap my brain around his scheme. "Pete—my magic—it's so unpredictable. I can't—"

"That's why I'm going to help you," he returned, calm as the Pacific.

He moved toward me but didn't reach for me, seeming to sense my momentary aversion for touch. How many times had Briar missed similar cues? He could've taken a page out of Pete's book.

"We've still a few weeks left on our journey. We can spend that time training."

"*Training*?" I laughed, scraping my hands through my hair.

"Aye." His voice gentled. "You must train to brandish your magic like the weapon it's meant to be. And I'll teach you to fight—if ever the need for defense arises." He might as well have said *when* the need arises. "Please, let me help you, and when we're done, you'll be a force to be reckoned with."

I squealed and doubled over. *Goddess, save me. This can't be my life.*

"He killed your father, Shorty!" Pete exclaimed in a spurt of passion, his cool flying the coop. "And whatever he wants you for now, in the end, he'll damn well kill you too!"

"I know that! That's why I don't want to go there, Pete!"

He set hands on his hips, shaking his head at the sky. "Even if I were to set you free right now, and you ran off to whatever home awaits you, Gentian *will* find you, and the second harbinger will come with a death ordination."

I plopped down in the grass, a tempest raging in my head. As frantic as I was, it took me a moment to realize a tiny tornado of pollen and petals was spiraling about me. It took me one more to realize I was causing it.

Pete knelt, determined, and met my eyes through my storm. "Even if you somehow evade that harbinger, get away with your life, he'll never stop hunting you. The curse won't allow it. Do you really want to spend the rest of your life running, always looking over your shoulder? The threat of death always at your back?"

"Pete—"

"Or would you rather take a chance on a bold move that would not only free *you* from this curse, but also *thousands* of slaves from Gentian's cruelty, oppression, and abuse?"

Chills raced along my limbs.

The Aurora is what the prophet named her, Olea's voice echoed through my head. *She's meant to be a savior, to break the shackles of those enslaved, to ease the toiling of those living in squalor and poverty, and to bring justice to those suffering from oppression.*

But it couldn't be me!

"Maybe you don't think your own soul is worth the risk of fighting back, but aren't all those others?"

I glared. How dare he put that weight on me! "Says the man who wanted to sacrifice my soul to save his own. Only days ago."

Pete gulped, glanced away. Was that shame on his face? "Aye," he agreed, his voice harsh. "That was before I'd had time to think like the man I once was."

You won't feel sympathy for him right now!

"I concluded that aiding you is not only moral—but necessary. Unlikely though it may seem, *you* are the only one in all the world who stands a fighting chance of killing the Shadow Prince." He clasped his hands together, pleading. "You're my only hope, Amy."

My breath stilled at the sound of my true name on his lips.

"You're your only hope too."

Silence stretched between us, my emotional cyclone dwindling as we sat there, facing each other in charged suspense.

Sionna finally broke our stare, wagging over and butting my hand with her nose. I lifted my hand to her silky neck, expelling a shaky breath.

"You won't face him alone," Pete brogued. "I'll be right there with you, fighting. And if we go down, we go down together."

There they were—the most romantic words ever uttered to me. Even though he didn't mean them to be.

"At least we'll have tried," he concluded.

But what if we did fail? Then I'd be dead. And there'd be nothing standing in the way of the blood curse and Vi.

I physically shook myself. "I need time to think. Please."

Pete snatched my arm, wrenching me back to my feet, gruff as a grizzly. I stumbled when he released me. He barely noticed, swaggering back to Bob. "Mull it over. We'll train in the meantime. You need control, regardless. I don't relish the thought of dodging fireballs every time I pique your temper."

I snorted, joining him by the wagon. "You could just stop saying shit that makes me mad."

The devil was in Pete's grin. "Now who's asking the impossible?"

Flung to the ground like a frisbee, I rolled away in time to evade Pete, who seemed intent on flattening me. Panting, I pushed up to a crouch, anticipating another attack.

Barely winded, Pete rose back to his full, rather intimidating height. "Well done, Shorty." His eyes gleamed, always assessing, strategizing. Part of his predatory prowess, I guessed. "You found your feet that time."

I gripped my knees, seeing stars.

We'd paused in our travels to train, and we'd been doing just that since dawn. First, in the art of magical control, second, in combat. I guessed it was near to two in the afternoon, and I was drained to the point of exhaustion and quaking from low blood sugar. Plus, I suffered the pain of numerous cuts and bruises from fending off a tireless behemoth.

"A break—*please*," I gasped, lights flashing around his head.

"No. You have weak stamina. In a fight for your life, your attacker will lend no respite. They'll batter you until you succumb. I'll do you no favors by going easy on you now. You must learn to push past your limits. You'll go further than you think capable. Believe me, Shorty."

Nauseous, I spat between my feet, then forced myself upright. "Fine," I growled, glaring. "But just so you know—you suck."

A shoulder to my midsection punctuated the insult. The last thing I saw before I blacked out was a fuzzy thimble fae on a violet.

I awoke hours later in the back of Pete's wagon. Aching, I sat up to discover we'd abandoned our training camp. Now, Pete was building a fire beneath a lone elm in a small clearing amidst a wild wheat field. The suns were setting, the breeze cooling.

Hearing me, my trainer/tormenter turned about. "You woke sooner than I thought you would."

I sneered, crawling out of the wagon and hobbling over to him.

"You're moving better than I assumed you would too."

I sniffed, kneading a sore spot in the small of my back. "Sorry you didn't paralyze me."

He chuckled, dropped the bundle of sticks he'd been holding, and approached. "Again, I needed to push you to your limits, and I did. Maybe tomorrow you'll last a mite longer before you swoon."

He wasn't joking. He expected me to pass out. Was that the only way a training session would end?

I stiffened further when Pete slipped behind me, grabbed my hips. "Uh, what are you doing?"

"Easing your back pain," he said, and I shivered as strong, callused thumbs nudged beneath my top and pressed into my spine.

Even in a massage, Pete handled me like vulcanized rubber. He massaged me with the finesse of a billy goat, assuming my flesh would bounce back. And, *ooh*, did I enjoy being touched like a durable substance instead of spun glass.

I realized that I might like it too much when Pete's grinding fingers slid to my lower dimples. My body melted into his hands, and Pete's fingers slowed to a firmer, more deliberate pressure. Almost cajoling. Almost seductive.

Pete must've felt the shift too. He dropped his hands, and I missed the rasping warmth of his fingers. "Hope that helps." He returned to his chores with a crooked grin, his cheeks now a shade darker.

I watched as he knelt to regather his kindling. "It does." I gulped as my eyes locked onto the toned curve of his ass. "Thanks."

"Why don't you eat some of the jerked riggit Olea packed for us, then have another lie-down? There's something I want to do tonight, and I can't have you wilting while we do it."

The ghost of his touch lingered on my back. "What do you want to do?"

Pete templed his sticks. "We're a brief stroll from Glynlea—where the Goblin Market will appear come midnight. Thought you might enjoy seeing it."

We were going *shopping*?

"You earned a reward for your efforts today. Let me know if something catches your fancy, and I'll give you the seeds for it."

If gleeful at first—to see the mythical market, to do something normal and commonplace—suspicion quickly followed. "Why?"

"I told you—you did well today." He looked innocent enough—or as innocent as Pete could look. "That's all."

"You wouldn't be trying to bribe me, would you?"

"Bribe you? Why would I do that? Waste a sum from my own purse on the slim chance that I might sweeten you into helping me kill Gentian?" His mouth quirked. "The thought never crossed my mind."

Oh, you wheedling rascal—

"If this reward you're offering has strings attached, then keep it. Your gifts won't affect my decision—whatever it is in the end."

As I strode back to the wagon to scrounge up some of that jerky he'd mentioned, I heard him say, "We'll see," under his breath.

The moon was full and bright in the sky when I awoke again, a wet nose against my neck. I giggled up at Sionna, scratching behind her floppy ears as Pete towered into view. "Up and at 'em," he said. "The market has opened."

Despite being warm and semi-cozy in Pete's bedroll, I sprang to my feet, ready for bargain hunting.

"No, Sionna," Pete gently scolded his hound, who seemed as excited for shopping as I was, when she made to follow us into the wheat. He stroked her head. "I told you—you stay here with Bob, keep watch of our camp and our belongings. We'll return in several hours, maybe with a treat."

That seemed to mitigate her disappointment, though she harrumphed as she curled into Pete's bedroll, staring after us as we left.

"Why couldn't she come?" I asked Pete as we forged into the wheat together. "She wouldn't cause any trouble."

"Aye, but the Goblins may." Pete took the lead, tromping down fronds, so I could walk unhindered.

How gentlemanly, I thought. *And unexpected.*

"Goblins have a taste for dog," Pete said. "While I'd wager most have sense enough not to steal their supper from a harbinger, I'd best not tempt fate."

I grimaced, picturing Sionna rotating on a spit. "Yeah, that's probably wise."

"She's sore with me now, but we'll be fast friends again when I return with a hearty slab of bacon."

I smiled at his fondness for her. "How did you find her?"

"I didn't." Pete glanced back at me. "She was given to me. By Gentian."

I shook my head. "Handing out puppies—doesn't seem like his thing."

"It's not. Customarily, harbingers select their hounds from Gentian's fighting kennels—mostly gigantic war hounds called pawlers, who've already seen a few matches themselves."

I hated that thought.

"But upon me—the harbinger he most detested—he foisted what he considered the weakest, feeblest, most skittish mutt in his collection. I suppose he thought it a fantastic joke. My overseer snickered like a jester when he dropped Sionna in my arms—said she was hopelessly immune to training and bid me a sarcastic good luck before he left me to the task of making her a snuff hound."

Pete smirked. "Little did they know, but he'd handed me the best hound I could've asked for."

His words warmed my soul.

"At first, I was beside myself. Sionna was skinny, mangy, and fair afraid of me, shivering in the darkest corner of my bunk. She wouldn't let me touch her for a full week and would only eat the food I offered her when she knew she was alone. Couldn't rightly blame her, of course. The way the masters train Gentian's hounds—it's a good deal of screaming and beating."

How could anyone treat a sweetheart like Sionna so cruelly? "Let me guess—Sionna responded more to positive reinforcement."

"If you mean she preferred a gentle hand and a kind voice, then aye."

"Exactly what I mean."

"Once we'd become friendly enough to attempt training, I realized Sionna had a mind quicker than a minnow can swim a dipper. I'd repeat a command two, maybe three times, and she'd master it. Against other snuffs, she's always the smartest, the fastest, and her nose is *uncanny*. She's indispensable to me now. She still quails at her own shadow, and bigger hounds easily bully her, but she does her job, and I wouldn't change her for anything. It's taboo to say so among fellow harbingers, but she's my family—or the closest thing to it I've found in this world."

Goddess save me, I loved the way he loved her.

"Anyhow, after we left those hellhole barracks and established camp, Sionna popped right out of her shell. Mostly."

Hadn't Briar said I'd done something similar after moving to college? "Sometimes a change of environment makes all the difference."

Pete nodded. "Aye."

"Then I was right," I said more to myself than to Pete. "You do live at the camp with Olea and everyone. That wagon I stayed in that night—it was yours."

"Indeed it was, Shorty. How'd you like your sleep?" He winked. "I've a soft bed, don't I?"

For once, I was glad for darkness. He couldn't see me blush.

I cleared my throat, ignoring his suggestive question. "How long have you lived there?"

"Roughly nine years."

"I'm still shocked Gentian allows his harbingers to live outside the Shadow Court."

"He doesn't pay much mind to where we choose to lay our heads. In fact, he prefers that his harbingers strike out on their own. Then he mustn't waste seeds on our upkeep. Not that he spends much on that, anyhow. I lived several years in the harbingers' barracks. We mostly had to fend for ourselves there as well."

"But doesn't that make it hard for Gentian to keep an eye on all his minions? I mean, if they're free to roam—"

Halting, Pete knelt to touch one of his ankles. A shadow tether, much thicker than mine, appeared in silvery moonlight.

"So, when you said you had no allegiance to Gentian other than the shadow tether that binds you—"

"I meant this." He gestured toward the smoky loop, night highlighting his glower. "This is how he tracks us no matter where we've roamed. If he sees fit to visit, he can follow the tether. Or he can send his punishers to do his visiting for him—if he thinks we've gone rogue."

Though as thick as a ship rigging, his tether was only pure shadow—no streaks of anything like ossified emerald. So, why not better his situation? And mine in the process.

Realizing why my face had grown pinched, Pete grabbed my hands, folded my fingers—looking caught between wanting to laugh and wanting to hug me. "If it were that simple, Shorty, I'd have roasted the damn thing years ago."

"It can't be burnt?"

"It can." He squeezed one of my hands. In thanks, I guessed. "But burning it off won't win me my freedom, for then I'd be a hunted man."

"Have any other harbingers tried to break free?"

"Aye, two that I know of. They were both captured and beheaded with the utmost haste. Their rotting bodies are displayed on pikes in the barracks dooryard."

Yikes!

"So, I'm afraid I must decline your help, though I appreciate your kindness."

Swallowing at the timbre of his voice, I withdrew from him, the feel of his skin too pleasant—becoming too familiar to me. Pete merely smiled at my brush-off, like he understood.

I cleared my throat, recomposing myself. "Is that tether the source of your own shadow powers?"

He exhaled, motioning me forward with him. "Honestly, Shorty, I don't ken. After Gentian dosed me, a chasm swallowed me until I was completely overcome."

"A chasm?"

"Well, that's what I've called it when questioned by those who care to know. It's not a fitting description. Words hardly explain the reality. Not that anyone wants to hear that desolate truth, anyhow."

I watched him, wondering how I'd cope with losing my soul, however briefly, if I didn't have somebody to talk to about it. "You can tell me if you want. I mean—" I shrugged, chuckling. "Words don't scare me."

Pete searched the sky like he was asking Danu how to answer me. Or maybe he just couldn't bear to look at me as he choked, "It's like a stagnant lake—a lake that's only ever used for drowning."

Gooseflesh spread along my arms.

"You can't—your *soul* can't—find a way to breathe in there, this inescapable vacuum. But you just keep swimming for the surface, hoping, only to be crushed back down—until you can no longer hold your breath. Then you've no choice but to inhale, and that's when the evil swells into you—fills you with cold. And you become a crock full of the worst parts of yourself.

"That—that's the bit I tend to keep to myself. That evil—it came from within *me*—these hidden slivers of latent depravity. The poppy's poison—it merely bloated those tendencies of mine until there was room for nothing else. And I sank under the weight of my own badness, wholly unbalanced and demonic. Still to this day, I grapple with knowing the monster dwelling in the bowels of my soul—he was always there, just in smaller pieces."

Chills burgeoned along my neck as well. Not from fear of Pete, but because gazing at him right then—I was looking in a mirror. Didn't I also see a monster whenever I dared to peer inside myself—an angry, scared, ugly, unworthy monster? Didn't I amplify all my flaws until they obscured even my greatest assets? Didn't they drive me to act shamefully at times? Like whenever I spurned strangers who might judge me, even when they'd never been unkind. Or when I set fire to people who called me a bitch. Hadn't I, for one split second, been glad when I'd heard Scully's excruciated death yowl? Didn't that make me a cold-hearted killer?

Pete and I had more in common than I'd guessed.

"Sounds like death poppy inflates the id," I remarked after several moments' thought, recalling snippets from my Psychopathology course.

Pete's distant expression focused, sharp as a tack. "The id, you say?"

"Yeah. It's part of a theory on personalities developed by—"

"I've heard of Freud, Shorty," Pete interrupted, chuckling. "I'm just baffled you hold stock in his theories. Wasn't it he who claimed women envied men their cocks?"

I burst out laughing. Because he was right!

"Of all the preposterous notions—" Pete grumbled, smirking. "Envy, my arse. Any female with a cunny can have as many cocks as she pleases. For breakfast, lunch, and supper."

Tears squeezed from my eyes. "Don't forget dessert!"

"Oh, indeed—the best meal for cock."

I snorted, paralyzed. Pete caught me before I toppled over.

"Oh, Goddess," I groaned, dabbing my tears. The man who kept causing them chuckled as I righted myself. "I forgot about penis envy—such bullshit."

"Aye—that's why I questioned you."

"I didn't say I agreed with the dude, Pete. I just find how he classified parts of personalities clever. The id is basically a person's primitive impulses—your selfish urges and your basest desires—your need to have exactly what you want *right fucking now*." I paused to shrug. "And anyone's a demon if that's all they're functioning with."

He grunted, his lips pursing.

"I'm just saying—that monster in you is no worse than the monster in everyone else. The death poppy just took away your ability to control it."

He quieted, considering me with such an avid gleam that I found myself closing the distance to him. Like a moth drawn to a tall, dark, and rugged candle.

Shaking myself, I skipped aside, out of his bubble. "Anyway—you—you were explaining how you got your shadows. Remember?"

"Ah, right." Pete grinned like a male who knew he'd ruffled a female—and was gratified by it. "Well, when I finally came to, cold to my core, I had my shadows." He shrugged. "I don't recall a moment of receiving them."

"Hm, not nearly as informative as you usually are, Pete, but I'll give you a pass on this one."

Pete chuckled. "Appreciated, Shorty."

"As long as you do better with my next question."

He rolled his eyes.

"So, say Gentian told you that he'd release you from servitude, that he'd remove that tether and let you go—that you'd never have to see him again. If you knew that would also mean renouncing your shadows, would you still do it?"

His eyes sharpened. "In a heartbeat, Shorty."

I chewed my lip, debating his honesty. Most men in history would've rather given up their lives than give up power.

Noting my skepticism, Pete sniffed. "Would I miss my shadows? Aye, most likely. They've helped me through many a stramash over the years. And this—"

I yelped when darkness enveloped me. Black velvet surrounded Pete's wry face—the only thing I could make out in his temperate oblivion.

Just like in my dream.

"This cloak has kept me out of many more stramashes." I jerked into Pete, wisps caressing my back—shadow tethers. But at least he kept his hands to himself. "It has also helped me woo many a fine beyn in want of discretion." His lips took a lazy curl, his eyes dipping along me.

I folded my arms. "Are you done trying to make me forget what we're talking about?"

Laughing, he freed me to the moonlight, and we moved along. "I'd renounce *all* my powers if it meant true freedom, Shorty. My magic is what got me here, and I've never been one of the fools who reveres his chains."

I reeled back. "I've read that phrase before." In fact, it was in the forward of one of the political books Daddy had given me.

"You've read Voltaire?"

"Not really, but I skimmed through a compilation of his works. My dad gave it to me."

"You should've read it from cover to cover." Pete peered up at the stars, diamonds swimming the aurora majesta's surf. "He was a brilliant thinker. Witty as well."

"Wasn't he also a major hater of Catholicism? I'm surprised you're okay with that."

"What makes you assume I'm Catholic?"

"The rosary I found by your bed. Don't know why else you'd have it."

"Very shrewd of you." Pete veered to the right, and I followed, close on his heels.

"You don't mind Voltaire's criticism of your entire belief system?"

Pete shrugged. "I've also never been the fool who hates those who disagree with me, especially on the matter of religion. For on Earth, we were all just guessing. Aye?"

"Still, how did a nice papist boy like yourself, who was probably raised to believe every word of the bible as fact, cope when he got here and learned that the almighty God he'd been worshiping his entire life was actually—" I gasped for dramatic effect. "Dum dum *dum*—an almighty *Goddess*?"

He smirked. "I thought it made more sense—females being the bearers of life. Logically, the creator of all should be of the same fair and glorious sex."

Now, *that* was a downright stunning answer.

"What?" he asked at my dreamy expression.

I shook my head. "Are you sure you're from the 1770s?"

"Aye. As much as you're from the 2010s."

"Yeah." I chuckled, then stopped. "Wait—*what*?"

TWENTY-TWO

"Is this some kind of joke?" I glared at the front page of a newspaper Pete had found me at the market. "It's got to be. You're playing a vicious prank on me."

Pete grimaced at the Washington Post issue. The paper looked and felt genuine—so soft its print transferred to my fingertips—but it *had* to be fake.

"I'm afraid not, Shorty. As you can well see, it's now the year 2018 on Earth. Obama completed two terms as president. Then the pendulum swung too far the other way, and—"

"Buy now or drop now," a voice groused at us. I peered up to find the Goblin owner of the stall we perused glaring at us beneath a fringed Victorian oil lamp.

Goblins looked just as I'd expected. They were slender, olivey little creatures with pointed ears so big they flopped over at the arch. Hooked noses marked their elongated faces—even the unfortunate beyns'. The feyr before me had beady black eyes beneath bushy yellow brows. He was bald but for a smattering of blonde puffs behind his ears, and he smelled like peat moss.

Offering the grumpy Goblin what I hoped was a disarming smile, I set the newspaper back down on its pile amongst a hodgepodge of human contraband and outlawed fae goods.

"You're saying I somehow skipped over the past 10 years?" I asked Pete.

He led me away from the crotchety trader, and we continued weaving through the largest, most elaborate outdoor bazaar I'd ever seen. Stalls suited for horses and lit with fae asters overflowed with minutiae, and a variety of fae in search of a good deal.

"In a manner of speaking," Pete answered. "I'd wager you crossed the portal with a chronopath."

My incomplete understanding must've shown on my face.

"A chronopath is someone who can travel through space and time on Earth. I think that you were born here in the year 1998, but when you crossed to Earth, someone ensured you wound up in the past, years before you were born."

"*Why?*" This question was purely rhetorical. How could Pete explain something he couldn't know? Still, he gave it a go.

"Likely to frustrate Gentian from following you." He regarded me like an uncracked riddle. "Harbingers can easily track you through the human world, but they can't follow your scent into the past."

When I'd touched Angel Oak, had I not only opened the portal to those bogeybats but also guided them through to the correct time? *Ugh.*

"If I've heard true, chronopathy only works on Earth, so when you returned years later, it was to your proper time."

"But I'm still 20, right?" I glanced down at myself. Was everything still in its proper place?

"Aye, Shorty. Those years skipped past you like they never existed." He shrugged. "You're just not a babe of the '80s, I'm afraid."

This I couldn't swallow. The trends of the time in which I was reared had shaped so much of my personality. I mean, without *Late to Class*, *The Baby Sitting Diaries*, the Perfect Princess classics, Gem Pops, and Virtual Pets, would I still be me? Hell, if we'd crossed to earth in real time, I would've been far too young to appreciate the whole pop explosion of the late '90s. I would've missed out on the voices that sang the soundtrack of my life.

I shook my head. "No, I'll always be a baby of the '80s. No matter where or when I was born."

"Suit yourself, Shorty."

I was wondering which of my family members was a chronopath when Pete gasped like he'd seen a ghost. I glanced up to find him ogling an object in the next booth. An object nestled in a bed of green velvet like a precious gemstone.

His hands clenched as he said, "A Kentucky flintlock pistol. I had one just like it. Lost it, ken. To the slaver who nabbed me."

The gun was a perfect historical specimen, something you'd see in a museum. Though I wasn't a fan of firearms, I could admit it was pretty—carved in ornate filigree from handle to barrel.

"I'm surprised I haven't seen more guns at this thing," I remarked on the market. "That's what the black-market on Earth sells. That and drugs."

Pete sniffed. "Guns are outlawed in this world."

"I thought everything from the human world was."

"No. But crossing a portal to earth without royal decree is, so excusing how you procured such earthly items to contraband sniffers would be tricky for the bulk of these Goblin traders. Guns are expressly forbidden, as are ammunition and gunpowder. They're believed to incite violence—embolden cowards."

"I'd think magic is a far more useful weapon, anyway."

Pete shot me a sidelong look. "For those with great power. Not everyone's a fire sylph, Shorty."

I smacked his chest. "Shut up." I eyed the bodies striding past us. Whether anyone had overheard, I remained a target of scrutiny. As per the usual. Even in such a crowded place, surrounded by the most grotesque fae features I'd ever seen, I was somehow still the anomaly in the bunch. "We're keeping that secret."

Pete dismissed my concern with a wave. "The masses are too engrossed in their errands to give a wit about us."

That's when a passing Middling with peacock feathered wings ran into a nearby post for his efforts of gawking at me. Clearly, his errands weren't engrossing enough.

Irritated, I twirled back to Pete. "Let's just go ask about the gun. I know you want to."

When I started forward, Pete barred me, sheepish for once. "This is sure to infuriate you, but I ken that trader—goes by the name Osnots. Which, if I recall correctly, means something akin to *Anti She* in Goblesh. He likely won't deal with me if I've a beyn in tow."

I sighed. "Then give me some slack on the damn tether, and I'll go browsing while you haggle with Mr. 'Big-Man Beyn Hater.'"

Amused by my reference without getting it, Pete added length to our smoggy connection. "Don't stray too far. If there's one thing Goblins fancy more than dog meat, it's a good toss with a pretty lass."

I harrumphed before sauntering off. *Pretty? Psh!* Maybe I'd do for a screw in the dark. With everyone staring like I was Pennywise from *It*, I didn't think they'd ravish me for my looks.

I rubbed the chill of the clear night from my arms and strolled through the throngs, trying to ignore the relentless discourtesy directed my way. I first stopped when I spied a message board, bulletins nailed across every spare inch of space. Their flowing calligraphy did little to lessen the impact of the hate speech imparted.

I stared down the inked apparition of a snarling nightmare. It's vicious muzzle bored back at me—red-eyed, bloody-fanged, and black-clawed. Beneath the sketch was a warning about Vampires—aggressive and homicidal, lusting for the tang of faelets' blood. Mainly, though, it declared them a radical, conceited people who viewed themselves as the superior race—alleged they conspired to overthrow Dananns as the ruling class (the benevolent masters that we were), yearning to subjugate the entirety of faekind.

Sedge would have me believe these accusations totally unfair. And I believed him.

There were similar broadsheets slandering numerous other Unseelie classes—Witches, Leprechauns, Werewolves, Hobgoblins, Banshees, and Fomorians, to name just a few. Regarding Fomorians, I suspected the board was dead on. The rest, however—well, I couldn't imagine half the fae realm consisting of demonic rapists, cannibals, thieves, and murderers. Honest observers would find good and bad in every race. Just as on Earth.

Disgusted, I stomped over to another stall. There, a family of kindly Goblins sold crystal spun into intricate forms. Their figurines glimmered inside like miniature nebulae and when asked about them, the mother Goblin told me they were frozen souls. By then, I was street smart enough to know she wasn't speaking metaphorically, but I wasn't about to ask how one would freeze a soul. I just hoped the souls in question weren't already engaged at the time of capture.

Worried I'd somehow end up on one of their shelves, I skittered to the next stop. The ancient, arthritic Goblin manning that stall sold discarded (or stolen) electronics from Earth: cell phones, laptops, keypad-less laptop screens, CD players, walkie-talkies, and numerous MP3 players. But how would one profit from such merchandise in a world lacking electricity? I goggled at a threesome of pixie-like beyns rummaging excitedly through a bin of old, scratched CDs. Some weren't even legitimately published but burnt at home on someone's PC.

I was still pondering their enthusiasm when a blinding flash several stalls away caught my eye.

What it was, I couldn't say, but it floated, scintillating, above a satin pillow like a star. If the frozen souls were mini nebulae, then this beckoning beauty was a supernova in a bean. Ready to burst.

My eyes locked onto its splendor, my heart damn near stopping.

I couldn't help myself. I beelined toward it. I reached with both hands, *needing* to hold it. Like I'd needed to touch Angel Oak, though the allure now was 50 times stronger. Mother save me, there was no one manning its stall. No one to stop me if I snatched it and absconded into the night.

It's not really stealing. It already belongs to me. Why else would it call to me?

The pulsating majesty was mere inches away when hands pinned my stretching arms to my sides. Whatever spell I was under shattered, the heat and strength of a flesh and bone man flaring against my back.

My arm hairs razored when I peered over my shoulder at Pete. He arched a brow at me, dark and dangerous. My heart thudded back into action.

"Life's not exciting enough with only one curse on your head? You need another?"

My eyes fell once more on the bean, my mind hazing.

Pete spun me to face him and patted my cheeks until my anger geysered, and I shoved him away.

"Keep your hands off me!" I rubbed a welt on my face.

Pete rolled his eyes. "Then stop being a damned fool! Have you learned nothing from your father's fate? Or did he also neglect to school you on how curses take root?" He pointed, accusing the glorious bean. "By touching seeds like that."

Oh, Goddess, am I an idiot?

Uncle Neel had aptly warned us how enticing curse seeds were to fae. Seeing one in person, I should've guessed what it was. Anything that bewitching had to be diabolical.

I frowned, still rubbing my cheek.

"You blasted Dananns and your wicked games," Pete grumbled, urging me from the would-be disaster. "Your kind loves setting traps like that. Not typically on one of their own—but you'd certainly suffice."

I shook my head, bewildered, as we walked. "Why would someone trap a stranger into a blood curse? Aren't those usually about revenge?"

"Aye, but I reckon that seed doesn't sprout a blood curse." Pete paused. "There are other kinds, ken?"

I hoped my sneer masked my ignorance. "Of course—I ken that."

His heavy sigh told me he wasn't buying my act. He strode onward without calling me out. Although, he did continue educating me. "I'd wager that seed sprouts a trystic curse, which doesn't summon a harbinger, by the by. Most curses don't if you were curious. Only death and blood curses summon us."

We'd been spending too much time together if he could guess my thoughts.

"Trystics are for sport, to entrap some unsuspecting halfwit—"

I sniffed at the jibe, though I didn't expect an apology.

"—so the caster may commit sinful animal acts upon their victim without struggle. Did I not warn you to be wary of such things?"

My pout widened into stupefaction. "You mean that seed could've—"

"Subdued you into a meek lack for some lecher? Aye. It happens frequently."

Taking his meaning despite his unfamiliar vocab, I cringed, then shivered. *Damnit, what is* wrong *with this world?*

"On the whole, however, curses of that ilk are merciful."

Only a man would liken being magically roofied as merciful.

"In comparison, it's mercy," he amended, his mouth taking a grim slant. "At least with trystics, the victims return unscathed to their own lives—after a brief spell trapped under some rutting git, albeit."

Uck! Can he be any more blasé?

"Stronger entrapment curses—their victims endure much worse fates."

Was it wrong that I didn't want to know the details of those worse fates? Me, the supposed ruler of this sordid world.

"Why isn't someone doing something about it? Doesn't this place have something resembling police? You know, guards who protect the general public?"

"Some, though it's mighty hard to police something the crown sanctions."

I froze like I'd short-circuited.

"Would you keep up?" Pete snatched my arm. "You should distance yourself from that seed. Besides, I want to show you something."

I nearly stumbled as he tugged me. "What? Did you buy your gun?" I refrained from sneering.

"The seller demanded more than I can pay," Pete said, exhaling. "It's fair impossible to dicker with a Goblin who knows the value of his wares. That pistol is likely worth thrice more than what he's asking."

I thought that unlikely with no ammunition. "Them's the breaks."

He shook his head at my idiom. "*Anyhow*—once I realized bargaining was pointless, I went in search of you and encountered something I think you'll fancy."

I sneered, his motives as clear as fresh rain. "Oh, yeah? What'd you find? Jewelry?"

I'm pretty sure I have vaults of jewels waiting for me at the palace you won't allow me to escape to.

"Nothing of the sort. Coddled you might be, but I haven't mistaken you as frivolous. You'll want something you can use."

I lifted my chin. "True. In my predicament, anyway."

"Precisely."

"What is it?"

"I believe it's a sauce."

I made a face. "A sauce?"

"Aye. Something to eat."

"I know what a sauce is. Just, why would you think I'd want it?"

"*Why*? Because you've done naught but moan about it for the entirety of our unfortunate friendship. You still won't eat a morsel of my woefully bland food without mentioning this beloved red sauce from earth. Christ, the way you speak of it, I'd think it was milked from the teats of angels."

Gasping, I jerked Pete into me, grabbed his smirking face in my hands. "If you're bullshitting me right now, I'm going to be *so* mad at you."

"What did you call it? I know it began with cat."

"Ketchup!"

"Ah, that's right—ketchup."

I scurried ahead of him, hands clenched, scanning the vicinity. "*Where*?"

Humming, Pete strolled past me. "Right this way."

He led me to a stall overflowing with human goods. Amongst a section of tins, cans, and boxes of food of varying freshness, stood a glorious bottle of Hinerz 59 ketchup. Torchlight sparkled upon its glass.

Oh, Danu, please don't let it be expired, I thought, ready to pounce, a cheetah on a gazelle. Pete caught me mid leap, wrangled me to my feet. "What's your *deal*, dude? You can't tell me there's ketchup here, then not let me have it!"

Pete tsked. "If you want a fair price for your treat, then acting as if your very life depends on it is the worst strategy to employ."

I stilled, finding the seller within random piles. He was diminutive, even for a Goblin, and schmoozing a trio of orange-skinned Middling feyrs in the market for human grade paper, which stood in an uneven, spiraling stack before them, weighed down by a rusting socket wrench. He was too engrossed with his current customers to notice my impatience, but Pete was right. If I rocketed right for the ketchup without browsing first, the seller would know he could rip me off.

Once I calmed, Pete released me and untied the worn leather pouch at his belt. "Would you like me to buy it for you, or do you want to try your hand at striking your own bargain?"

I narrowed my eyes at his amused tone. Was he questioning my capacity to get a good deal? I clicked my tongue. "*Please*, this ain't my first spin around a flea market. I got this."

"Very well." His lips twitched with dubious mirth. "What would that treasure cost you on Earth?"

I chewed my lip, laser focused on my prize. If those winged fae veered away from the paper and went for the ketchup, I'd freaking set them on fire.

"Like, two bucks."

"Here it's likely worth quadruple that." Pete's bear paw seized my hand and pressed several lemon seeds into my palm. "That sum should do. Now, remember, in haggling with

Goblins, be specific. They're wily little chiselers and will do their damndest to bamboozle you."

"Got it." I was getting that ketchup, and *no one* would cheat me out of it.

The glint in Pete's eyes expressed his continued skepticism in my abilities, yet he stepped aside. He wouldn't stop me if I felt was this something I should do on my own. Which, I totally did.

If I somehow got through this whole ordeal with the Shadow Prince and decided to take the throne, where I'd be in constant political struggle with the influential Danann leaders who'd been running the kingdom during my father's absence, then I'd better be able to negotiate with a single clever Goblin.

Pete nudged me toward the stall. "If you find you need aid, I'll be here."

Shaking off how his assurance heartened me, I then strode into the stall.

I'd never thought myself a spectacular actor, but I did a hell of a job nonchalantly perusing when I felt anything but nonchalant. I fingered a stack of mismatched lace doilies, ran my hand over the smooth plastic of a rotary phone with an extra-long cord, and tested several half-used tubes of drugstore lipstick on my wrist, none of them my shade.

No wonder I keep losing lip balms. They're probably all for sale in one of these stalls.

Finally, I made my way to the groceries, examined some of the cake mixes for sale. Four of them had expired more than twenty years ago. The last was just a month past its expiration. There were mossy cartons of vegetables; some I recognized, but some clearly weren't from Earth. Despite being vibrant and luscious, I distrusted their edibility after encountering the curse seed that night. Maybe the shopkeeper liked to poison foreigners for fun.

"Does lady find anything to like with?"

Gripping the counter before me, so I wouldn't jump out of my skin at the Goblin's gravelly voice, I glanced over my shoulder at him.

"Just looking for something to spice up supper," I answered in my best British accent. "What would you recommend?"

The shopkeeper's mouth spread into a wide grin, revealing numerous missing teeth. He waddled toward me in a hemp smock, scratching the back of one flopping ear. "I have many for spicing, Lady. Let you see."

As he waddled to my side, I spotted the Middling feyrs plodding past Pete, orange arms laden with blank loose-leaf. They seemed happy with the deal they'd struck. Would I be as lucky?

Pete now leaned against a signpost. He caught my eye, gave me a roguish smirk and an encouraging nod.

The Goblin pointed a knobby, grayish-green finger at the array of sauce bottles beside me. "Any this good spice."

I scanned the sauces, somehow avoiding the ketchup, though I sensed where it was. "Have you tried any of them?"

"Aye, aye, Lady. I yester-eve enjoy it here." He tapped the half-sealed bottle of hot sauce. "With good burn. Pleased to burn?"

I pursed my lips, considering, though I already knew hot sauce wasn't my thang. "Hm. No. I want something mild. Have anything tangy?"

"What tangy?" His brow furrowed.

"Something with a zip—a zing. Sweeter maybe?"

"Ah, might." He tapped the tops of two different brands of barbeque sauce, one of which had grown discolored, and at last—the ketchup.

It had never been opened, the bottle cap stating it wouldn't expire until October 2019. Holding my breath, I lifted first the unexpired bottle of barbeque sauce, examined its smudged label. Then, I finally grabbed the ketchup and did a side-by-side comparison. Although, there was no comparing anything with ketchup.

"What would you ask for each of these?" I peeked down at the seller in what I hoped looked like wishy-washy curiosity.

He twiddled his gnarled thumbs at his pot belly. "With dark sauce, I take 10 orange seeds."

Was that a fair price? I'd forgotten what an orange seed converted to in dollars. Regardless, I dropped the barbeque sauce back on the table. "Danu have mercy," I said to the Goblin, whose jaw dropped. "Am I buying a bottle of sauce or a golden goose?"

He blinked olive eyes at me.

Despite the overwhelming urge to clutch the perfect bottle to my bosom like my long-lost baby, I made to set the ketchup back on the shelf.

The Goblin raised a hand. "Wait, Lady. For bright sauce, I do good offer. I do take for thon five seeds in so median regard."

I assumed that meant he'd take what amounted to five 10s in Pittsburgh.

My nose twitched, though I celebrated inside. Pete had given me far more than what the seller asked. "I assume lemon seeds will do."

The Goblin grinned; the ketchup was as good as mine.

Once I spoke the right words, anyway.

I eyed the ketchup, then clicked my tongue. "Here's what I'm prepared to do." I paused, tallying specifics. "I'll give you four lemon seeds for this *entire, sealed* bottle. If I like how it tastes with my supper, then I'll return and give you that last seed."

The Goblin's mind ticked, his fuzzy brows wriggling.

"If that suits you, then you have a deal."

He massaged his jowly chin, then smiled like a cat. "Agreed," he croaked, and we shook hands.

Not a half hour later, after Pete had quibbled a butcher out of two pounds of the thickest, fattiest bacon I'd ever seen for a pittance, I skipped beside him on our way back to our secluded camp in the wheat.

He smirked at me, the ruckus of the market fading. "I've never seen someone so delighted over something fit to glaze an elderdeer."

What a scrumptious recipe idea! I wonder if elderdeer meat would make good burgers.

I gazed lovingly at my immaculate Hinerz bottle. Something I'd never hoped to see again. Its rich red color gleamed in the moonlight. "Just wait until you taste it, Pete. Then you'll understand."

"As a rule, food from Earth pales in comparison to food found here."

"Have you tasted much modern Earth food?"

"Aye, at markets such as this one. And I say what's become of food over the past decades on Earth is a travesty. Everything's so processed it's damn near artificial. It's either far too sweet or has had all its natural flavors sapped away. Nothing's fresh but preserved with chemicals. Christ, all that added nonsense always gives me a wicked case of the scoots."

I blinked.

"The shites, Shorty."

I cringed at the imagery, though his criticism was valid. "You just have to try it, Pete." At his sour face, I wiggled the ketchup at him. "Trust me. Just give this the tiniest taste. You won't be disappointed."

I, myself, already salivated at the memory of ketchup's heavenly tang. "You just *have* to."

His mouth quirked at one corner. "Well, if I must—"

I beamed. "Really?"

"Break the bloody thing open. I grow weary of your nagging."

I twisted the sleek white cap off the bottle with a satisfying pop. *He won't believe what he's been missing his whole life.* I tilted the open bottle toward him.

Stopping, his burlap wrapped hunk of bacon under his arm, Pete dipped an index finger into the bottle. It came out with a big glob of ketchup. I awaited his rapturous expression as he stuck his saucy finger into his mouth.

He floored me when he whirled about and spat into the grass. "Jaysus save me!" He gagged, hunching. "That rancid flavor makes me long for the days when I was forced to eat my opponents in the ring."

"*Excuse* me?" He didn't know how much he'd offended me.

"Here, I thought you were warming to me. Instead, you're trying to poison me." He pointed a damning finger at my bottle.

"What—I'm not trying to poison you!" I held the ketchup to my bosom. "I thought you'd like it!"

"How could *anyone* like that sludge?"

"Oh, come on." I dipped my own finger into the ketchup. "You're being ridiculous, even if you don't like it." I swiped a good dab of ketchup onto my tongue.

When a foreign grit settled into my taste buds, and I caught flavors of dirt, ground bugs, and decaying humus, I dropped the bottle and crumbled to my hands and knees, barfing the little I'd eaten that day.

Pete knelt beside me and pulled my hair back from my face. When I'd finished, he helped me right myself on my knees, his brusque fingers clearing tears from my cheeks.

Coughing and shaking, I wiped my nose. "It must've gone bad." My gullet spasmed again. I gulped to stave off another gush. "Terribly, *terribly* bad."

Pete retrieved the ketchup off the ground, held it in the moonlight. Gone was the cheery red delight I'd last seen in the bottle. In its place was a slurry reminiscent of excrement.

I gasped. "That's *not* ketchup!"

Pete's generous mouth twisted. "Aye, Shorty. I'd wager your sauce is still with the cunning cretin who sold it to you." He rubbed my back. "Looks like you got swindled at the Goblin Market."

"But I said I wanted the entire, *sealed* bottle! I made sure!"

"Aye, but you made no mention of the ketchup itself."

"But that's asinine! Who'd buy a bottle of sauce *without* the damn sauce?"

"Shorty, I told you to be specific." Pete rose to his feet, jerking me to mine in the process. "Your bargain must include every minute detail. That's how the market works."

I shook my hands. "But I asked for the *sealed* bottle! How the fuck did he get the ketchup out without breaking the seal?"

Pete spread his hands. "Do you seek a more complex answer than magic?"

I snorted like a warthog and spun on my heels to stalk back to the market.

"You may as well turn back toward camp, Shorty," Pete said, following. "Arguing with that weasel will serve nothing. He gave you precisely what you asked for."

I shoved a wayward strand of hair from my face, the breeze ripping around me. "I don't care! He won't get away with this without getting a piece of my mind!"

"Aye, that'll teach him."

Fuming, I barreled onward.

No matter Pete's reasoning, as the potential queen of this realm, I couldn't let a slight like this go unanswered. How many other fine fae folk had that Goblin conned out of their hard-earned seeds? He needed confronting.

At least, that's what I told myself to explain my piercing need for vindication. In truth, it was far more personal than that.

Which was why I should've listened to Pete and returned to camp. Maybe the storm would've passed us by.

TWENTY-THREE

"So, what?" I sulked, trudging around wheat stalks. "You're just never going to talk to me again?"

I wouldn't have thought it possible, but Pete's shoulders further stiffened. He prowled ahead of me, fighting off the wheat with a barely contained fury I knew was meant for me. His hands had fisted.

I frowned at his silence, already guilt-stricken enough.

We continued in the charged silence, the tension growing with each step until we finally came to the clearing where we'd established camp. On our return, Sionna rose from Pete's pallet, tail wagging, only to sense his mood and run to Bob for protection. I watched her cower under the masticating donkey and hated myself for what I'd done that night.

Pete stomped to the fire, its coals crackling in the silence, and hulked down onto one of the logs he'd set around it. He glared into the leaping flames as he flexed and unflexed his fingers. Then, on an afterthought, he snatched the bunched-up swath of burlap he'd stuffed in his belt—the one that once held a thick slab of bacon—and tossed it on the fire.

Biting my nails, I paused like a bundle of frayed wires a safe length from his side. *What can I say to make this better? How can I mitigate his anger?* So many good, humbling options sprung to mind, but what I settled on was a big fat, "It wasn't my fault."

He shot to his feet and rounded on me, teeth gnashing. "Then whose bloody fault was it?"

I stumbled back as Pete advanced, wrath fuming in his charcoal eyes. "If that asshole hadn't laughed at me, none of this would've happened!"

Pete shook his fists. "I told you all your faffin' about was pointless! I told you to bloody turn back!"

"But I had to do some—"

"No, you didn't, you eejit! You didn't have to do a fecking thing. You *wanted* to do it, and now look at the complete fecking bags you've made for us!"

"You think I wanted that to happen? You know I don't have control over it! It just comes out of me."

Pete's anger writhed through his limbs. He bared his teeth, towering like Everest over me, a mouse.

Though my chin trembled, I held my ground.

"You're truly going to look me in the eye and claim you had no notion whatsoever that there was a damn cyclone churning away in your veins?"

I gulped. "Well, I—I didn't know it was going to manifest like that."

"But you felt something coming, didn't you? Yet you went to lambast that innocent shopkeep anyhow."

"He's anything but innocent! Remember how this started?"

"He didn't deserve to have his entire livelihood scattered to the four winds!" Pete roared, his breath misting my face. "Nor did the twenty other marketeers whose stalls you destroyed in your fit!"

I winced, feeling like the crud on the bottoms of my boots. I'd terrified half the population of the market with my storm. After damage assessment, objects were the only casualties, but that included the entirety of Pete's seed purse.

The only reason I wasn't thrown into the thieves hole—a muddy pit in the ground—or taken as some Goblin's slave for my outrageous behavior, was because Pete had made it rain seeds. When his purse had dried up, he'd tossed me over his shoulder and fled. Livid Goblins had chased us, screeching, until they could no longer keep up. Clever little devils they might've been, but their wits had nothing on a harbinger's sheer speed.

After another silence, Pete swore something vehement under his breath and turned his back on me. He raked his already mussed hair.

I stood by in a mix of petulance and utter self-loathing, tears prickling the corners of my eyes. What would Daddy have said of me that night? If he'd seen me lose my shit over a bottle of ketchup? He'd have scolded me like the child I was and grounded me for eternity. If currently tuned in from the afterlife—wherever that was after being cursed—he'd deem Pete's hostility as warranted. He'd order me to make amends.

Huffing, I stomped over to Pete. "Look, dude." I threw up my arms. "I'm sorry. All right?"

Pete's lip curled. "Was that meant as an apology?"

I couldn't quit pouting. "*Yes.*"

He sniffed. "Sincere apologies aren't customarily accompanied by an eye roll."

I huffed again. "I'm sorry I forced you to give away all your seeds, but—"

Pete stomped to the other side of the fire by his pallet, began jerking himself free of his clothes.

"But it was just money, Pete! I didn't hurt anyone!"

"You've no idea what you've done." He yanked off his belt.

I froze.

Pete was from the 18th century. Yes, he was a rather progressive man from that time, but still—what if he thought the best punishment for wayward females was the strap?

I tried to contain my relief when he dropped his belt to the ground beside his pallet.

"I'm sure you didn't bring your entire net worth with you on the road," I said. *Goddess, Amy, now you're annoying even yourself.* "You probably have a safe full of seeds at home. It's not like you're indigent now."

"Aye, so should we just turn back and refill my purse?" he retorted stiffly. "You wager we'd make it there and back before word spreads to the Shadow Palace of a harbinger traveling with a powerful zephyrist?"

I bit my lip. *So that's what it's called. I'll just add that to my list of rare and exotic titles.*

"That'd be a poor bet indeed." He wrenched apart his jerkin toggles. "Now it's imperative that we reach the Shadow Court with all haste. Rumors of your power will run rampant. Your bounty will triple. It won't be long before other harbingers are on the hunt for the zephyrist from the Goblin Market."

Other harbingers?

"But wasn't my capture assigned to you? They can't just step on your turf."

"There's no honor among harbingers, Shorty. They'll fight me to the death for the bounty you'll bring." He unlatched his last toggle and wrangled himself out of his jerkin, dropping it beside his bedroll. "Just thank Danu you didn't spout fire tonight, or gossip would spur Gentian to send his whole bleeding army after your arse. You'd have destroyed all my plans in one fell swoop."

My throat constricted. Gentian had an army? Was it bigger than mine?

"How would they even know *I'm* the zephyrist? Couldn't it be any other harbinger's captive?"

He growled, tired of explaining such simple things to me. "Harbingers are harbingers for a reason, Shorty. We made it out of Gentian's cages, and in no small way was that due to our intellects. Any harbinger hunting you will question the marketeers you wronged tonight and get your description as well as mine."

I wrung my hands, now cursing my loss of control. "Then what can we do?"

My agitation barely mellowed him. "Right now, we sleep. With luck, I'll think of something over the night."

I bit my thumbnail, fretting we'd be set upon by a band of kidnapping harbingers. "Can I do anything to help?" I asked, knowing it a weak offer at best.

"Oh, no." He wrenched his large foot out of his boot. "You've done *enough* for one night."

Our conversations on the road the next day were like those of co-workers who only tolerated each other. Clearly, he couldn't forgive me for what I'd done, and I was so wracked by worry that I couldn't lend my mind to any stilted kindness he deigned to offer.

I sat in the wagon, quiet as a mouse, as we traversed meandering hills. Sionna sat with me, sensing my tension, and allowed me to pet her sunny head as I awaited an ambush.

Somewhere before midday, Pete jerked the wagon up a rocky berm and into a sparse forest. I knew this was an unplanned detour, for Bob brayed like the devil at being rerouted.

Though I wanted to ask where we were heading, I feared if I opened my mouth and further pissed Pete off, he'd turn demonic on me. His eyes had been black since dawn.

How can I create some lightness to balance him out? I wondered.

Fresh out of magic wands, I settled for several prayers to Danu—for Pete's soul, also murmuring some badly sung lyrics to the Delaney song he'd said he liked. Whether these things worked as intended, I didn't know, but they eased my disquiet.

Then I spotted a weathered sign stating a place called Humwater Dell was upcoming on the road we traveled.

As homesick as this city girl was for blacktop and 24-hour diners, I should've celebrated the prospect of passing through a town. However, my paranoia of attackers who'd make Pete look like Ichabod Crane was a bucket of ice water over any excitement. Right then, the mere thought of a populous area made my guts quiver. So, when the local citizenry thickened and the forest's towering trees served less as shade and more as domiciles, I flattened in the wagon, burrowing into the hay like a chipmunk hiding from a gang of cats.

Suffice it to say, I was dismayed when the wagon stopped only minutes past the town's social epicenter—rather crowded and rowdy from what I heard.

"What are you doing?" I hissed to Pete after he'd clomped through the leaves to the back of the wagon. I peeked at him from under my camouflage layers and hoped I wasn't imagining that his eyes had lightened. "Shouldn't we keep going? If we're being hunted?"

Pete worked at unknotting his bow from the wagon ledge. "As a matter of fact, that's precisely why we're stopping now." He jerked his bow free, his pointed eyes meeting mine.

Yep, they're totally lighter. Still angry but not demonic.

"I don't understand." Finally daring to sit up, I whipped my head free of my cloak, ignoring the sprigs of hay poking my neck.

Beyond the dense myrtle blossoms sequestering our tiny party from public scrutiny, I saw the form of a bustling town square and heard the thrum of commerce and chatter that always galvanized a city. They had me gritting my teeth. "Are you *nuts?*"

Pete wiped several trickles of sweat off his forehead, unmoved by my reaction to his decision to take a break *in the worst place possible in broad fucking daylight!*

"Why the hell are we making a pit stop at city hall? I thought you wanted to reach the Shadow Palace as fast as possible because of last night's shit show."

That he didn't immediately retort that it had been *my* shit show buoyed me. Still, his expression was granite. "Reaching the Shadow Palace with the utmost haste is imperative, Shorty, aye. The rub is, we won't get there without stopping."

"Huh?"

Pete shouldered his quiver. "In order to pass into Covenlen, we must first pass into Lithalaly. To do that, we must cross Crowcairn Bridge—which is heavily patrolled by Ogres who will, quite happily, crush our skulls like grapes if we try to make passage without paying their tithe."

I gawped at Pete.

"Which is 1,000 seeds from high order fruits, if you care to know."

I dropped my face to my knees. Of course, Evereostre had a fricking turnpike.

"Seeing as you've impoverished us on the road," Pete grumbled as Sionna wagged over to see if I was all right, "we're now faced with finding a way to refill my purse before we become sitting ducks in a slaughter. So, we're going to make a go at it tonight, whether you like it or not."

Already cringing, I peered back up at Pete's irate face. "*We*?"

His gaze sharpened. "Aye."

Without waiting for further complaints, he whistled for Sionna, who gave my cheek a comforting lick before leaping to her master's boots. "Make camp here. We'll return with meat. You'll need a full belly for tonight."

He was probably right, but I doubted I'd have an appetite, as nauseous as I was.

As Pete commanded, I skittered around the miniscule clearing he'd secluded us in—in the middle of a damn town—setting up our usual camp. His bedroll. My cloak. A small fire pit. I even unlatched Bob from the wagon, so he could graze unhindered. And every single time I heard a voice or footfalls drawing near, I'd freeze like a goat about to faint until I was certain Bob and I remained unseen.

I'd just finished checking the status of Pete's water skin when I overheard voices heading toward me on the road beyond the myrtles—straight from center city. Cursing, I huddled in the wagon bed, praying for invisibility.

My eyes popped open when one voice, a smooth baritone, clearly remarked, "Aye, well, you can't blame them for the brouhaha. Who wouldn't revel, seeing the convoy in all its finery? Sakes alive, the crown's own faelets be in it."

"*What?*" I shrieked, then barreled from my hideaway, knowing I was endangering myself if I'd heard wrong.

The unsuspecting Middlings strolling down the road both yelped when I leapt into their path. I grabbed the nearest of them, a burly scaled fellow of iridescent color, by his tunic collar. He boggled at me through long-lashed, sky-blue orbs.

"The convoy," I croaked, desperate and scared as hell. "You're sure it was royal?"

Understandably bewildered by my sudden appearance, my rudeness, my accent, my everything, the bulky feyr just continued gaping.

His friend, slenderer, though just as tall, scratched his feathered forehead. "Aye, lady," he answered for his dumbstruck pal. "They ride under the Larkspur banner. Heading onto the Spring Palace, I heard."

Why would they take such an odd path to the palace? I wondered.

They wouldn't, Amy! They're looking for you!

I grabbed the second male, downy as a goose, and got right up near his prominent nose. "You said the crown faelets were traveling in it." Mother, I hoped my hands wouldn't ignite and turn him into a drumstick. "Did you *see* them?"

From what Pete had told me, any inconsequential party conducting royal business rode under the Larkspur banner. And after hearing about the diverted river, I suspected there were factions in my father's court loyal to Gentian. Who else would agree to something

Briar hadn't even been consulted about? So, I had to know what cavalcade I'd now be racing toward like Phaedra, the loopy character on *Roomies*.

Birdman blinked. "Aye, lady. They waved at us. We spied the prince first, then the sweet princess. And the princess's wee moggie."

"Her *what*?"

The feyrs shared a look.

"You've not heard of a moggie, lady?" the hefty feyr finally spoke, the source of the rough baritone I'd first heard. "Er—um—a mouser?"

A living spasm, I released Birdman. "A cat!"

They stepped back.

"When did the convoy leave?" I was already sidling toward the swarms of Humwater Dellians thronging the deciduous town hub. The convoy must've ventured down the next road.

My Goddess! Is that really the tail end of a coach?

"It's there yet, lady!" Birdman called just before I left him and his friend in my dust, every hair on my body razor sharp. Yes, I was still petrified I'd be ensnared by some money-hungry harbinger as I darted into the teeming town square, but I was more afraid of missing my chance of rescue. Of missing my sister and brother. And the odds seemed good that if I reached them—and the security team that *must've* been with them—the harbingers hunting me would become a moot point.

"Wait!" I screamed so hard I thrashed my throat, shoving slower moving bodies. "Vi! Ace! *Wait!*"

I'd just made the central fountain of the town square, where masses gathered to hail their royal family, when the ground pulled back on me, a tablecloth under a plate. I went flying face-first to the fountain's cobbled steps, my right leg drawn as straight as a guitar string. When I spied the shadowy tendril shot through with emerald strangling my boot, I screeched, grabbed it like a rope, and yanked with all my might. I willed my tether to give. To stretch. To tear into tatters.

Somehow, I gained an inch. Then another. Then another. Then a foot. Two. Three. "Wait for me, *please*!" I cried as the forest swallowed sight of the last royal coach. An astronaut on Jupiter, I strained forward. "Guys, I'm coming!"

Just not fast enough.

By the time I'd stretched the tether five more feet, the convoy had clattered out of sight, and my energy was as good as sapped, my limbs quivering. I'd never catch them with the damn tether intact. I was as good as a chained mutt choking itself.

Whimpering, I plopped down on the fountain steps and hunched into my knees, weeping. I didn't care if passers-by judged my aberrance. How could they fathom my feelings right then? To have salvation so damn close, to lose it simply because I wasn't fucking strong enough. How infuriating! How utterly devastating.

I wasn't surprised to hear the familiar pant of a snuff hound, or to feel a wet nose against my hand.

Wallowing, I looked up to see Pete rushing toward me, winded and—frightened? I was bemused that he'd drawn his *scian*.

"What in Christ happened?" he asked, scanning the crowd. When he didn't find anyone menacing, he sheathed his dagger and knelt beside me. He palmed the back of my head in one bear paw. "Are you unharmed?" His eyes, now damn near back to normal, panged as they searched me for injury. "Did someone find you?"

I just stared at him—at his sincere concern.

"Tell me, Shorty." Pete gave me a gruff shake. "I must know if I'm to keep you safe. Did another harbinger come for you while I was gone? How in fecking hell did you get away?"

Finally, I shook my head. "No," I snuffled. "Nobody found me. I just—I—"

How the hell can I explain this without revealing who I am?

Pete wilted upon the fountain steps beside me, exhaling. "*Jaysus*, Shorty. You scared the living piss out of me. When I felt the tugging, then the wrenching—to the point where I was being dragged—I was fair certain you were being abducted."

I shook my head. "I saw someone I thought I knew."

He arched a brow, sweat beading his temple. "In this world you've only just stumbled into? Who?"

I glanced at my knees, shook my head.

Pete cursed, then rubbed my back like he was trying to rid me of frostbite. "Someone deceased, I take it."

Let's go with that.

"Makes sense, what with how hard you were pulling me. Wouldn't have guessed you had such strength in those bones, but you do surprise, don't you?" He chuckled, then spat, shaking his head. "Anyhow, sounds like you encountered a Púca."

"What's a Púca?" It sounded downright dirty.

"A mischievous Unseelie fae. They mostly mimic animals, but some find sport in mimicking images out of one's memories. If someone was foremost in your mind when you crossed its path, then—they might've taken liberties."

I stared at the departing crowds. They reminded me of Vi and me whenever we'd gone to a Bayview Boys concert. It was always so surreal, seeing our idols in the flesh. Now, all these fae were stunned that the royal family they'd merely heard tales about had just paraded through their ordinary lives.

Leaving their subjects thrilled and wanting more, the glorious royal convoy had departed. With my little sister and brother. And had left me behind.

Pete squeezed my shoulder until I glanced at him, forlorn. "I'm sorry your father's gone." His eye color took the last nudge back to fresh-baked cookies. "Truly, I am."

After a spell, I, too, extended an olive branch. "And I'm sorry for what I did last night. I may not have meant to do it, but I still did it, and I know we're in big shit now because of it." I rubbed the blood back into my face. "This really is all my fault. I should've listened to you. Next time, I will. Just—please, will you forgive me?"

Pete tipped his imaginary hat to me. "Now, *that*, Shorty, is a proper apology."

TWENTY-FOUR

Pete's scheme to replenish his seed cache had phases. Phase one—pawn enough goods to make a modest sum. Phase two—buy into a monthly card tournament. And phase three—swindle a royal slaver out of an ass-ton of seeds.

Once Pete finished detailing his plan, I dropped the riggit bone I'd been sucking the marrow out of and asked, "Are you out of your effing mind, dude?"

Pete grinned into the pot of stew he stirred—a pot he meant to barter once we finished cooking supper. "Aye, sometimes I am. With all my struggles, can you blame me?"

Well played. "What the hell can I say to that, if you're using the I-was-a-cage-fighting-slave-for-centuries-and-almost-lost-my-soul card?"

"It's my ace in the hole, Shorty." He winked.

Something fluttered in my belly as I stroked Sionna's silken head. She was napping, her head in my lap. "Speaking of cards—what game are we playing in this tournament?"

Angling my way, Pete added several more hunks of riggit to the pot, then continued his butchering. "Bachram, of course."

Of course. "I seem to remember you thinking my game play sucked the once we played."

"Which is precisely why I don't want you to play. At least, not in the traditional, lawful sense."

"Uh-huh." I'd figured.

"You'd be more of a pleasant distraction than a player."

"How?"

Pete's eyes danced, languid in their appraisal. "How does any female distract a besotted male?"

I stared at the idiot across from me.

"Plainly, I need you to finagle your way into the slaver's good graces, so that you're free to watch the hands he's dealt and signal me accordingly."

"That's just an eloquent way of saying I should shamelessly flirt until the slaver thinks he's getting laid."

"My eloquence aside, that's our diversion."

I scoffed. "Many beyns might be able to do that, Pete, but I ain't one of them." Just the thought gave me palpitations. "My Goddess, how would I even get his attention?"

"Simply walking past the bloke should do the job, but if you want to work for it, you could wiggle summat." He shrugged.

His plan sounded worse by the minute. "Obviously, you've never seen me wiggle."

I ignored the mockery in his eyes.

"It'd be like a stick figure in a mating dance."

He sawed through a riggit leg. "Do you mean stick bug?"

"Yep!" I tossed up a hand. "Either way, you get the picture, right? And it's not pretty. *I'm not—I'm not pretty.*"

The eternity he took in blinking at me was unbearably awkward. Then he shook his head and returned to his butchering. "God's truth, Shorty, it matters very little how you see yourself. So long as you have a pair of baps and an unoccupied cunny, he'll take to your advances just fine."

I soured. "Oh, do stop flattering me before I blush."

Pete laughed. "Then stop disparaging yourself unduly. Your looks notwithstanding, you do yourself no favors by making yourself feel badly, by shaming yourself." He opened his bloody hands, his gaze warming. "This is how Danu made you. There's no changing you. The sooner you accept that, the sooner those around you will too."

Now, it was me blinking. Speechless.

"Put simply, Shorty, if you strut into that tavern tonight believing you're the comeliest hen to ever flutter her feathers, that's what everybody will see."

I wrung my hands. "You don't understand. It's not just my looks. I've been on tons of dates before. When I get into a forced situation like that, where I know the guy is judging me for more than friendly reasons, I either clam up and can't think of words—like, any of them—or I end up spewing verbal diarrhea."

Pete cringed. "I pray that's not catching."

I giggled at the image he'd conjured. "No, it's just a metaphor for blurting out any thought that pops into my head."

Pete rubbed his furry jaw on his bicep, conceding, "Aye, if you do either of those things, you could damn us tonight. Still and all, I'd say you're overthinking this."

"But—"

"I assume it's safe to say these other chaps you—dated, as you say—I assume you wanted them to see you in a more than friendly light."

"Some of them, maybe. They never did, though."

Or they never had the chance to. *Thanks, Briar.*

Pete's expression slanted like he questioned those dates' intelligence. "Even so, this is a different gambit altogether, Shorty, because I tell you true—you won't care a whit if Ilex Howlite, slaver, finds you an interesting conversationalist. He and I have crossed paths many times on the road, but I chiefly recall him from my time cage fighting—when he'd gamble on matches. He's a consummate arsehole." He shrugged off the hostility rippling through his shoulders. "His profession is proof enough of that."

"Says the harbinger."

The corner of his mouth twitched. "Fair point. But as I've said, harbingers can be forced into their work. Slavers—they join their trade willingly."

"Hm." I imagined the breed of scumbag drawn to a job trafficking Danu's children—my subjects. Fury narrowed my gaze.

"See, the pressure's off you. You needn't worry if he likes you because you, yourself, will *despise* him. Tonight's only goal is to outfox the wanker. So, just act like the witty beyn who's come to vex me, and you'll do smashingly."

I arched a brow at the teased insult/compliment.

"And might I remind *you* of why I took issue with your bachram play." He smirked. "Only females with a mind to rob a man of his bollocks flirt the way you did that night."

"Psh!" Heat flared in my cheeks. "Hardly!"

"Deny it all you like, I was the recipient of your lash batting. I knew I was dealing with a vixen, and that's precisely who I want to slink into that tavern tonight and dupe Howlite out of his purse. That girl with the naughty eyes and clever tongue."

I shivered at Pete's brogue calling me a girl. Not a beyn—a girl. Was that how he saw me? I hoped so. Though I shouldn't have cared.

"One last thing to bear in mind with this plan, Shorty." He plopped the last of the meat into the stew.

Still ruminating, I twirled a strand of my hair. "What's that?"

Pete shot me a sidelong glance. "We don't have another fecking choice."

"**A**ll right, how do I look?" I finally emerged from behind the overgrown hydrangea I'd used as a privacy screen and tossed my hands skyward, resigned.

Busy counting the seeds traded for our most frivolous belongings (not my iBloom because I'd threatened to swallow it if he tried to take it from me), Pete glanced my way. And froze, his gaze lightning.

I blew the bangs from my eyes. "That bad, huh?"

Clearing his throat, Pete folded his arms on the wagon bed ledge. "Not how I'd put it, but—" Amusement bled into his expression. "I'll take a wild stab in the dark—that was Tansy's frock, no?"

"Yeah." I peered down at myself. "You probably won't get this reference, but I look like a cancan girl."

I totally did. Tansy had gifted me a dress for occasions when my togs wouldn't blend in. I hadn't tried it on. She and Olea had magically adjusted its measurements based on other outfits they'd altered for me, and Olea had folded and stuffed it into my book bag before I'd gotten a peek. Now, I wished I'd seen it. The violet bodice fit so snugly it would leave lace prints in my linen blouse, and the flouncy, layered skirt, which flared out at my hips and fluttered to a train, was slit clear up to my thigh on one side.

Biting my thumbnail, I cringed at Pete, waiting for his appraisal.

Several seconds passed before his brows rose, and he gestured at me. "Look at it this way, Shorty. You'll be certain to nab auld Howlite's attention—at the least. Only—" Reaching into his pouch, he then popped a small seed into his mouth like a Tic Tac.

His swarthy skin took on a crystalline glimmer. With one flick of his wrist, that glimmer floated my way.

A zinging shiver passed through me, my skin drinking magic. Gooseflesh stippled my arms, which I could now see, as my blouse vanished when the shiver crested. My bodice now clung to my bare skin, in danger of bursting apart if I breathed too hard.

No question, Pete slutting me up should've appalled me. And it would've—had I not been so intrigued by how he'd done it.

"How does that work?" I scurried to his side, eyeing his purse. Uncle Neel had explained seeds and their temporary powers, but I'd yet to see anyone use them in that capacity besides Pete just then. "Does each seed do its own thing when you ingest it, or can you adapt them based on your personal needs?"

Pete's strong fingers swirled through his seeds. "Some are steadfast in their purpose, others fluid."

"And the one you just used?"

His gaze was like the skim of velvet across my freshly bared cleavage. "Fluid."

Denying the wicked things his look did to me, I sniffed. "I should've guessed. I doubt there's a widespread need for a seed specifically meant to strip people." My jaw dropped when I finally glimpsed his current fixation. "Or to enlarge boobs!"

Pete snorted when I swatted him.

"What the hell? These better not be permanent, buddy!"

"Fret not, Shorty. It's a mere illusion—a bit of extra padding in your bodice."

I considered my breasts again. "Really?" They looked just about—average.

"Aye." His brow arched. "And not much, might I add."

"So, this—this is really just me?"

"Mostly."

"Then that's okay." I pursed my lips, squelching a grin. "Still, next time ask before you do something like that."

"Fair enough." As if I'd cued him, he selected another seed. "Mind if I pin up your hair?"

Biting my thumbnail again, I reached for the seed. "Can I try?"

An hour later, I slinked through the darkness behind the Ceridwen Public House like I was ready to do some high kicks, my hair styled back in my favorite pompadour ponytail. Pete prowled ahead of me, ensuring we stayed under cover. He didn't want us seen together. If anyone thought we knew each other, they might suspect I was helping him cheat. I assumed that would be bad.

The tavern resembled an ivy-roofed cabin built into a towering sycamore's trunk. The entrance writhed with fae folk, but I could hear peepers peeping in the rear. And like any bar in any world, the rear was meant for garbage and vehicle parking.

"I was right," Pete whispered once we sank down behind a set of massive crates that stunk to high heaven of decay. Compost containers? I wondered. "He's here."

"Howlite?" I searched the immediate area but didn't see anyone.

"Aye." Pete gestured toward a bronze domed carriage sporting the large etching I'd seen in my favorite nightmare—the ancient fae symbol for Larkspur. "That's his lorry, there beside the pond. He's likely already inside the tavern."

I blinked at the slaver's coach. The damn fool had left his wagon windows open—in a city. A fae city, but still urban in comparison to the vast countryside. In the human world, even small-town bumpkins knew not to tempt the dishonest—or the desperate, in our case.

"Hey!" I smacked Pete's chest. "Why bother with the tournament when we could break into his carriage and steal whatever seeds we find?" Even if Howlite had his seeds bolted up, the harbinger beside me probably had some surefire way to pick a lock.

Pete's mouth twisted. "Would that we could, Shorty, but Howlite never leaves his stash unattended in his lorry. That, he'll have deposited in his rented room." He shrugged. "We'll have to fleece him out of his purse. No getting around it."

Damnit. "Oh, fine. What does he look like? How will I know who to approach?"

"He'll be the Danann with a golden snake pierced through his eyebrow."

"A *snake?*"

Pete enjoyed my unmasked distaste. "Aye. He calls it Hydra, talks to it at times."

"Someone should've warned him how that would make him look. Since he's a slaver and all. He should've chosen a more innocent animal."

Pete clicked his tongue. "I'm fair certain the gobshite knows both snakes and slavers are widely betokened as evil and doesn't care. In fact, he's downright proud of it."

"Before I go in there to convince this douchebag that I'm hot for him, can you please assure me he has at least one redeeming quality?"

Mirth frolicking across his wide mouth, Pete thought a minute. "He customarily buys those he fancies ales."

"Oh. Well—that's—"

"But don't drink them, for he'll surely have dosed them."

I closed my eyes, shook myself.

"That reminds me—" When I met Pete's waiting gaze, he pressed several seeds into my palm. "If you find yourself in need of some Dutch courage, you'll have these at your disposal. Then you won't be forced to rely on Howlite's donations. I don't wish you to souse yourself, mind you. I need your mind sharp, Shorty."

I stuffed my drink money into my skirt pocket.

"Remember the signals we discussed?"

"Yep, and their corresponding hands."

We'd spent hours eating riggit stew and playing bachram at our camp, just so I'd understand the flow of the game and how consequential hands developed. He'd also tried teaching me the art of bluffing, but I hadn't taken well to that. When I had shit in my hand, my expression showed it. Of course, as Pete had already warned, I was even worse at pretending I had nothing when I'd struck gold.

"Good thing you won't be playing," Pete had chortled when we'd wrapped up our last round. "Those gleaming eyes of yours could sabotage a joker's wedding." This was the highest possible hand in bachram—two jokers, the queen and king of hearts, and the ace of clubs. Random, I thought, but the fae realm thrived on chaos.

Anyway, Pete was right. I should work on my tells. Not just for bachram purposes. Political negotiation, I assumed, oftentimes involved bluffing or slow playing opponents to attain one's desired goal. If I struggled with these things during a card game, then I was in real trouble when it came to being a queen of puckish fairies.

Again, I felt the sting of the Goblin merchant's treachery.

Tying his seed pouch back onto his belt, Pete nodded me toward the pub. "You go in first. I'll follow shortly."

Steeling myself with a deep breath, I rose. "Here goes nothing." I forged ahead, my off-brand Buggs my only comfort. Both hands and teeth clenched, I squared my shoulders and lifted my chin. *Be the vixen, Amy. Be. The. Vixen.*

"Shorty," Pete hissed.

I staggered back to him, worried I was being obnoxiously awkward. "What's the matter?"

"Nothing." He smirked, still kneeling behind the fetid compost crate. "Just curious—what's a douchebag?"

Snorting, I waved him off. "Tell you later." Then I flitted away, laughter settling my nerves.

The Ceridwen Public House looked much the same as the Thorny Rose Tavern. Moss and flowers festooned all surfaces, and fae asters hovered above the patrons, lighting the busy dining room with a buttery glow. A piper with stringy orange hair and knobby limbs pranced by the hearth in garb befitting Robin Hood, his warbles accompanying the chatter of carousal.

Surveying the space from the open doorway, I spied a vast variety of fae—Middlings, Dwarves, Trolls, tiny Hedge Gnomes, Giants whose heads touched the rafters—and, for once, several other Dananns. Somehow knowing I'd still be "the other," I exhaled and forced myself over the threshold.

I was the moon, and all eyes the oceans. My simplest movement commanded the tide.

Gulping, I feigned the confidence of a supermodel, then sauntered to the bar, singing "I Am Lovely" from *East End Epic* in my head the whole way. Trying to remember the showtune's next lyrics, I took an overgrown toadstool at the horseshoe shaped bar.

Numerous other fae waited there to place orders. Yet, the bartender, a slender Middling of average height and build with short black hair, silvery skin, and a pair of gorgeous navy-blue insect wings, addressed me first. "Here for the tournament, lady?" He gestured toward the batch of shroom-like tables to my right, where all the other Dananns mingled.

He must've assumed that I, being Danann, was only there that night for the thrill of gambling away my gluttonous wealth. Knowing what Pete assumed of my Danann-ness upon first meeting me, I'd take it.

"Only to watch," I replied in my phony British accent. "And to drink." I placed two apple-like seeds on the rough countertop before him. "This enough to buy me an ale?"

"O' course, lady." He flitted aside to fill a horn mug for me.

I lost sight of him when a Middling beyn stopped before me. She set a heavy tray down beside her on the counter, then swatted a tuft of long yellow hair from her creamy, lemon-hued face. One elegant hand on her hip, she grabbed a damp cloth with the other, wiped the bar with efficient pizazz. "What can I fetch you to drink?" she asked me, her upturned nose blushing.

I gestured toward the other bartender. "I'm already being helped but thank you."

Casting a quick glance over her shoulder at her co-worker, the beyn nodded my way. "Enjoy!" She darted onto the next patron, her hands a fluster of business. She circuited the bar like a machine. Before my drink found me, she'd taken all awaiting orders, then served them two at a time.

A chuckle drew my attention, and I glanced up to find the feyr bartender pocketing my payment. He'd set my ale before me. "Maggie's a tireless foofaraw. This pub would crumble without her."

"As would he!" Maggie shot over her dainty shoulder, winking a fringed eye. Her aery, knee-length dress shimmied about her round bottom as she scuttled, filling orders. "He often needs reminding!"

I took the handle of my mug. "Let me take a wild guess—you two are married."

"Astute of you, lady," the feyr said. "Can I presume you're married as well?"

"Oh, no, I'm not."

And I won't be for a while, I hope.

"I just—" I paused to smirk at my ale, thinking of all the romances I'd read in my life. "I just have a knack for picking out couples. Your banter tipped me off."

Maggie sent a horn of ale sliding to her last patron, a green-bearded giant in an archer's hat, and twirled to her beau's side. "Interesting gift, that. I've not met a love granger afore. Are you here to make a match?" Her sapphire eyes swept the dining room. "Who?"

I blinked, instantly equating love grangers with Cupid.

"I, uh, was kind of here for myself tonight." Though I simpered at first, I then cleared my throat and sat straight. Raised my chin. A vixen wouldn't be sheepish in looking for a date. Nor would a love granger, I suspected. And how did I know I wasn't one?

"Though I'm not looking for love, if you know what I mean." I waggled my eyebrows like a locker room hero and flashed her a sideways grin.

My Goddess, where did I learn to do that?

Maggie cooed in a glee that was nearly an overreaction.

Her husband chortled at my surprise. "Apologies for my ceyla, lady. After her sister married and moved to the next village, she's been hard pressed to find suitable prattle." He took up the tray Maggie had first carried over and dumped its cruddy contents into a large bucket of suds. "She'll no doubt natter your ears off if you keep seated."

Maggie giggled at his teasing, her cheeks dimpling.

"Shut it, Rye." She swatted him before facing me. "What's your taste?" She leaned on the counter, perusing her patrons. "Many of our finer regulars are here—beyns, mostly—though none as lofty in countenance as you."

I blinked. *Lofty in countenance?* I supposed she meant my Danann features. Did they really smack that hard of wealth and privilege?

"Feyrs are more my thing," I said, her casual acceptance of homosexuality refreshing after growing up in the USA, where gay marriage was still illegal. At least it still was when I'd left it. I hoped that had changed.

"Ah, then I can recommend several eligible swains what'll be visiting our pub this night. One, I've heard tell is fair marvelous with coupling."

I bit my lip on an immature *teehee* and took my first sip of ale. A party in my mouth, it was much sweeter than I'd expected. Was that honey I detected? Goddess, when had I last ingested anything containing sugar?

Still waiting for me to describe my ideal date while I debated how to subtly describe what I knew of Howlite, Maggie's eyes caught on something over my shoulder. Her yellow face glowed like a star. "Speak of the devil!"

I tried not to jolt off my toadstool when a now familiar laugh caressed the back of my neck. My hairs there stood.

Pete slid onto the stool beside mine. "You know better than to speak of me, Magnolia, if you wish me to remain in the shadows."

It took me a dumb moment to realize the swain Maggie had been hyping as the marvelous coupler was Pete. Which made my tummy flutter.

Bad tummy.

Maggie squeezed the roughened bear paw Pete rested on the counter. "Pete! Glad to see you, fella! I thought that was you I saw by the pawner's this eve! Told you, Rye! Lookie who's here!"

"Mother's love, I didn't anticipate you showing tonight!" Rye flapped with quick grace to Maggie's side. "Last I heard, you were long for the road again."

"Aye, well, I needed a wee break," Pete replied. "Sionna's fair tuckered as well. Finding myself in this neck of the woods, where a sporting card match and several pints awaited, I headed here straight away."

I envied how easily his lies came, slick as oil, never stumbling. Despite his penchant for brutal honesty.

"Happy to have you here," Rye said.

"Happy to be here." Pete withdrew his seed purse and untied it. "Care to add me into the tournament?"

Rye smacked the bar. "As you say." Winking, he glided off to fetch what Pete needed for the game while Maggie collected the appropriate pay in. Most of the purse, I saw with a furtive grimace.

An impish gleam in her eyes, Maggie gestured at me. "Was just talking with the lady here, Pete. She was saying as she'd be fond of some pleasant company tonight."

My face flashed hot, though Pete already knew the sort of company I sought that night. And it wasn't his. How would he skirt Maggie's suggestive intro? I was more than bemused when he didn't even try.

Chock full of swagger, Pete angled toward me. "That so?"

I sipped my ale. "Something like that."

"Allow me to assist you, darlin'." He offered me his large hand. "I'm Pete."

Considering him, beard to boots, I clasped his hand, so warm and callused. "Nice to meet you, Pete."

His thick brow arched, his debonaire expression sparkling. "And your name would be?"

"Rose," I repurposed my original alias, guffawing inside.

Pete's spreading smile was 100 percent genuine. "Such a fitting name for you—Rose."

My breath caught as he lifted my hand and his soft, full lips touched my inner wrist.

Goddess, they are just perfect! *Mm!*

He peered back at me, clocking how I'd flushed at the rasp of his whiskers on my skin.

Hands fluttering, Maggie squealed, "I'll leave you to get acquainted," and scurried off to fill more orders.

After several beats, my senses returned, and I tried withdrawing from Pete, but he held fast. "What are you doing?" I asked. "I need to be single, remember?"

Pete reached over with his other hand to pet the gooseflesh on my forearm. "Fear not, Shorty," he murmured, kissing my wrist again.

Gah! I wanted to erupt, shivering. *Stop doing that!*

"I failed to mention one pertinent thing about how to best attract Howlite."

"What's that?"

He gazed past my head, his pupils lengthening into a strangely feline shape—just as they did when we were training. "If he thinks I want something, he'll inevitably try to take it for himself."

"And that something would be—?"

Not a second later, Pete stiffened. I sensed a looming presence beside me and glanced up with what I hoped was a come-hither smirk.

Howlite wasn't a bad looking dude. About Briar's height, he was dark-haired, smooth-skinned, and had a pair of shrewd blue eyes. For a Danann, his ears were exceptionally pointy, his nose snubbed like it disdained all smells. He did indeed have a thin golden snake coiled through one eyebrow, and he seemed to enjoy wearing his official royal slaver uniform, a set of sleeveless, leafy coveralls, even on his off hours. To brag, I assumed.

I knew he sported his work clothes. An embroidered crown of golden twigs trimmed with violet-blue larkspur blooms embellished his breast patch. I'd seen that insignia before. On my father's business letterhead.

My throat constricted at seeing something so familiar and comforting on someone standing for something so heinous. My gut insisted Daddy had *never* sanctioned slavery. I prayed to Danu with everything I was that I could trust my gut.

"McKenna," the slaver greeted my captor in a thick Scottish-like burr. "Is it wise of you to squander your paltry bounties by coming here this night?"

I fought the urge to mouth *McKenna*, realizing I'd never asked Pete his last name. Instead, I tittered like the haughty Danann Howlite assumed I was, considering his first tactic to plunder me from the harbinger was to belittle his prosperity.

Ugh, I already hate him. This is going to be a loooong night.

Pete's eyes telegraphed, *I told you so*, before he said, "I'm a glutton for punishment, Howlite, what can I say?" His magnetic intensity recaptured my gaze. "Care to give me a spanking later, darlin'?"

My heart leapt in my scanty bodice at being so bluntly propositioned—by Pete. "Only if you're sufficiently naughty."

"Psh!" Howlite rapped Pete on the shoulder with undue force. The slaver's bicep flexed merely to impress me. I struggled not to roll my eyes. "You'd be lucky if you made it so far, as deep in your cups as you get, McKenna." Casting a sideways leer my way, he held a "secretive" hand to his mouth. "Prone to soggy bone, this one. I've heard tell most humans are." He squeezed Pete's shoulder in a way I guessed was meant to be jocular but looked more like he'd started a game of mercy.

From the terse twitch of Pete's mouth, I didn't figure he'd ever concede such a game. Nor did I believe he'd ever suffered soggy bone.

But the vixen wouldn't take that chance and potentially ruin her night, would she?

I clicked my tongue, slipping from Pete's touch. "Pity to hear that."

Pete's mouth twisted as I glimmered up at Howlite. "What about you?" I forced myself to ogle him. "Are you better at holding your liquor?"

Puffing like a rooster, Howlite became so smug it was unattractive. "Aye, lady fair. Spirits only ever stiffen *this* feyr's bones."

I covered my mouth before I spit out my last sip of ale. I offered Howlite my hand. "Then it's so nice to meet you, Howlite. My name's Rose."

His lips on my knuckles—uck! It was like being kissed by a slug.

"Care to join me, Rose?" Howlite asked. "You'd get to watch me slay this worthless human at bachram."

Howlite's insults drew my futile matchmaker's disappointment, so I decided against abandoning my own personality altogether. Maggie would become suspicious. Plus, the vixen Pete had met at the Thorny Rose Tavern had still been me. So, I remarked, "That was kind of rude."

Both males paused, Howlite blinking, Pete's mouth hitching.

I set down my mug. "Just because he's human doesn't mean he's worthless." I gestured at Pete. "I've met many fine humans before."

"Aye, you might have," Howlite agreed, though his skepticism was tangible. "But not this one, lady. This one's a *harbinger*."

The way he'd hissed *harbinger*, like someone paid to hump livestock had more honor, cued me to gasp. Nearby eavesdroppers muttered their disgust, then skittered away from Pete, the social leper. Even Maggie looked ashamed—maybe because she hadn't warned me I might've invited a slave to shadow to bed.

"McKenna's a leashed bitch, lady fair," Howlite continued, superior as all hell. "The lowest of the low, to be mounted at his master's pleasure."

Goddess, I didn't know how Pete remained so calm at Howlite's slander because I wanted to cut the jackwagon's tongue out of his mouth and shove it up his ass. Then maybe he'd get a taste of his own bullshit.

Stay the course, Pete's unwavering gaze cautioned me, though he looked carefully sullen.

Rob the fucker blind! I added with a hearty swallow of my ale.

Clearing my throat, I rose from my toadstool and proffered Howlite my arm. "Then I'd just love to watch you put this scumbag in his place."

Snickering, Howlite hooked my arm and led me to his place at the card table. Where he sat me down on his knee like a cat to pet, my skirt shifting to bare my leg up to my damn hip. I swallowed the urge to glare at the others already seated at the bachram table, feyrs who snickered about me—Howlite's new toy.

Several moments passed as tournament players gathered. I spent all of them wanting to escape back to camp until a friendly presence appeared beside me with another mug of ale.

"Oh." I gulped at Maggie, unsure how to reject the drink. I wasn't touching anything Howlite ordered for me if he was known for drugging beyns. "How nice of you," I praised my living seat, fingering his chest patch. "But I can't accept charity from a royal official. What would your superiors say?"

Howlite's brows rose.

"The ale's not from him, lady," Maggie corrected me, pressing the sweating mug into my hand. She gestured across the table at Pete, who was just taking a toadstool, arms full of poker chips. Apparently, Rye and Maggie imported human chips the way they imported Bicycle card decks. All from the black-market, I assumed. "This here's *Pete's* treat."

"Oh, well—" I shrugged. "Guess it can't be considered charity if it comes from someone so beneath me."

A cunning glint in her eye, Maggie spun away to complete her chores.

Pete gestured toward me while organizing his chips. "Thought you could use another draught, darlin', if you'll be whiffing Howlite's stink all evening."

Though anyone with a suitable fae nose could tell Howlite smelled of nothing worse than fresh cut grass, the other feyrs at the table chortled. Howlite laughed like grating metal, his canines more resembling blades.

The tournament, beginning shortly thereafter, progressed hastily. Perched as I was, I struggled to see Howlite's hands. And after five unproductive rounds, Pete hadn't won a single pot, and his irritation radiated like gamma waves. Not irritation at me, I guessed, but at the jerkwad foiling our whole plan to cheat him. Well, that couldn't continue.

Vixens wouldn't sit where they didn't want to.

As Howlite mulled over his sixth hand, I popped up, grinning at the Danann to my right. "Care to scoot over?"

Blinking, the rangy feyr did just as I asked.

Better arranging my skirt, I fluffed my ruffles before sitting on my own. If at first affronted, Howlite mellowed when I leaned in and trailed a finger up his forearm. A forearm tattooed in fae runes I was certain not even he knew the meanings of. "Can you show me how to play? I bet a clever feyr like you knows all the best strategies."

Wolfish, Howlite grabbed the edge of my stool and slid me so close that my bare knee settled into his crotch. I gritted my teeth, staying put. At least in this position, unnerving though it was, I had a clear view of his cards—the ace of hearts and the two of clubs. On Howlite's turn, he called the blinds.

Palming my chin, I watched the flop like a novice (which I was in reality). "What do you do with this?" I asked Howlite, guileless as an angel, though Pete had already explained what Howlite could do with a five of spades, a nine of clubs, and a four of clubs. He needed two more clubs to make a flush, and he also had a straight draw. But I hung on Howlite's every word as he whispered into my ear.

Even with such a potential wellspring in his fingers, Howlite bet a small amount, calling the three guys before him. Pete called too, glancing my way in anticipation of a signal. But I waited until the turn, which was a jack of clubs, before I scratched my collarbone.

Howlite merely called again when it was his turn. Pete folded, however, as advised. Good thing because Howlite took out two other players with that hand in the end. Yeah, Howlite was a total prick, but he was also a smart bachram player. Even when a joker ruined one of his hands, he still wheedled a win.

Plus, he had the advantage of a captive consultant. Pete hadn't lied about the slaver talking to his snake piercing. Hydra might've been its given name, but it also went by Chappie. And no, from what I witnessed, Chappie didn't talk back, thank Danu.

The night continued in a sluggish whirl of cards, chips, and ale. I'd imbibed so much of Rye and Maggie's sweet brew by the time the piper hit the hay that I'd grown accustomed to Howlite's groping and off-putting come-ons. I knew I should abstain, but I was giddy and having a blast. Not because of Howlite, really.

More because of Pete—and his tactics for throwing Howlite off his game.

He started with a cavalier remark regarding his preference for pocket eights. Then he stared at my half-covered boobs for a half hour, melting my insides—making Howlite glare like a territorial badger. Next, Pete teased me into cutting the deck for a token of luck between hands. When he got the higher card, he reached across the table, took my hand, and placed another titillating kiss on my inner wrist. Howlite had pounded the table for another ale, shattering the connection Pete and I were seemingly forging. The last time was just after Howlite boasted of punching his overseer in the nose over a beyn they both desired.

"Oh, my." I squeezed Howlite's arm. "Did that earn her affection?"

"Not as of yet," he slurred, having imbibed his fair share of ale. "But it will, mark me."

My heart skipped at Pete's deep chuckle. When I swiveled his way, he was again the dashing stranger I'd met at the Thorny Rose Tavern. "No wonder he didn't earn her, using his fists to impress instead of his tongue." Pete's eyes locked with mine. He lifted his mug to his mouth and licked foam off its rim.

Why, mercy me, I thought like a southern romance heroine, close to feeling the vapors.

"It's always been my experience that females favor a male who knows the value of a silver tongue." Pete's brogue had never sounded sexier. "Or am I wrong, darlin'?"

As tipsy as I was, I nearly said I'd need a demonstration.

His delicate feyrhood bleeding in his bloodshot eyes, Howlite tapped his cards upon the tabletop. "Is that what you used to please your masters in the Shadow Palace, McKenna? You remember—all the lusty Dananns Gentian lent you to as a novelty—for a pittance?"

Pete's smile calcified.

"Tell me, friend, just how many arses was your silver tongue obliged to lick?"

The two other players left at the table shifted, averting their gazes from Pete.

But I couldn't tear my eyes from him, from the pain and rage mingling in his darkening gaze. So, I didn't see Howlite's cards before he tossed a heavy handful of chips into the pot, raising everyone a fortune. When I looked, the brute had already set his hand face down on the table. Had he even checked them? I had no fucking clue!

But I *did* know that Howlite meant to bait Pete into going all in. Which Pete would need to do, should he call. As would the other two suddenly stoic players.

As smoothly as I could, I tapped my lips. Telling Pete to fold.

Testosterone throbbed in Pete's throat as he shoved his every chip into the pot.

WTF!

Howlite caressed my lower back, making my skin crawl. "Fret not, lady fair. The fates would never allow such a tramp to prevail over me."

I bit back a frown, praying like hell he was wrong. And that he'd stop touching me.

He didn't. And he wasn't.

After the river, Pete had a measly pair of 10s. Howlite had a fucking full house!

Pete's glower only intensified at the loss. His irises bled ink.

Whistling, the Danann to my right pushed back from the table. "Heated match, lads. Have a fruitful morrow."

Shit! I stared at the chips Howlite collected between glugs of ale. *That's the end of the tournament. We've lost everything!*

Everything!

Howlite breathed in my ear that he'd be back, pinching my hip before sauntering away to cash in his chips. I glared at Pete, wanting to shake him until his balls fell off.

Until I saw the ghosts in his eyes—the phantoms of shame from hundreds of years of abuse and assault that even Rye and Maggie's potent ale couldn't drown. And I made my own foolhardy decision, drunk as I was.

Howlite had humiliated and degraded Pete. And though I couldn't rightly call the harbinger a friend, I did care enough about him to want revenge. So, I was going to get our seeds back. And all the seeds the slaver currently had to his name.

Darting off from the game table, I shot Pete a pointed stare, which he merely blinked at. Then, I strutted over to Howlite, who chugged yet another mugful of ale, and grabbed a honking handful of his ass.

Startled, he gawped at me.

"I'm eager to see how liquor stiffens your bones," I purred, batting my lashes. "Like you said."

A trickle of ale meandered down Howlite's chin. For a moment, I feared he might do a victory dance. Instead, he slammed his frothy mug down on the bar with such force he made Rye and Maggie jump as they cleaned their quieting establishment.

"I'm eager to show you," he damn near belched, then grabbed my elbow and rushed me toward the wisteria laden staircase, right past Pete.

With one last glance at my accomplice, who'd risen from his seat, flushed and disbelieving, I nodded up the stairs—the subtlest hint I could give him—and scurried to the second story, Howlite panting against my neck.

Shadow swallowed us as Howlite grabbed me, backed me against an ivied wall, and kissed me like he meant to suck off my face. At least ale had sweetened his mouth. Besides that, the encounter was like eating a bowl of soup with my hands tied behind my back. Sloppy, wet, and my nose was way too involved.

Struggling to breathe, I inched along the hallway, pulling him with me. "Don't you have a room?" I managed beneath his seeking mouth.

"Of course. I always sleep in luxury."

While his slaves slept chained in cages. Or worse.

"Which door is it?"

He grabbed a handful of my skirt, probably expecting to feel a butt beneath it. Little did he know—

Howlite groaned deep in his throat as he pressed into me. "Doubt I can make it there. I must have you now."

I yelped at the intrusive hardness against my stomach and grabbed his chin, forcing him to meet my eyes. "Do I look like a strumpet to you? Have you mistaken me for the kind of beyn who has sex in dark hallways?"

Howlite blinked, somewhat returning to his senses. And his manners. "Oh, no. No, that I haven't, lady fair."

"Then please show me to your room—where you can have me." I croaked the last part, crossing my fingers.

Humming in anticipation, Howlite fiddled in his pockets. For a key, I assumed. "You won't regret your choice this night, lady fair. And come the morn, I'll be happy to tell my unworthy rival just how much you enjoyed my attentions. So, he'll know too how your choice satisfied you."

Weird.

"Oh, would you please do that for me?" I cackled, my British accent slipping. "I'm sure he'll want to hear every sordid detail."

Thankfully, Howlite was too drunk and aroused to intuit my sarcasm. He found his room key and staggered to his door, tugging me, still giggling, behind him.

Watching him try to unlock his door was like watching an infant try to solve a Rubik's Cube. He just couldn't seem to get the dang key in the right place.

Which doesn't bode well for tonight's exploits. Poor vixen just can't win, can she?

"Are you sure this is your room?"

His answer a mere snort, Howlite embraced me again, breathing like a beast against my mouth.

I rolled my eyes. "Not until we're in that room, buddy." Where I'd have access to his seed stash.

Whether he heard me or not, I didn't know, but his arms constricted me, his kiss suffocating. He slammed me against the door his fumbling fingers couldn't unlock.

A tumbler clicked. I squealed as the door swung away from my back, and Howlite and I careened to the floorboards of his well-appointed rented room like a pair of dominoes. He landed on top, flattening me.

Can't end up here! I realized in panic as the snickering hulk above me squirmed to get his hands under my skirts. *Shit!*

"Um, I also don't have sex on floors." I needed to get up! To find something heavy enough to knock him out with! "*Aah*! Hey! Please don't touch that! That's—hey! Knock it off! Get your face out of there!"

Struggling like a fly caught in a web, I didn't understand what made Howlite slacken upon me. Then, heaving, I found Pete standing over us, a heavy lacquered candlestick in his clenched fist.

"Took you long enough!" I shoved Howlite's heavy, drooling head out of my cleavage. "Oh, ew! Get him off me."

Laughing, Pete placed the candlestick back on the hearth mantle, then nudged Howlite off me with his boot. The slaver faceplanted into the floor beside his bed.

Pete reached to help me up. "Either you're mad or dangerously audacious, Shorty."

I chuckled, sweating, as he yanked me to my wobbly feet. "Or I just knew I could rely on your help."

Pete's brows rose. "You're calling me, a *harbinger*, reliable?"

I scanned the suite for a treasure trove. "Yeah, I guess I am."

His mouth quirked aside. "Huh."

"Where should we be looking for his seed stash?" I waved my hands about the room, which any resident of the Hundred Acre Wood would love. "And how big will this thing be?"

Pete had already unburdened Howlite of that night's winnings. "His coffer doesn't need to be big—or hidden for that matter. It's likely spelled, so thieves can't open or break it."

"We'll hash that out later."

"We have more than enough now, Shorty." Pete motioned toward the door. "We'd best count our blessings and steal into the night."

"No!" I stomped, drunk and righteous. "All that money in that coffer—he made it by selling people, didn't he?"

Pete expelled a breath. "All of it, I'd wager."

"Then we're taking it," I insisted, impressed by Pete's honesty—even when being so didn't benefit his case. "Every last seed."

"How does us filching it right any wrongs?" Pete debated, though he'd started aiding my search. "It's still—"

"Found it!" I grabbed a gilded box, the size of a large men's shoebox, off the furthest nightstand and plopped upon the bed. The perfect size for a slaver's coffer, I decided.

Whether Howlite had spelled it against thieves or not, I couldn't say, but I doubted so once I grazed the haft and it unlatched. The lid flipped open as if commanded. Pete gawped at the seeds galore in my lap.

"Ever see this many seeds together at once?" I removed a handful of assorted colors and illuminations, let them spill back into their nest, a glittering waterfall.

"No," Pete croaked, padding around the bed to me. "Shorty, it hardly matters who holds that coffer. No matter the nobility of our cause, if we spend those seeds, we're spending the blood of slaves. We'd be no better than Howlite or anyone else supporting the trade."

My stomach sank like the Titanic. *Please, Danu, don't let Daddy have supported such a thing.*

That's where I discovered that intense, troubling thought combined with a gallon of honey ale created two sparking fire sylph hands and a freshly ignited coffer.

Pete barked a curse as I screeched and leapt to my feet. "The hearth, Shorty! Christ, put it in the hearth before you catch the tavern on fire!"

So, I did. Then we two watched in conspiring silence as the coffer of blood seeds burned to ash in the slaver's rental room fireplace.

TWENTY-FIVE

"I thought I bade you not to souse yourself," Pete groused as I twirled into our hidden camp, still giggling as Sionna rushed me, her wagging tail propelling her hind end in the air.

"I gave it my best shot." I knelt before the harbinger's hound and barraged her with smooches. "Those ales you kept buying me were too good not to drink, Pete."

Pete gave Bob's backside a firm pat. "I wouldn't have bought you so many had you simply slowed your pace."

"Psh!" I grabbed my cloak from the wagon bed, the crisp night chilling me. "You could've let me buy my own as we'd planned, but whatever—we got what we needed, didn't we?"

He grinned in concession, removing Howlite's purse from his belt. "Want to count our spoils before bed, Shorty?"

"Yah huh!" I skipped to the cart and hopped up to sit beside Pete in the moonlight.

I never knew how it happened—the metamorphosis of moments. That night was no different. One moment, we were co-conspirators, hardcore into tallying what we'd stolen and debating the best uses for our new cache. The next, I could've been having a heart-to-heart with Olivia on a snowy Saturday night. Eventually, Pete and I lazed together in the wagon, chuckling about that night's events.

"Lord, I thought Maggie's eyes would bug out of her head entirely when she saw me heading up those stairs after you," Pete chortled, sucking on a leftover riggit bone. His head rested back upon the arm he'd bent behind him. "I wonder if she thinks I joined you."

I coughed, nearly spitting out the water I'd swigged from Pete's canteen. He'd told me to drink it all, that he wasn't in the mood to "meet the harpy you'll become when you feel like boiled shite." Un-hungover Amy was headache enough, I supposed.

"Like a *threesome*?" I squealed once I found my voice.

Pete epitomized my idea of a dark rake. "Is that what it's called now?"

"Wow." I shook my still inebriated head down at the water skin. "Only weeks ago, I was a virgin with my own private reading nook at the library. Now people suspect me of banging two guys at once. Jeesh."

"I take it that's not something you fancied doing tonight."

I blew a raspberry. "Not unless you subtracted a guy—and you also replaced Howlite."

When Pete's grin spread like warmed butter, I realized my careless verbiage may have admitted I was down for a twosome. With Pete.

"That's not what that meant. That's just how I say things sometimes. I say 'you' as a general 'you.' Doesn't necessarily always mean the person I'm speaking to. You know?"

"Is that right?" Pete's eyes did the tango.

"Stop looking at me like that!" I swatted the long leg sprawled beside mine, my heart leaping at my own slip up. "Stop!"

Pete shifted to evade my violence, hollow though it was. "Fret not, Shorty. I'll take your word for it. When you say 'you' in that context, 'you' could likely mean anyone."

"Right!"

"Like your fella, Briar."

Well, that was an emotional jab to the guts. I winced. "Oh, Goddess, you went there, huh?"

"Straight to it." Pete wiggled his foot against my hip. Did he even know he was bumping me when he did that?

"Honestly, no," I admitted to Pete—and to myself. "I wouldn't mean Briar in that context. Not tonight." *Maybe not ever again.* "I don't know why I'm telling you, of course."

He shrugged, as easygoing as I'd ever seen him. "Because I asked. And because sometimes it suits to unburden yourself when the moon is high and you're scuttered enough to do so."

I smiled, grateful to him. For allowing me the forum to vent. I hadn't had a proper gab session with a friend in weeks. Since my life had collapsed like a tower of twigs. I needed to get some stuff off my chest. Or as much as I could, given my limitations.

Or could I confess the truth about myself?

Don't make that call while you're drunk, you moron. You know he hates *Daddy. Telling him the truth right now will just screw with the pleasant vibes you've got going tonight.*

"Mother save me, Pete," I finally breathed a truth I felt safe divulging. "I really don't want to marry Briar."

The words thus spoken, they gonged through the pluming mist.

Acting as if this wasn't the be all and end all of revelations, Pete lifted a hand. "Then don't, Shorty."

If it were only that simple—

"If you dislike him, why would you honor such a betrothal?"

Because as heir to the dang throne, I might not have a frigging choice.

"Dislike is probably too strong a word to use." I gazed past wisps of fog.

Man, the heavens were bright, the stars diamonds in the sky. Some streaked across my plane of vision into the rollicking waves of the aurora majesta—which grew more vivid by the night.

"Briar *is* a great guy," I went on. "He's smart. He's funny. He's fun. I mean, he's got flaws, don't get me wrong, but I can't say I detest the guy. I just—"

How could I swim this quagmire?

"Do you fancy him?"

"Do you mean, 'Am I attracted to him?'"

Pete's expression was an unspoken *obviously*.

I chuckled, wistful for my girlish crush. "I always was."

"*Was*? Has your opinion on the matter changed?"

"Kind of, yeah."

Pete nodded. "Can't blame you, Shorty. After hearing your woeful tale over supper, I'd say he shouldn't either."

I snorted, recalling how I'd almost ruined story hour's merriment.

Humor welled in his molasses eyes. "When I'm so lazy with a toss, I expect to meet such disfavor."

I appreciated Pete's admittance of past laziness. Lazy nights happened here and there, I guessed. Yet, it would take more than one instance of laziness in bed for me to suddenly see the waggish man before me as unappealing. Likewise, I couldn't say Briar's cursory attentions were the sole cause of the new light I now viewed him in.

"Why the long face?" Pete nudged my hip. Maybe he *did* know he'd been wiggling against me.

I couldn't meet his eyes as I peeped, "What if—what if my woeful first times weren't woeful because of Briar? What if it was really me? What if I was the problem?"

"Don't start lamenting on your looks again," Pete groused. "If a bloke already has you on your back, you can rest assured that he finds you just dandy."

Cheeks no doubt flaming, I giggled. "No, that wasn't it." For a change. "The problem was that I didn't know how to tell Briar—to tell him what I liked—when we were doing stuff." I fidgeted with my cloak. "I didn't have the courage to speak up about it, I mean."

After several silent beats, I dared to peek up. Pete's habitual rakish charm had receded to rakish kindness. "Did he ask you what you liked, Shorty?"

I blinked. "No."

"Then how could he expect you, a virgin, to know how—or even to feel comfortable enough—in conveying such intimacies?"

Valid point.

"Unless he was a virgin as well? Or telepathic?"

"Uh, no." Briar would've been the oldest virgin in existence, and I knew for damn sure he couldn't read my mind.

"Didn't figure. Still an' all, good lovers ask—especially during a deflowering."

"Have you ever deflowered someone?" The question tumbled off my tongue without a bashful hitch. Probably because I was drunk. Maybe because conversing with Pete that night was effortless. My thoughts simply became words.

"Aye," he admitted, smirking at the stars. "In fact, a fair portion of the beyns Howlite so kindly reminded me that I'd been purchased for were virgins."

That he'd broached that subject after seeming so tormented by it earlier surprised me. "Did you have a reputation for being gentle?"

"Can't say as I did. I'm afraid even when I try to act the lamb, I wind up becoming more the ram. Truly, I think the youngbloods were so fond of me because I always endeavored to discover what would madden them with lust. That often routed their misgivings."

Ignoring my suddenly erratic pulse, I tittered. "And what would madden them?"

"Everyone was different, but I always found something to do the trick." Pete nodded my way, his amatory capacities revealed in a gaze, thorough as a resume. "I'm certain that if Briar had taken the time to learn your body, you'd not be sitting here, questioning your bed-play courage." His eyes glimmered. "You'd have been too far gone to care."

I cleared my throat. And my naughty mind. "I *was* pretty much in my head the entire time. Both times, actually."

"Mm." Pete's voice evoked images of shower steam. "See, I'd ensure you spent time in the rest of your body as well."

My breath shook. To cover up, I shimmied beneath my cloak. "Chilly, isn't it?"

Pete considered me for a moment before peering up at the moon. Then he inhaled like he was about to dive to the ocean's depths. "I kent what was being done to me. At the Shadow Palace—with Gentian's acolytes."

I held my breath, guessing he'd never made such an admission. Even to himself.

"I kent it was rape." His Adam's apple bobbed. "I suppose I simply chose not to see it that way, not to see myself in the light of a victim. Christ knew I was a victim in so many other ways." With a humorless laugh, he shook his head. "But for certain times like tonight, I rarely feel the indignity of it. Can't say I was always opposed to being sold like a prized stallion either. Especially to the virgins. They weren't as haughty or demanding as the more seasoned Dananns. Mostly, the youngbloods didn't even ken why they were at the Shadow Palace until I was delivered to their chambers—as a gift."

"That must have been awkward." How would I have reacted if a strange man had moseyed into my room for the sole purpose of taking my virginity? Probably not well. "Did any of them turn you away?"

He sniffed. "Gentian's brothelers don't precisely like refunding seeds, so I had to do what I could to inveigle the nervous ones. Making them feel safe was customarily all it took. Unless, of course, we were being watched. Then my task became a complicated game."

Had I heard right? "*Watched?*"

Pete shot me a sidelong glance. "Your kind has an affinity for voyeurism. That's why so many patrons pay second-hand stud fees—so they can watch."

"I swear on my father, I've never heard that." I could've gagged. "That's fucked up."

"Agreed, Shorty."

I shook myself. "Ick!"

Pete's grin faded. "My judgments are generally sound, but I should give him the benefit of the doubt—is your intended also ignorant of this world?"

"Oh, no, he'd lived here for a while before we crossed to the human world." I rested back against the wagon ledge, setting the water skin aside. I couldn't drink another drop. "He's much older than I am, though he doesn't look it, does he? He's a reverter, I guess. Actually, he grew up with my mother, which is just—so weird." I grimaced. "And I didn't know any of this until the day we crossed the portal. After my father—you know."

Pete sobered. "Then I'm right, Shorty. Don't marry him. I suspect you won't like what else he hasn't told you."

I stretched my arms high as I yawned, liquids jostling in my belly. "You're probably right about that too."

Pete stretched as well. "The night's waning, Shorty. We should sleep."

Nodding, I uncurled, the bracing air filtering its way beneath my ridiculous skirt. My teeth chattered as Pete helped me out of the wagon.

After we'd both relieved ourselves, I puttered around our camp in search of kindling. Our fire had died while we gambled, and mist now clung to my skin.

"We should've thought to do this earlier," I remarked as Pete shook leaves off his bedroll. "Now, we won't have the energy to get a fire going."

"We won't be setting any more fires tonight, Shorty." Pete angled my way. "Not after your last."

I stared at the cold, damp ground, then back at him. "And you're worried about me being hungover? Do you have any idea how uncomfortable I'll be, sleeping on the hard ground without a fire? I'll complain for a week."

His gaze rolled skyward. "I don't doubt it, Shorty. That's why you'll be joining me in the shadows tonight."

Oh, will I?

"When Howlite wakes, he'll be on the hunt for you. He'll know it was you who roasted his coffer. You were the last with him, don't forget."

I cringed, feeling foolish. "I hadn't thought of that."

Pete's twinkling eyes said he could tell. "A fire's smoke would betray our camp. Moreover, I wouldn't put it past the vengeful sod to send the dell's law force after you. As a royal official, he has that authority. So, you'd best sleep under dense cover."

Before I knew to scurry away, Pete's velveteen shadow cloak swallowed me whole, arousing both my claustrophobia and my fear of being lost to a vast and unending void. My only buoy in my welling panic was Pete's face, which glowed a yard away.

"Fret not," he dismissed my strained expression. "This isn't a ploy to debauch you. You need not sleep too near me. Think of the cloak as a tent."

"Not the problem, Pete." I fisted my hands. "How can I see your face so clearly when I can barely see myself?"

"Magic." His lips quirked boyishly.

I swallowed hard. "Right."

"What's the matter?"

I bit my lip, knowing I'd sound like a child when I answered, "I'm—I'm afraid of the dark."

"You didn't seem frightened the first time I showed you my cloak."

"I wasn't faced with spending a full night in it the first time, and your nightlight face was much closer then."

He arched a questing brow. "Then you do wish to sleep near me?"

Man, did I ever.

"To the light," I corrected him—and my reckless libido. "And I may need to listen to one or two songs to relax because I can't see my *freaking hands!*"

Pete swooped closer, chuckling as he grasped the invisible hands in question. Our fingers lit in his cozy, supernatural radiance. "That better, Shorty? Do calm down."

Taking his advice, I inhaled.

"As for the songs—I haven't the foggiest why you think I can sing."

"Not songs from you. Songs from my iBloom."

"That little whatnot you wouldn't sell to the pawner?" Clearly, he still thought me frivolous for refusing to sell it.

"That little whatnot holds hundreds of the best songs ever created on Earth, buddy. No pawner could pay us enough for it."

"Really?"

"Yeah!"

"Prove it."

"Huh?"

"I didn't mumble. Let's hear these *tours de force*. Perhaps that strain you incessantly sung to me on the road this morning?"

My breath stilled. "You heard?"

"Aye, I heard. What do you think rebalanced my magic?"

"My singing?"

"Aye. Or, I should say it gave me a nudge in the right direction. I finished the job myself."

"Good. I thought you could use some help in the lightness department. Didn't know if it would work." I clicked my tongue. "How—how exactly *does* it work? I mean, I remember how another person can directly affect someone's balance—like the siren you told me about. And I remember you talking about creating residual magic. You never said how those residuals affect people technically. Like, my song put out light magic, right?"

"Aye."

"Did you have to reap it to rebalance yourself? From the Community Chest of magic?"

He grunted at my colloquialism. If he knew how to play a game like Poker, he may have heard of Monopoly.

"I know you said fae can draw magic from that chest, but Sedge's story about Adam and Eve made it seem like sometimes those residuals can affect a person without them wanting it to."

"Sometimes it can. Not always. It depends on the magic—and the person. What residuals affect me might not affect you. Of course, in Sedge's case—I think it's safe to say that *anyone* standing too near soulmates should expect a drastic imbalance. Their magic would be *that* potent."

He rolled his eyes at my lovey-dovey expression.

"But to answer your *first* question—"

I shrugged, my questions doing more to distract from my fear of the dark than a tranquilizer.

"In the end, I reaped the residual magic your songs put out. In the beginning, you pushed me from the void without me doing a thing. And—I'm grateful to you for it, Shorty."

Was it just my imagination, or had his glow softened like candlelight?

"Some strong light magic must be veiled inside you for a simple song to push me that far. A song sung by a very, *very* bad voice, might I add."

Unoffended though I was, I blustered and swatted him. We both laughed.

"I never claimed to be a good singer either, Pete."

He yielded with a nod, then gestured toward something I couldn't see in his tenebrous dome. "Shall we get comfortable? I must hear all this music that's too wondrous to pawn."

"We can't really listen to *all* the music. I was only going to waste enough battery for a couple tracks. I want my iBloom to last for as long as possible." Danu knew I'd need a lyrical pick-me-up somewhere down the rocky road to Covenlen.

Smiling like the damn Cheshire Cat, Pete delved into his oblivion and produced a shimmery pomegranate seed—the equivalent of an American $100 bill, I'd been told. "Pomegranate seeds, when eaten for temporary power, allow one to draw the essence out of something."

Halleluiah! I thought, clapping—nearly leaping.

Pete chuckled at my excitement. "If used correctly, this tiny pod could power your music box without expending a fig of your battery."

Now, all those electronics being sold at the Goblin Market made sense. Electricity became moot with pomegranate seeds at hand. Finally, I'd found a reason to appreciate magic!

I closed Pete's fingers over the seed. "You better do the using. I'm afraid I'll screw something up, somehow delete all my data."

Pete shrugged. "As you say."

A brief eternity later, I bubbled like a shaken champagne bottle beside Pete on his bedroll. Laying as far from him as my earbuds allowed. Sionna snuggled between us, adding more heat to our already cozy midnight. Pete's face flickered within the dusky torchiere of his face. Mood lighting, I imagined.

"Ready?" He held the pomegranate seed to his broad mouth.

Man, was I ever? And as soon as the funk of one of my R&B favorites blared in my ear, the champagne bottle popped its cork, overflowing.

Spooked, Sionna rose from our nest. Pete settled her with a murmur, wide-eyed at my cackling.

"Jaysus," he said as Sionna calmed, her doe eyes still searching for danger. "If this is the best Earth has to offer, I'm sorely disappointed. We should've sold this bit of scrap for a measly grape seed."

Clicking my tongue, I snatched my iBloom from him. A paranormal aura now radiated from its smooth pink metal. Clearly the seed's doing. "Just you wait, mister man. It'll only get better."

"Goddess willing."

We surveyed song after glorious song in search of the ballad Pete had originally requested. He disliked a majority, sometimes snubbing a song altogether after just the opening verse.

"You've *got* to be kidding me, dude," I argued after he'd vetoed another song. "This song is iconic—one of the best pop songs ever—and you won't even hear it the whole way through?"

"Next," he repeated, bored to death.

I huffled but moved on.

"These blokes *again*?" Pete grumbled after a time. "Such mediocrity. Why must you keep subjecting yourself to it? Are musicians so scarce on Earth?"

"No. This group just happens to be my favorite, so I own every song they've ever sung."

"And what, pray tell, do they look like, Shorty?"

Clearing my throat, I lifted my chin. "Not important, Pete."

"Mm-hm."

"I love their voices." Their handsome faces, toned bodies, and charming personalities influenced *nothing*!

Pete's gaze shifted away, rife with skepticism.

"I do!"

"Uh-huh."

"Just—shut up!"

He rumbled, amused, as I skipped forward in my playlist.

As the song surfing drew on, the two of us grew quieter, our eyes heavier. When at last I heard the dulcet piano chords beginning "Know My Love," I had enough energy only to bump Pete's shoulder and whisper that this was *the one*.

His long-lashed eyes already shut, he grunted once in reply and angled toward me. The change in his wide mouth was infinitesimal. I wouldn't have noticed it if I wasn't all dreamy-eyed and studying him. His lips curled in the faintest display of tranquility as Delaney's sultry tones graced the earbuds. Peace descended on his body. His every muscle relaxed—his tension melting like cheese over a burger. After that night, I sensed that even in finding the ballad as sublime as he did, he'd never let his guard slip in the presence of anyone else. He only did so now because he was with me.

Because he trusted me.

My Goddess, Pete *trusted* me.

I supposed that made sense. After all, I'd saved his life. Once from the Fomorians, then again from infection. He'd also confided things in me that Olea insinuated most other harbingers wouldn't. Things I hadn't recoiled from—the lethality of the predator or the blood on his hands. Or from the demon lurking inside the murkiest parts of his soul.

Most of Pete's past would repel people. But I could accept the things he'd been forced to do in his past, the things he was forced to do now, for the sake of the man I'd come to know. He'd done the same for me, after all. Listened to my deepest anxieties and responded with acceptance and understanding. Maybe because he'd sensed the same thing I had. That on some level, we—an unladylike princess and an assassin with a conscience—were kindred spirits, both of us thieved of our previous lives and striving to find ways to cope with the grief of our new ones. Our hearts forever searching for home. For family.

That's when I realized something profound. And startling. As we lay there, an arm's length apart with a wriggling dog between us, surrounded by an unfathomable darkness that only grew closer the sleepier Pete got, I felt more connected to the harbinger in that chaste moment than I'd ever felt with anyone else in my life.

I fell asleep with this thought echoing above the refrain still crooning in my ear. And when the dark finally devoured me, I welcomed it like a friend.

TWENTY-SIX

The hysterical bray of a donkey woke me at dawn.

Disoriented at first, I flailed until I ripped the clinging oblivion off me like a sheet. I then goggled up at a tangerine sky bordered by blooms that looked as if they'd been painted with watercolors. My head fuzzy and aching (my duly earned hangover, I presumed), I took several moments to find my way off the bedroll. No sooner had I stood than was I tackled back to the ground by an enormity of heaving muscle.

"Don't make a sound," Pete panted against my ear, his rough hand muffling my screech. His beard scratched my temple. "Don't fight me, Shorty."

What the fuck are you doing? I wanted to demand as I kicked beneath him. *Get the hell off me!*

For goodness sakes! If he'd wanted to pounce on me, why hadn't he just done it the night before when I was drunk and giving him sex eyes? His morning sneak attack made no goddamn sense!

Until I saw it—a tiny, glittering beacon floating through the departing mist. A celestial gift sent from the devil just for me.

My gaze locked onto it, every fiber of my being itching to grab it. To take it. To eat it. To have it plant itself inside me and grow within my body like an unstoppable vine. To become nothing more than a vessel for germination.

"Remember what I told you," Pete whispered as I gawped at temptation itself, which sailed on a breeze wafting my way. "About the worst entrapment curses."

I stopped breathing when the curse seed paused just inches away. My reflection in its golden shell looked crazed with both yearning and fear. It peered back at me, hovering—waiting for me to give in. Not that I could, with Pete locking me down like a pro-wrestler.

Eventually, the seed realized that I'd somehow resisted its allure, and the damn thing got angry—started raging in convulsions. Next thing I knew, the burning itch I felt was in my veins. I was about to experience the hell my father endured when he'd been compelled to touch a curse seed.

"Christ!" Pete swore when he saw I was going to freak the fuck out. His shadow tethers constricted around me like restraints on a violent criminal. He gasped for forgiveness when he shoved my face into his forearm, silencing my agony, for fire ants were eating me from the inside out. I'm sure I hurt him back when I bit into his flesh. His salty blood welled in my mouth as I fought to claw off my skin and tear out my hair.

"Just hold on, Shorty," Pete begged while I bawled. "I promise I'll not let you go. Just hold on until it stops."

Goddess, please *make it stop! PLEASE!*

I couldn't say how long the torture lasted. I wasn't in my body for all of it. There were times I was back in Daddy's bedroom, battling bogeybats and watching him die. Then others when I stood in the cabin on Avalon Green, reliving Briar's expressions of not-quite-loving me. Moments where I knew I'd be butchered for a hearty Fomorian feast. And times where I mewled in a meadow of wildflowers, alone in a foreign world.

I was half present when Pete gritted a curse of shock. The blood rash had strengthened my urge to submit to the seed, and my warrior's skin was helping it. Yet somewhere in my barrage of suffering, I clung for dear life to Pete's voice.

The sound of which towed me into brighter flashbacks of a night spent in camaraderie beneath a colorful midnight sky, where a piano melody bonded me with the dashing rake smirking at me over a pair of Bicycle playing cards. Where he'd broken the dam of my pent-up despair with the power of laughter. That same rake then grew smug as he spoke harsh truths to me, brandishing a bottle of ketchup intimating, *Who knows you like I do?*

No one, replied my soul as I knelt in a storm, the rake gazing past it. To me.

If we go down, we go down together, he brogued over the whipping wind.

Yes, I clung to Pete. And that painful itch I couldn't scratch retreated like a wounded animal in the face of him.

The curse seed, admitting defeat, dropped to the loam, a dead thing.

Pete breathed a fervent oath as my body loosened in his stranglehold. My ribs ached from his unfettering tethers, cold sweat saturating my clothes. Pete, too, dripped like a soda bottle, hissing at the puncture wounds I'd made in his arm. My canines must've been hella sharp.

"It'll be fine," Pete assuaged my dismay. "You clean your teeth more than is holy, Shorty. I doubt you'll poison me."

I wanted to argue that even the cleanest mouths harbored bacteria, but that's when I registered the general commotion happening in town. At the break of dawn, even cities were quiet, so the shouts, wails, and screams for mercy were well out of place.

I wasn't the only one in Humwater Dell to be visited by an entrapment curse that morning.

"Please, sir, I beseech you with *everything* I have. Set her free of this!"

My arm hairs stood as I met Pete's horrified stare. Was that Rye's voice, so ragged and desperate?

"Shite!" Pete rushed to peer through the brush enclosing our hidden camp. His shoulders stiffened at whatever he saw.

Seized by some commanding instinct, I brushed Pete aside to see what was happening with my own eyes. The town square teemed with beyns of every race, organizing themselves in straight lines like automatons. More were unwittingly joining them.

Shit on a shingle! Is that what that curse seed would've done to me?

Most of the beyns were youthful and lovely. Several were ten years from elderhood. More than a few were in mid-puberty. All of them were still in their bedclothes, and none of them spoke as the team of armed Dananns I'd seen at the tavern last night, now all dressed in the uniform of their profession, chained them together with glowing ropes.

I searched for Maggie in the ranks but couldn't find her. The cursed were too numerous.

The keening we'd heard came from the beyns' loved ones—ceylas, parents, *children*. At least the ones who'd seen what was happening. The rest would be shattered to wake and discover a family member or friend had been cursed and taken as they slept.

"Please, sir!" Rye entreated, breaking my heart. He wore only a pair of breeches, his intricate navy wings flapping double-time beside one of the bustling slavers—a disheveled Howlite. "You can't turn Maggie slave! You've known her for years!"

"Aye!" Howlite snarled, spinning on Rye and stopping him short. "And this is how my decades of friendship and patronage are rewarded? I'm attacked in my private chamber, my entire year's earnings burnt to cinders! Tell me, *friend*, how long have you and yon ceyla been sheltering abolitionist foes under my nose?"

I jerked toward Pete, jaw hanging.

Sure, I understood why Howlite would be angry about what I'd done to him. He wasn't that far off, deeming me an abolitionist who'd weaseled her way into his room to deprive him of riches and make a point. Whether that was my original intent when I'd met him, that's what I'd wound up doing. But never in a million years would I have guessed he'd blame and seek to punish anyone else for my behavior. Let alone a whole fucking village!

"Tell me this isn't what I think it is," I croaked at Pete, whose face had drained of color, his hands clenching hilts of both *scian* and sword.

"Maggie and I have done no such thing!" Rye shook frustrated hands. Obviously, he'd already denied their involvement. Maybe more than several times, his words falling on deaf ears. "We'd never met that lady afore last night, sir! We knew naught of her intentions for being there! And we did *not* aid her in her plot! Now, set my ceyla free of your curse!"

Howlite sniffed, his lip curling. "I'll set her free as soon as you turn over that conniving harlot."

"I don't know where she is!" Rye was losing his shit. Understandably. "If I knew, I'd tell you! What else can I give you? I'll give anything. How much in the way of seeds did the lady burn? If I must, I'll sell the pub to recoup what you've lost. It'll be worth nothing without Maggie, anyhow. Just—*please.*"

I clutched a handful of my rumpled ponytail, wishing I hadn't woken up.

Howlite sneered. "Your seeds are worthless to me. I. Want. *Her.*"

My throat constricted. Vengeance was Howlite's only desired recompense. Shaking myself, I bid farewell to my freedom. "I've got to stop this." I took the first step toward zombiedom.

Pete clamped my shoulder, pinning me in place. "Don't be a damned fool, Shorty." His growl wasn't for me, but for the wolves among the lambs. "We must do something, aye, but your sacrifice won't save Maggie."

His breath, so close to my ear, sent shivers sweeping down my neck. "But you heard him!" I exclaimed. "He—"

"He'll enslave Maggie anyhow." The harbinger's face flared with the rage of a man once sold into bondage. "He'll enslave them all whether he has you or not. His greed knows no scruples."

"But he just refused Rye's offer." Wouldn't a tavern's worth of seeds slake anyone's greed?

"*None* of this is about what you did last night. Howlite and his cohorts are using that as a convenient excuse for gleaning half of all Humwater Dell, but you haven't caused this, Shorty." He withdrew from me and began pacing, squeezing the life out of his own mouth in his stress.

"Then why are they doing it?"

Pete raked his fluffy locks. "Howlite must be sniffing after a promotion." He uttered this more to himself than to me. "This must've been sanctioned."

"You mean he'd planned to do this?" My throat closed on an upwelling of nausea. "Before he even met me?"

Pete stopped, something potent and dangerous rippling through the set of his broad shoulders, then through the blade-like mind whetting itself on primal magic beyond those fresh-baked eyes. He fisted his sword hilt like he was already adding several royal officials to his kill tally. "Close your eyes, Shorty."

I recoiled at this request. *What* was he going to do?

When I failed to comply, Pete flung another shadow my way. Blindfolding me.

"Pete!" I pried at the tether. "Don't *you* be a damned fool either!"

He didn't answer me for several nerve-wracking minutes. Minutes in which I imagined him descending on the slavers like a ravening raptor. My heart hammered as I listened for the inevitable screams.

Then the tether unbound my eyes, slithering off like a snake.

Blinking to resettle my vision to the light, I found Pete standing before me, peering through the crepe myrtles. "Sorry," he said. "I needed to retrieve something from my sphere."

"Your what?"

"My talismanic sphere." His gaze shifted, assessing. "It's what I use to store various necessities while on the road. Like the ossified emerald I wove through your tether."

So that's where he keeps his potions. "Like an invisible backpack?"

"More like a closet—for professional use." Anger twitched through his mouth. "Each of the slavers has one, ken. It's where they store those gold tethers they're using right now."

My breath hitched. "You mean—their tethers aren't like yours?"

"Precisely, Shorty. Slavers' tools of the trade aren't rooted within them like harbingers' are."

Bile stung my throat. "These spheres—they don't stock themselves, do they?"

"No," he spat. "Every unrooted item kept there must be personally equipped. Every piece of food. Every blade. Every arrow. Every *slaver's* tether."

"And Howlite and friends couldn't have stocked their closets *after* he regained consciousness?"

"Not unless a royal armory was built in the Dell overnight."

My stomach curdled. "So, the hundreds of tethers they're using right now—"

"They'd already had them stocked and at the ready."

"They planned this," I repeated, almost numb.

"Indeed." Pete never felt the need for a sugar coating. "A slaving entourage carrying more than 20 tethers between them would be considered excessive. This stockpile—the royal armorers would deem outrageous. And needless, like. Unless this was a sanctioned mission for which these tethers were specifically allocated."

"And by sanctioned—" The bile rose again.

"I mean the king," he rumbled like righteous thunder. "He's allowing this horseshite to happen in his name."

I buckled to the ground and vomited at Pete's boots. It was all too much. The sorrowful howling of the Humwater Dellians, the barely restrained hatred surging through Pete's every fiber, the fact that I'd made out with a feyr who'd been planning to enslave every pretty beyn within a ten-mile radius for Goddess only knew what purposes, and the fear that someone in my father's inner circle, who he'd entrusted with his sovereign powers, was abusing them in atrocious and irreparable ways.

The powers that I was destined to inherit. Should I choose them.

With things as they were, how could I not?

Fucking A!

Sionna pranced around me, whimpering at my condition.

Still stiff as hell in his justified wrath, Pete took a knee beside me, laid a hand on my back as I barfed. He soothed Sionna with his other.

"Drink." He pressed his waterskin to my sour mouth when I'd finished.

Tears streamed down my cheeks, my fingers trembling, as I guzzled the dregs of Pete's water. When I'd washed away the noxious taste in my mouth, I returned Pete, the stone-faced cage fighter, his water skin. "Th-thank you," I croaked, wiping my chin.

"You're welcome." Pete grabbed my elbow and hefted me to my feet. "Are you through retching?"

I glared at his sudden deviation from compassion. "I think so."

"Good. Because I must do *something*, and I need your help."

Looking skyward, I said a silent prayer to all that was holy. For everyone's sakes. Then, rapping Pete on the chest, I trudged to the wagon for my book bag. "Give me a minute to change. I'm not getting in a fight wearing a fucking cancan dress."

I found Rye on the edge of the slaving lines, searching for Maggie. I'd done a cursory sweep for her too and hadn't found her. For all I knew, she wasn't even there. As personal as Howlite was making his beef with the publicans for simply encountering me, it didn't seem above him to lock Maggie up somewhere until the herds were ready for shepherding.

Stealthy as I could manage—given that I was close to shitting my pants—I grabbed Rye, clamped his mouth, and dragged him, wings flapping, into an evergreen alcove where shadows dappled us like leopards.

Rye's eyes blazed in recognition when I spun him to face me. His breath sawed as he opened his mouth to snarl at me for what I'd done, but I held a finger to my lips. Then I unsheathed a very large dagger from under my hair and held it out for his inspection.

The publican blanched. Pete was right—Rye recognized his *scian*. Maggie must not have told him Pete followed Howlite and me upstairs after the tournament because he gasped. "Where did you—?"

"Shh." I trembled, eyes darting toward the town square for slavers. If any of them saw me, I was toast. "He gave it to me for protection. We're going to try to help."

His shock fading, Rye scowled. "Did *Pete* have a hand in what happened to Howlite's coffer?"

I grabbed Rye's sweaty arm to quiet him. "What happened last night was an accident," I whispered, which was true. For the most part. But Rye's silent castigation pricked my guilt—the bleeding wound that it was. "And that's *not* why this is happening."

This, Pete had assured me. And I really needed to believe him right then.

"How are just the two of you going to help?" Rye gestured toward the slaving lines and their new hawk-eyed masters.

I bit my lip, sheathing Pete's *scian* between my shoulder blades. "Is there somewhere nearby that we can hide people?"

Rye's brown eyes clouded further.

Pete's plan wasn't a fix-it-all. We could only diminish the damage being done to the Dell—unless we wanted to become outlaws for killing royal officials. For me, I didn't foresee that charge sticking—being the crown princess, and all. But for Pete—well, that wouldn't be ideal. And I couldn't help *anyone* without him.

As if this thought had signaled him, I heard Pete gripe above the beyns' wailing families, "What in fecking hell is happening here?"

Rye and I peered around the tree trunk wall we hid behind, watching Pete prowl toward the slavers, all of whom had abandoned their posts to deal with the threat in their midst. The threat Howlite knew had spent centuries kicking ass and taking names. The disheveled, ornery, hungover predator whose hand hovered by his sword's pommel. If he blew his lid over their culling, they'd need all hands on deck to quell him.

Just as Pete had predicted.

I yanked Rye from the shadows. Together, we dashed to the closest grouping of bound beyns and led one of its chain gangs away. The cursed moved like marionettes, gazing ahead but seeing nothing. We deposited them in an alpine building reminiscent of a post office.

"What of the tethers?" Rye asked as we hustled back to continue our rescue. "How do we remove them?"

"Cold iron." Adrenaline racing through my veins, I skimmed for slavers and found only hopeful bystanders—too scared to aid our endeavors but willing us to continue. "You freeze an iron blade, then cut the tether. That's what Pete said."

"And their curses?"

"A Witch can remove entrapment curses."

Rye's face dropped. "The Dell was purged of Witches four decades ago!"

"I know." I frowned, wondering about the purge. "Pete told me."

Swearing, Rye took wing. "I'll move faster in the air."

"Stay low!" I gulped as he flitted off. At least when we'd been working side-by-side, I didn't feel as exposed. But I mustered on, my help meaning freedom to someone.

"You're seizing every bonny female in the Dell, you rotter!" Pete groused in the background at Howlite, who waved him off, all puffed up like a strutting, power-tripping turkey. "You take them, then who's to warm my pallet on my next pass-through?"

Good idea, Pete—playing the horny dog. Something Howlite can relate to.

The asshead slaver chuckled. "You'll wank it or make do, McKenna."

"Make do?" Pete harrumphed. "With what? The hogs in Exotic Enid's pens? I ken you and your ilk have already laid claim to several of their hindquarters, but I don't share your crooked appetites. You like the snuffling, dirty ones, don't you, buck?"

Howlite fisted his hands at Pete's impertinence, but several of his fellow slavers couldn't contain their laughter. He knocked one of his underlings aback the head.

"Funny you should mention dirt, McKenna," Howlite said. "Have you seen that bony bitch I fucked last night? I've a score to settle with her."

He did not *just say that!*

Seething, I ducked behind a boulder a breath away from the next chain gang, my chest expanding with flame at that magic word—bitch.

Get your shit together, Amy! You can't firebomb every person who calls you that! Even one who lies about sleeping with you!

I did as Pete had taught me during our initial magic lesson—breathed in through my nose, out through my mouth. He claimed ninety percent of controlling one's powers was simply breathing properly. So, I meditated for several heartbeats just to forestall physical flames, then scurried to the chain-gang and nabbed their tether. Knowing it wasn't flammable.

I rushed them to safety as fast as their hapless feet allowed. Pete could only keep his distraction going for so long, after all. My job was to work fast. And not get caught.

Sadly, I failed on that second part. Because someone dimed me out.

"She's the one what your gaffer's after, isn't she?" a homely beyn cried to the slaver she'd dragged over. I'd noticed her at the tavern the night before, having what looked like a girls' night with 3 of her besties. Apparently, she'd noticed me too. Now, she stood pointing me out as I halted by the fountain, gritting my teeth on a scream. Thankfully, I'd been on my way back to retrieve more slaves and hadn't had any with me. So, the slaver wouldn't know what I'd been up to and go hunting for hidden slaves.

He only knew I was wanted by his boss.

"You, there!" he bellowed. "Hold!"

"He'll release them all now, won't he?" The beyn clutched the slaver's leafy coveralls. "He'll release my Daisy?"

When the slaver ignored her concerns and shoved her away, I knew Pete was right about this whole situation. Those cursed beyns were as good as lost even if Howlite had me where he wanted me. I wondered who at the Spring Palace I needed to kill for orchestrating this clusterfuck as I raced off, deeper into the city—before the slaver gandered Rye flying our way, another line of slaves in tow.

The slaver tore after me, blowing a whistle of such high pitch that it shredded my inner ears. "Stop in the name of the king!"

Danu must think she's so funny, I mused at the irony of the command as the slaver blew his whistle again. I clutched my head, wincing at the dissonant warbling, and scrambled over tree roots and through corridors, having no idea where I was going. With my head throbbing, my eyes only worked in flashes.

Not long after the first whistle, a symphony of metallic shrieks pierced my eardrums, and my brain was 10 seconds away from rupturing. I wept for Danu's mercy and staggered to the verdant ground, crawling for my life when a hand snarled in my hair.

I screamed, that hand wrenching me to my feet, jerking me around to face its owner—the devil incarnate. Tears streamed down my cheeks as I glared at him.

Hydra glinted through Howlite's eyebrow in the golden morning suns. Several of his fellow slavers sprinted up behind him, whistles still in mouths. Pete was nowhere to be seen.

"Where's Maggie, you evil shithead?" I hissed.

That's all I could think to say at the time, and I got rammed in the nose by a hairy-knuckled fist.

My world fractured into stars, a furious crack reverberating through my face, my jaw, my eyes. I dropped to the ground like a bird with a broken wing—just the kind of disadvantaged creature the devil would revel in tormenting.

The first kick booted all the wind out of me. So, I couldn't even breathe to cry for help when the second got that tailbone the bogeybats had splintered.

"I want my bloody seeds, you fusty cunt," Howlite seethed, lumbering after me as I army crawled through the dirt, bleeding from my nose. "And I'll get them from you one way or another. Even if I must sell you at market to the highest bidder, you'll recoup my losses. Where do you think you're going, anyhow? How did you evade the curse?"

A wracking sob finally escaped me when Howlite aimed to kick me again. I managed to get ahold of his foot to unbalance him as Pete had shown me. But I couldn't remember how to counteract Howlite yanking my hair until I let him go. Or what move would've prevented him from flattening my hand to the ground and stomping on it, the straight-up dick that he was.

This time I screamed, my bones pulsing in shock as I gripped them to my chest. Tendrils of smoke were beginning to fume from my fingers.

No fire, no fire, no fire! I promised, I promised, I promised!

"Need another curse seed, cap?" some other slaver called.

Hyperventilation was a real possibility for me. *Wind*! I demanded of my magic. *Give me my goddamn wind!*

"Nay need, Bain." Howlite snatched me by the bicep and lugged me back to my feet. "Just the paralytics for this one. I want her to ken what's happening when we take her."

Something resembling a grenade pinged to the ground a yard away from us. Howlite saw it the same moment I did and bellowed to his comrades to take cover.

Just as the tiny canister exploded in a solar flare of fibrillating light.

The force of that light flung slavers and citizens alike. I, myself, was propelled skyward and slammed into a mammoth tree trunk. The collision must've knocked me out, because I couldn't recall what happened to me between impact and when Pete swept me into his arms and spirited me away.

"This is precisely why you need combat training," he chided, breathless, as I bleared up at him. "If you kent how to defend yourself against pricks like Howlite, I wouldn't have used my sol-scuttle."

I groaned as he bounded over a boulder, jarring all my injuries back to awareness. "You threw that grenade?" Just talking seared after having my nose crunched in. Goddess, I hoped the damage wasn't permanent. "You could've really hurt me."

"Aye, well—I did tell you not to get caught."

I huffed a laugh, licking a trickle of blood from my lip.

"And better a few scrapes than slavery."

That, I couldn't argue with.

"Hold on tighter, Shorty." Pete darted around bracken, joggling me as he went. "We must reach Sionna and Bob at the passage before the slavers catch us. There'll be no more pleasantries if they do. They'll come to fight and, well—"

I stared up at the coniferous canopy in mute alarm, knowing how that battle would end. Pete may have been mighty, ruthless, and cunning, but the slavers had curse seeds. And paralytics. Something that might render even Pete useless. And that was a gamble we just couldn't make.

As it happened, we did reach Sionna and Bob at the road, right where Pete had doubtless told Bob to be. Pete plopped me in the back of the wagon beside a fretful Sionna, then clicked at Bob to, "Leg it!" The enchanted donkey clattered off down the mossy road like Satan had caught our trail.

Pete hauled himself into the wagon with me before we picked up too much speed. First, he patted Sionna's bobbing head, then he grabbed me by the back of mine, which now felt like a cracked nut in need of shelling.

Ready to curl up and pass out, I moaned and swatted at Pete. He ignored my complaints, though, gauging my injuries. "You've broken your nose." He sighed. "I'll have to mend it."

I leaned as far back as I could with him holding me in place. "Do you have a potion for that?"

His mouth quirked. "No."

"Then how the fuck are you mending it?"

"Sorry, Shorty."

What followed was a lot of blistering pain and vehement cursing. From both of us. In the end, I sat in a defensive squat in the far corner of the wagon, pressing a rag from Pete's belt to my throbbing, readjusted nose. And Pete hissed at a row of fresh scratches I'd left on his neck.

But instead of lingering on the scuffle, we silently—and mutually—decided to move on. Let the unpleasantness between us fizzle into the sunshine.

Eventually, Pete relaxed back against the juddering wagon ledge—once he thought us safe from pursuit, I assumed. He draped a long arm over Sionna, who sniffed his wounds until he flicked her nose away.

Tears still pooling in my eyes, I croaked, "You really think the crown is behind the mass culling?"

Stupid question, Pete's answering look retorted. Because if royal slavers were doing the culling, then who else was behind it if not the king—or his proxy? But I didn't want my family embroiled in this. In any fucking way!

"It just doesn't make sense, though, Pete. I mean—they're enslaving half a fucking city! As prized as female fertility is in this world, doing shit like that is just begging for rebellion. The crown would have to know that. I mean, come on!"

Pete just stared at me, unspeaking.

"What?" I glanced down at the rag I'd been using on my nose. The bleeding had thankfully slowed. "Cat got your tongue?"

He chewed his lip for a beat before saying, "No, Shorty, I'm just hesitant to answer."

"Why?"

"Because I don't want to lie to you, but the truth might very well influence your decision to help me kill Gentian. And as much as I need your help, I want your choice to—"

"You think Gentian's involved in this?" This immediately enraged me. For *so* many reasons. "Why would you say that?"

"Because his unholy name is written all over this." Pete spat over the wagon ledge, that unholy name a toxin on his tongue. "I can't tell you what's happening at the royal level—arguably some lucrative bargain. But I ken how Gentian works, and he has his oar stuck firmly in this one."

I stopped breathing as he continued.

"And it's highly suspicious, ken, that Gentian's lover—Dewina—his favorite, mind you—is a Witch who was born in Humwater Dell. A Witch none too happy that her family was expelled during the Dell's Cleansing—as history named it."

I thought I'd be rather peeved about that too if I were Dewina. "So, Gentian made a bargain with the crown to enslave nearly all of Humwater Dell's beyns as a *gift* to his girlfriend?"

"I'd wager it has more to do with seeds than Dewina, though pleasing her certainly helps Gentian keep her to heel."

"But why just the beyns if the whole Dell was complicit in the cleansing? It—"

Something dawned on me then. Something heinous.

"Gentian's renowned for brotheling, Shorty—especially in the art of womb servility—where a beyn under an entrapment curse is bought for the sole purpose of breeding faelets for her owner—as heirs, or for vanity, or to be slaves themselves. I told you entrapment curses were terrible fates."

"Fuck my life!" I clenched my eyes shut, shook myself, but the nightmare he'd conjured didn't fade. "What dystopian novel are we living in?"

Pete grunted at that. "There've been rumors around the Shadow Court that the crown has been seeking a way into those sordid markets—seeking someone to help them manage such a venture. And Gentian's really the only feyr for that job."

"The crown procures the slaves then? And Gentian sells them? Gets a cut of the action?"

"Aye, well, there must be an intermediary to fool the Divine Cadre. A bargain like this is explicitly against the royal charter. But aye—that's the gist of it."

My hangover had suddenly returned. It took me several minutes before I quavered, "Did Rye ever find Maggie?"

Regret shone in Pete's eyes. "Not that I saw, no." He paused, watching me. "How many beyns did you save, Shorty?"

He meant the question as a boon for my sadness, but it only served to embitter me. "Thirty. Thirty out of hundreds."

"We can still help the hundreds. Royal slavers always take their quarry to the Spring Palace first—for inspection and sale. The process takes months. If we kill Gentian before the beyns are sold, then the king might come to his senses and rethink this whole enterprise."

At that, I wept. The king would've *never* struck such a bargain with Gentian—the feyr who'd killed his wife. I couldn't say the same about the rat running the show in his absence. Or about who'd be doing it now that Daddy was gone.

To say I was morose for the rest of the day was putting it mildly. Pete was melancholy too—quieter, less apt to joke—and once he deemed it safe for us to slow our pace, his usual stride on the road seemed to slog. But he didn't wallow. No, that was *all* me. For several miserable hours.

And then I got *angry*. So angry, in fact, that Sionna wouldn't come near me as I fumed in the back of the wagon, the air around me sulfuric.

Who the hell was this rat—or rats—bargaining with Gentian? Betraying my father, my entire family. Were they in league with Gentian when my mother died? For how long had they been working toward this plot for mass bondage? For sex trafficking? For *womb* trafficking? For this abomination to begin so soon after Daddy's death—it wasn't a coincidence.

And how dare Gentian! For seeking to ruin my life! My family! The safety and happiness of my people! How fucking *dare* he think he had the right to corrupt, and manipulate, and punish, and enslave—and *rule*!

Who the *fuck* did he think he was? This was *my* kingdom! Mine to protect! And I'd be damned if I'd allow some pompous, arrogant, narcissistic, avaricious, cruel, immoral motherfucker to take his overblown, petty sibling rivalry out on my subjects without meeting furious retribution.

The Shadow Prince was asking for it, and I was going to give it to him.

"Stop the cart!" I snarled around dusk. "Stop!"

Pete was just halting our progress to the obnoxious irritation of Bob when I stumbled from the wagon and hobbled, still rather sore from that morning, toward the rocky mountain wall rising sharply to our right. The road we traversed had grown much steeper, more precarious. Ferns and boxwoods dotted the stony path, tall trees now scarce.

Without explanation, I paused just feet from the wall and clamped my lips. Then I funneled all the fire I'd suppressed earlier into my fingers. I chucked a burning ball of turquoise at the hilly rise, a petulant child throwing pebbles. Luckily, the ball didn't ricochet but burst apart like a firecracker.

Pete stayed back with the cart and the animals as I threw ball after fiery ball at the wall, trying to spend all my rage, resentment, and devastation like a bottle of lighter fluid.

Finally, I threw a massive bomb that blazed up and set the drier shrubs on fire. It boomed as I clenched my hands and shrieked at my nemesis in a voice so jagged it tore my throat, "What the *fuck* did we ever do to you? What did those beyns ever do to you?"

My fit only stoked the combustion inside me, and my wind broke from me without my permission. It whipped the flames I'd created into twisters, their heat barely phasing me. They could've licked the skin right off my body, and it would've made no difference. My pain couldn't be any greater than it already was.

I clutched my ears. "Why won't you just crawl back under the fucking rock you came from like the fucking worm you are and leave us all the fuck alone? *Why!*"

Another firebomb exploded out of me just before Pete grabbed me like an idiot and swept me into his damn flammable arms. "Shorty!" He clutched my sweltering face in his already blistering hands, concern wild in his eyes. "Control your fire before you burn out."

My breath gusting, I cried, "I want my life back, Pete! I want my home and my family and my friends! He took everything from me! *Every* fucking thing!"

I heard my flames lashing, smelled the smoke choking the air, but Pete's flushing face was the only thing I saw. "Breathe," he urged, still not pulling back despite the sweat beading his forehead, soaking his unkempt hair. Dear Goddess, if he didn't get away from me, he was going to melt.

Trying to stop myself from hurting him, I shuddered inward. Deeply. Which was like catharsis. And a broken dam.

"I want him back!" I exclaimed. "I want my dad. I want my dog. I want my cats. I want my books and my own clothes and my own bedroom and a goddamn toilet with toilet paper! I want iced coffee and pop concerts and movie theaters and game nights with my friends. Oh, *Goddess*, I want my friends." *And Vi and Ace*, I thought, my tears crashing. "I just—I want to be a *girl* again! I don't want to be a Danann beyn fae whatever-the-hell-I-am! I want to be a girl—a woman—without magic. I just want to be *me*!"

My heart now bared, my passion fizzled. My firestorms slowly calmed.

"He took that from me," I whimpered to Pete, who simply stood with me—hearing me. "Gentian took *me* away from me."

The most painful part of it all.

Pete's Adam's apple bobbed, his eyes swimming. "That's what he does, Shorty."

"That's what he'll do to those beyns who've been culled," I gushed into my palm, my fingers trembling. "That's what he'll do to Maggie."

Pete's lips quivered as he pawed away my tears, gentle as a bear. "Not if we stop him."

I knew Pete would say that. I also knew what I'd say in response. That decision had made itself the moment I'd seen those innocent beyns, fae with lives and families, lined up like broken fillies for sale to the highest bidder. Unconscionable, yes—but that wasn't the only factor working in Pete's favor.

Shuddering, I gazed up at his grave face and thought that now, in this barbarous land, I had a friend—someone who had my back. And it wasn't weird that I'd forged such a bond with the guy sent to kidnap me for the creep trying to destroy my life. Not anymore. I stopped checking the warmth I felt toward him. Because I now trusted my own instincts, my own goddamn dreams entreating me to have faith in him.

Yes, Pete had said he wanted my help killing Gentian because he wanted me to save myself from the certain hell awaiting me at the Shadow Palace. But hearing him and believing him were two different things. Fear and paranoia had prevented me from seeing his intentions as anything other than selfish. But right then, as Pete comforted me without seeking escape from my dangerous, volatile state—something even Briar hadn't managed—his compassion enveloped me as if it were a hug.

Now, I understood that Pete, with his whole heart, didn't want me to live the horrors he had, that he dreaded that fate for me. And that he wouldn't ask such impossible feats of me if there were any other options. That in forging this plot against Gentian, he was risking his life—his soul. For me. And the millions upon millions who were under the Shadow Prince's thumb.

"Then let's stop him," I finally answered Pete, my voice as raw as my heart. "Let's stop him forever."

TWENTY-SEVEN

Two weeks later, Pete and I traversed the sandy footpath weaving between massive, pastel banyan trees, their feathery leaves arcing over us, shading us from the increasingly hot suns. The Summer Court, my mother's home, loomed on my horizon.

"You're improving," Pete said as I plodded beside him, counting my many bruises. Training that morning had been arduous. Productive but arduous. I only had a spring in my step because I wasn't the only one sporting new injuries.

Not that I'd wanted to hurt Pete, but that's just what happens when a guy plays with fire sylphen. And now I couldn't help smirking at the rough-hewn bandage on his neck, or the hairs singed off his manly knuckles. He seemed pleased with his battle scars too.

"If you don't quit taunting me while we're training, you'll see a *lot* of improvement out of me."

"Aye, Shorty, but I meant the fire you sparked when you weren't apparently angry. We need you to control your power no matter your emotional state, and you were doing just that near the end." He chuckled. "That's how you got me in my neck. Without your eyes glowing red as embers, I wasn't expecting that last bolt. Took me quite off guard, you did."

"I do that every now and then." I smirked at him. Which made him smirk right back.

Wonder what color my eyes are now.

Even after he'd turned away, I would've bet money he could tell me from memory.

"You're improving too."

Probably thinking something along the cocky ass lines of, *Can't improve upon perfection,* Pete arched a brow. "Am I?"

"Yeah. You're not nearly as big a drag as you were when we started this trip."

He eyed me. "Thank you?"

I didn't explain my idiom, his mystification entertaining.

Suddenly, Pete emitted a strident whistle that made me jump in my boots and Bob bray to a halt. Seriously, the literal ass would rupture my eardrums if he didn't stop making such atrocious sounds.

"Sionna, stay on the road!" Pete called, but she merrily zigged into the woods. "Sionna!" She didn't zag back out.

Cussing, Pete clomped to the back of the wagon, began untying his bow.

"Has she done this before?"

"Aye. She's caught the scent of some rodent, no doubt." Shouldering his quiver, he plucked the bow free of its bolt. "Should make sure that's it, though, aye?"

I started toward the coppice Sionna had wandered into.

"Where do you think you're going?" Pete chuckled as he fell into my step. "And unarmed, to boot?"

"*Psh*! Unarmed?" I snapped, my fingers sparking like a lighter. "Please."

Pete sniffed. "That fleeting ember couldn't light a candle, and you think it'll help us vanquish whatever evil lies ahead?"

Though I slowed, I didn't stop. "You think there's evil ahead?"

"Damned if I know, Shorty, but I doubt you're capable of defending us if there is."

Sneering, I flipped my hair at him and stalked ahead. "We'll see about that. Don't even think about trying to stop me."

Pete dogged my heels. "Why would I do that? Whatever you attempt, it'll surely be a fine thing to watch."

Whatever Pete hoped to watch, it didn't matter. Sionna hadn't gone far, and she hadn't scented anything nefarious. In fact, she'd nosed out a pair of youthful beyns nibbling from a basket of bread and berries in a wagon with a broken wheel.

At first glance, I pegged them as Middlings, but as we drew closer, I realized they were different racially. While Middlings shared a similar musculature with humans, these beyns' bone structure was more otherworldly. More like the sluaghs that hijacked my first traveling companion, though quite a bit larger. They were both blue as toilet bowl cleaner with eyes too large for their faces—Bratz dolls with wings. Their skin was so clean it shone, but their clothing was filthy and tattered. If not for the assortment of chests and bric-a-brac surrounding them in their wagon, I'd have thought them paupers. And they were more than generous in offering Sionna morsels of their lunch.

"Blue Caps," Pete murmured before we stepped from the drapery of purple Spanish moss concealing us. "They dwell under the hill."

"What hill?"

I wasn't the only one who delighted in making cryptic references. His lips quirked, Pete replied, "The phrase 'under the hill' is a generality for mines. Blue Caps work in mines."

That explained the dirty clothes.

"They're more deposit diviners than miners, however. Their skills are coveted widely. They make a fair living. Much fairer than the miners do themselves."

"Do they travel often?"

He shrugged. "I've seen them about on the road, though not too often. I reckon they go where the work is, aye?"

Made sense. "Anything I should know about them?"

The corner of Pete's mouth quirked higher. "Starting to think like a harbinger, are you?"

Should I be flattered or alarmed by that remark? I couldn't decide.

"I'd wager most Blue Caps are upstanding fae folk, although they're reputed for being opportunistic. Mind what you say to them, Shorty. We can't risk them selling information about us to those on the hunt."

"Then what should we tell them about why we're traveling together? We can't really say you're a harbinger, and I'm your captive. If the Goblin Market story has gotten past us—"

Pete watched me in patient pleasance as I hashed out our cover story.

"We could say that you're doing what Briar was doing—that you're seeing me safely to my distant family after my father's death—that you're a longtime family friend who's protecting me on my journey."

Problem solved!

"Hm." He rested a casual arm over the tip of his bow. "You suppose they'll swallow that?"

"Why wouldn't they?"

He clicked his tongue. "Firstly, because it's highly unlikely any Danann feyr would befriend a lowly human. They'll take your claim that I'm a family friend to mean I'm truly the family slave. And secondly, no discerning Danann father would entrust the care and protection of his daughter to the slave who's no doubt forced to clean his piss pot."

I cringed. "Oh."

"Not to scorn your cock and bull abilities, Shorty, but I think, in this instance, it's best if we employ the simplest possible explanation for our unlikely association."

"And what's that?"

"That we're lovers." He grinned as he passed me, the devil jigging in his gaze. "And you've run away with me."

I was still staring after him when Pete swaggered into view of the Blue Caps and waved a jaunty Irish hello.

Knowing my cheeks had flushed, I cursed Pete's raffish name. Then, feigning nonchalance, I tugged down the hem of my leather vest and glided after my "beloved," who was already chatting it up.

"Aye, she's my hound," Pete answered the Blue Caps hand-feeding Sionna, who'd invited herself to their luncheon, the shameless beggar that she was. "I do hope she's not intruding on you."

I stopped beside Pete. "Don't you mean *our* hound, sweetums?"

"Forgive my thoughtlessness, darlin'." He cast a wry glance at me. "Of course, Sionna is yours as well."

I sniffed at the apology, then smiled at the beyns. A couple, I presumed.

One of them sat curled in an adorable ball as she tongued a berry I'd yet to encounter. She had crimson hair, braided in intricate rows down to the gauzy wings protruding from her shoulder blades. The second had orange hair so short it barely covered her arched ears. She was a smidge broader about the shoulders, her wings taller and plainer, and if it weren't for her full bosom, I might have judged her an adolescent ryn. Even her voice was husky when she replied to Pete, "She's no bother to us. We adore mongrels." She fed Sionna another hunk of bread.

"Looks like your transport is fairly well banjaxed." Pete gestured toward their front right wagon wheel, which had busted apart into several different pieces, the boulder their overgrown hog had stranded them on the obvious catalyst. Of course, if that boulder hadn't gotten them, the twenty others surrounding us surely would have.

"Good eye, fella," the first beyn tittered before popping another berry into her sensuous mouth. "And we can't fix it, neither." She lifted a blue leg so lithe I couldn't help picturing her as a ballerina Smurf. Her elegant toes nudged her companion's hip. "Tibbs here forgot to pack the smithing dust."

Pete couldn't very well explain what smithing dust was if we wanted to maintain our backstory, but I guessed it could repair broken objects. Clearing my throat, I turned to Pete. "Would we have any to give them?"

Pete coughed, his hardening eyes insisting he handle the talking. "Afraid not, darlin'—as it's a rare and costly commodity for simple men like me. Please excuse my love, gentlefolk." He bowed his tousled head to the Blue Caps and patted my back, unnecessarily brusque. "She's sorely ignorant of life outside her father's grand house."

If he had to be condescending, at least he'd slipped in some educational details. So, I didn't stomp on his foot like I wanted to.

He sighed. "Would that I had a vial of that heavenly Dwarfish mineral, I'd offer it in a pinch."

"Wouldn't be right to ask it of you, anyhow. We'll make do." Tibbs grimaced. "Somehow."

The hardness I'd stirred in Pete's eyes vanished. "If you don't mind me asking, why were you fine fae avoiding the road? Are you on the run from someone?"

"Oh, in a way," Tibbs said. "We're onto our next hill, and with all our bits and pieces along, we thought a less traveled road wiser, what with the threat of possible bandits."

"Aye," the first Blue Cap agreed, her huge gray eyes widening further. "We've heard tales from our brethren—where every last scrap of wealth was taken from them—whole families left naked on the road—the faelets too."

Jeez.

Tibbs rolled bright eyes. "Rhoswen likes to exaggerate, but we *are* aware our kind are targeted hereabouts, hence our rutty course." She took another bite of bread, ruminating for a moment. "Would you happen to know of a wheelwright in the vicinity?"

"Can't say as I do," Pete replied.

"Didn't figure." Tibbs exhaled. "Never hurts to ask, o' course."

Chewing on the unspoken solution skulking amidst the small talk, I turned a pleading look on Pete. Yeah, I knew charity was against the law, and yeah, I knew these were strangers we'd have to maintain appearances around, but the thought of leaving them in such a bind unsettled me. Pete wanted me to stay silent, but I had to at least offer help. Whether he agreed with me or not.

His gruff hand squeezed my shoulder just as I opened my mouth to speak, warning me to hush. Offended, I almost wrenched out of his hold. Who the hell did he think he was, telling me when to speak? My ethics may have been out of place in this world, but offering aid to those in need would *always* be—

"Would you gentlefolk care to ride with us?" Pete shocked the hell out of me. And the Blue Caps, it seemed. "We're headed toward the Summer Court—Lithalaly."

Rhoswen nudged her speechless companion again. "What say you, Tibbs? We're heading that way as well." She glanced back at Pete. "Shanerie's our destination—not too far out of your way."

"We couldn't," Tibbs argued, though the temptation to accept Pete's offer shone in her eyes. "We can't accept such mal-alms."

"You've misunderstood me," Pete lied. "It's not charity I'm offering."

Tibbs eyed him. "No?"

"Of course not." Pete thumped his heart in a show of sincerity. "I'd never insult you so. But a bargain, aye? That's more what I'm proposing. We'll give you and your belongings a ride to Shanerie, and in return, you'll cook us a delicious supper tonight. I have it on good authority that your kind are wizards with a cauldron, and Shorty, while skilled in so many useful things, turns every meal she makes to ash."

I didn't even care that he'd just insulted me, an image of three hungry Middling faelets springing to mind. If Pete had been in Briar's place at Avenshire, I suspected little Gail and her brothers would've "gotten away" with the food I'd bought them.

How did a man who killed people for a living have a better moral compass than Briar?

"A bargain then?" Tibbs clarified. "And a meal's all you ask of us?"

"Aye." Pete's smile was so innocuous it turned him boyish. Or the closest he could come to it with the beard. "Do you accept?"

The Blue Caps conferred, then Tibbs finally said, "Aye. Shall we shake on it?"

After Pete led an ornery Bob between trees and down off the road, we helped the Blue Caps load their goods and chattels into our wagon. I took a seat in the bed with Rhoswen and Sionna as Pete led the way, yanking our blaring donkey back to the road. Tibbs assumed the rear, swatting the jaunty buttocks of their giant, snorting, spotted hog. His name was Oats, and he was about as talkative as Bob, though much less abrasive—which Bob proved by throwing a conniption when we veered off course toward Shanerie. Pete had to threaten to geld him before Bob shut up and trucked on, but Oats just trotted, snuffling, to wherever Tibbs wanted.

We covered as much distance as we could before dusk, which wasn't far given our heavier load and slower pace, yet Pete seemed satisfied with our progress. "We should reach Shanerie by supper tomorrow," he informed our wagon guests once we'd stopped to camp for the night in a woodsy glen by a rocky, rushing stream.

"Piminy!" Tibbs exclaimed. "That's even sooner than we'd planned."

We divided the chores. Pete fished for supper. I gathered kindling and wood to make a fire. The Blue Caps foraged for dinner ingredients. Sionna did the sniffing. Bob did the sulking. And Oats—he flopped over in the mud by the stream and went soundly to sleep.

He didn't stir even as I bumped his haunches while building my fire ring. Which was good, because I wanted no unfamiliar witnesses, not even livestock, for my successful attempt at igniting a spark out of pure will.

Smirking, I sat back on my heels and added kindling to the baby flames I'd just birthed. I glanced toward the stream, where Pete reclined against a tree trunk, one arm lazing across one bent knee, waiting for a bite on his line bobbing in the stream.

"Couldn't light a candle, huh?" I snarked.

Even in feigning sleep, Pete didn't pretend he hadn't heard me. He grinned, devilish, disarrayed, and—proud?

After supper (mouthwatering, as Pete had foretold), the four of us weary travelers lounged about my gorgeous campfire, making conversation. Pete suggested playing bachram, which we did, using tree nuts as our chips.

"Where are you two from?" I asked our new friends once I collected the sizeable pot of nuts I'd won with my last hand—a measly two of hearts and a four of spades that had become a full house. How awesome was that?

"Tibbs has lived in Evereostre her entire life." Rhoswen took a tiny swig from the jug of sweet juice being passed around.

The Blue Caps had included the jug as part of the bargain but warned it was dangerous to drink it too quickly. Without proper pacing, it caused hallucinations. So, I'd simply passed the last time the jug wound up in my hands. I would the next too.

"Up north," Rhoswen continued. "Small mining borough in The Peaks—right snug against the Winter Court."

A mountain range, I assumed of The Peaks, picturing UPJ in springtime. Exactly what I'd left behind me when I finished finals. I refused to think too hard about never seeing it again.

"But I'm from Autumn." Rhoswen straightened like a queen on a throne, making Tibbs roll her eyes. "Mac Midhna Hummocks precisely, from where our race originates according to legend. Where there's a mine for every element—including the sorcery elements."

It was on the tip of my tongue to ask what the sorcery elements were, but Tibbs interrupted, gazing at Rhoswen. "I met this one at a hill closer to the Spring Palace. My competition, she was. Forever trying to one-up me."

Rhoswen smirked, almost feline. "Never had to try too hard."

They giggled, Tibbs swatting Rhoswen.

Chuckling, Pete dealt the next hand.

I smiled, wondering if their constant proximity was why they smelled the same, both a mix of honeysuckle and roasted acorns. Because I'd recently noticed that I smelled an awful lot like Pete.

Tibbs cast me a curious glance over her cards. "How did you come to know your man here? A human and a Danann—*that* must be a tale to tell."

I turned to *my man*. Us being lovers had been his idea, after all.

Pete cleared his throat, prepared. "I was one of her father's husbandman—bought and sold nary a year past. Can't say I felt very fortunate to be where I was—until I chanced upon Shorty one evening in the forest. We'd heard tell of a dangerous creature on the estate—a cantir, as it turned out."

As Tibbs and Rhoswen quaked with fear at just the creature's name, I pursed my lips at Pete. *Really?* I wanted to say but only threw my blind into the pot beside Rhoswen's.

The memory of my actual encounter with a cantir shimmered like starlight in Pete's eyes. He called the blinds after a cursory glance at his bachram hand and continued narrating our fictional meet-cute. "All able-bodied males were put to the hunt, but I was the lucky lad who found the cantir—along with Shorty, who was dallying under a tree, reading one of her sugary odes. She wasn't aware of the beast's true nature and thought he might make a fine pet."

My mouth twitched. So far, the Blue Caps thought I was an ignorant debutante. Their chortles said as much. *Hmph.*

"I killed the cantir just as it was readying to pounce, startling her, like."

My descriptors now also include spineless. Great.

Pete's mouth twitched upward, brimming with secrets. "And I spent the rest of that evening *comforting* her."

Oh, let's just add easy to that list, shall we? Ugh, men and their flawed concepts on romance.

As the Blue Caps tittered, Pete laid down the flop, wherein another ace appeared.

Woot!

"And that was that." Pete shrugged as he considered his cards, and Tibbs checked. "We've been inseparable since."

Rhoswen checked as well. "Lovely tale, that."

"Hm," I remarked, knowing that this avid romance reader could tell a better love story than that. "It would be, yes. If it were true."

Though his laid-back expression remained, Pete's gaze betrayed how much he'd like to shake me. "How have I spoken falsely, darlin'?"

Smiling to myself, I bet a small number of nuts. Too many would've scared everyone else into folding. "For one, you act as if we hadn't seen each other before that night."

His brows drew together. In annoyance, I supposed. What else was new?

"We hadn't." He called my bet, too irked that I'd risk jeopardizing the plausibility of his story to give my gameplay just consideration.

"You may not have seen me before that night, sweetums, but I'd seen you." I sighed at the Blue Caps and lifted a shoulder. "You say I was sheltered, but I'd say I was caged. Like a bird—to be freed only upon marriage, when my ceyla would put me in another."

Tibbs frowned for me.

"The monotony was endless—constant etiquette lessons, gown fittings, embroidery socials, luncheons with other vapid young ladies with no interest in anything other than wealth, looking pretty, and popping out faelets. Oh, and the occasional awkward encounter with a suitor my family decided was a good match for me."

I wasn't totally lying, which was why my audience stared so intently for the rest of my tale.

"I was so damn tired of my life not being my own. I'd fight with my parents daily for control." I groaned inside at memory of all the altercations I'd had with Aunt Aylie and Uncle Neel. "I know I'm clueless about many things in this world, but I'm not complacent about it. I fought every day to better myself."

Pete's furrowed brow had smoothed. Had he detected the shards of truth in my deceit?

I'd captivated Tibbs so well that when Pete dealt the turn, she thought only a moment before making a modest bet, keeping me her focus. Or maybe she had good cards and was playing me. But I doubted she had three of a kind.

"That's when I saw him." I gestured at Pete. "I'd been storming through the gardens after yet another fight with my father, and I stopped to wrangle my temper. I looked up at the men working Daddy's land, who were being scolded by an overseer, and this massive, smirking hulk of muscle—this bearded bundle of irreverence and defiance—"

Pete barked in delight. Surprised, I thought.

Biting my lip, I feigned indecision before calling Tibbs's bet. Pete didn't drag his dark eyes off me, also calling.

"Well, he just took my breath away," I finished, making Rhoswen coo. "Our eyes met across the way for maybe a second before he went back to work, but I knew it right then."

"Knew what?" In Tibbs's suspense, she didn't even glance down at the river Pete dealt.

I almost danced, another ace appearing. "That he was my key out of my cage—my road to freedom. Granted, he had his own cage to escape, but it wouldn't hold him for long. He was meant for bigger things—just as I was. I thanked fate for bringing him into my life. For reminding me that there could, in fact, be more for me."

Enchantment had both Blue Caps betting nuts carelessly.

I called them, then angled toward Pete, whose mocking gaze had softened like a knit blanket on a rainy day. His acting ability was remarkable.

"To put it simply—I crushed on him for several desperate months before we had our first real meeting." My phony tenderness for Pete came so damn easily. Why wasn't a question I trusted myself to ask. "I wanted to approach him the instant I saw him but knew I couldn't. He'd never speak to me because of my father, who didn't want the help getting friendly with his daughter."

"As if that would've stopped me, darlin'," Pete said. "I'd have gladly taken the lashes to flout such unholy dictates. For how could anyone expect a wretch like me to spurn the suns finally shining on him?"

I gulped at his delicate, subtle, devastating compliment. Was I the suns in his metaphor? *Mercy me.*

I shook myself. "Regardless, I didn't wish to get you in trouble. But when I heard about the danger in the woods, that you'd gone to hunt it without an overseer, I set out to—stumble—upon you. Stumbling into the dang cantir first was just bad luck."

Our camp guests chortled, romanticism synchronized swimming in their eyes.

"Thank you, by the way." Pete's sweet words, hollow thought they were, had motivated my appreciation. I'd always been a sucker for a poet. "I never did say how grateful I was that you killed that monster before it hurt me. So, thank you—for helping me."

In the firelight, Pete's eyes were a decadent, dark caramel. They locked with mine as he tipped his head. "You're very welcome, darlin'. It'd have been a crying shame had the beast eaten a treasure such as you."

My breath whooshed out of me as we shared an effortless daze. A daze that weirdly felt like communing at spirit circle. Only *more* erotic.

"Golly." Rhoswen fanned herself in the balmy night. "No wonder you got to the *comforting* so quickly."

Our daze broke like an egg upon that comment, the secrets within mostly contained—but now in danger of seeping out.

Glancing at his cards, Pete became the crooked rogue I'd come to know. "She didn't take much convincing."

I smirked once more at my pocket aces. "Because I didn't need convincing at all."

My "beloved's" head tilted in question.

"I'm sorry. Did you still think our first time was your idea?" I tsked him. "Oh, no, sweetums, you gave me exactly what I wanted."

Profound exhilaration flashed across his face.

"Should I have just let you continue to take credit for it?" My heart thudded at the scent of his body on the breeze. "I hope I'm not tarnishing your manhood."

"By all means, Shorty, tarnish away." I *loooved* the way his mouth hitched in that moment, the way he chewed his lip, languid as fingers grazing rosy skin. "If it makes your eyes look like that."

I gulped again. *What color are my eyes?* I wondered. *And why do I feel like I've been reading smut all night?*

Had I drunk the sweet juice too quickly? Surely, I was hallucinating the connection suddenly sizzling between Pete and me. Yeah, a not so hidden (anymore) part of me yearned for him, but he couldn't possibly reciprocate. I mean, wasn't he the guy who'd looked at me like I was Medusa when he'd seen me naked? He'd retreated into the woods, his tail between his legs.

Even so, his predatory gleam seemed more than real as he eyed me up and called the bets. And raised them. Doubly.

Rhoswen whistled, folding. Tibbs did likewise.

Me? I bit down on a thumbnail and pretended to ponder my next move. All cards laid before me, it was clear Pete had a straight. If he didn't have a straight flush, which was doubtful, my four-of-a-kind was golden.

I glanced once more at Pete, at the challenge in his smile, and called him. Raising him double on top of everything.

Our camp guests murmured awed expletives.

"You wouldn't be bluffing me, would you, Shorty?"

Cool as a cucumber, Amy, I schooled myself. "Guess you'll have to pay up to find out."

Wicked—that's how Pete looked right then, a panther sizing up supper—or something more satisfying than food. Goddess, his dark eyes were molten. But I *couldn't* be turning him on. Could I?

I mentally noted never to touch sweet juice again.

"Hm." Pete strummed dirt-lined fingers against his cards. "You've learned some new tricks, I see. Can't rightly judge what that face of yours is telling me."

Something tightened in my belly. *Danu, I hope not.*

When Pete finally called me, I released a breath I hadn't realized I'd been holding and almost squealed with glee. Instead, I went, "Hm," the way Pete had and laid my pocket aces down for him to read and weep.

His mouth curved begrudgingly, his teeth grinding as he revealed his hand—a straight. "I'll be buggered," he growled, not even trying to hide his respect. "You beat me, Shorty,"

"I did it!" I giggled, collecting my pot. I didn't care that my winnings were worthless. They symbolized my first win at bachram—my first win at strategizing.

"Aye, you did," Pete admitted. "Artfully, too."

The vixen returned, suggestively batting my lashes. "I learned from the best, didn't I?"

This time the heat between Pete and I felt more like a coronal storm and had both Blue Caps tossing in their cards.

"I'd say it's long past bedtime," Tibbs remarked. She and Rhoswen shared a fiery glance of their own.

"It is getting rather late." Still on cloud nine after my win, I rose to prepare for bed.

After washing my face, brushing my teeth, and donning my night shift, using an overgrown bush beside the stream for privacy, I sauntered back to camp and grabbed my cloak from the wagon. I was spreading it out on a patch of grass dappled with dandelions when the Blue Caps unfolded a feather mattress on the other side of the fire. I watched them add a plethora of pillows to the mix.

Rub it in, would ya?

I sat upon my inadequate bed, which was in sore need of a washing, and tied up my hair in a messy top bun, hoping to keep the sweat off my neck while I slept that night.

"Something wrong with the spot I chose for tonight, darlin'?"

When I blinked up, Pete stood over me like a mussed sex god. He wore just his trousers and linen shirt, which also needed a wash, its sleeves rolled up to his elbows. His open collar exposed the dark fur covering his broad chest. Fur I wanted to lose my fingers in.

Cool it, Amy. You'll never sleep if you keep up those *thoughts.*

Indicating the Blue Caps with a subtle flick of his eyes, Pete gestured toward his pallet a yard away, where Sionna had been snoring since sunsdown. "Would you like me to move *our* pallet over here?"

Our pallet. Because we slept together. As lovers would.

What was it you said about sleep? I berated my conscience.

Swallowing, I nodded at Pete's pointed question. He went to fetch his pallet.

I stood, wringing my hands, as he nudged a sluggish Sionna off her nest. She trudged the few paces toward the fire, then plopped down with a great harrumph. I nearly seized in panic, realizing she was going back to sleep where she'd fallen. Wasn't she going to snuggle up as a buffer between Pete and I, like she had the night we'd spent in Humwater Dell? Wasn't she going to save me from having to sleep body to body with Pete?

Save you? Please, honey. Your loins are thrumming, and your nipples are pebbles. You don't want saved from anything.

Pete flopped his pallet at my feet, gesturing at it. "After you, darlin'."

Tucking a wayward bang behind my ear, I stepped onto the worn leather, still warm from Sionna, and sat as casually as I could manage—given that I was gulping on my heart with every breath.

Striding from the stream where she'd been readying for bed, Rhoswen waved as Pete's manly bulk settled onto the pallet beside me. "Good rest," she bid us just before Pete's arms engulfed me and urged me down onto my side, my back to his chest.

Afraid to move lest I bump something unbumpable behind me, I froze in that position, my head lying in an awkward, sideways angle as I stared ahead, an unblinking statue.

Chuckling, Pete tapped my stiff shoulder. "Care to make room for my arm?"

Gulping once more, I made an idiotic noise and lifted my head. His sinewy arm slid beneath my cheek, his bicep now my pillow for the night. My eyes fluttered shut at the warmth and comfort found there. His linen sleeve, though dingy and stale smelling, was soft against my skin, his muscles firm and supportive in the best way. Goddess, it was the most comfortable position I'd lain in since I'd crossed the portal, and I almost moaned at my abused neck's relief.

"No shadow cloak tonight," Pete murmured, his mouth so damn close to my ear arch. His other arm snaked my waist, his bear paw claiming my tummy. Why, oh why did I decide not to wear underwear that night? "Sorry."

Fighting the urge to wiggle as his deep timbre vibrated along the tendons of my neck, I clenched my fingers. "I figured. If you're not a harbinger tonight."

"Shh," he warned, his breath tickling my ear again, making me shiver. "Right. Tonight, I'm a simple bearded bundle of irreverence and defiance, aye?"

I bit down on a grin. *He liked that, huh?*

"You've a talent for storytelling, Shorty."

"Thanks, but I can't take credit for that. I basically plagiarized the plot of a romance I read last year. Wasn't even that good, but the story fit."

"But you drew some bits from your own past, aye?"

My mouth twisted. "Some."

"Then I suppose it's safe to assume your father—he'd have absolutely detested me as your lover." Dark as all hell, he chuckled.

"Says the harbinger who's captured me for the man who had him killed."

"Well—barring that, I mean."

I turned slightly toward him, Daddy's kind voice echoing through my head: *I want you to fall in love with someone* you *love. . . . Not someone you think* I'll *love. . . . Someone you'd trust with your soul.*

"Actually, if that had been our story, Pete, we wouldn't have had to run away." Now, I watched the stars twinkling beyond the undulating aurora ribbons and swore Daddy's approving smile appeared there, a constellation. "I think my dad would've liked you."

He scoffed. "Then I must seriously question his parenting instincts." His laughter rumbled, his lips deliberate in grazing the arch of my ear.

My gasp was uncontainable, though I managed to hold myself from bowing like a horseshoe, frissons spearing through my veins.

"Interesting," Pete hummed, trailing a finger over the goosebumps no doubt rising along my jugular.

Gritting my teeth, I kicked his shins. "Don't do that!"

After a throaty chuckle, he stopped teasing me. His arm returned to my waist, tucking me in tighter to him. To the heat and maleness nestled against my bottom.

Get it together, Amy, I ordered myself, inhaling a deep, relaxing breath.

"Suppose we should catch some shut eye before dawn," Pete remarked, his chin settling above my head. Only a man his size would fit with me so well. Only a man his size would make me feel so feminine.

"*Yes,*" I returned, terser than I'd meant to sound, my goosebumps still unnerving me. What had possessed him to agitate me before bed? The big jerk! "Good night."

"Mm."

Despite my body's clear reluctance to sleep with a hotblooded man wrapped around me, several deep breaths relaxed me into a drowsy state. I was damn near dreaming when the noises started—the dulcet moans of two Blue Caps making love across the fire.

I swore to Danu, Pete's heavy eyes popped open the moment mine did. And we both just stared into our mutual silence, neither moving a muscle as the sex susurration continued for an agonizing eon.

If either of us slept that night, it was only in winks between gasps and giggles.

TWENTY-EIGHT

"**W**ould you, uh, mind if I, uh, stepped in there to buy some soap?" I asked Pete the next dusk after we'd dropped Tibbs, Rhoswen, and Oats off at their mining site in Shanerie—a congested, muddy village carved into tall, grassy hillocks. Basically, a more cramped Hobbiton from *The Lord of the Rings*. We were about to leave town to make camp in a less populous spot, and I'd spied an apothecary that might carry replacements for my Dove products, now sadly empty. "Unless we can't spare the seeds."

Reaffixing Bob's harness after using him as a pack animal to get the Blue Caps' belongings to their new love nest, Pete glanced up at me, astonished. Probably because I'd broken our day-long silence. After the sleepless night we'd spent together, both of us were acting self-conscious. Hard not to. Every time I looked at Pete now, I heard sex noises. Which made me crave something I shouldn't—him.

I doubted we were on the same page with that. He wasn't as jittery as me, despite his reserve, and I hadn't been the recipient of a single evocative look all day, evidence that his lustful gazes the previous night were just part of our act.

"I believe we can spare a wee sum." After rooting in his purse, Pete offered me several seeds.

"Thanks." I let him drop the seeds in my palm, touching out of bounds for me right then. He replied with the hint of a smile. I smiled back, forgetting how to move. *Aaawkwaard.*

"Do—do you want anything?" I gestured toward the shop. "Any, um, oils or—lotions." Did they have lotions in Evereostre? "Any soap for you?"

"Taking umbrage with my scent again, Shorty?"

I giggled. "Just heard there was a blue moon tonight."

Pete waved me toward the shop. I took that to mean *buy me whatever you think I need* and scurried inside.

A suitable camping spot was situated just outside Shanerie near a lazy lake surrounded by rolling hills, towering foliage, and night lilies that glowed like the moss in the Nixie's cave—not that we needed further illumination. The moon wasn't blue, but the light coming off that massive globe in the sky was so bright it bleached us silver as we dined on leftover fish and my bachram winnings.

Despite us barely speaking, things felt almost normal again after supper. Afterwards, Pete skinned yet another fuchsia chipmunk for Sionna, and I excused myself to pee and change into my shift. Then, it was laundry time!

The soap I purchased was a chunk of tallow, milk, and something called kelpie ash. I was clueless how it would work as a detergent, but the apothecary had assured me it was scentless, so I bought it and hoped for the best. I was just retrieving the waxy hunk from my backpack when I sensed Pete's approach.

My heart lurching, I stuffed my panties into the folds of my cloak. *Please don't let him see my dirty underwear!*

Pete stopped beside me. "Mind if I add a garment to your wash load?"

His nearness, his citrusy musk—*damn*, was it intoxicating. "Of course." *Maybe a joke will alleviate things.* "But you'll have to wash your own back, mister." I blinked like an idiot at Pete's stunned expression. *Nope.*

Finally, Pete tugged off his linen shirt—my pillowcase the night before—exposing his broad, glorious torso as a feast for my oversexed mind. "What of my other parts?" He winked.

My voice was tellingly breathy. "I don't do *parts*. Sorry."

"Then I want no complaints if I don't cleanse them to your liking." Smirking, he mercifully broke eye contact, peered into the wagon. "The soap?"

My hands jerked into my book bag for the other hunk of soap I'd bought—this one infused with orange peel—and offered it to him. Chills raced up my spine when he took it from me, his rough fingers touching mine.

"Much obliged, Shorty." He gestured over his shoulder with the soap. "I'll bid you adieu for a spell. Nature calls."

Refusing to watch his perfect ass walk away in those snug leather trousers, I bundled my laundry into my cloak and fled down the trodden grass trail to the lake. Sionna tramped after me between glowing lilies, content after supper. She skittered off to sniff the beach's every petal as I worked.

My resolve to scrub my fingers red dwindled after mere minutes of sitting waist-deep amid the lake's dark eddies. The water was so warm from the day, as mellowing as a hot tub, and clouds of steam skimmed its surface, radiant with moonbeams. Letting the laundry soak, I listened to the peepers and the snorting hound progressing down the bank, sluicing my leg with my soap. I was just as in need of washing as the clothing, after all. As was the shift clinging to my soppy skin, titillating my nipples with its filmy caress.

Would you puhlease *stop equating everything with sex?*

Why? answered some deep-dwelling voice. *It's only natural that you're wondering what Pete's hand might've felt like last night if he'd just moved a few inches and squeezed your tit like a stress ball. Mm, probably pretty fucking good with those calluses of his.*

I tried to shake the image and its resulting longing. Which didn't work. At all. Disastrous thoughts flooded me without my consent.

What if I'd found the courage to turn toward Pete last night during the complimentary bedtime concert? What if he'd wanted me to? What if he'd been waiting for me to make a move, just as I'd been secretly waiting for him? What if neither of us had been faking our attraction last night? What if—?

Something moved in my peripheral, and the neon lilies along the lake's edge bobbed like tiny boats. I scanned the scenery, finding nothing and no one. Had a fish jumped? Why had the peepers suddenly gone mute? Where was Sionna? Had she gone to check on Pete? What was taking him so long? He'd said he'd return to camp shortly. Doubtful though it seemed, had the man with predatory prowess gotten lost? Did he need me to find him?

Stay, that secret voice advised. *He'll come.*

I shook myself again, disturbed. *What the—?*

The sight of a dog's wagging butt protruding from a flowered bush cut my thought short. A high-pitched squeak for help sounded from within the branches.

"Found herself another cherry marmot, did she?"

My heart leaping, I glanced aside toward Pete. He'd appeared with his trousers cuffed up at his shins, the soap I'd bought him in hand. His broad, furry torso was still naked, his firm abs etched in moonlight. As if they weren't obvious enough already.

"Yeah," I spoke once I'd squelched the need to fan myself. *If that's what they're called.* "Although, I can't tell if she's trying to eat it or make friends with it this time."

"Let's just say friends. Then I won't have to gut it after I've bathed, aye?" With another dashing wink, he waded waist-deep into the tranquil water.

Danu have mercy, I tried not to look. I went straight back to washing the clothes—and myself—as Pete splashed in the water like a great, shaggy dog. I even considered gouging out my eyes when the urge to watch him strengthened, but that corrupting voice in my head whispered, *A peek won't hurt.*

So, I glanced. Then I gazed. Then I ogled like a wolf drooling over a fresh kill.

Pete faced away from me, brawn rippling across his massive back and down to his narrow waist as he soaped his silvery, scarred skin. My breath stuck when his soapy hand slipped down his trousers, cleaning his man bits as discreetly as possible while I was present.

Discretion may be the better part of valor, I mused, slicking soap over my belly. *But he'll never get completely clean if you don't peel those pants off those rock-hard buns for him.* Short of breath, my body howling, I clenched my eyes shut. The lascivious thoughts persisted, anyway. *How else will you help him?*

My sudsing hand delved lower than it should've, gliding over an unquenchable searing ache. I began imagining all the sultry, naughty, seductive things I'd do to Pete if only I had the guts. *Be the heroine you've always wanted to be, Amy,* that voice coaxed. *Embrace your lust. Be spontaneous. Abandon your inhibitions. Take control. Lick him wherever the hell you want.*

"Wh—what are you doing, Shorty?"

Only after his stammer did I realize I was standing in bust-deep water with my hands on Pete's warm flesh, attempting to relieve him of his soap. When and how had I gotten over to him? I wondered. But then my libido took control again, and I didn't want the answer.

Gusting, I trailed my fingers over the planes of his chest, let them comb through the hair on his pecks. My other hand cajoled the soap from him. "You missed a spot," I purred like a sultry tigress.

Did that sound just come out of me?

His lips took a roguish curl, though his brow furrowed at me, questioning. "Have I now?"

"Let me get it for you."

Pete's next sound wasn't nearly so chill—as I'd tugged his flies loose. He clasped my wrists, tried backing away from me. "What's gotten into you, Shorty?"

Eyes on the rugged prize, I advanced back into Pete's bubble, trapping our hands between our bodies. "I was hoping *you* would."

Pete's amusement faded. His Adam's apple bobbed. His grip around my wrists lost some resolve. "This—this isn't like you."

"Mm," I hummed, transfixed by the divot between his collarbones. I went up on tiptoes in the watery sand and pressed my pulsing lips to that very spot. I touched my tongue to his skin, so hot, wet, and salty. "Right now, there is no me without you."

Pete stilled like I was a carnivore who'd only see him if he moved. But I saw *all* his magnificence anyway.

My head spinning, I snared his eyes in an all-encompassing gaze like the ones we'd shared the night before. The soap fell from my hand, plunking into the lake, forgotten. I took Pete's handsome, strained face, his dripping beard scratchy against my palms, and moaned with yearning as I rose again to quench my thirst and taste his lips.

Shuddering, Pete wrenched back. "Shorty—"

I tried again. *Needing* him.

He jerked aside. "Amy. Stop." Pete had to be in denial because even as he rejected my advances, his pulse throbbed in his neck, his breath grew heavy, and his eyes blackened with panic-infused hunger. "You don't want this."

"Yes, I do," I whimpered, managing to kiss the corner of his mouth. "Don't you?"

"I—" He rasped and turned his head aside. His lethal fingers bit into my skin. And it felt *so good* not to be handled like glass. "Something's wrong. Something's *very* wrong."

My voice hitched as I answered, "But it feels so right." Our lips touched like the flutter of butterfly wings, and I shivered, nudging his ribs with my peaked nipples.

A more than sexy growl rewarded the nudge. "Damnit, woman—"

Oh, fuck me. He called me woman.

"I cannot allow this—"

I strangled his gallant rejection into an animal groan by cupping his manhood. Hard. And, oh, he most assuredly *did* want to do this. The heat and power of him through his leather trousers burned my hand like a branding iron.

I swore I heard the whiplash of his snapping restraint. I barely had a moment to catch my breath before the predator I'd unleashed fisted his hand in my damp hair and crushed my mouth with his.

My heart did a cartwheel as Pete devoured me like milk after cookies. His demanding tongue surged past my lips, flooding my senses, making my mind reel. And lord save me, my soul sang out in joy at such a thorough kiss. At being kissed how I'd always wanted to be kissed. At how he groped my ass and pressed his blatant arousal into my stomach. There was no gentleness between us. Just raw, aggressive, primal passion.

Growling myself, I clung to his neck and leapt to wrap my legs around his waist, squeezing his ripples and ridges between my thighs. I nearly trilled like a gospel soloist when he responded, squeezing my naked bottom. And I didn't spare a thought for what Pete might think of the little there was to hold. For he seemed pleased as punch by the shape of me as he hiked my soaked shift higher off my ass, groping me. The shift became a rumpled scrap of linen between us as he bore me toward the shore, water churning in his haste.

I did sing out when we careened to the sand together. Pete's massive bulk locked me beneath him, the ground conforming to my body, and I reveled in the breathtaking weight of him upon me. Goddess, I *loved* that he wasn't scared he'd break me.

But *I* was scared. Scared in a way that thrilled me, like I was in line for a roller coaster. The predator above me was a force to be reckoned with, and he had me on my back and vulnerable to what seemed a ravenous appetite for dominion. I felt it in his consuming kiss, the way he yanked my shift above my breasts, and in the way his hips ground into me. He was going to take me, conquer me. And I was going to fucking *love* that too.

Gripping Pete's unkempt hair, I arched against him, surrendering to him. To myself and everything I'd always wanted but had been afraid to ask for.

Both Pete and I frenzied to get his trousers down off his tensed buttocks. The saturated leather resisted despite his loosened flies. Pete snarled an oath at them against my throat as I tried shoving them off with my toes.

Those damn pants were the only reason we didn't end up in full on missionary before the torrent of water hit us. Not from the lake. From a cauldron. And the deluge was so cold, it made Pete and I gasp and break apart.

Both still stupid and wanton, we gawked up at the cauldron wielder—Sedge. He hunched over us, heaving, his gleaming fangs bared. He dropped his iron pot—our iron pot—the one we'd bought with our stolen seeds from Howlite, and I'd used earlier to sterilize us some drinking water. "Get up, you dolts!" he scolded. "Before you draw the entire pack!"

"The pack?" Pete croaked, his eyes glazed.

Nostrils flaring, Sedge nabbed something off the ground by his feet. A head. A hideous, grotesque head with gray, wizened skin and curling ram horns. It's droopy eyes had crossed in death, its throat severed in a jagged, gory line. Its enormous tongue lolled from its slackened jowls.

I stared in horror, sex haze shattering.

Cursing, Pete rose off me. "Incubi."

"Aye." Sedge dropped the head at his feet. Wiping his brow, he bent and retrieved a blood-drenched short sword. "Took all my shadows to subdue it, Pete. You two must have been feeding it well."

Reality destroyed me. That voice in my head—it hadn't been me. Although it had known all my basest desires.

"Mercy on you, Pete," Sedge spat, unyoking himself of alarm and worry. "To think you'd let your guard down by one of the druidic lakes—and with lust in your heart, no less. Even I scented the fervor, and I don't feed off it. You're a lucky bugger that I was looking for you and got here as the wight was weaving its spell 'round you. Before you'd gotten snared completely. Gripes, you'd have been lost at that. And to think how I'd have explained your death to those reliant on you: 'Oh, Pete? Aye, he died. Fornication until starvation, it was.'" Sedge sniffed. "What a pathetic end for you."

Pete's mussed head bowed at his friend's rebuke, but I knew what had happened wasn't his fault. It was mine. The Incubus had found the lust in *my* heart, not Pete's. For it was me the creature had duped into propositioning Pete. Me, who'd ignored Pete's pleas to stop. Me, who'd drawn him into an act he'd clearly wanted no part of. Me, who'd just behaved no better than all the other Dananns in the Shadow Palace who'd used his body for sport. And now, as he knelt over me, I saw the stricken expression on his face and felt like a lecher in a dive bar.

Pete reached to help me cover myself. But I wrenched back, righting my shift myself. "Don't touch me," I cried before fleeing him and the hoax of our passion.

Desperate to sort out what had just happened to me, I donned Tansy's dress, not caring that I looked like a drowned streetwalker—or that I was on other harbingers' Christmas lists—and stormed off down the road. Though Shanerie really wasn't too far away, I shouldn't have made it the whole way back to the bustling village. Had Pete realized I needed space and given me extra length on my tether? Thinking so only made me feel worse—for taking advantage of someone so understanding.

It wasn't you, I told myself. Or tried to. *You'd never have done that stuff if the Incubus hadn't made you do it.*

Yeah, but it was all stuff you, in your heart of hearts, wanted *to do.*

What was worse, now that Pete and I had had this compulsory, untimely encounter, a real romantic moment between us was now out of the question. Not that Pete wanted a real one, anyway, as homely as I was. And not that I should even entertain the thought of a romance with the harbinger sent to capture me. But to know that it wasn't even a possibility now, that I'd ruined any shot at it—Goddess, it was depressing.

When I barreled past the muddy sign welcoming me to Shanerie, I was pouting like a child. Not even the welcoming candlelit windows and merry pipe music emanating from all the nighttime hotspots lifted my spirits. Although it was the first place I'd seen in Evereostre that reminded me of Pittsburgh—atmosphere wise, anyway.

It was a blessing, though, that I was so forlorn. In my self-pity, I didn't notice the usual staring, the whispering about me. Until one dude was so obvious about it that he circled me three times to get a closer look. On his fourth circle, I lost my cool.

Baring my teeth, I advanced on the young male Dwarf and grabbed him by his dusty smock. "*What* is your problem?" I shook him, wanting to shake all the people who'd *ever* gawked at me. Wanting to shake Pete for looking so goddamned sorry that we'd hooked up. "Don't you know it's rude to stare?"

The stocky feyr goggled, roses blooming on his round cheeks. If he weren't such a jerk, I might've thought him handsome. "I—I—I—"

I shook him again, my kettle close to boiling. "I have feelings, too, you know! Just because I look like this doesn't mean it doesn't hurt to be laughed at!"

"Laughed at, lady?"

"Yes! Or are you more horrified than amused?"

The Dwarf's jaw slackened just as a set of bear paws, the very ones that had been fondling my ass only an hour ago, snatched me off him.

I whirled on Pete. "Get off me!" Pushing him did nothing.

Sour-faced, he spared me a glance before rumbling, "Run away," at the Dwarf. Which the feyr did with judicious speed.

Pete's hair still showed signs of my gripping fingers, but he'd covered the naked chest I'd been kissing by donning his jerkin without his shirt—presumably still bobbing in the lake, half washed. His eyes were on the brink of onyx. "We're going back to camp."

I jerked away from him again. "I'm not going anywhere with you."

"You are with your eyes *that* color."

"I don't give a fuck what color my eyes are. You've no right to tell me what to—"

I shrieked when Pete swept me off my feet and threw me over his shoulder like a rug. My face smacked into his back, flooding my senses with his freshened scent and recent, mortifying memories.

Suddenly hating him for not being able to see past my body, I pummeled Pete's shifting back like a punching bag, which was about as effective this time as it had been the first time he'd tossed me over his shoulder. But I kept it up until we were halfway to camp, where Pete dropped me on my feet.

Stumbling into a viney tree trunk, I wiped at my cascading tears.

He was breathless, as if he hadn't stopped running since I'd left him at the lake. "Care to explain why you ran off?"

"You know *exactly* why," I wept into my palm.

Something wriggling in his jaw, Pete closed his eyes as if to calm himself. Then he glanced back up, earnest as a news anchor. And yep—there was that regret again. "I suppose I do." He ran a restless hand through his hair. "Regardless, Shorty, that's hardly cause to take your wrath into town, threatening innocents with a potential firestorm."

"That's not what I was doing!"

"What would you call throttling unwitting chaps just happening by, your eyes the color of rubies?"

"You don't know what you're talking about. That guy had it coming!"

How many times in my life had I let someone gawk or snigger about me behind my back without confronting them? How many times had I hid from scorning eyes like a misshapen hunchback? How many times had I ignored disrespect, let it roll off my back, though it stung on the way down? It had always been my burden that I didn't fit in. Well, not tonight! Not after the Incubus aftermath. Now, I demanded to belong. To someone.

"That pipsqueak about to piss himself? What in bloody hell did *he* do to you?"

"He just couldn't get a close enough look at the Martian." I folded my arms over my chest. Blocking the cleavage Pete clearly found unappetizing.

Pete shook his head. "Come again?"

"The Martian," I growled, gesturing at myself. "Or Sasquatch as the kids at school knew me. Or Grendel from Beowulf. Oh, that was a favorite in sophomore English class, let me tell you."

Realization dawned in Pete's eyes. Incredulity followed. "You mean to tell me you were close to losing control over your secret, *deathly* powers because some stranger *looked* at you the wrong way?"

"He was *staring*! Like I was some mutant! The way kids look at mole-rats at the zoo. They're so ugly that you just can't look away. And I've put up with the same offensive *bullshit* since kindergarten, Pete!" I paced, my hands open, imploring. "I mean, what's so wrong with me, huh? So what if I'm tall and gangly and my eyes are too big, and my face too sharp? So what if I'm too skinny and have no hips or ass or breasts?" I gripped my hair, wanting to scream. "Why does any of that fucking matter? I mean, please tell me, Pete."

Why don't you want me? I needed his answer, even if I wouldn't like it.

Finally, Pete shook himself, then scoffed. "It *doesn't* matter, Shorty. To anyone but *you*."

I flinched, though I knew he was wrong. Physical appearance had mattered more than *anything* for the bulk of my existence. I had no reason to hope this had changed. "Then why do they all stare?"

"I can't say! Because I don't fecking see you as everyone else does!"

"What the fuck does that mean?"

"It means that I know you!" he exclaimed. "And the closer I've gotten to you, the more beautiful you've become to me!"

Not the answer I'd expected.

"Save it, Pete," I said after several blinks of silence. "I'm not looking for bullshit right now. Just tell me the truth."

"It's not bullshite! You *are* beautiful. At least to my eyes."

I scuffed my boot against a rock. "Yeah—whatever."

Why did my friends and family shower me with false compliments when I admitted to feeling like a living carbuncle? They never seemed to realize how much they sucked at buttressing my pitiful self-esteem. Mainly because everyone else I'd ever met told me the truth. Though things became more civil in college, the belittling looks I attracted still ensured I knew the harsh reality about myself.

"When have I *ever* been dishonest with you, Shorty?" That gave me pause. His bluntness was what I liked most about him. "I don't patronize people. Never have."

"Then why didn't you say all this when I told you how insecure I am? Before we went to the bachram tournament, you didn't—"

"Christ, Shorty, you expected me to confess I fancied you? When we've done little but battle each other from the start? You can't see how that would disadvantage me as your captor? For you to know you could tempt me?"

I gawped, my neck hairs prickling. *Pete thinks I'm beautiful?* "But—"

"Damnit, Shorty, I've no cause to lie to you—especially now, after you've all but declared your disinterest in me."

Huh?

"In truth, you're the loveliest female this old boy has ever seen. In any world I've lived in. Although your hair is a rather dull shade, and I don't care for your choice of footwear over much—"

Blinking, I clutched my deceptively brown hair and glanced down at my snow boots.

"But every other part of you does wicked things to me."

HUH?

"Your eyes, for one—I'd surely have kept you bound and gagged the entire trek to the Shadow Palace after you turned my *scian* on me if it weren't for those dazzling rainbow eyes of yours. And I'd never have left you the day you escaped me if what I saw when you tore off your clothes didn't make me want to mount you like a buck in rut."

Goodness, I've forgotten how to breathe.

"And those lips—" His gaze caressed my mouth. "They make me want to do wicked things to *you.*"

Oh, please do them. All of them!

"If that's how you really feel, then why—" I stopped, wary of his answer. And to bring it up.

Pete's expression warmed. "Why did I try to stop you tonight?"

My throat tightened. "Yeah."

His gaze shifted back to molasses. "Because I—" He cleared his throat, glanced down. "Because I find your soul even lovelier than your face."

Be still my beating heart!

"And I think I've gotten to know you fairly well. You're simply not the provocative type, and when you came upon me like that—I *knew* something was wrong. That you'd feel violated if I—" He let the rest of that thought fade into the night.

"I—I thought it was because I—because I'd pressured you into something you never wanted to start."

Pete's mouth quirked at one corner. "That's not how Incubus spells work, Shorty. They draw power from sexual energy."

"I don't know many things about this world, but I *have* heard of Incubi before."

"Yet, it's apparent you haven't heard that their spells only work on *compatible* pairs."

Stars swirled in my heart. "Then the tension I've been feeling—"

Though he smirked, he did so kindly. "It's been tight on my end, too"

So, what happened that night wasn't my fault. Or not *just* my fault.

"Why would you think I'm disinterested in you then?" I asked. "If you know how Incubus spells work?"

He arched a brow. "Because you raced away like I meant to eat you for dessert."

Ooh, that sounds fun!

"And infatuation doesn't necessarily mean a person intends to act on their desires. Or even wants to, truthfully. And I thought—perhaps that was your plight."

I shook my head, moving toward him. "No, I just thought that you didn't want *me*."

Lust glazed Pete's gaze. His voice deepened, asking, "How could any male not want you?"

My breath shuddered. I reached for him.

He stopped my hands, the light in his eyes dimming. "I do want you, Shorty, but I'm still what I am."

I gulped. *A harbinger. A human.*

"And I'm still what *I* am," I murmured. *A Danann. A would-be bride. And what he doesn't know—a princess—a queen.*

The urge to tell him the truth about myself was so potent, my lips parted around the words. But I stopped. *Not right now. He'll hate you like he hates Daddy.*

"Whatever this is between us," Pete said. "It won't end happily." His rueful smile broke my heart. And that regret I'd seen earlier—these hurdles had caused it all along. "So, can we come to an understanding, that we'll do what's wisest? For ourselves—and our plans? That we might flirt, and tease, and look—" The rake reappeared. "But we won't cross that line into lovers."

My heart outright rejected Pete's proposal, but that didn't make him wrong. In my head, I knew getting romantically involved with a harbinger was the stupidest thing I could do right then. *Can you say bad boy complex, Amy?*

Problem was—I always thought with my heart.

Still, I swallowed my feelings and offered him my hand. "Friends?"

Pete's tousled hair glinted like tinsel in the moonlight as he shook my hand. The feel of his calluses still made me shiver. "Friends."

TWENTY-NINE

Pete

Heavy-eyed and heavy-limbed, Pete hunkered down by the fire beside Sedge, who poked radiant coals with a stick. He'd just gotten Shorty settled upon his pallet, where she'd precipitously passed into the Land of Nod, and had finished hanging their sopping clothes out to dry. Now the exhaustion from too little sleep and his daylong disquiet slugged him, a fist to the face.

"You look like death," Sedge said. "You should sleep. I'll keep watch in case another Incubus tries his hand at preying on you."

Pete dropped his weary head into his palm, his arm propped upon his knee. "Or any prowling harbingers?"

Sedge snorted, too incensed to meet Pete's eye. "You were smart to divert course, at least. The Leprechauns are after you, the blighters. They don't have as sharp a nose as I do, but they'll eventually stalk you down, you ken?"

Pete had already guessed as much, but his gut still sank.

"She's a zephyrist?" Sedge nodded toward Shorty, alongside who now slept two bloodhounds. The second being Sedge's blonde pawler (a behemoth compared to Sionna), whose name was Kit.

Pete scraped his face, relieved his friend wasn't about to lecture him for taking his mark on an excursion to the Goblin Market, when all harbingers knew to deliver their quarry straight to the Shadow Palace.

"By God, Sedge—I don't know *what* she is." That was the goddamned truth. Most magical fae Pete had encountered developed just one principal power. Which was usually plenty. Shorty had two—that he knew about. Seeing as she'd nearly overcome him that tragic morning in Humwater Dell, he suspected she had more.

Silence reigned as the Vamp's preternatural gaze affixed on the sleeping mass of hair and tumult drooling on Pete's pallet. Sedge's nostrils flared as he wielded *his* principal power—the ability to glean a person's strengths and weaknesses within a heartbeat. It made him a spectacularly efficient killer.

"You haven't told her of—?"

"No," Pete interrupted, afraid Shorty still might hear them in slumber. Although, he sorely wished she knew he was more than an assassin with a drive for self-preservation.

Clicking his tongue, Sedge faced Pete again, his surveillance complete. However, if the twitch in Sedge's pale cheek were any indication, he hadn't gleaned much. "She carries secrets, Pete. Substantial secrets, though something obstructs her mind from my breed of magic."

"Spellcasting's not in Shorty's repertoire, Sedge." Yet. "The obstruction wouldn't be her doing."

"Well, whosever doing it is, they're mighty powerful themselves. Because I can't sniff out the nature of her gifts either, though I'll tell you now—they're formidable."

Grim, Pete grunted. "Aye."

Sedge exhaled. "Are you going to make me say it?"

Pete cast a droll glance his long-time chum's way.

"The Leprechauns are on your scent and will kill you without blinking for the bounty I heard tell she'll fetch. Unruly as she must be to unleash a twister in public, she's a liability to you. To all the good you've done."

"We're working on that." Pete watched the coals in the firepit smolder like Shorty's eyes when she was near to combustion. "I've been teaching her control. She's doing well with it, frankly."

"You *must* cut her loose and let the Leprechauns have her."

Resolved, Pete clenched his teeth. "I can't do that."

"You most certainly can."

"Fine," Pete snapped. "Then I *won't* do that."

"Damn you, Pete. I ken she's a sympathetic case, but you can't save her. You know that!"

"Hush," Pete hissed. "You'll wake her." Shorty had uncanny hearing, evidenced by all the times she'd smacked him in the dead of night for waking her with his "loud breathing."

Sedge's mouth clamped in a hard line.

"I know I can't save her, but she's capable of saving herself." She had to. "That's why I've been training her. As you just noted, she's powerful enough—and she's agreed to help me kill Gentian."

Sedge's fathomless eyes rounded. "Have you gone mad, man?"

He sounded beyond mad. He sounded idiotic.

"You'll get both of you killed! Then what of your grand plans?"

"We've got to try, Sedge! Change requires action. And someone must do the acting." Pete shrugged, his gaze sweeping Shorty. "Might as well be us."

"*Us,*" Sedge repeated. "Has she become one of us?"

"No, and I don't want her to. That's the point."

"You've grown too attached to her."

Something in Pete's chest panged. "No. *No.* I—"

"If you fall in love with her, Gentian will scent it on you the next he sees you, then black eyes or not, he'll realize you've managed to overcome the death poppy. Demons lack the capacity for love, Pete."

"I'm aware." Pete glowered. "Which is why I'm currently sitting here bickering with you instead of plundering her treasure trove."

A trace of humor wormed through Sedge's mouth.

His eyes falling shut, Pete inhaled a cleansing breath—what he'd always done before gracing the confessional as a mischievous youngster. "I've been fighting her allure for a time now, all right? Tonight was the only buckling of my resistance, and it wouldn't have happened without the Incubus's influence. You'll no doubt be pleased to hear that after I found her in town, I informed her the rapport between us can go no further. That the impediments to us becoming—whatever it is we'd be—are too numerous, too immense."

A small pool of blackness welled within him. The demonic scourge rebounded at more than just anger. Gloom had the same effect.

The gloom he now faced at turning from the suns finally shining on him.

"She agreed," he stressed bitterly.

Though he nodded in approval, Sedge understood the weight of Pete's sacrifice. "On the bright side, if you manage not to get the both of you slaughtered—and *if* you somehow succeed in dispatching the Shadow Prince to the underworld—then you'll be free to pursue her in any vein you so choose. With my full support."

Pete offered his friend a weak smile for the attempt at optimism, but he knew Gentian's death would make no nevermind in his association with Shorty. He was human, she, Danann. Fae mores were rigid—neither the two should mix.

Amy

"No, I agree with you," I corrected Sedge the next day. Our cart jolted down the road out of Shanerie, now en route to the Summer Court. As Pete and Sedge strolled on either side of Bob, I knelt in the wagon with a panting Sionna and Kit, the latter of whom had a chewing compulsion and was currently working on an Incubus femur.

Pieces of the Incubus's body lay scattered throughout the bed for Kit's hiding and seeking entertainment. Its grotesque, decapitated head sat in one corner—a souvenir of his kill, Sedge claimed. He thought bagging a parasitic wight, as he termed it, a profound accomplishment. Trophy or not, though, I did my best to stay away from it.

"Prostitution should totally be legal," I continued, pushing out all thoughts of the head joggling feet away from me. "If people want to make money by selling their bodies, it's their decision. No one else's business—literally. There must be restrictions on *other* people seeking to make money off sex workers. Like brothels shouldn't be legal. And sex trafficking—no way should that be tolerated."

Sedge considered me, jabbing his walking stick into the sandy path. "Is a brotheler's enterprising spirit any less essential than anyone else's? Why should their potential profitability be scuppered?"

"Because their potential profitability hinges on exploitation."

"Not necessarily."

I snorted. "Not necessarily—but realistically—come on now."

Pete grinned at his friend, who'd now be traveling with us until we reached the Shadow Palace. Although I hadn't heard what role, if any, Sedge would play in Gentian's demise.

Sedge's black, triangular brow arched. "You'd have whores each running their own affairs? What if they've no mind for business? If they did, I'd wager they wouldn't be whoring."

Both males chuckled at this.

I rolled my eyes. "If they're smart enough to realize they've got a product that costs them nothing but their dignity to offer, then they're probably smart enough to take an accounting class."

"An *accounting* class?" Sedge laughed.

"Yeah—you know, bookkeeping? Maybe a little economics. With the schools and colleges I'd have set up—"

"Colleges? For whores?"

"Yep." I raised my chin. "And for anyone else who wants to learn something."

I hadn't asked Pete, and Briar hadn't told me, but I suspected that only the wealthy could find an adequate education in my kingdom. And that was not cool with me. In any way.

"The world according to Shorty," Pete teased. Although, by the twinkle in his eyes, I thought he might've enjoyed that world, the progressive colonial that he was.

Sedge's sharp teeth glinted in the dappled sunlight. "A fearsome prospect, that."

I narrowed my eyes at him. "By the way, we would've died of dehydration."

Puzzled, both males glanced my way again.

"Last night, you said Pete would've died from fornication until starvation," I reminded Sedge. "But we'd have both died of dehydration long before starvation. It's the rule of three. I don't know how it works with Vampires, obviously, but for humans—and other fae, probably—we can live for three minutes without air, three days without water, and three weeks without food."

"Really?" Sedge asked.

"Yep. And you know where I learned that?"

"No."

"College."

Pete's amusement erupted boisterously, scaring flying creatures from their feathery banyan nests and making Bob yowl. That I could elicit such delight from him exhilarated me.

"This is what happens when you educate a beyn." Sedge winked, belying his snark. "Mouthiness."

"If that means I'm a smartass," I said. "I'll take that as a compliment."

Sedge snickered at Pete. "You Earthers and your college learning."

I perked up. "You went to college?" Though I'd seen tomes of many varieties stocked in Pete's home, I hadn't pegged him for a scholar.

"Aye," Pete answered, mirth still choking his voice. "College of Philadelphia—now the University of Pennsylvania, I believe." He shrugged. "My parents encouraged it. Waste of my time, however. In your jabbering, Shorty, I've gathered that colleges of today run much differently than they once did. In my time, they taught little more than conservative church laymanship—which didn't particularly suit me."

Sedge chortled again.

"But after that, I took an apprenticeship with a lawyer who'd studied at Oxford—became one myself."

"You're a lawyer?" I boggled at the rugged scoundrel before me. He looked more like a potential client than a lawyer.

"I was, aye."

"But—" I shook my head. "You're so honest."

"Didn't say I was a good one, Shorty."

Sedge sniffed. "Don't let him fool you, lady. He knows how to lie when needs be."

I suddenly remembered the easy falsehoods Pete had spun for Maggie the night of the bachram tournament, how he'd misled the Blue Caps about our acquaintance, and when he'd convinced me he was a simple thirsty hunter the night I'd met him. He *had* been awfully smooth about it.

Pete shrugged. "I lie by omission, mostly."

Me too, I thought, stomach knotting. Pete and Sedge traded jokes as we jolted down the path, oblivious to my turning mood.

You should tell him, I scolded myself, the dishonest friend that I was. *He deserves the truth.*

The relationship I'd formed with Pete, though weird, was real. If nothing else, there was trust between us. Or at least he thought there was. And I was betraying him every day by keeping the crux of my plight from him. He was bound to find out the truth when we reached the Shadow Palace, anyway. I doubted Gentian would allow my identity to remain a mystery. And if Pete found out in such a fashion, without warning, that I was the daughter of the king he so detested—the king who'd overlooked him when he was so grievously suffering that he'd surrendered to Gentian directly thereafter—would he suddenly change his mind and sell me out—leave me to fend for myself in Gentian's clutches?

But if I cued him in ahead of time, told him everything, maybe he'd come to terms with who I really was before we reached those clutches. And I knew with time he would.

Because Pete found my soul more beautiful than my face.

Even if he couldn't find it in himself to forgive Daddy, he'd forgive me. I just needed to ensure that happened before Pete did something regrettable. If that man needed less of one thing, it was regret.

Later that day, when Sedge went off with Kit to hunt (what he was hunting, I didn't want to know) so Pete and I could train, I made up my mind to do the right thing.

Between my physical and magical training, I wiped the sweat from my brow, shoved my braid over my shoulder, and faced Pete on our makeshift battleground—a sandy forest enclosure where palms outnumbered banyans.

"Can I talk to you about something?"

Pete glanced up from setting aside his sweaty jerkin, the heat too much for him after our workout. "Of course, Shorty. Praise upon my skillset is always welcome."

Forcing my laugh, I bit my lip.

Pete quit the playful act and exhaled. "What is it you need to say?"

Still biting my lip, I approached him. The fact that his Adam's apple bobbed as it had the night I'd been compelled to seduce him flattered me to no end. I still questioned how the rest of the universe saw me, but Pete really did find me sexy.

I shook that thought away.

Friends, Amy. He just wants to be friends.

Maybe not even that after you confess.

"I—I haven't told you everything," I stuttered. "About my life. About who I am. And I think I need to—if we're going to be friends. And it—it might put a strain on us. On our friendship—our alliance."

His expression was like the dawning suns, spreading warmth over the cold dread in my guts. "Friendship doesn't mean I'm owed your secrets, Shorty. It means I must respect that you have them, for they're yours to keep."

I stared at him, caught off guard.

"I've taken much from you in our time together. Your freedom. Your totem. Your pride at times."

All that was true, but Gentian had forced him into it. Mostly, anyway.

"If that hasn't put a strain on our friendship, your secrets won't."

I cringed, certain he was wrong about that.

His chuckle was as good as a warm hug. "There's nothing you could say that would change—what we are."

I wondered what he'd really wanted to say.

"And given that, I don't want or need an admission you're neither ready, nor willing to make." He waved away my gasp of argument. "Now, stop delaying your lessons and spray that dead tree over yonder with fire."

So, that was my attempt at telling Pete who I was. His reaction had me humming a classic Bayview Boys song later that night.

The dream changes again. This time, when Pete wafts into my room, shadows rippling, I leap toward him, throw my arms around him, and we kiss like gentle lovers. Or as gentle as a man made for violence can be.

His shadows envelop me as they always have, but instead of terror, I feel warmth and safety. And joy. I feel like a woman who's been searching for a place to belong, to call home all her life, only to realize there was no need. Because her home was always going to find her.

When the chill in the air becomes ice, I grip my harbinger and grit my teeth. More phantoms darken my doorway, their shadows snaking toward us like mustard gas. Snarling as the melody always haunting the scene crescendos, I shove Pete and his tethers behind me.

I spin on the new threats with a feral gleam, now guarding Pete along with my siblings. I'm the only thing standing between them and certain doom. And I'm *going* to be enough.

"Run!" My voice shrieks in the background as I advance to destroy the world. "Just *run!*"

We reached Crowcairn bridge two days later and pulled the wagon off the road into a palm copse upon a scenic overlook. The shade was relaxing after hours spent baking in the near summer heat, but both harbingers with me were as tense as I'd ever seen them, their muscles poised for a fight as they watched the crossing like hawks through the leaves.

I watched too, but more because I couldn't take my eyes off the breathtaking panorama before me. The bridge was a massive arc of stone over a frothing pink river that flowed between mountainous, grassy hills like a fjord. Teeth-like standing stones, sparkling like quartz, fenced in both sides of the structure, and great vines of flowering ivy curtained its edges. I'd never seen anything so majestic in real life.

Of course, I could've done without the added visual of the four Ogres guarding the bridge. Just as I'd pictured, they were mammoths with bald, domed heads, beady eyes, and mouths of protruding teeth. They wielded spiked clubs the size of me in their dragging fists, bullying every traveler passing through—which was many, as the bridge connected the main thoroughfares from Spring into Summer—until they obtained their tithe. Most travelers scurried on after that, wanting as little interaction with the goons as possible.

Around twilight, sightseeing and people-watching now boring, I lazed in the back of the wagon, petting both Sionna and Kit, when I heard a vehement curse from both of "the boys." I peered over the wagon ledge to find Pete glaring through branches, Sedge standing beside him, unaware he'd bared his fangs.

"Glashtyn," Pete growled, his sharp gaze knifing the horizon. How keen was his predator eyesight if he could see at such far distances? Evidently keener than a Vampire's. "And Pecks—*damn* him."

"Envious rat." Sedge fisted his sword hilt.

"No sign of the Leprechauns."

Leprechauns? Like the little dude on the cereal boxes?

"They could be lying in wait."

"Maybe." Pete thought on it, then shook his head. "We'll wait until the moon is high to know for certain."

Wait for what? I gulped.

"Dando and company are too impatient, too restless to stay hidden so long," Pete said. "Even under shadow cloak."

"Aye, but they'll know to be careful in this. Dando's strategic—and he kens he's dealing with you."

Pete smirked in a fleeting show of arrogance before he was once again the stoic sentinel.

My heart thumped in my ears as I clutched Sionna, whose eyes were already darting. Sedge's nostrils flared several times, probably detecting my fear. Whenever this wait Pete requested was over, we were going to do something dangerous. Maybe dangerous *and* stupid. I could taste it in the air and grappled to contain my panic.

I'd say I failed at that when static electricity crackled in my hair. A storm was a-brewing. Was *I* the real danger looming?

Finally, the sky now a navy ombre, Pete approached the wagon. I nearly swallowed my tongue, asking, "What's going on?"

He rested a rough bear paw on mine, where it lay over Sionna's sable head. For just one moment, I worried he wouldn't tell me. That he thought me too hysterical or timid to handle knowing. But then—

"Other harbingers," he murmured. "They're waiting to ambush us. Down by the bridge."

My throat damn near clamped shut. But I forced out one breath. Then two.

Pete's paw moved up to squeeze my arm. Comforting me. "This is what we must do now—you, Sionna, and I are going to hunker down in the back of the wagon. It's very dark on the bridge. If we stay out of the torchlight, they won't see us under my shadow cloak. Sedge will lead the wagon across the bridge. Kit will stay in the back and lay over us—as much as we can stand."

She was a *big* puppy, after all.

I chewed my lip, my fingers trembling. "Will that work? I mean, they're harbingers too. Won't they assume you might be using your cloak to disguise us?"

"Aye." He grimaced. "That's an apt concern." No sugar coating, as usual. "Kit will, of course, attack should they uncover us, and—" He swallowed hard. "If that should happen, I want you to run."

I shook my head.

"I want you to run as fast and as far as you can. Run and find higher ground. Climb as high as you can, so—"

"Pete, I'm *not* leaving you and Sedge to deal with this! This is my fault! I caused this! And I can help. I *can* fight!" Even as I argued with him, I felt the wind whipping low in my belly, roiling for freedom.

"You might have to, at that." Bleak, that's how he looked. "I'm not asking you to scurry off like a mouse. I'm asking you to give yourself a head start, an advantage. To split the wankers up, like. Though if you do fight, unleash your wind upon them."

Did he also sense my stirring storm?

"Please remember to pace yourself—control your breathing. You'll need to fend them off at least until Sedge or I can reach you."

I continued gnawing the hell out of my lip. "All right. I—I can do that."

Goddess, I hope I can do that.

Something dark quivered in Pete's mouth as he glanced at Sedge. Then, causing me chills of both excitement and anxiety, he bent to whisper, "And I know I need not tell you, Shorty—if we don't reach you, use that fire."

The only way they wouldn't reach me was if they were—

No, I'm not even going to think it!

His next words were slow, punctuated. "And if you use your fire, *no one* gets away alive."

Because there could be *no* witnesses to my fire.

"Even if we don't get our chance to kill Gentian—" Because of Pete's death. "You still can't risk him learning you're a fire sylph. He'd slaughter his own cadre to get his clutches on you—the weapon you could be. So, you *cannot,* under any circumstances, let him find out."

"I get it. I—I won't let you down."

Pete pulled back to offer a small, encouraging smile.

"Wait! What about my tether?" I glanced at my boot. "If I'm supposed to run as far as I can, then I'll need more length. How will you know how much to give me?"

Pete blinked at me. "Shorty, I untethered you the moment you agreed to help me kill Gentian."

To say I was bowled over was an understatement. "That was weeks ago!"

At least I'd managed to make him look less serious. "Aye." He chuckled.

"And you didn't think you should *tell* me?"

He laughed again. "Christ, Shorty, I thought you knew. Didn't you feel it slip off you?"

I blinked down at my ankle. By Goddess, it did feel lighter. "I was a bit emotional at that moment! I wasn't exactly being observant!"

Pete sighed. "And here I was, thinking I'd made a symbolic gesture. I suppose I'll get no credit for it now."

"Maybe." I studied him, gauging his sincerity. He was an honest SOB, for sure, but something didn't make sense. "You really untethered me?"

Unbothered that I'd question him, he nodded.

"But—where—where's Andy? Where's my totem, Pete?" That, I'd remember him returning.

Enjoying some private joke, Pete twisted to open his satchel. Seconds later, he held a rumpled Raggedy Andy doll. "You mean this tuft of fluff?"

I gasped in disbelief as the harbinger sent to capture me for dark and foreboding sources tossed me my totem.

Pete shrugged. "Was merely keeping him safe for you."

Tears welling in my eyes, I clutched the tuft of fluff to my heart, not caring that the latter might burst. Also not caring about boundaries, I flung my arms around Pete's neck and hugged him with the strength of my relief. And the strength of my desire to free him from his own tethers.

Pete froze in my embrace, confused about how to be. Then, with a shake of his head, he wrapped his arms around me. And he hugged me back—really *hugged* me—a fortress of testosterone.

Our hug lasted a fervent length—possibly an uncomfortable length for Sedge—before the two of us receded from each other. Then I wiped my tears and gazed down on Andy's geometric features. He was a sight for sore eyes, but now wasn't the best time to be seeing him.

"You know what?" I said to Pete, who scratched the back of his head, flummoxed as a teenage boy. "You keep him for now."

Pete's brows drew together. "I—what?"

I offered Andy back to him. "You keep keeping him safe for me."

He stared at the doll, then at me. "Shorty, you don't know what you're asking—"

"I'm asking you to hold onto him in case I get captured by these assholes." Why wouldn't he retake Andy? Was he running out of room in his satchel? "If they need my doll for some weird blood curse sacrifice, then let's separate him from me." I shrugged, wiping my nose. "Doesn't that make sense?"

Pete gulped, then took Andy. His thick fingers strangled my old pal's cotton body.

"What's amiss here?" Sedge strolled to Pete's side, sniffing the air like something smelled odd. Pete gulped again, still choking Andy.

"Pete gave me back my totem, but I told him to keep it for now, so the other harbingers won't get it if they catch me."

And I presume they will.

Sedge's brows leapt into his hairline. "And you've entrusted the care and safekeeping of your *totem*—to Pete?"

"Yeah." I cringed, now afraid I'd made some major faux pas. "Something wrong with that?"

Pete coughed, stuffing Andy back in his satchel. "Not at all." Blinking as though he meant to purge his face of all emotion, Pete faced Sedge, who lent his friend a pointed eye. "Shall we get on with it?"

"Hmph." Sedge gestured to the wagon bed. "By all means. Stoop into the shadows together. I'll manage the rest from here."

Agreeing, Pete tossed Sedge his purse to pay the Ogres' tithe, then buried his belongings—weapons, mostly—in my grassy wagon padding.

Pete chuckled, relieving his tension. "For once, Shorty, I'm happy you treat my lorry as a barn loft."

"I'll remember you said that," I said as he hiked his bulk up into the wagon with me and the dogs. "So I can throw it in your face the next time you bitch about it."

We didn't speak after that. I laid down, spooning a cagey Sionna to my belly, and Pete did the same to me. He raised his cloak around us, trapping me in a lightless abyss where nightmares reigned unchecked.

Clenching my eyes, the dark literally blinding, I gripped Pete's arm like my only lifeline. He gripped me back like I was his.

Sedge clicked, and Pete and I hiccupped as Kit plopped across our thighs. Sionna, at least, was able to ball up like a hedgehog to escape the pawler's weight, but we endured Kit's careless heft as the wagon rocked into motion, the river beneath our spy perch crashing in the offing.

When the wagon stopped, the ground shook under massive footsteps, jostling us passengers like corn kernels in a hot pan. I gripped Sionna, muffling my fearful squeal in her neck. Pete clutched me harder, swearing every time Kit resettled herself.

"Evening, lads!" So nonchalant, was Sedge in speaking to Ogres. Of course, he'd crossed their path before, a frequent flyer to the Shadow Court. "Business running smoothly tonight? Hope you haven't flattened anyone."

A voice like thunder vibrated through my bones, a series of booms reminiscent of God in any old biblical movie following. The words "not yet" echoed across the firth.

Good damn thing we'd stolen Howlite's purse! Facing these goliaths with empty pockets would've been suicidal.

"But we've been tempted, Vampire," the Ogre grumbled. "Your friends down aways—they paid but have been flitting around our necks like fleas since noontide."

Sedge harrumphed. "They're no friends of mine." Another beat passed. "That should cover it, lads. Count it."

While the first Ogre counted, a second one, softer-voiced, warned Sedge, "If you've seen that McKenna fella hereabouts, I'd tell him to duck out for a time. He's who these fleas thirst for."

"Hm." I pictured Sedge scratching his boxy chin. "I'll pass word along next I see him. Much obliged."

After several more moments, the first Ogre grumbled again, making my belly quiver. "Half these seeds won't do, Vampire. There are bone-apple seeds in here, blame you. Who needs more bone-apples at the now?"

"All right," Sedge said. "Let me find something more to your liking."

"Bloody chiselers," Pete griped in my ear, making me giggle despite everything. "Shh."

"*Well*—?" The voice boomed again, inciting riotous noise from nearby fauna.

"Patience," Sedge cautioned. "You'd probably loathe becoming my supper as much as I'd loathe tasting you."

This amused some of the Ogres, and what a daunting symphony that created.

"Here, now that should suffice." Sedge meant it would—or else.

Even being one of the most feared monsters in pop culture on Earth, could Sedge, a puppy compared to the Ogres, really intimidate them?

The Ogre took his time deciding but then groused, "Fine, fine, you pale devil. Put those fangs away."

"Of course," Sedge agreed with all cordiality. "As you've been so amenable."

The Ogre sniffed. "Be gone with you." He lumbered away, jolting our wagon.

"Hi-ho!" Sedge spurred Bob into motion.

Our wheels rolled over the smooth, stone bridge, progressing in a wavy line to avoid torchlight. I held my breath. Waiting. Dreading. Preparing. Pete seemed to be doing likewise; I hadn't felt him breathe since we'd passed the Ogres.

The wagon halted abruptly, Bob braying like a bullhorn, his hooves clattering as if he'd reared up on his hind legs.

"Bullocks!" Sedge exclaimed, Bob still beside himself.

Pete held me closer, doubtless smelling my fear. Lord, I hoped the other harbingers wouldn't detect our scent. Maybe Kit's doggy stench disguised it.

"What in bloody hell do you two mean by jumping out of the bushes like that?" Sedge snapped. "Just about pounced on you, I did! Would've torn out your bloody worthless throats!"

"Such vitriol, Sedge," one of the ambushers responded, slick as oil. "Is that any way to greet your mates?"

"Mates, is it? Last I heard, Pecks, you were defaming my good name about the barracks, whining of how I stole your last bounty, when you know fine and well that ordination was mine."

"It was my turn, Sedge," Pecks replied. "If you people would follow any sort of decorum—"

"I don't have clout enough with the Shadow Prince to pick and choose ordinations, you lout. They're sent to me as he sees fit, and I complete them as he sees fit, or it's another bloody whipping. That's the decorum *my people* follow."

"You ken well it's unwritten custom to trade ordinations when—"

"*Enough,*" the second ambusher barked. "Sedge, tell us where McKenna is, and we'll happily let you pass."

"McKenna? Haven't seen him in weeks." He sighed. "What hijinks is the damn fool up to now?" His exasperation sounded genuine, and I sensed an eye roll behind me.

"He's in the lurch," the second ambusher said. "With something he can't handle, it seems." Me and my cyclonic powers, I presumed. "We've dispatched ourselves to aid his plight. To lift his load, so to speak."

How kind? I sneered into darkness.

"Mm," Sedge grunted.

"Just tell us where he is." Pecks's silky malice evoked images of all our deaths.

The breeze kicked up outside our cocoon, and I hoped the ambushers were too dense to realize their coveted zephyrist was in Sedge's wagon, losing control.

Pete shook me, unable to scold me.

"As I said," Sedge returned, unperturbed. "Haven't seen him."

Several agonizing moments passed before the second ambusher spat what sounded like a loogie. "Rare, isn't it, Sedge, for you to travel with a cart and mule."

My blood curdled. *Shit!*

Pete shared the sentiment, muttering in my hair.

"It's normally just you and your mongrel."

"Aye, normally it is, Glashtyn. This time, however, my course is set for the Kirk of Cara on an ordination of capture. A bevy of its druids have been raving about the coming of the next goddess, as the aurora's painted the night sky."

Were there really druids—holy fae, I assumed—raving about me in the streets?

I mean, maybe *me,* I corrected myself.

"Gentian wants them brought to his cadre for inquest." In my mind's eye, Sedge shrugged. "Pete lent me his cart last we met, so I could transport my marks more easily."

"We've heard tell of no such ordination," Glashtyn rasped.

"I doubt Gentian wants his plot for capture widely known," Sedge returned. "The druids might scatter into hiding if word gets loose. And we all know your companion here can't shut his yap about such things."

I imagined Pecks's snarl unmasking the beast behind his dignified speech.

"Easy, now," Glashtyn cautioned Pecks with an icy chuckle. "No need for such aggression. If Sedge is being honest, then he'll have no objections to us searching his cart for—stowaways."

No, no, no, no!

"*Feck!*" Pete hissed.

Sedge clicked his tongue as boots clipped toward the wagon. "I wouldn't do that if I were you—"

A scream threatened to break from my throat as the wagon shifted under a rising weight, but I clamped my mouth, and Pete gripped both Sionna and me just as Kit surged up and snarled at the invader, ferocious as a lioness. Whichever ambusher had tried climbing into the wagon wisely fell back.

"As I was telling you," Sedge continued, Kit's feral warning still churning. "My pawler's lording over a recent kill. She'll bite your heads off if you should even attempt—"

"Yet we see no corpse," Glashtyn snapped, the wagon bouncing again.

Kit barked like a mad dog and pounced. A ghastlier snarl, I'd never heard.

A vehement oath preceded a physical struggle between fae and canine. The iron tang of blood saturated the close confines of Pete's cloak, Kit doing her damndest to gnaw off one of the harbinger's appendages until he dislodged her gnashing fangs.

"Call off your bitch, fucking fanger!" Pecks's inflection painted the word *fanger* as a racial slur.

Unruffled, Sedge answered, "You ken I would, but there's no reasoning with her."

"We've snuff hounds too! We'll let them take turns shredding her!"

Sedge scoffed at Pecks's threat, alleviating my fears for Kit. "You mean the beasts cowering in the ferns?"

"Our hounds don't cower, fanger," Pecks seethed. "Especially not from one lone bitch."

"Perhaps not." I heard an inhuman (and infae) purr of menace, like a dinosaur acquiring prey. "Perhaps *I'm* frightening them."

That noise made me a little frightened of Sedge too.

"Enough of this rubbish," Glashtyn grumbled despite Sedge's turning mood. My blood frosted at the *sching* of an unsheathing blade. I jerked to jump up and race away, feet circling the wagon, but Pete held me down—even as a sword jabbed between the wagon slats, limning the immediacy of our doom.

Kit bounded about, attacking the slashing blades, giving Pete and I the flexibility to juke into safety, though tears burst from my eyes at every single evasion. How long could we really skirt the death blows?

At a startled noise behind me, I feared I'd found out. Pete's fingers dug into my belly.

"I hit something!" Pecks's sword sliced to and fro, Pete his pin cushion.

I cried into Sionna's neck, curled in Pete's protective arms like a pill bug, and did *nothing* to help him. I was too damn scared.

"What in the Isle—?" Pecks then screamed like a little girl. His assailing sword clattered off the wagon ledge, something thudding wetly in its wake.

The Incubus head! He'd stabbed the Incubus head! Not Pete! I wanted to sing exultant songs to Pete's *Jaysus.*

"What is it?" Glashtyn's footsteps scrambled to reach his comrade. "Bloody pox on a Goblin!"

"Oh—*that*?" Sedge was dang close to snickering. "That's Kit's kill, as I warned you."

"Jesus, Joseph, and Mary!" Pecks exclaimed, suddenly quite Christian despite his attempts at outright murder. "What *is* it?"

"An Incubus," Sedge answered. "Kit's made quite a shambles of the wagon with its carcass. Bone shards everywhere, you see. I suppose I must clean up afore I reach the kirk. The bones will only boost the druids' powers, ken. Can't have that."

Were shivers contagious? Because I could feel our ambushers' skin crawling.

"Are you satisfied that Pete isn't tucked away in the wagon?" Sedge asked, bored as hell. "If he was, you'd have just stuck him like a pig at any rate."

Several heated beats passed before Glashtyn grumbled, "Fine, you can pass."

Pete exhaled. The first sound I'd heard from him since Pecks had uncovered the Incubus head.

"But I warn you, Sedge," Glashtyn hissed. "If we should discover you've deceived us—"

"You'll *what*?" There was that prehistoric rumble again.

When no reply came, I figured the ambushers knew when they'd pushed Sedge far enough.

"I'm about fed up with your threats, *boys*."

I gulped.

"Get the hell out of my way before I drain you both to husks."

Muttering insults, both harbingers backed off.

As Sedge spurred Bob back into motion, Kit plumped back down atop Pete and I, still snarling as we left Pecks and Glashtyn to the Ogres.

After what seemed like miles into the balmy Summer Court, Sedge finally drew us to a stop. On the road's shoulder, I saw, when Pete unshrouded us, freeing Sionna to shake off her fear like rain. Sedge leaned against the wagon bed, its ledge now knife-nicked.

"By Goddess, Pete!" Sedge chortled around the fangs still out for blood. He stroked Kit's neck as she sniffed the Incubus head on her front paws. "For once, your carnal blunder has actually saved your sorry hide!"

The moon bleaching us like milk, Pete and I made eye contact and burst into laughter.

THIRTY

"I thought those dudes' whole point was to capture me for my bounty," I remarked the next morning. We were packing up camp, discussing the now humorous events of our jaunt into Lithalaly.

Pete wiped sweat off his brow. "Aye, that's the gist of it, Shorty." He shouldered his bedroll, marched it to the wagon.

"Then why the hell were they stabbing through the wagon? They could've killed me—ruined their shot at those seeds."

Sedge glanced up from dismantling our fire ring. With the harbinger hub so near, we now needed to erase all traces of our existence anywhere—so no one could track us. "They weren't thrusting hard enough to kill."

"They still could've wounded me severely," I replied to Sedge. "Even if they weren't aiming to kill. And without medical attention, I'd still have died—just slower."

"Medical attention?" Pete remarked. "You'd have gotten *magical* attention."

I scoffed, folding my dusty cloak, which I wouldn't wear again until we reached the Shadow Court. Summer was as I'd imagined—hot, humid, and stifling. Once Pete finished his chores, he'd stroll into town and procure us more suitable attire for the current climate. He refused to take me with him—on account of the other harbingers—so I hoped we were on the same page as to what "suitable" meant. Because when he'd used that word, he'd smiled like a wolf with a lamb, his gaze dipping to my body. "One of them have healing powers? Like Olea?"

"Goddess, no," Sedge said. "Glashtyn's powers are for brute killing—he can transform into a *tarbh*."

At my cluelessness, Pete said, "A bull, Shorty."

"Ah—okay."

"And Pecks—he has no powers save to talk you in circles," Sedge snickered.

I arched a brow. "Can't imagine that would be very effective in a cage match."

"Hmph," Pete grunted. "It is if you're gifted enough to convince the matchmakers to pit you up against the weakest opponents."

"Sounds like cheating to me."

"To us too, Shorty."

"Anyhow," Sedge steered our convo back on course. "We harbingers have healing potions, mixed by Gentian's most skilled alchemists. They'll make short work of a near fatal wound." He glanced my way. "At least for a time—until you reach a healer."

"Ah, yes." I remembered Pete talking about fortifying potions after our Fomorian scuffle. "The potions you keep in your invisible stock closets?"

"Aye," Pete answered after a moment, ignoring the arrow-sharp look Sedge shot him for divulging trade secrets.

Couldn't see why it mattered if I knew, though. How would I even break into said invisible utility closet? By design, I couldn't see it.

"Whatever," I said after a semi-tense lull. "Still seems like those douchebags were being reckless."

Sedge snorted.

Pete leaned back against the wagon and folded his arms. "You never did explain that term to me, Shorty—douchebag."

I blinked again, reluctant to educate him right then—with Sedge there.

Pete shrugged. "It's only fair. I've been translating for you."

I gasped at the mocking cant of his head. "You already know what it means, don't you?"

"No, I quite sadly don't." Somehow, he managed to look both provocative and imploring. "Please, tell me all about it."

My cheeks flaming, I tossed my cloak over his smug face. "Suck it! That's what I'll tell you!"

Both males guffawed while I stormed over to swipe our breakfast pot off the ground. Sedge met my eyes as I barreled toward the stream. "And you can kindly suck it too."

"*Me?*" Sedge sputtered. "I'm not the one deviling you."

I pursed my lips, my gaze narrowing at Pete, who'd pulled off my cloak. "You're guilty by association," I informed Sedge. "Pick better friends."

Their amusement converged as I plopped down in the sand and dipped our cauldron into the thin flow of pink water delving between vibrant jungle plants.

"See now, Pete," Sedge griped. "Here I am, paying once more for your misdeeds."

"I'll find a way to make it up to you." Pete's satchel buckles jostled. "Need anything from town?"

"Nay, sir." Sedge paused. "I need not tell you to be cautious, aye?"

"Aye." Pete whistled, and Sionna, off sniffing the camp perimeter for game, pranced over to follow her master. "Be back as soon as I may."

I didn't spare him a glance over my shoulder. But I bet his smug ass looked damn fine as he swaggered away.

Pete

Pete relished Shorty's flaming flusterment the entire trek into Keitha Ronan, for he loved watching her milky skin flush like a rose in bloom. A rose he couldn't pluck, but a rose still and all. And who didn't love looking at a rose?

Imagining Shorty's shock when he finally confessed knowing what ketchup was, Pete filtered into the foot traffic along the main promenade through town.

Keitha Ronan teemed with merchants and travelers alike. One to sell the goods, the other to purchase them. He never journeyed anywhere without stopping there. Many of the shopkeeps knew him by name and offered him goodly discounts for his charm and good humor. They didn't even mind his profession, as he didn't stomp about brooding or dragooning—behavioral habits of most harbingers.

Firstly, Pete graced the clothier's shop, and Mistress Petunia was more than tickled to welcome both he and Sionna. She helped Pete choose sensible—and fashionable, she asserted—Summer Court garb for Shorty and gave him the lighter weight jerkin he wanted for half price. Before he left, she offered him something not commonly in her inventory, and Pete, once again, feigned that he was too in a rush to enjoy the receipt of that particular luxury.

Secondly, Pete visited the tackle supply shop. He was low on hooks, and his stock of silk line needed replenishment as well. Wooly, the hirsute house-fae, handed Pete a basket of artful lures to peruse, then led Sionna into his smokehouse for a bite of dried fish.

While admiring the craftsmanship of the lures he couldn't afford to buy just then, a new aroma upended his felicity. That aroma—bitter myrrh. Pete knew of only several fae who smelled of that biblical spice—remembered their detestable scent well. He'd once shared a barracks with them.

Prowess flaring, Pete cursed Wooly. How much mackerel was he feeding Sionna? He whistled for her, and she emerged—when she was good and ready. Huffing at her pretty black and tan face, Pete laid payment on the counter. "That'll be all for me, Wooly."

Unfortunately, Wooly was as meticulous as ever in packaging Pete's goods, and by the time the fellow had finished to his satisfaction, the scent of myrrh had overwhelmed the fug of glow-grouper and sea-dragon roe.

Outwardly equable, though braced for a skirmish, Pete turned to face a fellow harbinger he'd been at odds with since they were both cage fighters.

"McKenna!" Dando's friendly rasp (a parody of his own fine Irish brogue) greeted him—the way Judas must've greeted Jesus that night in Gethsemane. "How you be, old boy?"

Battling a sneer, Pete leveled the ginger Leprechaun with a mild expression. "I'm well, Dando. And you?"

Eyes slitting as he grinned, Dando revealed a set of pointed teeth. He shifted toward the shop counter, resting a scarred arm upon it in a way that made his bicep bulge from his much too snug sleeve. Dando wore typical Lithalaly hunting togs, complete with jagged collar and knee-length trousers. His orange hair, unkempt and tufted, curled around the brim of a crimson tricorn hat. A hat topping a big, round head that reached just to Pete's stern mouth.

"I'm jolly good, McKenna. Jolly good." Dando's features hardened. He sized up Pete like they were meeting in the ring again. Neither of them had ever been able to kill the other, though they'd both tried their damndest. As Gentian hated stalemates, this had always irritated him. And Pete and Dando. "Been looking for you."

As Sionna skittered behind Pete's legs, he assessed his situation. Though Dando made Pete long for the reek of fish, the Leprechaun's stench was singular. So, his entourage wasn't with him, though they no doubt prowled near enough to join a fracas should one arise. And while Dando's sudden presence bothered him, Pete found no malice in the ruffian's demeanor.

Waiting for Dando to tip his hand, Pete loosened his stance. "Why ever for?"

Dando's laughter was often artificial—this time, no different. He massaged Pete's shoulder in a condescension that made Pete want to break his wrist. "Such a hawkish look from you. Now, now, Pete, settle yourself. I'm not here for your zephyrist. Or, not anymore."

Strange that he should reveal his intentions so openly, Pete mused. *What game is he about?* "Aren't you?"

"Not after the news of this splendid, *splendid* morn."

Pete glanced Wooly's way. The shopkeep looked inordinately busy for one with just two customers. Avoiding the Leprechaun, he was. *Wise,* Pete judged.

"What news?" Pete asked, not giving a fig. He just wanted Dando to make his fecking point. He always had one.

Dando's eyes—the color of tortoise shells—rounded. "You haven't heard? Oh my, Pete, you'll be happy as Larry to hear it. Though it boggles me you've dodged the news 'til now, what with the broadsheets nailed about town."

"I've no mind for ballyhoo, Dando."

Likely, the broadsheet Dando referenced vilified some class of Unseelie fae, perhaps spewing lies of a village slaughtered by Vampires. The last story was falsified; Gentian himself had sent his cadre to decimate that Middling hamlet, sending out broadsheets blaming the Vamps afterward.

Pete sniffed. "If this news comes from the Shadow Court, you'd do well to question it."

"That's the best part." Dando looked like he wanted to dance the *Ceili.* "This news comes from the Spring Palace."

Pete stilled, chewing that tidbit. "The crown has made no formal proclamations in years." He wouldn't foster hope that their incompetent sovereign had declared war against Gentian. Finally.

"Aye, well, they were obliged to make one now." Dando's bushy eyebrows wiggled. "King Laurustinus—he's dead."

Pete's heart stopped. Memories he'd tried to bury long ago writhed upward, phantoms in the darkest pits of his mind. "The king is dead?" he restated, fists clenched.

"Indeed. That blood curse finally claimed him." Smug as a cat with cream, Dando produced a creased parchment from his pocket, smacked it on the shop counter. On it was the image of a Danann beyn with sharp, ethereal features and long, flowing hair. "And his daughter—untraditional heir that she be—is missing."

Now, Pete's heart leapt. Fleeing the devil. Because the image looked strikingly similar—

It can't be—

Certain features were all wrong if it depicted Shorty. She was much more beautiful with a thick forelock the image lacked. Besides, Shorty had mud brown hair. The princess had copper hair, something he knew without the broadsheet's description.

Dando fingered the gilded calligraphy, reading, "Handsome reward for Princess Amaranthine. Last seen a week past Beltane at the Thorny Rose Tavern."

She can't be!

Shorty had been living on Earth for more than a decade before he'd captured her. How she talked and carried herself was evidence enough. And she'd been living there with her *father*. But the king hadn't left the Spring Palace since—

Oh, he wouldn't drudge up that memory.

Regardless, the king had been in Evereostre during Shorty's life on Earth. Hadn't he?

And he'd never have sent his firstborn through a portal with a chronopath to a different time and world. Without protection against the blood curse she'd inherit when he passed. The prospect was ludicrous. Simply ludicrous.

Still—

After an age, Pete cleared his tightening throat. "I take it you mean to collect that reward."

"I'd rather collect the bounty Gentian's offering for her."

Of course, Gentian would outbid the Spring Palace for its princess. Its queen.

Still, this reassured Pete that Shorty and the princess were different people. Why would Gentian send him a private ordination to retrieve the princess—if Shorty were, in fact, her—only to later open the ordination to the rest of his harbingers before Pete's job was done? Aye, Pete was dragging his feet delivering Shorty, but he was still well within an acceptable timeframe for ordination completion. So, they had to be two separate marks with two separate blood curses. Hadn't they?

"How much is he offering for her?"

Dando's fangs glistened. "An entire estate in Lithalaly. Five-hundred bloody acres, Pete, and a lordship atop it."

Faith and begorrah!

Pete didn't know how to react when Dando smacked him like a wayward brat and snatched back his broadsheet. "That's why you can keep the zephyrist, McKenna. I've got bigger fish to fry. My party leaves for the Shadow Palace today to catch her regal scent. Rumor has it, the bogeybat what did in the king brought it back with him."

Dando turned on his buckled heels and strutted from the tackle shop, leaving Pete a speechless wretch in sore need of whiskey.

Amy

Pete looked like he'd rushed back to camp. His tan face had gone ruddy in patches, and his usual stride was more like storming. Panting, Sionna scampered right to the stream to wet her whistle, ignoring Kit, who splashed about, playing.

"We've already got the wagon packed and ready to go," I allayed Pete as he passed me on his way to the wagon. "You didn't need to hurry back."

The corner of his mouth lifted, though his expression lost nothing of its tension. "Your dander was up again when I left. I thought I'd best return posthaste with your new garb."

I arched a good-humored brow. "Thought you could buy my forgiveness, hm?"

The second corner of his mouth lifting with the first, Pete handed me a linen-wrapped package. "Can't I?"

"Maybe." Giggling, I ambled over and snatched the parcel from him, needing fresh, dry fabric against my skin after sweating the morning away in leather. "Thank you."

Pete gestured toward the copse of palms I'd designated as my private quarters. "Go change. We're wasting sunlight, aye?"

Grinning at Sedge, I skipped on my way.

I had to say, Pete's choice of outfit for me—pretty damn perfect. The top was a dark-green leaflike material sewn into a mesh lining, forming a crop tank top—both comfortable and flattering. And the bottoms were heaven-sent. With the feel of absorbent cotton and the look of crepe wrinkle linen, they ballooned out from my drawstring waist into something resembling gaucho pants, cuffing my legs just above my knees. My boots didn't exactly go with the ensemble, but they were the only shoes I had, and they hadn't yet rubbed me the wrong way.

Delighting in the breeze against my bare parts, I gathered my other clothes and headed back to "the boys."

They stood just where I'd left them, neither speaking. Sedge's pallid brow creased as Pete tinkered in his satchel, stiff as Aunt Aylie being backtalked. Had they had a disagreement? Why did Sedge look mildly troubled?

"Well, they fit," I broke their silence, dumping my old togs into my open bag in the wagon. "You did good," I praised Pete.

Pete's cocky smile didn't quite reach his eyes. "Finally, I've earned some credit with you." Chuckling, I zipped my bag.

Pete offered his water skin to me. "Care to finish off these last drops for me, Shorty? Then you can refill it." He knew how much I hated being thirsty.

"Sure." Without reservation, I took the leather pouch from him and uncorked it. Taking a swig, I sauntered to the stream, so pink and fresh it didn't need boiled for drinking.

"How long 'til we reach Covenlen?" I wanted to judge how much time I had left to gain full control over my powers. Maybe we had longer than I assumed.

I downed two more gulps of Pete's water. Delicious, though it should've been stale.

"I think we should get some training in tonight." So far, we'd only trained when Sedge left to hunt or relieve himself, thinking his ignorance of my powers could protect him.

I guzzled the last remnants of water, ousting a satisfying burp. Then I knelt to refill the water skin as requested. "Training will probably be more bearable after dark." I pressed the cork back into the skin. "With this heat, I mean. Does it get worse the—?"

"*Fecking mother above!*" Pete barked like a hornet had stung him.

"*Bugger!*" Sedge exclaimed.

"*What?*" I whirled, my heart in my throat. Were we under attack?

Neither harbinger reached for his weapon, though. In fact, they looked like they'd forgotten how to move at all. They only gawked at me. Sedge's jaw unhinged. Pete flushed like he'd eaten a ghost pepper, clutching his mouth.

Dear Goddess, is he going to throw up?

"What is it? Is there a bug on me?" I flapped like a bird. "Get it off! Get it off!"

"There's no bloody bug!" Pete stalked over and fisted the braid hanging over my shoulder. "It's *this!*"

At first, I didn't understand. There was nothing wrong with my hair. My braid wasn't even unraveling. Then I broke into a cold sweat, my heart fluttering too fast, my nerves going haywire. Because my hair was red. Bright, glinting, copper, red.

Tamsyn's potion wore off? Why didn't she warn me it was temporary? Why didn't Briar? Why—

My eyes caught on the water skin I still held. Pete's water skin.

I dropped it like a slug.

Clutching my braid, wishing to blot out its glaring shade, I wrenched from Pete's grasp. "*What* did you do to me?"

"I dosed you," Pete admitted, blunt as ever. Despite being an *underhanded prick*! "With my vial from the Well of Sincerity."

Sparks choked my voice.

"The well does more than compel honesty," Pete rasped. "It also uncovers masks cast on people."

Fire surged through me like an adrenaline shot. "I—you—this—*so*—!"

Neither judging nor understanding, Sedge looked to his jackass friend. "Why've you suddenly decided to pry when—"

"The king's dead," Pete cut him off, never taking his hot, darkening eyes off mine.

I reeled back like he'd slapped me.

Sedge blanched to an impossible shade. "That's astounding news indeed. But—what precisely has that to do with Shorty?"

Pete's whiskered jaw twitched. "Do you want to tell him, or should I?"

I struggled to control both my tears and my fire. "I *tried* to tell you before! I would've told—"

"Then tell me now." His nostrils flared, his expression stone. "What—is—your—name?"

A tear slipped past my glaring eye. The truth I'd offered him days ago tumbled from my lips without my consent.

"Amaranthine Ginger Larkspur," I spat with all the attitude I could muster.

Sedge's curse was a quiver on the wind.

Fire surged into my face. "My mother was Ginger Larkspur, fae queen. My little sister is Princess Viola. My little brother is Prince Acer. My aunt and uncle are Cornelian and Eulalia Larkspur. The guy you took me from is Briar Hawthorne, royal guard and Paragon in the Old Order. And my father—" My voice hitched. "My father was Laurustinus Larkspur, fae king."

Pete's nausea must've rebounded. He muttered a vehement curse and bent to clutch his knees.

"But I never knew him as that until after he died," my tongue persisted, and I hated Pete for making me do this *this* way. On his terms. This was *my* story to tell. Not his to compel. "I knew him only as Rus—a kindhearted middle-class banker who loved his children more than he loved himself. Apparently, to keep us all safe from the evil fuck who killed my mother—*tried* to kill him—he left his birthright to live in the suburbs of a strange world. He, my uncle, aunt, and Briar took us to Earth—to Pittsburgh, Pennsylvania. Daddy was sick as hell for the rest of his life because of that damn blood curse, but he was still a world-class father, who raised us all as humans amongst a community of Dananns *pretending* to be human. I lived like a semi-normal American girl, never thinking I was anything different.

"Until I unknowingly opened a door to a portal and let in a shit load of bogeybats, who eventually found my father and killed him like a rat in a gutter. I tried to save him, but he died in my arms. His last words were my name!"

My exposed secrets echoed in the silence, jeering me.

I sneered at Pete through my tears. "*Happy* now? Everything else I've ever told you was the truth, you *asshole!*"

Pete's eyes closed for a nano-second. When his lashes lifted, a maelstrom of ghosts roiled in that blackstrap gaze. His pulse raced in his neck. "That evil fuck you mentioned—you ken who he was?"

"Huh?" We all knew who he was.

Overstrung, Sedge said, "Pete, don't turn down this road again."

Sedge's plea fell on deaf ears as Pete leaned toward me, something awful in his gaze. Shame, I realized with a jolt.

"Shorty," he rumbled. "That evil fuck was me."

PART THREE

THIRTY-ONE

"What the hell does that mean?" Even in my rage at Pete, my whole being shook, refusing his confession. It couldn't be true. It just *couldn't*!

"I'm the harbinger Gentian sent to kill your father," Pete growled. "I'm the one who killed your mother!"

"*No!* No, you're not!"

"I am." He just wouldn't stop saying it! "I—"

"Gentian killed her, Pete," Sedge stated—the voice of reason. "Not. You."

Pete's mouth thinned. "It was my fault, wasn't it?"

Grim-faced, Sedge turned from his friend.

"I don't understand," I said, frustrated. "If you didn't kill her, how was it your fault?"

Pete's eyes shuttered. "Th-that's a tale for another time."

What the— Is he dismissing me?

He sure was. "We *must* get her out of here," Pete asserted, facing Sedge. "The Leprechauns and every other harbinger known to this world are heading home for her scent. I saw Dando in town. He's who told me—"

"Wait just a goddamn second!" I snapped. "You can't just tell me you think you're to blame for my mother's death, then not explain what happened!"

Pete's gaze daggered back to me. "As prone to half-truths as you are, you'll understand if I pick and choose what I tell you." He stalked over to tighten Bob's harness.

Burning, I stalked right after him. "Again, I tried to tell you, Pete! You told me I didn't owe you my secrets. Remember that?"

His hands jerked Bob's cinches. "If I recall, I said friendship doesn't mean I'm owed your secrets. But we aren't truly friends, are we, if I didn't even know—?"

"You did so know my name!" I stomped for his attention. Goddess, he was being so rude, not looking at me while I was screaming at him. "You knew it before we met! You told me so yourself, you prick!"

The insult rippled through Pete's shoulders. "I didn't know the name that matters."

"*Amy* is who I fucking am!" I shook my hands at him. "*No* other name matters!"

He scoffed, in need of a good smack, it seemed. "Will you say the same to the family pursers when you collect your inheritance, *princess*?"

I did smack him, right on the back of his thick ass head. "I'm *not* a princess," I seethed as he whirled on me, eyes flashing. "And that's not even what this is about, is it? You're not really pissed that I kept my goddamn last name from you. No, you're really pissed because of *what* that last name is! You're pissed at my dad!"

Pete just stared at me, black marbling his eyes.

Sedge cleared his throat. "Don't go down that road either, highness."

I huffed. "Don't call me that, okay?"

"You'd prefer your majesty?" Pete snarked.

"*Just—*" I scraped my face, hating what the truth was doing to us. "Look, Pete, I'm *so* sorry that my dad didn't help you when you were in need. He should have, and I'm angry at him too for overlooking you. But you can't take your beef with him out on me! Because I'm not him! I'm me. And I've always been just *me* with you."

Pete looked to Sedge. Dismissing me yet again. "We must split up. You take her old apparel—it still smells of her."

I watched Sedge gulp, apology in his gaze when he glanced my way. "Aye, then we might confuse at least some of the others, lead them astray."

"You head toward the Woebegone Wood, scatter her clothes within. If Dando follows, he'll be so desperate for her bounty, he and his henchmen will charge straight in despite the perils. Then meet me in our usual spot, aye?"

Sedge grimaced. "Your effects—" He paused, unsure how to address me. He settled on, "Shorty."

Sulking, I stomped to my book bag. I was shoving my pile of dirty clothes into Sedge's stark arms when Pete whistled for Sionna to hop to. We were heading out.

"This doesn't change anything, you know," I said to both males as they bid each other a silent farewell. "I'm still going to help you kill Gentian, Pete. I don't care if a whole army of harbingers is after me. I made you a promise, and I intend to keep it.

"I've seen what's going on in this world—seen what Gentian's doing to people—and I haven't forgotten about Humwater Dell. I can't *not* do something about it. We've got to stop him."

Nobody answered me, and as Pete, Sionna, and I rolled back onto the sandy jungle road, I had the depressing notion that Pete wanted to forget I was even there.

We traveled for days in silence. Or at least Pete did. I tried fishing for conversations numerous times. He didn't bite. Not that he was hostile toward me. Instead, he reminded me of the frozen section at the grocery store—that sudden chill you weren't expecting. And his inky eyes were too aloof for my comfort.

When I noticed Pete's remoteness extended even to Sionna, a creature he showed affection to on the reg, I became nervous that his anger had emboldened the demonic poison within him—riled it to take hold. So, I started singing more ballads to him as I rode in the back of the wagon through a thickening jungle that sometimes spooked me with its mysterious wildlife (I'd encountered a cross between a fanged spider and a scorpion multiple times, and lemur like tree huggers had thrown feces at us just before we'd made camp one harrowing night). I didn't stop singing until Pete finally barked at me to, "Bloody shut your gob!"

But he could yell at me all he wanted. I'd take that over his frost.

On the fourth day, the jungle was so dense that our path became impassable. Pete barely deigned to explain what was happening when he drew Bob to a halt and started gathering supplies from the wagon bed.

"Stuff your sack with whatever you can fit," he ordered, not bothering to look at me. "And put on your stockings." My socks, he meant. "Aye, it's hot, but we can't afford for you to get bog foot."

Trench foot, I translated for myself. *Ugh, he wants me to walk the rest of the way.*

"How much longer until we get there?" I asked after Pete had patted Bob's rump and directed him to head back home without us.

Having fashioned his bedroll, cloak, and several other belongings into a rucksack, Pete hoisted the pack onto his shoulders. "A while."

Once Bob had taken off with my only comfort, Pete, Sionna, and I trekked through what reminded me of the Amazon for hours, narrowly avoiding venomous lizards, flying monkeys (Briar hadn't lied about at least that), apelike bears, and angry pterodactyl-like birds that dive-bombed us in flocks. Finally, I voiced a niggling thought.

"I was told Covenlen was a wasteland."

No reply from the long-legged dingbat hiking over massive, mossy tree roots ahead of me.

"And I'm confused that the jungle is getting denser as we near it—not thinner."

Still, no answer.

I glowered at Pete's back. "You're not thinking of giving me over to Gentian now, are you?"

As if I'd chucked a rock at his head, Pete spun around. "*What?*"

I winced, his expression so caustic it shamed me. "Sorry, but you're just being so—shady—like you're planning to sell me out the second we see Gentian."

Pete scoffed. "Well, I'm not." He turned right back around and forged along through the underbrush.

Well, that *makes me feel better,* I thought, sullen as I followed him, Sionna traipsing at my boots.

The next morning, I awoke hugging a ragdoll with red yarn hair and a blue sailor's hat. I smiled at Andy's damp face, getting Pete's message even if he wouldn't say it.

No matter his anger, he would *never* betray me.

After I'd stuffed Andy into my already bursting backpack and eaten the basically raw breakfast Pete had snared us (some creepy amphibian with a meaty backstrap I couldn't even look at as I shoved it past my lips), the rain began. First as a drizzle, then as a shower, and in the end—a straight up deluge that made the slightest hill a waterslide. Which might've been fun if not for my fears of whatever lay at the bottoms of those slides: poisonous plants with no antidotes, jaguar-like cats ready to pounce on any moving body, or other parasitic fae like the Incubus with magic as deadly as cancer. I would've bet dangers far beyond my comprehension lurked in a fae jungle.

Sionna had her qualms as well—mainly the intermittent thunder rattling the sky, which we couldn't see beyond the canopy. Pete carried her for sizeable portions of the day, as she kept skittering away to hide in tree trunk hollows or other creatures' burrows. She writhed for freedom from him every time our butts hit the ferns.

Then sunsdown came upon us. The rain hadn't abated, and Pete hadn't slowed his pace to find shelter for the night.

"Shouldn't we be looking for some place to make camp?" Shouting was the only way he'd hear me over the torrents sheeting upon us. I tried again to clear my vision of rain. It worked for mere seconds, but I saw Pete glance back at me.

"We should press on!" he called back. "We're nearly there now!"

"Huh?" The Shadow Court was *not* in a jungle. Uncle Neel would've known that. Briar would've known that. "You mean we're near a place you usually stop on the way?"

"Night's falling!" he stated the obvious. "Muster up some flames if you want to see the path underfoot!"

If I *want to see? Does that mean* he *can see in the dark? Damn him and his predatory eyesight.*

Souring at his magical fortune, I concentrated until I felt a definite *zing* dart into my fingertips. Then, with a snap, I made of my hand a torch. A torch that an apparent monsoon couldn't douse. "*Cool.*" I marveled at my flaming fingers. My fire had never withstood water before. Was I just getting better at invoking it?

Answering that question for myself would have to wait. I splashed along to keep up with Pete because he, of course, hadn't waited while I conjured fire with my mind.

When at last Pete stopped, he turned back to watch as I drew near. Still pleased with myself for keeping my fire burning for over an hour, I smiled at his stony mug. Sionna was at it again, worming away in his restraining arms.

"I'll leave it to your discretion." Pete gestured at something beyond the bubble of light my torch created around us. "You can go down first, and I'll follow, or I can take the lead, though you'll need to wait a brief length before you follow—afford me space enough to reach the bottom."

"Another slide?"

"Aye. This one steeper."

I chewed my bottom lip. "How steep?"

His pointed gaze said all I needed to know.

Huffing, I prepared myself to do something stupid. "I'll go first. I'll just psych myself out if I wait."

If he knew what that meant, he gave no indication. "The downhill slope begins just by those berry bushes there."

I walked toward the bushes, as jittery as I was the night I'd stepped through a giant tree into a strange, enchanted land. Because I had no clue what awaited me on the other side.

"Wear your pack on your front," Pete advised. "Keep your arms tucked in, your legs together."

The obtuse angle my body adopted when I sat in the rushing mud alarmed me, though I knew a decline was coming. Afraid the swirling rapids might take me before I was prepared, I clutched at a branch, several berries bursting between my fingers. Thank the Goddess there were no thorns.

My heart galloping, I stared past my flames into utter blackness. I released a tremulous breath, whispering a prayer to Danu.

"Shorty—"

Spraying rain, I whipped toward Pete. He hadn't shown me the courtesy of using even that infuriating nickname since we'd split from Sedge, the worry creasing his brow now the only emoting he'd done besides grizzling like a bear.

His Adam's apple bobbed. "Be careful, aye?"

Unable to respond, I simply faced forward, clutched the bulge of my backpack, and slid into the looming unknown.

To my own credit, I didn't scream until I went airborne the first time. After that, I shrieked my throat raw as I careened down a twisting, undulating, spiraling, endless death flume. Leaves smacked me in the face, branches and rocks scraping my exposed skin as whoops from a cluster of some version of a tree ape taunted my descent. And given that I'd lost concentration the moment I'd gone down that slick, earthen shoot, my fire had flickered out, so I couldn't see what hurt I barreled toward next. Not that I had the control to skirt obstacles anyway. Danu had definitely taken the wheel.

On my last scream, the ground abandoned me completely. I flipped backward in a flailing summersault, positive I'd gone off a cliff and into a fatal freefall. At any second, I'd hit the ground and become something that would never be. Images of people flashed through my frantic mind—my family, friends, and anyone who relied on me—to take my place in the Spring Palace—to change the world.

Then, I saw Pete. Pete in all his varieties—the harbinger, the jester, the scholar, the friend, and the only male, besides Daddy or Ace, who'd ever seen me for who I was. The only one I'd never been scared to *let* see me.

As I'd done when the entrapment curse summoned fire ants in my blood, I clung to my memories of him—and a wind caught me in a cradle, rocked me downward like a baby.

Then dumped me like garbage in a pool of stinky, sandy mud.

Sludge on my tongue, I thrashed in the pit, a drowning duck, until I heard a gloopy splash and a deep-voiced diatribe.

"Pete!" I squawked. "Where are you? My fire's out!"

"Are you all right?" Slopping sounds preceded hands clasping my arm. "Are you hurt?"

I clutched his slimy jerkin, his body solid beneath it. "I'm fine. I almost had a heart attack at that last ramp, but I'm okay now."

"What in bloody hell were you doing winging around like a leaf on the breeze?" he shouted, his face stark and creased. "You frightened the piss out of me!"

"I—I—I—"

"I thought you were being abducted by another zephyrist!"

"I wasn't! I—" Wrenching from his biting fingers, I steadied myself in the mud. "I think I went off a cliff and—"

"There was no fecking cliff! I was on the downslide when I saw you soar up into the trees, cackling and flapping about like some Witch who'd lost rein of her broom!"

I bleared at his general shape. "I did?"

"Aye." He snatched his filthy rucksack out of the mud. "Since I can't scent anyone nefarious nearby, I suppose I merely witnessed a dimwit letting her powers run amuck. Praise heaven that you floated back to ground, for only Danu knows where you'd have ended if you'd kept on as you were."

Exhaling, I eyed him. My vision must've been adjusting to the darkness, for now I could make out the frown within his mud smattered, rain drenched face. "Maybe if we'd spent any time training this past week, I'd have a better grip on my powers, but we didn't—so that's what we get!"

His mouth twisted. "Have you ever heard 'practice makes perfect,' Shorty?" He waded through the muck toward higher ground, raindrops plunking down like stones. "You don't need me to practice what you've already learned."

I glowered, trudging after him toward a swampy meadow where Sionna already lay, hyperventilating after her trip down the ravine. She glared at Pete, rain washing her coat.

His jaw flexing, Pete reshouldered his rucksack. "*Females*," he grumbled. "Come along, both of you, so that I may see to your every comfort."

His sarcasm earned him another glare.

We did come along, as it was, and it wasn't long before we finally—*finally*—stopped.

Before us, amid an overgrown, wild jungle, stood a viny, crumbly, gated temple, so tall I couldn't see its peak above the canopy. The gate was a high, stone structure topped by heavy corbels and finials carved into fae busts rocking wizard beards. Its flora-twined archway, fashioned out of a substantial, arced tree, had a capstone wedged into its highest point—a statue of a regal pregnant female with elegant ears and flowing hair. An image I'd seen before on Uncle Neel's official circle center stationary—Danu, the mother of all. Beneath her glory stood a lanky feyr in substantial homespun robes.

Through the storm, I struggled to make out the stranger's features, but I saw long light-brown hair and bronzy skin that glowed in the torchlight. He raised a hand in greeting.

Waving back, Pete started forward. Sionna and I followed. One step, then two, and the rain ceased.

I boggled over my shoulder. Sure enough, the storm thrived behind us, thunder booming, lightning flashing, but we now stood in the still, dry night as if we were inside a snow globe, looking out.

"That'll be the elemental shields," the strange feyr said in a friendly tenor. "Without them, the rains would drown us."

I'd wondered how an epic flood hadn't submerged the temple, being at the bottom of a gorge. All groundwater would surely flow right for it.

The stranger, gazelle-like, walked toward us. He smiled, further defining the already knifelike features I hadn't seen at first.

After a moment's blinking, I realized he was Danann. A black Danann.

Dear Goddess, how had I never met a person like him before? Why had all the Dananns on Earth been of the Caucasian variety if we were a diverse race?

So, not only was my childhood a contrived farce, but it was whitewashed too. Great.

The feyr bowed his ochre head. "Welcome, princess."

I just stared at him. "How—how do you know I'm a princess?" Right then, I looked more like a wet cat than a royal.

"Myrrdin is a high druidic prophet, Shorty," Pete said, his resentment toward me restrained. For the moment. "He likely saw you coming."

Myrrdin offered a rangy hand. "And I knew your mother well, child. You look very much like her. Although, you have your grandmother's nose."

Chills stippled my arms. Wasn't that how Briar had described me?

Yearning to learn more about the two beyns he'd mentioned, I took Myrrdin's hand and gave it a good, friendly shake.

Myrrdin's eyes, an indistinguishable color in the night, sparkled with a humor I didn't understand until Pete also took his hand and placed a reverential kiss on his knuckles.

"Oh, I—" I cringed, unsure what to do now.

"'Tis an outmoded custom, anyhow," Myrrdin said. "I prefer your gesture. 'Tis more hygienic."

"Myrrdin is just as finicky about cleanliness as you are, Shorty," Pete said.

That, I could already tell. Myrrdin smelled like vanilla and nutmeg, and his fingernails were well-manicured, clear as holy water.

"How did you know my mother?" Couldn't have held in the question any longer if I'd tried.

"I was her stepfather's high druid. He entrusted me with her spiritual schooling." Memories flitted through his gentle expression. "She was one of my most challenging pupils—questioning everything, forever intent on thinking for herself."

She sounded just like—

"Now I ken where you get it," Pete said, making my heart sing.

Chuckling, Myrrdin gestured toward the ancient temple beyond the vines. "I'll tell you all about your mother, princess, but I'm sure you'd first like a good, long rest. You've had quite a journey getting here."

I blinked again. He spoke with finality, like I'd reached my destination. But wasn't my destination the Shadow Palace?

When I turned to question Pete, he nodded me on. "Go on, Shorty. There's no one here who'll harm you."

Besides Myrrdin, I saw no other signs of life. "Who else is here?"

Myrrdin was already striding toward the temple. "Come along and we'll acquaint you."

So, I followed Myrrdin down a torch-lined path. Pete and Sionna followed. The latter with jubilance (she seemed quite fond of Myrrdin), the former in moody silence.

Myrrdin opened a set of massive stone doors into a rotunda. Its cupola was stratospheric, arched windows offsetting every story and welcoming the moonlight brightening my way as I staggered across the marble floor into the temple's heart. My soft footfalls echoed like tap shoes.

"What is this place?" I angled right to find a massive frieze carved into the curved wall on our level—a merging of two heads.

"The Kirk of Cara," Myrrdin answered.

I vaguely remembered Sedge mentioning a place by that name.

"Once known as the Kirk of *Anam Cara*, but nobody calls it that now," Myrrdin continued. "'Tis a shame, though, as shortening its name mists over its significance."

I wracked my brain, having heard the phrase *anam cara* before—somewhere. I just didn't remember where—or what it meant.

"*Anam cara* is a Celtic term, Shorty," Pete explained, seeing my struggle to place it. "Roughly, it means soul friend—soulmate."

I *loved* knowing soulmates existed. "Any reason it's called that?" Myrrdin *had* said its name was significant.

Again, I studied the frieze's melding faces as Pete replied, "The ancients built this temple to demark Danu's creation—the first soulmates."

"But—Sedge said—" Breath abandoned me.

For the first time since he'd discovered who my father was, Pete's lips curled in a semi-smile. Moonbeams silvered his features and the wayward tips of his hair. "They were Adam and Eve. We're standing on the precipice of Eden."

Mind blown here! "But I thought Eden was on Earth."

Danann circle lessons never delved into the bible, although many of its parables crosscut ours. But I'd taken a college course, The Old Testament as Literature; the good book totally claimed Eden belonged to Earth.

Pete shrugged. "Thought the same myself before I heard it was here."

"Eden is just beyond the next doorway," Myrrdin confirmed, steepling his hands. "The garden—Danu's great test, if you will."

I blinked. "A test? For what?"

"To ascertain if her new children—her soulmates—were worthy of life in the great new world she'd created," Myrrdin said. "To see if they'd seek more wisdom than offered."

What a satisfying answer. I'd always felt Eve got a bad rap for what happened in Genesis. Who wouldn't want the knowledge of good and evil? For how could one understand the good in their life if they've never known evil? Without the comparison, Danu's "good" would be meaningless. "Danu *wanted* them to bite the apple."

Myrrdin nodded.

"But what about the serpent? If the Goddess *wanted* her guinea pigs to break her rule about eating from the tree, then the serpent was helping her, not—" I paused, chewing my lip. "Unless the serpent was actually Danu in one of her animal forms."

I knew Danu could take the form of seagulls, horses, and even fish, but I'd never heard of her becoming a snake.

Myrrdin hummed. "Just as insightful as Ginny too."

My heart was growing very warm, indeed.

"Correct, princess. Danu was the serpent. She tempted Eve, who passed the test—as you're aware. Adam—well, he—" Myrrdin chuckled. "He was wrapped around his beautiful companion's finger and would do just about anything to please her. Hence, they both ate, and Danu cast them out of Eden—onto Earth, her cherished conception—to multiply and be fruitful."

"If Danu was the serpent, *is* there a devil?"

"Oh, but yes, princess." The high druidic prophet sighed. "But *that's* a story for another night."

"Aye." Pete exhaled. "For now, let's get you settled."

Let's? Is he the concierge?

"After you, princess." Myrrdin gestured me past him.

On my way, I glanced at him. "Please call me Amy."

Myrrdin bowed his head.

Under the frieze on the opposite side of the rotunda was another set of stone doors. They opened automatically when I touched one of their handles. Magic, I assumed, and tromped into the night.

Outside was a small clearing where a circle of standing stones of the smoothest obsidian gleamed. At its center, a large stone altar boasted all the typical accouterments of spirit circle: a chalice, a decanter of wine, a jar of blue, chalky paint for exaltation, a bodhran drum and stick to keep the beat during chants, and a mortar and pestle with a selection of herbs on the side. In preparation for a sermon, it appeared.

Who the sermon was for remained to be seen. Even the jungle animals I'd been hearing since sunsdown had abandoned this place—this *holy* place—like a nuclear blast site. Like life itself had jumped ship after Eden's occupants departed.

Around the ring was a vast, run-of-the-mill garden comprised of blossoming shrubs, flower beds, and fountains spouting pink water. Sweet, but nothing to write home about. I was surprised Eden was so dang—boring.

No wonder Eve had sought something better.

As it seemed the males expected me to proceed into the circle, I headed onward. Before I'd reached the first stone, though, I tripped on something invisible and fell flat on my damn face.

"Ugh," I groaned into a patch of sandy, flowery grass before I struggled onto all fours and found that—I was in a different place entirely.

I popped up onto my knees in a jungle oasis swarming with all the best things mother nature offered: lush flowers, mossy trees, towering palms, curling vines, exotic critters, ripe fruits, joyous laughter, and happy faces. Animals whooped, sung, and chittered in the palms around me, phosphorescent bugs like the Nixie's creature form flying past.

Woodsmoke mingled in the air with incense, spices, and pollen, several fires burning throughout the mysterious town before me. A cozy, well established town of thatched, straw huts residing beside a splendorous, fertile beach. And beyond, a gentle sea, teal as a peacock's feathers.

Fae and humans alike occupied the village square in convivial calm, chattering as little ones scampered in clothes straight from Tinkerbell's closet.

I was gawking at paradise when a large, hair-dusted hand reached into my vision to help me off the ground. My eyes followed the hand up to a swarthy grin.

"Welcome to Eden, Shorty." Grabbing my wrist, Pete yanked me to my feet.

"How did we get here?" I asked, tucking my straggled bangs behind my ears.

Pete shrugged, adjusting his saturated rucksack strap. "The garden you saw is a decoy—the doorway to this time pocket."

"Seriously? We're in a time pocket?"

"Aye." He watched Sionna prance off to join the giggling children, lightning bug clusters parting in her wake.

"I'm not aging right now?" Funny, but I thought I'd feel different in a place where time stood still.

"No, since you have magic."

I shook my head. "So weird."

"Aye, well, it serves well as a safe haven at any rate."

"A safe haven from what?"

"From Gentian's curses. Mostly death and blood curses."

I stared at him. "You're saying all these people—they're refugees?"

Solemn, Pete nodded.

Oh, my stars. There must be hundreds. "Are there *whole* families here?" I watched the faelets Sionna now played with.

"Aye. Blood curses devour full bloodlines, ken."

Oh, I kenned. And he knew I did. "Gentian doesn't know this place exists?"

"Not at all." For a split second—or whatever you'd call it in a pocket without time—I glimpsed the smug man I'd befriended. "Besides those sheltering here, only a handful of people know it exists."

While dazzled and heartened to learn a sanctuary like Eden existed for people in my predicament, those feelings soured quickly. Because—why hadn't Pete told me? He hadn't told me *anything* about it.

And you thought he trusted you, Amy.

"Have I given you enough space to explain everything?" Myrrdin appeared, spurring Pete and I to distance ourselves.

"Aye." Clearing his throat, Pete looked from me toward the huts. "Everything pertinent."

Myrrdin gestured toward the eternal dusk. "Let's find you a bed for the night, Amy."

Yes, let's.

We all headed into the heart of town, me shrinking like a violet as people stopped and stared.

"She can sleep in my hut," Pete told Myrrdin. "She'll be the most comfortable there."

His hut. Made sense, I supposed. He'd need rest after his journeys to Eden. I guessed they happened often.

"Presumed as much," Myrrdin said to Pete.

"I don't want to inconvenience you." I shook my head when both males glanced back at me. "You can have your hut, Pete. I'll be comfortable anywhere. I mean, it's only for a night. Right?"

Pete turned away—not ready to tell me what we were doing there, it seemed.

Myrrdin side-eyed his acquaintance. I couldn't say yet if they were friends.

"I'll be fine," Pete said. "You take it, Shorty."

I chewed my lip. "Well—okay. But only if you're sure."

Their silence concluded the matter.

Pete's hut was by far the largest in the town—a Tahitian dream inside, like he'd paid for the diamond timeshare package. Its roof was thatched into a dome, fae asters flickering in its rafters and around a spectacular skylight, where smoke from a crackling firepit escaped. A lone window stood across from the doorless entry, draped in flower blooms woven together by their stems—gorgeous, but impractical as curtains. Through that window flowed a delightful, cool breeze.

I squelched upon a spongy moss carpet—naturally grown, not placed like sod. It crept from the floor up onto a palm stump table topped by a clay bowl and pitcher. Wooden stools surrounded it. The bamboo wardrobe beside the dining nook housed blankets, towels, and cloths for washing. I half expected to find hotel toiletries and tissue packs. And a mint on the pillows topping the oh-so-generous, fluffy, blanketed mattress before me on a shallow platform. I wanted to squeal when I saw it.

"Will this suffice, Amy?" Myrrdin asked, though I thought the answer apparent.

"Uh, yeah. This'll be good."

Pete gestured outside. "If you should need anything, you'll find me next door. The nearest privy is just down the path behind the hut. No need to gather leaves—there should already be some stocked."

I removed my backpack and set it on one of the stools around the table. Sionna moseyed over to me, sniffing the floor in search of crumbs. Finding none, she snorted in displeasure and tramped straight to the mattress. After several windups, she balled up amidst the covers to lick her damp paws.

"I'll find you some dry bedding and scrounge up some food—for you both." Pete frowned at Sionna, who evidently still had him on her shit list. "Shouldn't be long. I'll just have a brief chat with Myrrdin first."

He then looked to his acquaintance, something heated in his gaze, and gestured toward the door.

Myrrdin's lips hitched subtly at one corner. "'Til tomorrow, Amy." He then ducked back into the chirping night behind the harbinger, who'd stalked out first, stiff-backed, like he was ready to pick some bones.

THIRTY-TWO

I awoke facedown across the pillowy mattress, naked beneath soft sheets. My hair was wild, drool pooled from my mouth, and several of the dates I'd devoured before bed were stuck to my cheek. It was glorious.

Purring as the warm, floral breeze fluttered past the curtains, I pushed onto my knees beside the black and tan snuff hound still snoring beside me. Reaching to snuggle her, I turned and found a faelet in a pair of leafy shorts watching me from the foot of my bed.

I scrabbled for my sheet, clutching it over my nudity.

"Hallo!" The faelet waved. He was short and skinny with round, transparent wings fluttering at his back. His hair was raven black and styled in a pixie cut, his matching brows slanting sharply down over eyes that sharply slanted up. With a button nose, a dimpled chin, and round, freckled cheeks, he was the cutest thing I'd seen since the cantir. I just prayed he wasn't also fiending to make me breakfast.

"Hi," I finally answered, wondering why he was there.

His dark eyes glittered. "I'm Jet."

"Nice to meet you, Jet. I'm Amy."

"The warden says you're a princess."

I pursed my lips, wondering who the warden was. Myrrdin, maybe? "I guess I am. But I don't act like one, so you don't have to treat me any differently than you'd treat anyone else. All right?"

He smiled, eyes asquint. "All right."

Somehow, I resisted the urge to pinch his cherubic cheeks. "Why exactly are you here, Jet?"

"Because you needed a bath!" He shuffled aside, revealing a round wooden tub half full of steaming water. I supposed *teas* stones lay beneath it. A bucket sat beside Jet on the mossy floor, brimming with teal water.

"You just decided to get a bath ready for me?"

"Warden said I should."

"He did, huh?"

Now, I didn't care who the warden was. If he was using child servants, whether it was a socially accepted practice or not, then we were going to have words. "Where would I find this warden if I wanted to speak to him?"

Jet shrugged, taking up his bucket. "All over, Amy. He's always working on something when he's here. We keep him busy."

"You keep *him* busy?" I watched the faelet dump the remains of his bucket into the barrel. "You're not his servant?"

His giggle was as infectious as a yawn. "Nobody's a servant to anyone in the garden, Amy. We all work together. Warden does the most, though. Mama says he does too much, that he wants to take care of everyone—that it's his way of earning forgiveness for sinning. She says he should be kinder to himself."

"Hm." And there I was, doubting the warden's honor, when he was really an overzealous, self-sacrificing people pleaser. "Sounds like your mother likes him."

"We all do. Most of us would be dead without him. He brought me and Mama here years ago, before the death curses killed us."

I blinked. How could a child say something like that so casually?

"What's all this chatter?" a deep brogue asked from the doorway. A deep brogue I now heard in my dreams every night. "Didn't I say not to disturb the princess, Jet?"

Clutching my sheet tighter, I faced Pete and his rugged roguishness square on. A good sleep had done him good. His under-eyes had lost their dark smudges, and his tan skin had brightened. He wore a fresh linen shirt, untucked from his trousers, and his massive feet were bare, his nail beds cleared of dirt.

"*You* said?" I blinked in realization. "Are you Eden's warden?" The huge hut made more sense if he was. "*You're* the one in charge?"

Pete's frosty gaze took me in.

"Why didn't you *tell* me, Pete? About Eden? About the refugees? About your role in helping these people? About *any* of it?"

Pete rested his forearm against the lintel and shrugged. "Those in glass houses, Shorty—"

I gulped down my bitterness, knowing I'd had that remark coming. But Pete's flippant attitude still pricked my temper—despite all I'd just learned of his altruism. Or maybe because I had.

How was it possible that the same selfish man who'd meant to trade my innocent ass to Gentian to save his own hide from demonic possession had been sneaking his other marks and their family members to safety under the Shadow Prince's nose for years?

And why hadn't he wanted to save me?

"You know, I was having a good morning until you showed up," I blustered. "Did you just come here to piss me off?"

"As a matter of fact, I came to find out what other truths you've withheld." With a cool flick of his eyes along my sheet, Pete addressed Jet, who looked like he'd gotten caught in headlights. "Tub's full enough, lad."

Glad to escape, Jet grabbed his bucket, then fluttered under Pete's arm. Leaving us to deal with one another.

I shifted but kept my chin high under Pete's scrutiny.

"Meet me outside once you're decent," Pete said. "We've a meeting with Myrrdin and his clerics." His mouth twisted before he glanced back toward the oasis. "To discuss the depth of your powers."

That sounded an awful lot like a meeting Uncle Neel or Briar would've agreed to. "Are my powers other people's business now?"

The corner of Pete's lips twitched. Several times. "Aye," he finally muttered, then tramped off.

Though I wanted to take my time just to spite Pete and the other males entitled to know my magic's secrets, I bathed quickly, then donned a set of dry, clean clothes left upon the palm stump table while I'd slept.

Pete certainly had good taste in feminine apparel. The leafy top (more a bustier) and shorts he'd scavenged fit comfortably, if not a smidge skimpily. But I'd seen the other beyns in the garden. I was right on trend.

Leaving my wet hair loose, I clenched my hands for another argument and tromped in my semi-dry boots out into the morning—twilight?

I paused, stars winking down at me from a lavender-blue sky. Phosphorescent bugs square-danced about my head as evening creepers symphonized their chitters, knocks, and hoots, as they'd done on my arrival the previous night.

Or was it the previous night? How long had I slept?

"We're in a time pocket," Pete reminded me. He knelt by a stone wishing well, washing his hands in the bucket Jet must've left. "If time stands still, so do the heavens above us."

Supposing that made sense, I moseyed to his side. We didn't speak as he washed, and I people-watched.

Several fires roared in the square, where feyrs, beyns, men, and women alike breakfasted, feeding their young. Moms chatted amongst themselves, their kids scampering about their legs before heading into a pavilion for what I assumed was school. A bespectacled, gangly man (and I mean human) stood at the head of the makeshift class, scrawling with a brick of talc what looked like Celtic runes on a humongous slab of slate hanging from the truss above him. He wore a white powdered wig upon his bald, sweaty head, so at odds with the leafy clothes adorning his reedy figure. What beef did Gentian have with such a bookish fellow?

The village was abustle with choring. Fishermen canoed on the sea, spreading nets, while others cast lines out for lunch. There were washer people knee-deep in the water too, scrubbing heaps of laundry until their hands were red and honest. A group of pre-teens reaped what they could from an orchard to my far left, Furby-esque creatures with long, frond-like tails playing pranks on them as they worked, stealing fruit from grass baskets retaining their harvests.

A structure smaller than the school pavilion housed an open-aired cafeteria, where fae and humans worked together—by hand and by magic—to bake bread and other fae confections in a spacious stone oven.

Several males wielded axes in the jungle outskirts. I watched, amazed, as they felled one tree, something akin to a coconut, and its shorn stump sprouted back to its original state in a blink—overgrown nuts and all.

My mystification of little import to Pete, he rose with a groan. "Shall we be on then? They're no doubt waiting for us."

I cringed as Pete led the way. "What exactly do Myrrdin and his clerics want to know about me?"

If Myrrdin's a prophet, shouldn't he already know enough?

"They didn't feel it necessary to inform me," Pete groused. Was he as annoyed by their gall as I was? "Myrrdin, especially, only tells me what he *feels* I should know."

Oh, that's definite bitterness in his voice. Maybe his attitude that morning had nothing at all to do with me.

"Should I be worried?" I bit my lip. "That they'll find out—" I quieted as we neared several fae shooting dice in a circle. "You know."

About my fire.

Pete paused, softening for once. "Last night, I said there's no one here who'll harm you. I mean that still. Regardless, if you know that you've a power, Myrrdin's already privy to it."

I frowned, preferring privacy.

Pete's mouth bunched. "It'll be the bits you don't yet know that he'll wish to pry from you."

I gulped. "And how—how will he do that?"

"That, I can't say, but he and his brethren won't hurt you." Pete headed down the sandy path. "I'll make certain of it."

I rushed after his long legs and into a jungle outcropping. We walked several yards down a flowery hill, above which monkey-cats swung from vines, cackling like hyenas. Then, pushing past several overgrown ferns, another stone circle—Eden's *real* place of worship—appeared.

Situated atop a hill, tapered megaliths towered into the twinkling morning night, the henge they created more spacious than a football field. Ancient and weatherworn in appearance, the stones were hewn from some mossy blue rock, glistering in the starlight. Double rows of torchieres lined the path Pete and I traversed toward the circle. Various feyrs dressed in homespun regalia, much like Myrddin was last night, gathered off the beaten path beside a typical American log cabin. Smoke tendrilled from its stone chimney. Though it didn't quite seem his taste, I guessed Myrrdin hung his robes here at night.

"You're late, McKenna," a small, wiry figure rasped.

Pete simply replied, "Aye," but something about the other's voice raised my hackles.

I stopped dead, the world teetering on its axis, and once again felt the brutal punch of a hoof against my chest. "You!"

Both Pete and the hairy, wizened primate he'd spoken to turned to me, the latter now cringing like a criminal nabbed by police—like the phone thief nabbed by *me*.

He opened his mouth to speak but didn't form the words before I unleashed a wind that could've blown a tree into the air, roots and all. While I succeeded in whipping several people around him off the ground, including Pete, the phone thief stayed put, having clawed fast into the wooden fence circling the fairy hill.

How dare he defy my power! I vaulted myself at the little shit.

"Let's see you mess with me now!" I screamed, shaking the thief by his frayed linen collar. His dark, wrinkle-ringed eyes boggled, his leathery hands wrestling my grip. "What the *fuck* did you do to my father? How did you *find* us? *How* did you know what was going to happen? And *why* the hell didn't you warn me sooner if you fucking knew? You *knew*!"

"I warned you when I felt I should!" the writhing beast beneath me exclaimed.

"Yeah, and only after you played your sordid little fairy game with me!"

The beast had the nerve to laugh. "That's what we do!"

His levity endured even after I'd punched him, bruising my knuckles but also making his lip bleed around his snaggletooth. "That's more like it, princess!"

More like the fight he'd prodded me to show the day he'd stolen my MulBerry. The MulBerry he'd used to warn me of the bogeybats. Just a little too late.

Screeching, I clutched his throat, choking him, needing to hurt him. Because he was the precursor to all my life's horrors. "Don't—fucking—call—me—PRINCESS!"

Slashing the air, three shadow tethers lassoed my wrists and shoulders, tugging me back from my victim. But I strained against them, gripping the blearing thief's neck.

The tethers yanked harder. I yanked them back. And Pete hurtled into my side, knocking me off my enemy. From Pete's expression as he flipped over in the sand, I could tell he hadn't intended on becoming a yoyo when he'd bound me.

Waspish, I now sat a yard away from him and the phone thief, wanting another go at using my stinger.

Panting, Pete rose on all fours. "You all right, Morus?"

"Just fine, Pete." Morus spat blood, his skeletal ribcage heaving. "I need a good row now and again."

"Keep talking and you'll get another," I rumbled.

Pete pushed to his knees. "What in bleeding hell has gotten into you?"

Every muscle clenched, I hopped to my feet. "That *thing* stole my phone, then used it in some mind-fuck to warm me—at the *very last minute*—that my father was in danger! The night he fucking died!"

Profaning, Pete stood. "Firstly, he's not a thing. He's a Kobold. And while I agree his methods are suspect—" Pete canted Morus a look of repudiation. "He likely meant to be helpful. And he was likely working with orders, Shorty."

"Whose?" I asked, fed up with all bullshit. All of it.

"Mine," answered a smooth tenor. We all turned toward Myrrdin, who stood on the threshold to the cabin, serene as Eden's sea. "Kobolds are masters at crossing worlds, despite restrictions against it, so I sent him to the human world to warn someone that the portal at Angel Oak was ajar."

Morus looked even more horrendous frowning. "I tried. They wouldn't listen to me. My last resort was to warn you, Amaranthine."

My heart stuttered. "Who did you try to warn before me?"

Groaning, Morus sat up, shrugged apish shoulders. "Who didn't I? None would heed me. Neither would that fool paragon you were friendly with. I begged him to pass word onto your uncle, the high druid."

Uncle Neel was a high druid? Did the position of circle center even exist in this world?

"I suppose the good paragon decided against it. Until he discovered the open portal on his own."

I shivered. Could all my recent tragedies have been avoided if Briar and his guards had listened to this one ugly creature? I doubted it. "Why wouldn't they listen to you?"

"Because I'm a Kobold. A *thing*, as you said."

"Sorry." I glowered at myself. "I shouldn't have said that. I have no problem with your race. I have a problem with *you*."

Morus's snicker was nightmarish. "Fair enough."

"Nobody would listen to you about the portal just because you're a Kobold?" I folded my arms. "Or did you play games with them too?"

"No games with them, honest." He held up a pledging hand. "Forthright as a crossbow, I was. Yet, they wouldn't trust me because—well, they remembered me."

"Remembered you from where?"

"Your father's inner circle." Morus shrugged again at my surprise. "I served as his emissary to the human realm for four decades until—" His pit-like eyes swiveled toward Pete. "Until I helped the harbinger sent to kill him escape the palace."

Pete winced as if Morus had prodded a wound, one still festering after 16 years.

"Why would you do that?" I asked the Kobold. Had he saved Pete in malevolence against my father as my kinsmen thought?

Dry as a drought, Morus looked to Myrrdin, who finally floated our way, his golden-brown hair knotted aback one arched ear. "He helped the harbinger escape at my request. I'd deemed the man worthy of clemency, as he'd saved—"

"That's not your tale to tell, Myrrdin," Pete snapped, his eyes knifing the prophet.

I rounded on Pete. "Then *you* tell me what happened. I mean, if you saved something—"

"Not something." Morus blotted his bloody mouth on his sleeve. "Someone."

"*Enough*," Pete rumbled like a bear. "Both of you."

"What don't you want me to hear?" I asked. "You've already admitted the worst part! Gentian sent you to kill my father—which obviously didn't work."

He stomped away, but I dogged his back, ignoring the bystanders' disbelief. I could give a flying fuck who witnessed me harassing the already peeved harbinger. Living in the dark had gotten old, and I *wasn't* scared of him.

"Is this really just about the guilt you feel over my mother's death? You didn't kill her either, Pete! My uncle told me it was Gentian, and Sedge said the same damn thing. And I believe that!"

Goddess, I *needed* to believe that.

"Then you believe a lie," Pete growled over his shoulder, storming into the cabin.

I barreled after him into a minimalistic room lit by dusky fae asters. "How is it a lie?" I barked at his taut back. He poured himself a mug of something from a cracked stone pitcher. Something alcoholic, I guessed, from how fast he downed it. "Tell me, Pete! Did you deliberately and maliciously harm my mother with any part of your body, any of your magic, or any of your weapons?"

"No." He slammed the mug back down on the stump table beside its pitcher.

I shook my hands at him. "Then you didn't fucking kill her!"

Pete whirled on me, his expression both anguished and enraged. He bared his teeth and thundered, "She died because she saved me, Shorty!"

I stumbled into a stool.

"It doesn't matter if I harmed her! She still died because of *me*! Because I gave in to my demons and allowed myself to be used as a weapon by someone with no scruples or morals."

Chills raced along my spine. "The siren you told me about! The one who sang away the death poppy!"

Pete flinched.

"She was my mother, wasn't she?"

Pete turned back to the pitcher, poured another mugful. "You seemed so ignorant about sirens during that discussion, Shorty. Was that a clever act to throw me off your scent?"

"No, I really knew nothing about her powers. Nobody told me. Well, I guess Briar did tell me she had nocturnal premonitions, but nothing else. Honestly. Uncle Neel said she had a rare power, that Gentian wanted her for it, but I never knew what she was." I huffed, frustrated. "It was only through hints that I started suspecting she was a siren."

"She was," he croaked, drinking again. "And she sang her last song to blast me back to myself. Seared me right to my blackened soul, she did. Knocked me on my arse too. All to save her ceyla from me—the cold rotter there to kill him." He took another swig, his Adam's apple bobbing. "She died because she drained her magic to stop me. She had only enough left in her well to incant protection for the king before Gentian reached him. She saved nothing for her own defense.

"Gentian didn't cast the blood curse for her," Pete elaborated. "It was going to skip over her—she wasn't meant to die. But Gentian's rage at the protection spell—at being thwarted from the kill he most craved—it would drive him stark raving mad. She kent that much too. She also kent what he'd do to her. I could tell by the sadness in her weeping eyes." His own eyes fell shut again, his continued confession a torture for us both. "But she spared not a single thought for herself as she turned to me, the man who'd just tried to kill her ceyla—who she quite obviously loved more than herself—and begged me to, 'Save her. Please, save her.'"

Tears welled in my eyes, and I gulped to hold my emotions in check.

His mouth quirked without humor. "You remember—don't you, Shorty?"

Yes, I did. Because my dreams had always shown me I was there—even after I'd forgotten I was.

"You were so little," Pete choked. "You were hiding under your parents' bed, and I truthfully hadn't seen you until your mother pleaded for my help. With her powers guttering out, there was nothing she could do to stop Gentian from killing you if he found you there.

"And please believe me, Shorty, if I'd had any strength left after your mother felled me, I'd have saved her too. It still haunts me that I couldn't. And I ken that I'll never be able to atone for what happened to her. Because I was weak and abandoned hope."

I cleared my voice of tears. Pete didn't need them right then. He needed a friend. "It wasn't your fault, Pete. It wasn't your choice to be there."

"Wasn't it?" He stared down at his mug. "Didn't I choose to become a harbinger?"

"You didn't choose to become demonic."

Disagreeable as always, he sniffed.

"What did Gentian do, anyway? Trick you into drinking the death poppy oil, then teleport you to the Spring Palace when you came to?"

"Aye."

Ohmigoddess, I was being hyperbolic.

"He wanted to test me—test my obedience—to see how well the death poppy had quelled my defiance." Nostrils flaring, Pete swigged from the mug. "And it had worked well, Shorty."

"But why test you so soon?"

Pete shrugged. "Gentian now had a cold, hard predator in his control—with strength enough to take down his greatest enemy. Once he had me, he was all too eager to take what he felt rightfully his."

"My mother?"

"She'd have been an added sweetness, aye. But Gentian wanted to be king. Hence, he and the members of his cadre escorting me there. Gentian rarely, if ever, gets his own hands dirty. But he wanted to claim the throne the moment the king was dead." His mouth tightened. "His blood curse just summoned me to do the killing first."

"How were there no guards around to catch you all?" I asked. "It's a freaking palace, right? With a royal army!"

Pete shook his head. "Shorty, I've spent many sleepless nights pondering that question. Things might've gone very differently if there were only one or two guards outside the king's chambers that night. They wouldn't have survived me."

I gulped at his certainty.

"But they'd have slowed me—raised the alarm. Maybe given your parents warning enough to flee or given the rest of the royal guard time to reach me—to put me down like the rabid dog I was."

"But then you'd be dead."

His gaze angled toward me, sorrowed. "Better me than her, aye?"

How could I answer that question?

"Pete, if Gentian didn't use you, he would've used another harbinger. Then *both* my parents *and* I might've been killed."

"No, I told you—Gentian waited for me—"

"Bullshit!" I cut him off. "Gentian has hundreds of harbingers. You're telling me not one of them was as strong or as lethal as you?" I scoffed. "That just *cannot* be true."

"Believe what you will." His mouth twisted. "It's the truth."

My mind spun a tale untold. "You want to know what *I* think the truth is?"

"Does it matter?" he grumbled, swigging from his mug again. "You'll tell me anyhow."

Sure will, Buster Brown.

I folded my arms. "I think Gentian had been planning that night for a long time, that he was going to invade the palace that night regardless of your decision to become a harbinger. The fact that you gave in right beforehand was just a coincidence. Maybe he even decided to use *you* on Daddy's blood curse, just so Daddy would feel the irony of being attacked by the suffering man in the cage, who he hadn't helped."

Pete sniffed. "Your father forgot about me the moment he sat for supper."

"*No*, he didn't." Regardless of Daddy's actions, I knew his heart like I knew my own. "Whether Daddy did anything to help you or not, Pete, please know he wouldn't have forgotten you. Either he was still wracking his brain to figure out a way to get you away from Gentian, or he was tormented in knowing he couldn't. Either way—you weren't forgotten."

You were never a Forgotten, I wished to say but didn't think I should invoke Gentian's term for his slaves. Pete looked miserable enough.

"I'm pretty sure there's a rat in the Spring Palace," I barreled into my conjecture. "Someone high enough in the ranks to ensure there were no guards around when Gentian came to cast the blood curse. Someone who's still collaborating with him to do things my father would *never* agree to. Like mass enslavements—or rerouting a major river to the Shadow Court. Hearing about that even shocked Briar, and he was always in the loop about things like that on Earth."

"You mean Dragoner Rill?" Pete asked.

"If that's the one near Avenshire."

"It's now the primary water source for Covenlen. Heard tell it was done to promote crop growth thereabouts."

"In a wasteland? Have you seen any crop fields?"

"Not a one, Shorty."

"Didn't figure." I bit my lip on a snarl, thinking again of little Gail and her brothers. "But my point is—the rat and Gentian had that awful night with you and my parents planned out. He wanted Daddy at his least prepared—after a long journey in the dead of night."

Pete's Adam's apple bobbed. "There's no preparing for an attack of that sort, Shorty. The curse seed—well, you ken what they do to Dananns. Your mother even tried to wrestle him away from it when her siren song failed."

I recoiled, wanting no more details about what led to her death. I knew more than I wanted already. "Regardless, I believe they were going to attack Daddy that night no matter what. They'd have taken another harbinger, who might've succeeded. And even if he or she failed like you did, the odds that your replacement would've had the compassion and courage to save a scared faelet from under Gentian's nose are slim to nil, Pete."

His eyes swam, peering away from me.

"So, I thank Danu that it was you that night, or I'd probably be dead."

Several quiet beats passed before Pete said, "It wasn't only me, ken. Myrrdin—"

"How come he didn't know Gentian was coming?" The guy was a prophet, after all. Why hadn't he warned my parents of Gentian's plans? Why not just tell my mother, the beyn he claimed to know so well?

"Gentian voids all visions coming out of the Shadow Court. Myrrdin tries every day for a clear reading from that hellhole. He always fails."

Sounded like a network firewall.

"Myrrdin's soul is pure, Shorty. Of that, be assured. Irksome he may be." Hmphing, Pete took another sip. "But he means no one ill. And he came running to your mother the moment he heard the rumpus. What he found was me, huddled in the corner on the side of your parents' bed with you tucked into my shadows—shadows I barely knew how to use, ken. Which was how he saw us. I was doing a piss-poor job of concealing us from the wickedness just beyond that blasted bed. And you just *wouldn't* stop crying." He gulped, hard. "For your mam and your da."

I blinked back another prickle of tears. "But they couldn't help me. Only you could."

He set his now empty mug aside, regarding it like it was my mother's apparition, there to answer all his unasked questions. "I—I often wonder if that's why she didn't incant protection for you instead."

The same thought had crossed my mind.

"Maybe she knew there was no way I could help your father out of that mayhem. No matter what I'd have done. But you—you were tiny enough to keep hidden. And I sometimes like to pretend that—that she saw enough good in me when your family visited the Shadow Palace to ken that I'd do all I could, risk everything, to protect you."

One tear escaped my lashes. "Seems like she was right."

He cleared a thickness from his throat. "Was she?"

I flung my arms around him.

"*Shorty*," Pete huffed, stiffening.

"Thank you, Pete," I gushed, my tears cascading as I squeezed his every jagged scar. I pressed my cheek to his thrumming chest. "Without you—" The rest of that truth dispelled into silence, the words preferring to remain unspoken.

Exhaling, Pete settled his hands at my back, gripping me close. "Think nothing of it."

For just a second, his lips skimmed my forehead. I tipped my chin to meet his gaze. Molten molasses poured down on me in a sweet, slow burn. My breath caught. My heart stopped. My blood sang.

Oh—my—stars. Now that's *how you want a guy to look at you, Amy.*

Leave it to Myrrdin to stroll in and fuck that shit up for us.

Smirking, he said, "Sorry to intrude," and chuckled as we broke apart, ruffled as chickens. "But it seemed you'd reached the end of the story, and this business about your powers must be tended to, my dear."

Behind him streamed Morus and a bevy of clerics of varying fae races, all of whom avoided eye contact with Pete. He'd escaped back to the pitcher with his empty mug.

Jeesh. He'll be black-out drunk before we leave here.

"We weren't completely at the end of the story," I corrected Myrrdin as he directed me to a stool in the center of the crowded cabin. "Pete just got to the part where you found him and me, but he didn't say how you got us away from Gentian."

Humming, Myrrdin claimed his own stool by the door. "Ah, well—before Gentian took his spite out on your mother, she shrieked to alert the guards. A skirmish broke out in the chamber—which I assume was how our resident harbinger was able to crawl over to safeguard you, unnoticed." He glanced to Pete for confirmation.

My savior merely burped before downing another mugful of whatever was in that pitcher.

"I came through a secret corridor to your parents' room," Myrrdin said. "So secret, in fact, that your parents had no notion it even existed."

"Might've been nice to know about," I said. "In case someone broke into their bedroom and tried to kill them."

"On that account, Amy, we agree," Myrrdin remarked. "Alas, the corridor was built so long ago and along the centuries was forgotten. I only chanced to find it when I heard the commotion that night on my way to bed and cast an *Exemplar* spell to find a clear path to your parents. I raced through that abandoned passage until I shoved open a door hidden behind a flora tapestry hanging in your parents' chamber—where I found you and Pete." Myrrdin shrugged. "Through that same passage, I spirited the pair of you out of harm's way. Once I'd deposited you in your own chamber, Amy, I sought out Morus to help Pete evade the royal guard and flee the palace."

Morus strutted past me on cloven hooves. "He makes it sound much simpler than it was. We got caught, obviously—barely escaped with our lives."

Myrrdin waved. "Still, you made it out." Was he an optimist or just apathetic?

Chewing my lip, I crossed my legs, propped an elbow on my knee, and rested my chin in my palm. Settling in for an interrogation. Myrrdin's, not mine. "And when did my family pack up and head off to Earth?"

As though he knew I was delaying whatever probing magic he meant to enact upon me, Myrrdin sighed. "Several days later, after an ascension service was held for your mother—a custom—"

"A custom to usher a soul to heaven," I finished for him, waving. "Uncle Neel made sure we followed *some* Danann customs. Although, he would've called it the Isle of Apples here, right?"

"Correct."

"So, after my mom's ascension service, my family sneaked over to the human realm? Through the Angel Oak portal?"

"Yes. With a substantial entourage, though we managed to keep word of your departure secret."

"Bloody good secret," Pete commented. "I doubt Gentian himself knew."

I shook my head. "But he had to know where we'd gone. Somehow. How else would he have known to send the bogeybats to Earth?"

"He mightn't have sent them there specifically," Morus said. Lord, did I wish he'd stay out of the shadows. The light made him look less monstrous. "Gentian's bogeybats frequent known portals on the off chance of sneaking through. They'd have noticed the Angel Oak portal was open within days."

And I'd just ushered them right on in, I finished for him.

Juking that painful train of thought, I swiveled toward the Kobold. "Was that the portal you went through too? Angel Oak?"

"Nay, Amaranthine." Clearly, I'd taught him a lesson about calling me princess. "'Twould have taken too long to travel there."

"Such a trip was unnecessary for you, anyhow, as you ken the black-market portals," Pete fumed. Even in speaking to a phone thief, his mood swing seemed unwarranted.

"You must forgive Pete," Myrrdin explained at my wide eyes. "He's been in search of an open portal to the human world since I've known him. Irrespective of what's known to become of humans who return to Earth after spending too much time in our realm."

I blinked. *What's known to happen to them?*

Pete sneered Morus's way. "My search could finally be at an end if someone would simply *tell* me where—"

"I can't do that, and you ken it well," Morus snapped. "Kobolds aren't renowned for our honor, but we follow a code where portals are concerned. Besides, knowing where the portals are would do you little good, friend. Even if you managed to breach one, you'd never manage to navigate the time tunnels as we can. You'd get lost in the abyss between realms."

"Not if I found myself a chronopath as a compass," Pete retorted. "You ken they're out there."

"Rarely," Morus returned.

Pete gestured his mug in my direction. "Shorty has kin that manipulates time, Morus. How else would she have gotten to Earth ten years in the past?"

The Kobold glowered, licking his protruding tooth.

So far, the debate had only amused Myrrdin. On the matter of time manipulation, however, his interest showed.

So, he does know who the chronopath is. I jotted a mental note to discuss that further—after I dealt with my sudden heartache about Pete's argument with the Kobold.

"You're looking for a way home, aren't you?" I asked Pete, my throat clenching. "Back to your family? Your own time?"

The atmosphere between Pete and I tightened like a bow string.

Eagerness to flee back to a life he'd never wanted to leave, back to the people he belonged to, lurched through Pete's gaze. Along with a hearty dose of doubt. Because to leave the world that had chewed him up and spit him out like gristle, to find his ultimate freedom, would mean turning his back on all the other Forgottens suffering the same atrocities he had.

Would mean turning his back on the friends he'd made in this world. Would mean turning his back on me.

At last, Pete cleared his throat, glanced down at his mug. "It's merely a pipe dream, Shorty. I've never found a chronopath, no matter how hard I've looked. Likely, it may never happen."

Myrrdin hummed. "You'd be wrong on that account, Pete."

Both our gazes bulleted to the prophet, his tranquility smacking of smugness.

"Why do you say that?" Pete's voice rustled in the hush.

Shrugging, Myrrdin flipped up an elegant hand. "Because you've been speaking to one."

I almost choked on my tongue.

"And you've been traveling with her for weeks."

The revelation was a gut punch.

"*What*? I'm *not* a chronopath." I really didn't want to be. Not now that I knew I was in danger of losing Pete. "I—I don't even know how I'd know if I was."

"That's simple, Amy." Myrrdin empathized with me, I could tell, yet he ran his mouth anyway. "As Pete so aptly put it—how else would you and your family have gotten to earth ten years in the past?"

I gaped at Myrrdin. Pete gaped at me. Myrrdin just folded his hands in his lap and waited for his bomb to sink.

"Wait a goddamn minute." I raised a hand. "You're telling me that *I'm* the chronopath who took my family to Earth?"

Myrrdin pursed slender lips, lending a concise and startling, "Yes."

THIRTY-THREE

"I was four when we crossed the portal!" I exclaimed. "How the hell could I have transported myself to the past, let alone all those other Dananns?"

Myrrdin shrugged. "Because your powers were as immeasurable then as they are now."

I bristled. How could he have measured my powers?

"You transported the royal entourage to Earth, Amy. I watched you all disappear into that oak's hollow."

No fucking way! This has to be a joke.

"The time tunnel you stitched was so strong, it's held fast to you for 16 years," Morus said. "I simply had to think of you, then I scurried right on through to your time."

I frowned. "So, I'm the one who took us to Pennsylvania in the '90s?"

Myrrdin nodded.

"*Why*? Why there? Why that time?" It all seemed so random, yet perfectly designed.

"Pennsylvania was your father's suggestion," Myrrdin said. "He had a fondness for the birthplace of liberty—as he called it."

The former resident of that birthplace guzzled another mugful.

"But we didn't go to Philadelphia—where they signed The Declaration of Independence. We went to Pittsburgh."

Myrrdin lifted a hand. "Your uncle thought Philadelphia too obvious a hideout—if Gentian were ever to track you—given your father's known affinity for the place. But the timing, Amy—that was all you."

I shook my head. "They let a *four*-year-old make that decision?" No wonder it made no sense.

"They hadn't much of a say. You'd decided where you wanted to go, and no one, not even the king himself, could change your mind. You told your muse that you were 'following your music.'"

I gasped in disbelief.

"You were waving around some odd plastic tome." Myrrdin tapped his smile, eyes dancing. "With lyrics and a disc inside—"

"A CD jacket," I murmured, somehow recalling the exact one—Bayview Boys *Millennia Men*. "How the hell did I get that?"

"Your step-grandfather, I believe. Your mother's stepfather. He reveled in spoiling you. Every visit, he brought a new bauble for you. One time he brought you that little tome, and it became your very favorite belonging—your Bayside boys from Earth."

"Bayview," I corrected him. "Bayview Boys."

He bowed his head. "As you say."

"But wouldn't I still have gone straight to 1999? When the CD premiered?"

"Surely, had your muse—a beyn who'd witnessed Beatlemania—not suggested you choose an earlier year, so you'd be a stripling for this music sensation on Earth. A more appropriate age to appreciate its allure."

I wanted to thank that muse. "So, I *chose* to be almost 13 when *Millennia Men* came out." A laugh stuttered out of me. Then another. "I chose to take myself, my entire family, and hundreds of other Dananns to Pittsburgh in 1992—because I liked the Bayview Boys."

Myrrdin smiled. "I believe so."

I buckled in on myself, clutching my stomach, as profound and fear-laden amusement plumed out of me in hysterics, disconcerting everyone but Myrrdin.

All this time, I'd thought Uncle Neel and Aunt Aylie had plotted out my entire life. In reality, I'd chosen the life I'd wanted when I was a faelet—a faelet enamored with poppy poetry who'd sensed a world she belonged to—and I'd taken my chance to join it, no hesitation. Aunt Aylie and Uncle Neel had been relegated to damage control over a life *I'd* chosen that didn't fit my "acceptable" path. A life with progressive values and freedoms that they'd never wrapped their antiquated brains around. And now I understood their frustrations, their manipulations—the only way they could mold me into a fairy princess in a time and place where few believed in magic, fairies, or gender inequality. They'd failed miserably, and I was ecstatic.

Wiping my cheeks, I sat back up. "How—how did you know at that time that I was—a chronopath?" I managed between residual hiccups. "Had I done something to tip you off?"

Myrrdin expelled a heavy breath, moving onto much heavier discourse. "No, you hadn't, Amy. Your mother told me you were a chronopath." He crossed his long legs at his knees, clasping the one on top. "She'd seen so in a premonition before you were born."

My throat strangled any further laughter. "Did she see anything else about me?"

"Certainly, but not all of what she saw made sense. As you know, nocturnal premonitions have a way of being ambiguous, misleading."

Damnit, Myrrdin.

Sheepish, I risked a glance at Pete. "Yeah—I get nocturnal premonitions sometimes." *Mostly involving you.* "Sorry I didn't tell you. It seems like such a minor power compared to the others I have. Sometimes I forget it's a thing."

Pete took a hard swig from his mug.

"Are premonitions like that in general?" I faced Myrrdin again, blushing now. "Or are just nocturnal ones that annoying?"

"Oh, they all have their insufficiencies—their unclarities. They all need deciphering, which is half the battle of being a prophet, I'm afraid."

Great.

"But when it came to her unborn daughter, Amy, your mother was certain—she'd be staggeringly powerful. She'd be a beacon of fire in the pitch of Gentian's hell. She'd be what the masses had been waiting for. She'd—"

"Please don't say it!" I flailed to evade the burden he was about to heft upon me. "Don't you dare! Because I'm *not*. Okay?" I fixed Myrrdin with a death glare—knowing my eyes shifted colors as I sat before him. "I'm not *anything* like what I'm supposed to be if your insinuation is true."

"Because you're still learning who you are, child. Even Danu wasn't *Danu* at birth."

Of course, he'd sit there in the face of my panic and compare me to the All Mother.

I felt Pete move before he stepped back into view. "Exactly what bush are you beating around, Myrrdin?" His gaze flicked back to me.

Myrrdin lifted a hand. "She's a triple goddess, Pete. She's the Aurora."

He might as well have sucked all the air from the cabin. Neither Pete nor I breathed for a brief eon. We just stared at each other, stuck in the web of Myrrdin's proclamation, the truth as sticky for Pete as it was for me.

One of the clerics, a short and portly Middling, cleared his throat. "Forgive me, Myrrdin, but if the princess is truly blessed with that kind of magnanimous power, why can't I scent it?"

The rest of the homespun army hummed in accord.

"A valid question, Buxus." Myrrdin leaned toward me. "If Amy is willing to allow me the privilege of conducting her reckoning, then we shall hash that out right now."

Finally breaking my stare down with Pete, whose cheeks had turned chartreuse, I faced Myrrdin. "First tell me what a reckoning is," I croaked, having never felt as alien as I did right then.

"Of course," Myrrdin agreed, his clear gaze a small comfort to my burgeoning turmoil. "A reckoning is a simple spell we conduct on those who need or want to better understand their powers—or to discover what's hidden beneath. You see, sometimes secondary powers—or the underlayers of principal powers—may lie trapped beneath surface magic. And as with any immense energy, trapped magic tends to build up in pressure until it bursts forth, unbridled."

Ghosts probably had more color than I did right then. What the hell was roiling within me? Myrrdin made it sound like losing control of my powers would be tantamount to a geyser blow-out.

"A reckoning will show me what's lying in wait, so we can form a plan, together, for an easier summoning ceremony." Myrrdin cleared his throat, shifting. "In your case, Amy, any added ease during a summoning is a necessary mercy. In order to alleviate the pressure building in your arsenal, we must release it. We'll then funnel your freed powers back to you—as conduits. And to conduct the powers of a triple goddess—well, it'll require all our combined strength."

I glimpsed the clerics. "Could conducting a summoning for me hurt you guys?"

"Our safety is not for you to fret over," Myrrdin said. "We've all trained rigorously to conduct such things. Besides, whatever your powers might do to us, foregoing the ritual would be far more dangerous for us—and for all who reside in the garden."

There was the rock and the hard place, and me right in between.

"Think of yourself as a volcano," Myrrdin posed. "You're going to erupt, your immeasurable powers unrestrained. Summoning them, however, will harness the deluge—so you don't thrash everyone unlucky enough to be near when you explode."

"Fucking *A*." I scraped my face with both hands, now as nauseous as Pete looked. "Okay, do it." I tossed up a hand. "All of it. Reckon me. Summon me. Just make sure I don't blow the Garden of Eden off the damn map."

Myrrdin and his clerics chortled. At least they found humor in this daunting situation.

Inhaling, Myrrdin shimmied closer to me. He held his elegant hands out, palms up. "You need only take my hands for the reckoning, child. Relax and let the spell do its work. Be assured, while you may feel discomfort, the spell won't hurt."

I cringed, wary, but an encouraging nod from Pete, despite his green gills, calmed me. Pete had promised—he wouldn't let Myrrdin hurt me. So, he must've trusted the prophet's word. And I trusted his.

Barely breathing, I laid my palms upon Myrrdin's and waited, my heart drumming. A heavy silence mantled the cabin as Myrrdin's eyes closed. His shoulders loosened, his back straightened, and his chin lifted toward the ceiling. Then his lips began a low, measured, completely foreign chant—his strange, stilted whisperings quickening until they were all syllables of one enormous word. The nonsensical drone all but lulled me to sleep.

Then I felt a prodding. In my head. Like my mind was under attack.

While Myrrdin had been truthful with me—it didn't hurt—my gut instinct was to flinch from the spell's incursion. Which solicited more aggressive prodding and Myrrdin gripping my hands too tight. Resulting in something inside my mind—something defensive—snapping shut like a guillotine—cutting off whatever connection Myrrdin had tried to make and throwing him and his spell from my psyche.

Blinking, Myrrdin released my hands and sat back.

"Was that it?" I chewed my lip. "Is it over?"

"I regret to say, Amy, the spell had barely begun."

I cringed. "I'm sorry." Again, I offered my hands to him. "You can try again. I'll relax this time, I swear."

"I'm afraid it won't matter what you or I do." He then addressed his clerics, dry as toast. "I cannot perform the reckoning, but I've uncovered why her powers are undetectable to the senses. Someone has shrouded her—quite well too."

"What does that mean?" I asked.

"It means someone disguised your powers—probably to protect you from Gentian—or from anyone else you might've intimidated."

"Did my mom do it?" There must've been a reason she didn't tell many people she suspected I was the Aurora. And Briar had warned Uncle Neel my fire might scare the old heads at court.

"Ginny didn't have that kind of power." Myrrdin considered me, the conundrum that I was. "Have you happened across any Witches since you've been in this realm, Amy?"

I froze. So did my heart. "One. Briar took me to her—for a disguise—so we'd blend into this world. While we were there, I felt her trying to get into my head—like you were just doing—but it was only for a moment or two, and then Briar stopped her."

"A moment might've been all she needed. Depending on how skilled she was." Myrrdin lifted a hand. "Did you catch her name?"

For a psychic, he sure asked a lot of questions. "Yeah, her name was Tamsyn."

The peanut gallery gasped.

Myrrdin's serene mouth tensed. "Tamsyn of Timbermoor?"

Why did I feel like I was going to regret meeting her? "I think that's where she said she was from."

"Bullocks," Morus cursed, flusterment doing nothing to improve his appearance.

I swallowed hard. "She wasn't trying to protect me, was she?"

Myrrdin rubbed a crease between his brows. "Oh, I think she was. In her own destructive way. As a token of her love for your mother, I'd wager. She was one of Ginny's muses before she was relieved of her duties—she could be gluttonous with the crystal magics, you see." He flipped a hand. "Anyhow, well-meaning though Tamsyn might've been, she's created quite an obstacle for us in summoning your powers to you properly. She's a Witch of robust skill, as you might guess, so I suspect the shroud she placed on your powers is a permanent fixture now—without Tamsyn herself to lift it."

"Does that mean you can't conduct my summoning?" I really didn't want to obliterate all the souls they'd saved from Gentian when my powers combusted out of me.

"A summoning is still possible—and required—but it'll be a dicier affair if we're in the dark as to what powers are coming our way."

"What do you mean by dicier?"

His eyes didn't shift from mine, though they seemed to want to. To look at his clerics—his colleagues—his friends. "Costlier."

I shook my head. "Then—then we shouldn't try it. I don't want to risk anyone's life. I should just leave and hide in the jungle—somewhere away from anyone else so—"

"Nonsense," Myrrdin chided, patting my knee. "We'll simply put our centuries-old minds together and mitigate the possible damage. We may enlist the help of some of the garden's residents. There are several here strong enough to withstand hosting your powers for a spell." His gaze slid toward Pete and back again. "The more hosts we have, the more we can dilute the potency of your powers amongst us, and the less danger there will be."

"And the risk for her?" Pete jarred me with a prospect I hadn't even considered. What would the summoning do to me? "Is she endurant enough to withstand the onslaught of those powers?"

Myrrdin's serenity returned. "Danu rarely creates a being weaker than the force of its own powers, my friend."

Pete's nostrils flared. "That's a shite answer, Myrrdin, and you know it."

"If it pleases you, Pete, we can continue her training, shore her up for the summoning, but I have all the faith in the Isle that she's strong enough as she is."

I glanced down at my arms, more muscled from physical training than they had been, yes, but still spindly. I decided Myrrdin's faith was misplaced.

"Myrrdin," Pete said. "She's a fire sylph."

That tidbit of information was even more astounding—and horrifying—to the clerics than learning Tamsyn of Timbermoor had shrouded my magic. Of course, Myrrdin was unphased by the revelation. Pete must've been right—if I knew I had a power, Myrrdin knew I had it too.

"What's to stop her from consuming herself in her own flames?" Pete asked. "And anyone hosting them, for that matter?"

"We'll strategize on that as well," Myrrdin said, appraising me.

Pete's dubious ire had me chewing my lip.

Grave-faced once more, Myrrdin addressed Pete dead on. "I promise you, I won't allow her summoning to commence unless I see the fates have assured her ultimate survival. We'll help her scale these obstacles, and she'll gain the blessings of her powers—in full."

Blessings? What a funny thing to call them when they had every chance of killing me. I was a ticking bomb in need of diffusing.

A threat glittered in Pete's gaze. "Danu save you if you're wrong."

Myrrdin arched a brow. "If I'm wrong, Pete, then we'll all need saving."

The walk back to Pete's hut was tense, too quiet. He strolled beside me, the set of his massive shoulders weary, his profile, rounded and human, etched in deep, hard thought. Finally, I cleared my throat to lighten the weighty moment. "I'm shocked you're able to walk a straight line after binge-drinking an entire pitcher of liquor."

He flicked a wry look my way. "It was merely cider. Barely potent enough to souse a mouse."

"You still drank a lot of it."

"As you can see, it has a trivial effect on me. Maybe a slight dulling of my senses."

"Oh."

Another silence hung as we weaved through the villagers. Although, after having my mind blown—again—I wasn't in the mood for silence. Especially with Pete. I wanted to know he still saw me as—me. Regardless of my divinity.

"When do you think they'll do my summoning?" I figured getting a proper timeline of my future was key, so I'd know at what pace to prepare for the impossibilities. "Are we hanging out here until then? Or will we come back after we've killed Gentian?"

After we've tried *to kill Gentian,* I corrected myself. Odds were that we'd fail, and the looming issues over my summoning would become moot.

Pete didn't reply, the creases in his brow deepening.

"I meant what I said. I decided to help you kill the asshole. You discovering my last name hasn't changed that."

One corner of his mouth twitched, not into a smile. "Much appreciated, Shorty."

"How long will we be here before we move on to the Shadow Court?" I continued. "Because those beyns from Humwater Dell are still in danger."

"Aye, they are." Pete peered toward his hut, which we neared as we waded against the tide of fae heading to the cafeteria (lunchtime was upon us, if my nose was correct). "Maybe—maybe we'll leave in a week. Does that suit you?"

I chuckled. "Does what suits me matter to you?"

"Not truly. But I'd hate not to ask and risk another bout of your harping."

I smirked sideways at him. "You know you love my harping."

He smiled, albeit halfheartedly. His eyes, though—they remained cloudy. "I wouldn't say that, though I've forgotten how to go about my day without it. And I fear it has made me habitually cleanly."

I laughed at his sourness on that last point. And the sound dimmed the light in his eyes, reminded him of his sadness.

I couldn't pretend not to know what was bothering him.

By the time we reached the warden's hut, I'd resigned myself to being as selfless and giving as Pete was with all those he'd sheltered under his big, magic shadow-wing.

"I don't know when I'll be capable, Pete, but I—once I learn how to work my chronopathy, I'll figure out some way to—send you home."

I might as well have shocked him with jumper cables.

"If that's what you want," I forced the words out. "Then I'll do what I can to return you—to your former life—your family." I offered what I hoped was a happy smile—not a grimace of my own grief at the thought of losing the only real friend I'd known since leaving Earth. "I can't say I won't miss you. But you—you deserve to be happy—after all you've done for everyone else." My lips quivered. "And if I can give you that, then—"

"Shorty, that is—" Pete cupped my shoulder, his touch hefty, and shook his head. "Your generosity humbles me. But let's not speak of it for now—while it's little more than a daydream, aye?"

I understood why he didn't want to get his hopes up. Before I could do anything with my chronopathy, I'd need to learn how to wield it, and who knew how long that would take. Then there was the whole conundrum of how I'd send Pete back. Sure, I'd transported a shit ton of Dananns to Earth in the past when I was pretty much a toddler, but I'd gone with them. How would I send Pete back without going with him? I supposed I could turn back—*after* I went with him.

And just like that, I was tempted to go with him. And stay. To run away from curses, betrothals, and the weight of the world I might rule. Corsets, smallpox, and misogyny were hardly a deterrent when I'd be with Pete. And we'd be free.

So much for being selfless.

"You'd hate it there," Pete chuckled, reading the temptation through my eyes. "You'd be expected to be demure and meek—a proper lady."

I sneered at the prospect. "How boring."

"Indeed."

I folded my arms. "I could just say I'm a war widow. Didn't they have license to speak their minds and act a bit—unladylike?"

"Mm, aye." Imagining me in his time had brought his twinkle back. "But only the aged widows. You, being so young—you'd be thrown to a frenzy of suitors like chum and expected to bear sons until your youth and vigor dried up like a prune—or you died in childbirth."

Awesome!

"Ugh, you're right. I'd hate it."

"Unless, of course, you found a lenient husband—able to overlook perpetual guff, disobedience, and a fiery tongue." His grin looked delicious, like devil's food cake. "A husband like that might shield you from the worst."

He was only teasing me, I knew. Yet I so wanted him imagining himself as that lenient husband. Because I sure as hell was.

Pete cleared his throat, changing the subject. "Might you grant me a brief catnap before you reclaim my hut? Sleep was brutal last night; tree apes heckled me through the skylight next-door."

Then why did he shine like a brand spanking new penny? Was that Eden's doing? Did the water here make you look as well as feel refreshed?

"Hm. So, you need a nap because of tree apes? Not because of the pitcher of cider?"

"I'll admit, the cider isn't aiding my fortitude."

I chuckled.

"I shouldn't need more than an hour," Pete promised, his strong fingers plucking something out of the pocket tied by his hip. He held the item aloft, earning my shock. "Why don't you take this useless frippery to the hot spring down the trail past the privy? Give it a listen while I catch a wee kip. If I'm not up and about by the time you're back, you have my permission to shove my arse out of bed, for I don't mean to be dossing while there's work to be done."

My mind leapfrogged over all his Irish speak to focus on my MulBerry. My *actual* MulBerry. "Where did you get my phone?"

"Is that what this is? Morus gave it to me." Pete handed me the smooth plastic device. I marveled that it looked and felt exactly as I remembered, for it seemed like forever since I'd last held it. "Said he didn't want it anymore with you likely to throttle him over it."

My thumb swiped across the tiny keypad and pressed the power button on its side. Was it too much to hope my battery wasn't dead? Or had Morus drained it like a total dick?

When the screen lit, I whooped, "Ohmigoddess! It works!"

"I told Morus it had better." Pete tightened his pocket strings. "For his own sake."

"Oh, wow!" I wagged my screen at Pete. "I have 29 voicemails! And 44 texts!"

He didn't pretend to know what that meant. "I take it that's a lot."

"*Yeah.*"

He waved me on. "Head down to the hot spring, take a dip, and do whatever it is you do with those infernal things."

I saluted him with said infernal thing. "See you when you wake up!" I called over my shoulder, then scurried down the sandy path, lightning bugs lighting my way.

Pete

A strangling knot formed in Pete's innards as Shorty scuttled off in those ridiculous boots, her hair aflame amid the greenery—happy and free as Danu had made her. As she would remain, Goddess willing.

He clenched his fists, compelled to follow her. To the springs. To the end of the world. But he turned toward the warden's hut to gather his belongings. And to say his farewells to Sionna.

She might never understand his disappearance, go on looking for him for the rest of her life, but with luck, that life would flourish and linger for quite some time to come.

With luck—and the protection of that clod betrothed to her—so would Shorty's.

THIRTY-FOUR

Amy

The hot springs were as I'd imagined—steamy. Thankfully, they were also private, like nobody else knew they existed. Which couldn't have been true, as close to the village as they were. Maybe people were too busy during the day for a splash. As Pete had stated—there were chores to be done—and no one there seemed content to slack.

Except me. And I'd feel guilty about that later—after I'd gorged on human tech.

Kicking off my boots, I plopped on the edge of a teal pool and dangled my legs in its soothing, bubbling, salty water, scrolling with single-minded swiftness to my texts.

I started at the beginning—from the day Morus stole my real phone. I'd missed several inane texts from friends and family after the theft: Aunt Aylie asking me to buy more milk after my date with Briar; Vi begging for help with her American lit essay; Zahra asking if I'd "tapped that ass yet" (Briar's, I assumed); and one from Olivia inquiring about my schedule for June. She and Grace had discussed going to a Pirates game and wanted to know if I'd tag along—and if they could crash at my place while in Pittsburgh.

Sounds like fun, I thought, wistful. *Hope they went without me.*

The next message was from Daddy, telling me to have fun at my first Beltane, that he'd see me when I got home. That he loved me.

I skipped past any texts that came through the night of Daddy's death. Superfluous details of what led to that horror weren't welcome. Nor were reminders of what I was doing when the shit first hit the fan.

The next day, however, a slew of texts from my friends had flooded my phone. All in response to my cryptic parting message. They ranged in sentiments, but the gist was this: "What do you mean you're not coming back to school next semester? Are you okay? Are you crazy? You can't do that! What about your degree? Did you find a swanky job or something? Are you pregnant or something? Call us, we want to talk to you!"

My friends would think I'd ghosted them, and I felt horrendous about that. We'd been better friends than that. I should've followed Briar's advice and invented a story explaining my sudden disappearance from their lives—a sense of closure. But having just discovered that I'd been living a lie for the past 16 years, I couldn't bring myself to outright dishonesty. Omission was a purer option, I'd thought.

When I came to my most recent voicemail, however, I regretted my nebulousness. Because it was from all three of my college buddies, together. And they didn't live near one another.

"If you haven't already officially withdrawn from UPJ, don't," Olivia ordered a little more than a week after I'd crossed the portal. "Give us the chance to convince you not to."

"Don't even think about skipping town this weekend!" Zahra shouted in the background. "Because we're all coming to see you. Whether you like it or not, we're going to knock some sense back into your head. And if that hunky jerk you've been hanging with has anything to do with this reckless decision to leave school, then I'm going to tell him what's what!"

"I got your address off the History Club rosters," Grace piped in, giggling as usual. "We know where you live, and we're coming. Today. See you in two hours."

"Bye!" they all chimed together in varying tones.

I decided to go through the rest of my inbox later, the first voicemail a boulder in my heart.

I'd spurred my loyal friends into a wild goose chase that would only end in disappointment. Obviously, I wouldn't be there for them to find and lecture. And who knew how long they'd spend after their initial road trip trying to track me down? They were a persistent gaggle.

On the other hand, that voicemail was the last one I'd received, so maybe they'd decided to let me go when they'd arrived at my house to find it abandoned. They'd continue questioning what happened to me, but if they weren't still calling and texting—maybe I shouldn't feel atrocious for vanishing on them. Maybe.

Finally, I turned off my MulBerry and rose from my dip, toes wrinkly. Not waiting for my feet to dry, I grabbed my boots and padded back toward the village. I paused at the warden's hut, where Sionna lazed in the doorway, happy as a house pet. Beyond her, the hut was still, quiet. Pete was probably still asleep, although for once he was breathing quietly. He had half an hour left of his requested nap, so I set my boots by the door and moseyed off to find lunch, my stomach grumbling.

Food from the bakery was free. Relieving, since I had no seeds. Finding somewhere to eat was a trickier affair. Cliques had gathered around the various fires, and nobody welcomed me when I drew near with my bowl and cup. Very much the outsider, I wound up taking a stump by the least populated fire on the outskirts of the village square. The few there didn't speak to me as I ate.

I tried to relax and enjoy my lunch—a scrumptious stew of savory blue fish, spicy turnips, green potato, and something that looked like carrots but was called nullion—but I struggled to ignore the touch of eyes, the whispers carried on sea breezes.

So uncomfortable it pained me, I was grateful when a flock of rowdy, squealing children blundered into my circle and somehow managed to tramp out the campfire.

"Blooming hell!" the Dwarf across from me railed. He had a patchy black beard and a sourpuss face. The little ones huddled together as he shook his meaty fist at them. "Now we'll have to find more flint, you wee savages, and Master Hickinbottom haint into smelding afore he's finished his lessons!"

I blinked, wondering what smelding was.

"Pipe down, Bumble," a beyn with short, pitch-black hair and narrow, veiny wings scolded the Dwarf. Barely five feet tall and dumpling plump, she flapped into the circle, where two Middlings sat to Bumble's right, trying to eat while he blew a gasket. "They meant nay harm. No need to belittle the chits." Her stubby arms opened for the faelets scurrying to her comfort.

"Oh, no?" Bumble groused, setting fists upon his hips. He wagged his head, sassy as a teenage girl. "And how d'you propose we finish the dyeing, now the fire's stamped to cinders?"

As anxious as I'd been, I hadn't noticed the clay cauldron sitting on stones amid the fire pit. I supposed that's where the dyeing was, steeping in purple water. A large wooden paddle idled in a cooling soup of berries and fabric.

The beyn flitted the children away. They all scurried off like mice in retreat of a cat.

Regardless, the cat hadn't finished hissing. "And where the graces is Nettle? She's abandoned the linens, as you well see!"

The buxom beyn flitted to the cauldron, frowned at it. Wondering what to do about the mess, I presumed. "She's like to have gone for a gnash, Bumble. You ken she didn't know the fire would sputter. And the fire's not her charge, besides."

"Nay, but she might've stopped the unruly runts afore they wreaked their mischief!" Bumble was becoming downright haughty. "Mightn't she, Liatris?"

Liatris rolled a set of jet-black eyes offset by smile lines and playful freckles. "And so might've you, you ornery sod."

Bumble's bulbous nose turned crimson at the tip as his friends—or unlucky lunch mates—chortled.

"Who gives a fig who might've stopped the wee ones?" a sensible Middling said, breaking a hunk of bread over the bowl sitting in her lean lap. She raised a silver hand tattooed—or birthmarked—in twining green vines. "The fire's still out."

I blinked. "Can't you just shovel some burning coals out of another fire?"

One would've thought me a wraith who'd walked through a wall. A wraith with no business speaking.

I shifted, wondering why I felt like an ignoramus. They were the ones being stupid. "And the coals will get this fire going again." *Right*? "If you add extra wood."

Bumble scoffed, blue eyes glaring. "Oh, now why didn't we witless louts think of that?"

So, Dwarves could be sarcastic as well as cranky.

"Might it be because nothing in Eden will take fire without magic!? Look around, lovey! Everything's too green, too moist!"

"I was just trying to help." I decided against using *my* magic. Couldn't entrust the knowledge of my fire to someone so needlessly hostile. At least, not until my summoning when word was sure to get out. "Forget I said anything."

Clicking her tongue, Liatris fluttered over to me. "Pay no mind to *him*." She bulleted a reproving eye at Bumble. "He's needed a toss for a good decade, and his missus has been missing about as long. Maybe by choice."

Bumble snarled at her, the Middlings chortling.

I sobered, feeling bad that they were making fun of what must've been his deepest sadness. "Sorry about your ceyla."

Bumble sniffed. "I suppose finding Nettle is up to *me*." At that, he tramped off, swift despite his bulk.

I chewed my lip. "Is his ceyla really missing?"

"Aye." Liatris lowered herself onto the stump to my left. She tucked her short, corpulent legs beneath her tattered rag skirt. "Likely the Shadow Prince got to her before the warden could. Shame. Although, which is a worse fate remains to be seen—death at Gentian's hands or a centuries' long union with Bumble."

I did chuckle at that.

"From what I've heard, Lia, Bumble wasn't half as fearsome as his missus," the viny Middling spoke, doe eyes glimmering like a socialite with gossip. "Word is, she was just as ornery as he, if not more so—that she was known for her skills with a rolling pin."

Clearly, she wasn't alluding to pastry making.

"Mm," the other Middling, a feyr with owl-like down cresting his head, agreed. "That's how their curse came to be. Bumble, there, owned a working basilisk powder mine—a mine what Gentian ventured to buy—but no amount of wealth would sucker yon wee auld grouser into selling. The Shadow Prince then tried charming it from Bumble, and when that also failed—as impervious to charm as Bumble is—"

We all had another giggle.

"He tried intimidation. Well, Missus Bumble wouldn't have it. She fair clubbed Gentian out of her house, humiliating him before her household and supper guests. Less than a fortnight later, the Bumbles were fisting death curse seeds."

Damn. Gentian's ego was one huge, throbbing bruise that would never heal—no matter how many curses he cast.

Owly licked the corner of his rosebud mouth. "Now, with Bumble taking refuge here and his wife no doubt a chink on some ghastly harbinger's knife belt, Gentian's all but taken over the mine. More's the pity for Bumble's glen."

"Hm." This sounded like something I should investigate. "What exactly is basilisk powder, and why would Gentian want it?"

Again, I took the brunt of their baffled stares.

"If it's not already clear, I'll just tell you—I'm not from around here. I mean, I was born here, but then I spent 16 years on Earth, where—as far as I know—we didn't even have basilisks."

Both Middlings bleared at me.

Liatris clicked her tongue. "You don't ken who's speaking to you, Ivy? Larto? This here's the crown princess, in the flesh. If anyone could freely take up residence on Earth, I'd say it was she."

The Middlings went slack jawed.

"Gripes, you'd think neither of you had met anyone notable in your lives," Liatris chided their shock. She faced me, pressing a chubby hand over her bulging cleavage. "Forgive them, majesty. I know I speak for everyone when I say, 'Welcome to Eden.'"

"Thank you, and—just call me Amy, please."

Beaming, Liatris bobbed her head. "Well, Amy, I'm Liatris—one of the empaths abouts—and I'm pleased as plum punch to meet you." She fiddled with her skirt, perhaps wondering if she should offer a hand to shake. "I believe you met my son earlier. Wee fella, always following the warden like a shadow."

"Oh, yeah! Jet! I met him this morning. He's a cutie."

Jet's mother giggled. "That he is—and sweet as nectar. I'd have had ten others just like him if things had been different." She paused, almost distraught, but then shook herself. "But you don't want my tale of woe. Tell us—are you getting on well in Eden?"

"Actually, if you wouldn't mind, I'd like to hear your story." I glanced over at the two Middlings. "And yours. Everyone's, really."

To be here in Eden, they'd all fled their lives in evasion of a tragic ending. And their tragedies mattered. Because if theirs didn't, then mine had no right mattering either.

"And I still need someone to tell me about the basilisk powder." I turned back to Larto. "I should know these things."

Once Larto overcame his surprise, he explained that basilisk powder was a sorcery element derived from basilisk fossils (they were extinct now, thank Danu), used to adjust the pH balance in soil to grow certain magical crops. A mundane need for Gentian, I thought. But did he really require a whole mine's worth? And was that need connected to the diverted river? My gut said *abso-freaking-lutely.*

What the hell was Gentian trying to grow?

Then we got down to story hour. Or hours. Because once the Middlings finished telling me how they'd wound up in Eden, others joined us, yearning catharsis.

After about five therapy sessions, I realized I'd never remember all their testimonials without muddling the details. "I wish I had some way to record yinz." With a record, I'd have evidence that society required radical changes for those pricks running the world in my stead. "It would make one hell of an anthology," remarked the literature major in me.

That cheered Liatris, who'd begun wilting during the narratives of pain and loss. She was content to listen, but she had yet to express her own misfortune. "I'll run and fetch Nimue. She's our resident scrivener and has just what you seek."

Nimue, a diminutive, mute fae with a strong resemblance to Samara from the movie, *The Ring,* did indeed have just what I sought. Barely peeking at me through her wavy dark hair with gold, slanted eyes, she handed me a bark-bound book strung together with seaweed. Its numerous pages smelled of velum.

Taking it, I marveled at its heft. "Are *everybody's* stories in here?"

Nimue waggled her head side to side.

Liatris, reclaiming her seat beside mine, touched my shoulder. "I expect she means she took from all who offered. She's principled, she is. Wouldn't dare work her magic without a speaker's say so."

I flipped to the first page. Stilted, almost runic, script glinted up at me, entitling the makeshift treatise: *A Sanctuary from Shadow*. "Wow." I marveled at Nimue's long, neat penmanship. "Did you write all this down yourself?"

My patients chuckled—all now fully apprised of who I was and why the fae realm still mystified me.

"Scriveners need not write by hand," Ivy said. "They but will your spoken word onto the pages."

Well, there was one magical power I wouldn't mind having. Not that I wanted to be an author, but I enjoyed the thought of watching my words appear in print out of thin air. "Very cool."

The expanding group hummed at my approval.

Chatter continued around me as I flipped through several pages, skimming the many stories Nimue had recorded. A first name entitled each refugee's tale.

"You know, it's kind of funny." I shook my head as I turned the page on another narrative in which a curse had sought to consume a life. "All these stories, and I haven't come across one where the person was meant to be captured instead of killed." I shrugged. "Is that just rare?"

The crowd fell silent.

"What?" I asked.

Liatris cleared her throat, faced me. "Rare's not the word I'd use, but it's a—sticky matter—to be sure." She paused, rubbed the back of her neck, and cleared her throat. "My own ceyla—Rhamnus is his name—was sought by the Shadow Prince for his leadership and strategic acumen. When I took vows with him, he was a simple agrifae with a few fields to plant, but centuries before that, he led the crown's winged legions in the war against the Fomorians."

Whoa! Rhamnus' birthday cake would burn right to the ground!

"Is Gentian creating a winged legion of his own?" I asked, chest tightening. I knew Gentian had forces, but I didn't think they were that organized.

"I can't say. But Gentian wanted him, and when Rhamnus wouldn't go willingly, he cursed our family. For Rhamnus, he sent an ordination of capture. For me and our little one, he sent death curses. I imagine he wanted all Rhamnus' sentimental connections severed. He does so dislike not having someone's full devotion."

I sneered.

Liatris swallowed, her voice cracking. "Anyhow, the warden came for us. He took me and my sweet Jet to shelter—but Rhamnus—he was beyond mercy."

I stared at her like her head had fallen off. "Pete—he took Rhamnus to Gentian? When he could've let him stay here with his family? With his *son*?"

What the fuck, Pete?

Liatris's face pinched, her pain and sympathy for my cluelessness mingling. "As I said—the ordinations for capture are sticky. A harbinger botching a delivery to the Shadow Palace within a reasonable timeline is considered an ordination failure. And harbingers daren't fail more than once—if that. Especially one as effectual as our warden. He'd be risking everyone he'd already saved, wouldn't he?"

"But not killing the mark in a death ordination *isn't* a failure?"

She and all the rest of the group cringed. "That's the trick, dear Amy. We can only shelter here safely if the Shadow Prince *thinks* we're dead."

My mouth dropped open. And didn't close.

"We've all reluctantly relinquished our totems to Pete or the other harbingers who've hidden us here. They deliver them as ordained, and Gentian believes we've been dealt with—killed. Some of us may as well have been. You see, when the void feeds off one's totem, it can drive a person to blithering madness. For if it's not magic, it'll likely be destroyed. Even with healers at hand, the weaker minded few never recover."

I knew there was more to totems than them being freaking ID cards.

"I laid with stupor for months afterward. Altered me to a degree, honestly."

That cued a chorus of empathic noise.

"Jet, the tot that he was, didn't yet have a totem, and so was in the care of another mother until I snapped to. Praise Danu that we were in a time pocket—I didn't miss an inch of his growth."

Clearing her throat, Ivy touched her shoulder. "Lia—" She cast a consternated glance my way.

Liatris's hands fluttered. "Oh, aye—apologies, Amy—we Pixies do ramble here and there. But the point I'm building to is this—the void mustn't ken if we're truly dead when it feeds off our totems. Or if it does, it doesn't care overmuch. And Gentian mustn't figure anyone would be foolish enough to risk a cracked bean to evade death. He mustn't ken some aged healers can cure the afflicted."

Something awful hit me like a sledgehammer. *To evade death*, she'd said. The hairs on my arms stiffened. "Are you telling me—nobody here was supposed to be captured?"

"Aye," Liatris finished. By now, she and everyone else had guessed that I was. "You can fake a death. But you can't fake a capture."

Nimue's book toppled from my shaking hands as I jumped up and sprinted off. I now had a sinking suspicion—an infuriating, gallant, heartbreaking suspicion—that Pete had never laid down for that nap.

Eden wasn't just a pleasant pit stop on our journey to hell. It was the new destination. *My* destination. But for Pete—?

Oh, how I hoped I was wrong! Pete couldn't just deposit me in Eden for safekeeping and fail his ordination. He'd made it abundantly clear what would happen if he did.

Oh, puhlease, let me be wrong!

Finding Sionna still chilling in the warden's hut reassured me. For a moment. Until I realized she now snoozed on the feather mattress, which remained loosely tucked with linen sheets, the way I'd made it that morning after my bath. The sheets smelled nothing like Pete.

Heart pounding, I nudged Sionna awake. "Where is he?"

She only blinked up at me, her tan eyebrows meeting. But what else had I expected of her?

I whirled in search of any sign that Pete hadn't sneaked out of Eden. Would he really have left Sionna behind as he trekked off on another long, arduous journey? The hound he loved so much?

He sure as hell would, I answered myself. *If he thinks he's marching to his death. Or worse, his demonization.*

That's when I noticed my backpack. It still sat on the tree stump table where I'd left it the night before, but the zipper was open, and I knew—*I knew*—that I'd closed it after my bath.

My heart dropped to my bowels as I croaked "*No*," and scurried over to an open space where a redheaded rag doll once lived. "No, Pete, you *stupid* son-of-a-bitch!"

The damn fool was going to use Andy to fake my death! He'd claim something went wrong on the road, that he'd needed to put me down before he could deliver me. Would Gentian believe him? Or would he see the truth? That Pete was no longer demonic, and that he'd let his mark, the crown princess, go.

Still hopelessly rooting through my backpack for a rag doll that clearly wasn't there, I grazed a note scrawled on a folded scrap of unrefined paper.

Sorry I lied, Shortie, but your mother was righte.

Your humble servent, P.

I shivered, recalling Pete's hope from earlier that day—that my mother had left my rescue to him because: *She saw enough good in me...to ken that I'd do all I could, risk everything, to keep you safe.*

P.S., I wager the world according to Amy won't be so fearesome a thing.

Take care of Sionna for me.

Pete wouldn't have given me Sionna—unless he had no hope of returning.

The man of shadows from my dream—the blackened harbinger who'd captured me for a blood curse—was marching to the Shadow Court to sacrifice himself for my safety.

Damnit, Pete! You chivalrous dumbass! You can't fucking do this to me!

That world according to Amy—it couldn't exist without him there to guide its creation. Because I trusted him above all others. Even in knowing he'd just completely lied to me—so he could be true to my mother.

And I refused—I *refused*—to lose him the way I'd lost her! The way I'd lost so many others!

I snatched up my backpack. Tied up my hair. Then stomped into my boots. I had to move fast. I could hardly save Pete from his idiocy *after* he destroyed my totem, and I lost my mind—temporarily, I hoped.

"Stay here, girl," I bade Sionna, who'd risen when she saw me readying for war. "I'll be back."

Pete

Pete was seldom so lonely on the road. Without Sionna sniffing around his legs, without Bob clopping at his heels, and without the plucky jabbering of one royal pain in his arse, the jungle was far too quiet. Yet, he loped along at his normal speed, trying to fill his empty mind with several of those melodies Shorty had stamped into his recent memory. Of course, the song that stuck on him was one he detested.

Gah! he seethed at the pesty voices plaguing him. *Poets be damned!*

No wonder those blasted Brook Lane Fellas—or whatever Shorty called them—were so bloody successful on Earth. Their songs were as catching as syphilis and could drive a bloke just as mad.

Mother, where was a fifth of whiskey when he needed one? Myrrdin's cider hadn't quite numbed him enough.

The song's senseless lyrics, though he abhorred them, spurred him through the hissing, humid jungle—reminding him why he now barreled headlong to his peril. They represented the beyn he was doing it for as much as the rag doll in his rucksack did.

The rag doll of note sat tucked safely beside the detailed letter Pete had penned to the dolt promised to Shorty. No doubt a promise made before she'd been born. As was the way with royal marriages, both in the fae world and on Earth.

All Pete could hope for was that this Briar had genuine care for his betrothed beyond the allure of her crown. Pete was counting on him to come to her rescue. To the rescue of all in Eden.

He was under no misgivings about the danger of his plan. To him, to Shorty's sanity, and to Eden. His loyalties would be questioned, his demonism too. Demons didn't often slay marks when they weren't meant to, even if said mark turned said demon's own knife on him. They lacked the passion and fear that would provoke acts of self-defense. In truth, demons felt very few emotions—apart from the pleasure of sin. So, despite Pete's black eyes and pitiless act, Gentian would see through him like threadbare silk.

But Pete had no intention of drinking either from the Well of Sincerity or from a vial of death poppy oil. He'd swallow one of Olea's Wolver's Bite capsules before he'd give up Eden—or Shorty. Then he'd die swiftly, painlessly, for the sake of all those innocents.

Of course, he still fantasized that he'd fool Gentian. Would he believe Shorty had ended her own life rather than become the prisoner of the one who'd murdered her parents?

Most magic wielders, like himself, were plagued with an ever-endurant will to live. They'd suffer through centuries of abomination before they'd even consider suicide. Yet, the act wasn't unheard of. And Shorty, being from Earth, certainly had an unconventional way of thinking for one so full of magic. Perhaps Pete stood a better chance of convincing Gentian that Shorty was prone to human despair and had taken her own life than he did of convincing him that he, a supposed demon, had killed his mark against ordination.

At the least, the story's plausibility might afford Shorty's unworthy intended time to safeguard her at the Spring Palace before Gentian nabbed her. Even with a probable infiltrator scuttling around the palace, subverting her family, Pete gambled Shorty's odds at evading the oncoming horde of harbingers were far better there, surrounded by a trained army, than they were in a time pocket, where anyone with a notion to look could breach the veil of false security.

Still pondering this, he trod into the kaleidoscope post—an ancient copse of crystal willows populated by butterfly-like beings—the *dealan-dhè*. While they weren't precisely fae, they also weren't precisely insects, cognizant and large enough to make brilliant messengers. They were also far more inviolable than birds, few kenning them from actual butterflies, making message theft rare.

Accordingly, Eden's harbingers, himself included, had been partaking of the *dealan-dhes'* services since they'd begun populating the garden, sharing information amongst one another through the skies. Pete hoped one of the more robust flyers would purvey Shorty's whereabouts to the Spring Palace for him.

The larger *dealan-dhes* congregated upon the drooping boughs of a willow, drinking nectar from its blossoms, which sparkled like dewdrops in the sunrays breaking through the jungle canopy. His intrusion caused a commotion of fluttering, but he mustn't have proven too bothersome; few ventured to fly away.

A senior by *dealan-dhè* standards, an iridescent blue flyer fluttered off its meal and landed on Pete's shoulder. The creature eyed Pete in question: *How can I be of service?*

Pete already had his folded letter in hand. "This must reach the Spring Palace posthaste." He slipped the note into a velvety pocket hidden by a design on one of the messenger's wings. "Give this over to Briar Hawthorne's hands only."

The creature's black eyes blinking in what Pete surmised as accord, it took wing off Pete's shoulder to soar away on its errand. Pete watched it rise, calm settling upon him. Whatever fate awaited him, at least word reaching the Spring Palace meant Shorty would be all right.

That was all that mattered.

Suffice it to say, Pete's heart dropped to his bowels when a shadow tether lashed his messenger from the sky. Time slowed, the *dealan-dhè* plummeting to the ground like a maple seed. Pete's letter with it.

Pete pounced to procure his message, but a foursome of more tethers hog-tied him before he got close enough. The air shimmered around him, a restriction spell laming his own shadows. He toppled to the ferns with a roar, one thousand butterflies frenzying into the canopy.

When the colorful storm cleared, Pete found himself staring up at the jagged grin of a Leprechaun. The belated smell of myrrh choked his senses as the breeze whipped into his face—an odor he'd have detected long before then if he hadn't imbibed an entire pitcher of Myrrdin's cider!

Blast you, boyo!

"Jolly pickled to see you, McKenna!" Dando exclaimed, cheerful as a butcher inviting a pig to supper. His crimson tricorn cast a sinister shade over his heat-freckled, sweat-streaked face. "Been looking for you."

THIRTY-FIVE

Amy

"**S**ave your breath, Myrrdin." I marched toward the edge of the time pocket, where the prophet waited with Morus. There to talk sense into me, I supposed. Too bad I was sense-proof. "That jackass isn't sacrificing himself for me. No way, no how."

Another serene smile graced Myrrdin's slender lips. "I'm under no misgivings that you can be stopped, Amy. I'm but here to aid you in your quest."

"Oh." I stalled before the slender feyr and his ugly, wary-faced henchman—whose wounds had healed since I'd last seen him. "Help me how?"

Myrddin offered me a linen sack. "Provisions for the road."

Goddess, I was a moron, setting off into the jungle without food or water. I cringed at myself, accepting the bag. "Thanks."

Myrrdin's nod said to think nothing of it.

I pursed my lips. "You're really not going to try to stop me?"

"It'd be fair lunacy not to," Morus groused.

I considered the Kobold. Sure, he'd returned my MulBerry, but I still didn't trust him.

"I see no reason to stop you, child," Myrddin said. "Although Pete expressly begged me to keep you here at all costs."

"Hm. And I suppose that when he told you his dumbass plans, you didn't try to stop him either."

"O' course not." Morus scowled at Myrrdin. "That'd have taken too much effort."

"A wasted effort, more like," Myrddin returned. "Pete's almost as stubborn as our dear queen here."

"Almost," I agreed. "When you talked to Pete, did he tell you anything that would help me find him?" I knew my disadvantages in this chase. "Pete taught me some ways to track people, but we—uh—we've never tested my ability to actually do it."

Sharing a pointed look with Myrrdin, Morus exhaled. "Well, I suppose that's why *I'm* here—I can track him for you—so you don't waste precious time trying to find him your-self."

My arm hairs stood. "Is time precious already?" Not just for my sanity, I surmised.

"Oh, why yes, Amy." Myrrdin's brows rose. "Pete means to rush to the Shadow Palace to foil Gentian and his harbingers' hunt." He paused, mouth tightening.

I gulped. "He won't make it there, will he?"

Myrddin shook his head.

I strangled one of my book bag straps. "Then we better hit it." Forging onward, I waved Morus over. "Come on. Just don't try to steal anything else from me."

Morus's laughter was like jangling change. "Wouldn't dream of it, Amaranthine." He started after me, ambling much faster than I'd figured he would.

"One more thing, Amy," Myrddin stopped us before we returned to Mother Time. "One of your powers—if you haven't already grasped as much—is the *scorán* heart."

That explained very little.

"No door is locked to you," Myrddin stated.

Recent memories flitted through my mind: the pocket door blocking me from the Danann elders' meetings in my family dining room; Howlite's tavern chamber door; his seed chest—they'd all opened at my slightest touch.

"Can't imagine that gift will be very useful in the jungle," I said. "Where there are no doors."

Myrddin shrugged, fluid as milk in his robes. "Nonetheless, the fates have pressed me to inform you."

"Thank them for me," I said, brow arching.

The prophet bowed his head, amused despite the dangers lurking in my near future. At least he had faith in me. Otherwise, he wouldn't let me go.

Right?

Banishing that disastrous thought, I swung the sack of food over my shoulder and soldiered ahead. "Let's go, Morus. We're wasting time."

Pete

Blood oozed from Pete's nose, trickled from his mouth. He sagged like a sweaty trout against the shadowy bonds tethering him to one of the crystal willows. After the Leprechauns had sprayed him with Gentian's voiding potion hours ago, stagnating the bulk of his prowess, he'd given up trying to escape, needing what little energy and focus he had left to resist the temptation to give into the torture. He *couldn't* expose Eden.

Glaring down at his swollen fists, Dando huffed at one of his orange-topped bed-fellas, Lugh, and ripped the proffered canteen from his meaty hand.

"Fecking humans," Dando snarled after guzzling a river, making Pete's cottony mouth twist. Pete hadn't had a sip of anything since the cider that morning. Blearing up at the canopy through swollen eyes, he judged the blazing suns were now near to setting. "You just won't see reason, no matter the motivation."

Pete spat blood, hoping he'd missed his boot. "That's more an Irish failing, old chum. Loyalty—*that's* human, ken?"

"And what of your loyalty to your brothers and sisters?" Alys fisted her bloodied *scians*, eager to inscribe more of her undue wrath upon Pete's flesh. Pete's jerkin now lay at his feet beside his weapons and rucksack, where Shorty's rag doll still rested, undiscovered. His shirt hung in tatters from his stinging, mutilated trunk. "Aren't we harbingers more deserving of your allegiance than the spawn of the bastard who let us all rot in those bloody cages?"

Pete was glad he'd never occasioned to fight Alys in the ring. She was little, aye, but her rage would frighten Lucifer. "I'd rather lay it at hers. *She* doesn't kiss the arse of the devil who locked us in those cages."

Alys yowled and advanced to attack, but Dando barred her, tsking, "Not yet, you harridan." He swiped a healthy sweat off the back of his reddening neck. The tropics weren't Dando's climate. "We don't yet know where he hid the royal twit."

"Have you found the blasted moth yet?" Lugh harrumphed at Domhnall, the youngest and least hateful of their troupe. The lad angrily scoured the ground for Pete's message without success, nursing a split lip, an inflamed throat, and a bloody nose—the only Leprechaun foolish enough to let Pete get his hands on him before they'd voided his prowess to its nib.

Pete snickered, deliberately mocking—a distraction from the prone *dealan-dhè* mere paces from Dando. If Pete could keep the Leprechauns' danders aflutter, then they mightn't think to canvass the ground. Why their snuffs weren't there doing just that mystified Pete.

Were they off trying to sniff out Shorty? *Praise Jesus for elemental shields and their scent blockades*, he thought.

"I'm curious, Dando." Pete fought a wince, testing his legs. His lower left flank objected. With gusto. "How long was it before you kent that that zephyrist you couldn't be bothered with and that royal twit you needed were one and the same?"

Dando's mouth bunched. "See now, McKenna, I've had a wonder myself these many years."

Pete licked more blood from his lip. If not thirst quenching, at least the bitter taste distracted from his wounds. Exhaustion worsened his pain. The combination could cripple him if he dwelt on it. "Have you now?"

"Did you never question why none of us has ever betrayed you to Gentian?" Dando smacked the canteen back into Lugh's burly chest. "Why none of us has ever let it slip that the death poppy had lost its grip on you?"

Pete cringed as he lifted his head again. The many blows his face had taken throbbed. Especially the knot at his temple. "No, I kent your reasoning. I'd have been too bloody good a harbinger without a soul to hold me back. The lot of you'd have never measured up."

Dando's smile could cut iron. "Aye, well—you're right about your soul, at least. It's always been your greatest foible. But it's more than that, aye? See, we never finked on you, so that one day we'd have your fear of a demonic recurrence at our disposal, to hang over your fecking head."

Pete didn't like where Dando was going, but his grin held firm.

Until Dando bent to his bag and retrieved a small glass case. Inside, an inky death poppy sat, a venomous spider ready to pounce.

No!

Pete's innards squirmed at sight of that flower. At the oblivion it promised. And there was his satchel, a yard away, his Wolver's Bite capsule within. He had to find a way to reach it. To swallow it. Now! If he turned demonic this close to Eden—catastrophe! Because demonic Pete would feel no qualms betraying everybody kind Pete had already saved. Shorty included.

Help me, Pete begged fate. *Please let me keep them safe! Keep* her *safe!*

Dando savored Pete's horror, eyes alight as Elven Absinthe. "You've two options, McKenna. You can tell us where to find the princess, and we'll release you without a word to Gentian. Or—" He raised the encased poppy for Pete's panting inspection. "You can stonewall us, and we'll feed this bloom to you petal by petal until your soul decays. You'll happily tell us where we can find the princess then—Gentian's puppet once again."

His nostrils flaring, his agonized muscles straining on his bindings, Pete glared. "You run a dangerous gambit, Dando, wagering I won't just kill you all once that poison takes hold."

"Golly, we'll be well away before you regain your strength, fella. With the princess, by all odds."

Digging within himself for remnants of his prowess, Pete tightened his hold on the tethers binding his wrists. If he could yank them with enough force, he might well get free to fight. To reach his satchel and the quick death it held. But it was going to hurt.

Bugger, it would be *excruciating*.

"You know I've never liked you, man." An act of the worst sort—Dando's sympathy. "But, please, for your savior's sake, have mercy on yourself. Just tell us where you stashed the princess."

Growling as he stood tall, Pete clutched his bonds and bared his teeth like the predator he was. "What princess?" he rasped, daring Dando to try him.

Dando clicked his tongue, sighing. "I won't like this any more than you will." He flipped open the case's lid.

Gritting teeth coated in blood, Pete barreled into his pain, roared like a bear, and yanked with every ounce of strength left in his pounding heart. And the willow branches snapped.

Amy

"How did you do it, anyway?" I asked Morus as we trekked through oppressive heat. Thank Danu for the skimpy fashions in Eden, or I'd have sweated away my energy long before dusk.

"Do what?" Morus tottered ahead of me, chimplike. He'd taken possession of our travel provisions, the burlap bag Myrddin had given me hiked over his bony, furry shoulder.

"Make everything stop in Peregrine Patriot." Maybe this new tangent of conversation would distract from my panic. Morus said we were on Pete's trail, but would we be too late to prevent whatever awful thing would befall him? "The music, the lights, even my friend, Olivia—they all stopped before you stole my phone. Do you have powers that do that?"

"Ah, no, no. My powers lay solely in the sleight of hand realm—used them to swap your phone with a changeling, at that."

I sneered.

"To stop everything, as you said, I used a werethistle root. Eating one gives you the power to dampen the flow of matter—even electricity, as it were. Was meant to work on you too, you see." He cast me what I assumed was a wry look. "I suppose you have a natural resistance to it. Handy to know—for your future."

"Why didn't you warn me about the bogeybats *there*?"

Morus paused, sniffing the air. Scenting Pete, I prayed. "At that time, they hadn't stolen through the portal yet. I did warn you that it was open, remember? Though, I likely sounded rather cryptic. Didn't realize you were in the dark about your origins. Myrddin hadn't read that snippet in the stars until I'd already left for Earth. He was heartily displeased to see it, by the way. He'd advised your father to always keep you in the know. But I see how the good feyr could be too afraid for your welfare on Earth to heed such advice.

"And I changelinged your phone because—"

"What does that mean? Changelinged?" Common knowledge on Earth held that a changeling was a fairy baby left in place of a human baby, kidnapped by fairies. The changeling looked just like the human baby, but the parents always sensed something was off. Just like the glitching phone. "How did you know all my contacts? The numbers? Even though they were all screwy, they were all in there somewhere."

"I didn't know them. Changelinging human devices requires little forethought or preparation. You only sprinkle a mimic potion over it—and well, then you have your changeling. It's never a perfect mimic, you'll know, but it does well to fool even the most observant mark."

I sniffed. "And why did you choose to fool me?"

He had the grace to look ashamed. "Well, I happen to hanker for human devices of the like—but I also thought to warn you only *if* the worst occurred. Dreadful sorry it did, forbye. I did so like your da."

His regret soothed my temper. I was about to express my thanks when a breath nauseated me. "Ugh, what is that stench?"

"What?" Morus's snout flared, making of his face a bad dream amid the dimming ferns. "I don't smell anything frowsty."

I stepped to his side and took in a big, disgusting whiff. "It's like that incense priests use in church services on Earth, only nastier."

The Kobold stared at me, licking his snaggletooth in what I presumed was apprehension. "From where does it drift?"

Breathing in another lungful, I pointed ahead and to my right. "That way."

Morus wrung clawed, leathery hands. "Then that's where we'll go." He glanced up at me. "Certain you don't want to turn back? We'll lose that option if we continue much further."

Foreboding much, Morus?

I held fast to my book bag straps and my determination. I couldn't let Pete die. I couldn't allow the further fracturing of his soul either.

I *would not* fail him the way I'd failed Daddy.

This time, I knew how to fight back.

"We keep going." I peered into the distance, knowing Pete was out there, needing me.

Uttering some foreign expletive, Morus rubbed his wizened brow. "Then stay silent; stay alert. We'll meet the hounds first, no doubt. I can take them, spare you time to—"

A war cry silenced the jungle's chirping, birdlike creatures flapping from their nests. The hairs on my nape rose. Without even a glimpse Morus's way, I darted headlong toward the offensive smell—and the howl.

"This isn't silent!" Morus growled as I raced on, my zippers jangling, my breath sawing. "My word, you're faster than I took you for."

"Right back at you!" I called over my shoulder.

"*Shh!*"

Let them hear me coming. They still won't be ready. I hunkered into myself, reaching for my wind as Pete had taught me.

"Slow down! We haven't located the hounds!"

I might've listened—if yet another bellow of mingling anger and pain hadn't rebutted his caution. A shouted cacophony followed.

Time for a little recklessness. "Keep going straight and meet me there!" I called to Morus over my shoulder and watched his jaw slacken as I leapt into the sky. And stayed there.

See! I cheered myself, soaring off. *You could fly the whole damn time. You got this, girl!*

I closed my eyes and pictured myself floating on a breeze as I had toward the end of my slide down to Eden. I steadied my breathing, maintained an even heartbeat, and trusted my nose to chase the strengthening incense stench. When I opened them, I could taste the smell—and the tang of blood.

I hovered in the canopy above a group of frantic harbingers skirmishing to restrain a massive hellion struggling on the ground, so they could stuff what resembled a half-plucked flower into his clamped mouth.

The man was a battered, torn, sweaty mess, but I could tell by the set of his shoulders and the haphazard fluffiness of his brown hair that he was, indeed, Pete. *My* Pete.

"You're only making this harder on yourself!" The harbingers' clear leader squeezed Pete's whiskered cheeks to force his mouth open. "If you'd only see reason, you eejit!"

The only beyn in the bunch sheathed daggers caked in blood. *My* Pete's blood. "I'll get him to open his fecking gob," she hissed and clamped Pete's swollen nose.

Pete's gaze blazed open, so wide that I could see the whites of his eyes from my altitude. He writhed for freedom, but his body, so abused—he'd never break free of the four burly cutthroats pinning him.

The beyn grinned at her leader like the evil queen in any fairytale. "As soon as he makes to breathe, shove the rest of that poppy in his mouth."

The rest *of it? Oh, Danu, please don't let it have poisoned him already!*

Sweating streams, the leader snickered. "Only moments now, McKenna, before you're confessing where you hid the blasted princess."

Glaring, I dropped from the magenta sky, my boots landing on either side of Pete's head. "She's right here, douchebags." I kicked the raging shrew hurting *my* Pete right in the goddamn nose. She reeled back with a crunch, blood spurting everywhere.

Pete's feyr enemies goggled up at me, blinked several times, then pounced to grab me.

A wind whooshed out of me at Mach 60, whipping them backward like tumbleweeds.

Pete rolled onto hands and knees, blood dribbling from his welting mouth. He gasped for breath, his head sagging. "Shorty, get out of here." He spat. "*Now.*"

"No, you dumbass."

Even amidst his heaving, he laughed. Perhaps he hadn't ingested enough death poppy to do spiritual damage. Yet.

I bent to help him up, but he was exhausted, heavy as a dead elephant.

"Leave me." His breath rattled. That *sound*—so like Daddy's final moments—triggered me before I shook myself. "This is the only way to keep you safe."

"Like hell it is. How is *this* keeping me safe? How is you getting yourself killed going to help any damn thing at all?"

He attempted another breathless laugh. "Would you believe things haven't precisely gone to plan?"

"You think? Just—never mind. Morus should be here soon to help rescue you."

Where the hell is *he?* I thought of the Kobold, my heart galloping. My wind hadn't sent the harbingers far. I heard them regrouping.

"He can't help." Pete lulled to the ground, his arms, carven and bleeding, giving out. "They bound my shadows, voided my prowess, and I used all my remaining strength to fight the poppy."

Gritting my teeth against the fear of defeat, I hugged Pete around his lacerated middle. He winced, and I pressed my cheek to his damp neck. "I'm sorry." Tears stung my eyes. "Just hold on, okay?"

Imagining another wind—a gust able to carry both me *and* Pete back to Eden—I closed my eyes. My bangs ruffled, my magic obeying—our exodus already before us.

I should've known it wouldn't be that simple. It was me, after all. Everything in my life was a fight.

"Son of a *bitch*!" I screeched when something snaked my ankle and wrenched me down.

Barking profanities, both Pete and I hit the ferns. He reached for me, worried—when *he* looked like they'd used him as a punching bag.

"I'm okay," I assured him, shoving to my knees. Before my leg jerked out from under me.

"Shorty!" Pete reached again, just missing my hands as I was dragged back into the willow copse. I seethed the entire bumpy trip.

I wound up the center of a reeking harbinger circle, surprised I wasn't the least bit scared. Their many weapons, shadow tethers, and overall menacing vibes had no effect on my nerves.

"Princess Amaranthine," the harbinger leader chortled, strolling about me as I popped to my feet. "Lovely to meet you, your highness."

This guy is something else, I thought as he removed his ugly tricorn and bowed to me, displaying a fuzzy orange head.

"It would be our honor to escort you to the Shadow Palace."

"No, thanks." I brushed dirt from my scrapes. "I'm cool here."

The leader blinked. "At these temperatures? How can anyone be cool?"

"She means she's no intention of leaving with you, Dando, you daft rotter." Pete staggered through branches blooming tears. He fisted his hands—his only artillery after potions and spells.

Please don't let them know any spells to handle me.

Tickled by Pete's insult, Dando turned to chuckle with his comrades. The female found nothing funny, however, blood seeping from her inflamed nose. She seethed at me, promising misery.

"McKenna! Thought you'd have limped away with your tail between your legs by now." Dando shook his ginger head, plopped his tricorn back atop it. "Daft of *you* to remain."

Ignoring him, Pete fell into the willow trunk for support. How the hell was he even upright? Where had he found more strength? Then our eyes met, terror glazing his, and I knew I'd given it to him. Or his fears for me had.

"Shorty, are you—"

"Don't worry about me, Pete. Just get out of here. Go!"

Goddess, please go before they kill you!

They needed me alive, but him—they'd end him like an ant underfoot. Especially She-Ba, warrior bitch. Pete understood this better than I did, but his knuckles only whitened. "I'll be damned if I'll let them take you."

"They *won't*." I hoped I at least *sounded* confident. I certainly didn't feel so, even if I wasn't pissing myself. "Go."

"*No*," he flat-out refused, his gaze a black threat to anyone who'd dare harm me. A threat She-Ba didn't take kindly to. She unsheathed one of her blades and, with a feral screech, chucked it at Pete's heart like a dart.

I screamed, jumping in its way. "*No!*" Pete roared as I clenched my eyes, concentrated, and erupted.

My wind blasted the dagger back at the beyn, hilt first unfortunately. It hit her square in the boob before she sailed away, a feather in a storm. Her shrewish screams grew fainter the further she soared.

Pete collapsed on his hands and knees, drained to a husk.

I rushed to kneel with him, wanting to hold him, comfort him, but I couldn't without causing him pain. "Are you okay?" I shuddered, brushing back his hair. Pete moaned in reply, grabbing my hip.

Dando clicked his tongue, something unholy in his voice. "Oh, I see what's happened here."

I didn't like the look he gave me. Or the tone of his snigger as he swaggered toward me. I braced myself, a fortress over Pete, preparing myself for lethal tactics. At any minute, tethers would shoot out at me from all angles. I'd have to wind-whip them away. Tricky to do, yes, but if I stayed on my game, I could do it.

Goddess, now I wish Pete had trained me even harder.

Smirking, Dando observed Pete, who struggled to rise.

That's when Morus finally reached us, muttering, "Accursed Leprechauns," from behind me. A small comfort as I faced Dando's malevolence head on.

Looking nothing like any Leprechaun I'd ever seen (primarily on cereal boxes), he scratched his bushy, orange sideburn. "Forgive me, Pete. We assumed you were sheltering an ally in your hatred for Gentian. But now the question begs—you've lost your ordination—we've beaten you soundly and now have nay more quarrel with you. You're free to scurry off to lick your wounds. So, what the devil are you still doing here?"

Pete's breath quickened. I felt his heated gaze on my back—marking his territory.

I marked my own, holding my ground when Dando swaggered into my bubble. He would *not* wedge himself between me and Pete.

Dando was about my height, but he may as well have been a ten-foot wild dog as he leaned in, fangs flashing, and sniffed my collarbone.

I recoiled because—how dare he!

"Hm. Do I detect a hint of orange rind?" He took another whiff. "And lichen?"

My nostrils flared in remembrance of that distinct fragrance. In remembrance of Pete's skin. Pete's hair. Pete's clothes. In remembrance of the embrace I'd shared with Pete earlier that day, and the sizzling look he'd given me when we'd pulled apart.

Overjoyed as my face flushed, Dando clasped my shoulder and squeezed. A tangible wealth of fury rose behind me. Pete's, I knew. Impressive, that his surpassed mine as I jerked out of Dando's grasp.

The cretin rubbed his fingers together, relishing the feel of my skin. "Pete's gone dotty for you, hasn't he, lovey? Can't say as I blame him. Eyes like that could pierce a feyr's heart, they could, to say nothing of a man's. What shade would you call them?"

"I don't know," I snapped. Right then, I had no idea what my eyes looked like. Whatever color they were, though, I was sure they expressed my surging unrest.

Why was Dando so interested in Pete's attraction to me?

Slugs dwelt in Dando's voice as he mused, "And now I'm asking myself—has the princess gone just as dotty for Pete?"

Before I could react, one of Dando's cronies had a knife to Pete's suddenly bobbing throat. The younger one nabbed a snarling Morus by the scruff of his furry neck.

"You'll leave off the wind and come with us easy, princess." Dando reveled in my alarm. "If you want Pete here to live."

For once, I listened to my instincts, acted without thinking, and loosed a cyclone on Pete's assailants. I swept them and Dando off their buckled clogs, flinging them, blades and all, into the jungle like slops to a pig.

My vision blurred, the willows spinning, but I shook myself and grabbed both Pete and Morus, driving more power from my core. I'd need hurricane-force winds to lift us all together. If only Pete weren't so dang heavy.

My boots had just found purchase on a hardy gust when shadow tethers snared my arms, legs, and shoulders, grounding me despite my momentum. I was a chained rocket trying to blast off.

Dang it, Amy! You didn't keep your head in the game! You knew *they were coming!*

I landed with a running gait, relinquishing my grip on my friends, and flailed against my new bindings. I could understand a few more tethers than the one around my ankle. Maybe. Twenty—that was excessive.

Weird, how these tethers felt nothing like Pete's. His had felt like peach fuzz, forgettable as a well-worn watch. These, though—they were steel wool, strangling.

Morus scuttled to my side, clawing a tether. When that failed, he fisted the damn thing, gnawed it like a turkey leg.

"That won't work," Pete uttered, his voice tissue paper thin. He'd braced his sagging body against another tree. I met his watery eyes, knowing what he was saying. There was only one way to sever a shadow tether. And no witnesses could get away alive if I used it.

Dando smacked his tricorn into the ground, pushed to his feet. "I'm plum fed up with this shite! Where the feck is that spell harpy Alys? You gave her the blasted voiding spray too, didn't you, Lugh? You lummox!"

Guess you blew away the right Leprechaun, Amy.

Dando spat as Lugh's face flashed red. "We aren't bloody taking this one without using both—stroppy bitch that she be."

That was the exact wrong thing to say to me.

An ember kindled in my belly.

Suddenly, the breeze turned, and I realized with a start and a sniff that Morus wasn't beside me anymore. From the corner of my eye, I saw him scrabbling away into the brush, yanking a debilitated Pete with him. The last I saw of them was Pete's face, contorted, despairing.

He wanted us to fight together.

Tied like livestock to a slew of Gentian's worst, I wanted that as well.

Echoes of myself weeping, alone in a field, punctuated this thought. Destroying the cool I'd kept. Because nobody could rescue me from this mess—the one I'd barreled toward like a bull out for blood.

Damnit, Amy—what the hell have you done?

Gulping, I squared my tethered shoulders and faced my aggressors. "You won't take me at all," I declared, worried one of the harbingers might chase after my fleeing friends. Just because he could. "I'll make you kill me first."

Dando scoffed. "What a curious thing to say."

He sounded so calm, so impassive. That's why I didn't anticipate it—the shadowy noose that clamped my airway closed. Or the instant, primal panic I felt when I realized I couldn't fucking breathe!

"Know what happens when you die?"

I stumbled to my knees, frantic to claw away the tether choking me. But other steely tethers tugged back my arms. Denying me even the struggle for breath.

Pete! Morus! Come back! Help me, please!

I saw them in my mind's eye, hobbling toward some haven in the jungle, some refuge from my fire, thinking I'd unleash hell on the Leprechauns at any moment. Something I totally had the power to do! I *knew* I could do it!

Just not if I couldn't focus on that ember dying in my belly. And not if I wasn't in immediate mortal danger. Which I effing wasn't!

Dando wouldn't strangle me to death. He wouldn't get his bounty if I died. But he could render me unconscious, then bind or spell me into another lengthy captivity. And damn my sniveling self, but I didn't think I'd be able to stop him.

And there they suddenly were, as clear as the willows' tears—my every shortcoming laid bare, my entire life's insecurities splayed open. Right there, as I grappled for air under the snickering of devils, I could have had all the powers in the entire magical realm secreted within me, and it didn't make one fucking bit of difference. Because I couldn't get a grip on *any* of them, couldn't see past my own fears and anxieties to touch them. I could only see that I wasn't worthy of the weight of the Aurora legend. That I was, deep in my marrow, nothing but a weakling imposter who'd thought she could be more. For herself. For her family. For Pete. For anyone in the universe who needed saving.

But I wasn't enough for them. I wasn't strong enough. I wasn't smart enough. I wasn't brave enough. I wasn't royal, or mighty, or divine enough.

Though, damnit all, I *wanted* to be!

Dando leered in my bulging face. "When you die of a blood curse, dear princess—you ken the curse doesn't end with you."

Fire! Now! I need fire! I grappled for that deadened ember, black dots filling my vision. Mother's sake, smoke had been right there at my fingertips just *moments* ago. It had been *right* fucking there! Where had it gone? *Where?*

"It moves onto the next in the bloodline." He paused, tapping his lips. "And if recollection serves—that means your sister's next."

Even in strangulation, something deep inside me gasped. Vi's face flashed across those widening dots. She with her easy smile, shimmering young eyes, and warm heart. She as a toddler with golden curls, clinging to me on an ornate bed, little Ace snuggled in tight on my other side.

Breathing became an afterthought.

Maybe I wasn't enough.

But I was all they had.

Like a flint wheel on a lighter, I felt a loaded click, and that cold ember in my belly blazed up like a torch in a chasm of endless night. Through my panic, I cast my mind out as far as it could reach, and I snatched that torch like a lifeline out of hell. I glared at Dando, thinking, *Oh, no—you didn't.*

My torch flourished like heartburn, my lungs smoldering. My fingertips smoked in a warning the harbingers didn't catch.

"If you force us to kill you—well, I think I might vie for dear sister's bounty. What say you to that, fellas?" Dando's taunting grin turned my way. "Tell us, princess—your sister—does she take after you?"

My warrior's skin kicked in full force. I stretched those damn tethers restraining my arms to their limits, hooking two fingers between the noose and my neck. And I inhaled.

"Will she spread her legs as willingly for her captor?"

*Oh, no. You—*fucking—*didn't!*

My blood boiled, my firestorm roaring, and drowned out the Leprechauns' bawdy laughter. Then they weren't laughing at all—because my vision flashed red, sulfur permeated the air, and my fingertips sprayed sparks.

"*Run,*" a portentous voice, neither human nor fae, snarled out of me—fair warning. Baring my teeth, I set fire to my throat and watched Dando's tortoiseshell eyes round to moons. *"Just fucking run!"*

My noose now cinders on my chest, the harbingers tautened my fetters. I smirked at them, their comeuppance in the flesh, and turned their weapons against them, now more hissing dynamite wicks.

Dando clutched his tricorn and whirled for escape. *"Fire sylph!"* he bellowed. His boggling comrades clambered after his retreat, their impotent, ashen tethers with them.

Please, I scoffed, surfing a breeze, and soared over their heads. I landed in their path. They skidded to a halt before me, drenched in their own fear.

I stood back to my full height and lifted incendiary hands. A tigress with three mice, I purred, "What were you thinking of doing to my sister?"

Backing away, Dando stammered, "It—it was a mere jest, princess."

"I'm *not* a princess."

I combusted then, a flame-thrower on steroids, my leg muscles quivering for control as I conducted a shrieking symphony of third-degree whoop-ass. I watched, refusing to cower, as the Leprechauns danced the dance of hellfire and brimstone.

And I witnessed a living nightmare when Dando, his face a contorted vision of hatred and malice, stumbled toward me, his teeth bared, saliva bubbling, and reached for me with charred, flaming hands. One of them fisted a knife.

Spooked, I shuffled back into a palm trunk and firebombed his chest. Ghastly, was his wail, before he fell to the ground, rolling, and set the palms near me ablaze. Hot ash rained from the sky.

Still, I never looked away, never allowed myself the comfort of ignorance.

This was my gift—the most agonizing, violent death imaginable—and I wouldn't be sorry for it. Not even as the Leprechauns begged for mercy. Not even as they screamed for their mothers. I blocked their voices, breathing deeply, evenly, and with a healthy dose of righteous indignation until the threesome of wailing infernos quit writhing within my flames—the ones now consuming the willows I didn't spare a second glance for as I cat-walked into the oncoming night, a freaking boss.

Gone, was the innocent girl shrinking from the bogeybats who'd eviscerated her father. Gone, was the child mewling, alone in a field of orphanhood and friendlessness. Gone, was the hapless youngblood who'd burnt herself out in a battle with ravening Fomorians. Gone, was the ineffectual abolitionist who'd gotten her ass kicked.

She'd been a victim then.

She'd never be a victim again.

Now, she was the only thing standing between the void and those who needed light. And she *was* enough.

I had *always been* enough.

THIRTY-SIX

Smoke and glowing ash choking the air, I scrambled through the rising night to find Pete and Morus. With me, I hefted Pete's blades and rucksack. His jerkin had gone up in flames.

I found them by a pink, trickling stream, only yards away from the flaming willows. Morus stood over Pete, who knelt at the stream's sandy bank, palming water into his battered mouth.

I cringed at my harbinger friend's brutalized face. It had seen better days.

"Any sight of the beyn? Of Alys?" I asked, first thing. If she were still out there, I needed to deal with her immediately. Couldn't risk her guessing I'd started the jungle fire. She'd totally wonder how.

"Taken care of," Morus assured me. "Clawed her gullet out when you flung her into me."

I blinked at the Kobold, not even grossed out by his report. From what I'd seen of Pete's graven flesh, dear Alys got her jollies by causing others pain. She'd deserved a gruesome death. "Guess my aim was lucky then."

"I'll say."

"And the snuff hounds?"

Morus shrugged. "No signs of them. For whatever reason, they mustn't have come."

Thank our lucky stars.

Groaning, Pete lumbered to his feet and faced me, hands out. "My baggage?"

"Yeah, right." I tightened my grip on his belongings. "I'll hand these over, and you'll try bolting off to the Shadow Palace again."

He soured.

"That's what I figured. What the hell is wrong with you?"

Pressing the heel of his hand to his pummeled temple—pounding, no doubt—Pete shook his head. His only response.

Suddenly, I thought his face needed more pummeling.

"Squabble later," Morus crowed. "Right now, we must race away before that fire catches us."

I handed Morus Pete's gear. Then I trod over to my boneheaded friend to help him walk. As fast as his long, bungling legs could carry him.

At first, the prospect of escaping the wildfire seemed impossible—with an injured man and a surly Kobold straining to breathe soot   and with us dodging fleeing stampedes, prey and predators alike.

Once, I did try to help. High from my victory, I felt like the master of all nature. So, I stopped before the formidable wall of fire devouring trees that had probably stood for centuries—until me—and whipped a great gale at the greedy flames to drive them back. This resulted in me dashing back past my hobbling friends, squealing, "I made it worse! I made it *so* much worse!" The fire roared on, taking double what I'd tried to wrest from its ruinous maw.

After that, flight was our only option. I grabbed both Pete and Morus and whisked us to cleaner air on a sweltering easterly. I did this sporadically, landing to run constantly to conserve my wind, worried I'd drain myself before we found safety.

The last time I tried lifting us skyward, we went but a foot before our feet touched back down. "I'm spent, guys." I bent over, heaving. "Can't even blow a leaf."

"Just as well." Morus folded his tired, monkey arms upon a fallen tree. "We're free of it now, I'd say."

I'd have said so too. Yes, distant smoke still stung my nose, but the air where we'd landed was clear, the orange aura around the jungle canopy absent. Now, we stood in the chirruping, whooping moonlight, relief cleansing my troubled soul like a good book.

That's when Pete, who'd fared the worst in the fire, clutched his chest and crumpled to his knees, coughing like his lungs mutinied.

"He needs water." I ran to kneel with him. "I think he breathed in too much smoke."

"Not smoke," Pete wheezed. "Poppy."

I clutched my mouth. *How* had I forgotten?

Morus pushed off the tree. "What's that he said about a poppy?"

"The Leprechauns—they made him eat part of a death poppy. They wanted to turn him demonic."

"Sweet mother of Felias!" Morus swore.

I didn't know who Felias was, let alone his mother, but I swore an oath to her too and snapped my fingers into a torch. I held them up to inspect Pete's eyes.

Thank you, Felias' mom! Pete, eyes like ginger snaps in caramel, wasn't turning demonic. Great news.

But bad news—he had other problems. Besides the wracking cough and shortness of breath, his eyes were glassy, the heat of his arid skin scorched my hand, and he shivered against me when I drew near.

I goggled at Pete. "I think you're sick."

His gaze returned to mine, dry as his wheezing, which was beginning to scare me. He sounded just like every horror movie corpse who'd risen from the grave.

Had one of his countless open wounds already become infected? Even if it had, could he have already gone septic? Didn't that take days? Not hours. Besides, I scented no festering bacteria on him.

"Could a few death poppy petals make someone sick?" I asked Morus.

He examined Pete's eyes for himself. "No, Amaranthine. Even a minuscule amount would corrupt a soul with all haste. If he's not demonic now, then they didn't feed him death poppy."

"But they *said* it was a death poppy!" *What* had those carrot-topped assholes given Pete?

Morus's mouth twisted. "They'd likely confused it as such—the dimwits."

"Confused it with what?"

"Shorty." Pete fisted my shirt strap. "I can't smell you." His chest rattled, his eyes widening in panic. Because he wasn't getting enough oxygen. "I can't smell *anything*."

Something about that complaint struck a chord of terror within me.

"Did you see the bloom?" Morus licked his snaggletooth. "How did it look?"

"I don't know!" I squealed. "Like a black poppy! Oh, uh—it was green in the center. Lime-green."

Somehow, that disturbed Morus more than the threat of Pete going demonic. His black pit eyes rounded. "Death poppy stamens are gray, Amaranthine. What you're describing—a black poppy-like bloom with a green center—is known as a bane bonnet, a posy cultivated with corrupted magic to foster dark magic on earth—by spreading plagues."

"*Plagues*? Like the black death?" The disease that had killed half of Earth's population in the 14th century!

"Aye, well, bane bonnets did start that, but Pete's is likely a new breed—if Gentian was growing it. He thrives on innovation in killing."

Holy mother of Felias! I thought, puzzle pieces clicking together. The diverted river. The stolen mine. *Gentian's growing bane bonnets!*

"We must curry Pete back to Eden and our healers as fast as we can." Morus took Pete under one arm to heft him up. "If he's in this condition now, he'll likely be dead by dawn."

No! No! No! No! No!

"Wait!" I grabbed Pete and shook him to get his faltering attention. Because I now understood why Myrrdin's fates thought I should know about my *scorán* heart. "Pete, stay with me, dude!"

Shit! Are his lips already blue?

"Do you have *anything* in your talismanic sphere that could help you?" I squeezed his head, trying to keep him alert.

His fatigued, swollen eyes dawned with a moment of clarity. "Locked."

"Not to me it isn't." I smacked his cheek when his eyes rolled back. "Will anything in there help you?"

"Maybe—" His voice drifted, as did his awareness.

I smacked him again. "Maybe *what*? What, Pete? *What*?"

Jarred by the violence, Pete bleared, then whispered, "Breath—breath of life—"

"Huh?"

"A potion!" Morus wrung his clawed hands. "It's a potion to restore vitality—at least for a time. If he has a vial of it, then we might be able to spirit him back to Eden before the worst occurs."

Gritting teeth, I laid Pete down in the ferns, praying his lungs would hold out until I'd found what he needed. Then I danced around him in a circle like a frenzied mime, desperate to lay fingertips upon an invisible door to a secret closet.

Piece of cake, right?

"What does the potion look like?" I questioned Morus during my freestyling. The Kobold knelt over Pete, counting his respirations. Despite their arguments earlier, they must've been pretty good friends. Pete's declining condition had Morus praying to any deity who'd listen.

And me—Pete had me close to a nervous breakdown.

Not Pete! Not Pete! Not Pete!

"It should be indigo in color." Morus touched his forehead in some silent invocation. "That's its primary ingredient."

The air beside my left hand shimmered, outlining a dark oval. Crying out, I waved my hand in the same spot until it happened again. Then I pressed my palm against something flat and solid, and the atmosphere around my hand pulled apart like theater curtains.

"Yes!" I surged into Pete's talismanic sphere—an earthen burrow lit by fae asters. Which is where I squawked like an angry chicken.

Because every item Pete had stored in his sphere—every weapon, article of clothing, special tether, case, foodstuff, and potion—lay scattered in voluminous piles with absolutely no rhyme or reason. Like a teenage boy's dirty clothes! Now, I liked to live in organized clutter, but *nothing* in Pete's sphere was freaking organized. Which seemed like an error on his part when there might've come a day when someone unfamiliar with the sphere would need to break in and find something that might *save his goddamn life!*

"How does someone *live* like this?" I squealed, going berserk on his piles, chucking things. Finally, I emerged back into the jungle, arms laden with liquid indigo.

Morus paced, hands scrabbling across his furry head, when I clambered over to him and Pete. I bit out the cork of one vial and pressed its mouth to the latter's split lips.

He didn't drink it.

"Shit, Pete!" My shriek echoed for miles. I shoved my armload at Morus before rising on my knees over Pete's slack, unresponsive form and started chest compressions. I thanked Danu I'd sought a comforting mantra—30, 2—after Daddy's death—because Pete wasn't fucking breathing! "Come on, you big jerk!" Tears streamed from my eyes. "I'm going to be *so* mad at you if you don't breathe for me! Right now!"

After 30 compressions, I tilted Pete's chin upward, pinched his nostrils shut, and blew the sputtering dregs of my wind into his mouth.

He surged up off the ground and into me with a wheezing cough, then crawled onto his hands and knees to vomit out the death he'd just tasted.

Morus collapsed, praising some other divine entity I'd never heard of. I didn't have time for prayer, though. Trembling, I wiped my tears and yanked Pete back over to me, pouring that dang potion down his gullet before he could almost die on me again.

The potion returning some of his strength, Pete was then able to stand and put one foot in front of the other, but he still needed us as crutches to hurry him back to Eden. After six Breaths of Life and more than a few close calls, we had one vial left. And miles before we'd reach the kirk.

We'd never make it. Pete's lips were already bluish again. I could tell without trouble in the light of dawn.

Refusing defeat, I shrugged out of my book bag and handed it to Morus. "I've got to fly him the rest of the way."

"Have you regained enough power to carry him?" Morus asked. "If your stores flicker out mid-flight—"

"Yeah, I know," I snapped, tired and damn near hysterical. "I'll crash to the ground like an asteroid and die along with Pete." Shaking my head, I uncorked the last Breath of Life vial. "I'll stay as low to the ground as I can. And when you meet us back in Eden, Pete will still be alive. Okay?"

Morus didn't reply as I stomped over to Pete, who rested back upon a vine-draped palm while I prepared for another desperate act.

"I heard," he wheezed, shivering, when I opened my mouth to explain. His eyes heavy, febrile, he reached for the vial. "I believe in you, Shorty." Then he downed the last vial and wavered back to his huge, unsteady feet.

I thought if I soared as fast as I could, I could get us to Eden before my wind—quite slow to rebound without rest—died out. This wasn't so. Apparently, using magic worked the same way gasoline did in cars. Going faster only used up twice the gas to get you the same distance. So, when I finally spied the Kirk of Cara on the horizon, Pete and I dipped down, my engines sputtering.

It took all my strength to heave us back up above the canopy before we smashed headlong into a rock wall, where nesting tangerine cats hissed at our intrusion. I tightened my grip around Pete's torso, his body so hot my breasts were sweating. He hadn't made a single sound during our near miss, but I felt his chest expanding and contracting in my arms, so I thought, given the circumstances, he was doing fine.

We stalled three more times, each scarier than the last. In hindsight, I should've just landed while I still had enough control to coast. But we were so dang close to Eden, and I wanted to land as close to the kirk as possible, questioning Pete's ability to walk. Having to drag him might waste valuable time.

Of course, so would a freefall to the ground, which is what happened the last time we stalled. Nothing I did brought another wind to my sails, and we plummeted, a pair of downed fowl. Screaming for Danu's grace, I clutched Pete to my chest and willed him to hold on.

The best Danu could give me was to land us in a mud pit. The one Pete and I had careened into from the natural water luge two nights before.

On impact, I lost grip of Pete. And slammed sideways into a bed of jagged rocks hiding under the mud.

Now bleeding, shaking in shock, I flapped through the mire until I located Pete, then lugged him to shore. Breathing in stilted gasps, he was unconscious again, and no amount of poking, smacking, or shouting woke him.

"Goddess, Pete, do you have to be so fucking difficult?"

With no other recourse, I hauled ass out of the mud and grabbed him by his limp, slimy wrists. I lunged backward with the little energy I had left, my punctured side screaming, my legs stiff, aching.

Growling through my teeth, I towed Pete's leaden bulk to the kirk, past its seemingly abandoned gate, and through the gorgeous rotunda beneath Adam and Eve's watchful gaze. The moment we tumbled into everlasting twilight, I fell on my ass beside Pete's sagging head and shattered paradise.

"Help us!" I screamed, gathering Pete in my lap. "Somebody help! *Please!*"

All of Eden came to my call. Several fae of differing races knelt with me in the flowering grass, their hands glowing white. Stem healers.

I wept when a kind-eyed drey touched my muddy, bleeding arm. "You've done right by him, child. Let us do the rest."

THIRTY-SEVEN

"**G**ood morning to you, Amy!" Liatris called, fluttering past me on my jaunt through Eden. I waved as lightning bugs danced over my shoulder on a tropical jet stream. Carrying a foraging basket, I bustled past numerous friendly faces, all greeting me like their longtime neighbor. I was well known by that point, as it had been six weeks, if I'd tallied my sleeps correctly, since I'd taken over the warden's responsibilities.

Because the warden himself was still down for the count.

"That particular bane bonnet germinated a phage—what Earthers call a virus," Cissus, one of Pete's many healers, had told me the day after I'd dragged Pete into Eden. We'd stood at the foot of Pete's infirmary bed, where my friend hacked into a medicated cloth a hedge healer was soothing his lungs with. "A deathly phage too, I fear," Cissus went on, gentle but forthright. "And while phages pose us no issue in fae sicklings, we've never cured a human of one. At this point, we can only manage Pete's symptoms until his body trounces the illness."

This had panicked me, so Cissus—a tall, charming Middling with a clavicle birthmark—had reassured me, "We'll keep him alive, but it'll be a battle."

Cissus hadn't been wrong.

On his worst days, Pete spent his few waking hours in bouts of coughing fits, vomit, and febrile delirium. After Alys's spell had worn off on Pete's tethers, things became dangerous for anyone trying to help the hallucinating SOB; he'd attack anything that seemed remotely threatening.

"He's returned to his cage," Morus remarked to me when I'd first seen Pete so lost. "Stay well back."

Pete had torn his infirmary room apart, equating those helping him with Shadow Palace gaolers because they wouldn't let him leave. If they had, Pete would've died. He'd needed a stem healer on constant call to purge his lungs of the pestilence suffocating him from within.

So, feeling trapped, Pete had devolved into his former hell. Hunched over his rumpled cot, he'd wheezed threats of evisceration to anyone who dared touch him. Angry as snakes, his shadow tethers had writhed about the shambled room, ready to enact his scared, frantic, brainsick will. Nobody, not even Morus, had the idiocy to approach him.

Nobody but me.

I couldn't have said I knew what I was doing. Or that I was even being courageous. I'd just seen Pete falling apart, become so sad I burst into tears, and my heart spurred me toward him. I'd made it all of three steps before Pete had snared me in every velvety tether he had. He'd wrapped me so tightly, he could've broken bones or disjointed me with a jerk of his hands.

"You damned fool!" Morus had hopped on hooves. "We warned you, didn't we?"

Others had leapt to help me.

"Stop," I'd breathed, halting them as the predator's black and blue eyes squinted at me over his scarred shoulder. I'd trembled, feeling hunted, but relaxed in Pete's tethers. I'd become so pliant, so docile, that he'd realized I wasn't there to fight him. His labored breathing had quieted. And he'd cautiously, curiously, tugged me toward him.

Only inches between us, Pete had studied me. I'd held my breath until, blinking, he'd shaken his tormented head. "Shorty?" My blood had rushed to circulate when his tethers unbound me. "What are—what are you doing here?"

Here had meant the hideous mirage he was living in—Gentian's fighting ring.

Tears dripping from my chin, I'd set my hand in Pete's mussed hair, whispering, "I'm not, Pete. I'm safe in Eden, and so are you."

He'd become as tame as a kitten after that.

Until his next delusion.

Eden's healers hadn't fought this battle alone. Spell casters had canvassed the infirmary, crafting charms to keep Pete's fluctuating balance from skewing demonic. His rancorous ravings and explosions of violence had kept them quite busy.

Simple things, like getting Pete to eat, were a damn nightmare. Without smell, he'd had no taste, so he'd wanted *nothing* that we'd served him. He'd started dropping weight alarmingly fast. Eventually, Pete's scary outbursts had subsided to crippling fatigue and long, terrifying lengths of frailty. Morus, the healers, and I had forced Pete out of bed every six hours to maintain his muscle tone, but he'd become winded after only moments and need another prolonged recovery.

Now, six weeks in, the hardest part for me was still the uncertainty. Some days Pete seemed to be on the mend, and others he was knocking on death's door again. I worried every minute of every day that he'd never get better.

Thankfully, for the last week or so, there'd been more good days than bad, and I'd eased up on visiting the infirmary to get more work done around Eden. Pete had a hefty list of duties as Eden's warden, and while I knew little about carpentry, fishing, hunting, or *anything* about the running of a thriving village, I was willing to learn from those who did know, help where I could.

Today, though, I really was needed for a major project that all the other zephyrists in Eden had been working on for a while—damage control to quell the forest fire I'd started. It still burned in places, and they'd grown desperate enough to solicit help from me, a newbie. I hoped they were willing to teach me from their collective knowledge. Having met them all before at various times, I knew they'd be kind to me.

"Ah, Amy," Myrrdin said as I tramped into the *Anam Cara* rotunda, where five other zephyrists of varying fae races congregated. "Right on time."

I smiled at Myrrdin and his convoy of cherubic children, including Jet, who sung a gleeful, "Hallo, Amy," flitting around with his friends.

The little ones spent time in the kirk and its surrounding yards each day, so their developing bodies could age a few hours. Still, some of them had been children for more than 16 years.

"So, where are we doing this?" Setting down my basket, I joined the zephyrists, psyched to flex my magical muscles that day. Lately, I hadn't been doing much flexing, what with all my chores—and all the time I'd devoted to Pete's bedside.

"The observatory, to start," Riordan, Eden's most senior zephyrist, answered. His long, spring-green finger pointed toward the glass dome rising leagues above us.

Not seeing a stairway, I asked, "How are we getting up there?"

In a group of zephyrists, that was a stupid question. Two other beyns took my hands, giggling, and gazed upward.

"Oh." *Duh, Amy.* "Sorry. Still forgetting I can fly." *So weird.*

"Have a safe flight," Myrrdin said before herding the children into the sunshine. We didn't catch much vitamin D in Eden.

"Ready?" Riordan asked, raking his jet-black hair.

Each of us called up a wind. Halfway to the top of the dome, I looked to the beyn on my left, Imogen—one of two other Dananns in Eden. She had friendly eyes, olivey skin, and a crop of wavy hair, two-toned from brown to gold. "Is there a door up there?" I called, hoping we weren't going to bust through the etched glass dome like assholes. Yeah, the kirk was just a decoy, but it was a beautiful decoy.

Imogen answered, "You'll see." Then she pulled me into her wind, and we both squealed as our combined magics shot us above everyone else. Nearly ten feet from the dome, the suns magnified through it, Imogen squeezed my wrist. "Call up a second wind! Blow it at the glass!"

I bit my lip, mentally pushing along beside her.

The glass dome separated into petals, us zephyrists slipping between them. We hovered above the dome for several moments before it closed again, and Riordan directed us to land upon the pristine glass.

I cringed, hoping not to leave boot prints.

Then, gazing out at the world beyond—the jungle and all its peaks and falls and foliage—I forgot I was even wearing boots. I stopped breathing.

But we weren't there to sightsee. Riordan got down to business.

The dome's etchings weren't just decorative. They projected the map of the fae realm—Mag Mell.

Well, don't you feel like a straight-up ignoramus, Amy? Why would you just assume your new world had no name?

Mag Mell boasted a ring of four massive continents with a large central ocean and another on the outside. Countless islands peppered these massive water bodies, even the tiniest land masses represented. Yet the Shadow Court, Covenlen—nowhere to be found. Yes, the place was a blemish, a wasteland, and the beating heart of evil. But pretending it didn't exist felt like a copout. Because it did exist, and we *all* needed to remember that.

After gathering us around Lithalaly, the southernmost continent, Riordan sprinkled a red powder over the lands between us. Figment flames shot up on the map wherever my jungle fire still blazed, even after rainfall.

I winced at the widespread devastation I'd caused.

"After we suppress the flames, Amy, the terra sylphen will repair the destruction. They can't regrow the lost vegetation, but they can awaken soil elementals to do it for them." Riordan offered a kind smile, shutting his powder canister. "Fret not."

Easier said than done, dude.

"All right," I said. "So, how do we suppress fire?"

He rubbed his hands together. "You'll know wind fuels fires, aye? Well, our task is to siphon that fuel from the flames."

I blinked. "You mean we have to *suck* it out?"

The other zephyrists chuckled.

"Aye, Amy," Riordan confirmed. "It's just that simple."

"Damn," I said. "Guess I could've done that the night I started the dang thing."

"Can't blame yourself for what you didn't ken," Riordan replied.

From there, we broke into pairs. Riordan chose me, the one in need of instruction, and we flew together to the closest wildfire cropping. Being any further from Eden while Gentian's harbingers had their noses to the ground, trying to sniff me out, was flirting with disaster.

I shuddered, landing before a sweltering wall of gluttony. Having devoured everything for miles around, my flames subsisted on the coals they'd shat out like greasy fast-food. Sulfurous ash crackled in the air. Cinders coated my lips, and I tasted the tang of my fury at the Leprechauns, now rampaging to flank us.

Jeesh, I thought. *Now* that's *conviction!*

Already coughing, Riordan shielded his green face with a wrinkled, homespun scarf. He handed me my own before beginning with, "Siphoning's a simple concept, mind you, but that doesn't mean it's easy." He cleared his throat, blinked eyes reddening in the dry heat. "Novices often find things go muzzy. If your head starts reeling, take a wee breather. Mother knows you'll need it.

"Now, this is the most stubborn finger of wildfire we've encountered. Water scarcely quells it. We've been siphoning here from the start. Somehow, we've held it at bay but can't seem to douse it. So, we'll likely be at this until sunsdown."

My mouth twisted. "Nothing like giving the new girl the tough job, huh?"

Crinkles appeared around Riordan's green eyes, his scarf hiding a grin. "I've been assured the new girl is worthy to the task."

I heaved a sigh. "If this is going to take all day, then we better get started." The pull of Pete's bedside was very real. Even with him showing improvement, I could barely stomach the idea of leaving him for an entire day. "Show me what to do."

"Aye, then." Clearing his throat, Riordan tugged down his makeshift mask and inhaled.

After what amounted to three hours of siphoning, I strolled, soot-streaked and smoky, through the kirk's gates, a siphoning maven. Sure, I got hella dizzy several times, but I hadn't needed the breaks Riordan thought I would. And together, with my boggling endurance and Riordan's mastery of zephyrism, we'd extinguished 20 square miles of wildfire, maybe more.

Comfortable letting Pete be for another few more minutes, I tasked my filthy, ashen self with pillaging the kirk's many garden beds of cantaloupes—or what resembled cantaloupes despite being aqua inside. Pete's recovery required a hearty consumption of vitamin C, also a scarcity in Eden. Seriously, it was a wonder Adam and Eve didn't have scurvy when Danu expelled them to Earth.

I was just yanking one of the bigger rocklike fruits off its vine against the temple wall when I heard a loud and urgent, "Amy!"

Imagining the worst, I grabbed my basket and scrambled back through the gate, where I found Cissus, beaming in his linen infirmary smock—only worn while doctoring.

I halted before the athletic Middling, unable to breathe.

"We've trounced the phage," he said, hazel eyes shimmering. "His fever has finally broken, and he's eating!"

Though it took me a moment to understand, once I got it—that Pete was *finally* in recovery—I squealed and flung my arms around the healer.

Cissus hugged me in return. "He's been asking for you," he teased.

Flushing, I scampered back to Eden, cantaloupes flying everywhere.

Pete grunted when I careened into him for a hug. He'd been sitting up, half-naked on his rumpled cot, chewing a piece of fish jerky, when I tore into his cabin-esque room, a copper-topped hurricane. I closed my eyes and pressed my cheek quite hard to his chest, which had lost a bit of its meat but none of its heart.

He squirmed against me, gulping like a prepubescent boy meeting the girl of his dreams, before his arms finally squeezed me close to his *normal* body heat. "I suppose now it's my turn to thank you," he croaked, his throat still raw from coughing. "For all that *you've* done."

I giggled out weeks of pent-up anxiety. "Any time, dude."

"And I'm truly sorry. For how I acted while—"

"I don't want apologies." I withdrew to stand over him, arms folded. The dim light of the fae asters highlighted his gaunt cheeks and unkempt beard. "I want an explanation."

Pete's dark brows lifted clear to his hairline. He stared, lost for words.

"Not about *that*," I corrected myself in a fluster. "I know why you acted the way you did while you were feverish. I mean—*why* did you run off to sacrifice yourself like that?"

Looking like he'd lost his regained appetite, Pete glanced away.

"Because you think my life is worth more than yours?" I supplied a terse answer and fell to sit at his side.

Eyes flashing, Pete faced me. "Aye, Shorty. Because it is."

"That's *so* not true!"

"You're the queen; I'm a fecking pawn."

I sniffed at him. "Don't use chess metaphors on me, you geezer."

Souring, Pete threw up a hand. "Fine! Then how's this? You're the *Aurora*, Shorty. The *fucking Aurora*! You're the savior of all the fae realm—and maybe the human realm as well, if Gentian's growing bane bonnets. And I knew if I didn't do *something* to buy you time, that other harbingers, or Gentian himself, would find you. And soon.

"And I was right, Shorty! Damnit all, I was right!" He glared at me. "You ken how close we still were to Eden when you caught up with me? The Leprechauns were on your trail, and they were *going* to find you."

"And I would've barbequed them if they tried to take me, Pete! Just like I fucking did!"

"Aye. And who knows how many refugees you'd have killed doing so?"

Ooh, that stings. He has a point, but it stings.

"Please, Shorty, you've got to be more prudent than—"

I clapped my hands in his face, startling him into silence. "Pete, I get that I'm impetuous sometimes, but don't lecture me about chasing after you. Because that means we'll be getting into a very deep discussion about who in this world is worth saving. If I'm the savior of all, as you just said, doesn't that include you?"

Pete's jaw hung.

"Uh-huh!" I hopped up to dance. "No comeback for that one, I see!"

He glowered.

Bloated with self-satisfaction, I folded my arms again. "Now, promise me you'll never do anything like that again—that you won't fall on your sword for—"

"No way in *bloody hell* will I promise you that!" Pete harrumphed, his flat-out refusal heartwarming. He'd make no false vows to appease me, too bloody honest. "My life is mine to lead, Shorty, and it's been a good deal longer than yours, as you keep reminding me. If I choose an ending that gives it meaning, a purpose, then I'm bloody well entitled to it."

Softening, I sat beside him again, clasped the bear paw clenched in his lap. "How you *live* gives your life meaning, Pete. Not how you die."

I'd stumped him for words again.

After a brief silence, Pete scoffed, quirking one corner of his chapped lips, the bottom now faintly scarred—compliments of the Leprechauns. "Guess I'm buggered then, huh?"

Tsking, I reached up and tucked a brown tuft behind his ear. "No, Pete—you're definitely not."

The fisher fae and I often joked that we'd run out of fish. Because Pete was eating them all. He'd shovel four filets into his mouth at each meal, without swallowing, it seemed, and then look at me like a big, shaggy dog who'd lost his favorite bone.

"I wish we had some beef," I confessed to Morus one afternoon during my first fish cleaning lesson. I worked my knife through an opal trout's belly, trying not to cringe. "Has anyone ever raised cows here?"

"You mean kinera?"

"Sure."

"We have three now." Morus clawed the guts out of his trout and discarded them onto the ground beside him. Sionna, keeping me company that day instead of playing with her faelet friends, tramped over and wolfed down the innards. *Ick*! "Where do you think our milk comes from? We also have a bull and a steer."

"I assume you need the bull for making more kinera." I chuckled. "But the steer—you think we could convince someone to butcher it for Pete? Some red meat would do him good. He's a predator, after all."

"You'll have to take that up with the druids. They have it earmarked for your summoning."

Once Pete's life was out of danger and my mind less occupied by death, plans for my summoning had commenced hardcore. Now, they were gearing up to summon me in a week. A *week*! And I wasn't anxious about it at all.

Not.

"Why would they need a steer for my summoning?"

"Ritual blood sacrifice," Morus replied like he'd told me the time. "The steer's an offering to Danu."

I chewed on this. "Can't we just save some of the pieces from the steer—while we're turning it into steak?"

The Kobold's prune-like face wrinkled further in amusement. "If you were readying to have any goddess, let alone the All Mother, to supper, what would you likely serve her? Day old stew?"

Souring, I exhaled. "No."

Morus let Sionna lick more fish guts off his claws. "You'd offer the best that you had, o' course. To display your deference. Your summoning's no different an affair."

The affair of my summoning would take place on the fire festival Imbolc, what we'd called Candlemas or St. Brigid's Day on Earth. I'd always thought Candlemas happened in winter, but it fell in late summer on Mag Mell's annual timetable.

Myrddin showed me their calendar for gauging the passage of time outside Eden later that day when he took me on a tour of the sacred stone circle where they'd conduct my summoning. There, I learned that a fae year consisted of 13 months instead of 12. Someone had carved these months into one of the standing stones in yet another circle (we fae—we liked our circles). A tree and a moon phase denoted each month. We were now in mid-hazel moon.

"August," Myrrdin clarified, helpful as always when I was pretending not to be clueless before his clerics.

"I've been here for three and a half months already?" My family probably thought I was dead. And my friends back home in 2008, who I pictured packing to return to UPJ for the fall semester, doubtless still hoped I'd come to my senses, changed my mind about dropping out of college.

If only I had that choice to make.

Clearing my throat, I faced Myrrdin's serenity. Maybe he'd rub off on me. "Is there a tutor here in Eden? I want to learn the little but important things about this world."

"I'll have Master Hickinbottom meet with you first thing in the morning. He's been offering to—"

The prophet's voice blurred into the background as my Danann ears detected a vigorous scuffle transpiring on the downslope of the fairy hill. Alarmed, I scampered to the edge of the henge. At the bottom of the hill was a rudimentary fighting ring constructed of fallen palms. Inside, weapons drawn, were three large males, the largest being Pete.

"What the hell is he doing?" I demanded. "He's still recovering!"

Although, watching the massive man right then, he didn't look like he was recovering from a deathly illness. Despite his thinner physique, which was filling in again with his constant gobbling, he still looked lethal, like he could crush a bear's skull in the palm of one massive hand. His body moved with such power, dodging and thrusting, that he made my heart—and other body parts—shudder.

Cool it, Amy, before you burst into flames. Anger was no longer the only emotion that riled my fire.

Myrrdin hummed as he glided to my side. "Trying to keep himself fit, I presume. He'll need to if he's going to help us in your summoning."

Startled, I whirled on Myrrdin. "He's what?"

"He's offered to assist us in conducting your powers."

That would only endanger Pete. Again! "But he can't do that! He's not—"

"He's stronger than anyone else in Eden, Amy—apart from you, of course—both physically and magically. And remember, we need all the strength we can muster."

"But he still coughs sometimes, and he—he gets tired too easily. He's been taking naps during the day."

Myrrdin chuckled. "Pete has always taken naps during the day. Even with all his undertakings, he finds time."

"I don't care. I don't want to risk it."

Myrrdin set a long, elegant hand on my shoulder, his voice a tranquilizer as he said, "He'll be fine, Amy. I assure you."

My pulse slowing, I scowled. "You better be right, Myrrdin. If he dies in this summoning, I *won't* be happy with you."

"Curious, but Pete said something similar to me about you." Myrrdin's crystalline eyes twinkled like water under moonlight, and I got the feeling he didn't find anything curious about what Pete had said at all.

Liatris's hands fluttered, as did her wings. "You look—" She beamed at me. "Exquisite!" Reaching for my hand, she spun me about in the warden's hut. "Just exquisite."

"You truly do, Amy," Imogen gushed from my other side. "You're a dream."

Unsure, I glanced down at my summoning garb—a strapless skater's dress with a frayed sweetheart neckline. Made of layers upon layers of the finest silk, so gossamer you could almost see the tint of my skin beneath, it floated around my thighs, deliberately tattered. My friends said it had been crafted of threads from enchanted silkworms, and two diligent sempstresses had magically woven the fabrics before they'd sewn them into the masterpiece. I wished they hadn't wasted so much effort on a dress I'd wear once.

How I looked in it—well, I'd have to take my girls' word for it; I had no mirror to see for myself. The dress certainly felt nice on me. Although, I would've preferred a longer skirt. I feared I'd spend the entirety of the evening tugging down my hem.

Of course, from how Liatris and Imogen had dressed, I figured nobody would yell boo if they spied my privates. Both beyns before me were pretty much advertising theirs in their fig leaf monokinis. Not for amorous attention, I guessed, as they were both still hopelessly in love with feyrs somewhere beyond Eden. No, they'd dressed to feel pretty, to feel free, to feel empowered for the celebration after my summoning. Because femininity was power, regardless of society's insistence that it should be meek.

Screw that shit.

"I daresay *someone* will struggle to keep his hands to himself when he sees you," Liatris giggled, her eyes crinkling as she led me to the tree stump table and sat me down.

"I-I doubt that," I stuttered. "Pete and I—we're just friends." We'd made a pact, and neither of us had mentioned breaking it. Though I'd totally been thinking about it. A lot. "We aren't like *that*. Lovers, I mean."

Imogen and Liatris shared a pointed look over my head. Their nostrils flared to take in my scent—somehow now entwined with Pete's. I couldn't even scrub it away.

"Yeah, I know how I smell, and how it looks—the way we interact—but really, there's been no hanky panky." Coerced, near hanky panky didn't count. And that felt like ages ago.

Imogen lifted a delicate paintbrush off the table and dipped it into a small canister of kohl. "Well, lovey, that doesn't mean fate has none in store."

Finally, my eyes winged with curly Qs and shadowed with seafoam-green and pale-gold—also the colors of my dress—I proceeded to the stone circle, where half of Eden—the strongest half—already awaited me.

The weaker half prepped the village square for the after-feast. Watching them work, I flashed back to the night of Beltane, pre-festival, a freak chill creeping up my neck.

Torches lit the path to the stone circle, a carpet of flower petals cushioning my bare feet as I climbed the fairy hill. A salty sea breeze floated a floral aroma to my nose, and I needed a moment before I placed it. Sweet William—the scent from my night terrors.

More chills.

I waved at the clerics gathered by the main gate, who bowed their heads to me in solemn greeting. They looked focused, ready for the task ahead. At least their gravity said they knew what they were getting into. In contrast, the volunteers I trod past jabbered like theatergoers before the prologue. I feared they'd all bitten off more than they could chew in agreeing to assist that night, and I hoped they all made it out of the circle alive.

Myrrdin found me before I found him, dressed in his usual robes, a headdress crafted of driftwood and bird bones crowning his golden-brown head. He set a hand on my back. "Right this way, Amy. We'll start the summoning as soon as all are in place. I know you want to get past this."

Goddess, did I ever.

As he led me to the circle center, we passed the steer, an intense shade of mustard, who munched away at the sandy grass surrounding the post he was tethered to, assuming that night would be just like any other night in his boring, but probably happy, life.

Sad for the steer, though I'd been plotting his demise days ago, I almost didn't notice who awaited us at circle center. When I did, my universe shrunk—just as it had when I'd first seen him at the Thorny Rose Tavern. Now, he was all that existed on that fairy hill.

Purple twilight framed Pete as we approached. Like all the other males in attendance, he wore a simple pair of black homespun pants, tied at his waist with twine. But unlike all the others, from that narrow waist arose a mouthwatering hulk of furred, rippled muscle, scars etching his broadness in the torchlight. Scars only recently healed. Scars I'd helped poultice while he was feverish and weak.

He showed no signs of malaise, now. Virile and towering, his massive bare feet firmly planted on the ground, Pete grinned down at Morus like the rake I knew. He'd trimmed his beard and had his hair shorn, though it remained devilishly unkempt. His cheeks, round and full again, were a healthy tan, his dark gaze a warm and glittering thing.

Maybe Myrrdin was right. Maybe I didn't need to fret over Pete's involvement that night. Maybe.

"Make ready, Pete," Myrrdin advised when close enough. "Won't be long now."

Pete glanced over at hearing Myrrdin's voice. Then he saw me. And froze. Like his heart had leapt up and choked him.

He hadn't expected to react that way. He'd have scented me or known I'd be with Myrrdin without thinking much of it. I'd become an everyday pest in his life, after all. Nothing special.

Except tonight *was* special. And my girls had dressed me for the occasion. Their handiwork had elated them. Now, watching Pete's jaw plummet, I supposed they had every right to elation.

I met Pete's gaze, barely cognizant of Myrrdin ushering me forth. Because Pete—his hunger, unbridled as a mustang, ravaged me.

Morus snickered at him. "Is there a punchline forthcoming, or—?"

Pete waved Morus to silence as we stopped before them.

If Myrrdin felt the heat rising between me and my harbinger friend, he didn't let on, diving into the details of my summoning. "You mustn't do much at all, Amy. Just don't fight the Goddess's offerings, no matter what they are. I suggest focusing on breath. That should calm you—to some degree."

I wrung my hands. "How long will it take?"

Myrrdin's mouth quirked. "That shall depend on how many powers you've been gifted."

"Oh, well—that makes sense."

"And Pete—" Myrrdin looked to him. "Yours is a more grueling lot. Not only will you serve as a filter for her powers—"

I nearly bit my tongue in half. "A filter? What does that mean?"

"It means I'm going to slow the flow of magic from the conduits, so your powers don't overwhelm you." Pete's smoldering cooled at the thought. "Because that might make you swoon while your gifts are still mingling among them. Then they'd need to keep them controlled until you came to."

I cringed, thinking of my powers as wayward toddlers. You'd never want them misbehaving at someone else's house. "Yes, let's not let that happen."

I fully believed Pete when he nodded, assuring me he wouldn't.

Myrrdin glimmered at us. "Pete, as Amy's anchor, you'll also keep her grounded in the onslaught."

I could've done without the word *onslaught*. "My anchor?"

Pete's eyes rolled skyward as Myrrdin said, "Aside from the threat of swooning, there's also the worry that you might forget yourself and soar away. Sometimes it happens with zephyrists. Wind sustains the Mother's Isle in the heavens, you see, and tends to call its vessels home."

"Home?" After a moment, I realized what he meant. "*Home*? Like the Isle of Apples, *home*?"

"Yes."

Pete shifted, his mouth bunching.

"Pete has to keep me from doing that? *How*?"

Myrrdin flipped up a hand, so nonchalant he was beginning to annoy me. "It's as simple as—"

"It's not simple, Myrrdin," Pete argued. "As I've told you, I'm not—"

"You *are*, Pete. I know you think otherwise, but I've seen it—you *are* her anchor. You, and only you, will keep her here. You've done it several times before already."

Oh, my Goddess. I thought I knew what he was talking about.

"But that's absurd." Pete scraped a hand through his hair. "Anchors are only meant to be those with whom you've formed an affinity bond. And we *haven't*, Myrrdin." He was so damn definitive that I knew he feared we had.

I might've taken offense if I didn't know Pete so well. He didn't fear for himself. He feared for me.

Pete looked to me for confirmation. "Have we, Shorty?"

I bit my lip, my cheeks warming. "Er, I—I think it happened that night we cheated Howlite. Maybe afterward when we were talking—and then when we were listening to my iBloom together—"

Because the next morning was when that curse seed had tried to enslave me, and the only thing that had prevented me from overpowering Pete and grabbing the damn thing had been him—my memories of him. The same thing had happened when I'd taken that slide down the ravine just before we'd first reached Eden. Without his visage to cling to, I'd have flown off to Danu only knew where until I was lost, alone, and in danger of nature swallowing me.

I offered a crooked smile. "Good music can make you do crazy things."

Guffawing like a monster, Morus ambled away.

"Damnit all, no!" Pete massaged his forehead. "This cannot be! I—I—I've spent *years* trying to avoid this very thing happening, Myrrdin. Years! I'm a *harbinger* for Christ's sake! And now—now you're telling me it might've happened when I wasn't bloody watching?"

"Yes," Myrrdin said.

Pete spewed a diatribe of what I guessed was Gaelic into his hands. I'd never heard him speak Gaelic before, but he was right—now seemed the appropriate time.

Heart aflutter despite Pete's mood swing, I peered over at Myrrdin. "This anchor thing—it's more complicated than Pete just keeping me grounded for the summoning?"

"Hm," Myrrdin hummed, amused again. "Pete will explain it to you later, Amy. Right now, all you need know is that he, as your anchor, will prevent you from a premature departure. And to do so, he must commune with you."

My guts somersaulting, I gulped. "Is that the same here as it was for me on Earth?"

"I believe so."

Holy shit snacks! That meant Pete was about to get up close and personal with my feelings for him, both romantic and sexual. He clearly wasn't down for that, as stressed as he was.

"Shall we get started?" Myrrdin asked, then simply moseyed off, leaving Pete and I standing together, avoiding eye contact.

Soon, the clerics had all the willing hosts organized into a circle around Pete and me. And the poor, clueless steer. A tense hush descended, all eyes on me.

I'd always hated being the center of attention. Now was no different, despite the kindness in the gazes. After a minute, I felt ready to burrow into my own hair, a sniveling mole. Then a bear paw nudged my hand.

Threading my fingers through Pete's, I marveled at his ability to know just when I needed a comforting touch. At his readiness to give it, despite his own tumult at our bond.

I was beyond grateful for his physical support when the clerics glided into a second, smaller circle around us, their robes reminding me of ghosts. Each wore a twine necklace bejeweled with animal bones. Joining hands, they peered skyward.

They commenced my summoning in a chilling, monotone chant, reforming the bones around their necks into vortexes of coruscant steam—smoke signals to the heavens.

Message received, I mused when lightning speared through the violet nebulae above, making me suck in a breath.

We were calling on the freaking All Mother. How, I wondered, would she make her appearance—if she'd literally appear? As the serpent of Eden? As a person? As a burning bush?

I jumped when lightning arced over the clerics, a sprinting reaper, and struck down the steer in a thunderous clap that made my eardrums vibrate. It left only a pile of ash and a single longhorn behind.

Instinctively, I pressed into Pete for protection like he could save me from the Goddess. And he probably understood his uselessness in that regard. Yet, he pocketed his current reservations for a later time and drew me closer.

"Praises be to our holy mother, Danu!" Myrrdin's voice reverberated. "We humbly summon your blessings and your tremendous magics in the name of your virtuous daughter, Princess Amaranthine Ginger Larkspur. We summon you in the name of the Aurora!"

No sooner had he shouted that last word—*Aurora*—than did the sky transform, rainbows streaking the sky. At first, everyone cooed at the splendor. At second, mass hysteria erupted when the streaks shelled the henge, shrieking like fireworks and rocking the ground.

"Remain calm!" Myrrdin commanded. "Stay where you are!"

Yeah, okay! I wanted to snark, the earthquake nearly knocking me on my ass.

Then came the asteroid, a veritable bomb with a tail of violet fire. I screamed as it blasted the hill in a mushroom cloud of sand and grass, bowling Pete and I over.

I coughed in the lingering haze, particulate stinging my eyes, and pushed to my feet. When the dust settled, I was the only one in the stone circle not kneeling in supplication, and three giant, semi-transparent beyns of startling beauty stood before me in a newly formed crater.

Their divinities glowed as shimmering auras around their breathtaking, stark-naked bodies. Even their elegant Danann ears scintillated as though sequined.

I stopped breathing when their omnipotence found me.

Pete gasped from where he knelt. "Holy Christ! It's all *three* of them!"

The clerics shared his incredulity, for more than one gaped over his shoulder as they scuttled to join the other conduits. Leaving me to face three awe-inspiring deities on my own.

When they approached me, I staggered back. One triple goddess would've intimidated me. Three put me in danger of peeing my pants. Pete's continued grasp on my hand was all that kept me from running away.

The first to speak had amber-toned skin and a soft, Botticellesque body. Her hair flowed like verdant rivers to her perfect feet. Flowers bloomed in her curls, and birds nested in her waves. She had the sweetest face I'd ever seen, her almond eyes slanted upward. Her regard, so imbued with tenderness and love, was a dead giveaway—*She* was Danu.

"My dearest, Amy," she tinkled, her voice a windchime.

She knew my name? Not my given name. My heart's name.

"We've been waiting for you to call on us."

"We've been watching you," the redhead to Danu's left spoke in a smoky lilt, her smile, sultry as the jungle, weirdly familiar. Her skin was as luminous as pearl, her hair a cascade of molten copper, fresh from a forge. "You've been making us proud, daughter."

Was she talking to *me*? *I'd* been making them proud?

The third goddess stood to Danu's right. She was much saucier, though no less beautiful. She had gleaming, walnut skin and prominent cheekbones, round and regal like an African queen's. Her hair, a voluptuous mass of raven ringlets pulled atop her head in a severe ponytail, fell over broad, muscled shoulders and arms accustomed to wielding swords. On one of those shoulders sat a large black crow, whom she petted as she burred, "The question we have now, little fighter, is: will you accept the destiny we've designed for you? Are you prepared to champion this world?"

Breathe, Amy. I jolted myself, the goddesses awaiting my answer. "Y-yes," I finally croaked, wide-eyed as a lemur. "Yes, I accept. I accept it all." And I did. Because *someone* had to do it. And I didn't trust anyone else to get the job done.

"Then kneel, Amy Larkspur," the third goddess ordered in a voice that meant *obey*. "For the bestowal of our blessings."

Yes, ma'am!

I dropped to my knees before Pete, who already awaited me, hands out. Shaking in fear of what was about to happen, I pressed my palms to Pete's, and his long, callused fingers wove through mine.

"Ready?" he asked, his neck flushed and sweaty.

Our foreheads touched, and I gripped his hands for dear life. "As I'll ever be."

THIRTY-EIGHT

Naturally, the All Mother initiated the gift giving. "I am Danu," she started. "Creator and mother to Seelie and Unseelie alike, and to all of humankind. Assured of your worth, my dearest, I shall bless you with my most favorite parts of myself."

She's blessing me with her own *powers? She can't mean that.*

My desperation to watch what Danu was about to do was killer, but I knew better than to break my concentration on Pete. So, I forced myself to stay focused, to relax my psyche so we could commune.

And, oh—*oh*! I knew it the moment I sank into his frequency. Because I *felt* him. The immense power in him, the unmatched strength in him, the yin-yang soul in him—they were all there for my mind to mingle with, melting my heart to a puddle at my knees.

And it was a good damn thing I hadn't wasted time watching Danu. Because she continued with, "I had many principals in my time, Amy, but I was fondest of my wind."

At first, nothing of note happened. I just started feeling like everything I'd eaten for the past year was escaping through my pores. It didn't hurt, and it wasn't uncomfortable, but I did become lightheaded, a little hungry. Because my magic was leaving me, so Danu could return it with interest. Like I was an updating computer.

Several hosts squealed. "Steady, now," Myrrdin cautioned. "Keep your heads, folks. Control is imperative. Funnel in small groups—take turns."

Pete's fingers tightened around mine. He grunted like he'd sat on glass, his shoulders bunching.

"You okay?" I whispered. *I never should've let him do this!*

"Shh," he hushed me, velveteen tethers snaking my limbs—extra protection from what he now knew was coming my way. "Focus on me."

Taking his advice, I leaned into our mental connection. Just before several breeze-like fingers tickled my cheeks, tugged at my hair in a come-hither flirtation. Inciting chills. I didn't dare open my eyes, but when ethereal voices whispered in my ear, I couldn't help imagining myself now flanked by wind seraphs—luminous in trumpet-shaped dresses like the angels Mrs. Crankle across the street hung on her house every Christmas season.

Come away with us, the seraphs enticed. *Come away to the clouds. To the stars. To freedom itself.* Never had I considered such a thing—going to heaven by choice—while I was still living. And I didn't think I'd consider it now either. But lordy, those breathy voices were persuasive. They made no bones about the Isle's wonder—a place absent of suffering, a land of eternal peace wherein all wishes were granted. *Don't you deserve that?* they cajoled. *Don't you deserve your dreams?*

And those dreams suddenly became illustrations in my mind. There was me in an old-world college classroom, laughing with friends. Me after graduation, working as a publishing executive in a skyrise overlooking a wind-powered fae city in the clouds. I saw myself at a pleasant supper with my family, both my parents there. Then, me curled up on a fairytale apartment's window seat with a steaming mug of coffee, surrounded by books, pets, and puzzles, listening to the best pop music any world offered. And I wouldn't lie to myself—I was tempted.

I winced, thrown from my reverie, when another image—a boy in breeches and waistcoat, his tousled brown hair tied back in a queue—pervaded the angels' visions. He squealed, a rakish little devil, dashing away from a short woman with golden-brown hair capped in linen. She chased him around a modest stone-built manse in her ponderous skirts, until she scooped him up and gave his round cheek a loving kiss. "Go wash up for supper," she lilted pleasantly and set him on his feet with a firm smack on his rump. "Ye wee hooligan."

Pete, I realized. He was the wee hooligan. And he wasn't in any of the seraphs' images. And if he wasn't there—

My Isle of Apples future lost all allure.

"Sorry," Pete said as I pressed closer to his hands and forehead. He must not have meant me to see that—memory? Strange, but I'd never received memories in communing with anyone else. I'd have thought the difference due to our increasingly lustful involvement if I hadn't had a similar involvement with Briar. I'd only *felt* things from Briar. I hadn't seen things.

Perhaps I'd seen Pete's memory because he'd yanked on my psyche when the seraphs were tempting me. Now, I was immersed in his mind, so deep that my being there would've been invasive if Pete hadn't invited me in.

Being there, snuggled like a bug in a rug with him, my heart purred, *Mm*, and I refused the seraphs beckoning me home. Even as Danu's winds became a maelstrom, I stayed grounded, gripping Pete's hands until I'd resorbed my first principal power.

Danu granted me two secondary gifts after that. The *scorán* heart, so no doors were locked to me, and chronopathy, a power which must've had some association to my dimples of Venus, my back a canvas for the Mother's art. I almost giggled. Aunt Aylie would be *sooo* pissed at Danu for defacing my skin.

Before the next goddess spoke, I experienced another hollowing. This one much more abrupt. This goddess lacked Danu's patience, for she drained whatever magic she needed from me in a blink, and I would've toppled over, dizzy, had my anchor not steadied me.

"*I* am Morrigan," she declared. "Goddess of war, advocate of kings, and defender of the people." I knew which of the goddesses spoke even with my eyes closed—the one who looked like a badass. "To you, little fighter, I give from my own arsenal: the warrior's skin, so that you may be harder to kill in battle, and my principal power—shapeshifting, so that no single form will constrain your glory."

Are you kidding me? Shapeshifting? I didn't like the sound of that right then. From his furrowing brow, I could tell Pete didn't either. Because what the hell was I about to become? And how would I turn back?

A ruckus of strain arose from the hosts. When Pete groaned with them, his hands strangling mine, I whimpered, "What's the matter?"

"She's given both her blessings at once."

Why? I wanted to whine. *Does she* want *me to pass out?*

"I'm trying to slow them, Shorty." Pete stiffened again. "I just don't know if I'll slow them enough."

I squeezed his hands. "I'll be okay," I probably lied. "Just do what you can."

Don't you dare hurt him! I wanted to squawk. At the Morrigan. *He's been through e—*

In the next instant, I *was* squawking. Literally. At a much closer distance to the sand. And—

Ooh, is that a bug? That'll make a nice snack. Come here, you little shit! I'm hungry!

Oh, no! Oh, my freaking *Goddess! Do I have feathers? And a* beak? *What the* fuuuuuck?

I had a conniption then. Fluttering like the *freaking chicken* I now was.

"Anchors away, Pete!" Myrrdin chortled. Many of the conduits chortled with him. Including Pete. Whose huge-ass hands reached to catch me. Just then, I didn't care to be anywhere near his huge-ass hands.

What ensued was a very unfunny (in my opinion) game of Pete and chicken. During this game, I was also resorbing the Morrigan's secondary gift. Because of that, Pete finally caught me. Croodled against his chest, I thrashed for freedom. His voice was a soothing rumble as he petted my feathery head with one of those huge-ass hands. *Bah!*

"Easy, now. No, no, Shorty. *No!* Leave off the henpecking—I like it less than your harping. Just breathe deeply as I've taught you, control the magic. Aye, there now. Come back to yourself, girl."

My, I do like it when he calls me girl.

And just like that, I settled back into Pete's consciousness, where I met him as a pre-teen boy on a woodsy excursion with a large, bearded man and a younger boy of Pete's own mien and make. All three held long rifles as they crouched behind a thatch of blooming mountain laurel. The man, sweating through his leather waistcoat and continental hat, spoke in a soft voice that sounded just like Pete's did now. He advised Pete on how to best shoot the buck grazing in the distance. But Pete didn't wait for the man to finish. He squinted one molasses eye, aimed, and pulled the trigger. His musket ball struck the buck right in the shoulder.

Though he gawped at first, the bearded man eventually broke out in a bout of silent, belly-shaking joy and mussed Pete's hair. "Well, I'll be dratted," he brogued, squeezing Pete's shoulder. "That's my lad."

By the end of that memory, I was my old Danann self again, standing to my normal height—my cheek pressed to Pete's bare chest. Our eyes met with the mutual recognition of how close he held me. I felt his even pulse in the roughened hand cupping my jaw.

We broke apart. Though, not abruptly. Reluctantly.

At last, Pete sighed. "Blast it, Shorty, please don't do that again."

I would've laughed if I weren't so shaken. Could I quit my summoning in the middle of it? It was on the tip of my tongue to ask.

Thankfully, Morrigan had finished with me, and she strutted back to Danu's side, smug as a cat in stroking her crow.

I whined when the redhead approached, literal flames lapping at her luminous skin. I knew exactly what gift *she'd* bestow on me.

"Fret not, my daughter." She smiled. "I'll start with my meeker gift before I broach the fire."

I slumped, relieved. "*Thank* you."

The circle of hosts had another chuckle. As did the redhead.

"Here, Shorty." Pete tugged my hand, drawing me to join him on my knees in the sand. He was right, of course. We needed to return to communing because another hollowing was already under way. And this time, it came with the bonus of nausea. My gorge rose not long after my forehead touched Pete's. I gulped back several mouthfuls of welling spit. "Just breathe." His voice was a sip of ginger ale. It helped, but only mildly. "Remember, you're so near the end."

He was right—I could do this. If I could survive mutating into a chicken, I could do anything.

The redhead's meeker blessing was the ability to protect those nearby from physical harm, the Allies' Aegeus. In resorbing this, a golden, transparent net whirled around Pete several times before leaping back into my unwitting hands.

I expected my queasiness to abate then. Instead, it got worse. My third hollowing was still ongoing even after the redhead's secondary blessing. So, how much freaking fire was biding within me? And how long would it take for her to purge it? Because I was two more gags away from tossing my biscuits, and one regurgitation away from passing the hell out.

"Look, look, look, Shorty!" Pete strangled my fingers like he could strong-arm my rejuvenation. "Look at this!"

"Huh?" I wanted to cry but didn't.

Because then I was watching two little boys—one taller and older than the other—competing in a pissing contest off a bench in a barnyard. Both their dusty breeches lay rumpled around their skinny, stockinged ankles as they giggled together. The older excelled at flooding thistles while the younger missed every single one. Still, the older boy praised the younger, "Well done, Paddy! Mam will be so tickled you've killed all the weeds!"

The younger boy beamed up at the older boy's approval with a bright brown twinkle. The older boy grinned, hiking up his breeches. "Last one home feeds the pigs!" He leapt from the bench and tore off. The little one scrambled down after him, breeches still sagging.

I smiled, breathless with the urge to spit up. "Did you really make little Paddy feed the pigs?"

Pete's reply was also wispy. Was his forehead sweating? "Oh, I still fed the pigs. Our mam made me."

Our mam. So, this *was* his boyhood I was glimpsing. "I like your family," I murmured, trying *anything* to keep my mind off my gnawing emptiness. "Your mother."

"Don't sound so surprised." If I'd been paying better attention, I would've noted his tension. "I seem to recall telling you my mother was a fine woman."

"You did." *Oh, Goddess, make this stop before I puke on him!* "But you rarely talk about her—them. I figured—you didn't—"

"I had a felicitous childhood, Shorty." Was his breath short? "I had a felicitous *life* before this place. Would you like to see it?"

So eager for his history, I failed to question his willingness to open that door to me. I also failed to heed the rising temperature of his skin, the hissing of the conduits. I simply answered, "Yeah," and Pete flooded me with snippets of how he'd become the man I knew.

He gave me the extended tour of his past, and I learned the minutiae of him, the tiny details, quintessentially Pete. From his favorite toy soldier to the worst horse he'd ever owned, and the quills he'd used in his legal practice that had always splotched his fingers black.

He also gave me an introduction to his extended family. Which was more than abundant and included uncles, aunts, cousins, second cousins, those who were "like family," and various furry friends. Seriously, the ship the McKennas had crossed the Atlantic on would've only had room for the McKennas. And that was just his father's side. His mother's side had stayed in Ireland, and they were quite the brood as well. In short, Pete grew up in a wellspring of love. With a wellspring of admirers.

Admirers whose hearts he'd often broken, I discovered. I doubted he'd intended this discovery. In wrestling with whatever was happening in his body, he'd lost control over his memories' flow.

Pete's discomfort brought my own corporeal distress to mind. I shook out of his mental slideshow to feel sweat pooling in my every nook and cranny, my blood nearly simmering, drumming in my ears. "I don't feel so good."

Pete drew our locked hands, mine smoking, to his chest. His sweat slicked over my knuckles. "Stay with me, Shorty. There's more to see, ken. Can't leave you there, thinking me some lothario."

"You aren't?"

"Judge me for yourself," he coaxed me back into his past.

There were lots of girls. Lots of ladies, too. Mostly pretty. Several homely. From the time Pete was 13 years old, he'd enjoyed their company. At least for short bursts. Pete's rampant mind bored too easily. Maidens of breeding were too damned agreeable, too pleasant and biddable. They were afraid of their own opinions, strong-minded females largely disfavored. Pete, however, sought an intellectual connection with the woman he must spend his life with. He needed someone skilled at repartee, who'd stand up to his wit without flinching. And when he'd pressed any of his options to expose her mind, she'd blushed at such "impropriety." At least, that's how Pete's mother had put it after one Miss Peggy Shippen had complained of his prodding—like he'd asked her to remove her blasted petticoats for him at the spring cotillion.

Once, Pete had thought he'd found *the one*. Lydia Lippincott, a lily among thorns—the cousin of his college mate. On their first meeting, she'd enamored him with a pithy discussion on the colonies' troubles with King George and parliament. He'd courted her like a right swain after that.

Turned out, however, that her cousin, his friend, had coached her into being what Pete desired. When Lydia experienced a stroke of conscience and confessed her cousin's plans to lure Pete into marriage—covetous as he was for Pete's merchant father's connections—she also confessed that she had no mind for politics, philosophy, or "men's matters," and didn't care to acquire one. She feared a life spent maintaining her cousin's lies would prove too toilsome, preferring to occupy herself with the running of a household, idle gossip, and being the proper wife and mother she was reared to be. If that was quite all right with Pete. Suffice it to say, his infatuation with Lydia hadn't survived that confession.

Soon after, Pete had joined the continental army, where his interactions with women had lain solely in the sex-for-money capacity.

Then, there'd been the Shadow Palace.

How fitting that after this blurred era of anguish in Pete's life, hellfire surged within me. To the point where I choked. On my own goddamn magic. As did everybody else in the stone circle. We were all going to die of smoke inhalation.

"I can't do this anymore," I sputtered like a candle. "Please, it has to stop."

"Not yet, Shorty." Pete sounded rougher than I did, but he wove his sweltering fingers into my hair and forced my forehead to his. Keeping me with him. "You can do this. I know you can."

"I can't breathe," I sobbed. "I'm melting inside. I'm *burning*." My fire had never hurt me before, so why did I now feel every searing lick? "Pete, are your cheeks blistered?"

"Don't fret about me." His breath rattled, his hands preventing me from jerking back to look at him. "I'll be right as rain once you see us through this."

"But I can't!" I cried again, my internal blazes intensifying. By my estimation, we weren't far from tied-to-a-pyre pain. "We're all going to die! We're all going—"

"Don't talk like that." He shook me. "Don't *think* like that."

Was the air flickering? Several conduits screamed—wailed—to answer this question. I was about to beg the redheaded goddess to stop the madness when Pete wrapped me in a stranglehold hug, pressing not just our foreheads together, but our bodies as well. He growled through his own torment, determination in the grit of his teeth, as he murmured against my burning skin, "There's something else I must show you." Then he wrenched my psyche into his, refusing me the distance for failure.

Now, I wasn't just inside Pete. I *was* Pete. And I was staring, entranced, at a girl with resplendent eyes and an arresting smile, wondering how in Christ I'd complete my ordination now.

Of course, she wasn't a girl. She was fae—a Danann, no less. At least, I tried rationalizing that. But, God's tooth, she acted nothing like a Danann, everything about her—the way she talked, the way she moved, the way she cared—screamed human. She was so different, so peculiar and audacious—a challenge, a fascination at every turn. And boyo, could she make me angry—and laugh.

Christ, after some time, she wasn't even scared of me. From naiveté or bravery, I couldn't sort out. Perchance an exasperating blend of both. And how could she be so endearingly unsure of herself whilst also being so bloody certain about everything else? She was the height of natural femininity with the forthrightness of a male, and a menagerie of riddles I'd never ever solve. Danu save my jaded, foolhardy, blemished heart, but I was so beguiled by that.

She was a vixen unawares, a constant temptation for hungry eyes, and I wanted to ravish her slender lines and watch her eyes flood with impassioned rainbows. I fought the draw for longer than I thought possible, and then I fought some more. But in the end—well, I was the scoundrel I'd always been. And she did beg his appearance.

We never did come to the ravishing part, and for that I was in turns grateful and discontent. But to hold her, to kiss her—that was to glimpse heaven, her lips, her breasts, her thighs the holy grail. For I would forever be suspended in those moments when all that I was, was hers.

She was right, of course, though I'd been furious with her at first—for she was everything in this world that I was not. Yet, in the end, her royalty mattered naught. Her destiny mattered naught. Whether she was a queen or a triple goddess with awe-inspiring magic was irrelevant. To me, it was the sweet, lost girl I'd met in the Thorny Rose Tavern who mattered. The girl with the bleeding heart and hopeless romantic's soul was who'd give all of herself to save this wounded world. Now, *she* was a worthy reason for damnation.

So, I'd gone without a farewell, knowing that if I could save her, all would be righted. Instead, she'd saved me, with boggling ferocity and doggedness. I was no better than the mud beneath her revolting boots, a man who'd killed thousands in the defense of his own trivial life. What in hell did she see in me that was worth such a furor? I still didn't know, but she was so bloody certain (as always) that she did.

And now it was my turn. Again. To save her as she'd saved me. To show her the truth of herself—her strength, her significance, her worth. To keep her from destroying herself and the entirety of Eden. Even if her fire engulfed me, burnt me to a pillar of ash as I knelt, clenching her tight, I knew with utter ferocity and doggedness that I'd never let her go.

If we were going down, then we were going down together.

THIRTY-NINE

When the smoke cleared, my sweaty face was squished to Pete's equally sweaty shoulder. I trembled, no longer from pain but wonderment, ineffable and infinite.

How naïve was I? I'd believed communing with Briar, the eroticism of it, had been the peak of personal connection. But with Pete—oh, there was no peak. Only transcendence and an intimacy as astral as the stars. Our passion had pierced my fiery heart, and now I not only felt desire thrumming between us, but also a mutual understanding—we meant something vital to one another.

Pact or no pact, we were *way* beyond friends.

My fingers shaking, I grazed Pete's inflamed cheek. He looked like someone who'd fallen asleep for hours in a tanning bed, his beard crispy, his clavicle blistered. But he was alive, peering down on me in a way that tightened my belly.

"Eh hem."

We bleared at Cissus, having forgotten where we were—that anyone else existed.

"Thought I'd mend you two first," Cissus said as Pete helped me to my unsteady feet. "So you can carry on."

I peered over the stem healer's shoulder. There, the redheaded goddess still stood, waiting. "There's *more*?" I whined.

"*Argh!*" someone in the circle griped, clearly regretting volunteering.

"Yes, daughter," the goddess replied. "But there are only several more gifts to bestow, and they are of gentler dispositions, I assure you."

I sighed, my burns tingling under Cissus' glowing white hands. There were so many questions I wanted to ask the goddess at that moment. Why did the fire hurt me when it never had before? And why the hell would she give me a power like *that*?

Instead, I blurted, "Why do you keep calling me daughter?" I might've expected that of Danu, not the others.

The redhead chuckled again, a pleasant sound reminding me of someone I couldn't place. "Why don't I answer your unspoken questions first?"

Of course, she can read my mind! Why wouldn't that be a thing?

"We gave you my fire, Amy, because we knew you could withstand it, as you were honed in The Before to wield it in the battles to come."

Pete's healing wounds glowed as we shared a grim glance. Yeah, we both knew there would be battles.

"And while you'll always be immune to the effects of your fire, we decided you should experience how it feels to burn this once, so that you realize the magnitude of the destruction and pain you can wreak if you use the fire too liberally. We pray you'll exercise discretion."

"I will," I promised. "We're working on my control, so I won't firebomb people when I'm mad. Which, I've only done once, but—"

Pete squeezed my arm, his gaze saying, *Shorty, shut your gob.* Taking his advice, I clamped my lips.

The redhead's smile spread. "And I call you daughter because I'm Brigid."

At least that made sense. Brigid was *the* fire goddess. My summoning was being held on *her* day. But that didn't explain why she'd call me daughter.

"I'm the Dagda's daughter, and you, Amy, are my direct descendant."

"Ohmigoddess!" I smacked my own head, making Cissus chuckle before he moved onto other patients. "That's right! I knew you were somewhere in my family tree. I just never put it together—that you and I are linked like that." I shook my head, Pete's exasperation compounding. "Does that mean you're, like, my dad's great-grandmother to forever?"

Tenderness softened Brigid's divine face. "Not your father, Amy."

"Huh?"

I nearly swallowed my own tongue as another willowy female, who looked very much like me—as I'd always been told—stepped from Brigid's wild, blazing mane and strolled into the night. She glowed like a moonbeam, stars alight in her long copper hair. Exquisitely gowned in trailing midnight-blue, she glided toward me, her orange-green eyes joyous. She had a broad, round nose like Vi's, and the tilt of her head very much reminded me of Ace. But that smile of hers—it was all mine.

Pete gasped in recognition the moment tears spilled from my eyes. "Mom?"

Without hesitance, she rushed to me, took my teary cheeks in her long, slender hands. And she was *real*. I felt her skin, warm as if she'd never died. I could hear her breath and see the baby fine hairs behind her pointed ears. Mewling, I burrowed into her, and her arms came around me, a security blanket.

"Oh, my sweet little love," she burred, her voice so beautiful, so devastating, that my bones poised to do her bidding. But she uttered only love as she stroked my hair, breathing, "How I've missed you."

I gripped her like she'd disappear. "I—missed you—tooooo." I hiccupped. Several times. "So much."

She thumbed away my tears. "I've been watching over you, Amy. We all have in the Isle." She chuckled, a row of dimples in her right cheek. "We can't wait to see what you'll do next."

I sniffled. "I'm a sit-com star up there?"

"Something like that. As your father likes to joke, you're big in heaven."

I shuddered out a breath I'd been holding for months. "He's with you up there? I was so worried that—because of the curse—because of Gentian—"

"He's there, Amy. He was never destined for anywhere else."

"Is he here with you?" I glanced toward Brigid, my hopes soaring. "Is he hiding in your hair to surprise me too?"

My hopes crashed at Brigid's sympathetic expression.

"He couldn't come, little love," my mother said, caressing my cheek again. "Only females can visit the living after death. Males can't breach the veil between."

Containing my disappointment was a lost cause.

"He's given me a message for you, though. He says, 'Keep thinking with your heart, kiddo, because a heart is what our people need.'"

My lips quivered. "Can—can you give him a message from me?" Because I knew she would go back to the Isle. Though I longed for her to stay with me, never leave me again for the rest of my life, I knew Danu wouldn't let her remain. "Tell him—" I wiped my drippy nose. "Tell him he was right. About Briar."

He's not the one, Daddy had decided.

After that night, I thought maybe—just maybe—I knew who was.

Her eyes dancing, my mother brushed my bangs off my forehead. "He'll be pleased to hear that. He's always pleased to hear when he's right."

I laughed, gushing more tears.

After several more heartwarming moments, my mother's smile dwindled. "I'll have to go soon, Amy. My being down here will soon disrupt the order of things."

I bit back a vehement cry of *no*. "I figured."

"But before I go, I have three more gifts for you."

The circle of conduits damn near mutinied.

So, my mother called out, "Be assured, I think you'll all find these magics much tamer than the others!"

They'd only have to be, right? But *three* of them? "I didn't think you had that many powers, Mom."

"One of them is from your father, Amy. A hereditary gift." Stepping back, she lifted a hand, and a crown of starlight appeared. "The sovereign's soul, so that you may always have the strength and bravery to lead, even when all else oppose you."

There was no hollowing this time, maybe because the power was genetic. Whatever the reason, I was grateful to feel whole as my mother placed the dazzling crown on my head. It tingled, my hair absorbing it like conditioner.

"And from me—nocturnal premonitions." At my snort, she smirked—getting it. "I ken your feelings about it." She glanced Myrrdin's way.

He looked a little worse for wear after hosting my fire, but a hedge healer was balming his burns, and he grimaced at his former student—poignant as a Tragic Fiddlers song.

"It's an infuriating gift—premonition." My mother turned back to me, unadulterated joy sweeping across her gaze. Her own voluptuous lips trembling, she brushed back my bangs. "But sometimes, my little love, it can be an unrivaled blessing." Pressing her forehead to mine, she released a bit of her glow, and we shone together like moonbeams.

When the glow subsided, she took several steps back, wringing her hands at her waist. Rough-voiced, she said, "And lastly, I have something for you—a weapon—that may have some use to you in the war to come."

I liked the word *war* even less than I did the word *battles*. But I listened.

"My siren song." Her chin tipping skyward, she opened her mouth and sang a haunting melody in the most *gorgeous* voice that could've ever existed in eternity. A voice that I'd heard a hundred times before. In the refrains of a dream.

"It was you!" I exclaimed, chilled, when her song ended. An orb, so brilliant it hurt to look at, glowed within her long, elegant throat. "*You* were the voice!"

With a misty smile, my mother turned to Brigid, who strode over, dwarfing my tall, ethereal mother, and plucked the shimmering orb from her throat. Gently, she placed it in a woven case like an egg and shut its lid. Accepting the case, my mother brought it to me.

"It may not be your fit, Amy," she spoke now from inside the box. "But that doesn't mean you can't use it."

Gulping, I took the case when she brought it to me. "Does this mean you won't be able to talk now? In the Isle?"

"Only until you need my voice no more. Then you can gift it back to me. In the meantime—I've other ways of speaking my mind."

I clutched the box. Her voice still glowed through the cracks in the case, like it was ready to burst forth and control some minds. "I promise I'll take care of it for you."

"I know you will, Amy, but be careful with whom you entrust the knowledge of its possession. Gentian would stop at nothing—and I do mean nothing—to have it for himself. And you do *not* want my voice being used against you."

I gulped again. "Got it."

She sighed, almost relieved. Maybe in knowing a part of her would stay with me even after she left. Then she grabbed my face, kissed my cheek, and fled back to Brigid, who took my mother's proffered hand.

Before she disappeared into Brigid's flaming hair again, Mom glanced back over her narrow shoulder with a kind smile. "I knew the truth of you long ago, dark one."

Astounded, I looked to Pete, who'd shuffled aside, almost in shame, during our reunion—and to whom my mother was now most definitely speaking. His whole face flashed in stone-cold stupefaction.

"I pray one day you'll know it too."

Her words were forgiveness itself, and Pete's eyes welled as he bowed his tousled head to her.

My mother caught my gaze one last time. "I love you," she murmured, blowing me a kiss. Then she and the goddesses shot back to the stars in a thunderous whoosh, leaving me windswept, emotionally bedraggled, and responsible for multiple magical weapons of mass destruction.

And the night wasn't even over.

T he party started immediately. Tribalesque drumming began before I'd even given Myrrdin my mother's voice for safekeeping. By the time I'd reached the town square, the wine was already free flowing, folks were already feasting, the bonfires were already blazing, and Eden ran rampant with revelry.

My summoning celebration was nothing like Beltane. Nobody was debauching themselves on the altar of the horned god, Cernunnos (yet), and I wasn't apprehensive at all to join in the fun. I drank, I ate, I sang, I danced—all without the slightest inhibition. Because I felt secure. For once in my life, I felt full and complete and comfortable in my own pale as hell skin. Who cared what anybody thought of me? They could accept me as I was and to hell with them if they couldn't.

Because I'd made it through my summoning. Because I'd met all the greatest legends in Danann herstory. Because my father was at peace in heaven. Because I'd hugged my mother for the first time in 16 years, and she'd gazed at me with unreserved love and pride.

Because I'd seen myself through Pete's eyes.

What he did while I grooved the night away, I couldn't say. But the potent aroma of oranges and oakmoss said he was near.

Once, I did glance up from spinning Jet around like a whirly-gig, Sionna scampering between us in exuberant play, and I caught sight of him. Cissus had done an excellent job healing his wounds. Pete's refreshed skin glowed in the firelight as he partook of spirits with Morus and Riordan. Maybe sensing my gaze, he peeked up from his frothing clay mug. And my word, I thought he'd smoldered at me before my summoning. That was nothing compared to how he looked at me now.

Shivering, I'd spun around and tossed Jet into the air. The scrawny Pixie squealed and flapped his wings to stay afloat. Panting, Sionna pranced beneath his tiny feet. Then, not one to be left out of the fun, she jumped up on her hind legs, her front paws landing on my belly. She wanted a dance with me just like everybody else.

I grinned down at her, waggling her floppy ears, and cooed, "He's still watching me, isn't he?"

She glanced aside to confirm, then smiled at me, stretching her back. I cuddled her head close. "You're my favorite, Sionna."

Her response was a good cheek licking. I wondered if she could taste my happiness.

Eventually, a massive group converged to jig along to the pipes, drums, and fiddles. Anyone who didn't join the masses was forcibly drafted in. Including Pete, who Liatris dragged into the jubilant scrum, where he two-stepped with a wryness clearly meant to mask embarrassment. His cheeks flushed as he swayed like a redwood above a field of shrubs. I knew exactly how *that* felt.

To his credit, though, Pete stayed on the dance floor, and after a bit, his body loosened, and he swept one of the cutest little female faelets I'd ever seen up onto his shoulders. Shrieking in delight, she clapped her tiny violet hands together before burying them in Pete's unruly fluff.

And on Pete's shoulders is where the tiny ryan remained until Jet and his friends decided to go for a swim. Then she dropped from Pete like a pinecone and flitted off to join them, her silvery ringlets bouncing as she ran.

"You'll be ridding your bum of those breeks before you soak them!" Liatris called to Jet, fluttering after him with hands on buxom hips. "Brine's nay good for them, ken!"

After that, the music slowed, and the dance floor thinned, leaving a few left dancing—including Pete and me.

Across the distance, we smirked at each other. He like a wolf, bonfire light flickering over his tan expanse, and me like a vivacious coquette (I hoped), twisting a strand of my hair. Then Pete swaggered over to me, head bowed slightly aside. When he was close enough that I could trace his scars with my eyes, he took my hand and twirled me like a ballerina in a jewelry box until I burst with laughter.

My tipsiness evident now, I gleamed up at him. "From how you looked a minute ago, I didn't think you liked dancing."

"I don't. Especially when it's no more than hedonistic gyration."

"Come on now, dude. I saw what your young adulthood was like on Earth. Hedonism comes second nature to you."

"Mm." What a deep, belly-fluttering sound that was. "Then I simply lack the grace for such free movement." He was a *big* guy, after all. "Christ, I've struggled to keep up with the slowest, most structured dances. My cousin once tried to teach me the minuet. I hobbled her so that she couldn't dance at her own wedding."

"I've never hobbled anyone, but I get having two left feet. I usually avoid dancing in public."

"In public, hm?" Pete's grin slanted. "Does that mean you *do* dance in private?"

Whoo! I fought the urge to fan myself as heat flamed up my neck—and as Pete pulled me closer. "Yes." I smiled like a doof in the framework of his arms. "All the time, actually. In front of my bedroom mirror, using my hairbrush as a microphone, so my droves of invisible fans can hear me sing along to my iBloom."

"They have my sympathies."

My amusement burbled again. Either that or a string of burps. Perhaps both. I'd had a good amount of some fruity, fizzy libation that night. I didn't know what it was made of, but I'd made sure it wasn't moonberries.

Who needed an aphrodisiac, anyway? Emboldened by the glory of the night, I palmed the smooth, warm, sinewy globe of Pete's bare shoulder. Goddess, I wanted to bite into it.

"You know you wish you were a fly on the wall in my bedroom," I teased.

Snap! went the tension between us, though I was baffled it could get any tighter. And those molasses cookie eyes—they hummed, saying Pete might prefer to be closer than the wall.

My breath shuddered as I watched the pulse accelerate in his neck. I nearly trailed my hand up to graze it. "So—about this affinity bond—"

Pete huffed, peering skyward.

"What's so significant about it? Besides it making you my anchor—which you very obviously are, if you haven't—"

"I saw it, Shorty. I kent I was grounding you through the summoning, though, aye, I doubted Myrrdin at first."

My lips pursed. "I don't know about that. I don't think you doubted him so much as hoped he was wrong."

He exhaled again.

"So, what is an affinity bond and why don't you want one?"

Resigned to explaining the matter, something he'd clearly hoped to put off until forever, Pete grumbled, "It's a connection formed between kindred spirits, Shorty." Whether he knew it or not, his hand at my waist snugged deeper into that subtle curve. "It means that on some level, we each feel deep and spiritual empathy for the other."

"Oh." Pondering his explanation, I shrugged. "That doesn't sound like anything too heavy."

Pete's mouth twitched.

"What?"

He loosed a breath. "Formed affinity bonds were how white magic fae kent that a pair could be mated—when they were permitted to mate them."

My breath rushed out of me. "You mean *soul* mated?"

He nodded.

"Wait just a second! Didn't you tell me only *humans* could be turned into soulmates?"

"Aye, well—" He grimaced. "I'm human, aren't I?"

"But *I'm* not. Which is quite obvious now." After I'd met my almighty fire fairy grandmother, how could I deny it?

"As Myrrdin described it to me when first we'd discussed my being your anchor, mating souls isn't as cut and dry as I'd always been made to believe, Shorty. As he put it—your physical body is Danann, but your soul—" He harrumphed—damn near a profanity. "Christ, Shorty, your soul is more human than most humans' souls. It's not just how I see you. It *is* you."

Something in the core of me shimmered like a diamond. "Was I born a human in a Danann body?"

"I can't say. Potentially that. Or potentially your upbringing transformed something *about* your soul, made it more human. They're plainly a messy business, souls." His expression took a mordant cant. "Myrrdin wasn't about to waste his breath detailing it all for me when he didn't feel I needed to know."

Goddess, he's so cute—all perturbed and shit.

"Pete, forgive me for being—well, me—but I don't see why you wouldn't want that kind of bond with someone else. I mean, isn't that the kind of thing 99 percent of people living in any world are looking for? Someone they can feel that close to?"

Goddess, that's what I'd been searching for since I watched Orrin and Talulaha's first kiss on *Kid Meets Life*.

"Aye, Shorty, and I was no exception—until I was abducted into this life of pain and suffering and darkness. And now I'm a harbinger, to boot. I'm a walking bout of heartache for anyone unfortunate enough to be mated to me. Soulmates *need* each other, Shorty. Long separations bring melancholy and misery, and I *live* on the road. And death—" He gulped, trying to contain his emotional response at the idea. "To lose a soulmate is to lose your very heart, and I couldn't place such an onus on anyone, knowing my life is Gentian's to take whenever he has the whim. And my soul?" He shook his head. "My soul will always be tainted with death poppy. Who kens what that might do to a potential mate? And what if Gentian learns I'm no longer demonic? He'd fix that in a blink, damning me, and I suspect, my mate.

"So, there you have it. That's why I've been avoiding such a bond. That's why I've spent decades avoiding the affections of other humans. Because I feared for their happiness, for the sanctity of their own souls. Now, is that a sufficient explanation?"

Warmth bloomed like a rose in my heart. "No," I said.

His laugh smacked of frustration, his gaze intensifying. "Damn you, Shorty. You *madden* me."

Now, there was a line from a novel if I'd ever heard it. Said by the hero right before planting a good one on the heroine. The heroine I rather saw myself as that night.

"It's a moot concern for you right now, anyway." I tried not to let my exhilaration show. Not only was he a closet romantic, but he had so much compassion for the person he might one day love that he'd surrender his own future happiness to safeguard them. He was an Oliver Saint love story with hair—and lots of muscles. "Yes, we have an affinity bond, but we haven't been made soulmates. Right?"

He was slow to agree, suspicious of where my thoughts were going.

"You said that approval is needed to make a couple into soulmates, that the powers that be aren't sanctioning them."

"Aye."

"Then there's nothing to worry about." My breath trembling, I closed the scant distance between us, slid my palms to his warm, fur-dappled chest. I made Pete's breath tremble too, when I batted my lashes the way he *loved*. "We're free to define our own relationship—be whatever we'd like to be to each other."

At his blank expression, I feared I'd been too subtle with my proposition, that he hadn't read between the lines as well as I'd assumed he would. I was about to be blunter when Pete took a sudden step back.

"*No*, Shorty!"

I bit my lip as he shook himself, vexed to his marrow with what I'd offered him—at how I'd tempted him, knowing what he wanted after he'd opened himself so completely to me. Was I taking advantage of his vulnerability? Maybe. But I wasn't sorry about it.

Seeing my delight, he gasped. "You wily little fox! We agreed! We had an understanding! *Friends*, you recall? We *shook* on it, for feck's sake! You gave your word that we'd *never* cross that line!"

He gestured back and forth between us. "We will certainly end in disaster! Whatever bond we've formed, whatever desires we harbor, they—*I*—could only do you harm, you brash little minx! Think, would you? I—I—I won't entertain this impulsive, reckless, foolhardy, shite change of heart of yours to—to wheedle me into sullying my own word! You may have your pretty little red head on arse backwards but—"

Pete ranted in a tangle of scolding and flattery like that for quite a while. I listened without comprehending a single word. Because my heart was pounding too loudly. Because I knew nothing he said would make a difference. Because I knew what I was going to do whenever he shut the hell up.

"I'll thank you to forget this lunacy of yours! And stop eyeing me up like I'm the only slab of meat in the larder!" He ended with a huff, his blackstrap gaze now invoking fantasies of our bodies entwined. "It's indecent, Shorty!"

I gave him my best flirty side-eye. "Are you going to kiss me already?"

Pete huffed, exasperated. His jaw grinding, his eyes sizzling, he fixed me with a delicious, begrudging smirk. "Aye," he rumbled, then advanced on me in one breathtaking, ground-shaking step.

I gasped as he grabbed my face with those rough hands of his and slanted his soft, wide mouth over mine in a firm, sensuous deluge of passion. And just like the night an Incubus had almost driven us to savagery, the man did not waste time with small kissing, which was totally a thing (e.g., Briar), but went right in for the *oh-my-stars* kill. I tasted ale on his tongue as he stroked a resounding response out of me that I hadn't even imagined possible. I'd been aroused before, but this—this was *something else*. And damn Pete's amused grunting, but he knew it too.

As did everyone else in Eden. The raucous cheering made that clear enough.

His own awakening heavy in his breath, Pete withdrew from our kiss. "You can still change your heart back, ken?" His fathomless gaze begged me not to.

Fiending for another hit of his warm mouth, I moaned and reached for his nape. "I won't. I—"

His crushing lips smothered whatever inane thing I was saying. His whiskers tickled my chin as he squeezed my ass in his huge, hot hands. He hiked me up against his ripples and ridges, my legs dangling from his hips as he wended us through the newly swarming crowds, still showing my lips what was what.

"We'll see to Sionna tonight," a voice said, chuckling. Imogen's, I thought.

There was no mistaking Morus's grizzly snigger. "You mean the next several nights, don't you?"

Whistles heralded our departure from the town square. We took our party straight to the warden's hut.

My conviction to act the vixen lasted until Pete and I stood on the threshold to his hut. The moment my toes touched ground again, old but untiring anxieties riddled me.

Am I kissing him right? Is that too much tongue? Should I be more vocal? How should I touch him? Should I take the lead again? Just because he knows what he's doing doesn't mean he wants to do all the work for the rest of the night. So, suck it up, buttercup, and say something sexy to get the balls rolling!

Then I gulped through our cooling lip lock, knowing whatever I'd say next would be the stupidest shit I'd ever uttered.

I stared up at Pete, mayhem in my face. He caressed my cheeks, smiling with a kind sort of understanding, then clasped my hand and spun me the way he'd done on the "dance floor." I giggled like I'd gone on a swift dip down a rolling hill.

My goodness, he is good at alleviating jitters, isn't he?

Pete then hooked my waist and pulled me back against him and his heat. My bangs snarled in his beard.

"Get out of your head," he murmured deep in his throat against my temple. His hand snaked up my body to take my jaw. My heart sped into a gallop when he tilted my head aside and fastened his greedy mouth to my neck like a famished Vampire.

I shuddered as he devoured me. Goddess, his tongue had so many good uses.

"Hm," he grunted when I'd grown content to sport his hickeys. Now I got why people let them happen. "Not there?"

Huh? Yes, please, there!

He began to nibble up the curve of my jaw—also rather nice.

"Hm," he grunted again, then moved his mouth, husky breaths and all, to my ear.

He might as well have tazed me. Electric lust cabled through me, hijacking my every nerve. Gooseflesh itself, I bowed back into Pete's solidity and cried out, *"Eeeeee,"* when my quivering legs gave out on me.

Pete scooped me up. "There it is," he murmured against that ear as I bucked in his capable arms. "Thought that was it."

"Oh! *Oh,* my Goddess!" I shuddered, my neck arcing. "If you keep doing that, I'm going to have a heart attack!"

"Oh, Shorty, I can make your heart skip faster than that," he rumbled against my arch, liquefying me. "You like it, don't you?"

"*Yes!*" I gasped in accusation.

"Then trust your body. Stop thinking. Just feel. And watch. And taste." At that, Pete's mouth seized mine again, and he conveyed us to the feather mattress.

In all honesty, I was ready to get down to brass tacks before my summoning had concluded. Pete couldn't pretend otherwise, his fingers delving between my dewy thighs the moment they had access, precise as heat-seeking missiles. Which made me squirm back against the rock-hard length barely contained by his pants. But he wasn't keen on beginning the main event until I was a senseless, sweaty, shivering, panting puddle of goo in his arms, driven insane by that artful mouth of his, which seemed intent on tasting every inch of my blushing skin.

Mindlessness, though, was a blessing. Not even in disguise. Pete was right. I wasn't capable of bashfulness when he peeled me out of my dress and bared me to his searing, feline gaze, his greedy hands. I couldn't worry that my breasts were too small, my ass non-existent as I lay nude beneath him, being suckled, groped, and fingered at once. In fact, I had an out-of-body experience when those fingers, so rough and strong and dexterous, buried themselves inside me, and I didn't give a damn what he might think of me when I moaned directives on how I wanted it—hard, slow, and now. He only chuckled against my ear, "That's how I like it too," before he untied his drawstring and offered his hot, tumescent, drool-worthy goods to my curious touch.

It was all just so easy, that scintillating leadup. Then, I suddenly found myself sprawled upon the rumpled mattress, my calves resting on Pete's shoulders as he and his mouthwatering body rose over me. And then it just happened. Naturally, effortlessly, breathtakingly. There was no awkward bumping or gritting of teeth. Pete and I, we just breathed together and converged.

There was a word for what we did after that. A word I overused, for it could fit in almost any sentence. But in the context of sex—well, teehee. Just thinking it made me bashful. That didn't make it any less fitting, of course. Because Pete didn't cosset me like a porcelain doll. No, I was modeling clay to him, something that could take the weight of him and reform. And I reformed over and over as he drove into me, every impact like the punctuation of his name inside me—Pete, Pete, Pete, Pete, Pete, Pete, *PETE*!

I couldn't get enough of his name.

Of knowing it was him.

Of knowing it was his voice murmuring in my ear.

"Oh, oh, oh, oh!" I cried, my pleasure coarsening my voice as I clutched Pete's elbows, now straddling him. My head fell back as I arched into him, gooseflesh cording my neck. My breasts shivered in feverish exaltation as he licked them, nibbled them. Fire surged in my core as he clutched my ass, worked me back down on his pulsation. "Oh, Pete, *YES, please*!"

Feasting on my abandon, Pete wove his fingers through my hair. "Look at me, Shorty." His bass brogue was like roasted honey, his smile lazy and dark when I assented. "I want to watch your eyes when this happens."

I moaned, unbridled. Because, *freaking mother above*, it was happening.

Then *it* happened. With such piercing, euphoric power that I convulsed, my nerves haywire with sensation. Pete clenched me tight like he meant to hold me together. And he did watch in glazed voracity as rapture crested in my eyes. What color they turned, he didn't say, but from his awe, they must've been something spectacular.

When I finally collapsed into him, twitching and panting, Pete kissed me with arresting tenderness. He bore me back upon the mattress and rocked me to euphoria again. He rocked himself there with me that time, his thrusts savage—echoing in my bones. And I happily submitted to his will, giving over to his predation like a lioness in season. I found myself just as transfixed with his surrender as he'd been with mine.

At once bestial and helpless, he gripped me so hard in those last crushing, sublime moments that I felt his fingerprints in my soul. I was moved by everything I'd ever felt for this glorious, kind, cranky, irreverent, honest man—for my Pete—and lost my hands in his fluffy brown hair, kissing him like an old school movie star, my heart igniting.

Afterward, we lay together, limp. Smoke tendrilling from my fingertips. Pete's beard scratched my forehead as I hummed against his red hot, throbbing neck. I didn't know what I was humming. I didn't even know why. I just felt like I needed to, so I did.

His laugh a rumble in my nether bits, Pete groaned and rolled to his back. "Is that one of the travesties from your squat little music box?"

I snorted. "No, but I could hum you one if you'd prefer."

"Quite all right, Shorty." Smug, he smacked his lips together. "You've expended your voice enough on my account."

I was rather hoarse, I'd give him that. But I was nowhere near expended.

I popped up in our love nest. Pete blinked as I climbed atop his ripples like a warrior on her mount. His sweat slicking my thighs, I pinned his wrists by his handsome, disheveled head. "You're silly." I nipped at his nose, my rosy nipples grazing his firm pecks. And lower—I could feel he was still game. "I'm not done with you yet."

His molasses eyes blazing, Pete licked his reddened, smirking lips and folded one arm behind his head. "Go on then, Shorty. Ride me 'til you set the bed afire."

Now, I didn't set the bed on fire. But I came damn close.

FORTY

Beyond Eden, the suns might've been rising by the time Pete and I succumbed to sleep. I dozed off first, one leg slung across Pete's hips. Weary as I was, that tiny bit of contact was good enough for me. But Pete gathered my limp parts into him. "That's more like it," he grumbled once I lay nestled back within the spoon of his body, my head tucked under his chin and resting on his bicep. I fell asleep happy, tears pooling in my eyes.

Because I'd been searching my whole life for a man who'd hold me in my sleep.

Days passed. Maybe weeks. I lost track. Pete and I spent our waking hours choring, socializing, and training. At days' end, we always retreated to the warden's hut for another night of *oohs, ahhs, and oh, yes, theres!* I was content for things to remain that way forever. As things could remain in Eden. And Pete—as relaxed as he seemed in his day-to-day with me—I was *not* just imagining that he felt the same way.

Leave it to Myrrdin, though, to burst our bubble.

One night, as Pete and I were finishing up dinner with some of our closer friends, Myrrdin traipsed into our campfire ring. Just in time to overhear Imogen say cheekily to me, "Blimey, lovey, what have you been about these past few days, hm?" Her brown eyes sparkled with good humor. "Rolling about in a vat of orange rinds if your scent is to be believed."

Everyone laughed, knowing Pete to be the vat of orange rinds in her playful jab. But Myrrdin barely cracked a smile as he asked Pete and I for a word.

"I've been having unsettling visions." Myrddin was calm and measured when we'd convened with him and the clerics, though his crystalline gaze had clouded. "I don't yet grasp what they're telling me, but *something* is happening in the world outside Eden. Some form of corruption has taken hold of the Spring Palace."

I glanced aside at the woven case sitting in the corner of Myrrdin's cabin, where my mother's voice glowed, a captive star—silenced by a rat and a Shadow Prince. "Didn't we already know that, though? I mean, we all had to guess that someone in the Spring Palace is working with Gentian. And has been for years."

"Yes, Amy." Myrrdin sat at his tree stump table, dropping his sharp chin into his palm. Was it a trick of the fae asters, or was his bronzy-brown skin a bit sallow? I wondered if he'd been sleeping. "And we know who at least one of those duplicitous louts is—your grandfather."

He might as well have smacked me.

"Your mother's birth father, Lord Luxovious Staghorn, whom your lovely and benevolent grandmother revoked her vows from while your mother was still a faelet. He's closely affiliated with Gentian. In fact, he affianced your mother to Gentian before—"

"I know," I interrupted, growing impatient. "Uncle Neel told me the story. Do you think he's the traitor?" Did Myrrdin think my grandfather was the one responsible for "fixing" my parents' security detail the night my mother died? Did he think my grandfather aided his own daughter's murderer?

"I can't be certain, Amy, but I sincerely doubt it."

Something tight inside me unwound.

"He's too blatant in his leanings to sabotage the inner workings of court life. Anyone with a pinch of intelligence at the Spring Palace would know to prevent his dealings in anything vital. He's a member of the Danann elders, yes, but he has no sway, his credibility questionable."

This conversation was starting to irk me. I knew why but was ashamed to admit it. "All right—so, how is this new corruption any different from the *old* corruption? I mean, why are you suddenly so bothered by it when you weren't before? And what exactly do you want me to do about it?"

Myrrdin and the clerics shared a wry, almost reproving look.

I pretended not to see it as Myrrdin took in a patient breath. "Amy, this new corruption, whatever it is, seems to be affecting the decision makers at the palace now. Someone or something is distorting their judgment."

I gulped. "Who—whose judgment?"

As terse as I'd ever heard him, Myrrdin replied, "You already know who."

Of course, I did, and I did *not* want to think about him. Not while everything I'd ever wanted stood so close behind me, his hand at my back.

At my stricken expression, Myrrdin softened. "Child, I know you're frightened of losing what you've found here, of facing what you've—"

"Thank you for the warning, Myrrdin. But until you know more about what's happening at the palace, I can't help. So—" I spun about, grabbed a stunned Pete by his collar, and towed him from the cabin. Away from the yoke of my uncertain but prickly future.

"J aysus, there's really nothing back here," Pete teased later, looping an arm across my hips. He'd been caressing my bottom for several minutes, sporadically kissing the new triple spirals Danu had branded me with during my summoning. My dimples of Venus featured as the epicenter in each triskelion.

Failing at not thinking about *things*, I barely managed a giggle for Pete's joke. Not because he'd offended me. Coming from someone else, that remark might've cut deep. But Pete—I knew he found my lacking derriere cute.

"It's my non-butt. It's really just an extension of my legs."

Pete chuckled. "Aye, I like it—non-butt." Still chuckling, he trailed a line of kisses from my tailbone to my shoulder, his beard tickling the whole way. If I weren't in so sour a mood, I'd have been shivering by then, just as Pete intended. As I was, however, none of his tricks turned me on.

After several more erotic but fruitless shoulder smooches, Pete emitted a leaden sigh and sat up, naked. As we always were in that bed. "Do you want to talk about it, Shorty?" I loved how he asked me for my thoughts without demanding them.

I pouted into my folded arms. "No."

"Aye, all right then."

I turned to peer up at him, chewing my lip. "What are *you* thinking?"

His wide mouth quirked. "About your arse there. About these lips here." He thumbed my bottom lip, making me flush. But he didn't defer my question.

"I mean about what Myrrdin told us. About the corruption. There's nothing I can do about it right now. Is there?"

Pete raked his hair, souring. "Shorty, I don't know. How can I say one way or the other? We don't even know what Myrrdin meant by 'corruption.'"

"But that's what I mean. If Myrrdin doesn't know what he's talking about yet, then how can I do anything about it? Does he just expect me to fly off to the Spring Palace? To go on a wild goose chase in search of this mysterious someone or something?" I paused, my heart cracking open. "Why are you looking at me like that?"

Pete's mouth twisted. "Because you're not asking for my thoughts. You're asking me to agree with you."

I stiffened, sitting up with him. "And you don't?"

Cursing, Pete jerked up from the mattress and strode, nude muscles rippling, past where Sionna snoozed on her own new feather bed, sprawled on her back in an odd contortion only she could find comfortable. He swept over to the table where we'd left a pitcher of water and some mugs. "What is it you want me to say?" Pete plopped upon a stump in the shadows. His hairy legs spread wide in casual shamelessness. "You want me to tell you to forget the Spring Palace even exists, that you can relinquish your crown, your duties to your people, and your destiny, so that you may spend eternity here in Eden playing house?"

I flinched. Because I wasn't playing; I hadn't thought he was either.

Fuming, Pete poured himself a mugful of water. "I can't do that, Shorty. And I can't believe you'd want me to either."

Tears blurred my vision. I turned away from him.

"You told the goddesses you were ready," Pete murmured. "At your summoning."

Sniffling, I swiped one tear away. Ten more replaced it. "What the hell did I know? I didn't know at that moment, that you—that this—that *all* this—"

"Aw, *Shorty*."

I couldn't even bring myself to look at him when he returned to my side. Or when he hooked an arm around me. Instead, I snuffled into my hand like a pig. "I didn't know I'd be so happy here. In my life, with myself, with—with you."

"Shorty—"

"No, listen, Pete!" I faced him, my cheeks dripping. "I *like* myself when I'm here! I *like* myself when I'm with you! Because this person you know—she's me! And I can't be her at the Spring Palace! I can't—" I despaired just imagining my life without him beside me. "I can't just give her up to be whoever they *feel* I should be. How can anyone expect me to do that? Least of all you!"

Pete held me as I shuddered in remembrance of all the etiquette, all the decorum, all the politics I'd have to surmount. *You'd be ridiculed as weak, ineffectual, hysterical, [and] dimwitted,* Uncle Neel's warnings echoed through my mind, shredding my newfound confidence. I pictured myself at court—mocked, sneered at, and degraded for merely accepting my birthright. "Oh, Goddess." I dropped my head into my hands. "Pete, they don't even want me to be queen. They want me to be a figurehead."

Pete stiffened. "*Who?*"

"*Everyone!*" I cried. "My aunt, my uncle, all the elders, probably all the gentry, and the council. Probably tons of other factions I don't even know about! Just because I'm female! They all expect me to marry Briar and give him all the power! They all view me as a baby-making factory who should sit in the background, smiling and looking pretty."

The corner of Pete's jaw twitched. "Briar included?"

"Probably. I mean, he gave me the choice of taking the throne if I wanted it, but he never really let me think about it. He kind of decided he would take it for me."

"What do you mean he *gave* you the choice? Was that choice his to give?"

I paused. "Well, no—"

"Whose choice was it?"

My lips trembled, more tears cascading. "Daddy's."

"That's right." Pete shifted on the mattress. "You know I have my—animosities—where your father's concerned, but I'll give the auld lad one thing—he knew what he was doing when he handed you that crown."

And, Goddess, I hope I don't disappoint him.

"He knew he was giving it to the right person, Shorty. The *only* person who'd right all the wrongs and dislodge Gentian's grip on his subjects. He knew you were strong-willed enough to fight for those who couldn't fight for themselves."

"But I'm scared," I wept into his neck. "And so fucking tired of fighting."

Pete withdrew to eye me, brow arched. "You ken who you're talking to, don't you?"

"Ugh." I smacked myself in the head. Had I just whined about fighting to a man who'd done nothing but fight for well over 200 years? "I'm such a cry-baby."

"Aye." He smiled. "A little."

"I'm sorry."

"Forgiven." He kissed my forehead. "But so as we're clear, it matters naught where you are, Shorty. You'll always be you—even if those wankers at court try to stifle you. If there's one thing I know about Amy Larkspur, it's that she'll eventually burst out of her shell in a blaze of fire—especially if someone dares call her a b—"

I pressed my finger to his lips. "Don't you speak that evil."

His eyes glimmered. "As I said—if they start haranguing you, it's at their peril. You'll show them the error of their ways."

That harkened my father's voice. *You're not a passive person, Amy. Don't act like one.*

"But they still want me to marry Briar. He still wants to marry me." As far as I knew. "What should I do about that?"

Pete blinked at me, dark eyes growing darker. "Don't marry him."

I almost deflated in relief. That wasn't just advice he'd given me. Or even a request. It was a full-fledged directive. "I—I won't," I promised.

His eyes instantly lightened.

"But they'll try—"

"Nobody can force you into marriage, Shorty, and they can't force you off the throne. No matter what they tell you. It's all in the royal charter. I've read it. Front to back."

"What? When?" *I* hadn't even read the royal charter yet, this crucial document that dictated major portions of my life.

"On the road somewhere during a shite. Printed on a pamphlet, it was, in tiny script. But I have mighty sharp sight, and I like to occupy my mind during a shite. Otherwise, it's just me squatting there, watching the clouds, and counting my farts."

And just like that, we'd reached the stage in our romance where not everything he said was charming. Or even necessary.

"Way too much detail about the shitting, dude. Can we get back to the charter, please?"

Pleased with himself, Pete agreed. "If memory serves, it states that a sovereign has the final say in their own marriage, though there may have been nuptial agreements formed prior to said sovereign's coming of age. And well before that, it also states that succession will fall to the sovereign's first born, and none shall dispute the heir's claim unless the sovereign does so formally at court. And in your case, Shorty, your father did not dispute you."

I smiled. "He didn't."

We delighted together in these revelations, but the heavy subject matter soon weighed upon us. Eventually, Pete exhaled. "I ken you don't want to be queen. That you'd rather live here in peace until you'd choose to join your parents in the Isle. I cannot and will not fault you for that. Christ, I've wished the same peace for myself. But we *need* you, Shorty." Something painful flitted through his gaze, and I felt like he'd forced himself to say this. Forced himself to say the words that would make me leave him. "The people here are suffering. Remember, too, all those beyns from Humwater Dell. They need you. *Maggie* needs you."

Wanting to cry for *everyone*, I whimpered, "I know."

"And if Myrrdin thinks there's something you can do to prevent more strife from befalling people like me, then I say, *yes*, Shorty. Yes. Fly to the Spring Palace and do your damndest to stop it." He opined this with such conviction, such passion. Such grief.

"I'm afraid I must leave here soon, anyhow." His shoulders slumped with the declaration, and my guts clenched.

He was going whether I decided to leave or not?

"It's near the time now that Gentian will realize I've rebelled, if he hasn't already, and he'll be on the chase for me." Grave, Pete shook his ankle to bring his shadow tether to light. Inky tendrils like snake tongues licked his skin before vanishing. "I must make the fatal move and burn this off—run for shelter—before he follows it. If he finds me here, everyone in Eden is done for." He rubbed his forehead, a bit droll in the face. "Seeing as you've forbidden me to sacrifice myself for you, I think I'll make my way to the Winter Court. I've heard the governing reeve there detests Gentian. Mayhap he'll grant me asylum."

My breath stuck in my throat as Pete fell silent, assessing his options. He seemed so resigned, so calm. But I was already freaking out. What if the reeve of Winter didn't grant him asylum? Then he'd be a sitting duck in a pond full of harbingers and death poppies.

What if he had no intention of going to the Winter Court at all? What if he was still determined to martyr himself for my safety and had posed this story of asylum as a smoke screen? I glanced aside at my book bag, lying slumped on the floor beside Sionna's bed. Was Andy still lounging inside? Pete didn't lie easily, but if he thought he was saving my life—

I wasn't about to let these shit questions haunt me. Mother save me, I knew I shouldn't go where my mind had led me, that I shouldn't broach this subject now when we'd never discussed it before. I knew I shouldn't get my hopes up. But I also knew I was going to do all these things. Right then and there.

"For the sake of argument," I started, my eyes doing a nervous bounce from him to my knees. "Let's say I'll go. That I'll pack up and head off to the Spring Palace to take on this corruption, Gentian, and anyone else who wants a piece of me."

Pete laughed. "Interesting adage."

I gulped. "If I did that—"

He waited, blinking and clueless.

"Would—would you follow me? If I asked you to?"

I might as well have walloped him with a frying pan. He bleared at me as if I had.

Could a person strangle themselves if they swallowed with enough force? I feared I'd find out if he didn't say something soon.

A range of emotions flitted across Pete's face, my hopes straining further with each moment. At last, I couldn't take it anymore.

"Just—never mind." Turning from him, I frowned down at my hands, my heart already breaking. "I know I have no right to ask that of you. You made it clear in the first place that you didn't want us to get too entangled, that we'd eventually be a disaster. I know I kind of seduced you into what we've been doing, and you don't owe me anything. Forget I asked."

Regarding me like a puzzle he couldn't piece together, Pete clicked his tongue. "You ken I didn't bring up my having to flee so you'd offer me safety from Gentian, Shorty?"

I rolled my eyes. "Whyever would you do such a thing? A male asking a *female* for protection?" I feigned appall. "How would you ever hold your head up again in a locker room?"

Getting the general gist of my snark, Pete smirked. "Aye."

I returned to my pout.

"And, aye, you did seduce me—the moment you told that first joke at the Thorny Rose Tavern, if you're curious. Long before your summoning."

I stared at him, flabbergasted.

"And though we'll likely end in heartache, I don't regret what we've been doing. Not at all. But consider for a moment our lot if I follow you to the Spring Palace. Do you ken what they'll say of us at court? The queen and her lowly human lover?" His mouth quirked. "They'll say I'm your concubine, your kept man, your doxy."

I grumbled, hating my ignorance of race relations. Hating that he was probably right. "I get it, Pete. You don't have to come if you don't want to. I just—" I swallowed my sadness. "I was just wondering what you'd do if I asked."

His brow furrowed. "Are you truly asking me?"

My voice went AWOL for a beat before I breathed, "Well—yeah."

I watched his expression slant, his tenderness devastating. "Then allow me to answer, woman, before you decide you ken my mind."

Wondering what in tarnation was going on in said mind, I watched as Pete cleared his throat, slapped his knees, and pushed to his feet. Then he proffered me a bear paw. "Stand for me, Shorty."

Blinking, I took his hand and rose before him, this harbinger who'd stolen me away in the night just to help me find myself. The torchlight cast him in diffused sepia tones, reminding me of the illustrations from my old *Grimm's Fairytales* anthology. The effect became even more surreal when Pete took a knee before me, still clasping my fingers. I half expected a diamond ring to appear when our eyes met. Of course, that's not what happened. Something deeper was in the works.

"I'd like to swear you an oath, Shorty, if you'll have it. I don't expect one in return, for I ken you'll likely be unable to keep it with the crown atop your head."

I wanted to argue but feared I'd stop the beauteous, romantic things pouring from his handsome mouth.

"But if you've no objection, I'd like to pledge myself to you. With an ancient oath my auld grand-da taught me. May I?"

I gaped at him like he was the densest man who'd ever lived. "*Yeah!*"

Chuckling, Pete kissed my knuckles. "Amy Larkspur—my queen, my goddess, my rainbow-eyed girl—I do solemnly swear in the name of our lord and savior, Jesus Christ, that you have my loyalty, my confidence, my friendship—and my heart—for as long as you wish."

My rainbow eyes misted when Pete dropped my hand. "And I promise you this—"
Hunching, he deftly hiked one of my legs over his brawny shoulder, his hands now palming
my bottom. I sputtered as he turned his mouth toward my inner thigh. "I'll follow you to
the Spring Palace." He nuzzled the delicate skin there, then grazed slightly left to do it again.
"I'll follow you to the Shadow Court." He moved his mouth again.

And then—

"Oh, mother above, Pete," I moaned, my neck arcing back as he continued his oath,
marking each new vow with another exquisite nibble.

"I'll follow you to the end of days—"

"Mm—"

"I'll follow you to war—"

"Are you for real right now?"

"I'll follow you to ruin—"

"This is the best promise *ever*."

"I'll follow you through fire—"

"You really weren't lying about that silver tongue."

"I'll follow you to hell itself—"

"Oh, *Goddess*! Your *grand-da* taught you this?"

His laughter vibrated through my core, and I shuddered as he finished with, "I'll follow
you *anywhere*, and I won't leave your side until you ask it of me."

Pleasure thickened my giggles. "Fat chance of that after *this*."

Stilling, Pete grinned against me. "Even so, I mean it, Shorty." Sincerity sparkled in the
gaze angled up at me. "All that I am is yours until you don't want me."

My heart expanded near to bursting. Here he was, this hardened fighter, being so vulnerable with me, just as he'd been in the deepest throes of our communing. His inner monologue
now echoed through my mind: *for I would forever be suspended in those moments when all
that I was, was hers.*

Where was a bluebird to sing to when a princess needed one? "Oh, Pete," I breathed at
his silken sentiments, his silken lips. "I'll never not want you."

At that, he set me on the edge of the mattress, my thighs snugging his kneeling warmth.
"Do you accept my pledge?"

I smiled. "*Yes.*"

My eyes fluttered closed upon a vision of Pete's hot gaze staring up at me, his tongue
parting the seam between my legs. It looked as sinful as it felt.

Then I lay back, a quivering mess, as he sealed his oath with an utterly *perfect* kiss. No
magic in the world could've ever enchanted me more.

"Why are you so certain our relationship will eventually end?" I asked Pete later. I lay in the crook of his arm, playing with his chest hair, the sea breeze caressing our entwined bodies. "We're so good together—and we have an affinity bond. Is it just because you're human, and I'm Danann?"

Eyelids drooping, Pete angled to meet my gaze. "Aye, but not in the manner you mean. I ken well enough what the tossers at court will say of me being human, and their insults won't bother me a fecking lick." He snorted, kissing my forehead. "You ken, I've likely been called worse. Christ, it'll take more than a little degradation to turn my head, Shorty."

"Then why is race such an insurmountable obstacle?"

"You recall our talk that night we supped with my harbinger kin?"

"What about it?"

"Do you recall why so many Danann beyns paid for the use of my body?"

I cringed, hating every single one of those beyns. Pete wasn't a freaking vibrator. "Yeah, you said it was because they didn't have to worry—" My throat closed.

"That they could become pregnant?" Pete finished my thought. "Aye, Shorty, because humans and fae *cannot* conceive."

I stared, blindsided.

"I'll never be able to give you babies. Or faelets. Or anything in between. And I find it difficult to believe that someone with a heart such as yours has never harbored dreams of motherhood."

I bit my lip, consternated. I did harbor those dreams. But my dreams of him were much more vivid.

"One day you're going to get that itch I can't scratch, and then—" He lifted a hand in the poignant sentiment: *what will be will be.* "Then the pain will fall in torrents. Upon us both. In the end, you'll realize you must move on and find someone else—someone who can give you the family you deserve."

He still must not have grasped how stubborn a chick I could be. I'd spent my whole life fighting for things I was told I couldn't have.

"And you're certain that we can never—?" I wiggled my fingers.

"As certain as hundreds of years of illicit behavior can make a man."

I grunted, thought just one more minute, then sighed, cuddling into him. "You know, Pete, I don't see this issue bothering me in the future as much as you think it will."

He kissed my forehead again. "Spoken like the 20-year-old nitwit you are."

"*Hey.*" I pinched his nipple—an action that made him yelp like a Saint Bernard puppy.

When Pete settled, he bundled me against him and murmured, "You'll see."

We fell asleep that night snuggled close in our mutual contentment, our eyes wide open. Nothing we saw in the distance made us want to blink.

FORTY-ONE

Pete

Aloud, "Eh hem," woke Pete. How long he'd slept, he didn't ken, but he felt well-rested. Shorty dozed skin to skin with him, drooling on his bicep, her hair tickling his ribs. Rubbing his eyes, Pete found the source of the disturbance at the foot of the bed—where Sedge stood, peaky and sardonic.

Partially sitting, Pete glanced down at Shorty—Aphrodite in slumber. His lips hitched into a smirk. He couldn't even feign remorse.

Sedge tossed up a hand. "What was the *one* thing we agreed you shouldn't do, Pete?"

After searching his soul for a sheepish reply, Pete settled on a half-hearted, "Oops."

Saying something unsavory under his breath, Sedge stalked to the doorway. "Come find me when you're decent. And wipe that shite grin off your face, or I'll do it for you."

Later while Shorty was bathing (it was a wonder she still had skin as frequently as she scrubbed it), Pete went to find Sedge—fully clothed, as ordered.

He found him, half-clothed himself in the warmth of Eden's eternal gloaming, restocking the garden's tool shanty, which stood beneath an enormous fae fig tree with bright red leaves. Sidestepping Kit, who lay in the grass, wolfing fallen fruits, Pete approached Sedge as a blaring donkey bray rankled the tree ape communities.

"You found Bob," Pete started, smiling at his auld, cantankerous beast. He patted Bob's dappled haunch until he calmed. "However did you manage to get him down the ravine?"

"Didn't." Sedge hoisted a crate of agricultural tools out of the wagon bed. "Took the long way. And Bob found *me*. Must've been avoiding the Leprechauns. They were nosing around nearby when he and I crossed paths. I'd led a handful of other harbingers into the Woebegone Wood, as you said, but the Leprechauns—they wouldn't take my bait. Anyhow, had to kill their hounds, I did, before we could give them the slip."

"Ah, that explains that."

"Explains what?"

"Why their hounds were missing when they caught me."

Sedge froze, then dropped the crate by the shanty. He set his lethal hands on his hips and eyed Pete, a parent tempted to box his child's ear. "Tell me all."

So, Pete told him—from discovering Shorty was the Aurora to the night of her summoning.

Afterward, Sedge sighed. "I suppose we owe the princess a debt for saving your sorry hide."

Pete leaned back against his wagon, arms folded. "Aye, she did." Frankly, the effort she put forth to do so still mystified him. If not for her constant, pestering presence, Pete might've let Gentian's plague take him. Because Danu knew, he'd suffered something fierce. As anyone whose lungs had turned against him would.

Now, Pete suspected that he wasn't only Shorty's anchor. Could she also be his?

"But how is an affinity bond even possible betwixt the two of you?" Sedge asked. "She's fae."

"Her body is. Her spirit, however—well, I've been assured it's human."

Sedge's triangular brows rose. "*Human?*"

"Mm-hm." Pete smirked. "Imagine my surprise."

After several moments, Sedge finally chuckled to himself. "Maybe that's what I scented on you two—the scent that drew the Incubus—that bond."

Pete's own nostrils flared, whiffing the tang of sweat, citrus, and oak moss as always, just now mingling with notes of morning dew and fresh pears. A heady, potent combination. Much stronger than it would be from just having a ride. "Sorry if we offend your senses."

"Nothing amiss with my senses. Yours, however, are lacking—at least in your head."

Pete grunted, mostly agreeing.

"Tell me true now, mate—have you fallen in love with her?"

Lost for words—maybe willfully—Pete turned up a hand in response.

Cussing, Sedge pinched the bridge of his bulbous nose. "Blast you, Pete, you're a dead man—or a demon—when next you venture to the Shadow Palace. You ken that, don't you?"

Cringing, Pete raked his hair. "About that—"

Then he confessed the pledge he'd made to Shorty just hours before.

Sedge's coal black eyes bulged from his head. "*Christ*, man! Were you pickled when you vowed this?"

"No, I—" Pete shrugged. "I just wanted to do it."

Suddenly, the Vampire's skin drained to gray, making Pete wonder how his stock of human blood held up. "Wait just one blighted moment. What does she ken about her totem? About what it meant when she gave it over to you?"

"She kens nothing about that," Pete assured Sedge. "And it meant *nothing*. It was as sentimental as anyone else in Eden giving me—or you—their totem."

"Aye, so we can feed them to Samain's Passion. Shorty gave hers to you for *safekeeping*, and you well ken the difference."

"I returned her the poppet soon after, anyhow."

"Good. Wouldn't want *either* of you clotheads imagining that now you're wed. Because where I come from, entrusting your totem to someone is all it takes."

"It was a harmless, innocent gesture, Sedge. Don't make a dither about it."

"You think *I'm* making a dither? Remember, Pete—you've formed an affinity bond with the crown princess—the *betrothed* crown princess."

Pete couldn't keep his mouth from twisting.

"Imagine the dither you'll incur when you try to claim her for yourself."

Pete was suddenly too warm for comfort. "I'll make no claim on her. Because, aye, I have no claim on her. But neither does *he*."

Shorty's intended—the worthless milksop who'd allowed her abduction—he could bugger the feck off.

Sedge scoffed.

"She's a blasted triple goddess, Sedge. She's the Aurora." And he was damn proud of the spirited beyn—the woman—he'd watched come into her own. "You don't make claims on her. *She* makes claims on you."

Sedge's mouth bunched. "You ken that's not how this world works, Pete."

"Aye, well, she's going to change this world. And, *Christ*, isn't that what we've been striving for all these years? Isn't she *precisely* what we've been waiting for?"

"I don't know, Pete! And neither do you!"

"Aye, I do, my friend. Because I've seen what she can do."

"What she can do? Are we speaking of the beyn who's too squeamish to skin her own supper? The one whose arms are too weak to split a log in twain? The one who shrieks whenever she encounters a new bug? That one?"

Pete grunted. "Aye, well—even fire sylphen have their flaws."

Sedge's mouth slowly rounded into an O.

"Did I neglect to mention how Shorty killed the Leprechauns?" Smug, Pete kicked a skinkcrab snapping at his boot. "She roasted them like stuffed geese—set fire to the whole bloody jungle."

Pete had never seen his friend so shocked. "*Shorty* caused that wildfire?"

"Aye."

"Gripes! You ken that's why I haven't shown 'til now? Couldn't get past the barricades for weeks—the palace tasked all Lithalaly's high officials with containing the blaze. I heard tell water wasn't even of use in some parts."

Pete watched the crab skitter away. "As Shorty learns more control over her fire, it's getting harder to douse. Her moods play some role in it as well—and the kind of fire she sprays."

"She has more than *one* kind of fire?"

"Aye, and fire's not even her only gift."

Sedge rubbed his forehead. "Aye, she's a zephyrist too. I recall."

"She's more than even that, Sedge. Shorty has three principal powers. *Three*. And six secondaries, as well. What's more, they're undetectable because some ingenious Witch shrouded her when she crossed the portal. So not only is she astonishingly powerful, my friend, but none of her enemies will ken what's biding in her, so they'll *never* be prepared if they're foolish enough to challenge her. Which, rest assured, they will be."

Sedge blinked several times, stupefied.

Pete arched a brow. "Still skeptical?"

"No." Sedge thought for a moment, his pale face lighting up. "No, I'm actually thinking—I'm thinking Gentian might just meet his match."

Pete clicked his tongue. "*Please.*" Dear lord, had he just mimicked Shorty? "Gentian's no match at all for our Aurora."

Amy

I stared at the most beautiful tree I'd ever seen. Surely the most beautiful tree to exist in time. More than double the diameter of Angel Oak, its heavy branches uplifted outward like a child reaching for its mother. Not a single limb touched the ground. Its rich, green leaves resembled those of a catalpa tree, large and droopy, and served as shade for the myriad of whimsical fae creatures I spied scurrying up and down its knotty boughs. Somehow the tree was both flowering and fruitful. And the fruits—they were big, juicy, ruby-red apples. So luscious they might as well have sported signs saying, *Eat me.*

Chills raced up my arms as I padded over to Myrrdin. He knelt before the tree, peaceful and introspective. I'd gone looking for him at his cabin, and his clerics had told me I'd find him here if I continued down the path. They hadn't told me I'd find *this* as well.

My fingertips throbbing to touch nature's ultimate glory, to learn of its everlasting secrets, I stared up in awe. "Is this *the* tree?"

Myrrdin's slender mouth curved. "The tree of the knowledge of good and evil?" He exhaled, his eyes closed. His brown skin seemed to have lost last night's sallowness. "Yes, Amy."

I stared at one of the lowest hanging apples, salivating. How long had it been since I'd had any food also found on Earth?

"Feel free to partake," Myrrdin surprised me, chortling at my scandalized look. "You won't harm anything, I assure you. We've already learned all we can from the tree, anyhow—many thanks to Eve." When I still seemed reluctant, Myrrdin rose back to his full height and plucked the apple nearest his head. He took my hand and placed the fruit, familiar and smooth, in my palm. "We eat from this tree regularly. The wine at your summoning celebration was made from it."

I supposed it was only fitting that the wine in Eden be made of apples.

Smiling my thanks, I set the apple in the woven basket I always carried for gathering purposes. Then I sighed and faced Myrrdin, sheepish.

"Sorry I was such a brat to you last night. You were right—I was scared. But then I talked to Pete about it and—" I paused, wondering how to tell him that I planned to bring my human, harbinger lover with me when I ventured to the Spring Palace to wrest the reins of power from my erstwhile fiancé.

"Pete assured you your fears were for naught," Myrrdin finished for me. He smiled, his eyes crystal omniscience. "Even if I hadn't seen so, child, I'd have told you that he would."

I blinked at him, surprised he wasn't giving me the same stern, judgy look he'd given me the night before. "You're not going to tell me what a monumentally bad idea it is to bring Pete with me when I go?"

"Why would I do such a thing?" Myrrdin chuckled. "I don't think it's a bad idea."

"But I thought you were upset with me because I was letting my feelings for Pete stand in the way of my destiny."

"No, I was concerned you were avoiding your destiny for fear of confrontation. With Briar. With your family. With anyone who'd oppose your rule."

I cringed. "Well—you're not wrong."

"I rarely am, Amy."

I arched a wry brow.

"Will you have an easy go at court to begin with?" Myrrdin posed. "Decidedly not, and likely *because* of Pete."

Was it too much to hope that he'd surprise me with an answer I hadn't expected?

"But I believe you'll eventually consider the troubles he'll breed as blessings."

I wanted to ask him to elaborate on that ambiguous point, but then he inquired, "Did Pete ever tell you the story of how he began this venture? Creating of Eden a refuge?"

To say I was baffled was an understatement. "No, I—I didn't even know he was the one who started it."

Myrrdin clasped his hands at his waist. "Doesn't surprise me that he didn't tell you. He doesn't feel he deserves credit for all we've done here because he didn't discover the garden on his own. I told him where to find it, to safeguard him from Gentian after he and Morus escaped the Spring Palace. I feared Gentian would seek retribution against Pete for failing to kill your father. And if Pete had been caught on the run, I daresay he'd be long dead now. Quite gruesomely too."

I quailed at the thought.

"Pete had been locked in a cage for well over two centuries. He was malnourished, his predator eyes were overly sensitive to anything brighter than candlelight, his first reaction to any problem was to fight, and he had no notion of the fae world beyond the Shadow Palace. He *needed* our help.

"Morus led Pete here to Eden, mostly under cover of night to avoid royal guards and Gentian's lackeys. And their directions were deficient at best—I'd only seen the path through landmarks. Yet, with luck and prayer, they made it here to safety. And here is where I meant Pete to remain—in this sanctum from Gentian. For he'd surely suffered enough."

He sure as hell had.

"But Pete had other ideas, as he often does." The prophet's face canted toward droll.

"I'd have just burnt off my tether and stayed hidden in the time pocket."

"Yes, well—none of us knew how to remove his tether back then. Pete learned of that years later. He'd never have done so at any rate—for then he'd have given up his new purpose for living.

"He needed a purpose, you'll understand, for life after cage fighting. Morus remained as a mentor to help him find it—to help him heal. Yet our dear Kobold friend was still dismayed when, after only a paltry month, Pete looked around this vast oasis and decided it would do to shield more than just himself from Gentian. He'd simply have to put his own life and soul at risk again—and again—and again. And, Amy, he didn't hesitate. He laid out his plans, and regardless of what evil might befall him, he'd see them through. For the sake of those in need of saving."

Just when I think Pete can't get any better—

"Morus tried to talk him out of it, of course, but that was a futile effort. After that month, Pete made Morus return him to the Shadow Palace, where Pete wore his demon mask to become a harbinger, full-fledged."

"And Gentian didn't punish him for failing to kill my dad?"

"He tried." Myrrdin cleared his throat. "To maintain his act—or maybe just for revenge—Pete killed Gentian's punisher. Strangled him with his own whip. Gentian let Pete be after that."

Good for Pete.

"Then Pete and the few other harbingers he trusted began concealing their death marks here. For all intents and purposes, they founded a village in Eden, and I resigned my post at the Spring Palace to aid Pete's cause—which was, in effect, to save as many lives from Gentian as feasible.

"They know one day Gentian will discover what they've been about. He has too many spies. They hope to kill him before that happens, but they've yet to decide how to accomplish this. Or at least they *hadn't*—until you, Amy."

I grimaced. "Did Pete tell you about asking me to help him? Before he knew who I was?"

"No, *that* I saw in a prophecy."

"Would we have done it? Would Pete's plan have worked?"

"I can't say." Myrrdin's expression warmed. "Because even if Pete hadn't learned your true identity, he wouldn't have let you go through with it. At a certain point in your journey, he grew to care for you too much and could no longer stomach the thought of risking your life, even if you were the only person in all of Mag Mell who'd succeed at killing the Shadow Prince. Pete was always going to waffle on your agreement. You were always going to wind up in Eden."

A breeze frolicked around me, blowing my hair into my face. After a blink, I realized the breeze was my doing.

"I tell you this to illustrate why your choice to bring Pete with you to the Spring Palace isn't folly. It's never folly to keep someone with such compassion close. Someone who puts others first—who puts *you* first. Just as you put him."

Suddenly bashful, I glanced away.

"Affinity bonds don't simply happen, Amy, and the having of it can only strengthen the two of you. It's another power in your pocket—and in his. Just remember that in the future—when things become arduous." He paused pointedly. "And consider where a bond such as yours might also lead you."

My stomach fluttered at what I thought Myrrdin implied. Would Pete and I become soulmates?

Cool it, Amy, I chastised myself. *Sure, Pete offered you his heart, but you don't know if that even means monogamy to him. He has yet to use the L-word. Oath or no oath, he'd run for the hills if he knew you were fantasizing of mating your souls—something he expressly stated he didn't want.*

Reading my mind through my doofish eyes, no doubt, Myrrdin sighed. "Your future with Pete will depend on a series of decisions the two of you have yet to make. So, I don't know what you'll become to each other at this time. But before you were born, your mother shared with me a premonition she had of you—you and a shadow man. She saw that he was inextricably connected to you, Amy. And you to him."

I tried to bite back my smile, but my smile won.

"Now, what that means, I can't say. Because you're also inextricably connected to Briar."

Way to ruin it, Myrrdin!

I shook my head, certain of at least one aspect of my unwritten story. "I've already decided—Briar and I have no future."

Myrrdin's lips quirked. "Maybe not in a romantic sense, but he remains in the picture."

That might've been okay with me. I might've assumed that meant Briar and I would remain friends. But the way Myrrdin said the word *romantic* unsettled me. Because even on Earth, romance was an afterthought where royal marriages were concerned.

Mulish as Bob, I shouted so that even the fucking fates above could hear me. "I'm *not* marrying Briar!"

This time, I detected delight in Myrrdin's inscrutable grin. "As you say, Amy." Oddly, I got the feeling he wasn't patronizing me—that maybe he'd been testing me.

After regaining my composure, I cleared my throat. "About the corruption you tried to tell me about last night—"

Myrrdin nodded.

"Tell me about it again." I grimaced sheepishly. "I'll listen this time."

"Basically, Myrrdin said Briar has stopped making decisions based on logic and ethics," I told Pete later that night as we soaked together in a burbling hot spring. He relaxed across from me, his arms stretched out along the rocky, mossy ledge of the spring. "Instead, he's making them now based on fear."

Pete's heavy brow got heavier. "Fear of what?"

I shook my head, letting my hands float on an eddy of salty, steamy bubbles. "Myrrdin doesn't know, but the premonition disturbed him. He saw a large royal force preparing for battle."

Pete's eyes brightened in the dusky vapor. "Against Gentian?" He sat straight and leaned closer. "If that's the case, then—"

I grimaced. "If Briar *is* going to war with Gentian, Myrrdin got the sense he wouldn't exactly be successful."

Pete slumped back against the ledge again, expelled a breath. "Bugger."

"Yeah." I made a face at the blurry outline of my legs.

Several moments passed before Pete turned up a hand. "At the least, it shows Briar's trying to do right—even if he's doing it recklessly."

I wondered what was going on in my—ex's?—head. "If he's actually going after Gentian, then yeah."

Maybe. Briar was, after all, the male who'd literally taken food from hungry children in the name of doing what was right. "But we don't know if he is," I reiterated.

"Aye, but who else would he ready a force against? Is there anyone he—"

"Can we stop talking about Briar?" I interrupted, growing flustered at having to anticipate and analyze my betrothed's intentions. I'd never been good at that. And I *hated* that I was going to have to do it again very soon.

Pete arched a brow. "*You* brought him up, Shorty."

"I know." I pouted. "It's just reminding me of all the shit I'll have to deal with when we reach the Spring Palace." We'd already agreed, we'd leave together in a week. "And I just—I can't talk about him anymore."

Pete's expression softened. He waded across the pool to me and draped an arm across my shoulders. My body melded to his warm breadth. "Then we won't talk about him."

Grateful, I cuddled into him, tilting my damp head against his bare chest. Pete kissed the top of my head, and I smiled, content, as fireflies blinked through the mist, birds sung from their perches, and bugs chittered in their mating dances.

Goddess, I'm going to miss this place.

"Hey, why are we the only people who hang out here?" I asked Pete, watching our fingers entwine, a medley of opposites. "On earth, this place would be popping. I mean, people drop thousands on tubs that act like hot springs. They hook them up in their backyards and make party porches."

Blinking, Pete shook his head at me. "I'm garbled as to what most of that meant. Truly."

I smirked to myself, not feeling the need to explain.

Pete rolled his eyes. "Anyhow, while I'm in Eden, the residents refuse to visit the springs. They insist I be granted at least one luxury all to myself as the warden—especially as I insist on being equal in all else."

"That's kind of sweet, Pete."

"Aye, although it does grow tiresome, soaking here with no one to talk to." His dark gaze raked me. "Or look at."

I giggled, cheeks flushing, when his breath caressed my ear. He rumbled, satisfied, as gooseflesh dappled my neck.

"Hm." Pete licked his soft lips. Drops of water sparkled in his beard as he smiled down on me. "Ken what color your eyes turn when I do that, Shorty?"

"No." I tittered, waiting for him to do it again.

"Blue." He kissed the soft spot behind my ear, making me shudder. "As a midnight sky."

"Yeah?"

"Mm-hm."

I shivered at the delicate touch of his tongue to my ear arch. "And what about when I—" I bit my lip. "You never did tell me what color they turn then."

His mouth hitched. "The most vivid violet I've ever seen—a blend of your fire and passion."

"Sounds pretty."

"Oh, it's the prettiest color I've ever seen."

I bit my lip, offering Pete my neck to nibble on.

"But there's one thing I don't yet ken about your eyes." His lips brushed the curve of my jaw. I quivered at the tantalizing touch, giggling again. "I don't yet ken what color they turn when I do this—"

The attack was swift and ruthless—just the way a harbinger would do it. Pete's fingers went right for my waist, and I balled up like a hedgehog, shrieking for mercy from his tickles. We then thrashed together like drowning birds in the spring. I cackled. Pete guffawed. And regardless of the privacy afforded us, I doubted there was a single soul in Eden who didn't know what we were doing.

Later, I wondered if there were ever sounds like that in Eden before the fall.

Two days later, it happened.

We'd never have known it was coming, the dusky morning as normal as ever in Eden. Pete and I hadn't even packed for the Spring Palace yet; we didn't have many belongings. The cafeteria had started serving lunch, and workers were breaking from their chores to fill their growling bellies. Spirits were high all around. Even Bumble's, who turned out not to be so ornery once I got to know him. The gruff Dwarf offered me his spot in line for lunch, wouldn't take no for an answer.

Maybe because I looked like I'd been through the ringer, having spent that morning feeding livestock. The fleecers, especially, could be quite uncouth in receiving their meals. I'd gotten stampeded. Though I'd made it out of the pen unscathed, my braid was in disarray, I smelled faintly of dung, and my leafy ensemble needed scrubbed.

"What happened to you?" Sedge snickered on his way past me, both Kit and Sionna prancing at his heels.

"Bernard," I named the worst-mannered fleecer. "He *thinks* he's starving."

Still snickering, Sedge moseyed on. Or at least he meant to. He stopped dead in his tracks when the ground quaked.

Confusion was my first reaction to the screaming. Abject terror followed when a volley of whispering arrows filled the purple sky.

Sedge unsheathed his blades. "Run for cover!" he bellowed, then smacked Sionna's already trembling rump, spurring her to seek shelter, before tearing off toward whatever evil slung those arrows. Kit dashed after him.

"Gentian!" someone cried as they raced past. "He's found us!"

Frozen in place, I watched the barrage skewer those around me like hunks of meat, people I'd come to know, impaled in twos and threes. Bumble got speared through his thigh behind me. The mothers who usually chittered together over lunch were downed before they'd even jumped up to find their faelets. I saw Riordan, standing on the beach, cast a wind at the arrows, trying to blow them back. But whatever wind carried the volley was stronger, for Riordan's blast barely affected them, and I screamed, enraged, as he took an arrow through the hip.

My shock shattered, I scrambled through the escaping slews, reaching for every power I had—my hands already aflame.

If this was Gentian's doing, then I was going to find him and incinerate him like the piece of garbage he was. But when I finally encountered an invader, a large Danann warrior taking a sword to an unarmed Middling feyr of medium stature, I froze again. Horrified.

The invader wielded a lightsaber-esque sword. He wore gleaming, engraved armor and a horned helm. An apparition from a dream.

"*No.*" Chills rippled through my soul. This wasn't Gentian's doing. Those weren't his arrows. And those weren't his soldiers storming Eden like Vikings fiending for gold.

They were mine!

And now I knew why Briar had readied an army. Somehow, he'd discovered where I was and had tasked this force with my rescue, unaware I no longer needed rescuing. And he clearly didn't care how many innocents he slaughtered to save me!

"*Stop!*" I roared at the invaders nearest me. They didn't spare me a glance, rushing after fleeing refugees. So, I waved an arm and sent them all whipping back like tin cans. Some, I swiped completely out of the time pocket. Then I darted through Eden, compelling any invader I spotted to tumble through the air. None of them knew what hit them as they sailed away.

Intent on my work, I didn't notice until the last second—the sizeable feyr charging forth to impale me. Startled by his murderous snarl—*so* inhuman—I lost grip of my righteous fury. On all my powers too.

I was as good as dead. And if it weren't for the small, apish creature that leapt out of nowhere and onto the charging feyr's back, I would've been. Instead, I watched, breathless, as Morus ripped out the feyr's jugular, spattering my cheeks with his blood.

I shivered at my stupid luck as Morus jumped off the fallen Danann's body, landing beside me in the sand, gore dripping from his muzzle and claws. "You must find the leader of this rabble, Amaranthine!" he crowed up at my wide-eyed face. "This attack won't cease until he's assured—"

I shrieked, my heart ricocheting into my throat, as an arrow tore diagonally through Morus, its tip protruding from his belly.

Morus's black-pit gaze rounded in shock, his hands gripping the arrow shaft. When he crumbled to his knees, I crumbled with him, clutching his bony, hairy elbow to keep him upright. "W-what should I do?" I stuttered, helpless. "How should I help you?"

"This is no time for fussing." He bared his ugly teeth in mingling pain and rage. "I'll keep long enough for you to end this madness."

"I can't leave you right now!"

He let out a harsh laugh. "Unless you're a healer, Amaranthine, then that's all you can do."

"Then I'll find a healer! I'll take you to shelter, and I'll—"

A barked roar of, "*Bloody stay behind me!*" resonated in my marrow, and I whirled toward the school pavilion, where I found Pete defending Master Hickinbottom, a terrified number of faelets, and several of their parents from twenty aggressors in horned helmets.

Lightsabers circled the ground around Pete. As did strangled bodies, his tethers working double time. Ten invaders were currently writhing for breath, prying at their shadow nooses, but more surged toward him.

His tan face flashing red, Pete balled already swollen, bloody fists. He never wore his weapons in Eden—the one place in this entire world he hadn't felt he had to. "Let the others go!" he shouted over the faelets' fright. "They've done nothing to no one! Let them go, and you can take me for whatever you will!"

Whether Pete was being truthful, I couldn't say. He lied when he needed to, and right then a lie seemed more than necessary. But one of the invaders clearly didn't believe him. He hurtled forth like a beast with an unslakable hunger for blood and vaulted himself at Pete, sword swinging.

I clutched my ears in horror, Morus cussing beside me—just before Pete released one of his blue-faced victims and lassoed the blade from his assailant's hands.

His nostrils flaring, Pete grabbed the sword and had it hard against the helmed jerkwad's bobbing throat in a heartbeat. Fury pulsed through his reddening neck as he seethed down into the Danann's face. "You dare to tussle with *me*? You'd best take me by surprise."

"Fuck you," the feyr rasped—in an American accent.

I gasped, dropping Morus's arms, and stepped forward to watch as the helmed feyr raised his pale, shaking hand and squeezed his fingers into a fist.

The cool breath of mist hit me first, then surrounding jungle wildlife awoke in petrified screaming.

"Danu have mercy," Morus croaked, blood dripping from his muzzle, as we stared ahead at the sea.

Before us, the always tranquil waters had become a violent thing of nightmares. They'd receded from the beach into a wall, eclipsing view of the moon. A wall that would careen back toward Eden, crash down on the village to destroy everything. And *everyone*.

"*Run!*" a guttural shriek warned, the masses scrabbling for a shelter with no hope of saving them. Every instinct I had told me to join them, to flee for my life. But I'd die if I did that. So many would die.

Pete's face drained of blood, watching the tsunami rise. And I knew he was about to kill his assailant to quell his magic. And damned if I could let that happen. Morus was right. This attack wouldn't end until the invading leader knew I was safe. And his death would only mean more bloodshed.

"Go!" Morus wheezed, shoving me forward with his waning strength. "End this!"

So after one more glance of concern for Morus's welfare, I dug into myself and regained the reins on my wind. I shot into the sky just as the star-scraping wave bowled forward.

Screams for Danu's mercy punctuated my descent to the ground. I slammed down beside Pete and the helmed feyr. Pete stumbled aside—giving me enough space to whip the invader back on his keister with a savage wind.

The feyr landed with a clang of armor. His clenching hand flopped open, and he lost grip of his deadly magic. The tsunami halted at the beach like it had hit a barrier.

I stomped down on the feyr's plated chest before he regained control. Ripped off his helmet. Just as I'd suspected—Briar Hawthorne gaped up at me, lime-green eyes blazing, his auburn hair sweaty and matted. His expression went from indignation, to recognition, to awe. "*Amy?*" he croaked.

"Yeah!" I smashed his helmet to the ground by his dumbass head. "What the *fuck* is wrong with you?"

FORTY-TWO

"**E**xplain!" I demanded of Briar hours after the ceasefire. After I'd taken stock of what we'd lost.

Hundreds of refugees were wounded. Ten were dead. Including Morus, who hadn't kept, as he'd promised he would. And Liatris, who'd taken an arrow through the chest just after safeguarding Jet.

Sedge had found the little one crying over his mother's body, and I'd spent most of the last hour rocking him into a fitful slumber before storming to the Kirk of Cara to tear my so-called fiancé a new one.

Shamefaced in his shiny royal armor, Briar rose from a pile of rubble in the kirk. Royal forces had catapulted several humongous stone balls at the temple before they'd realized nobody was inside. Cracks now spider-webbed across Adam and Eve's frieze, but the glass dome rising above us had somehow remained intact. Moonlight filtered in through its etched panes, washing us in silver.

Hands out in supplication, Briar started with, "I'm so sorry, Amy. I didn't mean for any of this to happen."

"Then what the hell did you mean to happen?" Smoke wafted from my hands. My emotions were on Mr. Toad's Wild Ride, and my powers had called shotgun.

Behind me, Myrrdin cleared his throat, then I felt another's warm touch upon my sweaty back, doing more to calm me than a tranquilizer could.

Pete's still here, I kept reminding myself. *He's here. He's okay.*

Briar's Adam's apple bobbed in his throat. "We were trying to rescue you, Amy."

"You could've killed me too, Briar, with the crazy way yinz burst in here!"

Briar shook his head, his jaw clenched in denial. "No, we'd planned that out. We enchanted our arrows, so that they wouldn't strike a single prisoner. We didn't want to hurt any innocents."

"There are no prisoners here, Briar! *All* of these people are innocent!"

Briar's lime eyes scathed the two harbingers standing behind me. Obviously, he had his doubts on the matter of innocents.

Neither Pete nor Sedge seemed to give a crap what he thought of them.

Myrrdin tapped his slender lips. "Briar, what led you to believe there were prisoners here?"

Taking a deep breath, Briar faced the prophet in something akin to relief. He clearly thought Myrrdin would have his back, as he'd been Myrrdin's former pupil, just as my mother had. "Because we had intel that said so."

"What does that mean?" I snapped. "Intel? Are you working with the CIA now?"

Briar's mouth quirked. "It was a message, Amy, detailing exactly where you were—that you were being held captive in one of Gentian's harbinger outposts."

I stilled. *Huh?*

"Who sent it to you?" Pete asked, his voice an echoing mallet in the rotunda.

Briar didn't even try to mask his sneer. "It wasn't sent. It was found. In the jungle while we were searching for her."

"You were searching for me?" How dogged had that search been if numerous harbingers had caught my trail, but no one from the Spring Palace had? Gentian couldn't be the only game in town for proficient trackers.

"Of course, I was!" Briar exclaimed, insulted. "I've been looking for you since I got carried away by those damn sluaghs! I even put out broadsheets offering a reward to anyone who'd deliver you safely home!"

I turned to my allies for verification.

"I did see broadsheets," Sedge confirmed, sour-faced. "They were everywhere for a time."

"Hmph," Pete grunted. "Doesn't mean he's who distributed them."

Yep, we're on the same page, man.

Briar certainly had a lot to gain from my absence. Since all the Dananns I'd met, besides my siblings (probably), wanted him to wear my father's crown. With me out of the way, it'd be much easier to take it.

"Thanks for that two cents," Briar snarked at Pete. "Look, Amy, I *have* been trying to find you. For months!"

"Why didn't you just assume I was dead?" I was curious why he'd told Jade from the Thorny Rose Tavern he knew I was still alive.

"I probably would've assumed you were dead. If the sluaghs didn't tell me straight up that they'd been paid to cart me off, so that some harbinger asshole could capture you for Gentian."

Pete laughed darkly.

Briar shot him a withering glance before continuing. "I'd almost given up hope that we'd ever find you when I got word that part of Lithalaly was on fire. I figured you'd tried to use your powers to escape your captor, and I sent a full battalion into the jungle to find you. It was during that search that we found the message. Half-burnt, I was told, but mostly legible."

"You didn't see the message with your own eyes?" Pete's amusement, stiff though it had been, had fled. "You just took someone's recounting of it as truth?"

"And who the fuck are you to judge my decisions on trust, *harbinger*?"

Pete sniffed. "I'm the arsehole who captured the princess for Gentian, as you said."

Disbelief and hatred wrangled for control of Briar's face.

I cringed, knowing this hadn't been the most appropriate time to let *that* bomb drop.

"But I'm also the one who wrote that missive you're referencing. The missive found in a copse of scorched crystal willows? A former kaleidoscope post?"

When Briar's ears perked, I knew Pete had nabbed his attention.

"Half-burnt it might've been," Pete kept on, growing more irritated with each word. "But it wouldn't have stated anything about a harbinger outpost. Quite the contrary. It stated that the princess was living in a safe haven from Gentian—a refugee camp, as she calls it."

Cursing, Briar hung his head.

"Every person residing in Eden is a victim of Gentian's curses. Victims I'd hoped would be granted asylum after you'd read my message. Not attacked like criminals. Or slain like mongrels before their children, their friends!"

My lip quivered at the pain in Pete's voice. As we'd only discovered our friend's death minutes before our meeting with Briar, his grief over Morus hadn't finished brewing. He was noticeably still in shock.

Thank Danu for that, I thought. *Otherwise, he'd have killed Briar on sight.*

Briar peered skyward. Asking for absolution? I wondered. "I—I didn't know," was his pathetic response.

Anger wormed through my mouth again. "It doesn't matter if you didn't know, Briar—if you made a mistake coming here."

He frowned—at himself, I thought.

"Even if you had the wrong information, you still could've stopped all this if you'd just opened your damn eyes and looked around for a hot minute. Didn't you see all the smiling faces or hear the laughter? Didn't you see the goddamn *children*? The ones you tried to drown with your tidal wave?"

"I didn't know what to expect of a harbinger camp, Amy!" Briar shook pleading hands at me. "I've never seen one before! Why couldn't children live there?"

I almost hiccupped. "You think what you did would be acceptable if the children you tried to kill belonged to *harbingers*?"

"No!" Briar closed his eyes, shook himself. "No, that's not what I'm saying, Amy. I'm saying that I thought this was a harbinger camp, and that everyone here was complicit in imprisoning you. That the children were as wicked as the rest! That *everyone* was guilty! I'm not excusing those thoughts. I just—I thought you were in danger! I thought that they were torturing you! Or starving you! Or raping you! And I'd been assured they'd do all three!"

Despite his unmasked prejudices, the fear contorting Briar's face moved me. Made my guts clench.

What the hell would've happened to me had Pete not been the harbinger who'd gotten my ordination?

Myrrdin clicked his tongue, calm as ever while my heart thudded out of control. "Who assured you of that, Briar?"

"Huh?" Briar blinked, returning to himself.

"The people who assured you of the torturing, starving, and raping," Myrrdin clarified. "Who did the assuring?"

Briar blinked again, bereft as he racked his brain. "I—I can't remember exactly—"

"Mm-hm," Myrrdin hummed. "And the message found in the jungle—who told you of it?"

"Paragon Ledum—Ledum Waybread." Anxious, Briar massaged his forehead. As put together as he always seemed, seeing him so distraught unnerved me. He hadn't even looked this troubled when the sluaghs carried him away, leaving me, a lamb in a den of lions.

"You remember him, Myrrdin," Briar persisted. "He's not a dishonest person. You can't believe he'd fabricate a message, so that I'd lay waste to a curse sanctuary."

Myrrdin glided over to Briar, set a hand on his shoulder. Pacifying him. "I do remember Ledum, child. Kindhearted fellow, he was, yes. You and he have been friends for some time. Nevertheless, we must question him about the message."

Chewing his lip, Briar motioned to the helmed guards outside the crumbling kirk entrance. "Fetch Ledum, please."

So, they fetched Ledum. And after a minute of Myrrdin's gentle interrogation, it was clear something fishy was happening. Because kindhearted Ledum, who admitted relaying the kaleidoscope message to Briar, hadn't read the dang thing either. And he couldn't quite recall who'd found Pete's letter and told him what it said.

After dismissing poor, befuddled Ledum from the kirk, Myrrdin patted Briar's shoulder. "My child, I'm afraid you've been antegraded—Ledum as well."

Myrrdin could've told Briar the world was ending, and he'd have looked less astounded.

The prophet glanced my way. "That means someone has blotted out pieces of their memory—pieces that would no doubt incriminate the spellcaster as the one who's been polluting their judgment with baseless fears and hateful rhetoric." He sashayed over to me and my harbingers. "And there's our corruption, friends."

"It's Gentian's rat!" I hissed, hoping there was only one. "He's got to be a part of that battalion Briar sent out."

"Must be awfully high ranking as well to have both the ear of a Paragon and the interim king," Sedge said.

I was grateful he hadn't said *future* king.

"Aye," Pete agreed. "And now we must assume Gentian kens of Eden—of what we've been doing under his nose. Once he learns his spy failed at having Eden decimated, nobody will be safe here."

Or anywhere. Except—

"Then we'll *all* go to the Spring Palace," I decided. "Every last person here."

"Of course, Amy." Briar opened his hands. "You don't even need to ask."

"Good." I arched a brow. "Because I wasn't."

Briar stared like he'd never met me before.

Behind me, I could feel Pete's pride. I turned to glance up at him. "Rat or no rat, we *will* keep them safe there."

Pete's gaze softened at my promise, conveying trust.

Sighing, I plodded over to Briar. Yes, I wanted to wring his fucking neck, but now I knew his shitty decision making wasn't entirely his fault, he having been magically brainwashed. Still, it was a trial to be kind as I folded my arms and watched his tongue roll in his mouth—the tic I still found cute, despite his reprehensible actions that day. Damn him.

"You have a lot to atone for, Briar," I stated. "You led an army here, and they hurt people—they murdered people—they *orphaned* people."

Briar's lime eyes shuttered on a flash of searing pain. Searing pain that was 100 percent genuine. Seeing it heartened me.

"I expect you to move hell and earth—or hell and Mag Mell—to find the prick who screwed with your mind and put you in this situation. When you find him and bring him to me, so that I can watch him die in a pit of fire, then I'll forgive you."

Shocked by my ruthlessness—because old Amy didn't hold death grudges like that—at least not out loud—Briar slowly nodded his agreement.

"Speaking of fire," Pete interjected, scratching his beard. "Who've you told of the princess's power? You seemed to ken she's a fire sylph."

Briar refused to look at Pete. Instead, he locked eyes with me, reached for my hand. My gut instinct was to recoil, but Danu help me, he was already in such a pathetic state, and I couldn't stand for it to get worse.

"I promise you, Amy, I haven't told *anyone* about your fire magic. Except your uncle. And he wouldn't tell anyone either. We know how folks will react to that knowledge. We don't want to spook them before they've met you."

I tried not to look as sullen as I felt. Of course, he'd fret about the danger of me scaring people with my power instead of thinking of me as some secret weapon you wouldn't want your enemy prepared for.

"And the guards who saw her power today?" Sedge prodded.

"They've already been dealt with," Briar answered me, not Sedge. He gripped my hand tighter. "Before we departed the palace, every fighting feyr signed a muzzle order. Which means they've been magically contracted into never communicating about your gifts—to anyone—even themselves—though they'll retain the information. Cornelian had the contracts drawn up for me, so you *know* there are no loopholes. He does *not* want to risk your reputation."

Good ole Uncle Neel, I thought, close to sneering.

"Is it safe to assume that Gentian's rat also had to sign that order?" I chewed my lip. "That he can't tell Gentian what I'm capable of?"

Briar seemed not to fully grasp my concern on the matter. Questioning my capabilities, I assumed, though I'd taken him down without much effort. Still, he answered, "If he was in my ranks, then yes. He signed it—before five witnesses—including your brother, Amy. We wouldn't have allowed someone who refused to sign to come."

I glanced over my shoulder at Pete, who gestured to confirm that this was, indeed, reassuring information. That I remained an ace in the hole. And some tension in my muscles eased.

Briar must've misread my body language. His hand moved to my elbow, drawing me closer. He gave me a devastating smile, the kind that once made my heart go pitter pat. His eyes brimmed with unmistakable joy. As transparently emotional as he was, I didn't quite know how to reject him right then.

"I'm *so* happy I've finally found you, Amy," he gushed. "I've been so worried about you. So worried you'd wind up hurt or dead. I can hardly believe you're here with me now. That I can actually touch you." He caressed my cheek, and I gritted my teeth on a curse. "I know I have a lot to make up for after today. And I will. I promise. I'll do anything you ask me to if it'll earn your forgiveness. I'll spend the *rest* of our life together earning it if you want."

When Briar moved in to kiss me, I decided I'd rather break his heart than Pete's. Whether I was capable of breaking Pete's heart at that moment, I didn't know, but I wasn't chancing it. And I pulled back.

I didn't have to pull too hard. Briar's grip slackened. He let me slide right out of his fingers. His eyes narrowed. "Amy—why do you smell different?"

I knew exactly why. Many of Eden's residents had been teasing me about it. Just—I hadn't expected Briar to notice that specific change before I'd officially broken our engagement.

Don't you dare feel awkward right now, I scolded myself. *You never agreed to marry Briar. Hell, you hadn't even changed your social media relationship status before things got weird. You have every right to smell like whatever feyr—or man—you want to smell like.*

"*Amy.*" The edge to Briar's voice made at least one harbinger behind me shift. To fist his sword hilt, I guessed. A wordless warning that Briar didn't even register, as fixated on me as he was.

Finally, I huffed. "It doesn't matter how I smell Briar. That has no bearing on my feelings about our relationship. I decided long before I started smelling this way that I—"

At Briar's crinkling brow, I knew he had no idea where my train of thought was chugging. Hearing myself, I understood his confusion. But I'd never broken up with someone before. And I'd never thought my first time doing so would be in front of a holy man and two harbingers—one of whom I was already banging.

Coughing, I started again. "I decided, maybe before we'd even crossed the portal, Briar, that we weren't going to work out. That I don't want to be with you. And I'm very sorry, but I can't—I can't marry you."

Briar stared at me, his mouth a hard line. His jaw didn't drop, and he didn't look angry. He looked—resolved. Bitterly, sternly resolved.

Not the reaction I'd been expecting.

"We'll talk about this later, Amy," Briar replied, glancing briefly over my shoulder. *When we don't have an audience,* his look finished his thoughts.

I shook my head. "What else is there to talk about?"

His auburn brows rose. "Plenty."

"But you heard what I said, right? I don't—"

"Yes, Amy, I heard you." His interruption was so dang calm. He looked at me now the same way Aunt Aylie had the day I'd announced I was going to be a unicorn when I grew up. "And I'd like to talk to you about it. So, why don't we go to my tent, where we can do that in private?"

"Wha—huh? *Hey!*" I sputtered when Briar set a hand at my back and "ushered" me toward the royal guard camp. Where he intended to go on pretending I hadn't just ended our engagement.

He "guided" me ahead all of three steps when a shadow slashed the air and wrapped Briar's wrist like a Slap Bracelet, yanking my wannabe ceyla back by his arm—putting Briar in danger of breaking his damn wrist if he struggled too hard.

In Pete's quiet volatility, I knew he hoped Briar would struggle like a fiend.

I'd never seen Briar angry before. Not like this. His lime eyes seethed at Pete as he spun about, his Danann fangs flashing in the moonlight. Gone was the jovial party boy I thought I'd known. In his place was the most inhuman fae I'd ever seen.

Briar's breath came in an animal snarl as Pete curled a lip at him and warned, "You touch her again without her say so, I'll rip your fecking bollocks off."

Mother save him and his darkening eyes, Pete meant it. And I knew Sedge would be only too happy to hold Briar down, so Pete could carry out his threat.

"Now, now," Myrrdin mediated. "There's no call for violence, lads. Let's all let Amy be. There are heavier things to weigh just now."

Myrrdin might as well have been speaking to a wall. Because Pete didn't retract his tether. And Briar, nostrils flaring, angled his head toward the door and roared, "Guards!"

Seconds later, five royal guards swarmed the rotunda, spears out.

I leapt in front of Pete. "Briar, tell them to back off!"

Briar did no such thing. He continued glaring at Pete, who didn't give a flying fuck—his concern solely for me.

Pete clasped my hand by my hip, drawing me back from the spears. And from Briar.

Even as I moved into Pete's protective warmth, I shouted, "Tell them to back off, Briar! Or I'll rip your fucking bollocks off myself!"

I hope I know what bollocks are.

The reality of the situation clobbered Briar like a baseball bat to the mouth. He knew by my scent that I'd slept with someone (if he couldn't already tell that scent was symptomatic of an affinity bond), but I noted his shock. He'd *never* have guessed my lover to be a harbinger, let alone the harbinger who'd captured me.

"Amy, what the fuck did you do?" Briar's humanity returned with a vengeance. "Him? *Really?*"

"Briar, you don't even know him."

"I don't need to know him! He's a fucking *harbinger*!"

"Yes, he is," I snapped. "He's a harbinger, and he's human, and he's a predator, and he's the most honest, most giving, most selfless person you will ever fucking meet!"

Briar goggled at me. "He kidnapped you! For a bounty!"

"Yes—yes, he did. And then he saved me! He brought me here, Briar! When every harbinger and their mother was hunting me, he brought me here to protect me! Then he tried to sac—"

"That's such bullshit, Amy," Briar interrupted, his voice harder yet calmer. We were back to the condescending adult to child dynamic. "You're smarter than this, honey. You can't seriously believe he doesn't have some ulterior motive for doing what he's done. What's he asked you for? Asylum along with the refugees?"

"*No.*" I glanced skyward, shaking my head. "He—he didn't have to ask. I offered it to him."

Briar groaned into his hands like he might be sick. "*Amy.*"

I bit my lip, feeling I'd lost control of the conversation.

Beside me, Pete cleared his throat. "Still want me to follow you, Shorty?"

Ignoring the face Briar made at my ill-fitting nickname, I whirled on Pete. "*Yes.*" Pete eyed me, and I sniffed. "It's going to take a lot more than *this* for me to free you from your pledge, buddy."

Pete's expression warmed, though it lost none of its dry humor.

"Pledge?" Briar repeated, baleful and tired. "There's a pledge now?"

"Mm, yes." Myrrdin moseyed over to my glaring ex—at least in my mind—and dispersed the guards with a simple gesture. "If you'll allow me, I can explain that and several other pertinent details about the princess and her harbinger." Myrrdin angled my way, lifted a slender hand. "If Pete would kindly unbind Briar—"

Pete arched a droll brow down at me, making it clear—he only took orders from me.

I couldn't help smirking as I said, "Let him go."

Winking, Pete retracted his tether from Briar. Its shadowy body wafted toward me, its velvety tongues tickling my shoulders on its journey back into Pete's hand.

"Well, then," Sedge said on my right. "Shall we go before another battle breaks out?"

"Aye," Pete agreed, his humor faltering at the memory of what awaited us in Eden—anguish and lamentation. "Let's be on our way." He offered me his hand.

"This isn't settled, Amy!" Briar called as I took my current lover's hand. I peered over my shoulder at my stern-mouthed, sharp-eyed past. "We still need to have that talk."

"We will." *When I'm good and ready, dude.*

Then I squeezed Pete's hand, leaned my head into his strong arm, and strode back into Eden.

E den, a utopian paradise where no one aged, gained a cemetery the next day. Us mourners dug ten graves around the stone circle where we'd held my summoning ceremony, and Myrrdin and his clerics conducted ten ascension services. I attended every single one.

I thought Liatris's service would be the hardest for me, as she and I had become as thick as thieves during my time in Eden. She was a ray of sunshine in that eternal dusk, always the optimist despite her life's sadness and perils. And she was, hands down, the best mother I'd ever met. Her love for her son had warmed my heart, reminded me why I was going to go to war. I'd miss her.

Still, I didn't flounder into a puddle of tears during her service. Mainly because of Jet. One glance at his weepy, freckled face kept my shit together. He needed my strength, the security of my arms. Not my tears.

But also because of Imogen, who'd been mothering Jet while I was off playing princess. She'd done such a fine job helping him cope that she'd alleviated a good deal of my sadness. Because I could tell by watching her with him—she'd never entrust the care of her late friend's son to anyone else but herself. She would stick by that little guy, and she'd ensure he grew up with love in a world so oddly cruel to orphans. And if there were any ludicrous laws preventing her from doing that, you could bet your sweet aunt sally I'd abolish them.

Given the circumstances, I made it through Liatris's service well.

Morus's service, however, was a different story. When I first strode upon his furry body all decked out in tropical phosphorescent flowers, his clawed hands folded over his heart, I hadn't expected to feel like someone had ripped my guts from my body. But I did.

Maybe because Morus represented the juncture of my old life with my new. Maybe because he'd barely known me before he'd joined me on a quest that could've killed us both. He was a ride-or-die friend if I'd ever known one. Or maybe it was because he'd saved my life moments before earning that fatal wound. Regardless, I was already bawling when I knelt beside his skeletal frame and touched his wrinkly, monstrous face.

I wanted so badly for him to turn to me with his snaggletooth and black-pit eyes and rasp, "Stop your damned keening. It serves nothing." But, of course, he didn't.

Sniveling, I wiped my eyes and pulled my MulBerry out of my leafy tank top. "Thank you for being a phone thief," I wept over him, clutching the smooth, bumpy plastic in my hands. "And thank you for telling me to fight harder. I've never gotten your words—or your voice—out of my head. Now, I hope I never will."

I kissed my phone's screen, then tucked it under Morus's folded hands. "You keep it with your stash for me, okay? I know you have one somewhere. Make sure you give it back, though." I shuddered into my hand. "Whenever we meet again."

Respectfully barefoot, I trudged back to the group of mourners circling Morus's grave. Even though my inner child was blubbering on a metaphorical floor by that point, I'd done a passable job keeping my shit together.

Then Pete took my spot.

I watched my big, hardened harbinger take a knee beside our small, Kobold friend's body, bow his head into his fist, and begin to cry tears he'd been withholding since we'd found Morus dead where I'd left him on the beach, Sionna whimpering and licking his unresponsive face.

I crumbled right to my knees, blubbering. So did several others. Because it was a devastating thing to watch a man made for bloodshed succumb to sadness.

"Thank you, friend," Pete finally gulped. "For helping me heal the parts of myself I'd given up for dead. You ken, I'd never have made it fully out of my cage if it weren't for you and your years of ornery counsel."

My heart shattered right there in that sand as Pete's time with Morus played across his face like a movie. I watched their every argument, in-joke, and deep conversation, his lips wriggling from frown to smile.

"Thank you for helping me remember the man I was." His smile lost ground. "For helping me remember the man I *want* to be. I promise you, Morus, I won't forget again."

I crawled over and clenched his massive fist in my hands. I kissed his temple as he drew into me, his wide mouth quivering into a poignant grimace. His brown eyes swam as they searched mine. He husked, "I won't *ever* forget."

A hush fell as we knelt there together like the posts of a lean-to. After what felt like an appropriate length, Pete sniffed and straightened. He wiped his nose, coughed, then expelled a heavy breath.

"Better do it now, Shorty," he croaked, scrunched up his trouser leg, and jostled the thick, smoggy tether about his ankle into visibility.

Because I needed to see it in order to burn it off him.

The others around us gasped in their grieving.

I understood why he wanted to do it right then. Before Myrrdin commended Morus's spirit to the Isle. If Morus had helped Pete escape his cage, then it was only right that he should bear witness to the breaking of Pete's final bond.

As I closed my eyes to concentrate on striking sparks in my core, I swore I heard the ghastly laugh of a jubilant Kobold. I smiled, assuring Morus, *He'll never be bound again,* then exhaled a long, controlled breath.

A plume of violet fire surged past my fingertips and into reality. It leapt onto Pete's tether and devoured it, gluttonous for more.

Pete fought a wince as my flames licked his hairy skin, but he didn't struggle. He fisted his hands and endured until the blaze vanished into smoke and his tether disintegrated into ash. Ash that a balmy breeze swept up and carried off, never to be seen again.

I may have been responsible for that breeze.

Inhaling a cathartic breath like he'd been living in a landfill, and this was his first dose of fresh air for eons, Pete grazed the charred skin around his ankle. He hissed at the burn, then chuckled, as giddy as I'd ever seen him.

Several more tears trickled down my cheeks. "There," I giggled, hoarse as a bullfrog. "You're free."

The others around us chortled, my silly remark helping to express their pent-up grief.

"Seems so, Shorty." Pete's eyes misted again.

"Eh hem."

We peered left to find Sedge eyeing us, brow furrowed. "I'm waiting for you to test your shadows now, you clothead."

"Ah," Pete said. "For an immortal fae, you're unduly impatient, ken."

"Aye." Sedge waved him to action. "Get on with it!"

Wryly, Pete raised a hand and flexed. Five bolts of shadow shot from his fingertips. Something tight inside me eased.

Pete observed the tethers for a moment, waggling the smoky threads here and there until he was satisfied nothing about his powers had changed. "Huh." He retracted his shadows. "Guess they're mine now."

"Hmph." Sedge stomped toward me and bent to roll up his trouser leg. "Give it a good blast, Shorty. I want Gentian himself to feel the heat."

My nostrils flared around sulfur as I raised my sparking hands. "Oh, he will," I promised, then gave Sedge's tether what for, more ghostly Kobold snickering in my ear.

On my last day in paradise, I woke up alone to a hot, steaming bath. I scrubbed my skin pink, washed and conditioned my hair twice, then air-dried in the warm sea breeze while I sat at the tree stump table in the warden's hut, eating a breakfast of figs and fish. When I was ready, I dressed in a leafy bustier, a crepey pair of shorts, and stuffed my feet in my knock off Buggs. I threw my damp hair up in a messy bun, shrugged into my backpack, and headed out for the road.

My walk through Eden depicted what the garden was like when just two people lived there. Because everyone else had cleared out much earlier that morning in preparation for the long journey to the Spring Palace. So, I heard every knock, every chitter, every whoop, every burble, and every cresting wave as I stopped in the village square to commit the details of that extraordinary, colorful, welcoming dreamworld to memory.

Though tragedy had found me there in the end, so many amazing things had happened to me in that place that I would always see it as my home away from Earth. And the only place I'd seen my mother in 16 years.

The Kirk of Cara was much repaired when I passed through. The crack in Adam and Eve's converging faces had been patched, the temple's rubble pieced back where it belonged. Magic, I supposed.

After one last appreciative gaze up at its magnificent dome, I forged out of the kirk and into the sunshine, where the enormous cavalcade to the Spring Palace awaited, a bustling village of its own.

"Ah, there you are, Amy." I glanced right to find Briar leaning casually inside the temple gateway beneath Danu's statue. Waiting there, no doubt, so I'd have no chance at avoiding him. He grinned, dressed in full armor except for his helmet, and the sizzling summer suns glinted in his auburn hair like rubies. Dashing though he looked right then, I struggled not to scowl.

Steeling myself, I forced a half-smile and trod toward him. Then past him.

Chuckling, Briar shoved off the gate and followed me, linking his arm about my waist. I stopped just to eye him.

"Glad you finally showed," Briar answered my look with his usual crispness. "Thought I might have to hunt you down. Again."

I wanted to say what a pity that would be for anyone who got in his way. "Did you want something?" I asked instead.

"As a matter of fact, I wanted to show you your carriage." He motioned ahead to a round, gilded carriage straight from a fairytale. Or a dream I'd stopped having.

Fit for a crown princess, the carriage was externally gorgeous with its scrolling carvings and whimsical construction. And its interior was even lovelier. It was plush, cozy, and spacious enough to sleep in should I tire before we made camp at night. I supposed there might have even been some semblance of a bathroom in there. I deemed it the most comfortable way to travel in Mag Mell. The equivalent of a private jet.

I took one look at it and clicked my tongue. "Nah."

Briar gawped as I skirted him. "Okay then." He fell into my step as I started past the rows of armored royal troops toward the head of the cavalcade. He grabbed my wrist to slow me. "If the carriage doesn't do it for you, Amy, then we have a horse for you."

I stared at him, disbelieving.

He motioned toward two snowy white horses just ahead of the carriage. One, a thoroughbred warhorse, had legs as thick as some tree trunks. His, I assumed. The other was daintier, prettier, and roses festooned her pastel mane. Her saddle was so thickly padded it looked like memory foam. Perfectly suited for any pampered, prissy ass to sit upon.

"You said you wanted to learn to ride," Briar reminded me, his lips slanting boyishly.

"Yeah—I did say that. But is now really the best time for learning?"

At my continued rejection, Briar shook his head as if shrugging off a bothersome fly on his neck. "Damnit, Amy, I'm really trying here."

That remark harkening another morning in a cabin in the woods, compassion overcame me. Compassion for him and the love he'd given up for the distant promise of a queen.

Exhaling, I set a hand on his plated shoulder. "Stop trying, Briar," I murmured at his questing lime gaze. Then, with one last tender grimace as my words' significance dawned on his handsome face, I plodded away toward the bray of a donkey.

At the front of the line were the harbingers, readying their own wagon to escort our procession to Evereostre. They knew all the best routes for avoiding Gentian and his henchmen. Doubtless the only reason Briar had allowed them to lead.

Kit met me first, wagging, and I patted her exuberant blonde head. She gave my hand a few sloppy licks before prowling after a cat monkey.

Reaching the wagon, I grabbed its ledge and hoisted myself up like I'd done a hundred times before, now standing amid scattered grasses, various weapons, bags of tropical fruit, and one happy, panting black and tan snuff hound.

"Hey, boys!" I called out. Pete and Sedge peered up at me from either side of Bob's dappled rump, both surprised I was there instead of riding in first class finery.

"*What?*" Pete called back, his thick brows meeting above devilish molasses cookie eyes.

I tilted my head, batting my lashes. "Mind if I travel with you?"

Amused, Sedge flashed a set of grinning Vampire fangs at his friend, deferring to Pete's judgment on the matter, it seemed.

"That depends." Pete swaggered around the wagon toward me. Licking his wide, delicious lips and scratching his bearded jaw, he rested his arms upon the wagon ledge to lend me a ribald smirk. "Will you whine, bitch, and moan about everything from the heat, dirt, and bugs to the stench of my sweat, the lack of a suitable bed, and the water level in my canteen? And will you harass me endlessly over the entirety of our journey until my eyes blacken, my teeth grind, and I quite seriously consider wringing your pretty white neck?"

I beamed, answering, "Yup."

Pete and Sedge shared a look of uncontainable amusement before Pete jutted his chin at me. "Aye, then—settle in and get comfortable, Shorty. It's a long way to the Spring Palace."

I bent down, grabbed him by his leather jerkin, and placed a delicate kiss on his soft lips. "Try not to make it too bumpy a ride," I teased, welcoming the gawking stares from the legions behind me.

His brow arching, Pete laughed. "No promises, Shorty."

At that, I chucked his scruffy chin and went to hunker down for the trip.

Just minutes later, we heard the official holler to roll out. Sedge whistled for Kit, and Pete clicked his tongue at Bob. "Giddap!"

The cart now rocking, I lounged in the back with my arm wrapped about Sionna's sweet, sniffing silkiness, the melody of "I Like it Our Way" skipping through the iBloom buds in my ears, and a shiny red apple—the one Myrrdin had plucked for me—poised in my hand. I took a big honking bite of the sacred fruit and gazed up at the suns beyond the jungle canopy.

Were my fans in the Isle of Apples watching me right then? Still wondering what I'd do next? Well, they could get in line because I was wondering too. But even in my uncertainty, I knew several things for sure. I'd have my powers, I'd have my family, I'd have my new friends from Eden, and I'd have Pete. So, whatever evil was coming at me when I took the throne, I'd handle it.

Smirking, I saluted heaven with my apple. "Don't worry, Daddy," I said, juice dripping down my chin. "I got this."

If you enjoyed *A Sanctuary from Shadow*, please take a moment and leave a review
on Amazon.com, Goodreads.com, or another platform of your choice.
Your feedback would be greatly appreciated!

TO BE CONTINUED....

Want to learn more about Eden's other residents and how they came to be there? Subscribe to Laura Irwin's newsletter to get your free eNovella, *Winds of Justice*—Imogen Rockrose's dark, tragic, and remarkable story.

She wants to save the world. But she'll have to save herself first.

Go here to subscribe:
https://author-laura-irwin.ck.page/6cf50a9289

ACKNOWLEDGMENTS

My journey as an author arguably started when I was 11, so there are a lot of people I need to thank. I'll just start at the beginning.

Mom and Daddy—I regret that you weren't able to read my first published book, but I know in my heart you were with me every step of the way in its creation. Thank you for never trying to squelch my wild imagination, even when my invisible friends were creating havoc around the house. Thank you for encouraging me to believe in magic and to never ever give up on my dreams. I wouldn't have certain wonderful things in my life without your voices always in the back of my head, prodding me to keep going.

Shannon and Mike—Thank you for your honest feedback throughout my writing journey. From ranking character names on a clipboard to reading random snippets, you are both always there to help when I need it. By the way, Noemi is still on the clipboard list, and one day I'm going to use it. We may not always agree or get along, but I hope you both know that I'll always stand up to the shadows for you.

Mr. Rosica—I will be forever grateful to you for changing up our class curriculum in 5th grade and assigning us independent creative projects. Without that, I doubt I'd have thought of writing my own books. I went through secondary education and 5 years of college, and you are still the best teacher I ever had.

Maria—Without you, I'd have lost my mind years ago. Couldn't have asked for a better friend.

Colleen and Big M—My found family. Thanks for all your love and support over the past sixteen years.

My critique partners, beta readers, ARC readers, and editors—Thank you all so much for your constructive feedback and helpful suggestions. Your input is integral to bettering my writing, and I always take everything you say to heart. I greatly appreciate all the time you've taken out of your own schedules to read Amy's story. You're all awesome!

Sierra—Thank you for being my writing buddy, sweet pea. You were the perfect sounding board, and I miss your pretty face.

And last but *never* least—my beer bottle cowboy and my little bug—you are two of my three dreams come true. Thank you both for always supporting me in my third dream, and for showing me the kind of immense and unending love I yearn to write about.

* 9 7 9 8 9 8 8 7 5 4 4 1 1 *